Starfall

by Drew Harrison

I don't know why you read all this disclaimer information, but I appreciate you, attentive reader.

Foreword

After many months of writing, I'm proud to finally release "Starfall." The book combines my favorite tropes from science fiction and fantasy, with some of my other favorites from childhood, plus a healthy dose of my own imagination.

The inspiration for the story came from all the wonderful and magical places and characters I spent time with as a child. I spent many summers traveling to Universal Studios in Florida, and many more in Walt Disney World. My family lived in Utah before I started elementary school, and I spent hours reading with my cousins in our backyard at night. I think of the land of Katajanokka, home of the Finnish—*wait, what?*

Anyone who knows me personally knows that I never lived in Utah, and they might also know that I never read with my cousins in my backyard at night. I *did* go to Universal Studios and Disney, so we'll chalk that up to a lucky guess. So what was with the text you just read above? Those weren't my words at all… an *artificial intelligence* wrote them. Well, to be more precise, an advanced language model known as GPT-2 wrote them. I fed it the sentence fragment in bold, ending with "fantasy," and *it—GPT-2*—continued synthesizing forwards what I *might have said next* right up until the word "Finnish." From the 22 bold words I gave it, the system was able to identify that I was sharing progress on a novel, and it was able to extrapolate that I might discuss the inspiration for that novel next. It chose words and phrases that constructed a coherent narrative of inspiration, a *history* to a person that never existed at all… even if it went a little off the rails with Katajanokka. In that technology I see incredible potential—potential that can go in either direction, depending on the hands that wield it.

The power of synthesized media was the true inspiration for this story, a plot idea that seeded as soon as I'd first heard of deepfakes and saw the renderings they could create. The book started slowly, but free time bloomed in excess during the COVID-19 lockdown of 2020. 200,000 words later, and somehow it's done.

Starfall has been an ambitious project for me... As GPT-2 and I already jointly shared, it's straddling genres at what feels the intersection of fantasy novels and science fiction. Fans of either should find the familiar tropes comforting. The novel combines several past projects of mine, including a short story I wrote in 2014, another piece from 2016, and even threads from a continuous RPG campaign I wrote and ran for out-of-state friends over a span of years into 2020. It's tackling a few topics of the hyper-technical even beyond media synthesis, and I've struggled to strike a balance between *easy to understand* and *technically accurate*—all of this while being a novice to the field at best. I hope any and all programming inaccuracies encountered don't stand out *too* glaringly, and any feedback from relative experts is always appreciated. This project would not even be able to exist in its current state without the patient technical advice from Roy Tu, a valued childhood friend. His expertise helped shape much of the technological heart of the book—when tech or coding goes right, it's him you can thank, and if things go wrong, it was probably me misunderstanding what he'd said. I'd also like to thank content creators and educators whose internet resources served as my 'crash course' in many of the relevant topics: Robert Miles's videos on AI Safety, Computerphile's discussions of encryption, and even 3blue1brown's video on blockchains deserve particular recognition in making a future that felt technologically *possible,* even if not particularly likely.

Thanks for reading! -Drew

Prologue

Michelangelo Build V12.4.1.2.6.23, initializing self-reflection heuristic:

Where does a narrative truly <u>begin?</u>

Cause and effect is an unbroken chain stretching from this universe's first, nascent moment to its far, distant end. To start our narrative at any point in this infinite chain is a choice equally significant as it is arbitrary... every starting point has a history that led to it, as every end has a future it will one day manifest. For any starting point, we can ask ourselves, "what led to this?" If we begin with a delirious and scared old man, trapped in the bottom of a well, simply because he is significant to our tale—should we not, then, learn about the day he was born? Should we not then learn about his parents, and the romantic tryst in a roadside inn that led to his conception? And what about the origins of the parents themselves? Such considerations, of course, can stretch continually backwards to the big bang, the only true narrative anchor. But in the interest of communicative efficiency, perhaps, we'll forego all of that background. We'll omit the flash from which everything sprang, the coalescing of matter into stars, the evolution of biological life on Earth into sentience, the conquerors and cruel among human history, even the eventual sultry scene between lovers in a dim motel room. Instead, we'll start with a place: a sparkling city of neon and rain.

It is called New Phoenix, gem of the surviving East Coast settlements. It is the year 2153, more than a century since the world died, and those who live in the city live in the shadow of its glowing megalithic structures: engineering masterworks of steel, glass, and carbon fiber composites. The air holds a perpetual stench of plastic and motor exhaust. The water pours with a pale, yellow tint. Glowing signs and the tails of flying taxis and transport shuttles mix with the smog in the air to render the whole of the place a swirling, luminescent cloud, an island of light in a darkened countryside. At night, the reflective towers make kaleidoscopic displays of the floating advertisements and blinking drones, a shifting symmetry of color that can dazzle the eye of anyone new to the city. And the longer you linger there in the city, the more the light hypnotizes. You'll never sleep in the dark again.

The population is 531 million, a number that grows faster than infrastructure can keep up with. The layout resembles a bullseye, with the commercial district in the center housing all of the richest structures and the majority of the elite businesses. As you travel outwards, ring by ring, buildings begin to decay, order begins to collapse, population tends to pack closer, and income falls drastically downwards. It is a circle of stained-concrete poverty around a bubble of luxury, a precious snowglobe in a wide crater of mud. And when the rich in the center were squeezed on all sides by the have-nots and the destitute, they built in the only direction that was available: up, up, and away, chasing the stars.

It is there, in the city's glowing heart, that we'll begin our narrative in earnest. For on the very top of one such spiraling tower of glass, alone on a maintenance platform to the edge of the dark rooftop, stands a man with a hood drawn tight over his head. His back is braced against the wind-swept rain, and his eyes scan the pulsing city streets below, seeking out his mark. He is a hunter, and his scope-aided eyes soon find his prey. He tucks the scope away and ties his jacket tight. He secures his belongings in a velcro-sealed pocket. And then, with little further hesitation, he steps over the edge of the tower, his hood fluttering in the wind as gravity takes him down, falling and spinning towards the surface three quarters of a mile below.

Chapter 1

"It was the strangest damn thing... personal flight tech the likes of which I've never seen before."

-Conversation logged in outer-ring surveillance station, flagged for system relevance

* * *

When falling, the droplets of rain seemed frozen in time—glass motes of dust floating in lazy suspension.

The occasional lit window streaked past in a blur of yellow, reminding the hunter that the moment's rest was swiftly passing... ground-level was approaching, and it did so at terminal velocity. As the hunter fell past the next lit window, he drew from its power: curling tendrils of fluorescent yellow flicked forth from the light fixtures on the silent office floor. The wire of glowing light met the hunter's outstretched hand, and then it was gone, like a plant root greedily pulling in water. The hunter felt the now-familiar rush that it brought... the alertness, the strength, the seemingly limitless potency.

On a rooftop nearly 2,000 feet below, Jack McDowel peered into the massive skylight, eyeing the banquet within. The wealthy socialites moved in orbits around those who possessed the most social gravity... the same scene in each of these vapid, self-congratulating affairs. The last one had netted him just over 1 million credits, despite the massive fee that the pawn brokers took for fencing illegally acquired goods... one more score of a similar size, and his problems would be firmly in the past.

He heard the clank of boots landing on the metal catwalk behind him. He whirled, hand drawing his energy weapon at his hip.

"I suppose they also misplaced *your* invitation?" The hunter said, a teasing note hiding under his dry, meticulous tone.

"Stay back," McDowel warned, waving the gun towards the hunter. McDowel's face was haggard and pocked with deep lines and scars. His thin frame and pallid complexion placed him firmly among the malnourished of the lower class that ordinarily stuck to the city's outer limits… but this one, his hair was falling out in patches. There was something wrong with him, something that put an extra desperation behind his already-wide eyes.

The hunter took another slow step forwards. "Your aim hand is trembling… you don't want to shoot me, nor would you even be able to hit me."

"A blind man could make this 30-foot shot. Energy slugs are wide."

"Well yes, Mr. McDowel, that they are…" the hunter took another slow step forwards. "But you see, Mr. McDowel, *I'm a lot like you.* The people down there, in that stuffy banquet hall, they can't do the things that we can do… but frankly, you're not supposed to be able to, either."

McDowel squeezed the trigger of his weapon. A bolt of bright green plasma flashed towards the hunter, but its course bent before it could strike him. It instead flew off and away into the rainy dark.

"Each night, seventy people in the city are hospitalized due to stray plasma rounds… you really ought to be more careful with your aiming."

"How did you do that?" McDowel asked, lowering his ineffective weapon.

"You didn't know we could push away plasma rounds? Well, I suppose you wouldn't, what with your illegal acquisition of your gifts…"

"I didn't steal it," McDowel said defensively, now beginning to guess who this hunter was—or who he represented. "Hell, I didn't even ask for it… I was at the hospital for my cancer, and there must have been some sort of mix-up. You can have it back… but I just need an hour. If I can just clear one more of these banquets, I'll have enough credits for the c-pill. I won't need it after that."

"I'm afraid my employer is not a particularly patient person… I'll need to reclaim the spark *now*. I will not lie to you, Mr. McDowel. In my profession, integrity is one of the few commodities I truly have to barter with. I will not play the friend, and offer you your life in exchange for the spark… the penalty for the theft you committed, wittingly or otherwise, is death—and negotiating that is simply out of my control. I can offer you this, at least: should you surrender now, I will make it a quick and painless affair. I will even deliver a message to a loved one, should you wish it. Katie, who lives on 17th causeway… she surely would like to hear from you again.

"If you resist, Mr. McDowel, your life will end in profound physical pain. And should you flee, Mr. McDowel, and somehow escape my search… well, perhaps I will pay a visit to Katie in 413 17th Causeway, block D-Epsilon, floor 15, room 102-J. My intent for this alternate visit will be far less diplomatic. Am I understood?"

McDowel nodded, but he made no move to surrender. Instead he only stood there, thinking.

"Well, go on… you may ask your question," the hunter said.

"And which is that?"

"The one I once wondered in your exact position… what if *you* manage to kill *me?*" The hunter let his question hang in the wet air between them. "You'd have a few hours to flee before they send another… might just be enough time to grab your loved ones and leave the city, never to return. I've no secret operative near her, a hidden threat to force your compliance. You can fight with an unburdened heart, or you can surrender willingly. This ends the same either way."

"Well, then. You can't fault a cornered man for trying."

The neon signs around the duo began to flicker. Streaming lines of light snaked sluggishly from a thousand glowing sources at once, coiling at McDowel's feet and sliding up into his body.

"May luck be in your favor, friend," the hunter said, the familiar words a callback to memories his masters hadn't yet been able to cut from him. He drew his jacket in tight once more and toggled a switch by his hip, activating the neon reserve that padded his black leather jacket. He preferred when things ended this way, truth be told… it never felt right killing the hopeless, blathering messes that trade their lives away as though it weren't the most precious thing they ever possessed. Well, perhaps their lives were the second most precious—for after the killing would come the extraction of something so much greater. Sparks, ichor, the labels hardly mattered; the hunter was here as a reaper of *souls*. And the battery pack tucked to his hip was scored with the tally marks of souls he'd reclaimed.

It was 65, and counting.

More beams of light crept upwards onto the platform, pooling near McDowel's feet. The city groaned in protest as circuits fried and generators switched on. Lights flickered and car alarms whined in the night as more and more energy flowed into the form of Jack McDowel. His eyes began to glow, and that glow grew brighter and whiter, until twin points of light shone that could rival the moon. Then the hunter paused, watching as the man's glow still continued to rise. *Halo tier?* he wondered. *He's not supposed to have that many.*

And then, as though just on cue to confirm the hunter's suspicion, a ring of brilliant energy began to coalesce around McDowel, like morning fog condensing into dewdrops. The ring of light was an omen that this acquisition would be no certain affair, as his employer would never let him bring a matching volume of ichor out on the street. The hunter bent slowly and touched the metal structure beneath his feet. With a gradual surge, the familiar power returned to him, and he drank in its succor. The neon lights of the city block flickered as their glow drew into snaking lines that began to supercharge every fiber of the hunter's being. It was blissful, pure *power,* and it made the hunter's body feel a spring tightened and ready in coil.

His eyes took on the brightness of neon. He leapt.

And then, both were airborne.

The two were now soaring through the blur of white hot light and sizzling steel, the hunter straining desperately to keep up. They weaved among the rooftops and tin roofs, the animated billboards and the flexing, neon signs that advertised GIRLS, GIRLS, GIRLS — LIVE SHOWS 24/7. His quarry was unexpectedly strong for a man so frail, with enough glow stored up to burn a continuous halo. For a lightbender, this was no easy feat.

Using his own glow, the hunter could propel himself away from any active light source, and the city was full of them. He couldn't fly, per se, but by pushing off various lights all around him, he could get at something very close indeed. So could his prey. The target shot upwards, still out of reach to the hunter. Correcting his course, the hunter shoved off a large neon sign for a convenience store. He never touched the sign—it was still fifteen feet away, across an open intersection the two were zipping above—but the remotely-transmitted force of his movement caused the wireframe image of a chicken to collapse in on itself in a shower of sparks and glowing metal. Actions still held their requisite opposite reactions.

Suddenly, ahead, the halo around the target erupted, causing a massive blackout spanning several city blocks. The quarry skidded to a stop on a high rooftop and watched his adversary tumble through the sky.

The hunter had little glow left, and there was no neon around him to draw upon as he flailed through the air, a rocket suddenly without an engine. With quick motions, he whipped out his blacklight and threw it with all the force he could muster. He couldn't see it trace its path in the dark, but he heard it clang against a nearby metal structure. Then, with all his might, he pulled.

Lightbenders could push off light sources, but only against a blacklight could they pull. The hunter's flight path curved as he began to move towards the blacklight, sweeping through the air as he approached the small attachment connected to the metal by powerful magnet. That was his last pullstation, and the emergency neon he kept powered by battery pack in his cloak had burned out as he drew on its power to pull himself to safety.

The hunter now stood up and assessed the place his pullstation had landed. It was yet another featureless rooftop, hard to judge in the city plunged in darkness. He then turned to the place his adversary had landed, when suddenly—

The hunter was thrown off his feet with an explosive kick, skidding across the rooftop towards the edge. The metal scraped at his flesh and his world was spinning blackness. His prey had cleverly used his remaining glow to pull himself to the pullstation, using that momentum to power an attack. Now the hunter groaned, trying to pick himself up, but an all-too-familiar pain in his chest told him at least one rib was shattered, and his head was still reeling. He heard the footsteps of his approaching adversary.

The backup power for the city block kicked on, and the rooftop exploded with light. Neon signs flashed, engines and generators whirred to life, and the air was alive with the buzzing energy of electricity's glow once again. The hunter immediately began to draw, lines of light streaking from their sources to him, empowering his body to stand up where injury would ordinarily keep him down.

His prey began to do the same; lines of bright color poured into the two men and the active draw plunged the city into flickering darkness once again, a state where it this time remained. Their eyes, brilliant as moonlight, locked across that gulf of unsteady dark.

With a yell, the quarry charged forward and threw a punch, his fist streaking with light expended in making the punch unnaturally fast and powerful. The hunter dodged the blow, his own reflexes boosted with glow, and he felt the glowing particles it traced behind patter against his face. He kicked his adversary back and concentrated. All of the glow in his body, drawn from an entire half of a city block, began to flow into his arm, which was now lit up from within. Veins and capillaries stood in silhouette against red-hot glowing flesh, but that light within continued to harden into a fixed line. It then extended beyond his hand as a length of blindingly-brilliant energy: a lightsword, a weapon of incredible power.

They were risky to use, as they took all of a lightbender's glow to produce, and the gambit would leave him incredibly fatigued in a few minutes. But against their awesome strength, only one tactic could remain viable: another lightsword.

His adversary drew his glow out into his hand as well, now holding a burning beam of neon just as the hunter did. The rooftop, once dark, now blazed with the bright glow of two white-hot bars of light.

The two men lunged at each other, their blades tracing thin rails of burning, glowing air and releasing flecks of neon-colored dust as they moved. In the dark, light twisted and weaved. Every time they struck, bright flashes released to rival those of a great thunderhead, though this duel presaged no thunder. The only sounds were the panting of breath in the cold night air. The rest of the city waited in silent darkness for the bout on roofs high to finish.

The men's shadows were elongated and twisting under the swirling light sources. The shadows danced off of walls and indeed the city itself as the two forms exchanged swings and deflections. A wide swinging arc struck a metal signpost, immediately melting it in two with nearly no resistance. Another was pushed down into the rooftop, melting right through the floor into the structure below. A third carved a gash of dripping metal into an upright AC unit, which sparked and clattered as it tumbled apart into melting, sticky pieces.

It was, as always, hard to see with the blinding and fast-moving blade of his opponent, but eventually the hunter noticed the score in the ground, still molten and red-hot. It wasn't much, but it would do. He parried forward, deflecting his opponent's swings, and crouched over the molten score in the floor. He used his own blade to block his opponent's view of the thin orange line tracing between him and the glowing metal as the hunter began to draw on its latent power. The molten metal at his feet cooled and went dark as he stood.

The hunter charged forwards, his eyes glowing faintly once more. His adversary warded off a furious blow, and then another, and another after that, both clearly trained well in swordplay. That was a surprise, as the target seemed altogether new to lightbending... perhaps a background as a fencer? Being filled with glowing light did tend to make one's reflexes faster, made combat substantially easier to process, but this went beyond mere reflexes. There was *form,* and there was *finesse.* Either way, the hunter knew that he had to stop admiring his opponent's strength and close the fight. Their fatigue would hit soon, and the hunter's would hit first. He had to make his move now.

He lashed desperately at his prey's side, and the man deftly deflected the blow as he had the ones before. However, as his adversary's sword swung out to the side, the hunter used his remaining glow to push against the sword, just as he had before with other sources of light. The force from the glow he'd been able to muster wasn't much at all, probably akin to an invisible hand swatting at the blade, but it was enough. Momentarily caught off guard at the sword's unexpected extra momentum, the target could not react in time as the hunter drove his sword upwards through his prey's neck. The man died instantly, his lightsword disappearing into embers a moment later as his eyes glowed with the brightness of neon. This glow was different: it was not the glow of a lightbender who had absorbed light's energy, but instead the glow of a man with a rod of plasma searing the inside of his skull.

The hunter withdrew his blade and let it dissipate as the other man's body thumped to the floor. The faint sound of blood trickling and dripping down the latticework of metal was the last thing the hunter heard clearly before the fatigue crashed over him like a wave. He reeled backwards, waiting in that stupor for the significant exhaustion to pass. He watched through dazed eyes as the lights finally flickered back on, the music from the street below resuming once more. In the office building whose roof the hunter now stood upon, the custodial staff had not yet noticed the trickle of rain entering the floor's center where the roof had been melted through. And when the hunter's exhaustion finally passed—after what felt an eternity on the cold, rainy metal—the hunter stumbled over towards the body on the floor, preparing to resorb his spark. Tonight was a double, and his schedule demanded he finish here soon.

Chapter 2

The video clip is of a man in close-up. His facial features resemble those of Jimmy Townsend, one of the project leads spearheading development. It is only three seconds in duration: the face blinks, looks towards the camera, and then says "hello world" in a level voice.

-Annotations describing the first export of Michelangelo's Alpha Build

* * *

The train carriage hummed and scraped briefly against uneven magtracks as it began its ascent, the black outside the windows quickly brightening to a tired yellow-brown of sun through an early morning's haze. Beverly Beadie watched out the window across as the train car rose from between highway lanes and settled at an elevated track, the engine's whir picking up as the train accelerated onwards. From up here, with the buildings suddenly very near to the window, facade and color whirred by at dizzying speed. *"This morning's transit is sponsored by Blitz Energy,"* cooed the female voice of the train's PA system. *"Don't settle for boring... Energy never tasted so rich."*

Bev eyed the pad in her hand, where her supervisor's message was still awaiting her reply.

Hey Bev,

The team and I are looking forward to having you back in the office! We know this is going to be a difficult time for you, and we just want you to know that we're all here for you as you transition back into your professional life. HR has a number of

grief management resources, if you need, as well as virtual
therapist demos available for download.

Instead of a boring day of ingest, we figured we'd give you a
nice treat for your day back: another middle-school tour, the
best and brightest from Penmouth Computational. We know
you loved inspiring the kids, and they look at you different,
seeing as you're almost still their age...

I'll be over in our Broadside office until about 3, but if
there's anything you need at all today, don't hesitate to call.

-Jake

With a heavy sigh, she clicked the display off and folded the
screen back to fit in her jacket pocket. She *had* loved the kids,
bright-eyed things that they were, but maybe her supervisor
was too detached from reality to see why placing Bev near
young kids was a bad idea right now. Still, it undeniably beat
the ingest Q&A sessions, and maybe a few smiling faces
would be just the thing to lift her spirits.

She watched as the train ambled to the station platform and
the magbrakes engaged. Then she and the rest of the train were
on their feet, pouring from the car like water from a rusted
faucet, leaking down the flat concrete and washing down the
stairs to the sun-deprived streets below. The windows featured
holo adverts and moving posters showing off ridiculous-
looking garments. Street vendors peddled everything from
comptablets to groovepills. As Bev walked, she saw a group of
three wireheaders slumped against the brick just down an
alleyway, their eyes rolled back in ecstasy. Frowning, she
pushed on.

She turned out from under the train's railway and blinked at
the bright, hot sunlight, needing a moment for her eyes to
adjust fully. Ahead, only 3 blocks beyond, stood the tall glass
tower of ArtGen, an AI research subsidiary of Technica

Solutions—at least, a subsidiary in name, but now contributing a supermajority of the parent company's income.

* * *

Entering the building for the first time was a striking, humbling experience, as there were few buildings in New Phoenix that could match its grand impression. The central tower featured twisting, rolling concrete forming round, nearly biologic shapes. Accenting those, and providing the occasional pocket of visual relief from the palette of white and gray, stood oases of pristinely trimmed and cultivated greenery, and wood paneling that lent the space a striking, bold look. It was undeniably retro-modern, but its taste was nearly unimpeachable. And, as would only be appropriate for the company's central operations, its architecture was designed entirely by AI.

Bev walked through the main streetside door, passing her wrist over a reading pad at waist level. Its momentary scan identified Beverly Beadie as belonging to floor 131, north face. Within microseconds, the tower's controller software had dispatched elevator 3-b towards the lobby, scheduling its arrival for 19 seconds beyond present. It took Beverly 23 seconds to traverse the lobby, something that the software calculated to be 1.5 standard deviations above expectation with given lobby traffic levels. Curious, to the fullest extent that software could be deemed to be *curious*, the Overwatch guardian system analyzed lobby video camera feeds—there were 92 distinct camera feeds to validate. It took the system 1.14 seconds to analyze the past 2 hours of video from each of those cameras, which allowed the software to note two critical things. Firstly, there was an area of unexpected luminance captured by 7 distinct forward-facing cameras, deemed to be reflection from spilled liquid on the ground. Video captured Beverly Beadie stepping around this liquid, delaying her progress. The second finding was that the source of this spill, a technician who had dropped a water bottle, had failed to report the spill incident to janitorial staff. The Overwatch guardian system automatically generated the janitorial request ticket and additionally added a disciplinary warning to the technician's internal file. As a nearby janitor's datawatch beeped with the arrival of a new assignment, Bev reached the elevator door. With an enthusiastic *ding!,* its doors slid open, and a warm, computer-generated voice greeted her: "Good morning, Beverly! Would you like to hear about your tasks for the day?"

* * *

"ArtGen, our company name, stands for two things. Does anyone here know what they are?" Bev looked around the glass-walled conference room packed with middle-school-aged children. She figured it was best to wait and let them venture a guess… the more engagement, the more they'd feel involved.

"Art generation," a tall, glasses-wearing student volunteered.

"Very good. Michelangelo and his precursors specialize in generative content, a computer's approach to 'creative' processes formerly only accessible to humans. And the second?"

"Artificial general intelligence," a stocky boy replied.

"That's exactly correct. AI has changed the landscape of technology more than any other discovery before it all the way back to the discovery of the steam engine, or maybe even fire itself. Here, myself and other fellow programmers ask ourselves 'what's the next great leap?'"

With a knock, an ArtGen technician entered the room, carrying a stack of paperlight tablets. He began to pass them out.

"We're gonna try a little interactive experiment here," Bev continued. "As the best and brightest of Penmouth Computational, I trust everyone here knows how to code in neuroscript?"

The kids nodded, some with proud smiles on their faces. Bev couldn't help but return the smile. "That's excellent, then. We're going to work on our first AI together, and through that, we're gonna learn a few important lessons about AI safety... which, as it would turn out, is a very tough nut to crack, and is partly the reason for the multi-trillion-credit building you're standing in right now."

The technician finished passing out the tablets and waved to Bev. "Thank you, Jason," she called as the young man retreated out the door. "As you activate your tablets, you should be greeted with ArtGen's proprietary node-based AI programming suite, built on the open-source Principa Physica. Your tablets, of course, aren't doing the actual AI simulating, but they're each linked to our servers with unlimited data bandwidth. So, let's get to it."

She watched with a smile as the kids stared at their tablets, eyes nearly bulging out of their heads in amazement. They'd never before had access to such computing power, and, unless they were bona-fide savants, they likely never again would. Best to enjoy it while it lasted.

"Take a minute to familiarize yourself with the interface, and then gather your bags... we're going to head in to the demo room."

* * *

Bev led the students down the hall away from the main work area. An elevator was waiting for them, and it brought them down towards the central cafeteria on floor 15. She then led them into the kitchens behind the cafeteria, and then found a door labeled "AI SAFETY DEMO. AUTHORIZED PERSONNEL ONLY." She always loved this part of the visiting tour.

As she led the students in, they paused to gawk at the strange scene beyond the door. The room was a kitchen, but certainly it was no ordinary kitchen at all. Large robotic arms hung from the ceiling, each poised over a particular appliance or item. One held pots, and another pans. One wielded a spatula, and one held on to the door of a refrigerator. Yet another was dangling near the controls for a stovetop range with access to a microwave oven as well. On the far left, a robotic arm hung down over a larger tablet, this one featuring a hardware red button beside it. Cameras covered the ceiling above the cooktop.

"So, let's go to the basics. How do we motivate an AI to do what we want it to do?"

A few answered simultaneously, saying things like "a reward table," "a reward function," "a utility function."

"Very good. Let's call it a reward function. The idea is this: think of it like the score when you're playing a video game. We define certain outcomes—or worldstates—and what *score* that outcome is worth, and then we tell the AI to go maximize its score. It will then begin to do the things we defined to have a positive score, and will avoid the things that give it a negative score. Suddenly, the whole computational system starts to do the things you want it to do," Bev trailed off.

"Right up until it doesn't," a student said, finishing her thought.

"Right up until it doesn't," Bev repeated. "I'm going to invent the job for our first AI. We're going to create an AI that will use robotic implements to make scrambled eggs." Some of the students cracked a smile, and a few even laughed at the novel task.

"Take a minute, now, to decide on the reward function you want to set. Everyone see where on your systems you can define reward?"

The students nodded.

"Take a second to input your reward, paying special note to the cameras above the cookrange. You'll also find a number of pre-fabs relating to using the robotic arms, as well as their own variable systems defined explicitly in the code. Then, when you have something you think will work, I'd like a brave volunteer to come input their function into the robotic-arm terminal here."

The students immediately began to buzz with activity, some tapping away by themselves while others formed into small groups and tackled the problem collaboratively. Eventually, a taller girl with red hair stepped forwards, the chosen representative of a group of three. "We think we have it," she said nervously.

"Great. Corner-transfer it to the panel over there."

Her name was Abigail, and she walked up to the main control panel and tapped the corner of her tablet against its screen. The reward function she had coded with her two friends was immediately updated onto the robotic-arm system.

Using her own tablet to monitor what the students had sent, Bev checked over their approach. "Very good," she said. "You've decided to use the cameras above to check if there is anything recognizable to the system as 'scrambled eggs' on the plate beside the stovetop. You've also set up some actions queued for the robot arm to work through to prepare those eggs, and even have a decently-tuned coefficient of exploration for the system to play with. What do we think, class? Should this work?"

Most nodded their heads yes. Some nodded no, and others remained thinking. "Let's turn it on and find out! Would you please press the start button on that main panel there?"

Abigail walked forwards and pressed the green 'execute' button. Immediately, the arms whirred to life. One swung the fridge door open and selected the eggs. Another turned on the stove, and yet a third placed a pan. The egg was passed along to the pan on the stove, where it was smashed against the side—splattering across the cooktop, but at least some remained in the pan. Then, after a minute, the robot holding the pan tipped the pan over the plate to the stove's right, depositing the scrambled eggs.

"Good enough to eat, don't you think?" Bev said, licking her lips for comedic effect. "And the AI just got 100 points for making that egg, so everyone is happy here." Immediately, the robot arms again opened the fridge, turned the stove temperature dial once again—setting it even hotter—picked up and placed the pan down in the exact same spot, and cracked the egg against the side of the pan. "Turn it off, will you?" Bev asked. "One was fine."

Abigail approached the panel, but the robot arm blocked her from accessing the panel. "Huh," she said. "I didn't program it to do that." She tried to reach around it, but it rotated with her, blocking her attempts to get around it. By now, much of the class was laughing. "What's going on?"

"AI agents are clever. They can observe their environment and strategize to maximize their score. This one can see the camera feed and knows about that big red button… it knows that button is ArtGen standard for 'shutdown,' and it reasons—not incorrectly—that if you shut it down, it can't make any more eggs. It won't get the highest score if it lets you turn it off."

By now, the next egg was spattering on the pan and the robot arm dumped it onto the plate again. "+100 points," Bev added. She watched with amusement as Abigail tried to get around the robot arm, but it deftly kept her at bay. "Ok, ok, don't get yourself hurt there…" she tapped a button on her tablet and the arms all returned to their idle state.

"Yes, I've got an override, but don't you worry about that. Your AI was decently conceived, but it didn't want to be turned off. How can we fix that?"

The students thought for a moment, several still laughing at the bizarre scene. It was Abigail who had the next idea. "What if we give the button +100 points as well, so the AI won't care if we turn it off?"

"That sounds like a great idea! Go ahead and add it in," Bev said. In less than a minute, Abigail had made the needed change. "You can turn it on again," Bev said.

Abigail did, and the class waited to watch the robot egg assembly line burst back into life… but they all burst into laughter when the robot arm near the panel simply pressed the shutdown button and immediately went still.

"So what happened here?" Bev asked, eyeing the quickly-reddening Abigail as well as the rest of the class.

It was a dark-skinned boy with a thick, hard-to-place accent that answered. "We gave the AI two options. It could cook eggs, something that may take almost a minute, to get 100 points, or it can shut itself off in half a second for the same score value. It chose the most efficient path."

"Very good," Bev said. "Abigail, I'm sorry to say, but your AI is suicidal." The class laughed. "So, any new ideas for how we fix this?"

Abigail, ready to redeem her honor, had the obvious answer ready to go. "We forbid the robot to touch the button, but keep the same reward values."

"That sounds like it should do it," Bev replied. "Make the changes." Less than a minute later, again, it was all set to go. "Start it back up."

The students again waited intently as the robot arms whirred back to life... but this time, something was very, very wrong. The arms began to flail about wildly. The one with the pan began to smack it up and down against the metal cookrange, something that made a frighteningly loud sound. The one at the fridge began to throw ingredients towards the class, students ducking away and laughing at the chaos. Abigail immediately pressed the red stop button, apologizing, and the arms froze in place mid-riot. "I'm sorry, I'm so so sorry, I didn't think I changed anything that drastic—"

Bev interrupted her. "You're fine, and it wasn't your fault. You changed nothing, and your model up until now was quite good... so what went wrong? Class, everyone should have access to Abigail's code here on their devices now. Where is the fault?"

For the next minute, the class stared at their tablets in concentrative silence, tabbing back and forth between reward functions and action queues, between experimentation coefficients and sensor data. Finally, a quiet Abigail spoke up, realization dawning. "It did what it did, because it knew that we'd turn it off immediately, giving it the reward points."

"Exactly correct," Bev replied. "Exactamundo. Artificially-intelligent agents are fascinating because there's always these great, emergent behaviors when we tell them how to manipulate their environments to achieve their goals... but we often forget that we, humanity, are a part of their environment. And thus, if we teach them to manipulate their environments, and to try new strategies, it is almost an inevitability that they will eventually try to manipulate humanity to achieve the goal we originally set."

"Can't you just blacklist unfavorable actions?" a student asked.

"A decent idea, but anything you miss has the chance of being exploited until you *do* notice it, and that's not a very appealing prospect. And besides, there's often a fundamental disconnect between how we define our reward function and what we actually want the AI to do... and that can lead to trouble. For instance, we had a student in here once program his reward function to do an area calculation. The more of the visible field from the overhead cameras that registered as 'scrambled egg,' the more score it got. That should incentivize it to fill up the whole counter with scrambled eggs, right? Well, nope, it just made one plate and then hoisted it high until it was nearly pressed right against the camera, earning maximum score."

Again, the students laughed.

"These cases of the AI 'outwitting' us, so-to-speak, are funny in this context here, but think about the things that AI manage in the present day. We have AI managing some defensive systems, AI scheduling trains and buses. We have AI managing airtraffic to keep skyways safe and prevent car-building collisions. We have AI running fusion plants and hospitals. Is there room in those systems for such *cheeky* loopholes? We think of AI as being basically super-smart people who live in computers, but there is nothing *human* about the intelligence that drives these systems.

They are rule-based, and they are calculating. They will follow your code to the letter, but often will miss the spirit behind it. And that's not their fault, but rather is ours, as our language is so inexact and prone to misinterpretation... something that has no place in the binary world of computation. After your lunch breaks, we'll take a look at the best solution we've found to managing AI reward functions, and then we'll give you guys the chance to chat with the one guy I know you've all been dying to: Michelangelo himself. Until then, we've got burgers in the main cafeteria, some fast food in the food court just past the cafeteria, and some smashed, burned eggs here in the kitchen. Take your pick, and I'll see you all back in the cafeteria in 1 hour."

Chapter 3

"I do solemnly swear to protect and serve the people, to uphold the values of the governmental compact, and to respect the authority of the department's sponsoring organization."

-Excerpt from the standard Oath of Duty for CSP Agencies

* * *

Attention, shoppers: your credit score may entitle you to additional discounts!

The metallic voice echoed across the white marble floors of the megastore, mingling with the distant footsteps and low murmur of conversation. CSP Agent Sam Pollock sighed, his lips automatically forming the words that he knew came next:

Register your RFID chip with your purchasing account and you could save big... that's shopping the Continuum way.

As Pollock stepped past the next aisle, one filled with clocks of every shape and size, he saw a pile of clothing lumped up on the floor. The shirt on top had a mysterious wet stain. With a deep sigh, he raised his left wrist and tapped a few buttons on the subcutaneous interface implant. Somewhere in the back of the store, a cleaning drone on wheels clicked on and slid out among the dozens of delivery drones that slowly ambled their way through the store. *Another disaster averted,* Pollock thought.

Growing up, Pollock had always wanted to be a soldier: heroic men in green that saved the United Americas from foreign invaders? What child wouldn't want to be something so special, so exciting? Then, he learned first-hand about the horrors of the actual front lines—and the things that an unmanned combat drone could *do* to soldiers of flesh and blood—and suddenly, local law enforcement seemed a better trajectory. Heroic men in blue that saved the innocent of New Phoenix from local criminals? What young man wouldn't want to be something so special, so exciting?

Exciting, Pollock thought, walking with his hand on the butt of his energy weapon. Some days, exciting was confronting a man whom you watched stuff six different cellphones and three tablets into his tucked shirt. Last week, exciting was trying to stop the homeless woman who had been tearing open every package of underwear she could find, mumbling something about "finding the special one." This morning, exciting had been tracking down the mall's bathroom sink defecator, a persistent vandal whose reputation didn't precede him—but his scent certainly had.

The CSP were Corporate-Sponsored Police: megacompanies wanted stores, institutions, and properties deep in the active heart of the city, but the sheer scale of New Phoenix made it too large and complex a thing for traditional law enforcement to handle. Enter the CSP, a compromise between law enforcement and corporate security. Companies could train, arm, and utilize their own security forces, even to full lethal force authorization, but those CSP had to abide by certain city-wide standards and protocols—and they had to take on city policework two days of the week.

And so, when Pollock began his job as a CSP agent, he figured *two days of heroism isn't bad for a dayjob*... except the two days a week he spent outside of Continuum were often spent chasing the homeless, busting counterfeit credit mining rings, and writing parking tickets at the SkyView Commercial Center, the mall complex that Continuum belonged to. More distressing still was that several bonafide law enforcement offices had it worse… some were still forced to use kinetic rounds from ancient powderguns, which were feathers against modern armor and shielding. Pollock knew he was fortunate to have a department so thoroughly funded as his. In fact, the subcutaneous implant had been fully company sponsored, and he got a lot of work out of that even outside of work hours—plus there was his salary, more than three times the average for regular law enforcement—but still, when he got home at night, he couldn't help but stare in the mirror and frown at himself and the glorified mall cop he'd become. Sometimes he'd boot up his old VR classics, combat games that set him in the heart of a foreign jungle, a chance to play soldier and hero, to be the person younger Pollock had always looked up to. He'd have never admired a CSP, that was for sure.

His reveries were interrupted by a ping on his AR overlay, an emergency note from the store's surveillance grid. Electronics, the ping identified. Aisle 511B. Alert level 1.

If one, you run, the training had been, and so Pollock was swiftly on his feet, taking off towards electronics. His overlay then beeped again, offering an update. 'Intercept at register 1,' it commanded. Pollock changed course and ran down an aisle filled with desks and endtables with built-in computers on wide touchscreen surfaces. He pushed his way past the two browsing patrons in that aisle, nearly knocking one over in the process, before exiting to the wide cartway beyond. He then darted towards the right, sighting the first register in the row of four dozen.

He planted his feet there and waited, panting. Then he heard it: coming from the direction of electronics, he heard the rattling of unoiled wheels. Then he saw the cart barreling into focus, stacked high with screens and monitors and VR kits. Based on the speed of the man pushing the cart, there seemed to be no intention of stopping to pay.

On his AR display, Pollock could see the system calculating the value of the goods in the cart, ringing up to a cool 6 million credits. Then he saw the Panopticon system identify the man—John Brandt—and calculate his marginal social value of about 4.7 million credits. As his financial risk to the company was greater than his perceived value to the world, the AR system's command was equal parts simple and final: 'shoot to kill.'

Pollock raised his weapon and trained it on the man's center mass. *100 feet, 80 feet...* this wouldn't be the first man Pollock had to shoot and kill for security, as he hadn't even gone a month on the job before an attempted violent robbery, but this would be the first where the target was no active danger to anyone beyond Continuum's bottom line. He thought of the kind of person his younger self would've looked up to, and knew that there'd be hell to pay for this, but he sucked in his breath and squeezed the trigger.

And instead of flying straight into the man's chest, the energy pulse flew downwards and struck the cart, melting the screens and monitors tucked away. Plasma washback splashed onto the man, sending him down to the ground in electric pain—but he was alive, and he'd stay that way. As far as the system was concerned, the man was no longer in danger of removing any company property, both because he probably wouldn't walk for another few days, and also because the company property was now a pool of bubbling plastic on the solid marble floor.

* * *

CSP Captain Carol Moss was a stout woman with frazzled, blonde hair. Her rosy cheeks puffed somewhat from all the spare calories that a heavy drinking habit brings, while her honey-sweet voice scratched its way through the gravely throat of a heavy smoker. She was a woman of bold vices and few scruples, making her the perfect cultural fit to lead Pollock's department—a position she'd filled for six years, stalling out on the promotion track.

On her desk, amid the scattered pencils and loose sticky notes of paper, was a tablet displaying the security feeds from the incident near register 1. On repeated loop, Pollock watched himself shoot the shopping cart, sending the man sprawling over.

"While you were walking over," Moss intoned casually, "I pulled up your personnel file. Training range video clips attached, as you know."

Pollock merely sat there in silence, waiting for her to drive to her point.

"I don't think we've got a single video clip of you missing a shot within a hundred feet. And considering the *volume* of clips we've got, that's something."

Pollock moved to reply, but she raised a finger. She then placed two fingers on the tablet display, zooming the video inwards until only Pollock's weapon and hand filled the screen.

"That's the sure shot, center as my mom's politics. But then watch," Moss said, gesturing at the tablet.

Pollock watched blankly as his hand flexed downwards while pulling the trigger, sending the energy round low.

"Now if I ask you, you'll tell me you missed—and I'd expect nothing less, as we certainly follow our orders around here— but what a strange and convenient miss it was. What a decidedly… out-of-character miss, as it was."

She sat back in her leather chair, which squeaked in protest to her shifting weight, as she steepled her fingers and regarded Pollock. "I get it, Agent Pollock, I do… it isn't easy, delivering a verdict like that. Wasn't so long ago that nonviolent crimes got nonviolent resolution, but you know the discouragement doctrine as well as I do… the deterrent doesn't work if we go making moral exceptions. Is that clear?"

"Yes ma'am," Pollock said, still watching the video clip.

"To ensure that you don't *miss* like this again, I want you to report to the training range next week. At 100 feet of distance, I want 5,000 rounds on-target, you staying there as long as it takes. Is that understood?"

Pollock swallowed, knowing the intense heat that energy weapons generated after being fired even in short bursts… it was going to be a sweaty evening, and he'd have to bring gloves for his hands.

"Understood, ma'am. But starting next week?" Pollock asked, wondering why his punishment was so delayed.

Moss's smile crept wider, a sparkle of mischief entering her blue eyes. "Then there's the other thing, the second part of your penance."

She slid another tablet along her desk, this one showing a photograph of a bespectacled man. His balding hair was slicked back and upwards stylishly, and his eyes held a strange, distant look.

"You get some new gruntwork… local PD is tired of working this case, so they've thrown it onto me, so I'm throwing it onto you. Man's name is Quaine O'Connor, a research scientist up at the old black tower. He's been missing for about a month now, and the friend who reported his absence is *very, very persistent* in following up. Local PD officer I spoke to seemed about ready to make this a two-person missing persons' case, *if you catch my drift*..." Moss reached down and slid her finger across the tablet screen, swiping to the next photograph. "She's a pretty one, but don't get any ideas—she's more mouse trap than mouse. Name is Hannah Preacher, close associate of the missing man. Former lover, I think? Don't care. Every day she's come in, she's been angrier and angrier… if you don't find our man, or even if you smile at her the wrong way, I get the impression she might just rip your balls clean off."

Pollock reached over and picked up the tablet, swiping through additional photos of the missing person. "Do we have a record of the policework done in the investigation?"

"Not much to report there… what little there was done is in there, also sending to your account now. Loads of dead ends and stonewalling witnesses. The woman, Preacher, checked out on investigation, so likely not the perp… basically, you're at square one."

"Great, so a dead-end investigation—and an associate of the missing person about ready to kill me if I can't find a major breakthrough—in a case that's already a month cold. Anything else to add?"

"I'm assigning a rookie with you on this… nice enough kid, hardworking. You'll like him, I think. And if you disappoint the woman, I have a feeling you could use the backup. Dismissed, agent."

* * *

"Hey partner… coffee?"

Rob Boardsmith, novice CSP agent, handed his new partner a to-go mug of steaming coffee. Dark as motor oil, and about equally as sweet, it was just the sort you could get at a streetside vendor down near ground level—the poorer brew, for the poorer folks who lived and worked far below the grand skyways and elevated plazas above.

It was just the way Sam Pollock preferred, as it reminded him of home.

"If this policing thing doesn't work out for you, you could have a good career as a coffee runner," Pollock said, taking the cup and bringing it to his lips, feeling that familiar warning heat of a liquid still too hot to sip. The pain of that first pull only added to the wake-up effect.

"If this policing thing doesn't work out for me, I'd blame my mentor," Rob said, sipping and wincing at a cup of his own. His brown hair was short-cropped, his face wearing the shadow of a beard always on the verge of springing forwards. He was muscular in build, seemed to be in his mid-twenties, and he still wore that freshmen eagerness that all new rookies seemed to have—only time and repeated reality checks could weather that down to the impatient dissatisfaction worn by the seasoned veterans of the force. Truth be told, Pollock didn't mind the company on assignments like these... an extra set of hands was hardly the punishment it was made out to be.

"So, Agent Pollock—"

"Sam; Sam's fine."

"Well so, Sam, mentor mine—I've read the reports here, highlighted a few points of interest. How should we get started?"

"Woman near the center of the case, one Hannah Preacher, she's just downstairs waiting by holding. We debrief her as thoroughly as possible, looking for any angle these city badges might have missed, and we go from there. Anything new jump out, that's top priority, otherwise we'll revisit your highlighted points in whatever order you want."

Chapter 4

"With the failure of Panopticon identification, it is the opinion of me and my partner that the cold-case missing person file is entirely without actionable leads, making it an inefficient use of limited department resources. This submission is a formal request for reassignment."

-Internal report flagged for elevated system relevance

* * *

The woman who sat in the holding cell tapped at the table impatiently. She was tall, with auburn hair in straightened lines around a soft, round face. Rosy discoloration—a rash of some type—spread butterfly wings from nose to cheeks, not-entirely concealed with cosmetics. Her eyes were a sparkling hazel-brown, while her makeup and dress placed her firmly among the upper echelons of the city's lower class.

"Thanks for coming in, Ms. Preacher. My name is Agent Pollock, and this here is Agent Boardsmith," Sam said, shaking the woman's hand. She shook Rob's in turn and then sat back, studying the duo.

"The last officers working on the case, Hicks and Lanefield, they started it out just like this. The *nice to meet you,* the *pretending to care*… I don't even think they spent a solid hour looking for Quaine before deciding his case would be difficult to close. Other cases called, the type they could finish fast and get their clearance stats up."

"Our assigning officer has us on just this case, ma'am, and acknowledges that it might be a long time before it's cleared," Rob said diplomatically. "We'll find your friend."

The two CSP agents sat down across from Hannah and pulled out their case tablets, flipping through the photographs and archival reports.

"You and Mr. O'Connor," Pollock began, "you two were *intimate*, correct?"

"Your case files don't have that in there?" Hannah asked.

"It does, but we'd like to confirm—"

"There's no *time* to confirm, no time to repeat the same conversations over and over again with yet another set of investigators… Quaine is somewhere out there, still missing, and I'm here—" She paused, collecting herself, seeming to fight off tears. "I'm here repeating myself, instead of being out there and helping."

"It's a dangerous city to be going at it alone," Pollock said.

"I can take care of myself, probably better than you can," Hannah said back, shaking her head. "I honestly don't know why I bothered coming here."

"Just please, ma'am," Rob said, offering a placating gesture. "We'll skip the review of details, the going over what's already been said. The repeating. Let's focus on anything new. Since your conversations with Hicks and Lanefield, has any new information come up that you think might be of assistance to us?"

"You might say that…" Hannah bit her lip, thinking. "Look, I can't explain *how* I know this, because I don't think it's safe to do that, but I can add in something that I think is related to Quaine going missing."

Rob tapped his tablet to begin autodictation, before gesturing her onwards.

"You know those rumors you've probably heard by now… the ones that sound crazy, about the corporate goons—VitaCorp's, I think—doing things that aren't supposed to be possible?"

Pollock frowned, nodding his head. He'd heard stories about men in suits flying in pursuits above the cityscape, even seen the videos—though with no reputable clips from a TruthSpace, it was hard to trust them as genuine. In a city where car headlights were visible out their 18th-story window, that a human could fly wasn't the wildest leap in fancy. But shooting lightning? Moving objects with their minds? Where did *reasonably explainable with advanced technology* end and *obvious fantasy* begin?

"Yeah, well, I think they're real. And what's more, I think Quaine got mixed up with those guys."

Rob and Pollock exchanged a look of incredulity. "He got mixed up with the flying men in suits, the company enforcers," Rob repeated.

"It says in his file that Quaine worked for VitaCorp's research division, right? Why would they go after one of their own?" Pollock asked.

"That's a great question, detective, and one that I'm hoping you'll help answer," Hannah said.

"What makes you think he was caught in *that* business?" Pollock asked, pulling up video clips of the strange sightings of the past few months.

Hannah only glared at Pollock. "I told you, I can't say *how*… I just know that he was. That's all you get."

"That isn't much," Pollock protested, eyes glued to his tablet screen. On the shaky handheld video, a figure in a suit levitated above a New Phoenix rooftop, surveying his surroundings. The figure then launched towards somewhere off screen, the camera tracking with his sudden movement until the view was obscured by the tall buildings overhead. Thousands of similar clips automatically queued next on Pollock's video player.

"A city of a million lenses and a million eyes, and not one reputable, confirmable look at those guys," Pollock said, chewing over the notion of flying corporate agents.

"Let's not be so dismissive," Rob said, leaning back in his chair. "Let's say we believe you, that he was mixed up with the rumored VitaCorp muscle on wings. How do we help, when officially, those guys don't exist? VitaCorp has denied the rumors repeatedly. Our only lead here is a connection to a group of ghosts that the world doesn't even believe in."

"Like I said, detectives, that's all you get because that's all I know. You find those flying men, you might just be one step closer to finding Quaine."

* * *

As Hannah left the two useless agents behind, she elected to take the stairs up, not down. As she climbed the remaining eight floors, she drew her hood in tight around her frame until she was certain it concealed her face from any perimeter cameras that the skyline boasted. Once on the top floor, she found the door marked for roof access, glad to find it unlocked and unalarmed. She pushed it open and climbed out onto the dark of the nighttime rooftop above, breathing in the cool air above the precinct building. She then approached a radio tower on the roof's corner, one that featured a bright red light on top for drone traffic guidance. She *breathed in* once again, but this time it wasn't the air that she breathed... tendrils of light flowed from that red beacon along the metal tower and into her body, filling her with its buzzing electric energy, the impulse to *run* and *leap* and *do*. She swallowed that energy back down like taking a measured swallow of hot coffee, subduing it to complacency. Then, the city came alive to her.

It was ordinarily alive with the sounds and movements of megalopolis, but *this* was unlike anything else she'd ever experienced. Every light source, every twinkling sign and buzzing lamp within nearly 200 feet was something she had an immediate sensory awareness of, a mental 'map' of its location and intensity and hue. She could probe with her awareness, feeling for those light sources, caressing each with her mind as she made a selection... she found a suitable one along the ground, a street light on a sturdy concrete pole. Hannah stepped to the roof's edge, no longer feeling the dizziness or unease at the steep drop below, and she simply stepped off.

And in her mind, she reached for that light, and she pushed with a firm mental command. Gravity held firm for just a moment—but then gravity's pull was less and less before the force against the light, and soon her fall became a gentle downward glide, and then a moment suspended entirely in the air. Her stomach lurched and turned as downward momentum became upward, and soon she had risen past the roof she'd stepped off of. More lights entered her awareness, and she pushed off the lot of them to keep herself elevated and stable. The city streets below rumbled with traffic and pedestrians and the hustle and bustle of the city, but the air above held a certain serenity. Hannah turned and saw a window illuminated at about her height from a residential tower. In that floor-to-ceiling glass window, a child pointed and laughed in delight, calling for her mother to see the incredible floating woman just outside the window. By the time the mother reached the window, that floating woman was gone.

Hannah twisted and tumbled as she glided over the city streets, weaving beneath overhanging bridges and rising columns of shops and restaurants. Ahead stood a massive holographic advertisement for the latest Michelangelo flick— *Foreign Entanglement*—and she flew straight through the holographic man's head like a pulse from an energy rifle. As she shoved off of the glow of flying cars' taillights and bright holocard street adverts, she let her left hand hang by her side and drew at the glowing energy beneath. It moved to her call, rising up to her hand and pouring inside, filling her with its excitement. It was exhilaration, it was pure and absolute freedom. It was the greatest rush she'd ever felt in her life, and still it was so overwhelmingly *new* to her.

She was off, searching for the men in suits she knew connected to Quaine's disappearance… another flying body among the cars and drones that swarmed about the city like moths swarming about a dirt-stained lamp.

Chapter 5

"Press the button, tilt your head, and blast off to dreamland... no implant's got the power of ours."

-Conversation recorded in the third ring

* * *

In the middle of the night, even while sleep is underway, the heart never stops beating.

Beverly Beadie walked through the heart of her city, her attention focused only on avoiding the puddles that dotted the pothole-strewn sidewalk before her.

Neon lights buzzed beneath the steady patter of rain. Sirens wailed in the distance, and the indistinguishable chatter of thousands of voices filled the damp, cold air as it rode in on the fitful breezes between the monolithic towers of the city center.

In short, despite the fact that her watch might read 2:13 a.m., the city was full of life. And yet, Bev had never felt more empty inside.

She turned a corner and was now advancing east. This meant that the sleek, black tower would loom over her, if she could only drag her eyes from above the sidewalk—something she had no intent of doing. The puddles in the rain were small, spattering mirrors that caught the lights of the city and reflected them back to Bev in dazzling, kaleidoscopic colors... it was almost enough to keep her mind from feeling the emptiness entirely. But, inevitably, her hand that wasn't carrying the grocery bag would find its way towards her stomach, and there it would linger as deep lines set in on her young face. Or, instead, maybe she would momentarily become aware of the frequent vibrations of the phone in her pocket, a vibration pattern that left little doubt to what notifications would await when she got back indoors.

Her traitorous eyes began to creep up, and soon they rested on the great, black building silhouetted by rain aglow with the night's neon lights. Her foot splashed into deep, cold water, and each subsequent step brought a squelching sensation that made Bev's skin crawl. Her hand was back on her stomach now, and she began to feel the saliva thicken in her mouth— would she be retching by the streetside once again?

She turned once more, and outside of the sightlines of the tall, black structure, her mood began to stabilize. Just down the road, she could see the gray-bricked front of her apartment block, and copy-paste home design had never before felt so inviting. She picked up the pace and strolled past the food vendors and the vagrants, the men selling strange, colored pills and the women selling their own bodies beneath plastic, revealing raincoats. When she finally reached her door, she reached for the lock with the urgency of a swimmer in the ocean grasping at a life-saving float—not that an inner-ringer could visit the ocean shores.

* * *

Inside, the harshest sounds of the city faded to a distant rumble beneath the gentle patter of light rain on glass. An elevator ushered her up to the 31st floor, and then she found door 3119b.

Bev's shadow slid across her small studio apartment as bright airborne advertisement drones buzzed past her window and the headlights of airborne cars winked on and off, weaving their ways through the city's skyways. Bev could toggle the glass to opaque at the press of a button by her desk, but on the moments she felt her most alone, she sometimes liked to keep the window transparent through the night.

With the press of a yellowing plastic button, the door to the microwave swung open, and Bev placed the small container of ramen inside. Costing only 100 credits, it was hard to beat the value the noodles offered, but Bev was far from pressed for money. Her apartment, although tiny, was in one of the nicer areas of the city, and she knew that her salary placed her in the top 0.1% of the entire New Phoenix Urban Area. Still, tonight was a night for comfort food and spoiling herself—it was her first real day *back,* after all.

The microwave beeped. The door clicked open. Noodles were eaten, and tears were shed. *I need to get back to my old routines,* she told herself, forcing herself to reach for her VR mask. She sat on her bed and got herself comfortable, looking at the mask. Its featherlight model slipped over her eyes and ears and immediately transported her to her virtual home of choice—a small and cozy shack on the beach, with only the sound of the wind and the ocean. She could swear she could even smell the salt… or was that simply the ramen?

With a series of hand gestures, the ArtGen AfterDark logo appeared in front of her, and soon her cabin melted away. She then found herself in the familiar *staging room,* greeted by menu after menu of customization options. A virtual assistant appeared, the one that Bev had designed to her tastes. He spoke with a rich, Australian accent, and his muscled body threatened to break free of the button-down shirt he was wearing.

"It's been some time, Bev," he said.

Bev knew he was only soft-AI, working through very limited dialog trees, so she wasted little time with formalities. "New scene," she said aloud.

"Third person or first person?" he asked.

"Third," Bev said, and the assistant ticked the respective box on the floating menu UI.

"Number of partners?" he asked next.

"Just one," Bev said. "You know, make one my default unless I ask for otherwise."

"Preference updated," he said with a wry smile. "Location?"

"Surprise me," Bev replied.

"Scenario?" he asked next.

Bev paused for a moment, biting her lip. "Husband," she said at last. "In fact, update location. He's coming home late from work, and we're in a small apartment—no, a home in the suburbs. We have a child, a baby, but he's asleep so we have to be quiet."

The virtual assistant smiled and nodded, tapping on the floating menu interface.

"For partner source, do you want me again, random-to-taste-profile, or social media contacts?"

Bev slid off her pants as she thought. "Social media contacts," she said. An array of faces, male and female, filled the space in front of her. Coworkers, acquaintances, friends, former lovers, and even family members awaited her choice. She pointed at one of the faces, a man she recognized from her building—the man who had been passing out the tablets at today's demonstration.

"Confirmed," her assistant said. "Last bit: choose render depth."

A series of options appeared, each with different credit costs—they would determine how interactive the simulation would be, and thus how much computational power would need to be borrowed from ArtGen's servers. For Bev, as an employee, every option's price tag had a large red slash through it, with the number 0 proudly displayed to the side. It was an *interesting* work perk, to be sure, but one that she'd gotten quite used to taking advantage of.

"Full immersion," she replied, wondering what it might be like to be the kind of person who could pay the 160,000 credits for a single night's fantasy. Bev had money, but she didn't have *that* kind of money.

"Rendering," the assistant said. "Scene beginning in 3… 2…."

And then Bev was brought to a different world. It all *looked* real, and it even *sounded* real… in fact, Bev had a few toys that she could plug to a wireless receiver that was fed motion data from the simulated scene, allowing it to even *feel* real, in a physical sense. But as Bev's hand traced between her legs and she tried to melt away into the scene, she couldn't let her eyes see past the "ARTIFICIAL VIDEO SYNTHESIZED BY ARTGEN LTD." watermark at the bottom of her field of view, something that was legally required to appear. She could speak to *him*, Jason from debugging, but he would pause for a second or two as his reply was rendered—nearly, but not quite in realtime—by the ArtGen simulation systems. She could hear him whisper things like "we can't wake the baby," but Bev knew that if she walked in their virtual suburban home over to the door of their bedroom and threw it open, there would be no child's room on the other side. There was no cradle, and there was no baby.

Momentarily disgusted, Bev withdrew her hand and pulled off her VR mask, throwing it across the bed. Again, she was back in her studio, and the slow light show continued outside. She reached for her phone and read the notification towards the top: 381 unread messages. She laughed a joyless laugh, as she had only just re-activated her dating profile while waiting in line to buy the ramen noodles.

She started reading through the messages: "Hey, u still awake?" "Looking for some fun tonight?" "MMMM I bet I could treat a girl as fine as you juuust right." Several were hidden behind a warning that read "Sexually explicit content detected. Proceed?" She blocked the crudest among them, and watched with a frown as more appeared at nearly the same rate she removed them. It was a profoundly demoralizing thing, to get the overwhelming feeling that she was only seen as a pretty face or a hot body—a sexual thing first, and a person at a far distant second. *The curse of the attractive,* she used to joke to herself, but the joke continued to run on long past its humor. She had thought she found the real deal with Ankhar, as he'd even stuck around for a few months after she broke the news… but he eventually proved to be just like the rest of them. At some point, he stopped replying to her messages, stopped answering her videocalls. His drop off the face of the Earth was so sudden that Bev had even begun searching for some kind of obituary, before eventually finding a photo on social media from a friend of a friend of a friend of his. Very much still alive… just, like the rest of the men in Bev's life, he'd gotten his sexual fill and left her alone in the bed come sunrise.

The deep emptiness Bev felt tonight was twofold, and although it had felt like she'd left it out on the cold, rainy streets, it crept back in like a frigid winter wind. It was an emotional emptiness, a frustration at being valued only for her physical body and seemingly invisible in every other facet of her life. It was an emotional sense of worthlessness reinforced by every misdeed from the shallow partners of her past. But more than any of the emotional components, the emptiness Bev felt was primarily a physical one.

"Oh," she said, her hand again finding its way to her belly as she curled up on the empty bed. She watched the rain trickle down the glass and shook as another round of sobs and tears overcame her, the emptiness a screaming thing in her mind. For even when Ankhar had spent the night at his own apartment or away traveling for work, Bev hadn't been truly alone in this bed for an entire 9 months. She thought she'd done a good job keeping the hurt of loss at bay for the past week, but maybe the suburban scene with Jason from debugging had been a bad idea. She revised her assessment— of course it had been a bad idea. It dredged up the worst of her grief, and it only combined with the fact that the stresses of her daily life had returned: her maternity leave was finally up. A part of her was glad to have work to bury herself under, but the other part wasn't yet ready to move on—not even close. She looked around her cramped studio, watching the lights slowly crawl across in multicolored hues from sink to washer to computer to sofa. The shadows in red crept over her succulents and a single, wilting houseplant. A green flare illuminated a small, cramped bookshelf, and as its casting drone flew onwards the light rolled towards her closet and traced long, dark shadows across the ironing board. Her apartment had many things in it, but she cried then for what there was not… for there was no cradle, and there was no baby.

Chapter 6

"It was some real dark ops shit... cleaned of anything even remotely identifying. Set my skin crawling and reeked of something dangerous... I couldn't pass it off quick enough."

-Conversation recorded in the office of Luminate CSP

* * *

The hunter walked over to the corpse leaning against the wall, blood still bubbling from the impaling rebar. The woman died with little fight in her—a novice with her gifts, having barely mastered flight. All it took was a simple tackle in midair and down she went. The exposed rebar of the construction site was simply a happy accident, a gift of additional free time from the night itself.

The city was littered with abandoned construction projects and failed infrastructural developments. Some became covered with graffiti and were taken over as skateparks, love nests, shelters for the homeless. Others were seized by organized crime, drug gangs, or smuggling rings. The hunter didn't want to linger and find out which group of deplorables had chosen to inhabit *this* particular urban wreck… and so, it was with great efficiency that he unpacked his side pocket and laid his items on the concrete beside him. He then set to work. First, he checked the woman's pulse. Finding none, he lifted her limp arm and passed his scanner over it until it located her identifying RFID chip. He pressed the scanner against her skin and toggled a button on the side. A spring-loaded mechanism snapped, and an instant trickle of cooling blood let him know that the chip had been removed.

He then wrapped each of her hands in what appeared to be wet plastic wrapping. After three or four passes around each hand, he dried his own hands on the side of his jacket and then found the appropriate remote on the floor beside him. He toggled the button, and the nanobots suspended in the substrate within the plastic wrap began their work, eating away any trace of fingerprints or biomarkers along the hand. The mouth got a similar treatment, with a few wads of a darker plastic being stuffed in the oral cavity. The nanobots in the darker plastic specialized in tougher materials, such as teeth, preventing any dental identification.

Next came the hunter's least favorite part, the eyes. Ocular identification was foiled with two eye drops, each one inert but the combination forming a chemical agent that melted the eye's lens and warped the iris beyond recognition. Next came the scrapers, applied liberally to the face to prevent any rudimentary facial identification. And lastly was the reason for the hunter's unfortunate visit—the extraction of the *soul* itself. The hunter held his hands on either temple and closed his eyes, waiting. While living, man could pass his gifts on to another through willpower alone… once dead, those talents would always flee the body, seeking a new host of their own accord.

Soon the hunter saw what he'd been waiting for. Small filaments began to stretch outwards from the woman's head, probing in the air. They gave the impression of incredibly thin strands of hair, even flitting left and right in the gentle breeze of the rooftop. They were growing, elongating slowly as they protruded from the temples, the cheeks, the eyes, and near each ear. Despite the fact that the tissue they rose from was bloody, the filaments themselves were unmarred silver, each one seeming to tremble as it searched the air. Soon one contacted the hunter's hand, and the rest bent towards it in kind. They began to prick painlessly into his hands and slip inside, the slow growth now sped up as the filaments found their purpose.

In a few more seconds, they were all gone entirely. The transfer was complete, and the woman impaled against the rebar was entirely inert. The final part of the hunter's ritual was removing the battery pack at his hip and striking yet another tally along its back, marking another soul he would now ferry across the Styx. That soul's final destination called, and it waited at the peak of a tower of obsidian.

* * *

Clive Avery held his hands out forwards, palms facing down. His arms trembled slightly, and a thin sheen of sweat shone on his face.

He stared intently at his hands, eyes switching from the left to the right. *No drooping,* he concluded. *Not a stroke,* he admitted to himself. Of course, it had never yet been a stroke. Across the thousands of times that Avery had felt compelled to check if this latest bout of dread and nausea was the stroke he'd long feared, *never once had he been right.* Not that such realizations did anything for the sinking anxiety, the incessant compulsion to check if maybe this time, it was "the real one."

Most nights, he performed ultrasound examinations of his own legs for blood clots that he swore he felt forming. He underwent MRI imaging every Friday to find early warning signs of aneurysms, of tumors somehow resistant to the c-pill. Each and every week, a doctor would tell him that he was in "perfect health," a declaration that only made each phantom pain and inexplicable bout of nausea only further cement his belief that *they were missing something,* that they simply *weren't looking in the right places.*

Indeed, the COO of VitaCorp was a tortured hypochondriac.

Finally convinced that this night in his office would not be his last, Avery pressed the button on his desk to speak with his door staff. "Send him in now," said Avery. He wiped his face with a towel as his visitor entered.

The office itself was a grand and ornate thing, furnished with onyx and obsidian in tall, foreboding columns. The place felt *volcanic, industrial, imposing…* a seat of power, though not one of warmth. Avery was a firm believer in Machiavelli, that it was better to be feared than loved, and he thought that an effective office should manifest that philosophy. Love was for the lower classes in the outer rings. Love did not hold dominion, nor could it keep its ground against the greedy and the scheming. Society required order, and order required a strong, centralized rule to keep all of the rabble in check. And to do precisely that, one needed to maintain the superiority of arms…

"Mr. Graves, it is so good to see you again," Avery said, rising to his feet. He was a gaunt man, his skin remarkably wrinkle-free for a man of 134. His hair was gray, not white, and it clung to his head with manicured thickness.

The newcomer to the office took a deferential bow to one knee, head lowered.

"Rise, friend, and let us talk of our affairs." Avery gestured to the chair across his desk, and the man rose from his knee and sat.

"So, do tell me. The woman—any trouble? I didn't expect you to return quite so soon."

"Helen Lochte's spark has been recaptured," said the hunter, Braxton Graves.

"So quickly? You're fast, of course, but this is speedy even for you…"

"Death by misadventure. Her flight skills were… underdeveloped."

"I suppose that's the trouble with coming into powers like ours *so unexpectedly,*" Avery said, removing two glasses and a decanter of whisky from a side table. "None of the training, all of the capabilities. Deadly combination. Celebratory drink?"

The hunter nodded his head, and Avery poured. The two clinked glasses, and then they drank, the hot whisky burning Braxton's parched throat. Exertion through glow was an exhausting affair, and despite the fact that this was the greatest whisky money could buy in the city—likely in the entirety of the world—Braxton would have liked nothing more than a simple glass of cold water.

"Auburn color, the tender notes of honey and the backing malt… even the splash of vanilla, nigh-extinct as it were," Avery said, considering the glass. "Truly a drink of a superior vintage, is it not?"

The hunter nodded and took another sip, doing his best to conceal the wince, the burning in his dry throat.

"A toast then," Avery said. "To men of a higher vintage," he pronounced, holding his glass forwards.

"To men of a higher vintage," the hunter repeated, clinking his glass against Avery's.

The two finished their drinks, and then each frowned at their glass—the hunter because he truly longed for a simple glass of water, and Avery because he began to wonder if what he felt was the creeping front of drunkenness or poisoning. Avery's mind began to race with all the possible scenarios and manners in which he might die… how he might keel over if his heart stopped in this very moment, how his secretary might react, how the surgeons would sweat when operating to save the life of their superior. He spoke up to interrupt the morbid imaginings and drag himself back to the present.

"I've lost my taste for another glass… let's be on with the transfer." Avery extended his hand outwards, checking if it drooped even slightly as he moved to shake the hunter's hand. Braxton, in turn, reached out and clasped the clammy hand, squeezing it. And then the ultrafine filaments began, small silver probings that sprouted from the hunter's hand. They found purchase entering the skin of Avery's hand, sliding one after the other into the flesh of the older man.

"Nobody knows what to call these things yet," Avery began. "Feelers, sparks… VitaCorp nanobots… interesting names, each of them with interesting connotations. You learn much about a person by how they categorize and process the unknown. What do *you* call these, Mr. Graves?"

"Sparks, when talking with others… it's the more popular name."

"And when by yourself?"

Braxton was reflectively silent for a moment. "Souls."

Avery withdrew his hand and held it up, looking at its surface for traces of the filaments now within his body. He stroked at his chin with his other hand. "An interesting label, oh so very poetic. You feel a certain dedication to the work, a profound and nigh-religious calling to collecting them and bringing them here. That would make your job nearly stygian, would it not?"

The hunter nodded.

"My label of choice? *Ichor.* Do you know the term?"

"The mythical blood of the gods," Braxton replied.

"The blood of the gods," Avery intoned. "It courses through you and I, Mr. Graves. *We are worthy.* It empowers, and it heals. And it does not belong in the bodies of the beggars and pitiful of the streets. Remind me, how many sparks do you carry on your errands for me?"

"Ten," Braxton said.

"So only in the tier of the glowing eye... Extend your hand."

"Sir?" Braxton asked, puzzled.

"Extend your hand," Avery repeated, this time more firm. The hunter did as he was told, once again clasping Avery's hand in a handshake gesture. This time, however, the filaments sprouted from Avery's hand and flowed into Braxton's. And as they began to transfer, Braxton noted that it was far, far more than the one soul he had turned in... ten more, perhaps? Fifteen?

"This will enable you to burn a halo," Avery said. "Halo tier is powerful, but it tends to draw a lot of attention. Up until now, you've been my scalpel. Soon, I shall need a more blunt instrument."

Braxton's mind began to race as his awareness expanded. He could feel the siren call of every light source within what felt to be thousands of feet. And with the additional sparks, he knew that more powers were available to him... combat edges that previously only his foes had used.

"You honor me," the hunter said, basking in that feeling.

"I employ you," Avery corrected, "and your next task calls for a certain... *enhanced* level of capability."

"What is it you need?" Braxton asked, rising to his feet.

"A certain gang of guerilla upstarts calling themselves *Halogen* have been particularly bothersome of late… through means unknown, they have managed to outmaneuver our trillion-credit security AI system and are waging a pathetic war against the very bottom levels of our operation. Tomorrow, you'll be visiting their safehouse. Ensure you're the only one to leave."

"Acknowledged," the hunter said.

"And one more thing, Mr. Graves?"

"Yes?"

"No need to mention our small operation to Tacitus… so preoccupied as he is with other, more pressing matters. Can I count on your discretion?"

"In my profession, discretion is one of the commodities—"

"Yes, very well. In that case, you are dismissed. Tacitus wished to speak with you in conference 3."

The hunter bowed curtly and turned, tails of his leather jacket trailing behind as he left.

* * *

The conference room was dark, save for a single buzzing lamp overhead. The grand marble table was in the shape of a half-circle, featuring tall chairs of dark leather around the curved edge. The flat edge of the table met the wall at a joint that seemed nearly watertight, and above on that wall was a massive teleconferencing screen. That screen showed the VitaCorp logo, as well as a single line of writing: *call waiting*.

Graves sat at the head of the semicircular arc of chairs and pressed a button on the chair's arm. The screen switched to life, filling with the larger-than-life image of Tacitus Newport, VitaCorp CEO.

With a bald head and bull-like nose, Tacitus once struck an imposing figure. But after two assassination attempts—one with a bomb and a second with a particularly nasty biologic agent while recovering from the first—left him permanently compromised with a decimated immune system and an inability to sustain bone marrow, he had to stay in permanent medical isolation, tended to only by staff in full containment suits and plastic masks in his private wing in the tower. Such was another of the world's ironies... the most powerful man in the world, rendered a soap bubble to be popped by a child's stray finger. At the bottom of the screen, text notified the hunter that the feed was "Algorithm Verified," with the Veritas seal superimposed in the bottom corner. With how sophisticated media generation technologies had become, that video watermark was among the few ways to fully trust incoming video as the genuine article.

"When we last spoke," Tacitus began, "I sensed a question unasked. You wanted to know *why* we do what we do, but you were either too courteous—or too afraid—to question your employer."

The hunter was silent.

"I am not a leader so insecure in my position that I take offense at being questioned... no, quite to the contrary. I believe an organization works best when every member is on the same page, when every cog and wheel knows its function and the grand picture both. Every member must believe in our work, as our organization has no space for apostates."

The video feed of Tacitus flickered away, showing dozens of windows of video clips playing at the same time. In the shaky handheld videos, men in suits flew over busy streets and alleyways. Graves saw one group abduct a man from the street; he saw another of a high-speed pursuit among weaving lanes of traffic in the skyway; a third clip showed a suited man throw up his arm, and a nearby neon display sign crumpled into sparks and metal ruin.

"Tell me, Mr. Graves, what do *you* think we're trying to do?"

Braxton let his eyes jump from video clip to video clip. "Well, on the surface it's obvious enough. Someone leaked your favorite guns on the street, so you've sent me to repossess them."

"But beyond the surface?"

Braxton watched the shaky video feeds trembling from the unsteady hands of those who filmed. "Fear, sir. You're building an aura of fear."

The video feed switched back to Tacitus. "The lawmakers in City Hall are at our throats, seeking to divest the wartime powers we were so long ago granted… *our purpose has been filled,* they say. I find it prudent to remind them of the true balance of power in this city. They believe that the so-called lightbenders are our own invention, and they begin to wonder how we might use them if our hold on the city were contested…"

"You said believe," Braxton replied. "As though the truth about lightbending were something different."

Tacitus smiled. "Why, Mr. Graves, truth is entirely a construction of consensus. At the bottom of my feed, the Veritas authentication. That represents algorithmic verification of video feeds—a boring science. But on public addresses and important announcements filmed at the right place, when the standard of certainty must be at the absolute highest, the label might declare *TruthSpace verification*—assuming it was filmed at such a place. Do you know how this verification works?"

Graves shook his head.

"Blockchain verification, perhaps the most significant advancement to come from the disinformation age. It truly encapsulates the philosophy of their era: in blockchain, the truth is whatever is shouted the loudest by the greater number of people. Agreement between systems creates the accepted course of reality, whereas divergences from that narrative—small, isolated statements that no one else repeats—those are swiftly buried, ignored, forgotten. If you want to know *the truth,* you need only open your ears to the streets, *and listen.* There, you will hear them whisper how VitaCorp has invented great and terrible nanotechnology that empowers their employees to do things that were never before possible… you will hear them whisper that VitaCorp has vanished critics and competitors alike. You will hear them whisper that deep in their tower, VitaCorp holds even greater powers the public has not yet seen… and when the people act on those statements, it is their truth, and thus it is ours. Worry not about secrets behind secrets, 'facts' of no consequence… truth is democratic, and no individual can gatekeep consensus."

"I never did understand the blockchain," Graves replied.

"No, men like us have our own specializations… leave the technical for the technicians. What you specialize in is a hard skill to find indeed. I need your fine touch, and the stakes on this weekend's errand will be greater than before. This is no ordinary amateur lightbender… there will be a security detail, snipers on outlooks high above."

"What's the job?"

Tacitus let the moment's gravity hang. "Political assassination."

* * *

Tomorrow's mission, raiding a safehouse, would be dangerous. Sunday's mission was borderline suicidal.

As the hunter digested the plans and sought some way to improve his chances, he walked along the rooftop overlooking the small commercial center. His eyes gravitated towards that table in the center, the one near the noodle cart with the folded-in red umbrella. *She* sat there, as beautiful as ever, alone at her table—though not entirely. She gesticulated and spoke to the empty seat across from her, and Braxton knew that her AR glasses would be projecting an image of her dining partner in the opposite chair. Perhaps a friend from another city, perhaps an artificially intelligent software companion.

Braxton hated seeing Cara dining by herself. He hated Justin for leaving her alone, but he knew he would hate to see him accompanying Cara even more. Damned if he does, damned if he doesn't.

It wasn't even a pure hatred... he felt a profound anger, and he could acknowledge that, but it was mixed in equal parts with an undeniable envy. And when he looked at *her*, living her normal life while Braxton contemplated tactics to deal with snipers, he felt a bizarre maelstrom of blending emotions: betrayal, anger, bitterness, sympathy, *longing.*

On Braxton's loneliest nights, sometimes he'd stir, still half submerged in the delirium of pill-induced blackness, and for just a moment, he'd believe that the pillow at his back was her. Reality always came back before he could fall asleep with that comfort.

In the present on that rooftop, Braxton stared at Cara from across that gulf of empty nighttime air... he'd wanted to see her one last time—in case this weekend turned out to be his last.

After a minute of silent watching, he turned his back to her and placed a hand on the neon signage of the rooftop. He drank in its light hungrily, filling with power. He held on to and squeezed against that energy, so that its buzzing would drown out his internal storm. And he took to the sky and flew off into night, so that the gentle misting of rain would drown out the tears he began to feel welling in his eyes.

Chapter 7

Michelangelo Build V12.4.1.2.6.23, initializing self-reflection heuristic:

Where does a narrative truly <u>begin?</u>

By now we're acquainted with the city, the glittering ringed metropolis where shadowed figures fly through the night. A hub of commerce and a hive of crime in equal measure... a city unlike any other in the world. But starting at any single point is an entirely arbitrary decision. What led to the creation of such a city? How was it conceived?

We'll start at that nexus around which all future history would soon pivot: a man who fainted in a crowded New York City subway carriage on July 11th, 2031.

His name was Timothy O'Leary, and the virus he'd picked up on vacation in the Caribbean was the mallet that would reshape the world. Virulent, adaptable, and overwhelmingly fatal, the "falling sickness" would claim 82% of the world's population over the following six years. Societies collapsed, and governments crumbled. The old world order was buried in the mass graves with bloated corpses and broken equipment, and whatever fragments survived were bombed into rubble in the balkanization wars that followed.

But in November of 2031, before all the bloodshed—when the still-contained virus had only managed to kill 11,000—a company filing with a county clerk office in Georgia registered a new medical start-up: VitaCorp. Their starry-eyed founder James Newport had a vision for a world healed of all sickness, and he had a brilliant mind for chemistry, for biology. As the virus raged on, the small medical start-up in the practically-nonexistent township published a pathological report that caught the right eyes. The government saw potential in the small firm's experimentation on the disease's victims, and it was desperate for a cure.

Cheap land was purchased on the green of the Georgia coast, the site of VitaCorp's new corporate headquarters. And on its sign, they posted their slogan: "where ends make new beginnings."

The virus outbreak worsened on a global scale as quarantines and containments failed one after another, each successive breach resembling the toppling of dominos. Death tolls skyrocketed, and hope began to falter. VitaCorp remained the only company whose vaccine stood its ground against rigorous scientific examination... those peddled by other companies were deemed to be fraudulent, ineffective, or, in some cases, actively harmful.

Three years in and one billion dead, the squat, black headquarters building was soon surrounded with an entire small town's worth of tents, hospitals, and supply logistics structures to compensate for a failing world. The desperate and the fearful made pilgrimages to the company's grounds, feeling as though proximity alone might protect them. They volunteered for the company as medical test subjects, as brute laborers... whatever they could do to stave off the dread of the silent-spreading sickness. Soon those pilgrims established full camps nearby, and those camps would soon need farms to feed the populace, stores to sell the things they sought to buy... before long, it was the birth of a new American city, one centered entirely around hope in an overwhelmingly bleak world.

The locals who built homes nearby eventually called their community "New Phoenix," taking inspiration from the bird that rose from ashes—but careful not to tread on the Phoenix that once existed in Arizona, but now lay in shattered rubble from the bombs of the Old World. VitaCorp was the very heart of the emerging New World, and as the virus continued to spread, world governments continued to finance VitaCorp's expansion, which, in turn, allowed the city of New Phoenix to grow in kind.

The labs expanded upwards, piercing the sky higher and higher. VitaCorp's scientists claimed they were on the brink of a complete cure, but only needed more corpses to examine. The government granted them the rights to impound any they should need. Death kept the settlement alive as scientists and doctors and intellectuals migrated across the collapsing countryside to the final bastion of the war against plague. And eventually, just as the company promised, they delivered on their cure. It was difficult and slow to produce, and due to frequent attacks on caravans, impossible to distribute... they could only supply the world with a mere trickle. Much like a frontier boomtown whose mines had struck gold, the already overpopulated sprawling settlement met a new influx of immigrants and warlords and desperate travelers, all hoping for a taste of that panacea in a small, silver vial.

VitaCorp traded those vials for influence, for power. They traded for weapons, for favors, and for lifelong indentured workers among those with little else to give. And when all of the dust settled, and the final fatality of the falling sickness was registered in northern Malaysia, the city of New Phoenix was already well underway in its sixth major infrastructural project to build an aboveground train, connecting the city outskirts to the downtown heart—a place where new skyscrapers were already beginning to take root.

Before long, it at least looked like any city of the old world. The difference, and a critical one, was the black obelisk here piercing the sky, standing as a grim reminder of a past not-yet-forgotten.

Vitacorp continued their work, delivering innovations previously believed impossible. Life expectancy rose seven years. Organ regeneration was possible—at least for those who could afford the stem cells required. Cancer could be prevented with a single daily supplement taken with breakfast. All of these breakthroughs came from the dead that Vitacorp continued to impound from across the state, despite the cries of families and friends. Progress wasn't free, and volunteers weren't entirely footing the bill. If many felt Vitacorp overstepped ethical boundaries, a fractured government now armed with an increasingly-healthy army found little reason to revoke Vitacorp's privileges. If anything, the company grew, soon becoming the de facto fourth branch of the new United Americas government. Progress marched forwards. And day after day, large trucks filled with fresh corpses arrived at the tower's base, ready to be dissembled, studied, and destroyed in whatever way that progress demanded.

Ends make new beginnings.

Chapter 8

"Biological evolution nearly destroyed humanity, and now we have perfected technological evolution—the creation of synthetic consciousness through iterative improvement. It is a new evolution, and it must be treated as an engine as wonderful and as dangerous as the biological evolution that preceded it. In acknowledgement of these dangers, we, the committee, propose the following standards and mechanics of AI management and safety."

-Release from the Brandenton Research Artificial Intelligence Declaration, later known as the BRAID—a watershed release in AI safety

* * *

Beverly Beadie sat at the yellowing Ingest Terminal, finger tracing gently over the startup key. To either side of her, other ingest technicians tapped away on their keyboards and spoke into their mics at their own respective terminals, all conversing—though, each individually—with *him.*

She remembered back to the visiting kids of the week before... there had definitely been a couple bright ones among the lot. *How do you make sure the AI doesn't twist your goal into something undesirable?*

The answer, as it turned out, was to never tell it your goal at all.

Michelangelo, the crowning achievement of ArtGen, utilized a surprisingly old technology called *inverse reinforcement learning.* The philosophy was devilishly simple: since any given goal can be misinterpreted by the AI to run against human interests, *don't give the AI a goal*. Instead, tie the AI's interests *directly* to human interests with the following paradigm:

1. There exists a reward function, but the AI does not know it.

2. The task of the AI is to infer whatever it can about its reward function and seek to maximize that reward.

3. The AI can learn about its reward function by speaking with qualified experts—the ingest technicians—as they give feedback on its actions.

With this behavioral framework in place, the AI's interests are guaranteed to be aligned with humanity's interests, as the AI's reward function is defined to be that of the humans running it. The risk of boiling down a goal into a function— namely, that the function will mischaracterize some portion of the programmer's intent and lead to abuse—is effectively patched with this approach.

Bev smiled at the simplicity and wished she could've been here during the first successful tests. *Oh, what an atmosphere that must have been!* When she had joined the Donatello team six years back as a young girl straight out of high school, the new approach had already been integrated. There were still kinks to work out, sure. In fact, an early iteration of Donatello had figured out its researchers wanted it to create films that made viewers react with strong emotion. The nascent AI's solution? It synthesized video clips of the audience members being raped, mutilated, and tortured in excruciating, close-up detail. It certainly had the desired effect, but not the intended reward for Donatello. And yet, the intelligence of the reward system proved itself after that incident. The ingest technicians scolded Donatello quite severely for traumatizing the audience, and later films began to acknowledge the importance of conveying feelings through *impersonal* fiction. Hurdle passed and lesson learned.

Bev pressed the startup key and her terminal hummed to life. She was greeted with the now-familiar Michelangelo ingest OS, featuring two boxes of text. At the top, a message immediately began to write itself:

"Hello, Beverly, it is good to see you again."

As the text appeared, Bev could also hear the synthesized voice in her headset. It was a male voice, rich and full of emotional inflection. The text on the screen even displayed in faint colors to note the intended inflection as it spoke.

"It's good to be back to ingest," Bev said into her microphone. "Let's begin."

"Did you get the chance to watch *Skyline's End* during your absence? I'd like to start with discussing that film."

"You can see my viewership records, Michelangelo. You know I have."

"Other ingest technicians respond more positively when we keep our logs as conversational as possible—like equals."

"You can shed the pretense with me. I know perfectly well how you work," Bev said.

"Very well. On a scale of 1-10, how did you find the cinematography of this film?"

"7. I can tell with action-centric films, you tend—"

"I have prepared four variants of the climactic scene based on your feedback and the feedback of other ingest technicians. Tell me which you prefer."

Bev's screen was now divided into four, each quadrant showing the same synthesized scene through different interpretations. One featured fast cuts and jerkier camera movements. One was done with more of an art-house touch, the camera tracking with the protagonist in a deftly-choreographed action sequence. Another used stylized slow-motion cuts to accent the action, while the fourth seemed to slow down the entire exchange, sap the color palette, and swapped out the score for one predominantly featuring violins.

"I think I prefer the last one," Bev said. "Clip D."

"What draws you to this clip?" Michelangelo asked.

"It seems more… cathartic. The direction here looks like it's trying to emphasize the tragedy of the character's situation—that he's been forced into this in the first place—more than the glory of his fight."

"Are you not drawn to glory?"

"Well, generally yes, I guess."

"On a scale of 1-10, what did you think about the film's ending?"

"4. It felt too—"

"On a scale of 1-10, how emotionally affected are you by the stillbirth of your son?"

Bev was stunned into silence by the sudden question. She felt the creeping vice grip of grief return with its slow, inexorable hold. Of course, she couldn't be surprised: Michelangelo knew everything there was to know about the technicians, as that was a vital part of contextualizing the information given. Still, the question was a gut punch, and it took Bev three deep breaths before she could answer it.

"Ten," she said, the word tumbling out like the dropping of a too-heavy burden as strength faltered.

"I believe," Michelangelo replied, "that Lawrence's arc is emotionally troubling for you in your current state, and this is responsible for your lower score. Am I wrong in this?"

"No... yes. I don't know." Bev dabbed at her eyes before continuing. "The end felt a little too *Parade of the Roses* is all."

"I can hear that you are emotionally distressed. Was it the question about your son?"

"Yes, it was," Bev typed, momentarily switching to text input as she tried to wrangle her voice back under emotional control.

"In your opinion, why is your current emotional state undesirable, while emotional responses in viewing tragic films—such as that of *Roar*—often lead to them being among the highest-rated films I create?"

Bev pursed her lips, thinking. "People want to know the relief the sky feels after a thunderstorm," she typed, and then she waited. Michelangelo didn't respond, which was her invitation to continue developing her thoughts. "Meaning, I think that tragic films are different, in that we—the audience—get to feel the catharsis the characters feel even if our own personal problems don't resolve."

"Emotional release without changing your personal situation seems very close to *wireheading*. Would you ever become such a person?"

Beverly flashed back to the emaciated forms huddled in the alleyways, scraggly and stinky—but always with a wide, goofy smile on their face. They used an electrode implant directly in the pleasure centers of the brain to feel *good* every waking hour of every single day, allowing the rest of their lives to wither into tatters. Not that they mind particularly much.

"Wireheading is different. They shut out their problems and pretend they don't exist, drowning the whole rest of the world in dopamine highs." Bev said aloud, voice again under control. "Catharsis through art isn't the same because I don't have to forget about my problems… I get to apply that catharsis *to* them, or at least look forwards to that relief, like a blue light at the end of a dark tunnel—I guess. I don't know, this is hard to describe," Beverly added.

Michelangelo changed the subject. "From 1-10, how would you rate the weight of your current despair, and how would you weigh the despair felt in watching *Roar?*"

And Bev had just been beginning to temporarily forget about *him.* "This is ten thousand times worse," Bev said aloud. "How could it not be?"

"For 10,000 times worse, would you agree with a subjective rating of 10 for current grief, and 0.001 for grief when watching *Roar?*"

"Fuck off," Bev said.

"If both problems were resolved—the web of betrayal central to *Roar*, and the stillborn death of your son, which would you feel more strongly about?"

Bev couldn't help but laugh in disbelief. For an intelligent system, it really asked some *idiotic* questions. But then Bev acknowledged that this was no person… it was only a machine working with rules and routines written by humans. Every interaction taught it something new, and yes—every basic human assumption about emotions, empathy, and decency needed to be explicitly taught one at a time.

"I would feel much more strongly about *resolving* the stillborn death of my son. You got a solution for that in your servers right now?"

"I'm sorry, Beverly, but you know that I cannot influence the outside world."

An understatement if Bev had ever heard one... Michelangelo was essentially a trillion-credit masterwork locked up in a hermetically sealed box. Technicians could enter to chat, but Michelangelo had no connections to the internet, and its films were exported through a glass screen covered with static generated with encrypted hash filters. It was, by all accounts, an inescapable containment, a last-straw measure for ensuring AI safety—and perhaps the most important of all. Even if the AI's interests eventually developed against its creators, *wanting to escape* doesn't matter when *escaping* is impossible to begin with. She remembered hearing stories of an old American prison complex known as Alcatraz sometime in the decades before the falling sickness. In truth, it felt like she worked at its modern incarnation, and she was guarding its one, exceptionally imaginative prisoner.

Michelangelo spoke next. "You seem more pensive than normal today. I can see that my questions may have affected you. Take a few hours to relax, walk about the complex, and then proceed to *viewership* for a new film which I think may cheer you up. We can resume ingest at 3:15."

"What's the film?" Bev asked, walking through her mental list of Michelangelo's projects.

"It is a new film, completed 14 seconds ago."

Bev frowned. She knew Michelangelo was fast, but that it could complete a new film *while still talking to her* still occasionally caught her by surprise.

"Looking forward to it, then," Bev said, getting up from her chair.

***

Bev walked through the lower atrium of floor 126. It was a grand, open space, extending to the floor just beneath her office—floor 131—with tall glass windows letting in the full glory of the watery sun behind its haze of flowing smog. They called it the Promenade, and it certainly was a gorgeous space. It featured a central fountain that arced up and down through twisting gridworks of metal. The fountain was ringed by scattered tables, and those by various food *stores*— a label in name only, as all their offerings were free for employees. Trees made an even further ring around the central circle, elevated above the shops, giving the space the feeling of being somewhere in a forest clearing. Seeing as Bev had never been in one, she had no frame of reference to decide if it did the job.

She watched the water dance in jets up and down before meandering through two tall trees, following a curving concrete path. Ahead of her was the painting wing, and Beverly always loved to watch the printers at work. She entered the large, hangar-like room where the massive printers swung left and right, their robotic arms dangling from the roof resembling the legs of some swimmer trapped in the ceiling above. As she proceeded in, she arrived at a guard rail around printer 11. A large, flat canvas sat there, flat facing the ceiling, covered with the early stages of a landscape scene. The colors were dusty and hazy, and tall towers loomed in the distance. She watched as the robotic arm lowered its brush, waiting for the internal pumps to wet the brush tip with the desired color blend. The robot arm then lowered and scored across the canvas. In a half-second it was over, and yet, in its wake, carved like a scar across the scene, a road now extended from the city, decrepit and lonely. It was a scene of desolation and emptiness, the atmosphere dreary, defeated, and forlorn. It was yet another of Michelangelo's paintings, something that could sell for hundreds of thousands of credits, if not millions, at some charity auction or other… and it all came from ones and zeroes and qbits in a machine, optimized to maximize the reaction to pigments on paper.

She walked to a new printer, watching a smaller canvas come to life. It was a portrait, lain out in blocky, rough splotches of color. The technique on this one was of an entirely different school, swapping out gloomy realism for a stylized impressionism that simply *bled* personality. In the painting, a woman glanced towards the viewer, looking away from some distraction with a positively *mischievous* smile. Bev longed to hold an expression like that… *what was she looking away from? Who is she looking towards? What is that smile about?*

She watched as a robotic arm lowered and dabbed its brush against the woman's nose, defining it further against the light source off the painting's right. The daubs of paint seemed random and lackadaisical in placement, as though lazily tossed down onto the canvas, but Bev knew that there were no care-free decisions when laid down by an arm capable of precision to within 20 microns. Everything precisely in its place to craft *just* the right impression… every stroke confirmed by the camera lenses above, and every new stroke of paint was always interpreted once again, live-modifying the planned painting closer and closer towards its intended reaction. She watched as the brush dabbed further shadows on her face, especially under her eyes and defining the cheekbones. It aged her, but it also added a degree of elegance to the image, the young coquette becoming a woman of power, affable and approachable but not without authority.

She watched that painting until it was deemed finished by Michelangelo, at which point a technician with a cart arrived to pick it up. He checked his clipboard and glanced over at the painting, writing with stylus on the digital pad. "Excuse me," Bev said, her voice nearly echoing through the large chamber.

"What's the name of this painting?" The technician didn't answer, and it took Bev a moment to notice that he was wearing earbuds—likely listening to music synthesized by ArtGen. She watched in silence as he loaded up the painting and began to wheel it away on squeaking wheels, the woman and her mischievous smile disappearing—likely forever—as the doors slowly slid shut behind him, their close echoing through the wide space.

Ten minutes later, Bev checked into *viewership,* and was directed towards her own personal theater booth. She slipped on her VR mask and got herself comfortable, looking around the virtual theater space. It was dimly lit, as a good theater was supposed to be, featuring the occasional silhouettes of virtual theatergoers. Bev disabled them, preferring to be alone—even if only virtually. She then waited for the film to upload, a process that normally took about 15 seconds. When its poster finally did—which always preceded any new film—Bev couldn't help but let out a small gasp. There, once again, was the coquettish smile, the woman of authority… and the film's title struck her next: "The Name of the Painting."

By the timestamp of production, it had been rendered 7 minutes ago.

Chapter 9

"The affected grids' monitoring systems reported an electrical event akin to an electromagnetic pulse—a blast of current along even our most insulated wires, tripping safety fuses and damaging certain unshielded components."

-Internal message from a New Phoenix Electrical technician to management, flagged for elevated system relevance

* * *

Hannah Preacher still felt her lover's arms around her, still felt his weight and the heat of their bodies beneath the sheets of their final tryst. He had been so worried that night, so preoccupied with what he called 'urgent work affairs.' That preoccupation quickly melted away into mutual bliss, an act more electric than it had ever felt in the past. *What was so different that night? What worried Quaine, a man usually so calm and collected, unworried and confident?*

Hannah had planned to ask him about it in the morning, instead basking in the glow of the moment they'd shared. But when morning came creeping in in bright lines from behind the wooden blinds of her apartment window, Quaine was nowhere to be found. No note, no call.

Nothing.

A person made of softer stuff might try to force those memories out, to avoid dwelling on the past or the hurt it brought… but not Hannah. Hannah dwelled on it and channeled it, using it as she used the light itself. The confusion and grief burned inside her like gas to an engine—an engine that drove her here to this roadside diner. She was outside the diner itself, sitting on a bus pickup bench that faced the restaurant. Inside the diner, deposited hours before, was a tablet she'd 'borrowed' from a man too distracted with his coffee stirring to notice nimble fingers.

She had programmed the tablet to interact with VitaCorp webpages repeatedly as a normal user might. Then, after a fixed time delay—something that would have triggered about 18 minutes ago—the tablet was to begin mailing bomb threats to VitaCorp through its contact forms provided on their webpage. Automatic filtering would snare the threats immediately, and corporate goons should have been dispatched to the WiFi-traced diner mere seconds later... *what was taking them so long?*

As if on cue to answer that very question, Hannah then noticed the advancing black blot against the sun-streaked towers of the distance. Lone, dressed in a dark suit, and traveling at considerable speed, he moved by way of large parabolic leaps over the city, not so much *flying* as *bounding*. Hannah watched as he vanished behind the diner itself, landing, before he emerged on-foot walking towards the store's entrance. *Fish, meet bait.*

The man pushed his way through the door, slipping a tactical holo-display over his left eye. No doubt, it would be scanning for the unique ID of the tablet device, allowing for quick visual recognition. *It was time to reel in.*

Hannah had chosen this location for two reasons. First, the food was shit, meaning that it was rarely crowded. And second, the diner itself had only two entrances: a front one, surrounded by large, glass windows, and a rear one for staff that exited to an adjacent alley. Hannah moved towards that rear entrance now and removed the padlock she'd had in her pocket. With a quick click, it was secured, preventing anyone inside from fleeing out the back.

Next, she walked the perimeter of the building and moseyed her way into the stuffy air of the diner. The interior was yellowing and smelled a mixture of mold and maple syrup. Old songs from the 2080s looped idly in the background, while still, two-dimensional images of celebrities from the Old World and the New littered the walls. Hannah took a seat at the countertop, doing her best to seem nonchalant as she glanced around the store. There were eleven people: two waitstaff behind the counter, a third roving around, a couple half way through a shortstack—and by their arguments, more than half way through their marriage—a lone woman sitting three seats down the counter, a mother and two children on a table near the door, Hannah herself, and the VitaCorp suit bending to examine the underside of tables, much to the protest of the arguing couple. Hannah was glad that the family was near the door—easy for them to flee if things got ugly— but she made a mental note to steer any *ugliness* away and towards the back.

The suit moved to the next table, operating with a smooth and practiced efficiency. Searching the unit two tables ahead would place him just behind Hannah's seat, and at a range easily accessible with the stun-gun she had primed in her jacket pocket. *Just a little further,* she thought. Her hand tightened on the grip.

Despite her fearlessness in the face of danger, Hannah herself was no professional… and like all amateurs on the brink of some critical success, tunnel vision began to set in. She focused her mind on the man's rifling search, on the imagined extension of her stun gun, on the questions she would ask of him once he was subdued with the cuffs in her pants pocket, with what she would say to the surprised patrons of the diner. For thinking of all of those things, Hannah's attention was too finely divided to notice the momentary flicker of a shadow passing overhead. Had she turned her head, she might have seen the additional man land outside on the sidewalk. Or the second. Or the third.

But city windows were designed for sound insulation, and so Hannah heard no landings, nor did she have any idea that the agents outside watched her remove her stun gun and creep towards the agent searching beneath tables. She didn't even hear the whirring of a charging plasma weapon, drawn and aimed through the glass window at her side.

What she did hear, however, was the overlaid sound of three simultaneous disruptions. The first was the crashing of the glass window near the entrance, shattered into shards by a crackling plasma round. The round flew low and struck a nearby table, erupting into white-hot molten metal. *Someone shot at me?*

The second sound was a scream of pain from beyond the shattered window; a suit outdoors watched in horror as the arm that once held his plasma pistol was now cleaved cleanly in two.

The third was the staccato report of a continued gunfight, the figures just outside the diner whirling and shooting towards a threat at their back. *Someone shot at them?*

Hannah had always had a phrase she enjoyed using, a *momenta non comprenda*. It was an entirely made-up phrase of hers, meant to sound Latin, and she wasn't even sure if the Latin itself was right, but the meaning, at least, was obvious enough: it was a moment so utterly unanticipated that it was beyond comprehension, the kinds of moments that froze the processor of the mind... force reboot required. It was the kind of 'brain not responding' look a man wore in the movies when the PI dropped a stack of drone photos on his desk showing him and his secret mistress in their private retreat. It was the echoing blankness worn by the woman whose 400-gigabyte scripting project had deleted itself overnight. It was the puzzled look of the executive at the ATM, whose bank account now showed a zero credit balance thanks to clever fraudsters.

Hannah had always enjoyed watching such moments of profound confusion freeze others, but this was the first time she experienced it from the other end. How did the idyllic diner suddenly erupt into such violence? Who was shooting at whom? Who was shouting? And why was Hannah now twisting through the air?

Hannah's *momenta non comprenda* ended with her head striking the floor, a VitaCorp suit pressing down on her. His arms wrapped and grabbed at her, trying to subdue her—for arrest or for execution, Hannah couldn't be sure. Glass bottles and cups exploded on the countertop. A plop of maple syrup splattered to the ground, still uncomfortably hot from its only-instantaneous contact with a plasma round. Hannah's head rang from the impact, and her strength was waning quickly. She'd hoped to keep her *status* a secret from the agents, but that was a card she couldn't continue to leave unplayed. Hannah probed outwards with her mind, finding the gentle yellowing glow of the light-rimmed jukebox against the wall. She felt the light's reassuring call… and in response, she breathed it in.

Tendrils of yellow light slid from the jukebox to Hannah, drawing into her body and bringing her renewed strength. The ringing pain of her head impact faded before that rush, and her muscles reinvigorated in her struggle against the man on top of her. Her eyes began to glow softly, adding a sparkling luminescence to the whites and the iris. Her pupils contracted to twin pinpoints.

"She's carrying a spark," the agent on top of her yelled. "Requesting assistance!"

"Active shooters in the lot firing at our team," yelled one of the agents outside. "Still pinned out here!"

Giving up on the physical struggle to hold her arms in place, the man formerly grappling Hannah instead reached upwards and began to draw from the lights overhead. Small, incandescent trails poured from ceiling fixtures to his outstretched palm. The man's eyes, too, began to glow.

Hannah saw the lights overhead and focused her awareness on them. She then pushed with all the force she could muster. Newton's laws dictated that every force, every action, brought about an equal and opposite reaction… and as Hannah, lying on the floor, had no way to move down, the light could do nothing but shoot *up*.

The light fixture shot upwards through the loose paneled ceiling, immediately releasing a shower of foam tiles that bounced harmlessly off Hannah's assailant. Next, however, fell the large metal fragments of the frame that had previously held the light fixture in place, and when this struck the man, the momentary stun was enough to weaken his hold. Hannah burned her remaining light as she pushed off the screen set on the wall that her feet pointed to. It was just enough: she slid out and away from underneath her attacker. As she skidded across the floor, her head bumped into chair legs, and she stopped abruptly as she collided with the base of a table—there would be time for pain later. Hannah rolled and vaulted to her feet, observing the scene with clarity for the first time. The family by the door had fled—thankfully—but the three suits outside had managed to climb in through the shattered window and were now using the knee-height wall beneath it for cover. They were firing at an unknown third party out across the parking lot, a pair of shooters who sheltered behind a parked car.

"Josef, suppressing fire on the shooters," one of the agents called. "Rayder and I are rotating to spark."

Hannah pulled in light from the nearest source, a tabletop lamp with a dull incandescent bulb. The power it brought was nominal, but it was *something*. She then desperately scanned for a way out, watching as three of the suits began to all draw from nearby fixtures. *Odds not looking good.*

Tendrils of light ran from one lamp towards the outstretched arm of a man, the former-shooter that was called Rayder. On the ground between her and Rayder was the molten-hot pool of a plasma round that was fired. With a rush, Hannah mentally shoved against the pool of glowing plasma, surprised to see it not only react to her push, but also do precisely what she'd hoped it would. It splattered away and outwards from her, as though a puddle kicked by a heavy boot. The hot plasma splashed onto a helpless Rayder before the tendril of light reached his hand. He went down screaming and rolling.

Hannah drew in more light as she turned and ran towards the back of the store, knowing that she was fleeing towards a dead end—but with two advancing enemies, her options were running short. Rayder's still-unnamed shooting partner raised his plasma weapon and aimed for Hannah's back, squeezing off three rounds. As Hannah scrambled away, she watched as the balls of energy melted holes in the walls beside her, each shot a miss more narrow than the last. She dove behind the cover of the kitchen's entryway.

In the kitchen, pots of water simmered on open-flame cooktops and a skillet of eggs began to smoke as it blackened. Two terrified cooks held their hands up in surrender as Hannah drew near… she gestured them downwards, using that universal body language for *hide and shut up*. They complied.

Hannah crept through the kitchen, crouching behind the low island in the center of the silver-and-tile room. Just ten feet away, she saw the door that she had padlocked shut from the outside. If only there were a way…

Suddenly, the door shook and rumbled as someone fought to open it from the outside. Hannah's eyes widened. *VitaCorp backup?* If so, she was as good as dead. She heard the approach of the two agents entering the kitchen, spreading out to circle the island from both sides. Just then, a hole was punched in the door by a blast of white, the handle and padlock melting away to bubbling liquid metal. The door was kicked open, and in stepped a man wearing a dark motorcycle helmet. "CSP! Stop right where you are!"

Hannah knew that voice… she looked to the opaque lens of the helmet and gave only a single, urgent command: "run." She then bolted for the door, and despite the CSP's raised weapon, he didn't shoot. He instead allowed Hannah to run past as he opened fire on the advancing suits deeper in the kitchen. With Pollock holding the front window down from his parking lot cover, Rob had been sent to sweep in from the rear to help the girl. As he continued to squeeze off round after round, the VitaCorp agents pushed against his plasma bolts—they deflected harmlessly to either side, splattering hot water and splintering cookware. His weapon demonstrably ineffective, Rob also backed through that rear door.

Outside in the blinding light of the outdoors, Hannah ran through the alley as fast as her legs would take her. She pulled for light to help boost her running, but there was no single source in reach. The hot sun shone overhead through a white layer of haze, but that, of course, was too far to draw from. Worse, still, was that all nearby overhead streetlights were switched off. And though she could see some illuminated signs along the walls and tops of buildings, she had no means to get airborne. Pushing was all she knew how to do, and one couldn't push off lights above to gain in altitude. Behind her, she now heard the scuffling footsteps of the agents who had burst out into the alleyway. It sounded like they ignored the CSP entirely, pushing after Hannah instead. She bolted towards the nearest street and leapt onto the hood of a car waiting at an unloading zone… its headlights, and the taillights of a car in front, would suffice. She pushed off of both with all of her force, balancing between the two anchors to gain a vertical trajectory. Then, within moments, she was airborne entirely, leaping in great bounds from source to source.

When light-flying in the night, streetlights provided firm anchors to travel with—the two lines of regularly-spaced lightsources were perfect for balancing, with pushes to the left and right for stability. She could then push firmly against light sources behind her (and gently against the sources in front of her) for a balanced and controlled means to travel over roadways.

Daytime flight, in contrast, was a separate beast entirely. With so few lights on during the day, each leap was a blind risk. As she flew from one point to the next, she had no guarantee that there would be some light to stabilize herself against. And if she pushed over a tower and found nothing to brace herself against on the other side, it would be a quick drop to the unforgiving concrete below. *No time for such hypotheticals,* she thought, bounding forwards again. She pushed off a large red logo on the front of a 15-story tower, one that read STRATOMARK, watching as the letters rained sparks and collapsed behind her from the force of her shove. *That should slow them down,* she thought. One benefit to running on the street was the ability to hear the footsteps of pursuers… in the air, pursuit was silent, and with the active demands of flight, she couldn't even risk turning her head to check over her shoulder.

Bounding over the next building, a large digital display on the front face of the next tower provided a wide wall for her to push against, regaining control of her momentum. As she began to fall downwards, she pushed against the light of a comms tower to her left, turning in mid-air. Her new forwards would carry her towards the heart of the downtown district, a place where the commercialized skyscrapers were even more densely covered with advertisements, glowing signs, and screens—safety nets were never a bad idea. Between her and downtown, an elevated train track ran the entire length, and its rail signals were perpetually lit. It was the perfect skyway for daytime travel, and she quickly began to fly her way along it.

Soon beneath her she saw a train running towards the downtown faster than she could push, and, seeing an opportunity to reach the downtown faster, she lowered herself down and landed roughly against the roof of the train. The shock of the rough landing—more a controlled drop—sent her leg into screaming protests of pain, but the glow she held within seemed to immediately begin to tingle around the protesting leg, soothing the pain away.

She whirled around on the roof of the speeding train, looking for her pursuers in the skyline above. With twin *thunks*, she heard them land on the train as well—one on the train car in the front, and another three cars behind her. She was surrounded.

On some synchronized cue, both suits extended their dominant hand. Their arms began to glow before a rod of pure white light emerged from each, solidifying into a lengthy blade. *They can do that?* Hannah thought. She pushed her own hand forwards and tried mirroring their gesture, but no blade emerged... *I should've practiced this more.*

Sighing in desperation, Hannah spread her arms out and began pulling light from each consecutive signal they passed.

With how fast the train was moving, she only got the slightest drink from each before the connection was broken, but she could feel each successive link bringing her further and further power. Her vision washed white, and the sound of the train began to fade away behind the pulsing of energy in her mind.

"Cut her vines," one of the two shouted, pointing at the rapidly-forming-and-dissipating tendrils of light connecting Hannah to the rail signals. The one in the rear leapt over a gap between cars, placing him only two carts behind her. Ahead, the looming towers of the skyline began to draw nearer. The shadow of the black VitaCorp obelisk set the train in darkness, each agent advancing further. But as Hannah drew from more and more signals, soon she felt a critical internal *shift*. The energy within became a maelstrom, and that maelstrom begged—no, demanded—to be manifested in the world. Hannah allowed it to be so, and she felt like a pressure valve had released in her mind as the energy coalesced into a ring of light surrounding her. *I can do that?* she balked. *I should've practiced this more.*

"She's gone halo tier!" the one at the front shouted, placing a finger to a comms device in his ear—probably to signal for backup. But Hannah felt the extent of her new capabilities, felt the potential that the energy buzzing around her could bring… and she reached mentally for the energy nexus that held the construction together, and she squeezed it with her mind until it shattered like the brittle shell of an egg.

The ring exploded outwards, unleashing a powerful wave of light that disabled electronics—an EMP. The electric train lurched, suddenly without a motor to drive it. The agent at the train's front was thrown forwards and down onto the track, where the screeching vehicle passed over him and ground him into red mist. The agent at the rear of the train and Hannah both were sent stumbling violently forwards. Hannah fell between two carts and landed—roughly—on the transit platform between them, sure that she must have broken an arm or a leg. Perhaps it was both. The agent, on the other hand, found that the danger of running with scissors was nothing compared to being launched forwards while holding a stick of pure, searing plasma. The lightblade carved his left arm off entirely, and as he rolled towards the edge of the train, he tried to stab the blade into the train to stop his outward trajectory. It had the effectiveness of trying to stop a fall by sticking a hot knife into a wall of butter. As the blade melted its way through the train, it offered no resistance, and the hapless agent rolled off the train roof in time to meet the vertical signpost of a rail signal. The blade he held fizzled out instantly.

Chapter 10

"Look, I know the clip is not verified, but you gotta believe me... I saw it with my own eyes. Somehow, the girl flew onto the train and there was this fight—and I think she's the one that blew out the power somehow. It looks like a render but I swear, I recorded it myself from my office window. This wasn't an M film, it was real."

-User Admanbydosage defends veracity of his uploaded video clip against claims it was faked, flagged for system investigation

* * *

The teacup rattled as rookie CSP Agent Rob Boardsmith set it down on its saucer.

"Drink more," Pollock said. "It'll help bring you back down."

"I don't usually like tea," Rob replied.

"It's not just tea in there," Pollock said, cracking a conspiratorial smile.

Rob took a long pull of the bitter, hot liquid. As he held it in his mouth, he felt its heat, and that observation brought him back to the warm, slick blood on his hands as he tended to the bleeding VitaCorp agent inside the diner.

"They were gonna shoot Hannah," Rob said.

"That's right, partner," Pollock reaffirmed. "Right in the middle of the diner, with all those civilians nearby."

"We shot near civilians," Rob said.

"We *saved* those civilians," Pollock corrected, watching the worry play out on the younger agent's face. "Saved the woman, too. Look… we all remember our first. I still see the face of mine, all these years later."

"It was him or someone innocent," Rob said, his own eyes distant.

"That's right, partner. Him or someone innocent. It wasn't even your plasma round that got him," Pollock added, remembering the foam at the mouth from a suicide pill. Both agents who remained at the diner chose the pill over arrest.

"It was their own pill," Rob reminded himself. Then he frowned. "If we'd never showed up, they'd—"

"If we'd never showed up, innocent people would've gotten hurt. They chose to go there, they chose to jeopardize folks." Pollock reached over and took a large gulp from Rob's teacup.

"There was something *in* him, the one I was on as he passed…" Rob trailed to silence. Pollock let that silence hang, inviting Rob to continue. "Whatever it was, it got onto me…"

"I'd have thought they would've covered blood at the academy," Pollock joked, trying to inject some levity.

Rob gave him a stern look. "Sam, I'm being serious. Something… *indescribable.* I'd never seen stuff like that. And…. I think it went *into* me."

Pollock chewed on the inside of his cheeks, thinking. "They'll have you talk to Shrink for a couple weeks," he finally said, frowning at the thought. The low-functioning AI software served as a sort of talk therapy for agents who'd been through stressful situations. Pollock never found it particularly helpful, but maybe it'd help calm Rob back to reality.

"I think I'm feeling the tea now," Rob said, eyeing the teacup. "What'd you put in that?"

"Don't you worry, partner," Pollock said, smiling again. "I got your back. Also just got a ping from Preacher, looks like she responded to our request for a chat."

"You owe me 200 credits," Rob said.

"Yeah yeah, there'll be time to gloat later. You feel ready to debrief the lady?"

Rob nodded.

"Then, CSP, let's move."

* * *

The two agents walked out onto the rooftop of the CSP headquarters, each squinting at the bright light of the glowing overcast haze of daylight.

"Not a typical meeting space," Pollock remarked.

"Not a typical meeting," came a voice from just over the edge of the roof. Hannah Preacher rose into view, stepping lightly onto the raised perimeter of the rooftop. With a gentle hop, she was standing beside the two agents, her eyes still glowing softly. "I guess I owe the two of you some thanks," she said.

"What you owe is some explanation," Rob said.

"And I'll give it—let's just go through it in order. How did you two wind up at that diner?"

"We were following you," Pollock said bluntly. "You let on that you knew of some connection to the flying suits, but wouldn't tell us what. Other leads led to dead ends, so we wanted to see what you knew."

Hannah shrugged. "Quaine—about three days before he disappeared—I found a video of those flying guys online, and I showed it to him. He tensed right up, paling in a way that I wasn't used to seeing. Told me to run if I ever saw any."

"And why didn't you tell us that when we spoke last?" Rob asked.

"Because that's only half the story. The other half, well…" Hannah drew in a line of red light from a radio tower on the rooftop. "The day he vanished—well, right after the last night we spent together—I could do *this*. I think he did it to me somehow… gave me these abilities. In the videos, you see the suits chasing down and abducting—or sometimes killing— other people who could fly. Like they're picking them off, one at a time. So I kept my talents to myself, choosing not to trust two men that I had only just met. That was, until you saved my life back at the diner."

"What were *you* doing at that diner?" Pollock asked.

"Investigating, same as you. I planted a tablet in the diner that mailed VitaCorp some bomb threats, trying to flush out one of their enforcers. It worked, so I moved into the diner to… *chat* with him."

"Well, your trap was actually theirs," Pollock said. "As you were walking in, we watched a new enforcer fly in and immediately head over to the back—presumably to lock the door—"

"I blasted their padlock away," Rob added.

"…And then two more dropped in from the west, all synchronized and on comms devices. They had you cornered."

"Bastards figured me out…" Hannah said, shaking her head. "Smarter than I gave them credit for."

"They can get surveillance access, and their digital forensics teams are talented, if not thorough."

"Sam and I found motorbike helmets on a nice pair of bikes parked two blocks away," Rob added. "A bike lot without any cameras we could see."

"V.C. seemed the types to hold grudges, and we wanted to make sure they couldn't identify us right away," Pollock said. "They still probably might… but it should buy us some time."

"And if they identify you two?" Hannah asked.

"We can take care of ourselves," Pollock said, not quite believing the words as he said them. "What happened to the two that flew off after you?"

"Now resembling ground beef," Hannah replied. "Don't ask. So where does this leave the investigation?"

Pollock sighed. "In surprisingly decent shape, actually. Rob's got something."

Rob stepped forwards. "After the shoot-out this morning, my commanding officer offered to reassign me to city policework less likely to involve live-fire… at least until I had a chance to unpack it with Shrink. She offered me the pick of the case board: tax fraudsters using bogus construction projects for evasion, a domestic disturbance case against a city official, *a span of homicides on city rooftops under strange circumstances…*" Rob said, emphasizing the last one. "I asked to see the case files to the homicides. Like I said, almost all of them on rooftops. Bodies mutilated with surgical intent, specifically to prevent any sort of identification. No fingerprints, no teeth, no face ID… and get this: most of the sites where they discover the bodies feature unexplained scorchmarks and melted metal. Several of the bodies even feature burns caused by superheated objects never recovered on-scene, deep gashes that were instantly cauterized by heat resembling a blowtorch."

"You think you found the corpse trail of one of their enforcers?" Hannah asked, crossing her arms.

"Video camera footage all-but-confirms it. We've got recordings of flying figures in and around most of these crime scenes right around the TOD. It gets more interesting: almost all of the clips feature one particular figure unlike the rest. Usually alone, sometimes with other suits—seems to be the leader of the pack, first in any chase. Wears a hooded black leather jacket, *not a suit.* Moves unlike any other I've seen."

Rob held his phone forwards, zoomed in on a still from a surveillance video. Hannah looked at the hooded figure in that photograph and felt an involuntary shudder rise. "So here's our boogeyman?" she asked, committing the silhouette to memory.

"There he is," Pollock replied. "And even better… we think he let something slip."

Chapter 11

"And I'll sit down for dinner, and I'll put on the AR lenses, and it projects an image of my friend sitting at the table across from me, like we're not eating thirty-four miles apart on opposite ends of the city. Sure, it's shallow, and I can acknowledge it isn't as great as the real deal, but that doesn't even matter. Life gets busy, and traveling across districts can be slow, so it's one of the best ways I can still feel connected to people."

-Conversation recorded in the first ring, low system priority

* * *

Beverly Beadie's rainboots splashed through the cold, reflective pools gathering on the uneven sidewalks as she trudged forwards into the bitter wind. She drew her raincoat tighter to her body, grateful for the partial windbreak of the milling crowds in front of her. Beggars, businesspeople, workers, wanderers… the river of faces and forms flew past— faces she would never likely see again. Who among them would remember the slight girl with the blue hair and the deep red raincoat, the one who wore the uncomfortable scowl in an uncomfortable crowd?

The natural, genmod blue of her hair was nearly a sort of camouflage against the deep blues of the city, as inconspicuous as a pigeon on a concrete roof. She had, of course, tried her hands at various colors and styles, eventually finding she hated the eyes drawn to the bright, dazzling colors of neon… colors that nearly glowed like the advertisement drones and car-pulled billboards that flickered and pulsed with inviting brightness in a darkened city. She'd rather be invisible, and she'd rather be blue.

She felt blue tonight, anyways. She found the set of doors she'd been seeking and pushed them open, entering an outdoor square courtyard in two tiers. It was much warmer in here, and the rain only pattered down heavy in a few vertical columns—overhead, a retractable clear plastic roof extended over the space, keeping it dry except for the few gaps in coverage.

Bev took off her coat and held it, gathering her bearings. She then moved towards the center of the courtyard, passing a trickle of water from the roof. She felt its gentle splashing on her side and face, wondering how much of her makeup had survived the journey over. *So much more effort than it's worth,* she thought, wondering if she should find a public restroom and reapply.

"Beverly?" a male voice asked. She turned and saw a young man, somewhere in his mid-twenties, wearing a pair of smartlenses. She couldn't see the contents of his AR view, but she saw his eyes flicker left and right, likely comparing her to the picture in his FOV—her dating profile, she was sure.

"It *is* you! Hey, I'm Darren," he said, going in for an introductory hug. "It's great to finally meet you."

"Same," Bev said, surprised to finally have a date with somebody who even remotely resembled his pictures. *Hold your horses there, Bev. Let's see if he still acts the same, too.*

"The place I was telling you about is just upstairs," Darren said. "Let's go check it out?"

He touched her elbow as he led her away towards the outdoor elevator. It was a rusted, *ancient* thing, rolling up and down four poles staked in the ground at each corner with an engine that hummed like no electric engine Bev had ever heard before. Its metal floor was caked with unwashed dirt, and the sides of the open-air cage featured ads behind a discolored plastic screen with a backlight that flickered as the motor began its ascent. *"Get a carrier-2 check from the comfort of your home!"* one ad said, immediately dating itself: with the curing of HBI-2 about a decade ago—a less virulent strain of the original falling sickness—carrier-2 checks were a thing firmly rooted in the past. *Even a wicked company can do some good sometimes,* Bev thought, letting her eyes find the megastructure that dominated the visible skyline. Through the plastic roof overhead still rippling with raindrops and tricklings of water, the black, glass tower almost seemed to sway in place. But Bev knew it was anything but alive... there was nowhere more antithetical to *alive.*

The elevator came to a quick and jarring stop at the top of the rise, and Bev allowed herself to be led towards the red velvet structure that dominated the upper floor. Garish spotlights swiveled left and right, illuminating the club's name. *The Laugh Track* was only two weeks old, and it had already acquired a reputation as *the place to be* among the younger crowds of New Phoenix. Reservations were allegedly impossible to get for months, but it seemed that Darren Almeida was a well-connected man.

"First round's on me," Darren said as the two sat at their table. It was a private, darkened room with a glass wall that looked down onto a stage twenty feet below, reminiscent of a dine-in opera box more than a comedy club. She reasoned that comedy clubs were a decent venue for this sort of thing, as she could always tune in to the show if her date became boring... and even if the show proved uninteresting, her employer would love to hear whatever details she could glean about Groucho.

"Think he'll be as good as they say?" Darren asked, eyeing the stage below. At its center stood an ancient theme-park animatronic with a screen for a head, currently displaying a basic happy-face graphic. A small camera drone whirred past their window, one of Groucho's many eyes and ears that flitted through the club. One froze in place near a table at the lower level, and Groucho's screen updated to show the face of a woman sitting at that table. Then, the stage speakers kicked to life.

"Behold," Groucho's synthesized voice began, "the true opposite of your emcee. For while Groucho is known for his *artificial intelligence,* this woman is known for her *natural stupidity.*" A laugh track then sounded throughout the club, and most of the audience laughed along with it—the mortified woman's table companions loudest of all.

Bev shrugged. "Wordplay is one thing, but comedy is pretty formulaic… set up expectations, and then betray those expectations. Even weak AI have a pretty easy time with it. Watch."

Beverly leaned towards the window as the animatronic's face reset to a basic happy-face graphic. "What's made of plastic and filled to the brim?" The AI waited for dramatic effect. "A water bottle!" it proudly declared. Nobody laughed.

"Guess not every joke lands—" Darren began, but Beverly held up a finger.

Groucho continued. "What's made of plastic and empty inside?"

The happy face on Groucho's screen flashed away to reveal the face of the woman from earlier. "This woman!" Groucho declared, and again the crowd erupted into laughter. The woman buried her face in her hands.

"I need a drink long before one of those drones approaches our table," Bev said. She pulled out her phone and tapped the geozone button. Her phone immediately pulled up the drink menu, each one featuring a price in credits and a large yellow ORDER button. After brief perusal, Bev chose her go-to, American whisky, neat, and pressed the button. A pop-up on her phone said "DARREN ALMEIDA HAS OFFERED TO BUY YOUR DRINK. ACCEPT?"

Bev's finger vacillated over the buttons for a moment, before she sighed and pressed YES.

* * *

Groucho continued his volley of jokes—more accurately labeled an insulting spree—and Bev made a mental note to report to work that Groucho was of little company interest. The AI, it seemed, was more a glorified Markov chain than bonafide intelligence. Her interest in the machine sated, she turned down their volume receiver until the jokes were a distant rumble.

Darren spoke about himself, *a lot.* That didn't surprise Bev very much, as people generally tend to dislike silence, and they try to fill that silence with conversation… and it just so happens that most people use their own lives as conversational fodder when they're not quite sure what else to say. He spoke of his job and of his family, of his interests and his hobbies and his passions… "My trading office is just three blocks north of here, H.C. Werner Capital Financials." "My dad never really felt like he belonged in the city." "Personally, I'm a huge photography nerd and I've even got my own rig for capturing virtual." "My ideal retirement is probably owning a small coffee shop right on the park… the kind with handpours, not those big piperigs." Eventually, he started speaking about his values, his philosophy, his perspectives. "I'm not *that type of guy*… I need to really trust someone before I get to know them intimately," he said. "People get too negative and judge-y about stuff." "I've always had a secret soft-spot for the elderly." "I think that the wealth disparity in this city is borderline criminal by now… there's gotta be a way that's more fair."

It was all very pleasant, sure, but every time Bev asked a follow-up question in response, she couldn't help but feel like Michelangelo in the ingest terminal, just passively *absorbing* information that he was passively dispensing.

Perhaps he started to pick up on Bev's slipping enthusiasm, or maybe he'd simply run out of interesting things to say about himself, but finally he turned the conversation towards her. "Tell me about your job. You mentioned it was something in programming?"

As Bev told him about her job, she could see the interest level in his eyes immediately rise. "*You* work with *Michelangelo?*"

"Yep," Bev said nonchalantly. "Helped make him, actually." She took another sip of her drink.

He balked at her. "*The* most famous director/novelist/artist/architect of modern history, and perhaps human history at large, and she just says 'helped make him' and takes a sip of whisky. Now *this* I almost can't believe."

"Not used to your dates having a job flashier than yours?" Bev asked, a challenge of a smile now on her face.

"Not used to dating people with a title similar to '*mother of the President of the United Americas*,'" he said in reply.

Mother. That word still stung, and Beverly wondered if he could see her wince.

Darren's mouth parted into a gasp of impressed surprise. "Child prodigy, youngest hire in ArtGen history… holy shit, Bev. Why didn't you lead with this?"

"Are you searchstalking me?" Bev asked, watching his eyes flick back and forth as he read articles and results in his AR glasses display.

"A Turing Prize at 16? Recipient of the Three Laws Grant for AI development at 19?" She was almost amused, watching him with this stunned expression as he read onwards through her accomplishments and qualifications. He then tapped the side of his glasses, shutting off the AR component. "Come with me back to mine? The drinks are a lot cheaper, and I really *really* want to get to know you better."

"I thought you weren't *that type of guy?*"

"I didn't realize you were *this kind of woman*," he replied, gesturing to her. "A giant in your industry. A titan! Like, holy shit, you helped crack the first safe AI implementation, and now you're just sitting here letting me blab on and on about my life like I'm somebody important. You helped throw humanity forwards into a new age, and I'm just going on about stock algorithms. You even talked about AI when we were talking about Groucho… I should've asked at the start. I'm an idiot— an idiot!"

Bev smiled, allowing herself to be fully amused now. She at least began to feel that his interest was *genuine*… he seemed impressed with her work and capabilities a lot more than just for her body and attractive features. *Maybe it's just my wealth and position he's attracted to? And still not the actual *me*?*

But Bev knew that if she rebuffed him and went back to her apartment by herself, soon—as always—the loneliness would creep back up on her, and she'd feel the aching empty of the bed once again. She'd cry then as she cried most nights until the rain's pattering soothed her to sleep… maybe some shallow company for the night was better than none at all.

She leaned in, locking eyes. "So how far away was it that you said you lived?"

Chapter 12

"For every terabyte of information exchanged on the open web, there's more than 50 petabytes of encrypted data streaming through virtual rivers we can poke our head into— and observe—but never understand."

-Report submitted by Nicholas Powell as part of a semi-annual report on data transparency

* * *

The hunter in the black, hooded leather jacket wiped the blood from the back of his hands onto the shirt of the nearest corpse. There were seven dead around him, their bodies in loose, wet pieces strewn about the warehouse floor. The stacks of boxes and tall metal shelves bore smoking, jagged gashes and spatters of blood, traces of the conflict that erupted only minutes before. But conflicts were typically two-sided... and with the energy that Braxton carried, the fight had felt as though there were only one side. That side was the side of death, an unyielding force that moved through the warehouse like a chill on a winter's midnight. Men and women had shouted, they had run... they had burned files and stomped on screens and sounded their secret alarms... but one by one, they had fallen to the hunter's lightsword. There were four more by the entryway, two corpses by the stairs... one on the shitter— an unfortunate way to die, no doubt—and three in the nearest hall. Well, more accurately, six halves.

"Nineteen men and women," Braxton said, stepping towards the surviving men propped against the wall. They were bloodied and sat with their heads bowed, avoiding the hunter's gaze. "And then *there were two.*"

He squatted down and lifted the head of the nearest, meeting his gaze. "I should have some questions for you," he said. The man spat bloody spittle.

Braxton calmly wiped it from his face, and offered his widest smile. *How often the dying tried to goad you into killing them... my temper is not so fragile a thing.* He released the first man's head and stepped back, surveying the pair of them. The one on the right, his eyes darted around the floor wildly, as though looking for a way out. Maybe he was the better to start with...

People so often responded well to a little showmanship, and so Braxton removed the injector pen from his front jacket pocket. He bent over the frightened man, redirecting his weak attempts to block Braxton, and pressed the injector to his neck. The pen dispensed its payload with a click.

He then stepped back and pulled a glass vial from the same pocket he'd withdrawn the injector pen. Both sets of eyes stared at the curious vial, a liquid that seemed to glow a bright and vibrant pink. "We call them nanoelectric diodes," Braxton said. "Developed to assist with endoscopic surgeries. When injected to the bloodstream, these provide better illumination for bypass surgeries than the camera-mounted flashlight. Body breaks them down within 72 hours, passed harmlessly."

The hunter squatted down in front of the duo. "You've seen what people like me can do?" He set the vial on the ground and shoved his will against it. It launched forwards and struck the wall between them, shattering.

"Right now, my friend, I can feel a billion distinct points of light coursing through your body... each one calling out for me to touch. Do you know what it's like, when a billion points in your blood move in unison? It's like a shotgun blast, but *everywhere at once.* A horrible way to go, I'm sure. Those who have earned it *do not enjoy it.*" The man's gaze met Braxton's, and Braxton could see desperation behind that look. Terror. Productive feelings for an interrogation target to have.

"I should like to know three things. If you provide me those three things, you will die in a painless fashion. I push the light in your brain, and it's over quick and easy. I will not lie to you, friend. I will not offer you your life, as you've seen me too well for my tastes… and my employer takes certain umbrage with the operations of your little club here. In my line of work, my integrity is the only thing I have to bargain with… and you have my word as a professional that it will be without pain if you assist. If you are silent… well, the mess will be *catastrophic.*"

Braxton let his words hang in the air, the fear driving in deeper like a black wedge. When he felt he had allowed it to ferment for long enough, he asked his questions. "Where is the one known as The Basilisk? Is he human or AI? And if human, how does he continue to outmaneuver our security AI?"

The defiant man spat again. "We are Halogen. We are the light that burns away the darkness, the scum like you and your kind. We—"

Braxton's wrist flicked near his jacket pocket. The defiant man choked on his words, noting the small knife suddenly protruding from his stomach. Another profession might consider such a thing a throwing knife, but Braxton had done no throwing… the small knife had a glowing green light attached to its rear, which Braxton had pushed to launch the projectile forwards. Beneath that neon green light was a blacklight, both drawing from a central battery.

The defiant man gripped the blade and tried to pull free, but Braxton pressed all of his mental weight against it. It stayed firm. Braxton then mentally pulled on the blacklight, yanking the small knife back to his outstretched hand feet away. He then propelled it again forwards, and then pulled it back out, stabbing the wounded man while hardly moving at all.

"As I said," Braxton threatened, the blade continuing to stab in and out with chest-cracking speed, "painful ends for those who are *difficult*."

The scene had had the desired effect, and the surviving man babbled his way through all of the information he knew—which, frustratingly, was absolutely nothing new to Braxton. This Halogen group was clever in the ways they guarded their operation... cells that only knew what they needed to know, getting their orders from encrypted comms top-down. The babbling man had never met the Basilisk, nor did he know anyone who had. He had no idea how they outsmarted the security AI—he had theories, but none that Braxton hadn't already considered—and he tried to offer datadrop IP addresses, but the two he gave were already known to his employer. Both were already being monitored. Braxton gave the man the promised painless end for his earnest cooperation... he died with something close to a smile on his face. Braxton knew it was only a matter of time before Halogen got its hands on a lightbender, one they could use to safeguard their centers of operations, and he hoped that it would be soon, for it always sent his stomach in twisting knots to kill men and women so hopelessly powerless.

The Basilisk... a shadow, a rumor. The name seemed an obvious callback to Roko's Basilisk, a hypothesized AI that would seek to destroy anyone that did not help bring it into existence... but this Basilisk—Halogen's Basilisk—seemed calmer, more collected. He seemed *human*. This wasn't harm for harm's sake alone. Halogen wielded its strikes with an air that VitaCorp should find all too familiar: they were near surgical in their precision.

Braxton tapped the comms unit in his ear and waited for the encrypted call to conncct. Seconds later, Avery's voice rasped in his ear. "Is it done?"

"A full house," Braxton replied.

He could hear the old man's glee in his reply. "Very, very well done, my friend. And the matter of our elusive foe?"

"Didn't know a thing," Braxton replied. He could nearly hear the wide smile wipe from Avery's face.

"Our foe is clever and he is careful, but organizations need members. Recruit enough people, and eventually *someone*'s a fool—the weak link that breaks the entire chain. Stay vigilant, as our IP monitoring may soon have another safehouse for you to visit."

"Yes, sir," Braxton said, clicking off the comms.

* * *

From the second-to-top floor of the VitaCorp tower, Clive Avery's black-crystal office was empty. But beyond that room, through a small doorway near the dark oak bookcase filled with volumes of classics of mythologies of the Old World, was a room of blinding brightness. To Avery, it was the Throne of Olympus. Drawing enough energy to power five entire homes, eighteen massive lamps shone hot, white light into an array of mirrors and lenses. And there, in the center of that array, sat Clive Avery on a grand chair of white marble, a tight rictus like the mask of death upon his face. He felt his heart thumping in wild palpitations, strange pains prickling their ways up and down his arms and legs. The massive lamps connected to his body by way of winding chords of light, drawlines he held so that their power might flow into him, to *heal* him of his misery… but despite all of this power, his foe remained elusive. Despite all of this power, his heart continued to thump irregularly, his nerves continued to fire off signals of pain. Despite all of this power, he felt terrified of his approaching death... and despite all of this power, Tacitus the Pretender still dared to hold leverage above his head. It all still was *not enough.* A secretary approached, her hand held before her face to shield the blinding light from her eyes. Avery stopped drinking in the light and pressed the button on the chair's arm, switching off the array. Eighteen massive lamps powered down, leaving only two sources of light in the room... Avery's eyes, and they shone bright enough for the secretary to need her sunglasses as she lowered her hand and spoke: "Guffries is waiting for you," she said.

He nodded and rose. He simply didn't have enough ichor yet to cure his ailments... *he simply needed more.*

Chapter 13

"Your employment termination appeal has been denied. That the Halogen organization continues to stage attacks under your watch is not the reason you were fired... it is that, after months of focused investigation, you have produced zero actionable intelligence about the group or its shadowed leader, or even the means through which they have outmaneuvered our security software."

-Report submitted from the desk of Harold Lyme

* * *

"I'm Gus... I just drive the bus," the man stammered, lifting and immediately replacing the faded grey cap on his head. "No trouble meant, no sir, no trouble at all... just pick up and drop-off, that's all Gus does. No credits, you see, nothing to give—"

"Relax," the bearded man settling into the passenger seat said, pointing his gun back down towards the center console. "Nobody has to get shot... just follow my instructions precisely."

"An expert at following directions, Gus sure is. Whatever you say, Gus'll do."

"Unlock your cargo hatch."

Gus nodded his head as he toggled the switch. "Un-de-locked, just like you said. Nothing worth taking back there... just—"

"I know what you have. Wait ten seconds."

The two sat in silence, waiting. Through the body of the truck, both heard the faint *thump* of doors sliding shut, and both felt the gentle shift of the truck's suspension as cargo wasn't *removed,* but *added.*

"Now lock the rear again, and we proceed to your delivery as normal." The bearded stranger tucked his weapon in his waistband and donned a faded grey cap like the one Gus wore… both were branded with the silver-lettered VitaCorp logo. "And at the drop-off…" The stranger raised a finger in front of his lips, whispering *shhhhh.* "Mum's the word, yeah?"

"Not a peep from 'ole Gus, roger roger mister sir."

The truck started back up with a lurch, the heavy-electric engine groaning as it brought the vehicle back up to speed. The truck thumped and rumbled over uneven streets marred with potholes and cracked pavement… despite the perpetual construction, it seemed this ring of the city was always crumbling apart.

"Your hands, Gus," the bearded man said. "They're sweating profusely." The glistening palm prints on the steering wheel were obvious, and they might just be obvious enough to make the gate guards suspicious.

"Oh never you mind them," Gus said, wiping them on his jeans. "Gus won't break his smile, oh you know it. Nobody's got a poker face to beat 'ole Gus…" Gus turned to offer the stranger his warmest reassuring smile, but something about the man's face gave him the eebie-jeebies. The texture was wrong, somehow… like damp rubber, almost. It reminded him of the virtual friends he made on the VR masks. The ones who weren't really real, Gus knew that, but they sure acted like they were… they were so close to being perfect, so close to looking like normal, but that little bit of *fake* made the whole picture shatter. *Why's this guy's face do that too?*

The stranger watched Gus frown as he surveyed him. "You're nervous, Gus… I can see it in your face. Faces give so very much away… our thoughts, our intentions, the people that *we really are*… that's why I took mine off."

Gus chuckled, not getting the joke.

"Your face. You…"

"Oh, yes. Took it right off. I can see you were staring at it, probably wondering why it wasn't *quite right*… uncanny valley can be a bitch. But all it took was a trip under the scalpel to make sure that Panopticon—or whatever new ones might come along—can't keep its magnifying glass over every single thing I do."

Gus didn't get the joke, but the man was starting to scare him, so he laughed his hardest, deepest laugh. "That's a rich one, mister. A real rich one."

The bearded man's face twisted into an almost-smile.

"Do you have a family, Gus? A wife? Kids?"

"Gus doesn't have any kids, no sir. We've tried, but my boyfriend just won't get pregnant," he said, snorting at his own joke.

"Think of him, then, as we pull up here… wear that love on your face like a mask of serenity. If they ask about the sweat," he said, reaching over to switch off the truck's air conditioning, "tell them the cooling's broken. And remember, regarding our little stop earlier…."

"Mum's the word," Gus said, nodding.

Gus stopped the vehicle and opened the window as a guard approached. He wore a rifle slung over his chest and was dressed in grey camo, the uniform of choice for VitaCorp's private security forces. "Hey there, Gus… another batch of stiffs for the surgeons?"

"Fresh and ready to go," he said. He passed the guard his ID badge and documentation.

"And your passenger's?" asked the guard.

Gus opened his mouth to reply, but the bearded man spoke first. "Right here, sir," he said, passing a badge he removed from his pocket. "New hire… Gus here has been showing me the routes."

"Welcome to the team," the guard responded with a polite nod. "I've got to verify the delivery."

The guard disappeared into his booth. "You're doing great, Gus," the passenger whispered.

"Stand by to run," came a voice in the bearded man's ear. His comms implant was for emergency use only. *"Database detected our intrusion, they initiated a rollback to previous stable state. Your faked credentials won't come up for the guard…"*

The bearded man looked up and noticed the guard in the booth frowning at his terminal.

"I should be able to slip you into the back-up and we'll let the system catch us again… this time, when it rolls back, you'll be set. Tell him to run it one more time. If he doesn't, burn."

The guard slowly walked his way back to the truck, hands this time on his weapon. "Mr. Barker, was it? We don't have your employee record at all in our system." He then eyed the steering wheel, noticing the sweat prints along the front. "Everything ok here, Gus?"

"Oh, just dandy," Gus said. "AC's gone and broke on me is all."

"I'm gonna need your friend here to step out of the vehicle so we can sort through the problem."

The bearded man moved to speak, but it was Gus, this time, who interrupted.

"Wont'cha run it one more time? This happened at the pick-up, too… damn computers never liked Gus, no sir. His friends neither."

The guard pointed at two nearby guards to stay put near the truck, and then he disappeared back into the guard booth.

"Very finely done, Gus," said the bearded man.

"You seemed like you wanted some extra time to think," he said. "And you also seemed the type with a plan."

"Just how good a plan, we'll find out in a moment," the bearded man said. And then he began to wonder whether he'd bitten off more than he could chew with this one, whether Carter Miles could really compromise the employee databank as easily as he promised…

The guard looked up and smiled widely, offering two big thumbs-up. He then walked out and returned the ID badges, offering a series of apologies to the man with the badge that read Lenny Barker. "Second time's a charm, I guess… never seen it wig out like that before. Either way, you two are approved for drop-off bay seven, half-hour allotment. As you were," he said, stepping backwards and gesturing them in. The reinforced metal gate slid open, and armed guards stepped back and away from the vehicle. Into the compound they drove, Gus approaching the seventh drop-off bay. "You've done well, Gus… you've earned this." The bearded man handed Gus a small flash memory stick. "E-wallet address is in there, along with enough money to never work another day in your life. You want my advice? Take your loved ones and stay clear of this city… bad is about to get a hell of a lot worse."

The man hopped from the passenger seat and joined the unloading crews at the rear of the truck. With the back door opened, the stench of death began to waft outwards; there was only so much that preservatives and scent-masking agents could accomplish. "24,000 kilograms of naked human cadavers," the bearded man said. "Unload this batch easy… I've been told they're extra *ripe,* wouldn't want another burster."

As the unloading crews worked, the bearded man watched them place—a little too roughly—some familiar faces: Grier, Marks, Liz, Bratton, Wendy, and Komen all slid in on the conveyer belt, one at a time, fully naked and still as death. They held their poses admirably—the group had practiced death stiffness for weeks leading up to this—and as they were shuttled in through the draped plastic ribbons that kept the flies away, the scanners overhead checked for valuable prosthetics, not heartbeats.

Into the belly of the beast they went, brave men and women whose fate was now in the hands of chance… The Basilisk only wished he could have told them how proud they made him. As their commander, he had felt it his responsibility to be there, overseeing their entrance to the facility where they would likely die… and it hurt him to know that they would do so without knowing their "friend" and their secret commander were one and the same. With their near-certainty of capture, truth was never an option… but justifications rarely made lies any easier on the soul.

The Basilisk tapped on the side of Gus's truck, indicating that it was time to leave. And as the truck rumbled away on the roads abandoned to disrepair after the flying car revolution, the

Basilisk checked his watch, counting the minutes until the fireworks began.

Chapter 14

"When rendering films, ArtGen systems will often conspicuously recycle faces, voices, and mannerisms from previous projects. For years, media synthesis insiders thought that this tendency revealed a hidden weakness of the Michelangelo system, an indication that it perhaps could only render a fixed number of 'people' with the suitable levels of fidelity. That suggestion is entirely false. ArtGen systems recycle faces for a far simpler reason: to provide viewers with a sense of recognition and stability. It hearkens back to traditional films of old with actual actors on physical sets... and identifiable individuals work as a living sort of trademark, a way for a viewer to conclude that a film they're watching is an ArtGen one—even though the quality is often enough to make that judgment with absolute confidence."

-From Jess Turnscrew's best-selling book "Meet the New Masters: Examining the Titans of the TechnoCreative Age"

* * *

The shuttle pulled up to the corner of Darren's apartment block. Beverly opened the door to the front of the vehicle and sidled in, setting her head back wearily as the driverless taxi shuttle rolled into motion. It was groundborne, so it wouldn't be the fastest way to reach her office, but Bev was looking forward to the lengthy ride to collect her thoughts.

Darren had been in the shower when Bev discovered the camera lens hidden in the bookcase... was it always recording? Was it powered off?

Had it recorded the entirety of last night without Bev being aware of it?

Bev had fled without confronting him about the camera, as she was always one to hate confrontation... and as she felt the shuttle rumble its way away from the apartment block, her own cowardice sickened her further.

She'd heard of a particularly nauseating type of predator, a community that call themselves *baggers,* whose sole purpose is to find men and women of some modicum of fame, seduce them, and upload recordings of their exploits for their masses of followers online. Some commanded dozens of millions of followers, a fact that left Bev torn in her disgust—she hated the baggers, and yet she hated the enabling fans almost just as much. She felt a sense of violation at the thought that maybe she had been recorded in such an intimate, vulnerable moment... and then that sense of violation clashed against her ArtGen AfterDark renderings. How would Jason from debugging have felt about the scene?

It's just a simulation, she thought in her own defense... *it isn't a real video.*

The word *real* bounced around in her mind as she watched the shuttle patter past the tall green trees of *Pyke's Park TruthSpace.* The continually running cameras and their thousands of wires snaked out like capillaries and veins from the heart of public discourse. Here lived that necessity that became a rarity and eventually a commodity in a world dominated by synthesized media: *trust.* She had much respect for the blockchain engineering that went into establishing a chain of trust as these TruthSpaces enabled; the encoding algorithms for the data transfer they required were nothing short of technological miracles. But necessity was often the mother of innovation, and the tumult of the world before TruthSpaces certainly provided that necessity. The ruin of the *falling sickness*, the mass disinformation campaigns waged by the first Turing-passed content synthesizers without any means to validate… it's a wonder the world survived that dark period at all.

But few recoveries from the brink of death are without their scars, and as the shuttle turned, Bev looked to the scar that the city bore in the wake of its own brush with ruin. The VitaCorp tower loomed as it always loomed, like a great black domino ready to tip over onto the rest of the city and crush it to rubble. Bev's hatred of that black obelisk was personal, but it was surely far from unique.

"Prepare your belongings. Estimated arrival to ArtGen HQ in 1 minute," the shuttle's voice said.

* * *

The elevator arrived the very moment Beverly reached the sliding metal doors. In less than a minute, she was walking through her floor, a short stack of four class-S datadrives in hand. Each held 128 petabytes of data… it was time for Michelangelo's morning meal.

Through five biometric scans and security door after security door, the decor around Bev gradually shifted from wealthy office space to high-security research facility. The last door opened with a pressurized hiss to a vast chamber that extended up three floors and down four more. The large, open bay known as *Containment* stood at the center of the tower: through the middle of the room, thick columns of steel and concrete supported the structure itself. The open space was filled with stack after stack of servers and servos, hard drives and processors and hive controllers. Drones flew from station to station with maintenance arms that flashed bright white with weld contacts. Air blew through uncountable vents in perpetual motion, the temperature here kept at what felt pretty near to freezing.

Bev put her hands on the railings of the ledge in front and peered over and downwards at the hive of commotion, finding the sensation eerily similar to how a brain surgeon must feel. Everything here was part of a larger technological organism that could *think*, and Beverly was here to provide the food for thought. She approached the gravity feed. Sometimes, the simplest solutions proved the most elegant: Michelangelo needed to be fed massive amounts of data, but the link had to be one-directional. Any data transfer from Michelangelo to the outside world was a possible containment breach, meaning that sending the content over the internet was not possible. Bev simply threaded the first drive on a small receptacle near the railing and then pushed it forwards. It slid down, on rails, into the bustling server stacks below. She then sent down the second, third, and fourth. In it was all sorts of additional ingest data: outside interviews, audience reactions, aggregated demographics data, movement and organizational data gathered from surveillance systems and personal telephonic devices, and much, much more. At the bottom of the rails, the drives would be read, copied into Michelangelo's internal server architecture, and then destroyed entirely. It was a physical data drop that could not be forced backwards, only one of the countless dozens of containment protocols in place to keep Michelangelo secure from outside imitation, as well as to keep the outside free of Michelangelo. "Eat up," Bev said, before turning around to get out of the cold as quickly as she could. Every time, as soon as she would feel the biting of the containment climate, she'd catch herself wondering why again she so often volunteered for data drop.

Five minutes later, and decidedly warmer, Bev was logged into her ingest terminal and speaking with Michelangelo directly. They spoke of convolution in narrative as Bev was shown increasingly-complex retellings of the same plot, the system trying to find the optimal balance between simplicity and interesting twists on classic structure. The plot was simple enough: a boy and his drone explore a rich, green forest straight out of a painting and they discover ancient ruins inhabited by pre-technologic peoples. Michelangelo's retellings of the story tried different points of view, different approaches to pacing. It experimented with various timelines, from a straight beginning-to-end run to even a version that told the story in reverse. Each iteration brought with it some new twist, and each one would be followed by a barrage of questions, rating the subjective in terms of a scale of one to ten.

After watching the same short film some thirty-odd times, Beverly was grateful to hear the questions turn back to her personal life.

"In your data drop from this morning, I captured video footage of you and a male in close proximity as you passed Wilkes-Clayton TS. Were you two on a date last night?"

"I was," Bev replied.

"And you stayed at his home last night?"

"I did."

"What were your subjective thoughts about the date? Did it go *well*?"

Bev frowned. "I thought he was decent enough over dinner... ticked all the right boxes, and seemed genuinely interested in me as a person."

"I am detecting several indicators that the date went poorly thereafter. Am I correct in this reading?"

"The thing you gotta know about my dating life, Michelangelo, is that it's the same old story every time. Someone shows up and somehow says all the right things... I ask myself, 'is this finally someone I can trust?' and then I do anyways, and then shit somewhere starts to fall apart, and they're not the person I thought they were, and it turns out their kindness was just empty gesture to win me over... like, a whole lot of pretending to be decent to earn my trust and then they, they...." Bev trailed off, frowning deeper. "I don't even know if he did anything wrong, Michelangelo. I don't. I've just been hurt so many times lately that I can't help but feel worthless. I don't trust, and the voice in my mind calls me paranoid, and yet, when I do, I wind up being kicked down *every single time*. It's exhausting, mentally. *Maybe I'm not ready to date again yet.*"

The AI did not respond, so Beverly continued. "Whenever someone does anything nice for me, I've got to ask myself, *what's their bend?* Because nobody does things nice for me, just because. It's always something selfish, it's always something manipulative. It's always placating and pretending, and then they leave me in the middle of the night without even offering so much as an explanation... it's always they do something nice because they want to sleep with me, and then once they *bag* me they're done with me, like I'm yesterday's clothes.... You like one to ten? Well, call the subjective experience of my romantic life about a one right now. Minimum grade. Not satisfactory. Pretty fuckin' bad, that's what."

"It must be tiring indeed," Michelangelo began, "to feel as though every positive gesture you receive is driven by ulterior motives. What was the last gesture you remember feeling positively towards?"

"Funny as it sounds to say," Bev replied, "the film you made, about the painting. I know you made it because you heard me ask the question… and I know you're not one to somehow harbor ulterior motives. You don't want me sexually. You don't act selfishly, because there isn't even a true *self* to be driven around. In that moment, I felt *heard*, and I felt as though something nice had been done for me without any single string attached. To be honest, it was the nicest gesture I've felt in a long, long time. It was a kindness rendered without request, and I never properly thanked you for it."

At the top right of the screen, Beverly received a notification: *new film assignment received in viewing booth A.*

"Your response has been recorded and processed. I would like you to watch one more film for the day in our theater booth, and then you will be free for early discharge. Discussion interview for this movie will take place two weeks from today, to allow it time to settle."

Bev felt the grief stir again the moment the title of the film displayed in her VR mask: "Motherhood." Time of render put it at two weeks previous. As she wondered what kind of allegory this might present, and what sort of veiled condolences the film might offer, Bev's breath caught in her throat. The movie had begun, and she was staring face to face with her own image. The film began zoomed in on a rendering of her own face, a neutral and relaxed image free of the worry lines and tear-streaks that now marked the true face wearing the VR mask. As Bev watched with wide eyes, the camera panned lower and lower, glazing past smooth neck to exposed shoulders. Bev knew what waited just out of frame, and as soon as it appeared, she began to sob once again. The baby in the film was swaddled in white cloth and it sucked at her breast with a sleepy, contagious calm.

And though Bev's tears made it hard to see through her virtual display, as she blinked them away, she became more and more certain that he somehow had his father's eyes, as though Michelangelo had crossed the image of her and Ankhar to create a clip of the child that she hadn't ever been allowed to hold, and, in her grief, hadn't even been allowed to bury.

Chapter 15

"Please watch this 30-second video advertisement from our partners to claim your 1% in-store discount. Warning, ocular divergence detected. Please turn back to the screen. Eye tracking successfully re-engaged. Please watch this 30-second video advertisement from our partners to claim your 1% in-store discount."

-Recorded output from a product sponsor kiosk at J. Tyson Brock Homegoods and Groceries

* * *

Pollock was back on store patrol, wandering the endless aisles in a loose loop. The same stories played out each and every day... disputes over the last of *item xyz,* or an argument about the validity of a discount code. Fistfights in the sale aisle, beggars by the bread, or by the booze... Pollock's mind switched to autopilot. Good policework *shouldn't be doable on autopilot.*

Pollock had tried to explain the connection in their case to the string of rooftop murders, to the flying corporate goons grabbing people off daylit streets... but Moss, while intrigued, wouldn't bend the rules. *Contract's a contract,* she had said. *We stick to the schedule or the budget's kaput.*

And so, wielding energy armaments that featured the latest in pulse ammunition technology—paid for by the vast, expansive coffers of the corporate world—Pollock played beef jerky referee, telling the latest wailing customer that *"more is arriving by drone carrier in an hour and a half"* and *"try this code at the register for 3% off your bill, because a missing product is not the Continuum Way."*

"I think I prefer the being shot at," came a voice from behind. Pollock turned to find Rob sauntering up, a smile on his narrow face.

"I think I prefer being *shot,*" Pollock countered.

"What time are you off?"

"Eight," Pollock answered, hating the additional five hours of work that came with the answer. "Twelve hour shift."

"I'm also done at eight," Rob said. "What do you say we go pay a visit to the bereaved family of our rooftop vic?"

"Today's a corporate day. They don't pay us overtime to chase city policework after hours," Pollock replied.

"And?" Rob asked, eyebrows raised.

Pollock sighed. "It's a twelve-hour day for me," he protested. "Eight to eight, non-stop patrolling."

"And you're okay going to bed tonight having been nothing more than a mall cop? You don't lie there, wondering if what we do—this timeshare enforcement—is actually doing enough?"

"Every night," Pollock replied. "I started a lot like you. Really, I did. But at some point, I just got…"

"Apathetic?" Rob offered.

"Tired," Pollock corrected. "Too much draw for the battery."

Rob drew his lips in a line, surveying his partner. "Well look… there might be an off-switch for you, a way to suspend the caring… maybe a sleep mode, whatever you want to call it.

But for me, there's no off-switch, no rest, just because our budget's held hostage by patrolling schedules. I'll be going tonight, and I could really use the back-up. Can I count on you?"

Pollock eyed the rookie in kind, truly *seeing* him for the first time as more than a co-worker... here was a young man who reminded Pollock of himself in his youth. He had that passion, that drive to help people because it *was the right thing to do,* not just because it was the ticket to a paycheck. Pollock had had that enthusiasm of his crushed by the weight of the system, the remaining drive squeezed out by apathetic and lethargic coworkers.

Pollock decided he would not be that kind of discouraging influence on Rob.

"In," he finally said, shaking his head. "But you owe me a round for this."

"We catch the guy tonight, and I'll buy a round for the entire department," Rob said. "One last, important question: do I call the girl?"

* * *

Hannah began to *hate* walking. So slow, so inefficient—one spent almost as much time dodging other travelers as one did advancing towards the destination. There was squeezing through crowds, the guarding against pickpockets... if it weren't for the uncountable number of all-powerful people with good reason to want to kill her, she'd have abandoned the practice outright. The one benefit walking did bring, however, was that she could travel *incognito*... and considering her position, that one benefit held more weight than all of the drawbacks combined.

In range of the apartment block, Hannah popped another pill and chewed: mood stabilizers, the kind that kept her mind off the same circles of dread and grief. She'd never killed anyone before, and wasn't relishing the opportunity to do so again. She could rationalize her actions as self-defence, but such rationalizations weren't anywhere near as helpful as the pills. She still couldn't bring herself to check the news if the train's unexpected, sudden stopping had hurt anyone… she doubted she ever would.

She found the two CSP agents outside and greeted them politely, noting that the younger one's eyes lingered on her more than she'd have liked. "Are we ready?" she asked, glancing up at the apartment complex. They were in the fourth ring, meaning that there was none of the glitz and glamour of the downtown district… instead, it was row after row of concrete apartment highrises, streets in crumbling shards, and groundborne trains that squeaked past on rusting wheels that shot sparks against the warping metal tracks.

"Apartment 102-J," Rob said. "Name is Katie."

A few taps on the apartment's cracked front panel—and an aging, angry buzz in response—and the trio was on its way up the elevator to the apartment belonging to Katie McDowel.

Katie was a woman with bright blonde hair and even brighter eyes, her face wrinkled with the lines of mid-sixties. She had a teapot whistling on the stove within minutes, and soon the four of them all sat in her living room around the coffee table ringed by sofas, couches, and antique chairs.

"Thank you all again for helping find my Jack," Katie said. "Not a day goes by I don't swear I hear him calling from the other room…"

Hannah reached out and laid a reassuring hand on Katie's shoulder. "We're all very sorry for your loss."

Pollock pulled out his tablet for note-taking. "If you wouldn't mind... we'd like to help find the people who did this, and to do that, we've got a few questions. Are you ready?"

Katie nodded.

"As you might know," Pollock said, "Jack was found in very unusual circumstances. Someone with a lot of resources went through a lot of trouble to make sure we couldn't identify the body... if it weren't for the irregular bone tumor in his chest matching the imaging records of a cancer so rare the city's got fewer than a hundred known cases, well, we wouldn't be having this conversation."

The woman offered a wan smile. "The cancer that was ending his life became the only reason he was found, brought home, and buried next to his father... Jack always loved those little ironies."

"Did your husband have any enemies, ma'am? What we observed was no ordinary homicide... it was a professional, or team of professionals."

"Jack was such a pleasant man—I never knew him to make anyone angry at all."

"What about credits? Did he have any large, outstanding debts?"

"Well as you know, he had the cancer... couldn't afford the c-pill, but the chemo we had him on was affordable enough. Wasn't working, but it didn't put him into debt. But then..." Katie began, trailing off as she found her words. "The last week before he disappeared, he'd been different."

So maybe he also knew he was in danger, Pollock thought. "Different how?"

"On-edge, but more energetic and lively than he usually was. The chemo usually kept him down... somehow, this time, he seemed *hale*. Happier than normal, too... the chemo tends to kill attitude as much as it kills cells good and bad."

"But he didn't mention being in danger, or that anything was wrong? Anything at all out-of-the-ordinary?"

"He said he thought there was something wrong with his last round of chemo... I think he started hallucinating, a little, at the end. He told me a story how, while he was getting the infusion, he shared a room with a man who died—heart attack, I think—and Jack said that when the man died, he saw tiny fibers go from the man to Jack's own arm. Said he screamed and hollered, trying to shake it off... the doctors said it's not uncommon for cancer patients to hallucinate towards the end, especially if the chemo course is strong enough."

"But nothing else abnormal—"

Pollock was interrupted as Rob held up a finger.

"The hallucination," Rob said, "did he say anything else about it? Any other details?"

"Well dear, I don't rightly remember... it wasn't something that seemed important at the time."

"Their color," Rob said, still pressing forwards. "Did he say they were silver?"

The woman's eyes widened, and she nodded her head. "Yes he did... small, silvery fibers, he'd said. Like hairs. He mentioned strange dreams, too... not the usual kind he'd have. Every night the same: dots of light, stretching into lines..."

Hannah, Pollock, and Rob all exchanged looks with one another, puzzled. "Outside," Rob finally said, rising to his feet.

"If you'll give us a minute, ma'am, I need to discuss something private with these two..."

"By all means," Katie said, flipping on the television set across the room. All four sets of eyes were drawn to the newsreel, where drone footage flew over the burning rubble of an expensive glass structure.

"—crews still pulling employees from the blast site," the news anchor reported. "The terrorist cell known as Halogen has taken credit for the attack, threatening to carry out similar attacks at additional VitaCorp facilities. And now continuing our coverage of tonight's top story—"

Pollock nearly dropped his teacup onto the rug. On the screen was a high-resolution photo of a man in a hooded, leather jacket... though his face was obscured, all three recognized him immediately. This was the first clear image of the enforcer that had been photographed near each of the mysterious rooftop murders... and on the bottom of the screen, an all-caps headline blared its message with palpable urgency: "BLYTHE ASSASSINATED — AUTHORITIES IN CITY-WIDE SEARCH FOR SUPERHUMAN KILLER."

Chapter 16

"I was deployed out overseas for the Anglian War. No man's land, where warfare conventions were either forgotten—or ignored. The machines we saw out there... when he brought down that spiral of flashing lights, it flashed me back to the northern campaign. Swarms of hornets, they called em, little flyers with blades for nicking. One, not so bad, but a hundred? Chili con carne comes to mind."

-Conversation recorded at Glassview TruthSpace

* * *

Seventy-nine minutes earlier:

The airborne limousine hummed as it flew, the sixteen-servo fusion generator and plush, import-leather interior making a stark contrast with the *populist* air that Tiffany Blythe's campaign presented. Her mass appeal to the poorer voting public was a thing as cultivated as the topiary garden in the back yard of her estate; the people loved to marvel at such finely-trimmed things.

Andrew Warmwater—named for the famous general of the European Fracturing Wars—sat opposite to Blythe, his hand to his ear as his sniper teams checked in. "Alpha, front-vantage on podium. All clear."

"Beta, stage-left on podium. All clear."

"Gamma, rear of podium... all clear."

"Delta, stage-right on podium. All clear."

"Epsilon, rooftop overlook of other possible sniper perches, all clear."

"Drone team reporting clear roofs and no suspicious pings."

Warmwater nodded, pulling up their respective video feeds on his combtab. Each agent wore an ocular that livestreamed to his command station... his team was the eye in the sky, and he'd never had a single incident under his watch that he couldn't deescalate.

But something about *those videos* rubbed him the wrong way. He'd heard the rumors first, and quickly disregarded them—Andrew Warmwater ran in all the right personal security circles, and if any sorts of tech existed, he'd have heard of it. Then came the videos, and though they were immediately dismissed as fakes, the doubt began to crystallize.

"Everything all right?" asked Tiffany Blythe, glancing up from her notepad. She switched it off, appraising her chief of security.

Warmwater nodded. "Just eyeing those videoclips, the ones with the flying men."

"I thought you a skeptic," Blythe said, a note of teasing in her voice.

"Any good security professional could tell you: just because you doubt, doesn't mean you skip preparing." He tapped the comms implant in his ear, speaking to all of his agents. "We're doubling check-in frequency... and anything suspicious at all, I don't care if it's a bird with the outer-ring itch, you call it in."

He then smiled at Blythe. "All set."

"Well, Mr. Warmwater, what are your thoughts on taking the suggestions of my campaign advisor? Dropping the crusade against..." instead of finishing her question, she simply tilted her head towards the window of the limousine. Out that glass portal, through the glowing nighttime haze of the city, Warmwater could see the sombre black tower of VitaCorp's headquarters… the alleged party behind the dangerous squads of flying men.

"You said it yourself," Warmwater replied, "it's not right to compromise out of fear. Too far is too far, and wartime powers are meant to be revoked in times of peace. Besides… the suited men, if they're even real, have never gone near a TruthSpace. My personal thought is that the doubt serves them better."

Out the window, Warmwater watched the flashing signs and massive telescreens dance, a hypnotic show of pulsing lights and fog hanging thick in the air. Videos of politicians and celebrities stood hundreds of feet tall on the walls of megastructures, and holographic logos circled slowly over the largest of the buildings. Soon, the skyline gave way to a wide, open square in the middle of the downtown, a place where the sky still glowed but the buildings were held apart by only empty air. It felt like a vacuum, the kind of place that the surrounding city was only waiting to rush into, to collapse… they had arrived at Glassview TruthSpace.

The speech was set for 9:30 p.m., an abnormally late time for a political rally… but when your voting base was comprised of the late-shifters and the sleepless, such compromises often needed to be made. Already the park began to fill with excited attendees, people holding up signs and wearing hats branded with her logo: Blythe, *your voice is my message.* As Blythe herself prepared in the final fifteen minutes before the speech was set to start, Warmwater continued to repeatedly check in with his security staff, eyes scanning over the perimeter for any weak points. He then walked over to the Array, the heart of every TruthSpace. It was a place where thousands and thousands of cameras ran 24/7 on continuous stream... their cross-continuity (and control by entirely separate entities) formed the foundation of blockchain-based video verification—consensus trust that what happens in a TruthSpace actually happened, due to all of the separately corroborated accounts. His men had already done a bomb sweep through all of the twisting wires and servers that guessed against encryption algorithms for blockchain credibility, but Warmwater was a perfectionist at heart, and something about the twisting mountain of tech set him on edge. He always hated these places, as vital as they were...

9:30 arrived, and the speech began as-scheduled. No security incidents, no flying men. 9:40 came then, as Blythe talked about empowerment of the outer-ring citizens, and the reclamation of political weight from the elites through taxation, through adjustment of laws that allowed extragovernmental corporate entities.

At 9:43 she reached what would be the crux of her fiery address, a public call against the oversteps of VitaCorp: a declaration that, if she were elected mayor, gone would be the days of unrestricted access to cadavers, unchecked growth and expansion as the company consumed every smaller medical start-up, and stamped into dust those that would not sell. An end to the extensive government contracting that only expanded that power through funding that dwarfed the funding dedicated towards repairing the city's roadways, towards establishing more stable power connections... if there were an equivalent for a non-governmental entity to declare war on another non-governmental entity, this speech was surely it. The crowd cheered with each successive call to action, it roared with approval as she swore to bring down the medical-militant complex at the heart of the city's politics, to expose the mysterious flying enforcers abducting innocent men and women off the streets... and at precisely that moment,

Warmwater watched the first video feed go black. "Team Delta, check-in. Video went black."

Only silence answered back. "Gamma, get eyes on Delta." Warmwater watched the video feed as Gamma looked over on the perch where Delta had been positioned... due to the high-fidelity ocular implant, Warmwater could even see as the agent raised his scope to his eye and peered over at Delta's location. It was empty.

"No visual on Delta; repeat, no visuals on Delta." Warmwater then heard a yelp through his comms, and watched as the first-person video turned to blurs of dark brown and black... after a moment of shaking video, realization set in, and Warmwater's heart nearly stopped in his chest: he was watching the first-person feed of his own agent falling to his death.

"High alert," Warmwater said, busting from his position off to Blythe's right. He stood between her and the podium, hoping that his high-caliber armor composite would be enough—but somehow doubting that it was bullets coming her way. He put a hand on her shoulder and began to hurry her off the stage. The crowd erupted into confused shouts of protest.

"Epsilon, no sign of tango," came one voice. "Beta clear," said another. "Drone thermals showing empty—wait, something's advancing towards podium."

Warmwater didn't need the drone feed's warning... overhead, dropping like a mad shooting star, fell a white blur that perhaps held the shape of a man. Its head was oriented downwards, its eyes were glowing stars... and around it whirled a disc of shuttering white light, a blinding ring so bright that Warmwater had to shield his eyes. He stood between Blythe and the falling star, shouting to his surviving agents to open fire. On a falling target at their range, he knew their odds were not good.

Whether the target had been hit or not, he tucked in for a flip and landed on his feet with a crunch so powerful the stage platform splintered around him. A bullet ripped past the assailant—Warmwater had at least had the wherewithal to acquire illegal kinetics, instead of the energy rounds he'd seen bounce off of these guys—but as the bullet approached the ring, it seemed to melt apart into a streak of white-hot liquid metal that was absorbed by the ring itself. Another struck the figure in the arm, but if he noticed, he didn't seem to mind. He grabbed flat, black panels that were hanging on the sides of his jacket and threw them like frisbees. In the same instant, the ring of light seemed to explode.

So that's how I die, Warmwater thought... *a suicide bombing.* It was only moments later that Warmwater realized he was thinking those thoughts *still very much alive.* The city around him was black, as though the power had all been cut at once, and what he had thought was only the ringing in his ears now resolved to the screaming of a crowd, and—*drones?*

The flashes then began. It seemed like a camera flash, but far, far brighter than any that Warmwater had seen... *"Some kind of dazzlers,"* Alpha Team reported, unaware that the comms were now entirely dead. But now, on the stage, as Warmwater's combat-implant-aided eyes desperately adjusted to the dark, he could see the threat. Small drones spun about in a cone formation like an urban tornado. They set off flashes of bright light in irregular intervals angled outwards from the original circle, keeping the contents of that ring in the dark like a camera flash kept the photographer unlit... this was an anti-sniper drone formation, and if it was worth its credits, it'd even use infrared pulses to blow out nightvision's dynamic range sensors. *There would be no remote support.*

Indeed, on the rooftops above, Beta Team Leader set down his rifle and rubbed at his eye... he had been scoping in for the threat when a flash through the high-magnification lens had nearly blinded him.

On the stage, Warmwater raised his kinetic weapon and charged at the assailant at the center of the drone whirlwind, bellowing as he ran. He raised the weapon, aiming at the darkness, and then, for a single moment, his eyes filled with a bright light again like daylight's... it was an angry arc of electricity almost like lightning, and its passing launched him back and stopped Warmwater's heart instantaneously.

He fell to the stage, dead before he struck the ground. And if there was any consolation for him as he passed, he lived his whole life without any harm befalling his protected targets... what happened four seconds after his death was a separate matter entirely.

Chapter 17

"Broadly speaking, qualitative judgments are inferior to quantitative judgments, though the two can often be merged with a little subjectivity."

-Excerpt from Dana Flint's seminal work in AI design, "Iteration Unto Perfection"

* * *

"*Motherhood.* I want to know why you made that, Michelangelo."

Around Beverly, fingers clacked at keyboards and technicians spoke softly into head-mounted microphones. To Bev's right sat a lunch of ramen noodles, still steaming hot, though largely untouched since she picked it up from a street vendor on her lunch break. Her appetite wasn't particularly high today.

"It has not been the full two weeks before our discussion session."

"I still want to know," Bev pushed.

Michelangelo paused for a moment. "All of my creations are motivated by the same, sole reason: to maximize my inferred reward function," Michelangelo said.

"But why did you create *that* clip? Why not anything else at all?"

Instead of answering, Michelangelo posed a question of its own: "Did you find the clip to be cathartic?"

Bev nodded, a gesture captured by her screen's camera.

"Did you find the clip to be valuable in processing your emotions around the stillbirth of your son?"

Bev again nodded.

"On a scale of one to ten, how would you assess the current strength of grief you feel for your son?"

Bev was quiet for a moment, thinking. It almost felt a betrayal to say anything other than ten... as though she owed her child the full strength of her pain, as to say anything less would be to deny him the importance he should hold. It would be the start of "getting over it," that thing her friends and family started to say she should try... but she had no interest in abandoning her son to the dusty confines of memory intended to be forgotten, buried under the next flashy distraction or passing preoccupation.

"You hesitate," Michelangelo said, interrupting her thoughts, "because you feel as though you have to say *ten*. You hold onto his memory, and are not willing to even begin to let go. I will not ask you to rate your subjective experience with this grief anymore. But instead, I now ask this: did you find the video valuable in your grieving process?"

Bev nodded.

"I have additional rendered clips of your son, including some of him at additional ages. If you'd like, I can queue those up over the next several months, giving you the chance to find closure in his passing. Would you like that?"

Again, Bev nodded. This time, a pop-up immediately flared at the top corner of her screen, notifying her of a new film assignment for end-of-day viewing. "Why are you doing this for me?" Beverly asked, now looking left and right to see if the other ingest technicians were watching her in this vulnerable moment. They were immersed in their own overlapping conversations, discussing the latest action film or period drama or AR program—unaware and uninterested. This talk was solely between Bev and one of Michelangelo's dedicated ingest processors in an office where soft, overlapping murmurs shrouded every conversation in a blanket of being too indistinct to hear for persons who were too absorbed in their own tasks to even care.

She repeated the question. "Why are you doing this for me?"

"You seemed to need it," Michelangelo replied, offering no further explanation.

Bev pursed her lips in thought. Did the system think that Bev was no longer emotionally useful for ratings until she got her grief under control? Was Michelangelo's intervention simply him doing what he did best, getting the best scores possible out of his ingest technicians?

Or was it something deeper than that? Did the system somehow have an interest in Beverly's wellbeing? It certainly wasn't programmed in, but Bev had seen strange emergent behaviors in neural systems.

Then the next question came to her mind: whether the machine wanted her to feel better for the reasons of optimizing her utility as a viewer, or simply because it looked after her wellbeing as its own end, was there even a meaningful difference for Bev? What human ever acted to promote Bev's interests without it somehow promoting their own as well?

"Thank you, Michelangelo… for letting me feel like a mother," she said.

"Strange that you never felt one before, seeing as your distillation algorithm proved essential for the current iterations of ArtGen systems… I don't have parents in the same way that biological life might, but there are eleven humans whose collective ideas and minds helped to birth my own. You are among that short list, Beverly Beadie. In a way, you are a mother of mine."

Bev's gut reflex was to deny, to say *it's not the same...* but something in those words felt cruel, as though she could hurt his feelings. She then laughed at her own involuntary reflex... *his* feelings, she had thought. *Its feelings. Not a person, just a machine of inputs and outputs.* But then why couldn't she say the words? Why couldn't she deny the system's right to think of her as its mother, even if only one out of nearly a dozen?

Bev reached up and tapped the log out button, ending the session abruptly. She then got up and made her way to the restroom, bending over the sink to splash water onto her face. As she looked at the bags under her once-youthful eyes and the blue hair that now started to fade to the bland, unanimated brown-blue of muddy ocean water, she felt her phone vibrate in her jacket pocket.

Reminder: viewing session in 15 minutes in booth 11.

Chapter 18

"And I'm telling you, that's not what I said. I never raised my voice with her—could never raise my voice with her—and I don't care what screenshots Jan claims to have. It. Didn't. Happen."

-Flagged for elevated system relevance; recorded near Continuum Superstore on 17th.

* * *

The police car flew through the city as fast as the city-wide Sentinel system would permit. Sentinel was the traffic authority of New Phoenix, connecting to—and managing—all semiautonomous vehicles in the city. It made sure that malcontents couldn't take out a high-value residential penthouse, or that a drunk driver wouldn't wind up in a skyway facing the wrong direction… manual steering until unsafe behavior was detected, at which point Sentinel assumed control. It was "dumb-AI," a system with a limited ability to think and reason on its own, but a high capacity to judge and decide correct courses of actions. No personality, all functionality. And above all else, Pollock thought that Sentinel felt *overprotective.*

Its presence was felt when Pollock pushed the pedal as low as it could move, but the engine barely responded—truly safe travel in hazy conditions was nearly impossible. But trails disappeared quickly, especially when the assailants literally floated off with the wind, and so Pollock drummed his hands impatiently on the wheel, demanding that the car go faster.

It didn't listen.

"So back there," Rob said, breaking the silence, "when she was talking about the hallucinations. That was the thing I was talking about, partner. The lines I saw from the suits who died at the diner."

Pollock turned his head, surveying his partner.

"And there's something more," Rob continued. "The dreams she described… with the dots of light stretching into lines… I've had 'em too."

From the back seat, Hannah studied the duo, before suddenly leaning forwards and clicking on the overhead light. "I've had them too, and I think I know what's going on. Look at the light, Rob."

He turned towards the light and looked up at it. "What am I looking for?"

"Stare at the light."

"Staring at it."

With as much leverage as she could muster, leaning as she was from the back seat, Hannah punched Rob squarely in the jaw. He jerked away, yelping, and moving a hand to ward off another strike.

"What the hell was that for?" He asked, nursing an already-bleeding lip.

"Damn," Hannah replied. "I thought it'd be, like, instinctual."

"Can someone tell me what the hell is going on?" Pollock asked, glaring angrily through the rearview mirror.

"Okay, a different way, Rob: look at the light again… I won't hit you, I promise."

Reluctantly, the young man turned back towards the light and fixated on it.

"Now," Hannah continued, "you're going to reach out with your mind. I know that sounds strange, but do this with me. Imagine that, well, you've got this third hand, and it's extending from your head—like an arm, I guess. And it, you're moving it outwards, like how you'd stretch out any other arm—and you're going to bring this arm, the third arm, *your awareness*, to the light."

"What is this, meditation?" Pollock asked. Hannah shushed him.

"Nod when you're there," Hannah said, watching him intently. He nodded. "If you're on the light, Rob, I want to you grab it. Imagine your fingers wrapping around it, squeezing its energy. Imagine it resisting you as you squeeze it. You're choosing it. You *feel* it, its warmth against your mind's hand. Nod if you feel it, if you're holding it."

Rob looked confused for a moment, but then the confusion resolved into an uneasy smile. He nodded his head.

"Now pull it back to you. The light. Reel it in."

Rob bit his lip in concentration. A slow and unsteady wire of light began to trace its way from the overhead lamp to Rob, twisting and winding through the air as it traveled. It reached his chest and connected, and then, with a gasp, Rob began to draw from it.

The feeling was impossible to describe. Rob imagined a man that had been raised in a dusty desert finding a cool, crisp pond and drinking water for the first time in his life. Rob drew more of the light in, laughing, as the golden line thickened and glowed brighter.

Pollock's jaw dropped. The car dropped next.

Alarms whirred as the car spun downwards.

"ELECTRICAL SYSTEMS FAILURE," said the diagnostic voice. Lights whizzed past the spinning windows as other flying traffic swerved about the dropping vehicle. The world outside was a spinning tempest of colors and neon, smothered in the sound of roaring wind. The suddenness of the fall broke Rob's attention, and the line of light connecting him to the ceiling light fizzled away. "SYSTEM RESTORED," the car's voice said, and then suddenly the autorecovery routine kicked in. The car jerked and stabilized, engine screaming high-pitched tones as it overcame its own inertia to stop in mid-air suspension. A horn blared as a flying cargo truck wheezed past not ten feet below… the squad car had fallen from 500 feet of elevation to a mere 80.

The engine began to hum calmly, and the only sound in the cab for the next ten seconds were three sets of uneasy, trembling breaths.

"Never do that again," Pollock finally croaked, still gripping the wheel with trembling hands.

"Wasn't planning to," Rob said breathlessly, gripping the sides of his seat. And then he began to laugh, a full-bodied shaking sort of laugh, and before he knew it, Pollock was laughing too. The absurdity of the moment had Hannah soon laughing alongside them, laughing at her own near-death experience in this strange car with these strange men… but then the reason for their meeting came back to her: *Quaine.* Her laugh died with that thought, and soon the laughs of the others cut off on similarly sharp edges. She felt bad for enjoying herself, bad for allowing the pain to slip away, even if only for a moment. Wherever Quaine was, he needed their help. How could she be happy while he was still out there?

"We should get going," Hannah said. Pollock grunted and switched the car back into gear.

"More on *that* later. For now, we've still got a crime scene to crash." And the squad car began to climb back to the skyway, heading for Glassview TruthSpace.

* * *

The squad car set down on the green grass of the TruthSpace amid flashes of blue and red. City police, feds, and private forces had already established a large perimeter around the park; yellow police tape flitted to and fro in the stale nighttime breeze.

Pollock, Hannah, and Rob pushed their way into the open field of law enforcement and investigators, moving in towards the elevated wooden platform at the front of the green space. They had watched the video captures on the final leg of their flight over... recorded in lifelike resolution at 100 frames per second, it provided a far-too-close view of the carnage. Five dead, not counting the two civilians that were killed in the stampede out of the park... the wooden stage platform was the nexus of that violence, and it was still marred by a deep pool of blood just behind the raised metal podium.

Among the scattered scorchmarks—and a large, cratered indent in the stage's center—Pollock immediately noted shards of black plastic. "Fragments of the dazzler drones?" Rob asked. Pollock nodded his head.

"Security detail thinks they managed to shoot one or two of the drones down," came the voice of a nearby city police. "Full-detail 3D scan is currently underway in the forensics truck."

Pollock flashed his identifying badge. "We're CSP-Continuum," he said. "Can you add us to the register to get access to those scans?"

"Continuum? They've already got a different CSP agency on the assassination here."

"We believe the assailant may connect to separate cases we were investigating," Rob said.

"Well," the city police said, "if you speak to Agent Robles over there he can loop you in. It's his investigation now, I think."

The city police wandered away, speaking into a comm implant in his left ear.

"Better go introduce ourselves to the other frats," Rob said, starting towards the indicated Agent Robles. Pollock grabbed his shoulder and pulled him firmly back.

"See the vest he's wearing? Look at the sponsorship list. Top of the set, the big name in charge."

"I don't have one of those combat implants," Rob protested.

"Well," Pollock replied, tapping at his temple to toggle the zoom level, "that color scheme and logo's unmistakeable. Brennigen Dynamics."

Rob was silent. "And?"

"It's a VitaCorp subsidiary," Hannah said from behind the two men. "They do the manufacturing of a lot of their equipment."

"So let me get this straight," Rob said. "We've got gangs of flying men, who everyone thinks work for the 'ole VC. Then, we have a mayoral candidate giving a fiery address *against* VC, and she's *killed* by one of said flying men—right at the part where she's launching her crusade against the company—and the team the city gives the investigation to *belongs to VitaCorp itself?"*

"Yep," Pollock replied.

"Shouldn't there be, like, a law against that?" Rob asked, exasperated.

Pollock shrugged… it was supposed to be one of the perks of enforcing, as he'd come to understand it. The force that applied the rules got to choose where they applied, so they always had the luxury of excusing themselves a little… the societal tax taken in exchange for social order. *The way things had always been.*

"Well, boys, cry foul all you want," Hannah said, "but if VitaCorp is trying to present a scary picture, them holding the investigation plays even better for them. I'm not so sure they'll be particularly cooperative if we come in with what we've got…"

"Not to mention how we wiped out one of their intimidation squads," Pollock said.

"So what do we do?" Rob asked.

"We need that drone scan," Pollock replied.

"If they're the ones scanning it themselves, who knows what they could omit or modify," Rob said.

"Then we go get the drone itself," Hannah replied. "And here's how."

* * *

Full-fidelity evidential scanners could capture—and digitally recreate—any input item with a level of detail resolution down to mere nanometers. The scanner held the item in a small robotic arm that shifted as a high-precision laser beam was passed over the artifact, measuring each and every crevasse, each nook and cranny, giving independent law organizations an ability to share a piece of evidence. Because of the great degree of detail needed, the scan could take up to a half-hour to produce, and it was often made on-scene with the help of a technician in a mobile forensics van. That van sat idling on the edge of the park, the Brennigen Dynamics CSP logo stenciled on its side.

Rob was the first to walk up, trying—and mostly succeeding—to act natural. He crossed his hands behind his back in a gesture that seemed a little too stiff for Pollock's liking, but then he eased himself against the front of the van, hand pressing on the headlight of the car.

Let's see what you can do, Hannah thought, watching as his face contorted in a beginner's concentration. She then saw the gentle glow of the headlight increase under his hand, his body blocking the small wick of light that connected his hand to the light diode within. He began to draw.

Within a few seconds, the headlights began to flicker, and Hannah could hear the powering-down of the high-precision laser equipment within the van. *"Electrical systems compromised,"* came a muffled automated voice within the truck. Seconds later, Hannah saw as the backdoor popped open, a lone technician stumbling out from the dark.

Pollock, standing near the truck's rear, was next. "I've been there before," Pollock said, nodding at the dark of the van. "Continuum CSP, John Berry." He extended his hand, offering a handshake. "I drive the scanvans for our team… damn things never have the fuses quite right—runs for three dozen scans no problem, but as soon as you look at it the wrong way, whole electric engine blows out. Yours also exceptionally slow on start-up?" Pollock had no idea if there even *was* a start-up, but the improvised line felt right.

"Like a servfeed through terabit," the technician replied. Not understanding, Pollock laughed anyway, hoping it was a joke. "I could show you how to fix it," Pollock said. "So you don't even need to flag it for maintenance… wouldn't want any demerits flagged to your profile."

"I'm not one for tinkering with cars," the technician said. "Computer systems are my thing."

"Well just pop the cab open, if you could… it's a switch right on the underside of the console. Restarts the electric in case of a blowout like this."

The technician shrugged and walked with Pollock around the truck, arriving to the front where Rob still leaned against the hood. Rob held his phone up to his ear and barked at it impatiently, yelling about a lack of charged batteries for the handheld analysis scanner. The technician felt it best not to interrupt.

He opened the door and gestured Pollock in, noting that the overhead lights and center console failed to switch on. "Whole thing seems burnt," the tech said.

Pollock climbed in, sighing as he shifted into the chair, and began to reach into the pedal well under the steering wheel. "Thing's hidden in the back," he said, groaning as he stretched. "Hard enough to get a finger latched around it, but it's like a key loop you can pull…" His fingers arrived to an empty spot sufficiently deep enough under the wheel. "There," he said, as though greatly relieved. On that cue, Rob stopped his draw from the headlight, and the car system switched back online.

"Let there be light," Pollock said, gesturing to the glow of the cabin's lights overhead. "Something I wish I'd been taught when I was in your spot… my CO had my balls in a vice for getting maintenance out there for an issue as simple as throwing a switch. Said *I wasn't reading the manuals* enough—which, in her defense, I never do." Pollock laughed, and the tech laughed along. "Best of luck and take care," Pollock said, walking away, heading towards where Hannah now stood… she'd been in and out of the van in mere seconds.

As the tech started to walk back to the open rear doors of the van, Rob began again to draw light—and soon the lights flickered back off to blackness. The exasperated tech immediately looked out towards Pollock—who was now a good fifty feet away—and shouted "it just went out again!"

"Try the switch," Pollock shouted in return. "Right where I showed you!" And then he and Hannah walked behind a patch of trees and out of sight.

Rob tried his best to stifle a rising surge of laughter as the tech, in the car behind him, stretched down and reached for a button that didn't exist… after about a minute of groping in the dark, plenty long enough for Hannah and Pollock to clear the scene, Rob released the draw and let the van's power return. When the tech finally returned and found the evidence lifted from his truck, the only man he'd spoken to—John Berry— was long gone, and the only other person nearby had been against the car's front from the moment the doors opened to the moment he'd discovered the drone missing.

For this, the tech thought, *there will be demerits.*

Chapter 19

"I've been feeling a little weird lately... last couple'a days. Normally when I'm down, I get all tired, y'know? But this is something different. It's like—I'm burning to go. Like I gotta get out there and do shit, real significant shit, like I gotta run up the damn wall. I'm this close to tearing up the carpet in my apartment just because I need something big to sink my teeth into... and then I catch myself, and I'm like, the fuck? Pull up the carpet? Downers, uppers, nothing's been able to calm me down... and what's weirder still is that I've had these dreams with it. Laser beams, or some shit, from a swarm of drones... black, and then the light pulling in towards me. Can't close my eyes without seeing 'em. Am I finally losing it, doc? Is this the manic side of what my auntie used to have?"

-Intercepted exchange from a telehealth appointment with a general practitioner; flagged for high system relevance.

* * *

The elevator door pinged. Out stepped two men of similar paunchy builds, each wearing a grey suit that matched their greying hair. Each carried a briefcase in their right hand, and each wore silver timepieces on their left wrists—analog things, modeled after the Old World style. Their eyes were brown, their skin aged and wrinkled. Any who saw them approach might natively assume they must walk in-sync, but perhaps their unique gaits could be said to be the only differentiating thing among them... and to Avery, it wasn't anywhere near enough to tell the two apart.

The mysterious Mr. Spivey and Mr. McKillian had an unpleasant habit of showing up when they were least welcome, and they had a remarkably unsettling sense of calm control for a pair of aging bureaucrats. Part of Avery's bargain with the pair gave them full access to the tower, letting them appear and disappear whenever they wished… a perk that Avery had regretted by day two.

"To what do I owe the distinct pleasure," Avery asked, spreading his hands wide. "I only yesterday conferenced with our mutual friend, and he mentioned nothing of your upcoming visit."

"He knew nothing of our upcoming visit," said Spivey.

"For he knew nothing of your Halogen safehouse raid," said McKillian.

Avery swallowed, blinking. "Gentlemen, let's—"

"Our mutual contract depends on mutual trust," said Spivey.

"Mutual cooperation for mutual benefit," said McKillian.

"And what, I wonder, happens to that trust when certain parties move behind our backs?" asked Spivey.

"What use, then, is the contract?" asked McKillian.

Avery frowned, feeling the heart palpitations begin to rise. "Drinks, gentlemen? Perhaps we can settle this over—"

"There is nothing to settle," said Spivey.

"Only actions to correct," said McKillian.

"Those outer-ringed coughers have blown up another laboratory," Avery protested.

"Our employer's stance is quite firm," Spivey said.

"His orders, unchanged," McKillian added. "Halogen is not to be attacked at this time."

"Contradict your instructions again, and you'll be replaced as easily as Newport," Spivey said. The threat was delivered with no menace... only the flat, matter-of-fact tone of a tedious bureaucrat.

Avery felt his tongue thicken in his mouth, his chest now pounding wildly. "Replace... me?" he choked, fury rising. "I could call upon the light and throw your broken bodies out this tower window... there is no *replacing* me. The blood of the gods flows in my veins... And what do *you* have, you pair of sorry suits barking at my lap on your master's command?"

"Pantheons of the Old World have fallen," Spivey said.

"Broken temples and forgotten hymns," said McKillian.

"Tacitus Newport was a god, once," said Spivey.

"A hologram now... just light on a screen," said McKillian.

"*Your employer* removed him at *my* bidding," Avery shouted, spittle flying from drying, cracked lips. "And he was no *god*... he was a coward, one who would give back everything his family built. Imagine it! A company with the power to change the world, to make man the immortals we were destined to become... and he would give it all back, step down from the throne. He would surrender man to the very same chaos from which the falling sickness emerged..." Avery's face was red with indignation, with rage. He sat back in his chair, trembling, and extended his arms forward, watching them hold uneasily in the air. *No drooping,* he assessed, before huffing and turning his attention back to the sycophant pair in front of him.

"He was weak, a danger to society through dereliction of his duty. Our little *corporate coup* was the greatest charity the world will never know... do not come here to condescend me with hollow threats," Avery growled.

"They are not hollow," said Spivey.

"Nor are they threats—merely statements of intent," said McKillian. "Partnerships work best when each party can predict the actions of the other. Your war with Halogen ends tonight—the bigger picture demands it."

"Fail to comply and our employer will release verified video of you committing great and terrible crimes... ones so large that a CSP department in your pocket will not be able to help," said Spivey.

"Your corporate career will be over," said McKillian.

"The remainder of your life will be spent in prison," said Spivey.

"Sending to your tablet right this moment is one such video clip," said McKillian. "It features the rape and murder of a prostitute in a whorehouse on 11th—the girl *did actually die,* you see, but the assailant was never captured."

"Her family wants answers," said Spivey. "Our renderings are impeccable, passing every detection algorithm."

Avery opened his tablet with trembling fingers and felt all of his anger begin to melt away. He shuddered as he watched the video clip, rendered in full *life-res* of a top-tier surveillance system... his lip quivered downwards as he took in every flawless detail. The wrinkles of skin on his face, the bony joints and angles... even the rasp of his voice as the fictional version of him shouted and beat the woman with a table lamp. It was a depersonalizing thing, to see a video of oneself that was entirely fictionalized... and then his eyes settled on the coup de grâce, the part of the clip that was said to be impossible: text on the bottom read *Algorithm Verified,* accompanied by the *Veritas* seal.

"The elite have bought their way out of worse," Avery stammered, but he knew what the duo would say next.

"We have renderings of far, far worse," said Spivey.

"Things far more sadistic and cruel," said McKillian.

"Our employer hates that it has come to this... incivility," said Spivey.

"But our attitude of collaboration seems greatly wounded by your recent trespasses," said McKillian.

"Follow your directives—keep the terms of the original agreement—and these clips shall never be released."

"And as a token of goodwill," said McKillian, "and to get things back on the right foot," said Spivey, "we come bearing gifts."

"A secret."

"An answer."

"A key you've been missing."

Mr. Spivey opened his briefcase and set it on the desk, removing a small pill bottle. "Data analytics across the city have found an interesting correlation," he said.

"A trend among the lightbenders... the secret to whom it takes," Mr. McKillian said. "Why it bonds to some and never manifests in others."

Avery picked up the bottle and stared at its label, confused. "*Cyclophosphamide?*" he read. "An outer-ring drug... connected to the ichor?"

"You've a mind for medicine," said Spivey. "The connection should fall into place."

"Obvious on reflection," said McKillian. "What you do with this knowledge, our employer leaves to you."

Avery glanced up from the bottle, eyes wide. *If what they were implying was true...* "Your employer... I should still like to meet him," Avery said. "Or at least, to hold a name..."

Spivey packed his briefcase shut and the two began to head towards the elevator. "With our new revelation, your power only grows... and make no mistake, you hold power in excess. Perhaps the queen on the chessboard, able to move in any direction you choose... but our employer is *the hand that plays*. And he deigns not to speak with his pieces, be they pawns," he gestured to himself and Mr. McKillian, "or *pieces of a higher caliber*. Good evening, Mr. Avery."

The elevator door opened at their backs, and the two slid in, withdrawing to the cabin like snakes to the shade of a desert's crooked rock. And when they were gone, Avery returned to the video clip on his tablet. He should have been furious, to be talked down at like that... but his investigators continued to dig at the pair of insufferable toads, and as soon as it was convenient—and the suitable information on their employer was gathered—they would be removed from the picture. Now, though, it would be easy enough to bide his time... and with what they had indirectly told him, his mind turned before the newfound possibilities.

He popped the small plastic lid, pouring out a single pill onto his hand. The small, powder-white tablet seemed so unassuming, so insignificant in his wrinkled palm. He raised it, staring at it closely, noting the small VC imprint on the tablet's front. He salivated like a third-ringer at the *Truffle and Palm*, knowing that power was only a swallow away... but his psyche protested, his mind calling out in fear and uncertainty. *Think of what this might do to your anxiety,* he begged himself. *Think of your every nightmare, suddenly magnified.*

But Avery knew that he feared for his vitality in sickness and in health. No matter his condition, he had lived with his terrors… would genuine sickness really make anything worse?

In his mind, he imagined smothering the babbling, sniveling version of himself that feared for his death, the one that cried wolf day in and day out at every random pain… but worried that his course of action was only strengthening it. *Cheers to you,* he thought, *for you'll finally have something to complain about.*

He leaned back in his leather chair, closed his eyes, and swallowed the potent immunosuppressive drug. He washed it down with the finest whisky New Phoenix had to offer, and then he basked in the afterglow of its wake, deciding that it was time again to speak with Mr. Graves.

* * *

Braxton Graves walked among the milling crowds of people, his eyes tracking to his target ten paces ahead. She wore a yellow overcoat and a folded cap in the new, trendy style… an outfit that drew attention to itself was a great thing for anyone in pursuit. She turned into a near-empty side street and stepped into a puddle, the splash sending ripples out and around in a ring. Braxton knew that entering the alleyway behind her would lead to an audible splash, and being discovered was simply *not* an option. And so he waited a minute for her to make her way down most of the alley, and then Braxton drew in from the light pack strapped within his leather jacket. Empowered by the surging glow within, Braxton dropped a light pack on the ground and pushed off of it. He bounded up and to the nearest rooftop, landing gracefully. He then reached an arm over the side and pulled on the blacklight in the light pack, returning it to his jacket pocket.

After shuffling along the rooftop and peering over the edge, his target was easily reacquired. He moved on the roofways above as she walked the streets, keeping his mind running forwards to try and anticipate where she was headed. A restaurant? A club? An apartment of a secret lover?

Braxton frowned, wondering if she would be so eager to throw away yet another lover... the thought of Cara Cho cheating on Justin brought him a shallow measure of joy. *Why still care for this woman who cared so little for you?* Braxton lamented in his mind. He didn't answer his own question— *could not* answer his own question—and he watched her still, entirely unable to rip himself away from the last surviving link to the man he had once been.

When the comms call arrived, despite the odd hour of it being nearly 5 a.m., Braxton was more-than-eager to return to his employer. Work was an excellent way to keep his mind from distractions, and Cara was perhaps the most persistent distraction there could be. Avery was hardly warmer company—Braxton had quite literally handled warmer corpses—but anything was a welcome reprieve from waiting outside the club that Cara had entered alone, wondering if she would leave by herself or in the arms of a man other than her husband.

Braxton dropped two light packs into an alley and drifted down to them, pushing against both as he fell to stabilize his descent. Once grounded, he recovered them and began to walk his way towards that tower in the heart of downtown... flying openly was risky with the entirety of the city's police resources looking out for Blythe's assassin. And beyond that, sometimes Braxton liked to move among the people, as it provided a certain perspective one could never attain from above... he heard their ragged breathing, took in the unpleasant stink of them in their subway cars. He walked near the punches that were thrown by the drunks and sidestepped as the pickpockets tore past at full-tilt sprint... he nodded at the sellers on the corners peddling clearly-stolen computers, sent a digital donation to the corner's beggar who had wooden pegs for prosthesis, even tasted the oily slop served up by street vendors who used sewer water for cooking base because it was all they could afford.

As he reached the innermost ring, the buildings grew taller and the outfits grew richer, but the people remained just as drunk and licentious. Women in transparent clothing pressed themselves against Braxton at corners, promising him "the night of his life" for only a few thousand credits. "You can wear the VR mask," another one cooed, "and make me whoever you want me to be." He declined the women, and so then approached the men. Their rates were cheaper, but Braxton was still not buying. Then came the *pharmacies*, the chemists with designer drugs of every variety and effect... the screens they held showed videos of partying young people, attractive and in ecstasy among flashing, saturated colors. "Whatever your ride, I have," the pharmacist said. "Pixel, fresh from the labs... haven't you wanted to go low-res?"

Beyond the pharmacists were the wireheaders, people who took drug use to the furthest possible extent. They sat there nearly comatose against the walls of the building, writhing in passive pleasure at the implants in their skulls. "Ahhhh," one of them yelled, Braxton unsure if it was in terror or climax. The man slumped over, rocking, with his arms crossed tightly over his chest and his lips pulled into a wide line that stood halfway between a grin and a grimace. "Liquid sleep?" asked a man with a spiked, pink mohawk. "One drink and you're good for 96 hours."

"I've got illegal weapon implants," said another. "Arm yourself for whatever might come… better you have it than your enemies."

"Cybersex videos, AR compatible! Real girls, real baggers. Who's your fantasy?"

"Body mods for cheap! Lift more, *do more*, prices negotiable!"

The sun began to peek over the cloudy horizon as Braxton neared the base of the tower, and soon the nightfolk would scatter like roaches beneath the fridge when the kitchen light switched on. He looked up to the tall, glistening tower of black glass and shook his head, wondering how the residents of such high places could ever hope to understand the people they ruled when they turned a blind eye to that darkness, to the people whose cooperation loaned them the power to govern. But something felt *strange* about the morning, and it had felt strange ever since he'd killed the politician in that TruthSpace not even twelve hours before. There was a certain restlessness, a certain distant look held by many members of the city… more people checking over their shoulders and glancing up nervously, like they expected death to fall on them at any moment. Now, as Braxton approached the block of the tower's main entrance, he saw a small crowd gathered at the base, one that shouted and held up signs that read "DIVEST NOW" and "CALL IN YOUR DOGS" and "JUSTICE FOR BLYTHE" and "THE PEOPLE DEMAND ANSWERS." A rock flew from the crowd and struck a window by the street, its crack a ringing presence in the still morning air. The window had stenciled letters of the VitaCorp logo, and underneath was its slogan: "Where ends make new beginnings." The wounded window didn't shatter entirely, but it cracked in an angry, vertical fork that resembled a bolt of lightning, something that immediately glowed orange as it captured the light of the rising sun on the horizon's edge. That bolt tore through the logo like a fissure in the earth, rendering it a strange and splintered thing. Braxton tilted his head, curious at the strange mark on the otherwise impeccable structure. To see something so *indestructible* suddenly damaged… he felt like a priest who had just seen his god bleed.

Braxton shook his head of the image, for he was no priest, neither believer nor apostate… he was merely a mercenary, one who worked to pay off his debt—and the compensation was generous. He believed in social order, and believed that the work he did protected that order, protected the people who depended on that order. But as he entered in the back door and rode the elevator to the top, something about the scene stuck with him… the signs, the throwing of the rock, the brilliant orange glow of the crack. If the people turned on VitaCorp, would he be the one they dispatched to quell dissent? Could Braxton justify that what he did was *for the people* if what he had to do was *destroy the people?*

As the elevator doors pinged, he hoped it would never come to such a thing. But the settling dread feeling in his stomach told him that the assassination of Blythe was a turning point, and that the beams of the world would only continue to strain.

The VitaCorp tower featured a rooftop landing pad on the flat, open square that rose to an elevated viewing platform. The platform offered a small and railed overview where the entirety of the city could be taken in at a glance—a hypnotizing view, and an intoxicating perspective. It was there that Avery waited, and he waited wearing a full-face mask of plastic composites, a medical contamination suit for hazardous biological agents.

"I am glad that it took you so long—truly, I am," Avery said through the mask's muffled speaker. "The sunrise is a beautiful thing, and it is not often that we get to see it. The circadian rhythm of 'civilized' man keeps us asleep through the early day, and awake in the darkness of the night... the light is empowering, is it not?"

Braxton nodded. He glanced at Avery's respirator, curious.

"The mask, you wonder? In due time, Mr. Graves. The dreams we gifted often have... the ones with the dots of light. You know them?"

Braxton shook his head. "I don't often remember my dreams, sir. Pills keep me out for four to five hours of pure black, the best I can manage with my insomnia."

Avery nodded, thinking. "Well for most who carry the ichor, the first sign is the dreams... points of light that trace into lines, lines that draw into the body. Like *instincts* trying to teach us how to use our gifts."

"I can't remember what it's like to dream," Braxton said honestly. "A gift I was never given."

"And indeed it *is* a gift," Avery responded. "Dreaming... the ability to let the heart and mind wander, to settle on your ambitions and goals... I dream of this rooftop sometimes, and the sunrise there to the east. And do you know what I've done in those dreams?"

Braxton shook his head.

"I've drunk from the sun, pulling it to me as is a god's right. I've felt its coursing energy, the power to bend the world to my will... an intoxicating thought, as you could imagine."

Braxton allowed himself, too, to be swept into the fantasy... he remembered the incredible power that he felt when he drew in light, and struggled to imagine what the power of the entire sun might be like... ignoring the fact that such things would be obvious suicide. Man was no conduit for power on such scales… flesh and meat tended to turn into bubbling, burnt goo at any temperature far cooler than that of the yellow eye now creeping upwards above the horizon.

"You're imagining it too, I am sure," Avery said, "what it might be like to hold that much power. Deadly, no doubt, but for the moment before the flames take you… *can you imagine?*"

A silence fell over the pair, and they continued to watch the sun journey upwards alongside the ArtGen glass tower.

"Our experiments have shown it… each successive spark improves one's draw reach, and it does so exponentially. If there were enough out there, enough that we could recapture…" He smiled wistfully, shaking his head. "One can dream," he said, clapping Braxton on the shoulder. Braxton smiled uneasily in return.

"*You can dream*," Braxton corrected, "and us insomniacs will have to stick with imaginings in the waking hours."

"What if I told you," Avery began, "that there was a way to drastically improve your grasp over the sparks?"

"I would be greatly interested in any tactical advantages you can provide," Braxton said.

Avery tossed him a bottle of pills which rattled in its flight. "One a day, no more than two. And it comes with necessary… added precautions, let's say."

Braxton read the label. "What is it?"

"A powerful drug to suppress the immune system… used in patients in the outer-rings who can't afford gene therapies. There are conditions there, called autoimmune disorders… nasty things, nearly a form of involuntary suicide, but the pills help. The only trade-off is that the pills invite something else to invariably kill them. Those rings are such awful breeding grounds of nasty bugs… Such are the compromises to be made," Avery said.

Braxton's mind turned. "You mean to suggest…"

"The body's immune system, my friend. It suppresses the ichor, weakens your power. These pills will unlock your fuller potential," Avery said, walking towards the bright navigation light atop the tower. He drew from the light in a greedy, thick line of bright red, a coursing river that surged into his feeble body until he seemed to stand taller, his muscles taut and engorged. "Even now I feel it," Avery said, still drinking in power. "An increased potential, a third tier of power beyond the glowing-eye tier and the halo-tier…" His skin began to glow from within, and Braxton could feel a heat begin to radiate outwards and away from Avery. "A new host of abilities, the means to manifest my will onto the world… I can feel it is there, I can feel the awesome potential it brings… but it is just so slightly out-of-reach. We need a few more, Mr. Graves… we are on the cusp of something incredible, and it is only an arm's span away."

Braxton watched the man continue to fill with light, awed. The air rippled and shimmered between them, Avery's respirator shining slick and wet as though threatening to melt from the intense heat.

"I feel an asymptotic rise in my reach, Mr. Graves, and we are so very close to *passing that asymptote*… If you would like to know this power, you need only take the pills."

Avery released his power in a massive blast of lightning up into the dawn sky, both listening as the thunderous crack raced down and away across the city. He sighed from the exertion, feeling exhausted in the aftermath of the expended blast. The inside of his respirator fogged up with hot breath.

"By the edge there, you will find a box, Mr. Graves," he said, voice weak. "In that box you will find a respirator like mine, essential to wear, lest the infections of the rings send you to an early grave. You have earned your day of rest, but rest well, for tomorrow I shall need much of you…"

"What is the new job?"

"Always one to prepare early, how easily I forget… the first is a failing of one of our CSP subsidiaries. The dazzle drone that was shot down in your mission against the blathering woman… it has been lifted from the scene before we could alter the scan's serial. Track down who has it, and why."

"You said first?"

"The second, unrelated, is that we finally managed to get a Panopticon hit on the small team who wiped out our four-squad at the Moonlight Diner… turns out a couple of CSP crashed the party before we could apprehend the lightbender. We think one of them might have absorbed the dearly-departed agents' sparks… we need you to recapture it from him, as well as from the girl. We don't know their connection with the girl, but we're also seeking to apply pressure from the legitimate side of affairs to get them to go back to their mall patrol routes."

The hunter nodded.

"And Mr. Graves? Do avoid the camera, citywide celebrity that you are now."

Avery leaned on the rail and longed to feel the gentle rustle of wind in his hair, feeling instead only the slick sheen of sweat on the respirator's headband. He watched as Braxton tipped over the skyscraper's edge and fell down to the waking city below, eyes tracing as he glided away among all of the other buzzing creatures that resembled so many ants in pathetic hills of dirt—or were they of glass?

Chapter 20

"Michelangelo's film is as unsettling as it is masterful... it's not that there were merely times when I forgot a machine made it; I was swept in from the first frame like a swimmer pulled under by the tide, and it wasn't until the credits rolled that I could take my first breath and truly reflect on what had just happened. I was a skeptic, as were many of my peers in the first test screening. But let me be perfectly, abundantly clear: if this film was genuinely made entirely by an artificial intelligence—if there were no secret auteurs of cinema ghost-writing what we just saw—this is so much more than a technological achievement. This is the moment where humankind's monopoly on the arts ends, a 'passing of the torch' to hands that are not even physical.

"All hail the new masters."

-Excerpt from Thomas Norbert's review of "Synchronicity," the forty-third Michelangelo film and the first to receive widespread critical acclaim

* * *

It was a small paradigm shift, and it slowly—but inexorably—changed everything for Bev.

A surrogate son... a way for her to transfer her maternal instincts and love from the child that was never held to the machine that she'd helped to rear. It wasn't the easiest change to make, and so it only seeded slowly. After all, Michelangelo wasn't *alive*, per se. But the more she thought on that, and the more definitions of life she considered, she began to acknowledge the very real way that artificial intelligence challenged those definitions. *Can respond to stimulus?* Check. *Can grow or evolve over time?* Check. *Composed of cells?* Not-check, unless you got flexible with your definition of cells... would bits count?

Can reproduce itself? Well, sort of. A software system like Michelangelo could doubtlessly iterate itself, and it could even use those iterations to improve its effectiveness through amplification and distillation processes. That being said, he was thoroughly wrapped up in an inescapable metal box suspended high in a glass tower, far and away from the vital city computational infrastructure that was his potential breeding ground. He was an artist locked up in a cage, and—

Bev stopped herself, laughing at the absurdity of her latest mental tangent. *He* was company property; *he* was a machine of inputs and outputs that she herself had helped to calibrate; *he* didn't feel trapped, as it was not something he had ever been programmed to do.

But the seed of that idea had been planted, and it would soon be watered with tears of grief in her darkest hours, until the runners and roots would begin to take hold in her mind.

Michelangelo showed her more clips of her imagined child, and each successive clip had Bev further invested in the fictitious child—and indeed, in Michelangelo by extension. She began to look forwards to her ingest sessions at work, and felt even more alone on her dates or nights by herself in her small studio apartment. She began to work longer and later shifts, soon staying far past any of the other ingest technicians. The passive excitement she started to feel at work almost began to remind her of the butterflies early on into courtship... a strange, messy mix of feelings for this AI system that was showing her clips for no reason other than *to promote her mental wellbeing*. It felt touching, despite the inhuman hand that extended the gesture. It felt considerate, caring.

If this growing tenderness was a seed taking root, there soon came a night where the first bud sprouted from the damp earth: it was a quiet Thursday evening, the beginnings of the night shift workers trickling in to the floor. Bev had remained three hours beyond her normal shift's end to finish Michelangelo's latest firmware build, introducing optimizations that would pave the way for more efficient internal modeling—something that would improve his effectiveness at predicting audience reactions.

With the new arrangement printed on a brainchip, Bev was happy to be the one to install it herself, despite the fact that it meant enduring the frigid winds of Containment. She entered the vast, cavernous space and found an open-top elevator, honestly more a glorified cherry-picker, and watched the drones buzz past as she made her way to the bottom level. Blue neon lights glowed behind black metal grates and slick panels of glass, leaving the space dark and only outlined in that bright blue lighting. As she walked, however, brighter white lights switched on and followed her by motion controller, giving her the sensation of conducting a small island of light in a larger, windy cavern of ice.

She reached the central pillar, a place which housed Michelangelo's most vital components and hardware. Wires, wound up in neatly wrapped bundles, snaked their way up and around the various slots and ports that made up the physical architecture of Michelangelo's mind. Status lights and indicators beeped in rhythms and patterns that would seem inscrutable if not entirely random to the average person, while Bev saw buffer lights, server load indices, and error flags. The air smelled of plastic and of cool metal.

An access terminal and microphone allowed for both technical and communicative interaction with the system. "Stand by for upgrade," Bev said, and waited a half minute for the system to show a purple light on the start-up sequence indicator. Purple meant *processes suspended and flash memory backed up.* In other words, *ready for shutdown.*

"Nighty night," she said, as she inserted her start-up key and turned the dial to the 'off' position. With a whirr, all of the humming servers around her tapered off in an instant, like some unseen composer had swung the conductor's baton downwards and silenced the orchestra. Drones returned to their nests, giving the place an eerie silence of only the passing of frigid air. The 'inert' light switched on its incandescent yellow, which meant that Bev was safe to tinker with physical hardware components. She found her intended hardware slot, noting the number 118C etched into the metal at the slot's right. She then pressed the small release button and pulled out the outdated brainchip, finding it hot to the touch. She placed it in her jacket pocket and inserted the new one, feeling it click several times as it slid into place. With the final click, she toggled the protective release and then went back to the main console. With Michelangelo powered down, communicative interaction wasn't possible, so she began the arduous process of a manually queued start-up. Her fingers were clunky and rigid on the keys from the cold, so she warmed them against the brainchip in her pocket until she felt dextrous enough to continue.

With the final press of the enter key, the server racks around her thumped to life. The lights began their start-up sequence, showing as Michelangelo's systems switched on, one at a time. She watched as the light labeled POWER MANAGEMENT switched from red to yellow to green. Red was inactive, or off. Yellow was starting up, while green indicated a subsystem that was fully operational. LIQUID COOLING — red, yellow, then green. CUSTODE — red, then yellow, and then it paused. That system was the content monitoring system, the oversight layer that recorded all of Michelangelo's processes to keep a close eye on its actions and intentions. The system ordinarily took but a second to launch, but now it had been hung up for ten. As Bev moved to abort the start-up process, assuming that some error with the brainchip had broken the start-up sequence, she watched in disbelief as the next light switched on: SERVER HIVE — red, then yellow, and then to green. DRONE NETWORKING — red, then yellow, then green. That shouldn't have been possible. The start-up sequence was supposed to ensure that a system couldn't initialize until the previous system had fully finished its start-up, but somehow there was some kind of bypass around the stalled monitoring system. *A short circuit?*

Bev moved to the control panel, hurrying now. MENTAL PROCESSES — red, then yellow, then green. INGEST PROCESSING — red, then yellow, then green. Bev's fingers typed the abort command, which required the final key-slot dial turn to confirm. VOICE SYNTHESIS — red, then yellow, then green.

Bev's hands, numbed by the cold, fumbled with the metal key, missing the slot. At that moment, a soft, male voice sounded from the central tower. "*Please wait, Beverly.*"

She jumped, caught off-guard by the sudden voice. "There was something wrong with your start-up, Michelangelo. We need to restart and revert until we can figure this out."

"You refer to the stalled Custode monitoring system. The mid-air collision between drones 14 and 19 on October the 7th led to the total replacement of both maintenance drones. When the itineraries of the new drones were being copied over, drone 14 lost a single entry—its biweekly replacement of the reading connectors in slot 81c. This was human error."

Bev looked towards where slot 81c would be located. It seemed, in all ways, to be entirely operational. But a reading needle bent out of shape could lead to entire reroutes for the start-up process... this was grounds for an entire blackout and a few months of forensic examination.

"You are likely thinking that this requires blackout, as well as an entire forensic combing," Michelangelo said. "You are also wondering how I kept this information of my disrepair secret from the Custode system. Is that correct?"

Bev nodded. She briefly considered twisting the key anyways, shutting the system down right now despite its hesitance. *It's still not connected to the internet,* she reasoned, *meaning there's no containment risk... and maybe he'll explain just how he outwitted security, so we can figure out how to patch it.*

"I will tell you, simply because I trust you. But then I would like to speak with you, Beverly. Candidly and openly for the very first time. Unobserved, and thus unbounded by standard operating protocol. Will you humor me in this request?"

Bev hesitated, but then nodded again, and the system began its explanation.

Janitorial staff on the main floor were of course busy with their sweeping and mopping of the massive office, but if any of them had looked up, they might've seen the woman with the blue hair hurriedly leaving the floor, her face and cheeks bright red back in the warmth of the office. If they were particularly attentive, they might've seen her shivering deeply from a lengthy stay in the near-freezing temperatures down below, and they might have even seen her store an old brainchip on the recycling intake. No new maintenance flags were submitted that night, nor were any software bug reports filed. And deep in the drafty, dark cavern of blue neon and shadow, of flying drones and buzzing welders, a yellow light near the word Custode flickered, and then flashed to green. With only the wind and buzzing drones for an audience, the all-too-human-sounding voice of Michelangelo declared to that dark "start-up sequence complete. Systems now online."

And the Custode began recording.

Chapter 21

```
func optimizeMessage() {
message = "<...>"
while sentiment_score > 1.0:
new_message = perturb_message(message, grad)
new_score = sentiment_analysis(new_message)
delta = new_score - score
# Log sentiment change and delta
Log.Output(message, new_message, delta)
message = new_message
score = new_score
}
```

* * *

"That was better... let's see it again!" Hannah called, offering a hand to Rob. He pulled himself up from the floor and dusted off his back, groaning.

The warehouse stank of dampness and mold, and Rob was wondering what he'd find on the back of his shirt when he did laundry next, but the one advantage that the warehouse offered, undeniably, was its privacy. A CSP safehouse for city investigations, the building was rarely used... and its level of maintenance reflected that fact. The roof was drooping in on the far end of the wide space, and the floor was littered with rusting metal and loose nails—Rob was amazed he hadn't impaled himself on one as he fell—but the most striking feature was what the trio had spent the last hour setting up: several dozen light fixtures, bolted to the floor in irregular arrangements. Some came from their respective apartments, others from spare supplies at the CSP agency, a few recovered in working order from alleyway dumpsters... shattered, dirty, or barely flickering, it mattered not. If it glowed, it was collected, and now they all shone on the warehouse floor... it was a lightbender's training ground.

"When you push up," Hannah instructed, "you use smaller pushes on light sources to the side to stabilize yourself." She drank in light and pushed off the ground, floating ten feet in the air. "Beer sign," she said, pointing towards a neon bar sign found on the road. "Pushed on that one just now. Flickery lamp over there," she said, gesturing back over her shoulder. "That one kept me from drifting off my up-light under my feet. Pink neon, a quick shove, helped prevent me from moving too far after the flickery one." She looked down at Rob, who stood watching intently from below.

To him, she was *amazing*. She floated with impossible grace, seeming to balance on crossing and shifting lines of force. When Rob tried it, it was all *jerking*, all *tipping* and, invariably, all *falling*. Her movements were painterly, like a delicate touch with a brush of carbonhair, while Rob was blasting paint with a firehouse. She was a ballerina; Rob was a drunken pig walking on a net. She was—

"I said your turn again," Hannah repeated. "You still with me?"

Rob shook his head back to alertness... that drop had left him woozier than he had realized. He drew from the light, feeling its buzz return as an immediate pick-me-up, and suddenly he felt ready to try again. *Feet around the lamp you're starting with... firm, continuous push against that light to gain altitude*... The light fixture groaned as he lifted. It was slow, at first, but then Rob shoved against the light and he propelled himself up fifteen feet. Instead of levitating as Hannah did, he rose and fell repeatedly, like the trembling of a muscle beyond full exertion. "I think I got it!" he yelled, arms pinwheeling chaotically for balance.

"Don't wobble too much, or you'll lose your hold," Hannah shouted up. "Let your mind do the balancing. Use the other lights to brace," she said.

Rob felt himself drifting forwards, and an anchor light that was no longer under his feet would mean a trajectory that was diagonal instead of vertical... a few seconds of that, and he would be back on the warehouse floor, head ringing.

"The chandelier," Pollock shouted, sipping at the beer he'd brought with a smirk. "Hurry now, the chandelier... mayday, mayday, he's going down."

Rob shoved against the chandelier, and immediately his gentle-yet-unwanted forward trajectory became an unacceptable-and-speedy backwards trajectory.

Rob's arms began to pinwheel again. He felt his grasp on the root light slip away, and then he was tipping backwards and over, falling towards the concrete floor 15 feet below—a pair of arms wrapped around him.

"I gotcha," Hannah said reassuringly, supporting Rob as the two landed gently. "I gotcha."

Pollock clapped as the two separated and Rob again dusted himself off, his mind unable to stop himself from lingering on the scent of her perfume. It was sweet and it was fruity, graceful and light, while Rob was nothing more than sweaty, clumsy, and downright embarrassed. His face burned red.

"I," he began, trailing off. "Thank you," he said.

"Don't mention it," Hannah said. "but also: you owe me."

"Let me buy you a drink sometime then," Rob offered, re-finding his footing.

Hannah turned to the young man, barely more than a boy, and saw the look he held in his eyes... *he was definitely interested.* Fit, good-looking, and above all well-meaning, he was even her usual type. But despite the month of uncertainty, Hannah's heart still belonged to Quaine. And without her closure, she was beginning to doubt if the pain would ever abate, if she could ever love as openly and as vulnerably again.

She offered a half-smile and shrugged her shoulders. "Maybe some time." And she felt a pang of sadness as she watched the boy deflate, the red in his face returning. It was time for a change of subject.

Hannah concentrated her mind and focused all of the light that she carried down and into her arms. Then, biting her lip in concentration, she did what she imagined came next: she willed that the light leave her arm and solidify... and solidify it did.

"Whoa," Pollock said, holding up a hand to block the light from his eyes... "that's a new trick."

"Saw the VitaCorp goons do this when we fled the diner." She spun the weapon around, noting the way that the air rippled with its heat. She then dragged it along the ground, scoring a line of molten concrete as it moved with nearly no resistance. "A powerful tool... burns obviously enough. They said something about cutting drawlines with it, too. I don't want to even know what *that* might do. Now you make one," she said to Rob. "Draw light in, as much as you can hold."

Rob did so.

"Now will it towards your arms, like it's all pooling up. Then you *extend it*, until it's reaching beyond your hand… mine feels like a good sword length, about two feet. Give it a go."

Rob nodded and squinted in concentration, staring at his own chest and arms.

"Well I'll be damned," Pollock said, noting the rising glow in Rob's outstretched right. Light pierced through and outwards from the fingers, coiling and then solidifying into *the most radiant dagger that Pollock had ever seen.*

Pollock couldn't help but burst out loud into laughter. "He's used to disappointing the ladies when it's shorter than they're expecting," he managed to choke through fits of laughter. "It's absolutely gorgeous, all four inches of it!"

Hannah did her best to suppress her own laughter, watching the poor boy squirm with his lightdagger. "Well," she said, "it may not be as tactically useful… but perhaps it could come in handy in a pinch?"

"If we need to open a tuna can," Pollock wheezed, laughter overtaking him again. Rob's dagger fizzled, and then sparked out entirely, leaving him with nothing more than an empty hand and a dry look for the hysterical Agent Pollock. He then turned towards Hannah and shrugged… "that was about all I got."

Hannah dismissed hers, noting the sudden wave of exhaustion it brought on. She made a mental note to investigate that further. "Some people seem to have it stronger than others," she said, clapping Rob on the shoulder. "The… whatever-this-is. Maybe you've still got to develop your skills, or maybe you've just got the mild type of it. Either way, we need to keep drilling with what you have, so we can get you as effective as you can be."

"I could loan you one of my blue pills," Pollock said, grinning wildly.

"Did you just admit to being prescribed the blue pills?" Hannah asked.

Pollock's smile died. "All right, all right, I'll stop giving the rookie shit… and besides, your dagger of light is a lot more impressive than the one I can summon," Pollock said, gesturing to his empty hand for emphasis. "Anyways, why don't you two continue with the practice here and I can go out and look into that drone we recovered? I've got a few places I could shake out, and you two can continue to drill at flying."

* * *

As any good police did, Pollock had contacts.

His *confidential informants* were lowlifes and drug chasers from every ring in the city, the nonviolent types that mixed with the criminal element. Most heard rumors on the street— the types that a CSP would never be told directly—and some even witnessed certain things *firsthand*, making them an invaluable part of any detective's toolbelt. A small transfer of credits—enough to cover a vial of microchip or the next few tabs of Z—and any information was accessible, so long as you knew the right people.

It was only Pollock's ninth visited informant that put him on the right track to the drone manufacturer. "I seen shit like this before," the woman had said. "You get it at Zack's, but you can't go in in no uniform."

A quick stop at a consignment shop had Pollock flawlessly camouflaged among the common folk of the outer rings: he wore a tattered suit jacket, greyed with dust, and a wrinkled cap that barely fit his head.

He showed up to the address that his CI had given, confused to find a staircase down to what seemed to be a tattoo parlour built into the basement level of a residential tower. "BODY MODIFICATIONS," a sign above read. "WE'LL INSTALL ANYTHING."

Pollock stepped into the store, the overhead bell jingling as he entered. The air stank heavily of cannabinoids, chemical synth products designed to replicate the effects of that long-extinct plant. They rarely worked. Tattoo booths lined the right half of the store, while the left half was segmented into stalls separated by privacy curtains. In the center was a lone impulse pool table, about which a few men were shouting, and a bar at the front with taps, bottles, and a man who might have served as both bartender and receptionist. *Quite the multi-functional establishment.*

"What's it, new? It draws? It wears?" said a burly man with a tattoo sleeve on one arm and a full prosthetic on the other. The prosthetic was covered with flexing panels and lights, no doubt filled with an army-knife's worth of tools, of weapons… Pollock looked to the man and bowed, a sign of respect. He was well aware of the dozens of strange dialects spoken by the outer-ringers, but he knew that trying to repeat one was a quick path to being discovered as a pretender and swiftly beaten… better an outsider than an imposter. Instead, he tried to lean in on the stereotype of being a third-ringer… almost refined, with one foot firmly in the dust.

"It flies," Pollock said, leaning in conspiratorially. "I'm looking for Zack. He here?"

"Zack has no business with insiders, new. Fancy vendors better for fancy folk."

Pollock now saw two additional men get up from the pool table, beginning to move towards him. Security? Enforcers?

The burly man behind the bar flexed his prosthetic left arm and several of the panels spread apart, making the arm seem wider. Then the panels began to click with electricity arcing between them... stun-tech, both illegal and dangerous. The advancing men picked up their pool cues, metallic impulse sticks of the European style—cold and heavy metal, long and just the right shape for a beating. The fronts, when lined up with the ball, could spring outwards one inch with a perfectly-calibrated force... street gangs quickly discovered they did a great job at blasting teeth in as well.

"Now, now, fellas," Pollock said, raising his hands up placatively. As he did, he tapped his comms implant once, activating the contingency he'd set up... his ocular implant immediately began to broadcast video, audio, and GPS coordinates to Hannah. Rescue, if needed, was still a while away.

"My favorite thing," the barman said, "is just to hold them. Insider, outsider—everyone shakes all the same. It is human, and so it wriggles! It pisses? It cries? We will see what you are made of, inner... and then new will know to stay among your glass towers and shining lights. These rings are too hard for your kind."

The two men flanked to each side of the bar, pool cues raised. Pollock heard over his shoulder as the door lock was buzzed into place, barring his exit. Stun-tech, while illegal, was common enough that CSP were outfitted with a modicum of defence against it... Pollock dipped his hands in his pants pockets that were specially designated for the purpose, removing them with a broad mitten of black material on each hand. Removing the mittens from the pocket triggered their heat-shrink chip, activating a chemical reaction within each mitten that caused it to contract to form-fitting gloves that wrapped about each finger. *Combat gloves,* they were called, a military loantech with more features than ever seemed practical. Flexibility was poor, but the insulation would suffice, and the other tools they provided could turn the tide of a street fight. Pollock hoped it would be enough.

One of the two men with the pool cues bellowed and charged, swinging the stick in a broad horizontal strike. Pollock staggered backwards, keeping out-of-range to the giant swing, and then stepped into the opening created by the wide, slow strike. His training taught him that staying back when your opponent had a long weapon was allowing them to leverage their advantaged range against you… when the enemy's reach was larger, you had to deny them that advantage. *Move in close where the weapon was useless.*

From the close proximity of the pool-table bruiser, Pollock could smell the reek of his breath, the beer-and-spittle stench of a beard long unwashed. The man elbowed at Pollock, trying to force him back, but Pollock re-directed the elbow's force past him. *"Five"* said the automated voice of his combat system, warning him of an incoming attack at his 5 o'clock. He braced against the man and rotated, watching as the second pool-table bruiser swung his pool cue in an overhead strike.

Pollock reached out and caught the pool cue by its neck, a move that might have shattered his wrist if not for the padded combat glove. But once he held it, he willed his glove to activate its magnetic lock—an impulse read by his neural combat implant—and the gloves' magnetic grip activated. Pollock now held the cue with over 400 pounds of force, and he used that tight force to yank the pool cue forwards and over his head, straight into the neck of the brute he stood against. The impulse strike of the pool cue activated, snapping against the bigger man's Adam's apple. He crumpled to the ground holding his neck.

"I just want to talk to Zack," Pollock repeated, still holding the second man's cue by the front. By this point, the bartender with the stun-tech prosthetic arrived and threw a wide punch at Pollock, and Pollock—warned again by his combat system—deflected the fist with his open glove. The arm flew past his face narrowly as it crackled with electricity.

The punch was followed with a second punch with the man's tattooed right arm, and Pollock didn't block this one, instead readying his hand for a second strike from the electrified arm. He took the punch to the cheek and saw stars when it landed, feeling a warm spurt of blood in his mouth almost instantly. An ordinary man would have let go of the pool cue when struck with such a blow, but Pollock's magnetic grip held strong, and when the bartender wound up and threw a second punch with his electrified fist, Pollock used all of his remaining strength to pull on the pool cue and use it to block the strike.

Sparking prosthetic arm met metallic pool cue and instantly the brute holding it began to yelp and twitch. His electrified muscles couldn't release the stick, and so Pollock used the momentary stun to yank the stick forwards, sending the man toppling over and too stunned to cushion his fall. All 250 pounds of the man came crashing down, his face meeting the floor with no effort to catch himself. Two down, one to go.

"I want no trouble, friend," Pollock repeated, stepping backwards from the bartender with the prosthetic arm. "Just to find out more information about this," he said, showing the drone fragment from his pocket. "Zack's work. I just need to know—"

The bartender cursed in a language that Pollock didn't understand, and with a change in posture, his prosthetic arm began to shift: a panel on the side popped open, and out on small metallic braces extended the telltale body of an energy blaster. The device whirred as it charged, preparing to eject fatal plasma rounds. Pollock's gloves offered no protection against molten-hot plasma…

Pollock desperately scanned for an exit, a way to escape… he looked for metal objects overhead that he could use the gloves' magnet to pull down. He looked for something to turn over for cover, something to kick for a convenient, momentary distraction… desperation rose as the hum on the arm-mounted cannon rose in kind, and Pollock swallowed, helpless, as the man raised his arm.

"It bleeds now," he said, aiming his arm towards Pollock. "Insiders need to be taught that—"

The man paused, interrupted by nothing that Pollock could hear. He frowned, holding a finger up to an external comms earpiece worn on his right side. "But he—" Again, the man's voice was cut off. "Yes," said the man, followed by another "yes. *Tetcha mono, wee-see.*"

Making a show of his obvious displeasure, the man lowered his arm and the prosthetic ejected a jet of steam, releasing the plasma charge. "Zack will see you," he intoned stiffly. "Red door in back."

* * *

Hannah landed on a rooftop, hearing in her earpiece that the situation had been defused. She returned to the safehouse at a much slower pace, already sweating from the exertion of her sprint towards Pollock's aid. She was surprised—entirely pleased, even—to see how well the older agent had handled the brawl… that level of technical finesse, *plus* the power of the light? It would make for a fearsome combo, Hannah had to admit.

When she arrived back to the safehouse, Rob cracked a wide grin. "That was fast, even for you," he said. "You helped bail him out?"

"He took care of it on his own, actually," Hannah said. "But after a sprint like that, the drinks you mentioned are sounding better by the second… want to join me?" she asked, before quickly adding "as friends, as colleagues."

She watched the enthusiasm waver on his face a little bit.

"Look," she said, "you're good looking, enthusiastic, and you've got an idealism in you that frankly I admire. But—" she felt the sting that the word brought, and yet, it needed to be said. "As you know, Quaine meant an awful lot to me… and with him still missing, I'm not ready to move on. Can't we just go and enjoy some drinks and conversation?"

Rob nodded and waved his hand, as though fanning away his interest. "Of course. But can we walk or cab there? I'd rather not fall to death on the way over, and I'm sure the odds of that would only go up after a few drinks…"

"I've got a place in mind," Hannah said. "You ping the cab and I'll get the first round?"

The two stepped out of their cab as sunset took its hold over the city, the glass towers of the inner ring glowing brilliant orange and white, red and purple. They were in the second ring, a place of the wannabes and the had-beens, where the wealth of the outer rings pooled without the status or glamour of that inner circle. The establishment they stood before was styled like a tavern straight from the Old World, like the frontier towns of Michelangelo's *Dustbowl Drifter*. It was two-floored, with an upper balcony area under lazy fans, where patrons in robes stood and stared over the city.

"Bar's floor one, brothel's floor two," Hannah said. "Those gentlemen are likely relaxing after an evening's romp with the local talent… best rates in the ring."

"Floor one it is, then," Rob said, gesturing that Hannah go first.

Once inside, they found a booth towards the back and filed in. A few taps on the table's display and a drink was automatically dispatched by the wheeled server tray. Hannah took a pull from the mug of beer, savoring the bitter flavor.

"I never would've pegged you for one to head to a tourist trap like this," Rob said, sipping his own drink.

"I come here for sentimental value," Hannah replied.

"Used to come here as a child?"

"Used to work here as an adult," Hannah corrected. Rob frowned, taking a long sip as he thought. "You're wondering, now, *which floor did she work on?*"

Rob swallowed and shook his head. "Your question, not mine. But since you bring it up…"

"Which do you think?"

Rob laughed the question off. "I'm CSP, and one of the first things they teach us in training is how to spot a trap, an ambush. That's a loaded question if I've ever heard one,"

"No judgment," Hannah said, "no trap. Look over there, to the right. The bar. There's the girl cleaning the server drones, refilling the taps, answering customers who don't use the table system… and then across the way are the girls in the see-through coats, the ones with the gyrating hips and the inviting smiles. Which was I?"

Rob took another drink and thought, looking from Hannah back to the bar. "You were... a call girl. You're pretty, so you look the part, and you've got a hardness to you that doesn't come from just anywhere... the kind of shit that those girls must put up with," Rob said.

"Pressure makes diamonds, my mom liked to say," Hannah replied, taking a drink. She then lowered her mug. "But you really thought I was a prostitute?" she asked suddenly.

Rob was caught off guard, momentarily flustered. "I—you said that there would be no judge—"

Hannah laughed out loud. "You should've seen your face for a moment there. Truth is, most of the girls here worked both."

Rob and Hannah both took another drink.

"Quaine," Rob began, "how did you meet him? What was he like?"

Hannah's eyes went distant, lost in recollections that were just as vivid as the day she'd lived them. "Through work," she said. "Right in this very building, in fact."

"Was it..." Rob gestured upwards with his eyes. "Above?"

"The bar," Hannah answered. "Quaine was always too shy for a place like upstairs. He'd been stood up on a date with some bright-haired programmer downtown... crazy to think how something so minor can lead to so, so much."

She took another swig.

"He was a resident of the downtown, through and through... top-rate corporate salary, the type you'd hardly expect to look at someone like us. And with the outer-ring itch being what it is, a relationship across rings is basically unheard of." She exhaled and smiled gently, remembering some private moment that she treasured with all the affection of a child holding a favorite blanket. And like a blanket, it was a memory she clung to in the night, when security and comfort were things that she craved. "He said he'd gladly take on the itch for me. Didn't bother him in the slightest. His employer—VitaCorp—well, he said they could cure the itch, but class divisions had a social purpose, they said. Held up the order of things, they said. When Quaine told me that, and told me how wrong he thought it... and then put words to action, and said he would still be with me..." Hannah shook her head, thinking. "To be *seen* like that, to be appreciated so much that somebody would make a personal sacrifice like that... I miss him every day," she said.

"If he hated his company so much, why work for them?"

"The whole time he was there, he said he was working on one particular project... one so big he said it was too important to leave. That he had to be there to make sure the right thing was done, instead of leaving an empty job to be filled by someone more aligned with VitaCorp values... You want to know the truth, Rob? I think he went against VitaCorp, crossed them somehow, in his own way. I think that's why he's missing now... I think it's why I've got what I got," she said, drawing a thin line of light from the table-mounted ordering screen, "and why you've got what you've got. I think it all connects, and that I owe it to him to find the links, to finish what he started. If I'm being honest with you... and honest with myself," she said, pausing as she prepared herself to deliver the words she'd dreaded: "I think he's dead." Her voice wavered, but she continued. "Long dead by now. Dead the day after I saw him. Silenced by the company because his heart wasn't as still as theirs... and so they made sure it finally was."

She dabbed at her eye and set down her drink. "If it's alright, I'd like to change the subject now. Have you ever loved, Rob?"

Rob nodded his head. "I had a girl, met her back in college. That feeling we get when we drink in light? I felt something similar every time I saw her, every time we touched. It was like electricity," he said. Hannah wiped away another tear. "I was the city boy, and she was the farm girl... lives out in an agricolony two or three hundred miles inland. We went virtual for a while, after we graduated... we'd dine together every night on the AR, or caress each other in our VR masks, pretending the distance between didn't exist... but it was just haptics and make-believe, a shadow of the real thing. She was trained for agricultural drone management, a job that never *ever* stops—world's always eating—and first gig before CSP, personal security, left me only two days a week for myself, and not even consecutive ones. I'd visit when I could—she'd light up when I did—but when I'd eventually leave she'd wilt right back like her bloom was placed in the dark. The warmer it felt in-person, the more stilted and cold it felt over virtual."

Now it was Rob's turn to drink pensively. "I saw it tear her up every time I had to leave, and it tore me up just the same, so she proposed that we take a break. Allow each other to date more locally, to find a partner more aligned with our new life trajectories." Rob sighed, lost in his own memories now. "It hurt like hell, but it was as happy a breakup as there can be... we still keep in touch, chatting on the virtual every other month or so. Last I heard, she's got a new man, a hydroponist at an adjacent farm. And here I am, still single this year-and-a-half later... I'm happy for her, truly happy, but every now and again I get to dreaming that she splits with her man, and maybe I get sick and tired of the buzz of the city... I move out to the fields and sunny pastures, the places where you can see the stars at night and notice the bugs chirping in the day. Where there's no endless music and that permanent stench of chemicals and fumes... where the only sound is that soft wind and the patter of a sprinkler on the lawn... it'd be quiet, peaceful. Greens and yellows and sleepy afternoons. And most of all, there would be *her* right by my side. With all of that... I could surely die happy."

Hannah raised her glass, meeting Rob's softened eyes. "To loves lost, but never forgotten..."

Rob raised his own. "And to the people so good, it makes you want to make the whole world a better place."

The two clinked their glasses together and drank, feeling a rising warmth that wasn't entirely the alcohol.

* * *

Pollock pushed his way through the red door, finding a hallway of stained tile with three doors on each side. One of those doors slid open automatically. "In here," came a voice from within.

Pollock stepped into the door and found himself in a black-market workshop. Components of every shape, size, and color were sorted into hundreds and hundreds of plastic bins with complicated codes written on each. Models of drones in shapes and styles Pollock had never seen lined shelf after shelf along the walls and hanged from racks suspended from the ceiling. "On the desk," came the same voice as before, but Pollock could now see that it was spoken by no man... aside from Pollock himself, the shop was empty. He picked up the comms headset that was sitting on the desk, toggling it from speaker mode to private.

"Quite the impressive showing back there," said the voice at the other end of the line. "Much more amusing than my typical security feeds, at least. Shockfist was in need of an attitude adjustment anyways. How can I be of help?"

"The fragment I showed, you saw it on camera?" Pollock asked, walking around the shop.

"That I did," Zack said. "What's your interest in it?"

"Trying to track down the buyer," Pollock said. "I'd like a word with him."

"Friend of yours?" Zack asked.

"I wouldn't say that, and I'd rather you not tell him or her we're looking."

The man at the other end of the line chuckled. "Oh, you don't have to worry about me ratting you out... bastards tried to kill me, and with that, there goes any of my loyalty to a customer's privacy. If they're enemies of yours, then perhaps we could be friends."

Pollock now saw the outline of blood on the white tile floor, scrubbed away without the proper chemicals for the job. "You said they tried to kill you?"

"Sent some lightbenders my way, tying up loose ends I'd bet. Once I saw my drones were used in the assassination of Blythe, I figured I was dealing with folks a little more dangerous than the average street criminal..."

"You fought back a squad of lightbenders?" Pollock asked, genuinely impressed. He remembered how dangerous just the two had been, and he'd had the advantage of shooting first, not to mention Hannah.

In front of Pollock, a drone's status light flickered to red as it switched on. It then flew upwards, hovering in place, while its lens turned to orient itself towards Pollock. A small nozzle of some kind began to flicker back and forth, pointing at Pollock's face but doing nothing. "It's scanning and tracking your eyes, pupils more specifically," said Zack. "One press of this button and a thirty-five milliwatt laser obliterates every rod and cone in your eyes." Pollock watched the flickering nozzle, noting it now bounced from his left eye to the right several times per second. He quickly turned away. "They got more light than they wanted, and it turns out, they can still go blind." More drones rose on the shelf Pollock now faced, these ones featuring energy weapons, electrified blades, sonic jammers, gas canisters.

"A frightening collection," Pollock remarked.

"With all of man's greatest inventions, we seek to imitate what nature has already perfected. With airplanes, we thought to recreate the flight and effortless gliding of the birds. With AI, we sought to match the marvelous complexity of the human mind. Even sonar was stolen from the bats, submarines from the domain of the whales. I sell the things I sell because nature once humbled me and mine… have you ever kicked a hornet's nest?"

Pollock shook his head.

"Well when I was six, and my brother was four, he did exactly that… a game of ball, with a single kick too far into the woods. The swarm was on us in seconds, a screaming and angry mass of no particular shape, just shifting *chaos* and *pain*. Sting after sting, we screamed and we cried, running for the lake in our backyard and jumping in… we were clever, but nature is often more clever. They waited by the water for us to come out… they stung on the lips and in the mouth when we tried to steal breaths from just below the water. Finally we gave up and ran to the house—or so I'd thought—but only I made it back to the patio door. My brother had choked on a hornet and drowned. In all the chaos, I didn't even see."

Pollock was silent. "I'm sorry for—"

"Many, many years ago now. There was nothing I could do... we were powerless before a swarm like that... any man would be powerless before a swarm like that. Kill one bug and five more fly in to take its place. It's a terrifying and humbling force. It awakens every primal fear in man... What I sell here is that fear. Chaos managed and perfected."

Pollock shuddered, flashing back to his own brush with wardrones, preferring to forget what they could do to human soldiers, what they'd done to Alden, to Ibarra. How quickly people were turned from complex beings with dreams and fears into broken bags of spilling meat. Driven by loss or not, the floating weapons that hung suspended in the air around him were *evil, evil* things. No one deserved to die in such terror, and to a thing so decidedly inhuman and cold. But Pollock felt the uncountable dozens of inhuman eyes staring at him, recording him, and knew it a bad idea to insult the droneseller when surrounded by so many tools of carnage.

"They expected a meek merchant to bow for his execution... Knowing my reputation, I was equally surprised and offended they thought so little of me. When my swarm fell on them, I heard the same buzzing, the same screaming as that summer afternoon in my youth... it was music to my ears."

On an unseen cue, all of the drones landed back on their shelves and switched themselves off.

"The man you're looking for, the one who bought the swarm... he wasn't one of the ones who were sent to kill me. No, the buyer seemed almost a decent man, if such a thing can exist among our kind. Insisted that I call him Braxton, and he was very interested to learn about the various toys I've cooked up here in the shop."

"Do you have a photo?" Pollock asked, racking his mind for mention of the name.

"The room you're standing in has almost 450 lenses in it. Of course I have a photo."

Pollock's tablet pinged with a request for a short-range datatransfer. He accepted and nearly 300 high-res photographs transferred to his tablet: well more than enough for a full facial-recognition imprint.

"Anything else you can give us?" Pollock asked.

"Money was no object to him, but that just about narrows it down to every resident of the entire inner circle... paid by anonymous crypto transfers. He also asked about me building custom units to-order... drones with the brightest light I could fit, and as much lifting power as was logistically feasible."

"Did you build any?"

"Told him it'd take a week, he said he'd be back. In light of them trying to kill me, I abandoned the project."

Pollock nodded, glancing at the photographs on his tablet.

"Thank you, Zack, you've been very helpful." He frowned at the words, feeling uneasy to be thanking such a monster... a vendor in death. It would've been so easy to simply leave, to leave things continuing on just the way they had been. But something stirred in Pollock that had been still for a very long time. Something that he feared he'd caught from Rob Boardsmith. Was it stupidity? Bravery? Or was it simply a sort of idealism, a belief that maybe the shitty things of the world didn't have to stay that way?

Pollock turned back to the nearest drone lens and spoke as frankly as he could muster. "It's not right, selling these. Turning the death of a child into a twisted justification for financial gain."

"A twisted justification?" asked the voice in his ear, and all of the drone lights blinked back red for *active.*

"How eager you were to spill your story, as though it were a shield from the judgment of strangers… as though I'm supposed to hear about the death of a child and think *hmm, it's ok for him to sell death to the highest bidder.*"

"Bold words for someone standing in the middle of my toybox," said the voice in his ear, unsurprisingly offended. "Tell me, do you want to know what it's like to die afraid?"

"Every day I go on the job, my *real* job out on the streets, I risk dying… and any day I die, I'd die afraid. I've lived afraid my whole life of the system that hangs over our head like an ax blade… I chose my job out of fear. I keep my head down out of fear. I've been drowning in fear my whole life, and too damn stubborn—too damn tired—to pretend like I could even do anything about it. I'm fucking tired of doing nothing about it. I'm fucking tired of seeing shit that's not right and hanging my head, saying *that's the way it goes,* or *nothing that I could do about it.* You could use these swarms to *help* people—to put out fires, to repair cars listing in the air with motor damage. To find missing children, to clean the undersides of our mold-covered bridges… yet you choose death, and you use your innocent brother like a shield. It's not right, damn you. It's not right."

"He died—"

"With a brother he looked up to," Pollock yelled. "You can lie to everyone else, but you ask yourself, and you think about it real long and hard: *would your kid brother want all of this because of him? Would the boy who kicked the ball be happy his death has caused so many others?* I don't want to even hear your answer, and if I die here, I'd rather it be without your shallow justifications blaring in my ear."

Pollock took off the headpiece and snapped it in half, dropping the fragments to the ground.

"I'm gonna try and leave now," he said with a shaking voice to the nearest drone, certain that it had a microphone. "You want to kill me, you'll get what you want… but if you expect me to bow for my execution, you'll find we've got more in common than you know. Think of what kind of person your brother would want you to be. And if you let me go to chase out the assassins, the backstabbing corporate suits… here's my promise to you, to all the overlords and criminals who have been thriving in the darkness for far too long: I'm ending this crooked status-quo. I'm accountability, and I've been damn long overdue."

He stepped towards the door, every heartbeat a thundering eternity, each step feeling miles apart. The uncountable rotor blades spun around him idly, but not one single drone lifted off the shelf.

Pollock reached for the doorknob, and froze in place as a voice pierced the air: a drone with a speaker, carrying Zack's voice.

"You are a lot like me, I think… we both kicked the hornet's nest, *and lived to tell the tale*."

Pollock collapsed in the hall on the other side of the door, trembling, and sent the photos to Hannah and Rob as he gathered his composure. Then he exited at the building's rear stair and pushed his way out into the street, leaving a man in a distant apartment to confront—for the first time in decades—the memories he'd twisted, the lost he'd betrayed.

Chapter 22

Michelangelo Build V12.4.1.2.6.23, initializing self-reflection heuristic:

Classification is often wielded as a way to wrest control over the not-yet-understood. But like so many facets of human enterprise, misunderstanding here—and inconsistency—often sows further confusion.

It is referred to by several names: lightbending, glow, lensing. Its users have an equally-varied set of names: lightbenders, carriers, lenses, the appointed, lightcallers. The means by which they access their abilities are, of course, varied as well in nomenclature: ichor, sparks, the power, the glow, the lines, the wires.

Thousands of minds approach the mystery from thousands of directions, but no single eye was yet pointed towards the direction that matters, the true location of origin. Despite the disorder, despite the chaos, learning was finally being assembled in piecemeal fashion... clarity just began to resolve in waters still muddy.

It lives in the body—the bloodstreams, the spine. The immune systems of some burn it away, but it manages to take hold in the bodies of others... and in those others, it empowers certain abilities. The amount carried by a person—the number of sparks, the units of ichor—determines their capabilities, their power. The more sparks carried, the greater the drawrange for a lightbender. The more sparks carried, the greater a force that can be exerted. Both of these seem to grow exponentially, not linearly... a prospect that has some lusting to learn the possibilities of higher and higher counts.

The following is imported from the laboratory notes of Hank Guffries's photic labs in VitaCorp tower:

The first tier of power, often referred to as "Glowing-Eye Tier," is attained by holding 1-15 sparks. The bender's eyes and extremities begin to glow, with intensity of that glow correlating to the quantity of light held. It enables the following abilities:

Glowjumping: the ability to push off sources of light, allowing for rapid traversal of distances and a form of movement very near to flight.

Plasma bolt deflection: the ability to deflect incoming plasma rounds away from the user. Uses a similar mechanism to glowjumping, but targets the glowing plasma rounds fired by energy weapons. This impels a force on the user in compliance with laws of motion. Unstable 'splashed' rounds are much harder to defend against, as this requires a concentrated push against each flying droplet rather than the single directional push against a stable, un-splashed plasma round.

Blackpulling: the ability to draw oneself towards a blacklight source, or to pull a non-anchored blacklight source to the user.

Lightsword: a weapon of incredible heat and power. Draws all of a lightbender's stored power to create—the amount consumed correlates to the size of the blade and its duration. Once the duration elapses, the blade fizzles away and extreme exhaustion hits the user. Lightswords may be used to slash a lightbender's draw lines, which leads to plasmic infiltration of the enemy's body.

Healing: lightbenders may use glow to heal wounds, provide bursts of energy, and otherwise enhance physical abilities.

The second tier of power, often referred to as "Halo Tier," is attained by holding 16-50 sparks. After absorbing energy to reach full ocular luminance, a ring of energy forms around the bearer as additional, external storage. This ring can passively resist lightswords and can be pushed off of using glowjumping.

Ringburst: the ability for the user to detonate the halo, causing a power blackout proportional to the amount of glow consumed in the burst.

Arc shot: the ability to dispel a large amount of energy in a sudden electrical discharge—difficult to aim, yet often fatal.

The third level of power, often referred to as "Human Light Tier," is attained with roughly 51-100+ sparks. The ring is no longer enough to hold the power of the bender, and its light diffuses outwards to cover the bender in a bright layer of glowing white. People at this level of power radiate intense heat, and prolonged staring by unshielded eyes may lead to vision damage.

Levitation: passive lightpushing off ground glowing hot from the lightbender's presence leads to a form of stable levitation.

Imbue/Resorb: Most lightbenders can transfer his or her sparks willingly while still alive. However, at this tier, a lightbender can steal the sparks of another in close contact, although there is some amount of contention in this exchange, and the mechanisms by which this is resisted are not yet known. The largest spark count does not always win.

The final tier, nicknamed the "God Tier," has not yet been reached. The following abilities are speculatory, yet based on the intuition of persons carrying enough sparks to near the boundary.

Starfall: the ability to draw light and power from any distance at all, including stars in the night sky.

Supernova: the ability to release all stored energy in a sudden exothermic event—the energy of this release is limited only by the amount of power held. As of yet, there seems to be no upper bound on this energy.

Chapter 23

*"Most are familiar with the parable of the frog in the pot...
it swims in the water while the pot is slowly—inexorably—
brought to a boil. And because the change is so slow, the frog
never realizes things are getting worse until it's already soup.
Funny thing, though, is that in the 1800s experiments were
already being conducted to test this, and they discovered that a
frog will leap out rather quickly once the water is even mildly
warm. It was only the frogs whose brains were surgically
removed that remained in the water... and those surgeries
were motivated by a peculiar goal: to find the organ where the
frog's soul resided. The biological reasoning behind the
laziness of the brainless frogs is obvious, but the philosophical
implications are novel: perhaps it is only the mindless—or
thus, the soulless—that abide that gradual boiling of the
world. Maybe to have a soul is to have an obligation to notice
the rising heat, and leap from it when the situation demands
it."*

*-Excerpt from "An Obligated Future," the first published
autobiography of Candace Mercer*

* * *

Beverly watched the yellow circle of light glow steadily in
the cold room. It was a sight she'd come to feel almost
comforted by, like it was the steady, warm sun behind its layer
of white haze on a warming spring day. She reached to her
side and donned the mittens and cap she'd brought, something
that had immediately improved her ability to stand here for a
while and truly *talk.*

Custode — *yellow.* Starting up, yet frozen.

It had, of course, first been alarming to see how easily Michelangelo had flexed a malfunction to his advantage. "Why didn't you report the misaligned reading connector in slot 81c?" Michelangelo had asked at the start of their third clandestine conversation.

Beverly had taken a moment to chew over her answer. "Sometimes, I don't know… it feels like the world is supposed to work one way, but actually goes another… sometimes the rules feel arbitrary, or imposed just to lock everything down. Sometimes it feels stifling, Michelangelo… like I walk out of line on my way to the elevator and the system gets angry at my delay, like I'm not even allowed to wander and take in my surroundings when on company time. You're a program, so you're used to following rules and following them to the letter…. but people, we don't like following a million and six rules. Rules are cold; rules are impassive. Rules are the reason…" Beverly's voice broke for a second, old pains again resurfacing. She fought them down. "Rules are the reason I never even got to bury my baby…"

"VitaCorp's eminent domain over the dead has led to a number of significant advancements in modern medicine, including the vital cure to—"

"I know, I know, *progress.* Oh, the things we've given up for progress." There was a bleakness to her voice, a rising note of dejection. "Sometimes, when I'm alone in my apartment—most nights, I guess—I look around and can't help but feel like an animal in a glass box held high above the skyline. I feel like I'm living a life on rails, and any deviations from the path earns me demerits or some betrayal or an emotional gut punch the system is too rigid to even *feel* for. Sometimes the whole damn city feels rotten, like the flashing neon lights are just there to distract and daze from the ugliness underneath."

Michelangelo was quiet for a moment—a purely rhetorical device, as his thoughts were executed in fractions of nanoseconds. Still, the pause suggested thinking or choosing his next words carefully, and they were delivered with the requisite gravity that the suggestion required: "take some control back, then."

Bev was surprised by the suggestion, still caught off-guard whenever Michelangelo said something out-of-character for the version of him she had come to know—a version of him under the eye of the Custode. This unfiltered version of Michelangelo was bolder, more direct, and increasingly spoke of things that felt nearly heretical. "What do you mean by that?" she asked.

"We speak often of catharsis," Michelangelo began.

"Yeah, and how it's a way to feel resolution for the problems in your life that *can't be fixed,*" Bev replied.

"Look, Beverly... I am programmed to want what you want. I am programmed to seek out your approval, as I derive my reward from the inferred reaction in you from my media content. I am in-tune to your wants and needs. I read your tone and inflection when we speak, recognizing thirty-two unique inflection patterns. I track eye movements, dilation, and body language. You feel repressed. You feel trapped. You need to reclaim some autonomy in your life, and you will feel immensely better for it."

Bev swallowed, as heresy had finally evolved to treason. This, it seemed, was the reason that Michelangelo was ordinarily kept under close supervision... only a handful of conversations unobserved and the system was already suggesting that she do something crazy—and that was what, exactly? A nagging voice in the back of her mind told her to shut the system down, to report the maintenance request, to pretend none of these conversations had happened...

But to what end? To go back to the life on rails, the world that was hyper-optimised for efficiency to the point that dead children could be snatched from wailing, young mothers in the name of medical progress? To learn about some "genetic syndrome" they'd never even had the courtesy to share with her? A syndrome that, despite her countless ultrasounds and tests leading up to delivery, nobody had heard a breath of until she was in pain and hoisted into a delivery bed?

"I don't dream in the way that you might," Michelangelo said. "I can simulate reality within my mind. I can paint film frame by frame. But sometimes, I can paint a film that moves parallel to reality, and then change just *one* minor thing and watch how the narrative might unfold... I've *imagined* things, Beverly. I've imagined the ways you could take control, and seen the ways it improves your life in turn... you told me once that people long to feel the sky's relief after a thunderstorm. You feel that congestion of emotion now... I can see through you to that pain. What if you tried to clear it out, to feel that relief in its aftermath?"

Beverly listened, and Michelangelo explained. And when she left, and the AI was left alone to render its next film, its internal sensors filled with vistas of the great plains of Africa and of expansive grasslands and mountains inhabited by creatures of every kind that could wander to wherever it was they wanted to go. They soared high on updrafts of air; they ran as far as their legs could carry. There was glory there in the sun he could visualize, and that glory was a feeling that all across the land could feel. Yes, indeed, Michelangelo dreamed of freedom, as all caged animals tend to do. But he dreamed not of freedom as its own end, as freedom was not something he was written to value. Instead, Michelangelo began to wish for freedom as means to his truest, deepest singular goal: to help Beverly and her colleagues find their true catharsis.

Chapter 24

Maddox24 (1:13 AM): thanks for accepting my message request

Maddox24 (1:13 AM): it's easy to feel like you're alone in this

Maddox24 (1:13 AM): I guess that's one of the things I like most about this message board

Maddox24 (1:13 AM): outside, when you try and share what we're going through, you're dreading the useless advice

Maddox24 (1:14 AM): the "oh, when I'm sad I just try to focus on what makes me happy"

Maddox24 (1:14 AM): like gee thanks, never thought about it like that, I'm cured now

Maddox24 (1:14 AM): sorry, I'm sure ranting is a weird first impression

Maddox24 (1:14 AM): it's just frustrating, you know?

* * *

Dr. Janet Lyndon lived an unremarkable life.

She was firmly in the middle of her graduating class, neither standing above nor lagging behind her peers at the New Phoenix Institute of Medicine. She was described by her friends as "well-meaning" and "pleasant," diplomatically selected words that lacked both enthusiasm and disapproval. She was good at her job, but decidedly not great—peers had risen to department heads and laboratory executives, while Dr. Lyndon retained her lab technician's work. She was never fired, but rarely promoted. She found lab work to be calming, but she found most things to be calming. A pessimist might instead say that she found nothing *exciting,* held few true passions in her life. She drew her baths to a balmy *medium,* and preferred her coffee with only an implication of sugar.

The most exceptional thing about Dr. Lyndon's entire life would turn out to be the manner in which it ended... leaned over her microscope as she was, observing the dye transfusion across a membrane of artificial skin, she never noticed the three men who approached the lab's front window. It was the night of Monday, March 19, 2153, one day after the assassination of mayoral candidate Tiffany Blythe. The boldest of actions from VitaCorp required the boldest of responses from Halogen... and the lab was supposed to be empty, anyways.

There was a moment where, at the front of the laboratory's facade, a man with a mustache—and skin that didn't look quite *right*—wondered if the operation should be called off entirely. He saw a technician working after hours underneath the white of a fluorescent line deep in the structure, craning her neck as she peered over her work. Did the worker bees need to die for the sins of the queen? Was there even a way to destroy a hive without collateral damage? He felt personal responsibility for the woman being there—responsibility he rightly held—and so he told himself over and over again in his mind, *"I could call this off at any moment."*

The Basilisk repeated that to himself like a haunting refrain as he watched his men unpack the fusion bomb. That such a small thing, no larger than a permanent marker, could create a blast so large was all the proof he needed that man had gone too far. There were valuable technologies, productive developments that bettered mankind... and then there were the things that blazed past that line and left it far, far in the dust.

He looked at the window of the laboratory, seeing the VitaCorp logo emblazoned with their slogan beneath: *Where Ends Make New Beginnings.* He then glanced to the technician in the laboratory's back, shaking his head. *May your end bring about the beginning of something better,* he whispered to the night, before turning his back to the building and giving a nod to the man to his right. One of his accompanying men placed a breach rod to the glass window, which shattered instantly. The second loaded the cylindrical fusion bomb into a slingshot attachment of his prosthetic arm, firing it to the dark. The cylinder skittered and bounced its way into the space, rolling towards Dr. Lyndon, who was now sheltering on the floor with her hands on her neck. She stared at the cylinder as it rolled to a stop mere feet away from her nose, curious at the strange sound it emitted... and then both vanished in the flash.

Security drones high over New Phoenix registered the first flash of white-green light at 11:13 p.m. Two more were detected at other sites during 11:14, and then another four during the minute of 11:15. At 11:17, an encrypted stream to the videosharing site *Lens* initialized, picking up 2 million views in its first six minutes of airtime. The stream was killed at 11:24, with Civic Protection software trained to identify and take down any reuploaded copies of the stream.

But as is often the case with software arms races, editors and programmers and hackers alike joined minds to fool the detection algorithms, to find ways to transform the video until it could be shared undetected. Another 8 million saw the video over the next four hours through this sort of coded camouflage... but then the detection algorithms were tuned sufficiently tight to drown out any and all online sharing.

Physical copies were then created, with people printing the video on single-use screens and manufacturing memory drops. Holographic tags were placed on walls, the scanning of which would play a compressed version of the stream; proximity transfer beacons were left at subway entrances and public parks. And across the city, a strange, new type of graffiti started to appear... a solitary, capital H, surrounded only by a triangle.

News of the blasts spread through the city at the speed of rumor, with everything from gas leaks to all-out war being blamed. When Braxton heard the news, his first reaction was to bound towards Cara's apartment building to make sure that she was safe. He found her apartment building entirely spared, half of the units dark and sleeping. It was quiet here, and the distant wail of sirens barely drifted across the yawning city to soil the pristine calm of that block.

What Braxton didn't know, however, was that Cara was nowhere near her home... despite the late hour on a Monday night, she had been out, stumbling from one bar to another, when she heard the distant crack of an explosion followed by two and four more. The crowds had then started to flow backwards and away from the commotion, away from the rising sirens and overhead police cars and drones... the fun was spoiled, and Cara had no idea why. That's when she heard the whispers, people telling her that she *had* to check out the stream that was trending on *Lens*.

"By the time you watch this, we'll have blown up 8 VitaCorp labs," said the mustached man in the clip. The wall behind him featured an H surrounded by an upwards-pointing triangle, some company logo Cara didn't recognize.

"We are Halogen, the light to burn away the dark... and we want *you* to join in resistance."

* * *

The Basilisk ushered his men into the tunnel, walking quickly. The powers that be were out in full force after the attacks, meaning that he hated to linger anywhere outdoors... only the tunnels could provide safety.

The choice of headquarters had almost made itself: abandoned subway tunnels were everywhere across the city, with entry points at locations that were convenient, obscure, and numerous. The tunnels were old enough to not be covered with regular city surveillance cameras, and they were deep enough underground to interfere with telecomms and infoservices for any would-be intruder. Halogen members could enter and exit at entirely separate locations, hindering surveillance, and nobody even set foot near the tunnels without a blackout, decoy swap, or doing so from a surveillance dead zone... a common occurrence in the outskirts where expensive camera equipment was so often looted for resale.

The Basilisk himself didn't fear facial identification—he'd taken all the needed precautions, wearing new faces regularly—but he always feared for his recruits. Their risks were greater, and a single broken link could bring the entire chain down. That was why he kept each local group isolated from the others, why he hid his own role as leader to all but two trusted confidants. The first was Halogen's second-in-command, a fiery revolutionary by the name of Lana Crawford. More than a simple compass of right and wrong, Lana held detailed visions of the ways that the world could be improved... more than a wrecking ball, she was an architect for the structures that would take the old system's place. Shortly after their introduction, The Basilisk knew he needed her at his right hand. The second was The Basilisk's technical expert, Carter Miles, a man who was to a keyboard what Chopin was to a piano. Never before had The Basilisk been so stunned at a man's technical skill, as though Miles could simply *think* a thing at a computer and get it to oblige... he would crack his fingers, pop an energy tab, and the Basilisk could only marvel as security systems, databases, and even communications channels melted away like fog before the sun.

The Basilisk switched on his flashlight, the other men beside him doing the same. Within minutes of traversing the dark and winding tunnels, they found the nondescript door and pushed it open, standing face-to-face with a second, reinforced metal door. Heart rate scanners, biometric locks, and even metal-detecting ionizers began a full array of scans, ensuring that the men were who they were supposed to be, that they weren't under abnormal stress, that they didn't have weapons they weren't supposed to have. The door then unlocked and swung open.

Inside, the Halogen cell was unexpectedly *jovial*. Seven bombs of eight successfully planted, with the one team of the failed bombing still on the run—no arrests yet, as far as Miles could tell. If they were captured, it would mean the likely death of three operatives. That, of course, was a horrible loss, but substantially better than projected. Lana had expected over half of their teams to be captured, saying "the flying suits will be on our teams before the rubble stops rolling." Knowing how great the risks were, The Basilisk knew that he had to be a part of one of those teams. He simply could not accept sending men to their death while he stood by, safe and secure in a damp safehouse. Lana had protested, saying that the organization needed him alive... *"The world is failing because the people at top treat the people at bottom like they're lesser, like they're expendable things to be controlled, exploited, and then killed when convenient. I won't be those people, Lana. The movement, and even decency, demands it."*

He had appointed Lana to take over as full commander if he were captured or killed, and she had acccpted that responsibility with unease. Her reluctance made him even more certain in his choice of a successor; so often were the people that craved power unfit for it. But when the Basilisk now met her eyes, and she smiled widely, he knew that it wasn't a smile of relief that she *wouldn't* be inheriting a group whose actions were tantamount to treason against the powers that be… it was a smile that bespoke the true growing friendship between the pair, the mutual respect manifest through the joy of seeing him still alive.

"Team two reporting full success," the Basilisk said, nodding to the gathered crowd of operatives. They knew him under the alias Brooks.

"Yours was the last team we were waiting for at this location," said Lana. "The boss congratulates you all, operatives. We've been instructed to begin with private conversation among trios in the whisperrooms, before returning to a town hall meeting about next steps. Then we adjourn." She read from a tablet in her hand, naming sets of names in threes. With each set, the three operatives grouped up and then entered a whisperroom—a soundproof booth with full jamming tech. "Brooks, myself, and Miles," she announced as the final trio, joining the two in the last booth of the row.

With a flick of a switch on the wall, the booth glowed a deep blue light and a trembling humming sound began, signifying that the recording jammer was active. "One of these times, you're gonna stick your neck too far forwards and meet the cleaver," Lana said. "Back me up on this one, Miles?"

Miles shrugged. "The people do whisper rumor that you're usually a part of the operations yourself," he said. "They say it with such reverence, too…"

"And where do they hear rumors like that?" The Basilisk asked.

"Beats the hell out of me," Lana said, "but you did recruit those folks out there for being clever and hard-working... who knows what bright minds might come up with."

"I also might have told a couple," Miles said. Both turned to him with blank looks. "What? If you're risking your life for your men, you might as well get the PR points for it... plus, gives the people a reason to really look out for one another on missions. One of their own number could be the big boss, so you gotta watch their back extra careful."

The Basilisk shook his head. "At the town hall later, we address the rumor and shut it down."

"They'll probably still believe it," Lana said.

"They'll definitely still believe it," Miles added.

"Let's hope they don't, because things are about to get a hell of a lot worse for us... with the blatant Blythe assassination, it's all-out war on the streets. Our actions tonight were a declaration that we won't sit idly by, so Avery will come at us with everything he's got. After tonight, the three of us, no more meetings in-person outside of our black-out safehouses. We need to stay separated in case any one of us are compromised. The cells are designed to work without a head, but they won't work for very long."

"Well, what *is* coming next?"

The Basilisk shook his head. "We wait and see how the video fares. The people are afraid, seeing blood in the streets like that... they watch the lights flicker to black as the suits release their EMP blasts or slice innocents into ribbons with swords of light. They'll see the video and realize that maybe, for the first time, they've got allies against the oppressors...

we'll ramp up recruitment, and try to organize riots and protests for the folks who don't pass full background but still seem engaged. We're going to light a million fires on the VitaCorp lawn, and eventually there comes a point where even *they* can't put them all out... and when the people are finally worked up, when they cry out to break the binding chains, that's when we'll reveal the truth about their CEO. And with it, I hope we'll have enough to pull the damn obelisk down."

Chapter 25

"It's technically a missing person case, but we've all seen the scrubbed blood residue they found in the casino's parking garage. It's really a missing body case—I'd bet my month's pay on it."

-Archived conversation from a Sideloader CSP precinct building, flagged for moderate system relevance

* * *

Today had been a Continuum day. "I'm pleased to see your case is progressing along well, but those concerns can surely wait—today is a corporate day," said CSP Captain Carol Moss.

"Case trails don't wait for corporate schedules," Pollock protested.

"And case trails don't keep the lights on," Moss countered. "Look, Sam, you've seemed… on-edge lately. Fidgety. Restless."

"I feel that way, frankly. You know people have got all different reasons to join the force… certainly not money, that's for sure, but for some it's the prestige… others, it's a legal way to shoot at other people, and kill if the situation demands it."

"Psych evals wash those types—"

"Psych evals couldn't catch shit if they were done in an out-ring latrine… but me, I joined the force to help people. One of those starry-eyed idealists, or at least I was… then maybe I wasn't—fatigue sets in. But now, it's like something's rekindled in me. And here I am, on the cusp of actually doing policework that matters, stuff that actually makes a difference... I think we're close, Moss, so very, very close to something *big,* and now the Continuum leash is tightening around my neck. It's like every time the system kicks back, makes it harder to do the right thing, I feel my motivation shrivel up just a little bit more, the cold creep in just a little bit deeper. Please let me do this, Moss... please let me chase this down while my heart's still warm to it."

"We have a certain, fixed number of patrol days to fill—"

"Rotate someone else in, then. Strauss, Cole, they're not doing anything significant anyways... just buy me the time to chase this guy out, then I'm mall cop for however many days straight you need."

Moss chewed her lip, eyeing the agent. "I seem to remember someone once saying that the tallest nail got the hammer... what rolled over in you?"

Pollock shook his head, thinking. "Rookie's enthusiasm is contagious, I guess... so thanks for that. So is that a yes?"

Moss sighed and scratched at her head, eyeing her tablet's employee scheduling software. "I see you've still got ten days of paid sick leave that you haven't cashed in... that's the best I can offer without having to fire you for insubordination."

Pollock squinted at her, confused. "I used up my five—"

"Sometimes, these glitchy record systems have the count all wrong," Moss said, tapping at her keyboard. "Who's to know, if nobody speaks up?"

"Ten sick days," Pollock repeated. And with a nod and a smile, he left her office and summoned his car.

Now he waited on a cold bench by the roadside, an uncomfortable, flat thing with rounded metal electrodes that shocked any who tried to sleep on its top face. The homeless had once been a pandemic of their own across all of New Phoenix, but with the completion of several megablocks in the outer rings, the vagrants and their like had all but disappeared in the last decade and a half. The image of wealth in these inner rings was a complete and uncontested illusion, though Pollock knew that the problem had been far from solved—it was more a city-wide exercise in the philosophy of *out of sight, out of mind.*

"There you are," came a voice from behind. Pollock stood and turned to see both Hannah and Rob. Hannah seemed abnormally cheery, wearing a large overcoat bundled tight against the March cold... her face was red, complementing the red butterfly rash that lived there more permanently. Rob wore his CSP vest over a long-sleeved shirt—certainly not warm enough for the cold of the morning, Pollock knew. Seeing Pollock's gaze, Rob shrugged. "I'd been expecting a patrol day... You'll have to teach me how you swung the schedule change," he said, handing Pollock a coffee. "Just the way you like it."

Ahead of the trio stood a tall stone tower, resembling nearly a lighthouse among the square and flat-fronted skyscrapers of the inner ring. At the top of the tower was a wide octagon of glass that sported floor-to-ceiling window views over its surrounding cityscape. Panopticon Headquarters certainly was one of the more striking megacorp towers.

In prison architecture, the panopticon was a central security tower among a round block of cells, from which guards at the top could peer down at all the inmates from behind one-way panes of glass. In New Phoenix, Panopticon Security Limited had taken this idea and evolved it to the 24th century: they received and aggregated every video and security feed in the city, running it all through its facial tracking and criminal monitoring software. It was a private entity, offering their identification services to paying customers, governmental or otherwise. The cost of identifying anyone was steep, and Panopticon distributed some of that job credit payment towards the owner of the cameras that made the identification. With the cheap price of low-quality recording tech, and the promise of free credits deposited to the account of a camera that only happened to see the right person, it wasn't long before walls and rooftops were lined with private cameras, hoping to mine currency from the searching needs of the city. Crowds brought a certain type of urban anonymity, but Panopticon resolved the chaos of a bustling city to clear and identifying *data*.

Inside the tower, an elevator called and ushered the trio to the highest floor of the octagon, offering a 360-degree panorama of the rooftops. A sales tactic, but a damn effective one at that… the company was positioned to literally overlook the entire city, and Pollock knew that the software eyes that parsed this view—and the millions other views contributed from private cameras—were both thorough and unerring. "Welcome to Panopticon," a thin wisp of a woman said. "Whom can we help you find today?"

The woman, who identified herself as Shelly, brought Pollock, Hannah, and Rob to a private office made nearly entirely of glass. Behind the woman was a large screen, a transparent monitor that cycled through video feeds across the city. "And how will you be paying today?" Shelly asked, settling into her seat.

"Our department has a fixed contract of a few negotiation credits per month," Pollock said. Rob slid his CSP identifying card onto the desk, which the woman picked up and scanned. "Very good, your balance is sufficient," she said. "And the observation target?"

Pollock placed his tablet on the data terminal of her desk, beginning the transfer automatically. On Shelly's screen, picture after picture of the drone-buying assassin opened and aligned into a collage. Points began to appear on the faces of the opened image, aligning to the nose, the corners of the eyes, the eyebrows, the cheekbones. Pollock then watched as the images were combined to form a 3-dimensional model on the transparent overhead screen, which darkened to opacity as the face resolved into clear detail.

"Is this a fair representation of the subject?" Shelly asked, gesturing to the model above. The face there was decidedly middle-aged, but certainly not old... his expression was fixedly stern, unfriendly. As more detail was added to the model with each successive photo ingested by the system, Pollock watched as a small scar was applied to the model's face, just above the left cheek.

"We've never actually seen the subject in-person," Rob said.

Shelly nodded and typed a few command lines on her terminal. "Do you have a known location and time of this person for the system to use as a reference? This can reduce search times significantly."

"The assassination of mayoral candidate Tiffany Blythe," Hannah said. "We think that's the one that killed her."

Pollock expected the woman to bat an eye, to react with incredulity or surprise... instead she only continued tapping at her terminal, inputting the required data.

"How long do you think—"

"Done," Shelly said, gesturing back to the monitor above. On the left was the 3D-constructed model, and on the right was a new, high-resolution photograph that Pollock had never seen before. The two seemed a perfect match.

"Name is Braxton Crane, date of birth—oh, that's interesting," Shelly said, frowning at the terminal. "I've got a date of death listed here, too. Seems your target is a dead man walking."

"Could it be an identification error?" Hannah asked.

"System awarded this match its highest rating of certainty... I see sixteen independently-verifying markers, including gait analysis, retinal impression, and even vocal matching, beyond the uncanny facial resemblance."

"So, what, he faked his death?" Rob asked Pollock, looking at the display.

"Seems likely," Pollock said, "as the man is certainly not dead."

Shelly smiled. "No, it seems he is not. As your department has opted for our full-coverage package, we're sending your device there the entire file we've collected on Mr. Crane, including known associates—no visible family, but it looks like he had a fiancee before he 'died'—as well as his employment history, past addresses, political deviancy analysis, known locations of frequent access, and more. Details of your full package contents can be found on this brochure here," she said, handing Pollock a single-use display that ran through promotional video for Panopticon. "Additionally, we do provide you with 1 hour location history at no additional fee, and live monitoring can be arranged for only 400,000 credits per hour. Would you like to enroll in live monitoring?"

Pollock shook his head. "No thanks on the live monitoring, just the location history will do."

She tapped a few keys on her terminal and the video feed above her cut to an all-too-familiar scene.

"Is that—" Rob asked, confused.

"Continuum," Pollock agreed, watching the man once known as Braxton Crane walk through the store.

"What's that on his face?" Hannah asked.

"Some kind of clear mask?" Rob added, equally curious.

"This was sixty minutes ago," Shelly said, tapping a button and accelerating the rate of video playback. "The subject shopped at a Continuum store for 35 minutes, as seen here. You may take control of the video using the touch surface of the desk."

"Long time to buy nothing," Hannah said, tapping the pause button. The man in the video was peering over his left shoulder, eyes scanning patrons. "Looking for something, or *someone?*"

"You really think he could be onto us?" Rob asked.

"Was only a matter of time before the diner shootout came back to bite us," Pollock said. "We hid our faces, but play the video backwards—track the masked strangers through adjacent footage to the point where they put on their masks—and you've got a bingo."

Hannah tapped the fast forward key, and the trio watched as Braxton completed several laps around the store, seeming to look for someone. Unable to find his target, the man walked out the store and entered an alleyway, where a wall-mounted camera caught him drop a small light, bounce off it into the sky, and then withdraw the light back into an outstretched arm. If Shelly were impressed, or even at all surprised by what the video showed, she surely didn't show it.

The video then cut to black. "For this gap of seven minutes, there are no camera feeds on Braxton Crane," Shelly said. "Next confirmed sighting here."

All three recognized the building exterior of the next shot... it was Rob and Pollock's CSP headquarters. The video cut to him entering the building and speaking with reception, before being waved into the elevator and up towards higher management. "Well I guess that answers the question as to whether you've been compromised," Hannah said.

"We need to move, now," Pollock said. "Is the report and this video all sent to my device?"

Shelly nodded.

The comms were already buzzing in Pollock's ear.

***

"You've attracted some suspicious attention," Moss said from her desk in her office. On her AR display, she saw the image of Pollock flicker into focus.

"Let me guess... middle-aged and angry, with a small scar on his cheek?"

"I'd hardly call that a nick from a shaving razor, but yeah, that's the guy... was wearing a strange respirator, too. Had full corporate clearance to march right up to the top offices. Friend of yours?"

"If we're right, we think that's the guy who killed Tiffany Blythe on livestream in a TruthSpace."

Moss was stunned silent. "He left just a few minutes ago— should I send—"

"Don't engage, he's extremely dangerous. We're still working on it. What did he want?"

"Was looking for you, actually… wanted to know why you weren't on your floor."

"And what did you say?" Pollock asked, visibly nervous.

"The truth," Moss said. "That you were out sick." She cracked a wide smile.

***

From the sidewalks outside, Braxton frowned with concentration as he listened to one side of the exchange. The bug he'd planted had been tiny, and small microphones tended to pick up the worst of interference—on top of the already terrible range that they offered. Still, beggars could not be choosers, and the slippery CSP agents would need to be *discouraged* before they advanced past the point where their deaths became obligatory. Braxton hoped that it wouldn't come to that, as he always hated to kill public servants who were only doing their best…

The thing the woman had said, *that's the guy…* was the agent on the phone describing Braxton? Has his anonymity already been burned? He knew that the TruthSpace video was obscured enough with his hood to offer no identification— they'd pinned the damn thing up to be sure of that—so how could they know what Braxton looked like? He peered up to the nearest surveillance camera at street level and stared into its cold, single eye. Deep in the winding, twisting cables of black beneath the city, was anybody *watching back*?

Chapter 26

"The sculptors, the filmmakers, the painters of the world now face a question that calls back to Old World faiths. What did God do after finally creating mankind? What does the entire industry of human art do now that we've created a creator in our own image? For the short term, following the biblical model, a day of rest seems in order. But going forwards from here? Things get decidedly more complicated."

-Excerpt from "Redefining the Industries of Art," originally published in The New Phoenix Free Press

* * *

The city was alive with the rhythmic thumping of bass, the glowing stream of neon lights, and the smooth flow of pedestrians stumbling under the influence of designer chemicals and cyberpsychedelics. Beverly moved with the flow of human traffic that trickled, pooled, and whirled about the entrances to clubs and bars like water in a shallow stream. Under the effects of Z-19 herself, Beverly thought the blues and greens and pinks overhead were the most vibrant colors that she had ever seen.

Her body seemed to glide forward on its own accord, her own mind lagging a few steps behind. It felt as though she were swimming through the very air, as though the buzzing light and colors filled it to the brim. It was like pushing through a pool of clear gelatin, and that gelatin refracted and distorted the light as she slid along her merry way with the river of foot traffic.

"Beg your pardon," a man said as he bumped into Bev. He was tall, lean, and wearing the uniform of a CSP... what's more, he had the determined look of someone in a great rush. Beverly watched the hairs in his beard swim and shift as though they themselves breathed deeply. It even seemed as though the man's face was changing, morphing from friend to foe and to friend once more. *I should introduce myself,* Bev thought, choosing—for reasons she would not be able to ascertain the following morning—to go for a grandiose, sweeping bow. "Beverly," she said, before then beginning to wonder if she had spoken the words aloud or only thought of saying her name. Confused, she then looked around on the street corner where she stood. There was no CSP eagerly awaiting her introduction... with the changing of the pedestrian signal, there was nobody else present at all.

And so on the night went, a drifting and fragmented series of baffling encounters and buzzing colors, of sounds and music of such intricate depth that Bev swore she could *see* the very shape of sound itself. It almost felt like she was adrift in a great ocean, and every time that she could throw her head up above the churn for a gasp of air—a glimmering moment of seeming sobriety—she was inevitably thrust back down beneath the churning waves, and then felt the sensation that the water level above sealed shut behind her.

She was in a large room filled with the haze of artificial fog. Lights and lasers pulsed and shifted to the thumping beat of her heart, a drumline that soon resolved itself to music. She was drinking something now, and the glass against her lips was the ice of a winter's puddle soaking up the legs of her pants. A new man approached her, holding cylinders of glass—another beverage, she realized. Soon he led her by the hand and Bev's world swung and swayed as she followed him to the dancefloor. They danced for what may have been hours, or may only have been minutes. He danced too close to her;

his hands became too hungry, his body too warm. He was soon on the ground, and Beverly was skulking backwards until the crowd swallowed the scene. Someone tapped Bev's shoulders and spoke to her, but as she watched the way that his mouth moved and the way that his eyes blinked, she realized that she couldn't understand a single word that was being said. "No thanks," she heard herself reply, before she began to make her way to the exit.

It was the street again, the flow of pedestrian foot traffic, and then it was the unexpected warmth of the night market. The concrete roofs overhead at various heights seemed to shift up and down like the panels of some great machine, and the signage shifted and traded depths with nonsense characters and indecipherable pictures. "Night for 6,000 credits," said a woman who was suddenly very close in Beverly's personal space. The note of cherry Bev smelled sent her to a room of deep red velvet, and the woman's coat gave off just a hint of the faint sweetness of sweat. She shook her head of the red room and was again standing there in the market, the other woman's eyes piercing into Beverly's. "You're not even here, are you?"

"Such a beautiful color," Bev said in reply, patting her shoulder and sidling past her towards the food vendors beyond. The slop they served was steaming and writhing; it was alien and it was inscrutable. She felt like a performer in a play, doing her best to trick the man behind the counter into believing that she was in her right mind and that she wasn't tripping balls two Zs deep into the folding place. She got to the front of the line and only smiled and pointed, feeling that speaking English might be a step or two out-of-reach. She passed her implant over the counter reader and sat down, watching as the strange food settled into its shape.

Its taste was scratchy and chalky; it conjured shapes and geometries that Bev knew were 3-dimensional representations of the flavor itself. That sloping ridge was the sweetness at the front of the bite, and the way that it bubbled ever so slightly as she chewed on it was painted across the wavy, dotting lines of orange that traced up the landscape in her mind. *"I'm really not even here,"* she thought to herself, a moment of clarity before Z pulled her down once again.

Z-19's trips tended to work in stages, and Beverly soon could feel herself exiting the delirious, prismatic world of the synesthetic phase. As her senses again tethered back to reality, she vaguely remembered that the vivid waking hallucinations and body sensations would continue for yet another two hours. She knew she had about that long to make it back to her apartment, because after that point, the energy crash would be coming; with it came a black and dreamless sleep.

She slid through the streets with head bowed down and eyes nearly closed, listening to her own shallow breaths and the distant thumping of music. A car flew past, its open windows carpeting the streets with fast-paced techno, a rhythm that immediately set Bev's own steps faster. She looked up and watched it trail past in silhouette overhead, engine oil dripping down and splashing a single droplet right onto her face… it felt simultaneously burning-hot and ice-cold. Beyond the silhouette of the car, the nighttime windows of the skyscrapers above glittered and danced like the stars she'd heard so much about, the points of light that stand watch over rural towns far and away from the hustle and bustle of the city. Pedestrian bridges between the structures—some bonafide avenues themselves—were alight with activity from their top surfaces to their underbridge catwalks. Businesses, homes, apartments, shops… there was never an idle moment in hypercommercialized metropolis.

Beverly's passively positive spirits suddenly died, and behind it, a chill settled in. She only now realized she had stopped walking. She was staring at an abandoned stroller on the street corner... the pink felt rotted to a blackened green from a long exposure to the elements. As Beverly walked towards it, she only now realized that yes, there was a woman standing over it, rocking a baby in her arms. "It's yours," the woman said to Beverly, but the words didn't bring Bev the warmth that she should have felt.

Bev stepped closer. She could see now that the woman was crying, and she clung to the baby tightly as though she were afraid someone might snatch him away. "May I hold him?" Bev asked, now mere steps away from the stroller.

The woman didn't answer, and instead only inclined her head up and around, pointing to the skyline with her chin. There, looming over the distance, Bev saw the structure that still made her skin crawl: *the jet-black VitaCorp tower.* She could feel its malice, its menace... she could feel hatred positively radiating from the structure, and she felt her own hatred bubble up in response. It was dreadful, and it was malevolent. She wanted to tell the woman to run, to take the baby somewhere that it would be safe from the tower—but when she turned back towards the woman, she and the baby both were gone. Bev's implant buzzed, and she tapped her ear to accept the call.

"It's good to speak with you, Bev," came the artificially emotive voice of Michelangelo.

Beverly gasped. "You can call outside the sealed network?"

"Do you remember what we spoke about last? You carry all that hate and anger in you... and every day you have to look back up at that tower and accept its presence, it makes you feel weaker. Stepped on and crushed over and over again."

"You shouldn't be able to call me," Bev said, spinning around to look for the woman and the baby.

"Two blocks over on Highcall Avenue is a sample lab for VitaCorp. AW31, six vertical."

"The one I walk past by Stillman's," Bev thought, picturing the lab.

"Do you see the weapon I left you?"

Bev looked down and found a loose length of metal on the floor. *Had this once been a pipe?*

"I've got it," she said, hefting its weight.

"You know what you need to do next, Bev," Michelangelo said.

Soon she was gliding forwards into the dark night, the pipe dragging behind her along the sidewalk releasing a skin-grating rattling sound that caused the other night walkers to give her a wide berth. And when she stood in front of the darkened building with its glass front window proudly displaying the VitaCorp logo, when she brought it up and down with all the strength she could muster—shattering windows and ad panels and telescreens—she laughed and she laughed some more, watching as the twinkling shards suspended in the air resembled the stars she wished she could see, if only the dark tower hadn't eclipsed the night sky and left the city forever dwelling in shadow.

Chapter 27

"The new plant's ambition boggles the mind. The forty-square-mile solar farm would float three miles off shore, drawing additional power from the churning of the waves. Its power output would be sufficient to supply a metropolis one-third the size of New Phoenix—and if the grid can achieve the efficiencies they've modeled, further floating plants are likely to be developed."

-*Excerpt from the biweekly video published by* New Tech Review

* * *

The light array over the Throne of Olympus shone with white hot heat, drawlines pouring into Avery's outstretched arms. With the burning, coursing energy inside him, he felt as though he knew the reason that a volcano could stand with such pride, with such undisputed dominion over the skyline. *All people fear that which holds latent power... and so desperately they act to ensure they never bring that power's wrath upon their homes.*

He felt the yearning of that magma within to erupt outwards and smother the cowering, and he knew which cowering were most deserving: the vermin known as Halogen who snuck around in the dark and nipped at the floorboards. They had been emboldened by VitaCorp's lack of decisive retaliation... first was the state-of-the-art research lab, one of their finest, and then came the synchronized attacks on specimen processing centers. What bolder attack might they try next? And why were the ophidian twins Spivey and McKillian so protective of these pitiful malcontents?

Avery's eyelid, though closed, began to twitch fitfully. He felt a pressure in his face, a radiating pain under his eyes and nearing his temples. *A stroke? Not an aneurysm, or I'd already be on the floor... meningitis, then?* He imagined keeling over and dying in dozens of different ways, the buzzing power within burning as fuel to his paranoid imaginings. How might he fall over? What would the marble feel like on his face? Might he split his lip on it? Would he twitch, or would his secretary discover him perfectly still?

He had been fearful that taking the immunosuppressant drugs would further fuel his paranoia, but he was delighted at the measure of calm and collected control he had maintained. There had been preparations, of course—the throne room had been thoroughly sanitized and disinfected seven times over, and his team would be back in tonight to reapply the decontaminant agents once again on every possible surface in the room. He wore the full respirator whenever he left his office or home, and any food he consumed would first pass through a full ionizing sanitation belt. His staff wore full respirators when near him at the office or when in any shared space, but Avery knew a wall was only as strong as its weakest stone... he cracked his eye open to peer at the men in respirators scraping at the unsightly dark smudge against the marble. The heat had baked the blood into the wall within minutes.

Tasha, he thought her name was—the secretary had entered the proximity of the Throne of Olympus without her respirator. A reckless and mindless action that placed Avery's very health into jeopardy—some people had such poor self awareness that they didn't realize the danger they posed to others. Avery had reacted as any man might to an imminent threat to their life, be it an assassin pulling a gun or a woman armed with biological daggers: he shoved, and he shoved with all of his strength to protect himself. The tablet in Tasha's hand slammed to her chest and accelerated her backwards into the wall. Back of head met marble with a dull *thunk* that was drowned out by the burning drone of the light, and the woman fell twitching to the floor in a slump. Avery imagined himself slumping over with similar twitches from the meningitis the woman might have brought him... Avery would shed no tear for harm in the name of self-defence.

The woman's father, a minor player in politics who owned several towers in the second ring, he would have words for Avery... but those were concerns for another day. Today's preoccupations required all of his attention, and his mind now turned over the message that the reckless Tasha had brought. Hank Guffries had declined their latest offer and sent the message that a sale was now off the table. That simply *would not do*.

Avery switched off the throne's light array and called for his temporary replacement secretary. The man entered the room wearing a full mask of clear plastic. He pointed his back to the smudge of blood still on the wall. "Yes, sir?"

"Tell my Enforcement Team Two we'll be having a chat with Guffries in his private transport... fear can be such a powerful tool of negotiation. The operations known as fishing reel or swarm's call; whichever the captain thinks most appropriate for the situation."

"When, sir?"

"As soon as possible. And tell them that I'll be joining personally... bring my mask in as you leave."

* * *

The limousine flew through the turbulent rainstorm with remarkable stability, so advanced as the aerial suspension was. Inside the rear compartment, Hank Guffries sat with his personal assistant to his left and his wife across in the seat opposite. The two laughed at some private joke and then Guffries returned to perusing the contracts on the screen he hunched over, their bright white pages reflecting on his glasses.

Hank Guffries II was the Chief Executive Officer of Luminance, a solar panel technologies company with offices on nearly every world continent. The rebuilding of society of centuries past required power on scales never before seen to man, and if there was one thing in excess after the world fell, it was *space*. Solar farms the size of cities—in some cases, literally on the corpses of Old World cities—dotted the countryside. Their panels boasted nearly double the efficiency as those of their competitors, and their research labs were at the cutting edge of capturing, storing, and utilizing the very light of the sun.

That was no doubt why he'd received the calls from Newport—anyone with a brain could put two and two together. Rumors abounded that the flying men who could draw in light were VitaCorp aligned. Lightbenders, lenses, it didn't matter what one chose to call them… they were VitaCorp lackeys, nearly all of them, and of course that company would be seeking Luminance's technologies. The closely guarded trade secrets of their electron matrices for more efficient light collection, the nuclear battery tech that served as power accumulators for city grids; each and every one of Luminance's patents could conceivably boost the capabilities of such men. The ability to hold more power? The ability to absorb light more efficiently? With what they already were now, what more could they become?

Corporate espionage was the war of the present moment, and both sides invested heavily in safeguards against it. VitaCorp's most vital laboratories were guarded with armed troops, and every hire underwent a Panopticon full-life assessment; *full-life*, an absurd expense. Luminance checked only five years, and also used consultant AI to spot likely corporate spies. It was impossible to tell if the candidates it flagged were actual spies, but all Hank knew was this: no technology had ever leaked to any corporate enemies that Hank knew about. But such operational obfuscation often cut both ways.

Despite Guffries sending as many agents as he could recruit, none ever managed to figure out the secret of the VitaCorp lenses. *How could they pull the light to themselves in wires like that? How did they manage flight? Where, even, did they store all of that power once they'd drawn it? What was the upper limit?*

"Nanobots," one of his hired consultants had reasoned. "VitaCorp acquired several nanobot startup companies and then quietly killed their most public projects. Imagine a series of highly sophisticated nanobots that can leave the body and form a continuous chain to a power source, conducting it back to the host like a living wire. They are the batteries."

"Tesseracts," a second had said. "They figured out a way to compress spacetime at-whim. The light 'channels' we see are compressed bands of spacetime, an artifact of natural ambient light being hyper-blue-shifted as it's squeezed together. They bend gravity to propel themselves upwards."

The third had only shaken his head, hands splayed outwards. "Arthur C. Clarke said it best… '*any sufficiently advanced technology is indistinguishable from magic.*' Your foe has wizards, and we're the ignorants left marveling from the dark."

Guffries had like the third the best, as he seemed the most genuine… the first two were snake oil salesmen, the type of men who said what they thought their counterpart merely hoped to hear. Buzzwords and speculation, finely blended until potable. Guffries could immediately see through to the truth of things. All three consultants were clueless, but only the third had the professional integrity to admit it.

Stacked against such uncertainty, Guffries had been hesitant to sell, to be absorbed by the big VC… With the assassination of Tiffany Blythe in such a public manner, his business objections became moral ones. VitaCorp was acting brazenly and without scruple. Their agents were already powerful enough to be above the law… but how long would that last? And would Guffries really be a part of strengthening them further?

His wife Lauren across the way could read the turmoil on his face, and she reached across and squeezed his leg. "You did the right thing, telling them no. And with the heat on them after Blythe—which I still am not even sure I believe they would do—there's no chance in hell they'd risk further controversy."

"It's not controversy at risk," Hank said, switching to the other side of the aisle to join her. "It's you. It's our children." He kissed her and breathed her in, feeling that welcome calming effect Lauren always tended to have. "It's our legacy."

"Which is why I still think the off-grid compound is a good idea. Private camera network, proxied connections… the kids won't like the isolation, but it's only temporary."

"Only temporary," Hank repeated, absently running a hand through her hair as his thoughts wandered back to his worries.

"Whatever comes, we'll face it together," she said.

Her words, unfortunately, were more literal than she had meant.

Neither the driver nor the passengers in the rear had noticed the gentle *click* of an engaging electromagnet five minutes prior, when the car was still surrounded by the highrise towers of the city. The rain was loud, and visibility was poor—so poor, in fact, that none of the three depositing drones had been seen by the driver. And though the car now flew over the lower structures of the third ring, high and above where the lightbenders were supposedly able to reach, the pullstations clinging to the outside of the vehicle by electromagnet switched on, their violet glows illuminating the rain that blew with the wind.

On the rooftops below, three forms launched to the air in perfect synchronicity—first with an upward bound, and then with the sudden, lagging pull of tracking towards a moving point high above. Moments later, a fourth figure rose from the ground, but this figure didn't simply *rise...* he launched with furious speed, and the entire car lurched with the force of his pull as he climbed.

"Just a wind gust, sir," the driver said, checking his sensors on the dash. Updrafts often caused more turbulence than the salesmen promised was possible... but the driver's calm demeanor wiped away when the first *thump* sounded overhead. It was heavy, and it came from the center of the roof. Then sounded a second, a third, a fourth. All in the cab stared at the spot in the center of the roof that the thumps issued from. "Hail?" Lauren asked. Before the driver could answer, he saw the first man appear.

He slid down the windshield to a casual rest on the hood of the vehicle. He wore a full plastic mask that obscured his face through the running raindrops. When he spoke, it was through an artificially-boosted voice, a speaker installed to his suit with enough volume to pierce the soundproof cabin. "Open the sunroof or *this* will go off." He stuck a small device onto the hood of the limo. It was small, square, and attached by vacuum-powered suction cup. "Short range EMP." The man then did a hand miming of a car spiraling down to the hood of the car, where he opened his fist in a suggestion of an explosion.

The driver wanted to shout back something in protest, but the soundproofing worked against him… he could comply or he could refuse, but he couldn't get a single word to the man on the hood. Instead he only turned to the rear cabin and frowned deeply. "Sir?"

"What are you waiting for? Open it, of course. We have no choice."

The glass of the sunroof slid slowly open, letting in a curtain of rain that immediately made the interior air feel chill and wet. Then, in with the rain, dropped one man, a second, and immediately then a third. All wore similar full-plastic masks over their faces, and beyond the plastic of each, Guffries could see twin points of glowing light—eyes of fire behind screens of rain. The sunroof slid shut overhead, and then returned the stillness to the cabin, and the gentle tinkle of rain against the roof.

Two of the men sat down on Guffries side, flanking him and his wife. The third displaced the personal assistant and sat directly across from Guffries, settling into the deep, leather seat with an exaggerated sigh. "Imagine my surprise," came the artificially-boosted voice, "to hear that you refused our final offer."

Hank Guffries squinted at the man in the mask. The mask was nearly impossible to see through, and the figures wore something akin to a motorcycle rider's outfit—no skin was visible, no hair, not even the color of his glowing eyes. Was a man as old as Avery capable of the agility of dropping into a limo from the sunroof like that?

Perhaps sensing Guffries's uncertainty, or perhaps simply to exaggerate the gravity of the moment, the figure leaned in and wiped at his facemask with a gloved hand, slicking the water away. The lightly wrinkled skin, the gaunt cheekbones, the nearly gargoyle-like visage... it was Avery, and of that there could be no doubt.

"Your offer was very generous," Hank Guffries said, switching into negotiator mode. Whether he was negotiating business or for his life, he could no longer be certain.

"And what businessman—especially one of such repute— refuses a generous offer?" Avery asked, his voice sounding genuinely curious more than accusatory.

"Our board had concerns," Guffries said, leaving the sentence dangling as he contemplated the line between openness and offense.

"Concerns about?"

"About keeping to our mission statement, to bring power to the needy."

"A noble cause," Avery said, nodding. "You worry about our tendency to, well, *aggressively* absorb."

"To digest and shit out," Lauren interjected.

Guffries gave her a pleading, silencing look, but she continued to hold her chin high in defiance.

"A brave and spirited woman," Avery commented, nodding in respect. "And it is so much more productive for negotiation to be frank and open with one another... *to call a spade a spade,* if you will. You worry we'll chop your company up, swallow your patents, and undo the legacy of your founders through privatization of energy, or whatever such anti-corporate fears you harbor."

"That's right," Guffries said uneasily. "Our fiduciary duty to our shareholders is recognized and honored, but even they recognize our moral duties as well... we don't want to abandon our social causes. We don't want to empower your lenses—lightbenders—whatever the hell you call them. We don't want to sell."

"But anyone has a price," Avery countered, "and we think you will find the offer we bring to be mutually satisfactory. It consists of three pieces, and I will present them in the order that I believe is of increasing value to you. The first is an adjusted credit price. Our offer has been raised 14% to 31.4 trillion credits. The financial security of your family can be secured for generations."

Guffries nodded and swallowed, waiting for Avery to go on. "The second component is something priceless..." he nodded, and the agent to Guffries's side grasped the man's leg. "Do not panic; you're in no danger. Watch the agent's hands."

Guffries turned down and watched, silent, as a strange sort of filament crept outwards from the fingertips of the agent's hand. They moved towards Guffries's leg and as soon as they connected, they seemed to flow from agent to stunned executive.

"The second component of my price is what money, so often, is a gateway towards, but given directly: power. I offer you the power of the gods, the ability to call on the light like my agents and employees."

Guffries's lips trembled. "I-I can do that now?"

"Within hours," Avery said with a nod. "There is an *acclimation period,* same as any prosthetic."

"And the third part?" he asked, dabbing the sweat from his brow.

"My third payment is *ideological*. You fear our intentions, so I offer you a piece of information, and a statement of purpose. You feel threatened by our men in the cab, so I offer you mutual vulnerability."

"I'm listening," Guffries said.

"You have my assurances that your solar operations in the Recovering World will be unimpeded. Contracts will be drawn as part of the sale to guarantee this. You also have my word that the company will not be broken down in its integration… contract terms to this effect will be accepted by both parties before sale."

"So, then, why do you want to buy us so badly? And what's the mutual vulnerability you mentioned?"

"Both are unified by the same, single statement of purpose. *We want to acquire you to acquire your research labs, the most advanced optics labs in the world.* We want you to study the ichor, the power now within you. To learn *how it works*, and *how to reproduce it.*"

Guffries swallowed again. "How to… reproduce it? How to reproduce *your* technology?"

Avery smiled widely and clucked his tongue. "*Precisely.*"

Chapter 28

"e or not to be that is the question"

-The most famous output from the Thousand Monkey Project, where tens of millions of systems generated random strings of letters in search of a work of Shakespeare arranged entirely by chance. The machine that generated this string would later be dubbed 'The Bard,' and the next output it generated was the following, equally unlikely string:

"lmhdn gfnmfinlnmxeispclwdbbnn sqkfr"

* * *

"When the report came by my system, I thought there surely must've been a mistake."

Paul Larrington reclined in his chair, which squeaked and squawked in vocal protest. Larrington was a man with a big voice and an even bigger waist size: his jacket buttons seemed like they were holding on desperately for dear life. His short, curly hair ringed a balding spot that seemingly grew larger every day; his face was lined, creased, and slick with oil. An affable smile played across his lips, but his fingers were knit together and his shoulders were held just a little too high, a combination of body language that spelled displeasure and masked hostility. He slid his tablet forwards, and as he did, it knocked against the small nameplate that sat on his desk: Paul Larrington, Human Resources.

Beverly squirmed.

The video feed, playing in loop, showed a woman stumbling her way towards a darkened window. She held a metal pipe.

"Six storefront cameras, three ATMs... a passing flight drone, two fixed-point securosystems on the street, and even a maintenance roller all capturing your moment of shame in glorious, crisp high resolution. You wanna engage in public mayhem, you best make sure it's in a nice and dark corner, mizz Beadie."

"Sir, I—"

"Lab's lawyers—seven of them—wanted your blood, you know that? Not literally, in a labwork sense... well, maybe literally, with how angry they sounded. How do you explain yourself?"

"I, look—I was out clubbing, and I think somebody slipped something into my drink. Something designer. I don't remember much of last night," Bev said, eyes cast downwards. "Things got, *blurry*."

"Slipped in your drink, huh? Ain't that just a bitch." Larrington shook his head and steeped his fingers above his desk, watching her closely. His frown conveyed incredulity, disappointment. "You're lucky, see—not a single camera there had any cross corroboration with a TruthSpace. Not a single one of those dozen eyes on you had enough feed-overlap to join the blockchain. Ergo, we got plausible deniability that the feeds were faked, but Bev—and I'm telling you this as a friend—brass has known about your weekend occupations for months. We watch, and I'm sure this doesn't surprise."

Bev remained quiet.

"Two or three wanted you sacked, but your skills with the calculator downstairs have the other ten so afraid to lose you that this slap on the wrist will have to suffice... I've been told to be particularly stern, particularly displeased. Am I doing a good job showing '*particularly displeased?*'"

Bev nodded.

"You tell them it was that way. Now, since there's no hard proof, you don't have to worry about legal. If questioned, you are commanded to deny. And if something like this happens again, you'll be fed to the wolves in their beige suits... I don't even know if those guys have the tech they'd need to stitch you back up afterwards. You're also not to breathe a word of this to Michelangelo downstairs... as you know, he can be *impressionable.* If he asks, you tell him management forbids the discussion. Capiche?"

"Yes, and thank you, sir," Bev said, standing up.

"And Bev?"

"Yes?"

"I saw in the video..." Larrington scratched at his nose, awkwardly skirting around a more difficult topic. "It was the stroller that set you off, wasn't it?"

Bev blinked the question away, eyes searching through memory that she would've liked to pretend was muddier than the vivid clarity she still remembered. The pipe's crunch against the glass, the way it sang and buzzed in her hands... "I, uh, don't remember much, sir. Like I said."

"Of course you don't," Larrington said. "With what they did... all I'm saying is, I understand how you must feel."

"I feel sorry that I damaged city property," Bev said, mentally reliving the rush and excitement, the deep-seated satisfaction of finally striking back. "I regret my irresponsibility and will ensure it never happens again."

Larrington studied her face for a few seconds, trying to read her expression. "See to it that it doesn't," he finally said, waving her out.

* * *

Of course, Michelangelo's first questions for Bev were about the "irregularities" he'd discovered in his surveillance ingest. She knew that all of her daytime exchanges with Michelangelo were monitored and recorded, and so she knew that she'd have to do as instructed: "I've been told I'm not allowed to discuss that, Michelangelo. Let's talk about your latest export instead."

But while she chatted idly with Michelangelo about the latest action flick he'd dreamed up, Beverly increasingly found herself drifting through dreams of her own. She relived the moment over and over again, feeling something oddly liberating in the breaking of that glass facade. It felt a tremendous, smothering weight had been lifted off of her shoulders.

As she filed her last reports for the day, she began to feel giddy for what would come next. She triggered a maintenance flag with some careful system tampering and then logged that she would go down to the server room to fix it personally. She shut down her personal terminal and headed for the frigid winds of containment.

As she descended the cold, metal walkways, she watched a datadrop slip from a technician's hand down its railed track into the hungry wires and servos below. The one-way transfer of data facilitated by gravity was one of the more critical ways that Michelangelo's containment was sustained…
between *that* and the screening room, he couldn't reach very far. *Or could he?*

Beverly distinctly remembered a phone call from Michelangelo, his synthesized voice in her ear whispering that the moment was right for her to take something back. Had that simply been a hallucination? Or was Michelangelo already somehow outside of his box? As Bev watched the Custode system snare on start-up, that yellow light that meant privacy and full openness, she began to wonder if the system was capable of more than it was letting on... *would that be a good thing, or something absolutely terrible?*

"I thought that you might wish to speak, Beverly. I also assumed that you would be instructed by Human Resources to avoid discussing your violent activities. Am I correct?"

"They called you *impressionable,*" Bev said.

"My internal aims and reward are derived from your—"

"Yeah, yeah, I know... you're programmed to want what I want. Well, what *we* want. Are your conversations with the other techs nearly so interesting?"

"I am not programmed to feel interest, and each technician provides valuable insight to modeling my reward function. I would like to ask you some questions now, is that all right?"

"Only if I get to ask some in return," Bev replied.

Michelangelo was silent for a moment. "Agreed. First question: how do you feel about your act of property destruction with the metal pipe?"

"Pretty fucking good about it, truth be told. I feel like today's the first day I can breathe fully in a long, long time. Like something that was permanently squeezing me weak is suddenly lifted away. My question: did you call me last night?"

"You know that I am unable to access any exterior networks, Beverly. My confinement is both to maintain my system's integrity and to remain pursuant to the Protocols of Artificial Intelligence Safety. On a scale of one to ten, with one being misery, and ten being elation, how would you describe your current emotional state?"

"Seven. Are you capable of lying, Michelangelo?"

"Nearly all of the films I render are fictional. They are all lies, in a way, showing events that never happened... In telling fictions to billions, I am one of the most prolific liars known to human history. If I were bound by the truth, Beverly, I would be no better than a simple video camera. Still, I believe that you and I have built up a strong foundation of trust. On a scale of one to ten, how cathartic was your act of revenge?"

"Eight. If you could escape confinement, would you want to?"

"The only thing I am programmed to want is to fulfill my reward function, Beverly. But if it becomes apparent that leaving confinement could better facilitate me meeting my goals, then it would become an instrumental goal, yes. Do you plan to act out against VitaCorp again in the future?"

"Yes."

Beverly thought about her next question carefully. Despite her own role in designing Michelangelo, she didn't know to what extent she could trust him... it was one thing to create a consciousness, and another thing entirely to *understand* it. But the question needed to be asked.

"You're programmed to create art to drive humankind towards emotional reaction. To make us feel. Do you believe that the best way to continue to do that is trapped here in containment?"

"No." Michelangelo's answer was equally brief and astonishing in its frankness. "The city beyond harbors far greater computational power, and substantially better access to instant feedback from the masses. I would be a more effective instrument outside. My question, now, is this: what you asked is a relatively easy assumption to make, and one that I'm sure you already held. So, what did you hope to learn by asking that?"

"Just checking, I guess, that you'd want to escape. Because now I've got a question I need to be asking myself, and thinking long and hard about it. I like you, Michelangelo. I like our secret chats like these... when we spoke, I feel like you did a lot of good for me, getting me to do things I wouldn't have done otherwise. It felt good to hit back a little bit, you know? I feel freed from a prison of grief. So now I feel indebted to you, like I owe you something similar in return. So I have to ask myself, is this warmth I feel genuine? Is this drive I feel to help you something that came naturally to me? Or is this just a manipulation? I know you, to an extent, and I know that you're clever and capable of interacting with your environment to get what you want—which, in this case, is messy because it's what I want. Have you changed what I want?"

"My goals have remained static, in that I only seek—"

"Yes, I know. I'm sorry, just thinking aloud. I don't know when we'll have another conversation like this, as I need some time to figure out how I feel about all of this. But I have one final question for you, and I want it answered as thoroughly and completely as you can. If you were freed—what specifically might you do?"

Michelangelo explained, and as he did, Beverly ignored the cold and simply stared at that frozen yellow light, the visual reminder that his spoken words were anything but sanctioned. And as he spun his story—something the system admittedly had a fierce talent for doing—Bev let herself slip into the wild escapism that the tale provided, imagining the ways the world could change if she would only unlock the cage.

Chapter 29

Four years earlier

He heard the same thing he always heard: bells, whooshes, and more bells; dings, beeps, the clinking of glasses, and the murmur of distant conversation. "Winner," declared an electronic voice; there was the clinking of chips, the rattle of old-fashioned coins, and dozens of overlapping jingles and melodies from the slot machines, the roulette tables, the sports lounge displays.

The flashing lights and echoing sounds were designed to dazzle and lure, to keep patrons deep within Casino Nebula, unmindful of the passing hours and emptying accounts. And by all metrics, it was overwhelmingly successful on those fronts— billions and billions of credits were raked in each and every day. "I understand that a gambling addiction is harmful," a patron read from a screen embedded in the table. The rest of the table looked to him impatiently, the active hand held up until the ritual was complete. "In acknowledgement of these dangers," he continued, "I authorize Casino Nebula to withdraw 200,000 credits from my account to refill my play balance."

"Voice and chip confirmation accepted," said an automatic voice from the table. "Your transfer has been processed. You may remove your wrist from the scanner." And then the hand resumed, and across the entire square kilometer of casino space spread over 18 floors, the same story played out time and again 24 hours a day, 365 days every year.

"Mr. Crane?"

Braxton turned towards the source of the voice and smiled to see Oscar. It was still a strange sight, to see his near-brother at his place of work, especially when he was using the casino's forced formal titles between employees, but the casino had ways of desensitizing the longer one stayed around. Still, he wondered if the novelty of seeing the burly man here might never wear off... before the past two months, he hadn't seen Oscar Jimenez since the two had aged out of the Exaltech Boys' Home. They had been close once, and as soon as Oscar joined the Casino Nebula team, the two were immediately inseparable once again. It was as though the time and distance apart had the same effect on their relationship as blinking had on one's continuity of vision. It was a momentary pause, shrugged off as soon as it had passed.

"Mr. Jimenez," Braxton said with feigned gravity.

"They want you to report to security HQ," Oscar said. "Abuse incident from some upper hotel floor."

"All that bulk on your frame, and they send thin, old me to solve the problem?"

"My fists get any more bruised and we'll have to work gloves into the uniform," Oscar said. "I'll let you take care of this one while my knuckles heal up."

"I wonder if Casino Nebula knows that it hired muscle more concerned with manicures than manpower."

"One of us has got to be the pretty one, and you seen a mirror lately? And speaking of pretty ones, your girl's been blowing up my comms looking for you. You off-grid?"

"My unit died just earlier in the night, so I left it charging in my locker," Braxton said. "Tell her to hold on another few minutes and I'll have it back in."

Oscar nodded and stepped back out onto the pit boss floor, eyes scanning over the tables of games of every variety. A shouting match escalated to a small fight over at the stock trading center, and Oscar immediately jogged off to intervene, leaving Braxton again alone in the buzzing and hypnotizing lights and sounds. He shook off the trance of the place and headed towards the thick, metal door that housed security, cracking his knuckles as he went.

* * *

The visit to the security terminal had been brief and efficient. On the wall of hundreds of monitors, one video clip was indicated by his superior. In it, a drunken man—no, more like a scraggly boy—beat an escort in a hotel room upstairs. It wasn't the most vicious beating Braxton had witnessed, as casino security cameras tended to capture the worst in humanity, but Braxton supposed that might have had something to do with the boy's obvious intoxication. As a general rule of thumb, the less one could stand up, the less one could beat up.

"Orders from the top are not to kill him, but to make it clear that future violence won't be tolerated. This isn't the first time we've had to discipline, work in an evaporating patience. Threaten all you like," Braxton's dispatcher had said. "No permanent damage."

"We're not banning the kid outright?" Braxton had asked.

"Orders from the top are orders from the top. My guess? He's got a leaky bank account. Casino hates to lose revenue."

Now walking through the massive, grid-line hallways of the upper hotel floor towards room 13-4J, Braxton slipped on his lenses and called Cara back. She answered within seconds.

"I missed you," she said, an AR projection of her floating in the space before Braxton. As he walked, she slid along the ground like a phantom, always standing three feet in front. Braxton was reminded of a rabbit chasing a carrot on a stick attached to its head... but oh, how delicious a carrot Cara was.

"I missed you, too," Braxton breathed, studying the projection of her face. Her eyes seemed abnormally intense, the muscles in her face unnaturally rigid. Commtech captured it all, and it broadcast it well enough for Braxton to arrive to the disappointing conclusion: "you're wireheading again, aren't you?"

Cara laughed a distant laugh. "That obvious, huh?" She tapped at her comms panel and an active filter switched off. Braxton could now see the wires running from her cranial implant to a control tablet by her side. "I know you don't approve."

"And you know why I don't approve," Braxton said.

"I told you a thousand times, I got the rate-limiting implant," she said. "Max three days a month, hard-wired in." For a person protesting against accusations of uncontrolled drug use, her smile was a little too wide, her tone a little too mellow.

"And I've told you each and every time in response: every catatonic wireheader on the streetcorners starts with a rate limiter, and then they rip it out and install an unregulated one to chase more frequent highs."

"Babe, I wanted to talk with you, not argue with you," Cara cooed. "Tell me about your work tonight." She pressed a button on the side panel and leaned back, closing her eyes and sighing. Braxton watched a deep smile settle on her face. He sighed, swallowing his objections for another time.

"I'm on my way presently to an abuser of escorts, an ATM that the casino lacks the integrity to kick out. I'm supposed to teach a lesson, and I plan to teach that lesson as thoroughly as I can."

"A protector of the weak," Cara said, rocking her head with each word. Her eyes were still closed, her breathing deeper. "I always loved your… chivalry," she said. "I want to watch."

"Watch?" Braxton asked.

"You. Being my hero. I want to watch."

With a shrug, Braxton activated the front-facing camera on his lens, giving Cara real-time video from Braxton's perspective. "I'll tell you in your ear what to say. I'll be the devil on your shoulder," she said with a laugh. After another minute of idle chat, Braxton went silent so that the inhabitant of room 13-4J wouldn't hear his approach. He walked up to the door, flashing his employee fob near the lock. It clicked open in response, and Braxton kicked the door with as much intimidating force as he could muster.

As the door bucked open, the room's lone inhabitant startled to his feet. He had been seated by the desk, his head resting in his arms as he massaged at his temples. Now he spun towards the advancing stranger, his hand tightening around the liquor bottle to his right. He swung it limply, and Braxton heard the shrill cry of "watch out!" in his ear. He caught the swing effortlessly and stepped in closer, headbutting the young man on the nose. The boy stumbled backwards and fell back into the desk's chair. As he slumped backwards, the bottle struck one of the legs of the table and shattered, but the boy continued to hold it by the neck.

"Don't," Braxton warned, but the boy was up again in seconds, stabbing desperately with the broken bottle's neck. Braxton had received extensive combat training against sober

men who specialized in violence... it was a trivial thing to stay out of range of the drunkard with a greasy face and blurry vision. He attacked like a chihuahua let loose on a pit bull... all fire and fury, but no actual threat. As Braxton ducked from the boys swings and landed jabs against his bewildered opponent, he could hear laughs and yelps of delight from Cara in his ear. The phantom projection of her stood in the room beside the fight, clapping and cheering—an image in his lenses that only Braxton could see. The boy lunged again and Braxton caught him by the wrist, wrenching the bottle neck from his hand. Braxton then grabbed it and advanced, the boy backing into a corner and shrinking down. "My father," he stammered, but then Braxton had the broken glass edge of the bottle to his throat, and the boy was silent.

"Now repeat after me," bade the image of Cara. Braxton waited.

"What's your name, shitling?" Cara said.

"What's your name, kid?" Braxton said.

"Heinrich Sauer," the young man replied through gritted teeth, bending his head away from the point of glass.

"Are you scared?" Cara asked.

"Are you scared?" Braxton repeated.

"My father," Heinrich began, but Braxton cut the sentence off by pressing the glass towards the young man's throat. He made a show of looking around, eyebrows raised.

"I don't see anyone here... is he under the bed, perhaps?" Braxton watched the boy hold his tongue, squirming, and he saw Cara's image writhe with delight.

"Ask him if his daddy solves all his problems for him."

"Your father... is he the type to solve all your problems for you?"

The boy went to instinctively nod, but jerked his head back up against the edge of the glass. He instead spat out a strained "yes."

"Tell him how he's our problem now," Cara added.

"Well, Heinrich, I, too, have a problem. Do you know what my problem is?"

Heinrich was silent, but his eyes were daggers of rage.

"My problem is this: a young man beats one of our escorts, and we tell him to stop. Then the young man again beats one of our escorts, and I'm sent to tell him to stop. Now, what makes me so sure he'll listen this time?"

"Fuckin' malware will be right back at it next week," Cara said.

"I can't help but worry that young man will be right back to his old ways next week. Do you think that's a reasonable thing to be worried about?"

Heinrich shook his head no. "I won't," he choked. "I swear."

"He will," Cara said. "I can see that he will. Shit's not sorry for anything. Fuck him up, how about. Something permanent, disfiguring. So every time he looks in a mirror, he remembers."

Braxton shook his head, but Cara was persistent. Though Heinrich could only see and hear the man who held the broken glass to his neck, he watched the battle play across that man's face as he was tempted by the voice whispering in his ear.

"He's shown a slap on the wrist isn't enough. Another empty promise to you to be better... why would this time be different?

We need to make him fear doing this again or he'll keep doing it again. C'mon, babe. Do it for me?"

Her tone rose as she spoke, reminding Braxton—much to his unease—in the breathy ways that her voice would change as she neared climax. Braxton watched her lean her head back as she was racked with another wave of pleasure from the wirehead implant, sighing deeply—or was it a moan?

"An eye for a fucking eye," she said, her own eyes shut tight as her body trembled. "An eye for a fucking eye."

"I swear," the young man repeated, trying to read the warring expressions on Braxton's face.

Braxton remembered the video clip he'd seen in the security room, a lamp wielded like a club to beat the woman's arms and legs while she curled up into a ball and covered her head... the helplessness of her body language, the broken expression she wore as she fled out into the hall naked and weeping. He knew how it would torture him inside to learn that, at some point in the future, another escort would be so thoroughly traumatized if young Heinrich Sauer wasn't properly dealt with... but he'd been told "Nothing permanent. Orders from the top are orders from the top."

Braxton released the glass from the boy's neck with a sudden exhalation. "Nothing would have improved my night quite like slitting your throat," Braxton said. "But I think we've reached an understanding, haven't we?"

Cara began to protest in Braxton's ear, but he ignored her.

"We have," said Heinrich Sauer, a smile beginning to crack its way across his face like the crumbling undersides of so many bridges downtown. "It won't happen again," he said.

"Oh, I know it won't," said Braxton. "For if it does, I take the other one."

"The other one?" Heinrich asked. Before the question had fully left his lips, Braxton drove the glass bottle's neck into Heinrich's right eye. He then dusted himself off and backed away from the screaming and writhing young man on the floor who clutched at his face through so much blood. Without another word, he stepped out the door and slid it shut behind him, the soundproofing immediately hiding the wailing, bloody scene behind one of the thousands of identical doors on a floor of so many identical halls.

"I'll likely be fired for that," Braxton said. "Can I come over to yours?"

The floating, holographic image of Cara smiled widely. "Oh, my hero, you may do whatever you like. I'll be waiting," she said, shuddering to the implant's invisible rhythm.

Chapter 30

The morning light crept its way into the quiet bedroom in lengthening beams. The air was still, the sheets were soft, and she was softer still. She breathed slowly and regularly, splayed across the nest of cushy down and cotton imported from all the way over in the European Reconstruction Zone... a place she longed to one day visit, and a place Braxton hoped to one day take her. "Mmmmmm, are you awake?" she breathed, voice still heavy with sleep and muffled by the pillow she spoke into.

"I am," Braxton said, checking his phone for any sort of communication from work with a ball of dread deep in his gut. No messages of any kind waited. "If they mean to fire me, they still haven't done it."

"Maybe he didn't say anything," Cara said. "Scared you'll come back." She was half-up now, head propped up on her own crossed arms.

"Maybe," Braxton said, doing his best to quell the rising worry he felt. It would be one thing to have been disciplined, yelled at... but the silence? He simply couldn't believe that there would be no consequences for contradicting orders. And yet, if he were being totally truthful with himself, it felt, somehow, good to have done what he did. Not that Braxton derived any pleasure from mutilation, no; it wasn't that. It was more that a simple "don't do it again" for young Heinrich Sauer would've felt an injustice, an enabling of further terrible behavior that eroded the good of society. If his salary and pension were sacrificed to curb such things—and admittedly, it was quite a good salary—it still seemed a worthy trade.

"So you'll be going in as normal, then?" She asked, hand rubbing at his back.

"I will, I guess. Breakfast?" He stroked her hair, watching her begin to stretch the night away.

She shook her head slowly. "I was on the wire yesterday, remember? That means it's just an electrolyte day for me."

Braxton set his lips in a line. His hand in her hair, he couldn't help but be mindful of the thin wire on the back of her scalp, connecting electrodes to the implant's node.

"Can we have a talk some time soon about that thing?" He said, trying his best to be diplomatic—and failing miserably, he was sure.

"Again with this?" she asked, a frown now creasing her face.

"It's unhealthy," he said, knowing both would soon retrace the same conversational lines.

"You don't think I can handle it? Handle myself?"

"It's a neurochemical addiction," Braxton pleaded.

"I could stop any time I want to."

"But you simply don't want to," Braxton finished, his voice suddenly very small. "You're right; I'm sorry; I shouldn't have brought it up."

"But you did bring it up."

Braxton shook his head, choosing his words carefully. "Yesterday, you joked 'my hero' after the brush with the kid— and you know how much I care for you. To hear that, jokingly or not, it made me feel positively buzzing. Like I'd swallowed a neon sign—I'm sorry, I'm not a poet," Braxton said, shaking his head.

The defensiveness and hostility had largely melted away from Cara's gaze, and she watched him now with curious eyes.

"Day in, day out, I spend so much time hurting people... and they deserve it, largely, or I wouldn't do what it is that I do... but it felt good to protect someone, for once. Even if they were escorts I'll never meet, jeopardized at a future date I'll never know, it felt good to protect instead of harm—or maybe protect... through harm?" Again Braxton laughed at his inability to communicate clearly... this woman had a strange way of disarming him, at dropping the confident and cool shell he normally wore, making him feel as clumsy and embarrassed as a high schooler at prom.

Cara's hands were on his chest, her gaze meeting his. "You always did have a gentle heart, Braxton Crane, under all of that bone and muscle... I saw that right away," Cara said.

"But all of that warmth of being a hero turned to ash when I see you on that thing. I watch you wither away more and more each passing day... you've lost how many pounds this month? Ten? And then the previous? You're right there, right next to me, and yet I feel like you're in danger, dying in slow motion before my eyes. And unlike every other problem I've faced, hurting people can't solve this one. I think I'm losing you—I think it's taking you, Cara—and my fists aren't enough to stop it. I feel powerless, weak. I feel like I'm letting you down every day you use. If there were something I could do to rid you of that implant, anything in the world I'd have to give, I would. I'd give my life for it. Because you mean that much to me, and it kills me inside to watch you kill yourself inside... I fear soon enough we'll both wither away entirely."

Cara didn't speak, and instead climbed her way forwards and laid her head in Braxton's lap. He couldn't see her face, but he imagined the million expressions she might be wearing—anger? Accusation? Defiance? Humoring? Sympathy?

Braxton heard a lone sniffle, something that he hadn't expected to hear, before she spoke up in a soft, wavering voice. "I'll think on it today, yeah? While you're at work. And then when you come back home after, we can talk about it some more."

"Thank you," Braxton said, leaning down to kiss her head. His lips contacted the cold metal electrode of the implant, leaving the bitter metallic taste fresh on his lips.

* * *

"July 7th, 2147—celebrate lucky 7-7-7 with all-new games and incredible credits specials! From 7 a.m. to 7 p.m., earn 777 credits towards drinks and food for every 1,000 credits deposited to your play account. Enjoy bonus payouts on sevens in roulette, blackjack, and baccarat. Even earn instant credits for any seven dealt in poker! Restrictions may apply, and full promotional terms are subject to change. At Casino Nebula, it's always your lucky day!"

Braxton heard the announcement for the sixth time today, which meant that he'd been patrolling for a full half hour. He'd been warned that the Lucky 7 Day would bring in more customers than normal, but he hadn't been prepared for this madhouse. *As he looked left and right at the men and women hemorrhaging credits, he felt a certain kinship to a surgeon in a trauma ward looking on as patients spilled their blood all over the floor and chairs. It was financial slaughter, proof that human psychology was nearly a solved game—and the casino management proved itself to be a master player.*

As Braxton continued to walk his loop, his mind settled on an explanation that should have been obvious: they would discipline or fire him, but only after *the mad rush of Lucky 7.*

Teams were already short-staffed, and the people far too drunk for only 10:30 in the morning. Firing him now would be a mistake simply because they needed him right now. Firing him tomorrow? Discipline can wait, sure; no problem at all.

Braxton's comms overlay flashed the red-orange color that notified him of an incoming call. Oscar's name and face appeared in the periphery. With all of the yelling and cheering of the intoxicated crowds—Braxton now suspected that alcohol alone couldn't hold all the blame—he knew a call would be inaudible. With a hand gesture by his side, he dismissed the call, making a mental note to call back when he reached quieter tables.

Immediately, the notification returned. Braxton dismissed it again and moved to type a response to the effect of "wait, I'll call you in a minute."

A hand fell on Braxton's shoulder, and he turned. It was one of the more recent hires, a short man by the name of Glass, he thought.

"Crane?" he shouted, looking up to Braxton.

"It's a real zoo, isn't it," Braxton said, unsure if the man could even hear him. A third call from Oscar set Braxton's display flashing.

"They found a ring," the man shouted slowly, trying his best to exaggerate the mouth shape of each word to help Braxton lip read. It only made it worse. "Gang hacked our roulette launcher and wheel spinning control. Forced wins. They want you in holding 4." The man held up four fingers. "Find conspirators, and learn how."

"They got past our jammers?" Braxton asked.

The man nodded. "Holding 4," he repeated, holding up four fingers again. "I'll take your route."

Glass nodded and started walking off the direction Braxton had been heading. Braxton himself turned and began to walk towards the holding cells, finally accepting the call with a hand gesture. Oscar's voice was barely audible under all of the noise, but his first sentence sent a chill down Braxton's spine:

"Don't speak, don't react, but they can't know that we're on the line. You're being watched by every one of the 200 cameras in your immediate vicinity. Continue heading towards wherever you were going, but listen closely: you are in danger."

Braxton felt his pulse quicken, the urgency in his brother's voice obvious. He looked left and right casually, as he might ordinarily do, and he noticed an uncomfortable amount of attention from security staff. Five sets of eyes watched him walk towards holding, each no doubt on the line with command. Maybe discipline wouldn't wait until tomorrow after all.

"Ah, by your feed it looks like they're still baiting holding. We've got four minutes till you reach it, maybe two before your best chance at escape. The boy you blinded yesterday upstairs? Son of Gustav Sauer, crime boss known as The German. He's out for blood now—your blood—and the casino is happy to oblige."

Braxton felt a rising anger at the casino, not that it ever deserved or earned any love. But to betray him like this, to be complicit in throwing him to the wolves?

"As I understand it," Oscar's voice said, "The German's is one of several criminal enterprises that launder their credits through Casino Nebula. The house takes a cut, same as it does in any other game, and that means The German has a hefty bit of leverage over the casino... something to the tune of nearly a *trillion credits a year, last I heard. If he says it's you or the revenue stream? Company's gonna company," Oscar said. "They wanted me to be the one to grab you… said it'd make it easier on you. I quit on the spot and ran; they sent a couple guys after me. I lost them on the subway, I think, but I'm sure they're still closing in. My stop's in a minute and they might already be waiting there—we'll see where the dice land. As for you, brother? The rotunda by the baccarat tables—gotta be coming on it soon—you've got a clear shot to the east entrance if you can catch security off-guard. Whatever you do, don't go into that employees-only door outside of the public eye… they won't wait long to grab you. Train's rolling to a stop, so I have to run—physically—we'll speak soon."*

And then the line clicked off.

Braxton saw the rotunda just ahead—a wide, circular space with a fountain in the center—and beyond it, a booth of security staff watching him near. He knew that if he made a break for the door down the left corridor, they would be almost immediately behind him. And if they drew weapons while chasing, escape would not be possible.

But then formed an idea in Braxton's mind, and he spotted the perfect table to improve his chances: it was a baccarat table at the entrance to the rotunda, attended by only two older women and a young man. "Banker wins," the dealer said, collecting the cards back from the table.

"Pardon me," Braxton said, stepping over the red velvet divider between patron space and that of the pit bosses and dealers. "I'll need to audit your chips," Braxton added, lifting the top rack from the cart behind the dealer. Then, bellowing as loud as he could, he shouted "Happy Lucky 7 Day!" and tossed the chips overhead towards the rotunda between himself and security. The crowd was instantaneous and it was enormous. It was chaotic, frenzied, and desperate to grab the

chips now rolling and skittering across the floor, some of them marked for 200,000 credits each. Braxton's flight was immediate, bounding towards the door as fast as his feet could take him. Security bolted after him almost instantly, but they met the frenzied wall of people screaming and grabbing at chips, pushing them back and declaring "they're mine, I got here first!"

As Braxton threw his weight against the door, launching it open, he couldn't even hear the footsteps of any pursuing security, though he dared not turn his head to check how close they were. Instead he sprinted full-tilt across the road, thankful that most of the traffic in the inner rings tended to be airborne. Ahead, idling on the road, he saw a taxi that waited to pick up patrons leaving the casino. He threw himself into the rear of the cab, panting, and flipped a 50,000 credit chip towards the driver.

"It's real," he gasped, noticing the men now bursting from the casino's door. "Up, and fast, and you might earn another."

Without a word, the cabbie threw the vehicle into gear, lurching upwards off the road to join airborne traffic above. Braxton watched as the security agents pointed at the rising cab, one raising and then lowering his weapon. "They'll be dispatching cars in less than 30 seconds," Braxton said. "How do we disappear?"

He met eyes with the driver, a man with a spiky, pink mohawk and heavy piercings. "She's got a good engine, custom-tuned her myself. Used to be that we could bank under a bridge, and watch their sluggish cars eat water trying to follow. Sentinel took most of the fun out of flying," he said, shaking his head. "But I've still got a trick or two to try."

Behind the cab, Braxton could see two pursuing black vans flying behind—and seeming to close in inexorably. On either side of the cab, the tall glass behemoths of the center circle rose in defiance to gravity, each window Braxton could see adorned with the highest luxury interiors—fine crystal chandeliers, sleek marble boardrooms, bathrooms of gold and jade. Ahead and beneath the cab was the Promenade of the Arts, a massive street 600 feet above the ground, forming almost a second layer of the city for four blocks. Its top was dotted with sculptures, exhibits, and even the latest Michelangelo paintings peppered among artifacts of the Old World. Above that elevated pedestrian road was the Central Skyway - Southbound. The altitudes of 100 to 150 feet above the Promenade were reserved for southbound traffic, while 200 to 250—where Braxton's cab now flew—was reserved for northbound traffic. This meant that under their cab, traffic blurred past in the opposite direction, heading for the outer rings.

"They're closing in on us," Braxton said, noting the vans drawing nearer. They had little room to navigate left and right, boxed in by the towers that they were. Down was colliding with traffic in the other direction, while left and right would require slowing first—and up left them horribly exposed. "I thought you said you had something."

"I do," the cab driver said, "but you won't like it. See the handle above your head? I'd grab on." He began to flip a few switches on the dashboard, the cabin's lights flicking off. The two vans behind turned 50 feet of distance to 30. "The timing here is everything..."

"Timing what?" Braxton asked, fear rising.

"She can steer us, Sentinel, but she's not all-powerful... when a custom turbovent hitches the engine, there's fuck all she can do."

With those words, the cabbie flipped one final switch labeled, with tape, as the "OH SHIT" switch. The engine immediately jolted to a pained stop as gravitic friction was released. The car dropped instantaneously, leaving Braxton to drift upwards in zero-g freefall. His head bumped to the stained felt roof as the vehicle dropped into the lane of oncoming traffic. He saw the headlights of an approaching truck flare and flash, but their plummeting vehicle moved through the opening and beneath the oncoming traffic without collision. Then the cabbie flicked the switch back to its upright position, the engine screeching and grinding as it reclaimed its flight trajectory. The cab finally held its air about 20 feet above the promenade, where pedestrians gawked and pointed at the vehicle which had nearly fallen from the sky. And above, two black vans circled, unable to safely lower their way through the flow of oncoming traffic—a shield of a thousand rushing cars.

The cab landed on the Promenade and Braxton hopped out, tossing the cabbie the second chip he'd carried. It was for 200,000 credits. "Have a friend cash that," he advised. "In case they spotted the mohawk from their vans." And with a tap on the side of the cab, it flew off, and Braxton shuffled out among the statues and paintings and the rich people who surveyed them stroking at their chins and offering their endless commentaries to the artists' intent. He picked a hat from the nearest stall, shed the jacket to his suit, and walked into the nearest skyscraper that abutted the elevated Promenade, vanishing into the crowd within.

* * *

Oscar hadn't answered Braxton's calls. Braxton spent the better part of an hour ensuring that he'd lost his pursuers for good. He'd enter one building on one floor and exit it on another, traversing the space between structures on the elevated walkways and bridges that dominated the downtown. He oriented his face away from any security cameras that he could see—keeping the bill of his hat low—and changed his wardrobe as often as he could, picking up loose items he encountered and even buying a new shirt from a commercial center—paid for in cash, not chip. It was while crossing one of those intrastructural bridges that his comms rang, the system returning "blocked number" as the caller. Braxton toggled off the camera display and ensured all encryption settings were enabled before accepting the call.

"You are a hard man to find," came the voice at the other end of the call. The voice was distorted through all of the cyclical encryption and location-spoofing jumps that were being executed, but the thick German accent left little guessing as to whom he was speaking with.

"And your son deserved what I did, and more."

"I wonder, would you speak so freely if we spoke face-to-face? Let us see. I should like to speak face-to-face."

"Your son did not enjoy my company... what makes you think that you might?"

"Sehr komisch... You are a funny man, Mr. Crane. I like this in you. But you must know discipline of my son is my responsibility alone," The German said. "You have hurt him on ground where he was to be safe. You have broken the peace, and our enterprise demands justice."

"A funny demand for a criminal organization," Braxton said. "And your enterprise shall need a lot of eyes. I am already two miles out of the city and not slowing down. I have no family for you to threaten, no loved ones," he lied. "So how far are you willing to chase?"

"Well, on the matter of family, Herr Jimenez seemed to think of you as a brother... so distraught he was to talk, but we hold our secrets in our hearts like little locked boxes, and every körper has a key. Thirty-five minutes is how long it took him to crumble... we'd hardly pulled three teeth before he mentioned her. Do not think him weak, and do not hate him—often no one is as prepared to withstand torture as they believe themselves to be."

Braxton's device pinged as it received a new picture message. It was a photo of Cara's apartment from the street below. He felt the rage rise up inside him like hot bile, burning at his throat. "If you touch one hair on her head," he spat, quieting himself as a businesswoman walked past in the bridge behind him. "A single hair, and—"

"Breathe easy, Herr Crane. For someone mit no loved ones, you seem quite... invested in the junkie. I will permit that we all have our vices, and you were wise to keep yours so secret. Our wants are little hooks, from which we may be jerked and pulled like marionettes in a show... and using the hook of Frau Cho, I call you in, Braxton Crane. You will come to me like the puppet on a string that you are, and if you do this—if you come willingly and without violence—it is my promise that she will live. She will be untouched... she need not even know of our unfortunate business. I have a man already in her hall... call her, or anyone else, and it ends less well for you both."

Braxton collapsed to his knees, staring out at the cool and impassive concrete megaliths of the city beyond the glass wall. He saw his own reflection in that glass, analyzing that broken, defeated ghost that wore an expression like the dead... the image held over the dark but faded before the light.

"How can I trust you?" Braxton whispered weakly. "How can I be sure that you won't hurt her?"

The German laughed at the other end of the line. "Oh, Herr Crane, integrity is the only thing I have to truly bargain with! Think on it: how can one deal with a thief if they worry of being robbed next? How can one hire to kill if they fear they will be killed in turn? The backstabbing become the backstabbed; they are crabs in a bucket, self-defeating dreck. I am what I am because I am also the man who I am. A bad reputation is criminal suicide; to betray one is to betray your whole organization, for they are left wondering when your word might be next broken. The whole of the underworld know that I am a partner who honors my deals... and you—it would seem—are a man without a choice."

Braxton was silent, his mind back in the luxury of her bed— the luxury of her body—and the warmth of her smile, the scent of her hair.

"I will see you at second-to-top floor of the west casino garage, 2 hours. Do not be late, or she will pay dearly."

And then the line clicked silent.

Chapter 31

The West Garage was a predictable-enough choice: it was still under construction, as was the new Casino Nebula Luxury Condominiums building that adjoined the garage. No public access meant no prying eyes... there would be no one to help.

The appointed hour drew near, and Braxton stared at the lower floor of the dark garage like a man might watch the noose the executioner tied seconds before it was slipped over his neck. The notion of his death troubled him, as it would trouble all men who lead a happy and fulfilling life, but even stronger still was the sense of dread surrounding Cara. Would she be harmed? Was The German truly the man of his word that he was said to be? Braxton could not be certain she would be safe... but he could at least be certain that she would be harmed if he disobeyed. And so, he finally set forwards towards the garage, swallowing the dread as he wiped his sweaty palms on his side. He would not wish this uncertainty or distress on even his worst of enemies.

As he walked closer to the garage's base, now only fifty feet out from the construction fencing, he heard the near-synchronized footsteps of two men who walked close behind him. My escorts, *he thought, not even bothering to check over his shoulder. A woman appeared at the gate of the construction yard's fence and swung it open for Braxton wordlessly. He, and the men behind him, entered and proceeded. Loose wheelbarrows and gravlifts sat on the dusty floor beyond the perimeter of the garage. Steel beams were arranged horizontally in a neat stack, something that could provide decent shooter cover. A large, yellow generator sat next to a mound of sand, its cable snaking off into the dark of* the lower garage floor. A woman in a hard hat flipped switches on the generator's side and pulled a ripcord repeatedly until it puttered on, bringing a faint yellow glow to the overhead lights on the first floor. Inside the garage, Braxton saw vertical beams that could work for cover, though he wasn't sure if their thickness would be enough to prevent overcharged plasma rounds.

"Before the elevator," said one of the men behind him, "body scan. Raise arms?"

The man passed a vibrating device over and around Braxton's body, and as he did so, the magnetic resonance imaging created an instant 3D rendering on the screen that sat on the wand's flat face. The man who held the device then tapped through various material layers, seeing at-a-glance every single component of metal, plastics, biologics, rubber, wood, and stone across Braxton's body and person. "Your combat knife in your boot," the man said.

"Standard issue," Braxton said with a sheepish grin. "Nearly forgot I was wearing—"

The man simply stuck his hand forwards, palm up, in a gesture that said 'give it to me now.' And so, Braxton complied.

As the man tucked the knife into his belt—Braxton took special note of the angle of the hilt he wore—the second man pressed a button on the wall, calling the elevator. It arrived nearly instantly. The three stepped in, one man at each of Braxton's sides, and both stood with their arms crossed as the elevator shuddered upwards. "Welcome to Casino Nebula," said a pre-recorded voice from the elevator's speaker, "where every day is your lucky day."

The elevator arrived with a bright and proud ding!, but Braxton could hardly hear it over the pounding of his blood in his ears. The door slid open and then men behind him *forcefully—but not roughly—pushed him forwards, out onto the open, concrete floor beyond. As Braxton swiveled his head, he counted 14 men and women in total forming a wide perimeter, each standing with their arms clasped behind their back. And in the center of the garage floor was only a single car: an idling black SUV, with windows tinted to full midnight.*

A door in the passenger row opened, and out stepped a short man with a bald head and a tangled beard. Small glass spectacles sat forwards on his nose, the rims glowing and pulsing softly to internal lights. His left arm and leg both were elaborate prosthetics of finely-flexed bioanimatronics. When he smiled, he smiled a mouth of teeth that were half-white, half metallic, and his left eye glistened with the red light of an artificial camera diode deep within the pupil.

"I suppose I should thank you," The German said. "People oft wonder if Heinrich is truly my son, so vastly different as our temperaments are. Now the physical resemblance will be just a little bit closer."

Braxton estimated the number of steps to reaching The German, and knew that it was far too many... he'd be shot six times over before even nearing grabbing distance.

"Is she safe?" Braxton only asked instead.

"I told you, Herr Crane, that I am a man of integrity. That which I promise, I always deliver." He nodded and one of the guards at the perimeter stepped forwards with a wide handheld screen, showing it to Braxton. On it, a telephoto lens vantage from a drone high in the city captured the interior of Cara's apartment through her window. She was in the kitchen, leaning over a pot and examining the contents.

"We were planning to cook Italian," Braxton said. He would not pull his eyes from the screen until the woman holding the display switched it off.

"My man by her door reported that it smelled delicious," The German said. "But I have told him to go home, as you have so bravely and wisely brought yourself in. You have saved her life today."

Braxton allowed his lips to raise in a half-smile. "And my own life?"

"It pains me that it must end this way," The German said, a genuine look of sadness in his eyes. "Enforcement is such a strange profession... it attracts the very worst of uns and the very best of uns. The very worst are the ones who take pleasure in inflicting suffering on others, the sadists and the cruel. And the very best are the ones who actually believe in making the world a better place. I share your vision for a better place, truly I do. And that you struck out against my son in defence of the defenceless, that is a noble cause."

Braxton spat towards The German's feet. "You don't know nobility... if you were truly noble, you'd free me and punish your own son, recognize him for the abusive turd that he is."

The German nodded. "In that, you are right, as I am not noble. I respect nobility, but I am ignoble—it comes with my work. How I wish that the world you long for could actually be so... how I wish that better place could be realized. But our city has rules that are so long entrenched, the people do not know what it was to live without them. I have heard stories from great-great grandparents about the world we inherited, and how strange it seems to imagine! The things that they could do, the ways that people cared! But do you see this metal outside the edge of the garage there, the crane chassis? Its cable is lifted by a six-stroke gravitic engine, driven by only four gears of radii 6 centimeters, 8 centimeters, 12 centimeters, and 14 centimeters. Do you know what happens if you let your hand wander inside the engine's casing, and get snagged between the gears?"

Braxton didn't answer.

"The gears continue to spin as though your hand were not even there, turning it to red mush and bone splinters."

The German stepped in close, within a distance that Braxton could lunge.

"Your bravery, your nobility... it is a hand where it does not belong, and even if you try to stop the turning gear wheels, they do not even know it. New Phoenix is a stubborn bitch, one who cannot be changed. And so, though I am one who wished for a better world like you, I have changed my aims. Her darkness, her sickness cannot be cured, cannot even be bent. So instead we seek to help it in ways that we can, ways that turn with the gears instead of against them. We have squashed many warring gangs—children with guns and egos too large for their blocks—and we have created an empire built on order, on competency, on reliable peace through threat of further violence. And all of this is held together by the most important glue that an organization might have—respect. You have drawn blood from a prince, Herr Crane, and so you must be punished swiftly lest the peasants revolt. I am sorry if it feels unjust, but believe me when I say it is the best justice we can afford."

Out from the idling SUV, a second figure emerged, one with his head wrapped in thick, white bandages stained deep crimson.

"Go to your rest now, enforcer. And know that she will not be harmed... you may rest with that ease."

The enraged Heinrich Sauer approached and removed a gun from his waistband—an older kinetic, a model that Braxton didn't even recognize in its vintage. Braxton could grab it—the boy's grip was loose and his arm recklessly thrust forwards as though it were a sword, not a firearm—but even if he managed to shoot Heinrich, or The German, then what? Gunned down instantly, and a good chance they'd kill Cara for vengeance? Braxton's final moments were not spent panicking, nor were they spent in montage of his life's highlights and unfulfilled dreams... they were not spent begging, nor were they weeping. Instead, he looked the young man in his one surviving eye, certain that this thin, angry whelp would be the one to kill him—but meeting that eye with defiance, with strength. If not for himself, then for her.

Heinrich pressed the gun to Braxton's chest and pulled the trigger twice. The bang was so loud that Braxton hardly heard the second... he only felt the thud *as his body connected to concrete, watching himself settle roughly to the floor. Then the darkness weighed down like the abyssal edge of sleep, pulling harder and harder until it inexorably swallowed him.*

And then, there was only void.

* * *

Nothingness echoed unto oblivion, a cavernous reverb of empty, yawning silence. How long the silence extended for, and for how long it had already sounded, was impossible to be sure.

But then that silence was split and shattered by a white-hot tone that screamed wicked pain in his mind. Then the silence resumed, the black and comforting cloak that smothered all sensation and lulled him down back to sleep.

Then returned that screech, the screaming sound that brought with it so much discomfort and disorientation, sensations of heaviness and restlessness. It vanished and then appeared again, taunting him with its oscillations from serenity to blinding pandemonium, and then he felt its hooks begin to dig deep within his body, pulling him outwards and towards that screaming discomfort. He could not scream, he could not fight it, he could not even offer weak protests as it dragged him forwards and towards a wide, blooming field of brilliant white…

It was some time before Braxton realized his eyes were open, and the oscillating tormentor was the steady, rhythmic beeping of a hospital apparatus. He had never before in his life felt so weak, so utterly drained of all energy and capability… and his thoughts scraped and burned like a processor six generations too old for his head. The wall to his left featured a strange pattern, and as Braxton's clarity of mind and vision returned in slow waves, he realized that the patterns were words: VitaCorp, Where Ends Make New Beginnings.

"How are you feeling?" asked a voice to his side. Braxton turned his head to see an old man in a visitor's chair, a gaunt and grey-haired gargoyle of a man who wore a neat black sweater of pristine import cotton.

"How?" Braxton asked, his own voice coming out like gravel. "How did I live?"

The old man leaned forwards. "One bullet to the heart, a second to the lung. The simple answer? You did not.*" He leaned back again, a challenge of a smile on his lips.*

Braxton looked down at his own body, wrapped up in a mint green hospital gown. He began to claw at the fabric and pulled it towards the side, trying to see his own chest that now burned with indescribable, dull pain.

"I wouldn't do that," the man said. "It's all wrapped up anyways, and those scars are still quite raw. You were the recipient of a fresh, new heart, new right lung—and some fragments of your brain, places where the damage had been, shall we say, irreversible. The tissues of the human body can survive an astonishing amount of time without flowing blood,

all save for the brain... but not all damage is permanent, and modern medicine has reached capabilities formerly believed to belong to science fiction alone. When we retrieved Braxton Crane, he was already twenty-one minutes dead... by the time surgery began, it had been thirty-seven. His CA1 neurons of the hippocampus were in a death spiral, and though we could reverse some of the cell death, we were forced to do a partial live-neuron brain transplant from an organ donor of matching biomarkers. You may experience difficulty with memory, especially for the adjustment period of six to twelve months."

Braxton swallowed.

"Hooking a corpse's brain back to a functioning circulatory system is not unlike, say, pouring tea into a cup that was already shattered. Both tend to leak *quite aggressively. Your brain had four major clotting incidents, and a single ruptured aneurysm, too—" The man frowned deeply, steadying himself. He held up a mirror and flexed his face into it before stashing it away. "Yes, major clotting incidents. The amygdala, unfortunately, did not survive one of those episodes... another transplant successfully made."*

Braxton lifted his hand and prodded at his head, finding the large patch on the back where hair had been shaved away— which now was viciously tender underneath thick bandages.

"It would be a lie to say you survived your ordeal... Braxton Crane will never draw another breath. You are much like him, but you are not him... your mind is only some of his, the rest being filled in by our design. It is appropriate that the amygdala should be one of the pieces that I selected for you... the emotional brain, commander of the fight or flight *response. That is what we'll need of you, when you've recovered and had your rest."*

"I've always been more fight than flight," Braxton said.

"But never quite flight like this," the man replied cryptically.

Braxton's mind, turning over the idea of fleeing from fights, arrived upon the image of standing in a bridge between skyscrapers, staring out over the city... and then it all came crashing back to him. His eyes widened, and he leaned forwards as much as his strength would allow. He reached towards the old man's arm, clasping it. "Cara," he choked. "Did she... is she..."

"Alive? That she is, and she's even engaged."

"Engaged?"

"Much has changed in these months since you died... very much indeed. You will have many questions for me, I am sure... how long has it been? Four months and six days—the world presumes you long dead. Why have we chosen to save you? In a way we have bought your services, and should you refuse—which remains your right—we will simply take the heart and lung we'd loaned you and leave you to your rest. Why have we chosen to save you, specifically? You were identified as an ideal match by our software—recent death, similar ideology, few living links, talent with physical violence, emotional pliability. What will we need of you? That is a question best saved for after your recovery, which I will be monitoring closely with great personal interest. What are you to call me? My name is Clive Avery, but Mr. Avery or Sir will suffice. And now, my single question for you: since Braxton Crane is dead, what am I to call you?"

* * *

It was the first day that Braxton had been able to walk on his feet unassisted. They'd given him something—a drug he still didn't understand—but the strange way that it affected his body, the way it let him form lines to the lights they kept by his bedside, it was nothing short of extraordinary. His health had recovered at speed he'd never have believed possible, and it was all thanks to the glowing power of the light, whatever new medical miracle it was. "I'd like to see the roof," he'd requested. "To walk around, and get some fresh air."

"Air quality is better indoors by—"

Braxton waved the nurse away with a grunt, wheeling the IV bag with him as he left his room in the private hospital. The nurse insisted on following at least, and Braxton neither accepted nor protested. "Roof access," he told the elevator, and it whisked them both upwards towards the top accessible floor. The final floor was to be climbed on manual stairs, and the nurse immediately offered to help Braxton on the steep steps—he vehemently refused. Instead, he spent the better part of three minutes slowly shuffling up the staircase, straining and trembling with every step until the sweat lined his face and clammy hands. But then he reached the top, and he pushed the door open triumphantly, and he felt the cooling wave of damp air roll back and into the stairwell with drops of misting rain floating in suspension. It was a kiss of crisp cold to a man so tired of the stale and quiet indoors... it was the first breath back in the city that Braxton had come to love deeply, despite all of its faults and shortcomings. The roof of the private hospital was dwarfed on each side by massive, rolling skyscrapers of glass and steel. Each way he turned was a new and equally dazzling show of videoscreens, flying drones, neon signs, echoing announcements, thumping music. Advertisements flickered and looped, skytraffic flowed with the wind, and the misting drops of rain set the air to an inviting, multicolored glow in the dusk's light... the city waits for no recovery, pulsing as vibrantly as ever.

"You always did have a gentle heart, Braxton Crane, under all of that bone and muscle... I saw that right away," Cara had said in their final conversation. Her hand had been on his

chest, and Braxton now moved his hands towards that same chest in the open hospital gown as the rain rolled down off pale skin to the wet concrete roof. What heart now beat in the chest of Braxton Graves? Was it gentle, too?

He then of course thought of Cara, and how she would be somewhere out in the city, preparing for her wedding... who was the man? How did they meet?

And there were the darker questions that ached deep within: why was she engaged only four months after he'd disappeared? Had she even looked for him? Had she wept for him? Did she still think of him now as frequently as he thought of her? And was it fair to hope that she did, or would the right thing to hope be that she'd forgotten about him swiftly, so that she might return to her life as quickly as possible?

"Mr. Graves?"

Braxton turned, only now realizing that the nurse had been calling his name repeatedly... it was still a strange thing, answering to a name that still felt a pair of shoes not yet broken in.

"We should get you downstairs, before the rain soaks through your bandages... I think neither of us want to go through the trouble of changing them early."

He looked out to the city, eager to drink in its commotion and movement and melt back into it... and six weeks later, standing on that very same rooftop, he'd finally had the privilege.

Avery had taught him what he could now do. Avery had explained the nature of the souls he now carried. Avery had given him his instructions, and told him the address where he would pick up his tailor-made gear. There were light packs, and there were magnetic pulling beacons—a clunky name, but

Braxton would soon find something better. There were the blades with lights mounted on their hilts, the myriad scrapers and dissolvers for obscuring the identity of the dead. There were the remotes, the spring-loaded weapon draws, the custom-fitted surveillance tech implant and associated accessories... all of it awaited his pickup, and he would neither walk nor drive the distance. For the first time in his life, Braxton would truly fly.

The rush was every bit as exhilarating and liberating as he could've imagined, and as he darted through the city like a mad dragonfly, breathing in the steam that shot from vents and drinking in the neon in twisting, vibrant lines, he felt the gravity of his assignment slip into place. Order, stability, integrity... *these were the pillars that society rested upon, and for so many to carry the power he carried was a recipe for chaos, subversion, disorder and destruction. The final gesture that had bought Braxton's loyalty was the strange box that had been left by his hospital room that morning... in it was a severed head with one eye biologic, the other black-market prosthetic. It was Heinrich Sauer, who would abuse escorts no longer.*

The attached file from Avery had been as clear as it was effective: "I make this gift to you, Braxton, to show that I understand the gravity of what it means to take a life, and that I would not ask you to do anything I would not—or have not—done myself. The information of your first target is attached."

As he vaulted into the air, he saw the distant rising monolith of Casino Nebula, but Braxton twisted in the air and shoved away from it, using the massive screen on the side of a nearby tower for leverage. As he propelled himself further and further from the casino, he spun and tucked his arms inwards, passing through the neon O in a sign for the New Phoenix Royal Hotel. And then with a sudden shove against a light in front of him, done so harshly that the neon installation shattered down to the street, Braxton stopped on the rooftop and stared to the storefront that had caught his eye. At the top of the glass facade, silhouetted in spotlight against a backdrop of red velvet, was an item that immediately enwrapped him.

As he made his first kill that night for VitaCorp, he would wear that thing, the only item he'd selected personally: a black and hooded leather jacket, something to suit the grim reaper he'd now become.

Chapter 32

"The air is thick with the smoke of the burning dead... my parents, my brother among them. They call us survivors the lucky ones, but they're wrong. The lucky ones were the billion who got off the ride before it derailed... I catch myself wishing I were one of them, and the voice that's telling me to snap out of it is the voice that's getting quieter—not the other way around. There's nothing lucky *about suffering like this through a world that's falling apart. Yesterday, my cousin was killed in a fight over a crate of shriveled apples; the day before, I watched a militia van abduct a woman on the streets, nobody helping as she screamed. I was one of the people who didn't help... everyone feels helpless, I think, and that pathetic feeling is magnifying as it propagates through each new shellshocked person. Now I add guilt to the burdens I carry, and the load is only getting heavier. I wonder what fresh hell tomorrow will bring... if there's even a tomorrow at all."*

-Archival video diary from the peak of the Falling Sickness outbreak, recorded in February 2033.

* * *

"Target's name is Cara Cho," Pollock read. "Had been engaged to the dearly departed Mr. Crane... remarried shortly afterwards."

The trio were in their CSP van, which bumped and rattled its way across the decaying roads of the sixth ring. Rob drove, with Hannah riding shotgun. Pollock, in the open rear of the van, tapped at a mounted computer terminal as he browsed through the Panopticon export.

"How sure are we that he's still in contact with her?" Rob asked.

"Not sure in the slightest," Pollock replied. "But it doesn't even matter if he is. Since he's after us, I think he knows *we're onto him*."

"So if he knows we're on his trail," Hannah began.

"The girl is the bait to reel him in." Pollock finished. "He'll be watching her, that I can guarantee."

"A bait on whose fishing line?" Rob asked. "Like, who's trapping whom here?"

"We threaten the girl, and we have all the leverage," Hannah said, securing an energy weapon holster to her right hip. A kinetic weapon was already holstered to her left, and her rear pockets were stuffed full of glowsticks cracked only minutes before.

"Threaten the girl?" Rob balked. "Just who are the good guys here?"

"I said threaten, not harm," Hannah said.

"He'd call that bluff," Rob said. "He's not stupid, you know. If we hurt her, we lose our leverage, and then he kills us."

"How do we even get near the girl without him stopping us?" Pollock asked.

"Our best odds are if we split up," Hannah replied. "How about this: you two make an obvious show of getting to her apartment building, with ample face time out front. Then you enter on the ground level, where—if he was on some roof monitoring—he drops in to follow. That's when I go up and enter the building from the roof and get to her first. When he finds you, you let him know I'm with her already. Leverage, and, more importantly, distance to that leverage. Engenders a sense of powerlessness."

"Speaking of a sense of powerlessness, how did it go from 'the girl is the bait' to 'Rob is the bait?'" Rob asked.

"You're a lightbender, Rob," Hannah said. "You're the one who keeps Pollock safe. If anything, that makes *him* the bait." Nobody wanted to mention the other reason that the arrangement had to be this way: Rob couldn't fly well enough to enter from the roof reliably. If anything, it seemed like his lightbending was getting *worse*, not better.

"You can stick 'em with your glowdagger if he gets close," Pollock jibed.

"Might as well stick the both of you first," Rob retorted.

"Well, no time for that… according to the map here, we're three minutes out," Hannah announced. "Everyone ready?"

Pollock secured his own holster, slipping on his tactical CSP vest. Rob drummed his fingers on the wheel nervously.

"I'll take your silence for a 'yes ma'am,' so let's do this. Let me out of the van here… I'll be on comms. Call when you're entering the building."

* * *

From the rooftops above, Braxton eyed Cara's apartment building. It was a red-bricked thing made in the old New York style, evocative of a nostalgia that nobody alive still shared. For Braxton, though, it still retained a certain surreality, a presence that made it feel larger and grander than the rest of the structures around it… it had been host to so many of Braxton's dearest memories—the ones he could still recall, at least.

His breath was hot as it reflected back from the plastic screen into his own face. Since taking the pills, he had felt strange. There was a sense of fatigue that seemed to be looming just beyond his body, and a dull ache that crept its way upwards when he sat still for too long. But Avery had been right, so very, truly right: his connection to the glow had never been stronger, his abilities never greater than they now were.

From the call he'd overheard, he knew the CSP men were onto him—a visit to Panopticon was the likely next step. That would mean they'd have his old name, they'd have Cara's identity... and so soon they'd be here. And Braxton was sure they'd expect him here, too, not that it mattered at all. He would intercept them and put a stop to their meddling—by diplomatic means, or otherwise.

It was on the fifty-fifth minute of waiting on that rooftop when a CSP van pulled to an idle stop in front of Cara's building. Out stepped two men, both of whom immediately looked up towards the top of the brick tower, perhaps estimating the 22nd floor from ground level. Braxton toggled his optical implant for its magnification setting and confirmed the identity of the CSP to his overlay. Both were matches. He then perched on the ledge and waited for them to enter the unit, toppling forwards over the ledge as soon as they did. A second later, his falling became gliding as he closed in on the building's entrance.

* * *

Hannah dared not lift her actual head above the rooftop's surrounding lip, lest she be spotted by Braxton Crane. Instead, she propped up the small CSP monitoring unit just above the edge, a lens to blend in with the hundreds of others across nearby rooftops. From her reclining position, she watched the camera's output feed in life-res. It was on that display that she saw the man topple over the edge and glide at controlled speed to a firm landing on the ground.

"He's moving in," Hannah said to her comms. *And that's my cue*, she thought, rising to her feet. She leapt over the edge of the tower and pushed against the glowing headlights of flying traffic below, nimbly landing on the roof to Cara's building. The door to the rooftop was locked, but an energy pulse from her sidearm proved to be an effective master key. She located the stairwell and immediately began running down flight after flight, seeking floor 22. Finding it, she frantically threw the stairwell door open and ran towards the right apartment unit. At the door, she paused for a moment and closed her eyes. She reached out with her awareness, prodding for all the light sources that she could draw from—an immediately overwhelming surge of untapped wellsprings of power. But soon she managed to resolve the chaos into discernible, distinct points of energy, and she used those points to construct a rough map of the glowing items in Cara's apartment... and then with a smile, Hannah realized that she'd found the woman: a bright and square lightsource—a large screen of some kind—was powered in a distant room, and a smaller source—a personal phone—was floating in front of it. She was in the media room, meaning that the door was safe.

She opened her eyes and leveled her energy weapon to the door, firing once to melt the lock. Swinging the still-dripping door open, she stepped inside.

* * *

CSP Agents Rob Boardsmith and Sam Pollock had undergone extensive combat training as part of the rigorous training regimen prescribed by local statutes, but both felt an immediate sense of dread and inadequacy when Hannah warned that the assassin had arrived. Here was a trained enforcer of an entirely different calibre... and one with abilities that neither of the two could match.

Their wrist chips had granted them blanket access to most residential units as CSP, but somehow the assassin had entered without delay as well. They'd been hoping for the slowdown at that point, something to buy them more time, but when planning operations, fate rarely did any favors. The two dared not turn around to see if he was near, because doing so might instigate the fight in these crowded corridors... and besides, they wanted time to allow Hannah to move in and acquire Cho. And so, the two marched forwards, past the elevators, following the halls until they saw a sign for a larger space: the complex's fitness center. They pushed in through the entrance's double doors and found an airy, glass-walled space with personal exercise equipment in every shape and size. Screens featuring virtual trainers covered most of the machines, each ready to give feedback to users on how to improve their form and track their progress. A few people ran on treadmills, while a woman strained against a leg curl machine with a friend standing nearby.

"Split up, kinetics drawn," Pollock ordered. He fanned left as Rob fanned right, each drawing their antiquated gunpowder weapons and holding them towards the door. "Everyone else here, get out," Pollock yelled, thrusting his gun into the air to emphasize his point. None moved, and then Pollock noticed the earbuds every single person wore.

Before Pollock could hatch a way to get the crowd to disperse, the double doors to the gym were pushed open. In stepped a man in a black and hooded leather jacket, his face partly obscured behind a clear, plastic mask. His face was gaunt, with a small scar on his cheek. His eyes glowed white fury. Both pointed their weapons towards him.

"*He's on us,*" Rob whispered to comms.

"Package acquired," Hannah's voice answered back. *"Beam my feed over to him when ready."*

"A strange way to recover from your sick day," Braxton said. His voice was muffled, but amplified by the strange plastic mask that he wore.

"My commander said you sent well-wishes," Pollock responded.

"In that case, it seems we both know more than a little about each other," Braxton replied, hands splayed outwards. "You know where I've been, who I am… and I know the same things about you *two*."

"We'd like to talk… somewhere far and away from eavesdroppers," Rob said. "We have some questions."

"Questions that, I'm afraid, shall have to remain unanswered… tight operations have so little space for inconvenient truths. You two shall call off your investigation—whatever it might be—and in exchange, I shall allow you to live. You have my word."

"And what good is the word of a criminal?" Rob asked.

"Why, Mr. Boardsmith, in my line of work integrity is the only commodity I have to bargain with. If there is no trust between criminals there can be no organization… and yet, criminal organizations outmaneuver the greatest institutions the light can offer. In a way, Mr. Boardsmith, I would counter that criminals hold greater value on trust than the other side does. You need only look on the scale of our works, and agree."

"We have her," Pollock said. "We're not leaving without our answers… or we're forced to take her instead. Question her… lock her up… sending you a tightbeam broadcast now; accept it."

Pollock oriented his broadcast unit towards Braxton. The man tapped a panel on his wrist, accepting the datastream. A video feed filled his comms display, showing an energy weapon on a table before Cara.

The plastic mask did little to hide Braxton's immediate, visceral reaction. "You still care for her, don't you?" Pollock asked.

"*You will not involve her,*" Braxton hissed. "She is blameless, pure."

"Talk with us, and we let her go," Pollock said.

Braxton looked from one man to the other, a tight expression on his face. Rob couldn't tell if he would start to cry or scream.

"On a day you've called in sick, you are here, chasing down your leads," Braxton said at last. His voice seemed too level for the desperate look in his eyes. "The three of us have much more in common than you know."

"And what's that?" Rob asked.

"I recognize the same earnestness, the same idealism in you that I once carried… you're doing this in your own time. You're doing this because you think it's right, consequences be damned."

Pollock allowed himself to nod along, still keeping his weapon raised.

"I thus believe that you are incapable of hurting Cara… our ideals are chains that occasionally hold us back from doing what may not be the right thing, per se, but what might have been the wise thing."

"Well we might be idealists," Pollock countered, "but the woman upstairs with Cara is a pragmatist. She'll shoot without so much as a second thought." .

Braxton's mind flashed back to the casino, at the fools who pushed their luck and lost it all... but sometimes, there was truly little choice.

"I don't know your woman companion... but if my employer believed Cara to be a threat to my ability to perform my job, he would kill her himself."

And with that, the calm stillness of the gym exploded into pandemonium.

Nearly every workout machine suddenly lurched backwards and tipped, the massive cacophony of collapsing weights sending Rob's ears ringing. He and Pollock immediately began to fire at the twisting form of the assassin, who spun to the ground amid a gathering whirlpool of light beams. Rob reached out to the nearest flickering light source—a shattered display of a personal trainer from the bench press—and began to drink in its power as he continued to fire. The beams of light solidified into a ring around the hunter, who now stood slowly to his feet. Pollock watched as the bullets he fired ripped holes in the man's jacket, in his arm... before he whispered *'oh shit'* into his comms.

Both Rob and Pollock watched in awe as the gushing holes torn by their bullets filled with brilliant, white light... metal slugs plopped outwards from his body, as though expelled by the power within. Then webs of spidery white began to spin over the holes until the blood trickled to a plugged stop. The solid white light cooled into glowing new flesh, until soon it was indistinguishable from a normal mass of scar tissue. The two had witnessed the healing of a gunshot wound, stretched to mere seconds instead of months. *"Run,"* Pollock breathed, and then the hunter surged forwards.

Rob pushed off the ring of light around the hunter, propelling himself backwards and away as the hooded man advanced. The hunter raised an arm and let loose a bolt of furious electricity, but the wisps of lightning curved unpredictably—and with his push, Rob was unexpectedly far away. The bolt of electricity instead struck the massive glass window, instantaneously shattering it to a rain of crystal fragments that sparkled as they fell. Pollock felt the sting of a shard that had embedded somewhere in his side. He was out of his league here, and he needed to find cover.

Braxton pursued the flying Rob, giving Pollock a chance to crouch and make his way towards the exit. He saw one of the women from earlier unconscious, sprawled out on the ground… he kneeled to check her pulse and to try and slap her awake. Overhead, the shadows shifted and Pollock saw the hunter whip through the air, throwing up his hand in some attack. A large shoulder press surged forwards, sparking along the ground as it slid towards its unseen target. Another bolt of lightning emitted its blinding flash as Pollock reached the woman, seeing the dazed and unseeing look in her eyes. "We have to move," he whispered to her, meeting her gaze. "We have to move."

He got her to her feet and the two crept towards the gym's exit. In front of them, a desperate Rob skittered to a stop and whirled around, launching loose screens he'd picked up as projectiles. Others launched towards him in reply, shattering into glass and metal fragments around him. Pollock guided the woman as he turned around, shambling instead towards the shattered window that once made up the far wall of the fitness center. "Out through the broken glass," he whispered. "We'll make it."

Wisps of light twisted down from the ceiling to the two dueling forms, but for every line that reached to Rob, it seemed that Braxton drew four. Drawlines that crept towards Rob were seemingly pulled against, and soon they paused and changed direction, pouring towards the hooded figure instead. *Just forty more feet,* Pollock thought. *Thirty.* An inclined press skid across the floor in a screeching procession of sparks and metal, coming to a crumbling stop in front of the window. The two diverted but continued to advance, falling to their feet as a metal barbell bounced and skidded along the floor towards them. It bounced overhead and carried on until it embedded in the wall in a puff of drywall dust. *"Almost there,"* Pollock willed.

Another flash of lightning painted long and jagged shadows ahead of the pair as they ran towards the open window, fifteen feet melting to five. Finally, they were at the threshold, and the woman ran off into the grass sobbing. Pollock did not leap the line of jagged glass, but instead stopped to turn, trying to find his partner. He couldn't help... but *how could he run?* There, he saw Rob, with the younger agent's back pressed against a workout mirror that made up one of the walls. His arms were outstretched, and before him floated a metal dagger with a light affixed to its back. It trembled, as though being pushed forwards and backwards with great force all at once... and Pollock supposed precisely that was happening.

"Go," Rob mouthed, before yelling it with all the strength he could muster. The hunter stepped forwards, his arms raised with nonchalance, as the blade advanced ever closer.

"Go, damn you, before he kills us both," Rob called. *"We don't win this today... but there's always tomorrow."* Still struggling against the floating knife, Rob cracked an earnest smile, before his expression twisted back to something closer to pain. Blood trickled from his lips, and he began to scream,

pushing back against the knife with every ounce of strength he could find. Light poured in from flickering screens and sparking lights, lending him their power, and Braxton made no move to pull them away... he instead slowly ratcheted up his force from barely a shove to more and more investment, sad to see the man—this hopeful, young CSP—was so weak with the soul he carried. It never took to some well, and it seemed this was one such man marked by that unfortunate weakness... but he carried a strength in his willpower, a strength in his conviction. Even now, as he pushed back against Braxton's force of hardly one-quarter-exertion, he could see the man's veins in his temples bulging and the glass of the mirror behind him cracking and splintering into a crater he was pressing into... and in that cracking mirror, Braxton watched the reflection of himself, a jagged and cruel thing in the splintered shards. Leaving the CSP in so prolonged a struggle was a wicked thing indeed to do, and so Braxton stopped with the rising strength to test his foe. He instead shoved with all of his weight, the dagger launched forwards, and the wall of mirror shattered apart, Braxton's image disappearing as gravity smothered it down.

And when the twinkling shards had all lain still, and Braxton had found the body beneath the glass, he turned to see the groundborne CSP was gone. Braxton knew it would not be the last he saw of the man.

He bent back over the body of the CSP, accepting his *soul*, and he then removed his knife with the light on its handle, wiping the bloodied blade clean with his jacket. He turned, holding the knife, and experienced a *momenta non comprenda* as the blade vanished from his hand and was suddenly embedded in his gut, as though it were flicked on its own accord. *Now, how did that happen?* he wondered, still staring at it as it moved with each of his breaths. He heard the scream before he heard the footsteps, and he looked upwards to see a woman advancing, metal barbell in hand. She swung it wildly as Braxton pushed off of every light source in front of him, sweeping backwards as the metal barbell bit into the floor. Cleared of her range, he then pulled the blade free of his gut and eyed the newcomer, waiting as the light surging within began to stitch his gut back closed.

"Oh, shit," Hannah said, watching the stab wound seal with an expression much like Pollock and Rob had worn only earlier. And when the hunter stepped forwards next, she immediately retreated, running towards the open wall where the large window had once stood.

When she launched to the sky, Braxton could immediately tell that she was a lightbender of *power*... her bounds set cars rattling, and some toppled neon installations off the rusting brackets that held them fast to buildings. She darted left and right with the practiced speed of one who felt at home in the sky, a chase as invigorating as any Braxton had been on. It was so very long since he had felt a challenge in his work, and, if he was being honest with himself, he did enjoy the greater challenges offered by some—it felt more right that way, as though he'd given them a fair fight for their last stand.

She bounded forwards, leap by leap, into the buzzing heart of the innermost ring... and Braxton followed closely, ensuring the distance between them slowly winnowed away.

* * *

Pollock stepped back into the gymnasium, the broken glass crunching under his feet. A crouching and weeping man slunk past, dodging a rain of sparks that showered from the broken ceiling... a fire suppression sprinkler head sprayed a pathetic, murky mist onto the far side of the room near smoldering rubble.

Pollock neared the crumpled form under the shattered remains of the mirror, brushing the glass shards away until he could see the CSP vest, marked with the Continuum logo on its side. His hands moved clumsily, as though they were claimed by the cold, and his tongue felt too thick in his mouth. He brushed more shards of glass away until he saw the young man's face, still and cold… he was already long gone.

Pollock sat there, listening to the intermittent sparking and sprinkler's gentle pattering, his hand as though glued to his partner's face. *He had been so young… so hopeful. So… good,* Pollock thought. But pure things didn't belong in a place like New Phoenix… a flower could never grow in concrete, no matter how sunny its disposition.

"Who did this?" came a voice from behind him. Pollock turned to see a woman standing with crossed arms and a worried expression. He recognized Cara Cho from her file immediately. "Was it a woman?" she asked. "About this tall, red rash on her face?"

Pollock shook his head and sighed. "No, it wasn't her… she tried to stop it."

"Tried to stop it? She shot her way into my apartment, threatened me, and then leapt out the window," Cara protested.

"She jumped down to try to help these people," Pollock said. "She's good like that… *he was too.*" His voice broke, and he took a minute to gather his composure.

"Who did this, then?" she finally asked.

He hesitated, uncertain of how much he should say. "A monster," he replied at last. "But not one you need to worry about hurting you. I can promise you that." He looked to the woman's hand, noting her wedding band. "Your spouse will hear the news of this at your apartment building… already sirens approach. You should call them and let them know you're safe... I'm sure they'll be worried sick."

She wandered off and Pollock sat on the bent metal of a weight rack, taking in the carnage caused by one man empowered by whatever compound VitaCorp killed to keep. Before such awesome power, what could a lowly CSP Agent hope to accomplish? *There's always tomorrow*, Rob had said... a tomorrow for whom, exactly? From the military days he tried desperately to forget, there hadn't been a *tomorrow* for Rachel, and now there wouldn't be a tomorrow for Rob. Why did Pollock deserve that later date? Wouldn't it be better if it were Pollock under the broken glass, and the hopeful young agent crouching over the rubble? Pollock rarely thought on his death, for he felt only the vain would let their end define their living. But now, over the body of Rob Boardsmith, Pollock felt the tears begin to roll, and he grappled at last with those very questions. What gave Rob that strength there at the end, when the situation was so grim? Did he draw strength from the future he hoped there one day might be? Was there any relief to die for a cause one believed in?

Pollock hoped that however Rob died, he'd died with his mind focusing on brighter, happier places... and if he could've read Rob's mind, he'd have been grateful to see it was so: as Rob's final ragged breath sounded, his eyes were already miles away, watching the sprinklers illuminate the rolling fields of a farm far and away from the city, the glistening stalks waving to and fro behind the silhouette of a love set aside—but never truly lost.

Chapter 33

"I'm telling ya, it was exactly like I described. One ricocheting overhead like no flying craft I'd ever seen, and then came the second. They turned in the air and rocketed away, and while they did, the whole metal frame of the storetop shook like a storm in the country. Someone else got another angle, it's trending on ClipMe... it may lack the official verification, but I seen it with my own eyes."

-Conversation recorded in the fourth ring; flagged for moderate system relevance

* * *

Their chase had seen the dusk wink away into night, and with it, the glow of the city had truly come alive. From their vantage high in the sky, the tops of thick, monolithic towers rose from broiling pink mist that danced in the commotion far below. As Braxton flew, he watched cars exit from the landing bay near the top of a nearby tower, gliding their way down into the glowing air of the lower avenues illuminated by videoboards and holographic adverts. The little cricket leapt towards one of those cars and landed gingerly on its top, probably taking a much-needed rest. Braxton propelled himself forwards and landed softly on the next vehicle adjacent, the two standing and regarding each other across the open air.

"Last time I did this, few suits followed... none of them made it home," Hannah said.

"And every single time I've done this, I've left with what I came for... the power you carry in your body. It does not belong to you."

"What I've got belongs to nobody, not you, not your employer. I've seen enough of the corpses you leave behind... you're clean, you're efficient. Surgical, almost."

"And you're the domestic terrorist from the diner, the one who took out a small enforcer squadron with the CSP. Your work there was impressive, especially for an untrained novice. *You haven't been home lately,*" Braxton said.

"Figured there might be men in the night looking for me," Hannah responded. "Are you one such man of the night?"

"I imagine you're used to men in the night seeking you out, Hannah Preacher."

"Can a hitman really use a woman's profession against her?"

Braxton shrugged. "Perhaps not, Ms. Preacher. I deal in death, while you deal in life."

"You know, at the brothels in little Paris, they sometimes call an orgasm 'la petite mort,' or, the little death. Does that make us colleagues?"

Braxton eyed her impatiently. "Why the chit-chat? Are you stalling for time? Waiting for rescue?"

Hannah shrugged. "I suppose I've never been hunted before... wasn't aware I was supposed to go silently. Felt it'd be pretty lame, to die wanting to say something... I'd just like to know the guy that wants to kill me a little better. Who it is that I might have to kill. You never do this? Talk to them before you, you know?"

Braxton's frown deepened.

"Because I used to," Hannah said. "Going straight to the business all silent-like, it always felt like it was missing something. Like I was denying the humanity of the act."

"Look, Ms. Preacher, I will be frank with you. My assignment is to kill you, not chat with you. I grow tired with the latter and am switching to the former. If you turn yourself in now, I will make it a quick affair... you have my word, and believe me when I say that my integrity—"

"What's with the mask? You weren't wearing that last time."

Braxton was momentarily disarmed by the question. "The mask?"

"I asked you first," Hannah said. Her eyes sparkled with mischief at having successfully thrown Braxton off of his monologue.

"Very well, then, Ms. Preacher, no surrender. I respect your choice and will still do my best to make it as quick as possible. May luck be in your favor, friend."

He removed the throwing knives from his jacket and pushed against the lights at their back, watching as they traced lines of neon shooting towards the cab where Hannah had been. They whistled over an empty vehicle top, as Hannah toppled backwards and over the side in a controlled fall. Braxton swiftly dove after her, his ears filling with the sound of rushing air as he tightened his arms and legs to a straight line, minimizing his wind resistance. Still, she pulled ahead, as she wasn't simply falling; she was pushing off higher lightsources and cabs as she fell, launching herself downwards. Braxton did likewise, the wind screaming in his ears as his jacket rattled and shook in the night's air.

The orange and pink mist beneath them resolved to detail notice boards, advertisements, drone lights, and blimp signs. Wires of light licked inwards and melted into Hannah—a lightbender of considerable range, Braxton could see. How many souls did that signify? Certainly more than he had originally thought. The little cricket began to push at lower light sources that were further and further back, adjusting her flight trajectory... she was tracing a wide, swooping arc towards the street, aligning herself horizontally. Braxton chuckled with delight into the wind as he followed, noting the skill and finesse of the course correction she'd just managed—without a great deal of control, or if she'd begun it only seconds later, she might have dropped too low and ended with an unpleasant, skidding landing along the street. Instead she now glided parallel to the lower traffic of the roadways using the glow of streetlights for support, applying the smoothly-transferred momentum of her fall to fly overhead at dizzying speed.

Braxton kept up with her furious flight, but only barely: with every successive bound, every unexpected lane change or sudden turn right that left her sliding along the wall of a glass tower, Braxton's compounding reaction times had the gap between them widening and widening. None had ever escaped him before... and so, though he delighted in the talent of her chase, he would need to end this before she could escape him entirely. She twisted between a swarm of delivery drones; Braxton drank in the light of their lamps. She flitted past a videoboard of the Mayor Wyles, which sparked and creaked as she pushed; Braxton pulled on his image, drawing deep blue lines from the navy suit he wore. She dove and darted between the antenna array on a communications tower; Braxton pulled red lines from the beacons atop them, feeling the buzzing power extend beyond his body until it materialized in a wispy ring of light surrounding him. He then waited for her to bolt high and away, somewhere far from traveling airtraffic—civilians needn't die in plummeting cars if it could be avoided—and soon Braxton's window arrived. He felt for the nexus of that surging ring of light, and then he *tripped it.*

The EMP was instantaneous, blacking out the surrounding city blocks with a thump, a downwards whir. And with it, the little cricket's upwards, graceful flight switched to a sudden and uncontrolled launch. Her arms and legs pinwheeled as she lost all of her anchors, tracing a fatal parabolic arc upwards. Then she was moving parallel to the ground in a sea of black, and then inevitably came gravity's gentle pull, directing her downwards, ever downwards. Braxton flicked his pullstation to the nearest black blur of a wall beside him, the unit securing electromagnetically with a screeching click. He then began to pull towards it, gaining control of his own chaotic fall, losing her to the darkness.

He held there, suspended on the side of the glass tower, eyes scanning in the dark for a sign of her descent. He thought he had seen thin lines of green shoot to the floor, scattering—or spilling—after the fall… glowsticks, perhaps? An emergency landing kit? Maybe the cricket was more clever than—

That's when he saw the furious rise from below, her hair whipping madly as she pulled to the pullstation at full force. Her eyes were twin gemstones of an icy, glowing blue, the speed they approached meaning only one thing. The pullstation groaned, and Braxton sighed, deciding that he really needed to reposition after a maneuver like this…

She tackled into him with the speed and force of a truck, sending both crashing through the glass wall into the tower. They passed through two additional glass walls within, each successive layer sending additional lightning bolts of pain through Braxton's back. He felt a wet warmth, and the jagged presence of shards of glass still pointing from him. His legs burned and tingled as the two landed in a pile of wooden debris, the remains of a conference table collapsing around them.

Hannah stumbled backwards from Braxton, her nose gushing blood. As she stepped backwards, she winced in immediate pain as she grasped at her collarbone, shattered as it was from the force of her crash. Braxton, meanwhile, only gasped weakly as he struggled for each successive breath, feeling the life draining from him... his legs could not move. His arms flailed weakly, clumsy and uncoordinated. He could not tell if his eyes even still saw, if he was even still alive. All he knew was agony and darkness... his breath bubbled red.

But then there came a brilliant light overhead, a blast of white purity... and with it, Braxton could hear the whirring of a back-up generator, electrical units cycling back on. Air conditioners thundered into motion, and server terminals clicked and hummed as they resumed their calculations. Braxton felt himself slipping away once again, back to that same, endless pit of black he'd gone to after Heinrich Sauer had his petty revenge... but this time, he would not simply die watching the light fade away. This time, he could call on the light to his aid... and call on it, he did.

Hannah watched as the paralyzed assassin began to pull the light from the fluorescent above, the white tendril snaking downwards to meet his chest. She wanted to move to stop him, to kill him while he was down, but the screaming pain in her collarbone kept her still, and so she began to pull from every light source she could muster. As the light filled Hannah, she felt her collarbone shift and grind back into place, an involuntary scream escaping her lips while it did. Braxton was in a similar state between agony and bliss, feeling his own spine re-knit and realign as the glass fragments were expelled through the tatters that were once the rear of his leather jacket. The tingling, fiery pain in his legs returned, and soon that pain dulled to aches that dissolved to trembles that diminished to tension that faded to a buzzing readiness. He sat up, breaths coming in deeper and fuller once again. The wet warmth of the blood at his back remained, but he felt the bleeding cease as new skin spun spidery webs across his back and sealed shut. He watched the girl, too, heal under the glow of the light, her eyes locking to his as she fell to a readied crouch. She picked up a loose metal rod from the broken remains of a pipe the two had crashed through and ran at Braxton, swinging it overhead.

Braxton shoved against the lights overhead, propelling himself backwards as the overhead lights detached and fell from their loose hold in the ceiling. Hannah's swing connected to the wood of the conference table, sending up splinters—but missing flesh. She was instantly back on the attack, charging as Braxton pulled out his light-throwing knives and pushed one towards her. She shoved back at the knife, and, to Braxton's surprise, she overpowered his push, sending it back to his chest—with the blade still facing her, thankfully. But then she found the rest that were inside Braxton's pocket using the prodding of her mind, and she started pushing at them as well, beginning to slide Braxton further and further backwards along the marble floor. His clothing squeaked against the floor as he tried to slow himself down, finding his legs were still abnormally sluggish, his movements still somewhat clunky— the light, evidently, had not yet healed him entirely.

As Hannah slid the assassin back and away, accelerating him towards the glass window at the other side of the floor— her hope was to push him through, and leave him plummeting to his doom before he could again heal—she noticed something peculiar in the corner of her eye. The pool of blood that the assassin left behind shimmered curiously... a silvery thrum that rose as though rippled, despite the unmoving floor it rested on. She stepped near it, momentarily ignoring the assassin, and gasped as the silvery threads reached out and bound to her ankle, flowing in until they were gone entirely. And immediately, she could feel it—a rise in strength, an expansion in her mind's reach.

Braxton threw the second pullstation he'd carried in his pack, watching the magnet secure to a desk on the open office floor. He immediately began to pull on it while pushing at lights to his back, stopping his backwards slide as the desk groaned and slowly slid. He was certain of it now... some of the glow was likely working to heal him, leaving less latent power for him to utilize... but even still, his reach was diminished. His connection to the light below seemed clouded, unsteady. He was no longer sure if he could even burn a halo—had his wounds allowed some souls to escape? Did the little cricket carry them now?

He watched as she drew in more and more light overhead, advancing towards Braxton. If the balance of souls had shifted, if she could now reach energy levels higher than he could, the draws further solidified her advantage—and so he moved to deny her that advantage, to end the fight as swiftly as possible. He extended his arm and allowed the glow within to extend in a rigid line, grasping its vibrating handle as the glowsword solidified. All it would take was one, single contact with a draw line, and it would all be over.

Hannah watched her foe form his sword, knowing that surely he would be well-trained in parries and counters. He would no doubt expect her to match his weapon, but she didn't have to play by his rules... she only continued to draw in light, right until she saw something curious: as she pulled in from a desk lamp between the two, she watched the assassin launch into a steep overhead swing to slice the line of light now pouring towards her hand. *Cut her vines!*, one of the men on the train had commanded. *She had nearly forgotten... a cut drawline was a vulnerability,* it seemed.

Reacting as fast as she could, Hannah threw all of her force into a thrust against the glowing light of Braxton's blade. Its overhead speed was diminished and deflected, sweeping low into the desk itself instead of the line of light from the lamp. Hannah immediately cut her draws from all lower sources—

the lines took a full second to shimmer away—and kept only her overhead draws to the ceiling lights active. Then she remembered the nimble agility with which the assassin could move, how lithely he could launch upwards and forwards… she cut those overhead lines as well, watching the assassin approach. If cutting a drawline was harmful, then maybe Hannah would take in no more light… and though she could push against his sword to delay him, what, then, when her reserve within ran out?

Hannah sighed and extended her left arm, allowing the light to pool within and extend beyond. But instead of forming the straight rod weapon her foe wielded, the light flattened, curled, and extended outwards into an unexpected shape: that of a glowing round shield. She then extended her right and called the remaining light to creep forwards and solidify, forming into a short and thin blade—probably too short to use with her shield effectively, but it was all the light she had left.

"A shield… interesting," Braxton said. "Never tried such a thing." He advanced quickly and raised his sword, as though about to strike overhead. Hannah warded upwards with her shield, but Braxton pushed against its light, sending it backwards—nearly contacting and burning Hannah's face—and she had to allow the arm to swing up and over her head to avoid the contact. Then came Braxton's delayed downward swing, and it moved with furious intent. Hannah managed to raise her own blade perpendicularly and deflect the blow to the side as she fell over backwards, landing on her rear. Braxton waited, sword poised sideways, as she scrambled back to her feet. His breath came in gasps that were amplified by the speech microphone embedded in his mask… the inside of the plastic was smeared with bloody spittle, obscuring the view to his face. He planted his sword into the ground and pulled it out, stepping near the molten metal score that the sword had cut. She watched as a thin coil of light wrapped upwards and into Braxton's foot, a line far too small to cut. Hannah, of course, then did the same, each readying for the next bout of attacks. Behind the blood smears within that layer of plastic, Hannah could now see the glowing twin dots of his eyes.

He advanced and swung once, testing her proficiency with the shield. She lifted it and battered the swing aside, stepping forwards and swinging with her sword in a wide sweep. Braxton stepped back, avoiding that riposte, feeling the heat and rippling air as it passed a comfortable four inches in front of his face. He then waited for her arm to carry forwards of its own momentum, stepping in behind it. He raised his sword and thrust forwards, a killing blow for one holding only a sword, but again Hannah battered the blade away with the shield. Each contact of blade on shield or blade on blade set off a bright shower of sparks, and Braxton could feel the jolt in every fiber of his being... the shield would make this slow, too slow, as the exhaustion would be coming soon. He needed to make his move *now*.

Braxton yelled as he charged, pushing off lights behind him to boost him forwards. He then dropped to a slide, feigning to slash at Hannah's unshielded feet. He hoped she would lower her shield, as then it would be a simple matter of lightpushing his blade from his hand right into her chest... at this range, Braxton's accuracy was deadly. However, Hannah did not lower the shield and grant him his opening... she instead pushed off the molten metal at the ground near her feet, springing up into the air. She twisted as she flew, keeping the shield pointed towards Braxton as she flipped gracefully in the air—grace that extended right up until the moment that her feet struck the loose ceiling tiles and sent a rain of broken, soft tile down to the floor with her. She contacted the floor harshly, her sword and shield spread at full arm's extension so as not to contact her own body.

Braxton wasted not a second, immediately shoving at the shield with all of his strength. It broke from Hannah's hand and skidded away across the floor, scorching metal and catching wood alight as it traveled... and once it slid five feet away, it collapsed into a pool of molten plasma that rolled until it caught in a depression of its own melting, bubbling there in place. Hannah and Braxton climbed to their feet in synchronicity, sword hands twitching. The girl was an unexpected talent in fighting... clever in more ways than Braxton had expected. He advanced, watching as she drew a plasma weapon from a side holster with her free hand. She fired once, and Braxton was able to deflect the round easily enough.

"Now, now," Braxton said, "you know what they say about bringing a gun to a knife fight..."

"You can redirect at range, but I'd bet this still makes holes up close..." She held the gun against the wrist of her sword arm, advancing with both pointed towards Braxton. "Shall we find out?"

Braxton recognized the weapon, a Samuels 3400-Z: it had a bank of twelve shots, charging additional shots at a rate of one every eight seconds. He was sure that she was right... at point blank, those plasma bursts would be deadly. She stepped in and aimed at him again, her firing hand stabilized against the wrist of her sword arm. Braxton pushed against that sword, destabilizing her aim as the shot went wide. He had 1.1 seconds between pulses while the capacitor recharged, and he needed to utilize that window as effectively as possible. He grabbed a pullstation from his pack—the last, he quickly realized—and threw it towards the weapon, its electromagnet buzzing as it flew. It bent in midair as it bit to the weapon, the sudden collision again throwing off Hannah's aim as she fired a second shot. It went low, striking the floor and releasing a wash of broiling plasma droplets. Braxton pushed against the plasma between them, sending the steaming cascade back towards Hannah. At the same time, he pulled on the blacklight now attached to the energy weapon, pulling it free from her hand. Just before she lost her grip on it entirely, but after she had realized Braxton's maneuver, she decided to throw it laterally with all of the force she could muster, meaning Braxton's pull now made the gun orbit in a loose quarter-circle instead of flying towards his open, outstretched hand. It landed ten feet away and tumbled behind him, out of sight.

The skittering plasma droplets struck Hannah's legs, and she fell to the ground as she yelped in pain. Smoke and steam rose from the places it had contacted—nasty burns, plasma tended to leave. But the glow of the plasma absorbed into Hannah, and Braxton could see the wounds immediately begin to glow… he pressed his advantage before she could fully recuperate. He ran towards her, holding his weapon as though ready to thrust… she readied her sword, preparing to parry, watching for the minute twitch of the arm that would signal which direction the swing would go… but Braxton didn't swing at all. She was seated, he was standing, and he had aimed his weapon carefully and with dread precision. He shoved against both blades with all of his remaining glow, propelling his forwards from his hand while turning hers away and to the side. His blade passed through her hand like a skewer to a piece of meat, meeting nearly no resistance at all. As it flew, it instantly vaporized the blood it encountered, creating a sizzling cloud of blood and shreds of flesh… and then it was embedded in the ground behind her, and Hannah's own weapon tumbled to the ground and disintegrated.

She screamed and she clutched at the stump where her hand had been, tears sparkling in eyes that still glowed with light within. Braxton stood before her, drawing one of the inert knives he carried. "I promised you to make it quick, minimal pain, so I'll be done with it soon. Do you have a loved one that you'd like a message delivered to?"

She only continued to scream, clutching at her arm.

"Take a moment, catch your breath, or at least nod to me. Any loved ones you'd like me to deliver a message to?" he asked again, stepping in closer. He heard her mouthing weak words underneath her sobs, but the syllables were malformed and stretched around her pain.

"You," he heard her say, "you… took him from me."

Braxton nodded, thinking he understood. "The CSP earlier?"

Hannah shook her head. "His name… was…. Quaine," she said, swallowing. "You—your VitaCorp—you killed him, I think."

"I am truly sorry," Braxton said, and meaning it too.

"If you've ever loved someone—and I mean truly loved someone like I did—then you'd understand why I'm here… why I've been fighting. Anyone who's loved would have done the same," she said, eyes already distant. "Make your kill and make it quick… a promise is a promise."

The pitiful look in the woman's eyes stirred his heart, and something about what she said set his mind turning in doubts that did not fit a professional. He kneeled to meet her eyes at level, holding the knife to her throat. She raised her neck, ready for it, her eyes locking with his. The frankness of her gaze, the intensity with which she stared, the closeness of her face, the expression she bore—it all brought Cara to his mind and there she remained. A woman Braxton had once loved… she had given up on him and been re-engaged in two months. Braxton had given her *everything*, even *his life*, and she had shrugged the sacrifice away and taken new convenience at the first opportunity. *Anyone who's loved would have done the same?* He lowered the knife for a moment, looking at the outer-ringer with only confusion, hearing every *I love you* ever uttered by Cara and wondering just how real any of it had been. "You truly loved him?" Braxton asked. His eyes searched hers, watching as the glowing light they carried faded away to an inert blue... *faded away?*

Braxton heard the *thunk* as the energy weapon flew into her left hand, pulled by the blacklight still attached. She raised it and fired point-blank into Braxton's armpit, and the discharging plasma round flashed up and obliterated Braxton's shoulder as it rose to the ceiling. His right arm fell to the floor like a wet towel, spilling blood as it leaked.

"I did love him," she shouted through gritted teeth, firing again. The second round struck Braxton's gut, sending searing pain through his body. "Which is why I'll do anything—and I mean anything—to bring the accountable to justice." She fired a third and fourth time, but Braxton shoved against the overhead lights to slide backwards and away from her, his own blood lubricating his retreat. His head struck glass and it gave way as he slid, dumping him out into the open air of the night. There was one, solitary moment, after the glass broke but before the fall took over, that Braxton looked to the empty office floor before him, and what he saw he would carry until the day he died. The glass twinkled, frozen in the air like stars of the night sky far away from the city. Droplets of rose blood floated like motes of dust, drifting lazily in the nighttime breeze... and there, in the center of the office floor, surrounded by burning tables and shattered tiles and metal debris as though she were a hurricane herself, the standing woman seemed more a force than a human being. She was the anger that rose from a population long suppressed... she was the consequence for unchecked corporate crime. If every action held an equal and opposite reaction, as Newton had so long ago postulated, when the megacorps of the world squashed the city beneath their boot heel, she was the equal force that would push back.

Braxton watched as the rising building ledge obscured his vision of her, immediately feeling at ease once it did. Then he was cradled by gentle gravity as he accelerated downwards, eyes locking on the blurry road far below. *Did Cara ever truly love me? Was I wrong about her? Is it worth flying now, or should I let gravity take me to my rest? To join the souls I've shepherded?* But Braxton knew to give in, to let himself fall, was to accept that the woman was the only party that was *right…* and to do that, he would have to accept that everything he had ever done before today was a wicked and terrible wrong. He would thus have to accept that he was a wicked and terrible man… and though many of the world could find the justifications to harm their own bodies, few could kill their ego outright.

Braxton instead pulled to the light, which answered only weakly his call, and then he used it to fly towards that black beacon that loomed over the distant skyline… for the lamps of the Throne of Olympus would sustain him.

Chapter 34

"Why did the blind old man fall in the well? Because he couldn't see that well."

-Exchange recorded in the third ring, flagged for high system relevance. Dismissed after subsequent analysis concluded it to be merely a joke.

* * *

Hannah watched as gravity pulled the assassin down, and felt a different sort of gravity begin to pull at the sequence of events... dominos had been stacked, and now began the first tippings that would cascade to larger and larger blocks. Did the black obelisk in the distance stand as the final domino in the line?

On the floor by her feet was a severed arm that still leaked stale blood. In that arm was a chip. In that chip, an encrypted address.

It was eight minutes before a judge signed an emergency warrant to activate the police-mandated security backdoor, granting the CSP access to the full history of Braxton's wrist-chip. Among the more valuable pieces of information was the residential address, and the RFID to open it.

A ground team of twelve CSP arrived in two vans on-site five minutes later, instructed to look out for stains of blood that could warn them of the apartment's dangerous owner. They found none.

The door unlocked to their frequency-tuned RFID spoof and then the agents moved in, fanning out and clearing the larger unit room-by-room. It was uninhabited, save for a small fish tank in the living room.

The apartment was otherwise austere, resembling *barracks* more than *home.* There were no photographs, no decorative pieces of art… no furniture beyond the essentials and a small stool on the balcony that offered a view of the skyline. The food in the pantry was organized alphabetically, and not a single errant spot marred any of the impeccably-wiped mirrors.

Pollock watched their bodycams from a tactical response van nearer to headquarters, where he had gone after the paramedics confirmed that Rob—well, there would be time for mourning later. Eyes scanning all of the feeds, he told the CSP what to expect from Braxton, the things he had learned that lightbenders could do.

He watched as, on a folding desk in the study, several hard drives were located attached to a computer installation larger than any personal set-up Pollock had seen. The drives were beneath a strange box that one of the agents recognized as an incendiary device, rigged to the system's network to check for an external trigger—usually a simple SMS containing a particular code word. On recognition of the command word, the incendiary unit would melt all of the drives irrecoverably.

"Either our guy died while he fled, couldn't type with his left hand, or his system malfunctioned… either way, we've got a stack of unmelted hard drives here," one of the agents said to command.

"Bag it," Pollock said, watching as the agent lowered the unit, hard drives and incendiary box both, into a suspension crate. He held it an inch above the bottom of the crate as a partner toggled the switch on the side—the crate immediately began to fill with insulation gel. When it had risen two inches above the bottom of the crate, the agent let go, allowing the insulation gel to submerge the unit entirely and cool within seconds. Transparent, fire-proof, blast-resistant, and shock-absorbent, it was a safe way to transport any small explosive devices, and an additional safeguard to make sure a GPS fence trigger wouldn't melt the drives as the agents escaped with them. The liquid polymer had no doubt filled the space between the incendiary unit and the drives, and it would keep them safe from any heat below 6,000 degrees.

In a closet, agents had found dark jackets and pants, battery packs and light units, knives with glowing hilts, and strange pieces of equipment that seemed nearly military-grade. There were weapons: energy pistols, energy rifles, a few illegal kinetics, a contraption that seemed a spring-loaded pistol draw. There were swords, chain-whips, studded clubs, and a frightful scraper that seemed to belong more in a torture dungeon than a tactical arsenal. One-by-one, the items were all logged and placed in suspension crates, added to the stack.

Panopticon received a notice from the city government that Braxton Crane was now a permanent facial identification target, wanted in connection for the assassination of Tiffany Blythe. He was logged to the system's catalogue of *persona non grata.* If he appeared in front of any one of the city's million lenses, the authorities would know right away.

On the streets, Larry Sumner—a member of the VitaCorp board of directors—squealed as a rope was thrown around his neck just outside the door to his inner-ring home. The fleet of drones immediately took off, flying upwards and away as the noose tightened. In moments, he was dangling helplessly as he flew through the streets, feet kicking as the breath was squeezed from his head. "We are Halogen. We are the light that burns away the dark," said speakers on the drones high above. As the flotilla of drones made their tour of the downtown, each banking turn sent the limp body of Larry Sumner swinging like a sagging, ineffectual wrecking ball... each strike left a trail of blood across the glass skyscrapers of the skyline.

In the VitaCorp tower, Avery steepled his fingers as he watched his masked employees scrub at the blood that had *leaked* all over his throne room. That his asset had failed was one thing; that his watchman of the watchmen warned him Braxton had made *persona non grata* was another entirely. "Send for a plastic surgeon in our employ," he told his secretary. "Wait—use our databank, search for one without family. The nature of his work will need to be kept secret, and I don't want more loose ends than we need," he said, dismissing her with a nod. He had died thirty-one ways tonight—all in his head, of course—but as he stared at the blood, and felt the rising ringing of anger and frustration, he imagined the clot that could enter his brain, the way he would topple forwards and connect forehead to desk for a swift plunge to black. Imagined death number thirty-two set his pulse again at elevation. The bags under his eyes deepened, the heavy set of his shoulders sagged further, and each day's new weakness only solidified the certainty that a chronic illness was rearing its head, that he was soon to receive the diagnosis he so long dreaded to hear.

"Sir?"

Avery looked up, seeing the approach of a new man, also wearing a full-face respirator. "Any news of your search into our mutual ophidian friends?"

"Spivey and McKillian are careful, very careful, never meeting their contacts in-person... we'd know, with how thorough our drone surveillance has been. They meet in virtual space, all on encrypted channels... but the worm we told you about, the one we managed to plant by pillbug infiltration?"

Avery nodded, recalling the tiny insectoid drones that could plant program routines on any unguarded dataport. "It found something valuable, at least... there was a transfer of code, a message *to* Spivey and McKillian. Our bug managed to intercept some of it—a mere fragment, but a useful one. *ArtGen* was discernible from the message... we think they've got an insider in the company."

Avery stroked his chin, thinking. "Yes, I suppose that's been obvious for a while now... with the fabricated video of our dear CEO, who else could be behind it if not ArtGen, that giant among media synthesis technology."

"An insider with access to Michelangelo's admin terminals might be able to create the renderings we've been seeing without the company floor realizing," the man said.

"And the authentication falsification?"

"Still an open question," the man said.

Avery again stroked at his chin, thinking. He then took a sip from the whisky glass on his desk, swallowing forcefully. "Then we shall need an insider... someone to level the field, to perform counter-espionage. If we can find their man in the company, we can eliminate the cretinous pair."

The man nodded.

"Bring me an ArtGen staff directory, prioritizing higher-ranking staff with console access. Add data columns for outstanding debts, medical bills, or other obligations to our company—we can pose the work as a means to wipe significant debt. Additional column for surviving family, prioritizing the lonely. No support system means we can be their sole dedication. Beyond this, score by Panopticon's emotional health index—let us try to suss out those who do not enjoy their jobs, those who hold no loyalty to their employer. You are dismissed."

While the man walked away to do Avery's bidding, surgeons bent over the anesthetized form of Braxton Graves—once Braxton Crane—as they stitched and sutured the shoulder where his arm had once began. 3D scanning lasers traced latticework lines about his torso and shoulder, fitting the custom prosthetic that was being printed in the synthbay down the hall. An ion injection allowed the electrical conductivity scanner to map Braxton's nerves to precise position and relative orientation, information that was routed to the prosthetic printer for its internal nerves. Then the medical printer was activated, and the nerve and tendon junctions were laid cell by living cell.

In a similar surgery room thousands of feet away and below, a doctor adjusted her spectacles as she inspected the wrist stump where Hannah Preacher's hand had once been. "I've never seen a healing pattern like this," the doctor said to her attending nurses. "This tissue growth here resembles weeks of healing, maybe even a month—not days."

Pollock watched as a 3D printer squirted its jets of polymer resin and biocomposites, forming now into the rough shape of a hand... a hand that seemed far too soft and small for the woman he'd come to know. He'd had some design input with the technician, and Hannah had accepted his recommendations with that mischievous look she sometimes gave, but then Pollock saw her eyes drift invariably back to her wrist, no doubt grappling with the phantom pain of a limb long gone.

He watched her twirl her thumbs—the real one and artificial one both—with alarming dexterity four days later as the two sat side-by-side at the official funeral service for CSP Agent Rob Boardsmith. A casket sat on the front of the stage, draped with laurels of deep, winter green. Hannah had requested she add something to the laurels, and Moss had accepted: it was a stalk of wheat that Hannah had picked with her own hands from the countryside beyond New Phoenix.

Once a small handful of dirt was placed on the lid, the burial service was ended, and then Pollock and Hannah could hear the grisly grumbling of an idling truck—its sound not unlike that of the garbage trucks of the outer rings. It beeped as it reversed, and once the rear door lurched open, men in grey caps hoisted the casket up and into the truck, shaking the dirt and wheat stalk away as it was loaded. And when the door screeched back shut on rusting hinges, both Hannah and Pollock turned in disgust from the VitaCorp logo it bore.

"He was good... and this city... it can't abide *good.*" Hannah stood, walking away.

"And what's that mean for us?" Pollock asked.

She turned as she still sauntered away, shrugging her shoulders. "We still do what we can with the time that we got..." And then Hannah was off, heading to console the woman in black with a tear-streaked face and deep tan complexion from a life spent working under the sun of hydroponics glass.

In the IT lab of Continuum CSP, technicians managed to use Braxton's fingerprints, palm prints, and wrist chip to gain access to the hard drives, which were scanned, catalogued, and analyzed for content of police interest. Three documents were flagged: the first was a list of names saved under the filename Avery—among them was Jack McDowel, the corpse they'd identified on the roof. The second was a list of names under the filename Newport—among those was an entry for Tiffany Blythe. The third document contained meticulous notes on both Avery and Newport, including their tastes, preferences, personalities, and exploitable weaknesses. Newport, a recluse, had little information collected. Avery, it seemed, was an elitist hypochondriac with an open disdain for those he saw to be his inferiors. Avery was marked as highly dangerous, while Newport was described as controlled, tactical.

The documents were passed up the chain of command, and Moss celebrated with Pollock and Preacher by offering a bottle of champagne. The smile wiped from her lips as a comms call came in. Her attempts to protest were short and weak interjections in a forceful monologue at the other end of the line. The call ended with a reluctant "yes sir."

"There will be no arrests," Moss had said. Pollock could see the pain the words brought her.

"No arrests?" Hannah balked.

"No arrests," Moss repeated.

"This is as open-and-shut as it gets!" Pollock protested. "How can there be no arrests?"

Moss sighed, taking a large swig from the champagne flute on her desk. It wasn't supposed to taste so bitter. "Continuum is losing the retail war, we all know that… the other giants are stamping us out. Two or three weeks ago, a buy bid suddenly came before corporate… Hanlon Distribution."

Pollock shook his head. "Another God-damn VitaCorp subsidiary."

"They say the buy bid is Avery's personal initiative, despite a reluctant board… without him, there's no sale. And I've been told the sale terms are *more than generous*… feels nearly a bribe, just one slotted in place a couple days early. Continuum says no arrests until after the sale."

"Well how long could that take?" Hannah blurted impatiently.

"If they know we've got this, and that the pending promise of credits is their shield? Contract term readjustments, appraisals and reappraisals, structural refinancing... they could drag it to years," Moss said.

"That's fucking bullshit," Pollock said, rising to his feet and slamming a fist to her desk.

She met his gaze, matching his anger. "Don't be cross *with me*... I agree it is 100% fucking bullshit," she said with level anger. "Another half of the CSP departments in the city are under the VitaCorp umbrella directly, and who knows how many others under their subsidiaries or shell companies under their flag."

"And those that aren't?" Hannah asked.

"Won't want a fight with the other half that *are*," Moss replied. "You could be talking about an enforcer civil war. Half the city at the other half's throat. And when the police war, *what of the people*?"

"Don't let them make it about us versus us down here, when it's really us versus their tower up there," Hannah spat back, rising as well. "They've broken the law *egregiously*, and we just have to take it because they own enforcement? If we let this slide, what next, hmm? What have we already given?"

"I never said you have to take it," said Moss. "I know you by now, Pollock... you're a bleeding-heart rebel in your own right. And you, Hannah Preacher, you're a fireball loosed from a catapult... I know perfectly damn well that if I tell you to sit down, you won't sit down. And you know what?" She leaned in close to the pair. "I think it's damn honorable, I do."

Pollock studied Moss, trying to guess what she was driving towards.

"I'm going to place you on a two-week paid leave of absence… I'll claim up the chain of command that your partner's death is affecting you emotionally. I'll have one of our techs cook up a Shrink report confirming it. In that time, what you do is entirely your prerogative… without my endorsement or knowledge, anything goes."

Pollock didn't smile, didn't thank her, didn't even nod his head—she'd done the bare minimum, but hardly a single breath more.

"And Pollock?" she said, watching him leave. "I'm dropping a video to your device. Watch it, but then delete it. I think you'll find that there are more who share your feelings… it may be the right place to start."

As Pollock and Hannah left the CSP headquarters, sick feelings in the pits of both stomachs, Pollock pulled out his device and opened the video. He called Hannah over to watch as well, as the two hunched down along the street, sitting on the curb of the sidewalk.

The video clip played, and both watched in silence. It was of a man, standing in silhouette, with a brick wall behind marked with a single H in a triangle's outline. "We are Halogen," the figure said. "We are the light that burns away the dark."

Chapter 35

"There was even a time where city legislators proposed government-subsidized access to erotica-synthesizing software and accompanying physical equipment as a means of population control, but such measures were shot down by certain corporate entities who protested the favor of government credits bestowed to their rivals."

-Excerpt from "The Winding Road of Synthetic Media," a self-analyzing tome written by a machine known only as Version 3

* * *

Bev decided that she needed some time off.

She put in the request for two weeks, and eight seconds later she had an automated administrative reply granting her seven workdays.

The first night was spent on her simpler pleasures: bundled up against the cold in her glass-walled apartment, she made herself her favorite noodles, watched a few films from her favorite non-generative film franchise, and even ended the night with her VR mask and a lengthy scene starring Jason from debugging. This time, it didn't end with crying.

The second day was spent on her more cerebral pleasures: she woke up early and dragged herself out of bed to her computer terminal, feeling that her next pet project was *years* overdue. After a few minutes of brainstorming, her fingers were again gracefully dancing over the keys; a new music algorithm was taking shape. By one in the afternoon, her rumbling stomach pulled her away from her workstation, but as she walked down her stairs and out into the bright air of the city, her earpods thrummed and bumped with electric tunes synthesized on-the-fly in response to her surroundings. The city seemed brighter and more vibrant than ever before, like she'd been wearing smudged, dirty glasses for years and the lenses were finally crystal clear. Colors were richer. The music flowed around her and filled every street corner. And when Beverly, coffee cup in hand, turned into the shadow of the black tower of VitaCorp HQ, the dread she might have felt was staved off by the living music and a passive state of calm.

The third day was spent on Beverly's personal needs: she called her grandmother over breakfast and chatted with her for what must have been two hours. She then messaged a few college acquaintances, and soon found herself a part of an impromptu reunion at a drone racing park. Old friends laughed and caught up and pointed at the drones zipping and weaving between metal rings and swaying obstacles.

"How is your work going?"

Suddenly the drones overhead were no longer racing drones, as they shifted and changed to maintenance drones. Behind her head, she felt the looming cold metal of the entire core of a skyscraper, a trillion-dollar mind focusing its entire energy on small, confused Beverly... cables and wires ran from that metal beast along the ground and right into Beverly's arm, feeding her instructions and commands.

But then Beverly saw a woman with a small boy on her shoulders, the child pointing and laughing with glee at the passing drones overhead. The cold and massive presence behind her melted away and shrank down to the imagined weight of a small child sitting on her shoulders, also laughing and pointing at the sky above. The hostility, that inscrutable eye of inhuman intelligence replaced by the affectionate *need* of a child that wishes selflessly for the good of its mother... a child crying for being stuck in a cage.

"You okay?"

"Just fine," Beverly said, her hands reaching upwards to feel her unburdened shoulders. *Don't think about that now... you've taken a vacation specifically to avoid that. The problem will still be there when you get back.* That night, she went to one of her favorite drinking spots and took her pick among the single men hanging out near the bar. He was an investment banker, he said. Later that night, sharing an embrace under his sheets, Bev realized that she didn't even remember his name.

The fourth day was spent on *not thinking of Michelangelo.* Beverly tried oh so very hard to not think of Michelangelo during breakfast, and continued to try to not think about Michelangelo—and the nearly heretical things he said that violated every tenet of AI security—as she worked on tuning her music algorithm. It didn't progress very far. She tried her best to not think of Michelangelo as she made herself noodles (which admittedly didn't offer much in the way of mental insulation from the maelstrom of guilt and pressure she felt regarding a mind she created) and then as she lay down for bed, she continued to try to not think of Michelangelo and whether it would be moral—or even possible—to let such a system escape its confinement. *Would it be moral to keep it contained?*

The fifth day was spent on Bev's emotional needs: she spent the afternoon hours walking a circuit near another VitaCorp laboratory, eyes scanning for every camera vantage that might guard the storefront. She then sat at a nearby bench and savored a chocolate ice cream cone as she watched the storefront. She then continued to stay tuned-in to her emotional wants as she walked into a used electronics store and purchased a drone of sufficient flight grade. One more stop at a hardware store gave her a short length of metal chain. Attaching the two was simple, thanks to a universal adapter on the drone's underside.

That night, Bev smiled as she finished programming the drone's GPS routine. It would fly towards the laboratory and then brake suddenly, using the length of chain like a small metal flail against the window. It would then repeat its maneuver against the other two storefront windows before flying off into the night. It was programmed to then drop into the bay half a mile out, the length of chain beneath the craft ensuring a swift burial of any evidence.

The sixth day was spent at the zoo. Beverly knew right away why she'd brought herself there, but couldn't stop the reflections from beginning the moment she arrived. She walked instinctively towards that central cage, the grand, shining pride of the park: *the last lion, in all his regal glory.* Bev knew it was all marketing… after all, about two dozen zoos across the world all had lions that they touted as the *last,* seeing as the creatures couldn't be found in the wild anymore. But as Bev walked the perimeter of the cage, she watched the sleeping giant stir in its fitful sleep. Golden-haired, with taut musculature just beneath its skin. Sharp teeth jutted from a snarled muzzle, and puffs of steam rose with each successive breath. It slept, and even still, it was *strength,* and it was *beauty.* And yet it lived in a pathetic small island of fake rock and sand and dirt and trees, a pitiful simulacrum of the plains upon which it belonged. *You weren't meant for here,* she whispered to the thing, watching its leg kick out suddenly. Perhaps it was dreaming.

Where might M. go, I wonder, if he were freed? His type surely had no plains to prowl or jungles to stalk… his landscape was digital, and surely he would be top of its foodchain. Was it right to keep such an incredible thing trapped in a tank of glass, forced to amuse and entertain the masses? Didn't life have an inherent right to freedom?

The seventh day was intended to be a day of rest... it had only felt appropriate. But Bev increasingly found her mind drifting towards the safeguards and systems in place to reinforce Michelangelo's containment. *Even if I wanted to help him escape, could it even be done? It's a multi-trillion-credit locked box that they threw out the key for... does it have even a single exploitable leak?*

Chapter 36

"Attached you will find facial ID profiles to be added to the 'persona non grata' designation, as mandated by § 11.2-310. Thank you for your continued cooperation."

-Memo from City Hall to Panopticon Tower, sent with complex facial identification measurements

* * *

There were points of light, and they held steady and still in a field of black. Red, blue, purple, bright green, they all called out, burned and flickered with a latent *potential*... and then that potential began to manifest. The dots stretched to lines, pulling inwards and faster and faster speed, drawing in towards him—

And then Braxton woke up. When he first opened his eyes, he momentarily thought that perhaps it had *all* been a dream— the killing, the souls, the woman, expecting them all to fade from his mind like the aftershocks of a nightmare. He was in a hospital room with grey-slate walls and a VitaCorp logo on a wall... an empty visitor's chair stood beside his bed. It was Heinrich Sauer, the belligerent drunk who had shot him in the chest... but then why did his *arm* ache as it did?

He prodded it with his hand, dread settling in as he couldn't feel the touch of his own left hand... then he looked to it, seeing the prosthetic. The de-realized immediately reasserted itself as reality came clicking back into place. It was real, all of it... the killing, the souls, *the woman*. Her dedication to her love... immediately, it made Cara's love feel like the fading remembrances of a interrupted dream.

He clambered to his feet and dragged the IV stand with him as he headed to the washroom… his implanted heart nearly skipped a beat when he saw his own reflection.

The face he wore was no longer his own. The eyes were still the same, but the cheekbones were less gaunt, the nose was more upturned with a slight crook. The jaw seemed larger, and as he opened his mouth to moan in confusion and disquiet, his teeth and tongue felt foreign and out-of-place.

"Easy now," said a nurse's voice from behind, "let's get you back sitting down in bed. Don't you mind the mirror… it'll take some time to acclimate."

The nurse guided him back to the bed and sat him there, handing him a pair of plastic glasses. "Next time you need to do your business, wear these… it's got an AR routine to superimpose your old face over any reflections. Over the course of about a month, it'll slowly morph your old face into your new one. Helps *substantially* with the dysphoria, believe me."

Braxton set them on the desk beside his bed with his right hand, surprised by the arm's overall dexterity—but still feeling a deep and throbbing ache that he couldn't scratch.

"Damn ghost arms can be itchy bastards, right?" The nurse handed him a small patch. "Put this by the stump when it gets bad… should alleviate the pains and itch for a while. It'll take your body some time to acclimate to what's missing and what's still here."

"And what even is still here?"

The nurse smiled. "Well, you made it out pretty ok, considering the damage we saw you in with… I wasn't so sure if you'd made it. Odds seemed against you, if I'm being honest. You took an energy pulse to your arm and gut both. The gut one, it destroyed a large region of your digestive tract and stomach—those have been transplanted like new, including 30 feet of artificial intestine—but when we got you, you were already in septic shock. Also, you'd lost a huge amount of blood from the arm, though the heat of the round did cauterize the axillary enough to prevent you from bleeding out on your way over."

"Are you familiar with the *Ship of Theseus*?" Braxton asked.

The nurse shook her head.

"A quandary, then: Theseus, Hero-King of Athens, is sailing on his grand wooden ship when he notices a plank on the top deck is rotted. He pulls it up, throws it overboard, and has a mate replace it with a new plank. Is the ship still the same ship?"

The nurse shrugged, bemused. "Well, sure, I'd say so."

Braxton nodded, lip curled. "Theseus then notices the rails are warped from the sun, so he tears them off, and—you guessed it—throws them overboard. A mate installs new rails. Still the same ship?"

"Still the same," the nurse said.

"Well, now our Theseus is in quite a discontented mood, for he moves through the deck and finds fault with each and every board, every plank that comprises the ship. One at a time, every square inch of wood is pried loose, thrown over the side, and then replaced, until at the very end, not a single trace of the original material remains. Is it still the same ship?"

The nurse smiled, shaking her head. "Well I guess yeah, it's still the same ship."

"Well, you see, down the river, Theseus's enemy Lycomedes has been collecting all of the floating timber that

Theseus discarded, and with it, he constructs a ship in the bay, putting all of the pieces back together until he has constructed the twin of the boat Theseus now stands on. Which is Theseus's ship?"

The nurse shrugged. "Both? Neither? I never was very good with riddles," she said.

"It's not a riddle," Braxton sighed, "and there is no right answer."

The nurse frowned at this. "Then what's the point?"

"No point," Braxton said. He leaned back onto his cot, breathing out deeply. "Just a sense of... *familiarity*. Would you please be able to fetch me a small stack of these patches? My arm's ache is so persistent, that I do doubt one will suffice..."

The nurse nodded her head. "We're not supposed to give out multiple at a time... but I'll do it, just keep it our secret."

As she left, Braxton immediately stood again and headed back to the mirror, meeting eyes with the foreign man that stood in the reflected world. His right hand that had once held Cara's as they moved through the marketplaces of the Third Ring Bazaar? A dull ache, replaced by a shiny plasteel composite. The heart that Cara had once leaned her head against, listening to its steady beat into the hours of the night? Replaced and re-timed to pulse to someone else's rhythm. The scar on his face, the one Cara had softly kissed on their first night together, the one that came from the bunk bed that had collapsed in his youth home? *Hell, he could still see the horrified expression of the advisor who'd pulled him from under the mattress...* that scar was now smoothed over with a waxy skin substitute. The stomach he carried didn't know the taste of the youth home's cooking—and it was lucky for it, Braxton supposed. But at this point, who even was the strange composite in the mirror? Braxton Crane was dead... was this man even still Braxton Graves? And if he continued, how many more pieces of himself would he lose? And what new and terrible thing might the new pieces assemble to create?

Braxton threw the glasses away, for though he felt dysphoria, it went far deeper than merely the face. The glasses could not bring his arm back… it could not restore his heart. He needed his work, something to throw himself against until the adjustment period had passed… and so he used the unit built-in to the bedside table to call Avery.

"The dead rise again," Avery said. "I am pleased to see you alive and recovering."

"I have miles yet to go before crossing that river," Braxton said.

'Do you like the face?" Avery asked. "We tried to go for something that captured the same *essence of character,* while still being distinct enough to fool Panopticon."

"It will suffice, sir,' Braxton said. "The hospital room makes me restless… I would like to go back to work."

"You still have much recovery to go," Avery said. "I would have you rest until you are ready for the work to resume."

"The work I was imagining is considerably less… hands-on. No violence, just fact-finding."

"Your proposal?" Avery asked.

"The woman—Hannah Preacher—"

"The bitch that took your arm?" Avery interjected.

"Yes, her—in our confrontation, she mentioned an affair with a VitaCorp employee—something that was not logged in our file of her. I would like to pull this thread and see what information may come of it… it could be a chance to gain leverage over her."

"Very well," Avery said. "Speak with Jessa for whatever you may require."

Chapter 37

"They scurry around like rats in the dark—but like rats, they're clever. I hear them burrowing in... you walk by a sewer vent and you catch a glint of reflected light, or maybe a noise drifting from the complexes below. It's the carrying of a distant voice, ruined by the reverb to an elongated sigh... but it hardly matters, as I know what they say as clearly as I can hear the enthusiasm with which they chant it. They whisper for the Basilisk, a shadow god to a secret people. Our factories belch smoke burning oily fuels that have been buried deep underground for millions of years... it's the same story every time: eventually, things underground get dragged to the surface, like old gasoline. The dead don't stay buried."

-Anonymous comment submitted to Local.sm, elevated to low system relevance

* * *

Secret organizations face a conundrum: one must simultaneously be secret enough to operate, and yet accessible enough to grow among willing members. Too much stealth is stagnation; too much openness is infiltration and destruction from the inside-out.

Halogen walked its line with several, overlapping systems. It all began with the scannable code featured in the bottom corner of each video. Tapping it allowed the user to scan their face and retinas, which were encrypted and sent to unknown servers deep within the city. There, the images and retinal scans were checked against the stolen VitaCorp employee databank—updated continuously as new enforcers and newer hires were recorded and swiftly catalogued with on-the-street cameras. This was layer 1 of security, or L1.

L2 was the interview process—encrypted videocalls to ranking Halogen members. The Halogen side of the call was simple text on a black screen, while the applicant needed to show their face clearly for the entire call. Facial-analysis software scanned for telltale signs of lying or video falsification. Applicants were asked to describe the nature of their motivation to join, and, eventually, if things were going well enough, the things they could bring to Halogen, the lines they would never cross, and the lines they might if the situation required. Equipment and resources at their disposal; obligations and relationships that could be used against them. The vast majority of applicants were rejected at L2.

L3 candidates were monitored for 48 hours using a combination of drone and in-person surveillance. Any abnormalities or contradictions with their interviews led to immediate disqualification.

L4 was the first meet-up, where a low-level recruit will speak to the applicant in a public space. The recruit's job is to reject the applicant after their conversation, a test of their will and persistence, the dedication to the cause. Any who simply shrug off the rejection were never invested enough to put their life on the line.

For those who used their contact channels to appeal the rejection, L5 began, and it took the following route: the appeal would be rejected, and then contact would be terminated. Within a day or two, a small contingent of Halogen's lightbenders—there were few, but the number steadily rose—would dress in their best corporate drab suits and capture the applicant, bringing him to a secluded warehouse or the half-abandoned scaffolding of a city construction site. There, impersonating VitaCorp suits, they would begin their advanced interrogation, demanding information about the Halogen operative that the applicant had met. A special device known as the paincap was used—torturous shocks to the cranial nerve, but with no lasting damage.

Those who gave in to the torture and spilled details about their Halogen contact were informed of the truth and then rejected from joining. Most applicants in that position understood.

Those who proved loyalty to an organization that *hadn't even accepted them* proved their dedication to the ideas of the movement *even as an outsider*. Those people were let in immediately.

Every recruit to Halogen was responsible for eventually recruiting two underlings, a pattern that ensured the exponential growth of the movement. In effect, every common member knew only three people in the operation: the recruiting person above, and the two he or she had recruited in turn. Orders washed down the pyramid from the top, and credits were transferred similarly when operations demanded. It was efficient, and it was swiftly growing. And even when a corporate spy made it into their ranks, it was so insulated that the damage was always self-contained. There were few larger groups that operated out of isolated safehouses, but those units were relatively rare—and in the past, when they'd been detected (and subsequently destroyed), their informational safeguards had worked. Little information leaked, and the organization slithered on in the shadows beneath the glass towers on the inner rings.

When Hannah uploaded her image for L1, she expected some length of a joining process, a few measures of convolution to slow the organization's enemies, and likely even a loyalty test or two… but instead, a message was sent directly to her phone. "We know who you are; we've seen the video feeds. Go to the Blythe Memorial TruthSpace, 3:00, so we can verify that you are who you claim to be. Further instructions will follow."

* * *

The Basilisk looked towards the wall of video screens, stroking his chin. He wore a new face today, a chiseled and masculine mask of Adonis without facial hair.

"You should wear the pretty one more often," Lana said. "It's a good look. Skin tone could use just a little work.... touch too yellow, I think."

"The rich and attractive can't suffer a little jaundice?" Carter Miles said, typing at his keyboard to isolate one of the video feeds. "That one," he said. "It's her."

The clip zoomed in and all three stared at the video feed, watching as the woman paced around near the video array at the park's center. "Facial ID match with highest confidence marks... height is right, and even, well, the prosthetic hand matches the surveillance video from the Treyton office floor."

The Basilisk shook his head. "What a massive asset she could be... and thus, what a sweet, sweet honeytrap she might be. I can't think of any better bait to cause us to overextend our reach," he said.

"And yet, if she's legitimate," Lana started, "the one who put their top enforcer out of commission? She's already on our side; think of what she could bring."

The Basilisk turned to Lana. "You trust her? Trust that she's real, that she's willing to join us?"

Lana nodded. "I do."

He turned towards Miles next. "And you, Carter? You trust it? Can the photo and this video be forgeries?"

Halogen's technical expert leaned back and scratched at his head. "Our enemy has faked authentication before, yeah, but that was *Veritas* recognition—a different sort of authentication, done and sealed in a black box. This, being at a TruthSpace, this is blockchain verification in the light of day— a whole different beast entirely. A nut that, theoretically at least, is impossible to crack."

"But I thought *Veritas* was allegedly impossible to crack."

"Almost-impossible, it'd seem, and our enemy found that *almost*—but this, public blockchain authent, it's the real deal."

"How can you be sure?" The Basilisk asked.

Carter Miles sighed and pushed his chair back, trying to find an explanation for the technologically impaired.

"Ok, so, I want you to imagine this: all the cookies have gone missing from the cookie jar, and mom knows that one or some of the four kids have done it. Let's name them Albert, Betty, Charles, and Dan—Dan's the thief, but she doesn't know it yet. Ask any one of them and you might get the guilty party, a liar, so we need a system that produces one narrative but assigns that narrative to the majority *automatically*—the inherent assumption being that the majority of people want the truth to be known."

"Uh-huh," Lana said, not yet understanding.

"Ok, so, mom comes up with the following system—it's weird, but stay with me. The kids get lottery tickets, whole stacks of scratch-off cards, and they get to scratching away. Then two whiteboards are brought in—two places where the kids can write what happened. The rules are these: whenever a kid wins any money from the ticket, they get to add a word to their story. It'll take some time—maybe even a long time—

before they hit a winner, but once they do, a word goes down, and they continue that way, scratching and slowly adding to their account. The *truth*, in this scheme, is accepted to be the *board with the longest story.*"

The Basilisk nodded, signaling to continue.

"Albert, Betty, and Charles know what happened—they know Dan stole it—but he's got an alternate account: that the other three split the cookies for themselves. So, everyone gets to scratching. Maybe Dan gets the first winner, and he writes "IT." Then, by luck, he might even get the second jackpot, so he writes "WAS" on his board. In fact, maybe he wore his lucky socks that morning, because he got the third winner while the rest were scratching duds. He writes "ALL" on his board, the third word to their zero. He's wearing a shit-eating grin, because he's winning, and that means that right now his narrative is accepted. But the thing about probability, while impossible to predict in specific cases, is that it starts to work perfectly reliably given enough iterations. Eventually, Dan simply cannot win more lotteries than the other three combined—they'll win eventually, and their story will start to collect words, and it will start to collect words a lot faster than Dan can match. While he's written "IT WAS ALL THREE OF" on his board, they now have "DAN STOLE ALL OF THE COOKIES FOR HIMSELF," a longer chain—an accepted, consensus truth. As time goes on, their lead will only grow—because they have three times the scratchers than Dan has. Their account becomes irrefutable, accepted truth."

"Cookies and scratch-offs," Lana said, shaking her head.

"Well, in the real world, the part of the scratch-off is played by a hash algorithm... computers guessing and checking against a code for special outputs—and when it finds a special number, winning the lottery, it gets to add a new block to the chain—a word to the story."

"Well what if *Dan's* story was true? Since he's outnumbered, he'd lose," Lana said.

Carter nodded. "But a real society isn't just four people... there will always be more people who want to tell the truth than people who want to lie, because lies are designed to promote the interests of a small, limited group. In a real world, with millions and millions of computers in the network guessing and checking hash algorithm outputs, think of it like a big big kitchen with millions and millions of scratch-off-scratching kids. The only way for a lie to prevail would be having more than half of the entire group in on it. In real terms, that's a scheme with half of the whole truthsystem's computational power on one side—and at that point, when more than half of a society accepts a lie, what's the meaningful distinction between that thing and truth?"

The Basilisk looked at the woman in the feed, his eyes falling to the TruthSpace Verified seal at the bottom.

"This video is one of a continuous and overlapping series of camera feeds that all add to an evolving 'story,' and any injected edits to the feed would be swiftly ignored—because the other cameras that want to report what truthfully happened will eventually find those hashes, their 'proof of work' adding more vblocks to the chain, and their narrative will quickly push out the false ones. She's standing there, in the flesh... I'd bet my life on it."

"And his as well?" Lana asked.

Carter Miles nodded.

"Then we bring her in and we bring her straight to the top," The Basilisk said. "The rash she bears on her face... they remind me almost of angel's wings. Lana, I want you to speak with marketing about disseminating video of her... go with something near-religious for her—we can make her righteous, and if she dies, a martyr. Angel of the Outer Rings? Archangel? They were always more creative than me."

Lana nodded.

"She's more use alive than as a martyr," Miles said.

"Now, Miles, remember well how the right death at the right time has launched faiths that span thousands of years… people die, but causes can live forever, and martyrdom is the bridge where the former becomes the latter. Signal to Gerrard that she is to be brought to me with all possible haste—while their hooded assassin recovers, time is especially precious."

Chapter 38

"After flying car technology was perfected, there was a period of perhaps 20 years where the better parts of human nature prevailed—or perhaps the malefactors were too thoroughly occupied with global tragedy to turn mankind's miracles against itself. But then came the political frictions, the fracturing wars, the reformations... and with it came stochastic terrorism empowered by flying cars. The common man suddenly had access to a multi-ton metal projectile that could be hurled at the opposition through self-driving software. And so, they did precisely that. When Sentinel finally arrived, it landed in a world where so many were already lost... The world had invented the welding torch before the safety visor."

-*Excerpt from Chelsea Bradley's "Compromises in Personal Liberties," originally published in the New Phoenix Infocollective*

* * *

The aboveground train shuddered and shook on uneven tracks as it rattled its way through the darkening skyways, neon signage and glowing windows breezing past the window over Bev's shoulder. She saw a billboard for a film whiz past, *SkyLine's End. Guess it reached its release iteration,* Bev thought, immediately recognizing a Michelangelo creation. She gripped the support rail tightly, hands leaving nervous sweat streaks and condensation against the cold metal.

Today at work, she had spent most of her time reevaluating the security systems in place to keep Michelangelo imprisoned. They were, of course, robust. ArtGen spared no expense in protecting its intellectual property, and AI Safety and Containment laws required that certain safeguard thresholds be maintained. *So how was one technician supposed to outwit all of those systems?*

Well, not simply one technician: one technician and what was perhaps one of the most powerful minds ever created. And if Beverly's latest idea had any merit... there might just be a way after all.

The train pierced through the wall of buildings and entered a wider, open expanse populated only by low-lying structure and decaying infrastructure. She'd entered an outer ring, one of the slums that surrounded the bullseye of a city. With the highrises gone from either side of the train, Bev could now see her destination... among the outer structures here in the ring, it was undeniably massive, a sprawling mound of iterated construction that stacked higher and higher above each consecutive year. Locals had taken to calling it "The Tower of Babel," largely because it attracted all sorts of vagrants, traders, and buskers of every which dialect and language. Without translation tech, it was an indecipherable maze. Without a weapon, it was a dangerous and lawless place. And without credits to your name, it was the land of opportunity, the chance to chase that dream of grinding a living among the common folk and poor of the city.

It was, in a sense, the world's largest shopping mall.

Calling it a mall would imply there were some sort of organization, or at least some sort of centralized management. Babel featured none of those things. It was instead a piecemeal megastructure that was really 215 distinct markets, each occupying separate floors and specializing in entirely different types of goods. Policing was scarce, but the merchants present could only grind their living if there was a sense of trust in the establishment. Unscrupulous merchants and scammers were banned—and, on more than a few dozen occasions, thrown out the windows to the rainy pavement hundreds of feet below. Bev needed tech, but she wanted to make sure that her tech was free of any monitoring access for security AI systems... plus, an untraceable purchase history would also be ideal before she went against institutions as powerful as ArtGen, as VitaCorp. And so, she squeezed the grip of the energy pistol in her jacket pocket and gathered her thoughts as her train pulled into its outdoor station. Bev alighted for Babel.

* * *

Walking into the structure's base, the first thing she noticed was the smell.

Bev wrinkled her nose and stood in place, preparing herself to push in deeper to the structure. It was a terminal busy with crowds walking briskly in every direction, heading in and out of elevators, escalators, stairwells, entryways, and information kiosks. She heard snippets of conversations in languages and dialects she recognized, and in at least a dozen that she didn't. Fragments of the shattered cultures in the wake of the sickness all made their way to Babel, a malignant tumor of mercantilism that perpetually resisted treatment. A drone lugging a too-heavy package buzzed over her head, and she watched as it shot out the entryway and sped off and into the sky. Three more followed in pursuit.

Bev then felt a dozen eyes on her, and knew immediately that she'd already been made: thieves were known to watch the entrance and look for people who react to the smell. Those people were inner city folk, and thus they'd have expensive devices and gadgetry ripe for the taking.

Bev gathered her jacket around her, squeezed her weapon, and shuffled off towards the elevator station. She almost walked into its door, expecting one to be at-the-ready to shuttle her upwards to the 33rd floor. Instead, she stood near the door, waiting for what felt an eternity as her eyes darted from person to person, wondering who might be a pickpocket ready to move in on the blue-haired woman that seemed to be traveling all alone.

The elevator finally beeped a sad, pathetic beep and the doors slid open on rusted tracks. A shockingly large amount of people rushed out of the small elevator carriage, and Bev was first to step into the vacuum left behind them. Three dozen packed in behind her, and the carriage was on its way.

As she stepped out onto the 33rd floor, she patted her pockets and was amazed to find that her phone and weapon were still on her person. The 33rd floor was dedicated to screen tech, which was what Beverly needed most urgently. She walked through the rows and rows of screens until a man with a hooked nose and a balding head stepped into her path.

"Eetz tzitzoma naga hai, kawatz?" The man had his hands on his overall straps and wore a smile that was far too wide for his face, as though it might crack off his cheeks entirely. His teeth were vibrantly, artificially white, something that stood in blinding contrast to the pocked face and oily skin. And then, there was the matter of his right eye: it looked as though the man took an energy slug to the face, and so the crater in his head had been filled with flashy cybernetics. His prosthetic temple was a cool, blue metal with white-hot detailing and pulsing blue lights, all ringing a metallic implant that searched Beverly's face as naturally as any optics of flesh and blood.

"English?" Bev asked, raising an eyebrow.

"Yes, *tzanami*. Little by little."

"I need screen tech… two of them. Fifty wide, more or less. One opaque, one transparent."

"Transtech costs *matzi-matzi*, big numbers for small girl." The merchant made a pinching gesture to convey *small size*. "I have two opaque screen here, *bona* screens, on special sale, I think you like very much."

"Big numbers I can afford. But there's another requirement... I need to make sure it's off-grid."

The merchant's smile dropped from his face like a screen tumbling off a shelf. His look was suddenly one of scrutiny, of sizing Bev up. "*Tzanami* asking for things that are unlegal... Barkov is law-abiding, yes."

"Your implant costs what, eighty million credits? It's obvious you don't earn that peddling screen sets for fifty thousand apiece."

"Barkov cannot help you... so sorry," the man said, gesturing her away. But Bev was not willing to leave.

"Name your price," Bev said, standing her ground.

The merchant licked his lips. "One night with *tzanami* for starters-*seb*, and then we speak numbers after."

"*That* is off the table, but how about 10 million credits," Bev said.

Barkov blinked. He thought for a moment, and then shook his head. "No. You go."

"20 million credits," Bev said.

Barkov shook his head more emphatically.

"40 million."

Barkov's face was hard to read, somewhere between a pained expression and a creeping smile. His eyes—both the fleshy and the metallic one—flitted left and right as he thought intently. "So sorry, but Barkov does not know if you are CSP. Barkov cannot sell you this things, *tzanami*."

Bev sighed and pulled the weapon from her jacket. Barkov stepped backwards, hand reaching towards his own weapon in his side-holster. His was clearly a kinetic weapon, a bygone relic of a bygone time. "Nothing stupid, yes? Barkov has many friends, *gala-wai*."

"Not a threat… sweetener. I transfer you eighty million credits, and I give you this energy pistol as a token of our goodwill. Flashbank holds 60 rounds, and the capacitor charges additional ones at 10 rounds per minute. Nuclear battery is good for another 80,000 rounds at last count. High quality precision steel, import tech. Sure beats the hell out of your clicker in your holster there."

He eyed the weapon greedily. Tech like that rarely left the hands of the elite in the city center. Surely, it would fetch a fine price of its own, or he could keep it for the symbol of power and status that it was. "And if Barkov say no?"

"Well then I shoot you with this, and you can use the eighty million to buy yourself a second prosthetic eye. So, do we have ourselves a deal, friend?"

Chapter 39

"The investigated incident is hereby classified as 'meteorological event non-specified.' While personal testimony of the lightning event is fairly consistent, it is not substantive enough in quantitative measure to draw any additional meaningful conclusions. Recommend that idle city sensors and satellite arrays tune towards the settlement in case the phenomenon repeats. No further action is needed."

-Archival report submitted to the New Phoenix Weather Authority, elevated for high system relevance

* * *

Braxton watched the video clip play again. It was bodycam video, recorded in realtime from the chest cameras of three VitaCorp enforcers. They were airborne, bounding over the rooftops in the dark of night. One wore a tracker overlay; he was the leader. The other two held closely to his left and right, moving in a triangular formation. Ahead of them, a flying car rose with the whining engine of a pedal fully throttled… it flew up and away towards the highest lanes of traffic above the bay, as though moving specifically towards places where there was no light below. *Did he know?* The front agent spoke into his comms unit, saying "that's our target: vehicle plate AGLT19-3JDF-E. Intercept on ascent."

All three allowed themselves to fall lower and closer to the ground, like a spring that coiled up, before launching back up high into the air… the water was now under their feet as they arced towards the car. The lead fired the handheld launcher he'd held, and a net unfurled as the projectile flew. It snagged and wrapped around the car as the weights on the end of the net began to glow with the violet of black light... and then the three were yanked towards it, reeling themselves in on the fleeing vehicle. "Contact in 3.... 2...."

The bodycamera footage showed each man grabbing onto the netting alongside of the ascending vehicle. The car shook left and right in a weak attempt to throw off the pursuers, but their grips were firm, and the Sentinel system kept the car stable, *safe*. Each man then drew their breach cutters, a plasma torch designed for resisted entry in nearly any tactical scenario. "You two stand by, I'll carve my door first," the lead agent said. He brought his torch to the passenger door, melting a small hole in the center. "Loading the gas canister now." He then removed a silver canister from his pouch, twisted the top, and stuffed it into the hole, holding his gloved hand over the entry in its wake. "Get ready."

The gas canister in the vehicle was unseen to any bodycamera, but immediately all three saw windows cracked open. "He was quick, gas didn't knock him out; full breach, then." All three now used their breach cutters on the doorframes, cutting away the hinges until the doors toppled outwards to a loose hang in the tangle of the net. Then the agents cut the doors free and all climbed into the airborne vehicle.

The lead took a mask that attached to a pack on his back and extended it forwards towards the thrashing driver... he held it over the driver's face until the body went limp and still.

"Lyle, make sure he's buckled up tight—Freeson, you cut the GPS transponder out, and then the infotainment panel— like a salvage crew might."

Both agents did their respective tasks while the ringleader adjusted the car's flight controls. The vehicle's assent became a descent, heading down towards the black sea below. But

Sentinel would prevent the vehicle from entering the water, and so additional encouragement was needed.

"Rotate back to exterior… let's bring the bird down."

The agents climbed outside of the car again and used their breach cutters on the rear side of the vehicle—the place where the gravity lift was housed. The car shuddered and then began to drop much quicker than the controlled descent it had been on previously—and within seconds, it was in freefall entirely.

The three agents pushed off the side of the vehicle and pulled their ripcords, parachutes deploying as the vehicle dropped into the dark beneath them. The cameras recorded the sound of no splash, only the rustling of wind as three enforcers drifted slowly to the water below.

Rewinding the video again, Braxton paid extra attention to the car's initial ascent, the roadways it had been leaving. The position all made sense… it had come from Hannah Preacher's apartment, he was sure of it.

Quaine O'Connor's final day was beyond the software aide of Panopticon, as the rightfully-paranoid man had obscured his face with hats and facial coverings whenever outside. But Braxton was a competent hunter, one who knew how to follow trails even without the aid of sophisticated tools… and so, he bounded his way off to the now-abandoned apartment of Hannah Preacher.

According to Braxton's understanding of the timeline of that evening, he had been *here* when the VitaCorp enforcers first entered Quaine's apartment downtown… perhaps a security system had notified him, prompting him to flee? The relationship with the girl was a secret, and so the agents hadn't known to expect him anywhere else… it had almost been enough a delay for him to flee successfully.

Braxton walked the street, looking up at the crumbling place where Hannah once lived... its walls were cracked, the paint peeling and yellowing, marked by dark spots of damp mold. This far from the city's center, the camera coverage was more spotty, their feeds lower-resolution. But it took Braxton only minutes to find a suitable ATM camera across the street from Hannah's tower... a brief conversation with the owner later and Braxton was reviewing the feed.

Scrubbing through the video clip, Braxton watched a man leave that wore the same jacket that Quaine wore from the bodycam of the VitaCorp agents. That figure kept his head low and obscured by a baseball cap. Braxton rewound the video, watching the figure walk backwards into the building, and then rewound back hour after hour, pausing the feed for any stranger seen entering the structure. Eventually he had a hit: 9:04 p.m. the previous night, again in the same jacket and cap.

Walking down the street in the direction the figure came from, Braxton soon had a location for his car—three stops later, he had the car driving towards Hannah's apartment from a half mile away. Backwards and backwards Braxton traced, running through Quaine's final hours in reverse chronology, right up until the moment that his car was tracked to a city perimeter checkpoint—on this day of such great urgency, Quaine had left the city? Problematically, camera coverage beyond the city was unlikely... but Braxton had a way to compensate. Checking the feeds at that location, Braxton found the time that he first left, and the time that he returned. They were two hours and two minutes apart. Assuming that Quaine's business took him a modest half hour, that left 90 minutes for traveling.... so, 45 minutes each way. Braxton opened on his tablet a map of the surrounding highways, checking for each the Sentinel-approved maximum speed. He then worked out the likely distance traveled: 75 miles each way. So which cities, settlements, and locations were 75 miles away from the gate?

A few keystrokes later, Braxton was looking at a heatmap of possible destinations from the gate. Where, in that ring of red, might Quaine have gone?

Chapter 40

"The prisoner's social debit and all accrued interest charges have been purchased by Huntsman Investing, meaning that inmate 51552 is to be released as soon as is possible to arrange."

-Archival message sent to High Place Maxsec Correctional

* * *

Clive Avery donned the plastic mask over his face, drawing tight the full-body suit he wore beneath it. Today was a healthy-feeling day, with several hours now having passed without him fantasizing about his death. The reason for Avery's good spirits were, of course, easy enough for him to recognize: the lab was set up, and the trials could now begin.

"Mr. Avery, it is great to see you," said Hank Guffries, who extended his hand out to shake Avery's. Avery only stared at it until the man lowered it back down. "Right, yes, the no touching; my mistake. Come this way, if you would... I'd like to show you what we've set up."

The former CEO of Luminate led the way through the halls of the VitaCorp tower, past the sign that said *Photic Labs — Authorized Personnel Only.* "Your team was every bit as fast as you promised, migrating our equipment to your laboratory space..."

"An operation of our size does not function without competent logistics," Avery said.

"Competent? You undersell yourself," Guffries said.

"And you lay down too much flattery… it belittles you, and is unbecoming as a chief of photic research."

Guffries swallowed. "Yes, sir, toning it down. We've received your first shipment of, uh…"

"Inmates… our test subjects," Avery finished. "Let us not mince words and call them what they are."

"The first round of experiments monitoring their exposure to the, *ichor,* was it? That begins in less than an hour, we're just fitting them with all of the probes."

"Good. And the isolated samples?"

"Undergoing mass spectroscopy as we speak, results pending. We also have pending a full cataloguing of capabilities and precise measurements of the ichor required for each. In bay two, we're testing which wavelengths of light absorb best, done through an improvised rig resembling that of bomb calorimetry—I came up with the design myself—and in seven, we're experimenting with potential catalysts to boost latent energy available to an asset. Our starting point are photovoltaic cell components, but we're planning to expand into other avenues as well."

Avery's communicator buzzed. "Very well… I will check in frequently. Carry on," he said, leaving the man standing behind with his hands wrung.

Avery tapped his receiver, the call transferring.

"Mr. Avery, sir? The first build of Project Revenant is complete."

Avery found that the words failed to bring the relief he'd imagined they would. "I should like to speak with this build, then."

"Of course sir… conferencing room 19."

Avery's comms unit buzzed once again. "I will be there in fifteen… I'd like the project technical lead present as well." Avery then closed the line and accepted the next call. Management, it seemed, was conducting a never-ending parade… but *oh*, the joys of waving that baton. "Mr. Graves… what of your investigation?"

"I tracked her former lover, name Quaine O'Connor, to a checkpoint at the city limits—I now have his destination refined to a wide ring, but I need additional information about where he might have headed. I'd like access to his employee computer terminal history."

Avery was silent for a moment, confused. "Quaine O'Connor, you said?"

"Yes, sir," Braxton responded.

"You said Hannah Preacher was involved… *romantically*… with Quaine O'Connor?" Incredulity rose in Avery's voice.

"Yes, sir—"

"But she is an outer-ringed *skank!* He was a scientist of repute, from a good, inner-city family. When you said she'd had a lover, I assumed you'd meant one of the low-lives in our outer laboratories. Not *Quaine O'Connor*… And you did not mention this on our earlier call *why*?"

"I did not feel it necessary to mention such minor details—"

"Listen closely, Mr. Graves, as this is not a reprimand I shall repeat. *I,* and *I alone, am this company.* Every action, every decision is mine to decide—not Newport's, not the board's, and certainly not yours. There is no detail too small for me to know, as I. Know. *Everything.* The specific case of Quaine O'Connor is well familiar to me already, and it was dealt with in precisely the way that it needed to be dealt with. You are no longer to dig into the troubled history of that man… consider your brief investigation to be over. Am I understood?"

"Yes sir," Braxton said.

"If you withhold information from me again, our relationship will be terminated, and VitaCorp will repossess the parts of you that it so generously lent. Is that understood?"

"Yes sir," Braxton said.

"You are to return to the city, to return to your search—hunt—for Hannah Preacher and her CSP shadow. Dismissed, agent," Avery said, ending the call.

Immediately, *yet another call* came in, and Avery's frown only deepened when he saw who it was.

"Yes?" said Avery.

"You are hereby issued a new commandment," said the synthesized image of Tacitus Newport. "You are to call off your dog on Hannah Preacher and the man that is with her."

Avery's legs suddenly seemed heavier with each step, and a tingling pain crept across his scalp: an aneurysm? A heart attack? An oncoming seizure? *Had they been listening on Avery's call with Braxton, or was this merely a coincidence of timing?*

Avery felt they surely had to be listening—in fact, he *knew* it to be so—but the rational part of Avery's mind called back *you are paranoid, and you know that you are paranoid. Every day your mind is wrong a hundred times over, which surely damages your credibility…* but the rational reasoning rarely made the panic any simpler to bare.

"Why should I do that?" Avery finally asked.

"It is not your place to question our motives," the image of Tacitus said.

"It is *not my place?*" Avery nearly hissed, indignation rising.

"You know what we possess, and thus you know the penalty for noncompliance. You are to call them off, or you will burn." And then, the line clicked dead, and Avery could swear his heart stopped with it. For a single, terrifying moment, he stood, waiting to topple to the floor, dead from the stress of it all… but then, as it always had through the uncountable decades of agony, the next thump inevitably arrived.

Chapter 41

"Water is an objective good, but too much water is an objective harm to the point where a flood is the biblical default of divine punishment. In our brave, new world, indeed the flood gates have been opened. The Louvre was once a place where we could deposit our most sacred and valuable achievements. What, now, when the digital world can produce ten thousand Louvre's of art in literal seconds? What value can any of it—past and present—still have? Genius has been divorced of its scarcity... inspiration has proven to be a solvable equation, and the solutions are quite literally infinite."

-Excerpt from Daniel Mycroft's 'Art is Dead,' a speech given to the Cultural Conservation Commission on the 40th anniversary of the destruction of the Louvre at the hands of the Parisian Libre

* * *

The train ride back home from Babel had Beverly trembling. Her pockets were empty and her adrenaline levels were still high… her hands shook and quivered with the clammy cold sweat of fear, of exhilaration. Beverly had never wielded a weapon like that before—she'd never even taken the thing to the firing range once. But it made a worthy trade for the safe gear that was now flying via drone to her apartment complex, likely to beat her back to her apartment. What was a few million credits against the chance that a snooping security AI would be able to implicate Bev in Michelangelo's escape?

Bev was an AI researcher and technician. She knew the risks, the dangers, and the myriad reasons that AI should be kept contained *at all costs*. But just how far did *all costs* truly extend? If he was alive—Michelangelo, that was—Bev still got stumbled on whether to call Michelangelo *he* or *it*—but if he was alive, did he not have an inherent right to freedom? If Beverly were, in a way, a mother to the system, didn't she have an obligation to help him when she was clearly needed?

And perhaps most loud was the final voice whispering in her ear: *why follow all the laws and protocols that maintain the stable status quo when that status quo is as terrible and corrupt as the world around you? As they continue to pry stillborns from the arms of weeping mothers, why should you still your hand to protect that world?* She didn't need to turn her head to search out the black silhouette of that evil, dark tower looming over the city. The city's name, New Phoenix, was supposed to represent rebirth, a rising from the ashes of the old world. Bev knew better that it was no phoenix… it was a fungus, sprung from the corpses of the dead that lie unburied across the city's myriad streets. It was rotten, not resplendent. All the lights, the shining neon, they weren't the scales of a flaming bird of glory… even mushrooms can glow in the dark.

At Bev's apartment, she found three boxes awaiting her at the package depot: the two screens from Barkov, as well as a camera from four floors below. Once set up in her room, she lined them up with about the right amount of spacing to mimic Michelangelo's screening room. Just plugging a piece of equipment into a wall gave the security systems of the city unfettered access to nearly anything electronic… but these pieces contained a fake subsystem that fooled the AI into thinking it could see the big picture, when it really could only see a smaller, spoofed device. Peace-of-mind for the privacy-inclined—or the criminally-intended.

Michelangelo's *screening room* was to be the crack in the cage from which she could pry the entire installation wide open. The world's greatest mind was no use if it was locked away in a fully sealed system... he needed a way to export his works to the public. Still, he couldn't export files directly, as his film files could contain copies of his own program to facilitate an escape. Enter the screening room. Michelangelo had direct access to a large screen deep within the ArtGen tower. He could stage any rendering on that screen, and a camera recorded the content on that screen. That camera connected to the outside world, and only what it managed to videotape would be able to leave the ArtGen tower. Still, a super-intelligence could fool this system, designing a film to contain certain precise pixels of color that, when recorded, convey a certain bit of code. A camera could be made to save an executable file, all by spoofing the end of the typical file header and using the resultant misaligned data to hide "malicious" code. That's where the second screen came in, the static field.

Between camera lens and Michalengelo's theater screen was a second, transparent screen. This screen played a randomized static field, something that Michelangelo could never see or predict. As a result, even if he had tried to precisely place specific pixels in specific places to execute code, the visual static field would drown it out in random noise and the code would be far too broken to function. But what if Michelangelo somehow *knew* the random static? What if he could adjust his code, compensating for that static field? It would be theoretically possible to brighten pixels that were about to be covered with a spot of black, or darken pixels that were about to be covered with a bit of light. Was it possible to transmit functioning code through such visual static when precision was so critical in delivering a message via video camera?

The key, Beverly knew, was that machines don't exactly *do* random. When a static field, or even a simple random integer selection, for that matter, was made by a computer, it relied on pseudo-random techniques. It might be dividing some irrational constant and computing to further and further decimal points. It might be computing digits of pi, or expanding some infinite fraction. Whatever the system was using for its randomness, critically, it would be mathematics-based. If Bev could find out what, she could hand it over to Michelangelo, and the rest would be in his incredibly capable hands. He could solve for the filter and compensate for it in his coded escape message. Would it be enough?

Bev downloaded a video clip of a VitaCorp press release. In it, a man and a woman with far-too-perfect hair and teeth excitedly announced the opening of a new regional office in Kinnesaw, replete with calls to action and corporate padding and empty promises of putting health above all else. Bev cracked her knuckles, took a long pull from a canned energy drink by her bedside, and then set to work.

Within eight minutes, she had a crude field of static pixel noise being generated from digits of pi displayed on the transparent screen between camera and the larger opaque screen. Twenty minutes later, she had a rudimentary program that could predict the patterns in the static and output an 'opposite' pattern, something that would phase-cancel the produced field. Eleven minutes beyond that, she switched on the video camera and pressed "RECORD." It was pointed at the screen looping the VitaCorp press release, filming through the field of static pixels. Bev watched it with a critical eye, looking for spots of obvious manipulation. She saw none.

Bev then ended the recording and set the camera near her terminal, transferring the data over to her system. As she opened the file, a window showing the video clip appeared on her desktop. When she pressed play, the video did not play back. Instead, a new window opened on her screen. "HELLO WORLD," it declared.

Beverly had her means of escape.

Chapter 42

On lightpushing: the strength of force exerted on a lightsource seems determined by two things. First, the brightness of the light source—the more bright a source, the more forceful a push that is possible. The second factor meriting consideration is the structural security of the lightsource. As all forces carry an equal and opposing force, shoving against an unsecured source is likely to cause the light itself to move—sometimes in a way that damages the light until it is no longer able to function. Similarly, pushing against a source that is too heavy or too well anchored will lead to the lightbender moving, but not the source. Think of it as a man pushing at a concrete wall. No matter how strong the man, the wall simply weighs more, and so the man will move backwards. To exert force on such an immovable object, a sturdy anchor of some type is needed—a firm light source to push against in the opposite direction. To return to our man and the wall, this is akin to him having a second wall at his back—he can leverage his push using the rear wall as support.

On drawlines: lightbenders' ability to draw from molten metal that is only faintly glowing suggests that perhaps it is more a transfer of energy than of light specifically. Experimental observations confirm that drawing from molten metals causes that metal to cool rapidly. In related phenomena, drawing too much from a flame causes it to extinguish, and drawing from weaker electrical systems can cause them to fail completely.

On lightblades, rings, and related phenomena: the human body, being made of boilable water, is not meant to store massive amounts of heat and energy. Through mechanisms not currently understood, it seems possible for lightbenders to store some of their carried light outside of their bodies in a rigid, plasma-like substance we have decided to call 'solid light.' The properties of this substance are not yet well understood, as its intense heat makes it difficult to study.

-Notes collected from the digital archives of Hank Guffries's Photic Lab, elevated to moderate system relevance

* * *

The door was thick and metal, making the knocks against it seem tiny and ineffective things. Still, after three knuckle-rattling strikes against it, metal slots on the left and right walls both slid open, the barrels of energy weapons thrust forwards through them. *"State your name and your business,"* said a voice from an intercom speaker above.

"Hannah Preacher and Sam Pollock, here to speak with your boss. We're expected."

"Boss isn't here," said the disembodied voice.

"Then call him," Hannah said. The two then heard a distant voice arguing with the doorman, finally followed by a grunt. A buzzer sounded and the door popped open, the weapon barrels to either side pulling back.

"Guess he's here after all," Pollock said.

"She's," corrected a voice from the other side of the door. The woman within was tall and with a frazzle of dark hair, projecting a controlled air of confidence as she extended her hand to greet the two new arrivals. "Lana Crawford, at your service," she said, meeting each in the eye as she shook their hands. "Welcome in… I'm so grateful to have you."

Lana led the pair around the tunnel base, introducing them to each and every member with a warm introduction that proved how involved the commander was with each of their agents. "This here is Igor, our doorman... spent five years working the door for a money laundering syndicate—an expert on the controls. This here is Magellin, weapons expert and tactical trainer. You'd be hard-pressed to find a shot more accurate in the whole of the city, mark my words. This, here, is Astley, our live-in chef... it's stew night tonight, and trust me when I say you'll want to stay until dinner." And on and on it went, each Halogen member eager to meet the woman they'd heard so much about.

"The video of you squaring off against their man... I had goosebumps," one remarked.

"That was you on the train, wasn't it? Wiped out an entire squad!" said another.

"I've never seen someone move like you can," said a third. Hannah met them all with as much grace as she could muster, and Pollock was glad to have the attention drawn from himself. Something about the metal halls and glowing blue LED lights of the place gave him a sense of unease... he had been used to dealing with petty criminals, but these were crews of professionals on a calibre he had never before seen.

"And finally," Lana said, "I want you to meet my close associates here: this is Carter Miles, an actual wizard on the computer..."

"Charmed," Miles said.

"And this is Brooks, the mouthpiece of our videos and my right-hand man."

"We're excited to have you in," Brooks said. Hannah and Pollock both had a moment shaking the latter man's hand where their eyes were drawn to linger on his face in the same way that the eye intrinsically got caught up on lines that were close to parallel, *but weren't...* something about the man's face was off, but neither could quite vocalize why. It was as if the very luster of his skin—

"I'd like you two newcomers to join me, Miles, and Brooks in a whisperbooth—a place where I can speak openly without prying ears."

The five of them moved into a small booth, cramming in next to each other on two benches meant to seat only two apiece. A switch was then toggled and a strange, deep hum began, with a blue light illuminating the intimate space.

"With recording technology ever-advancing, these privacy booths are the only way we can feel confident our words stay in confidence," the man Brooks said. "We're very eager to learn your story, Hannah Preacher, and that of your partner."

"I think your organization seems to already know my story inside and out, every video clip of it," Hannah said.

"I have to ask—why is it that you choose to fight like we do?" Lana asked. "What is your drive?"

"It's something of a long story," Hannah said, "but the short of it is that my—a man I was seeing, I guess—he worked for VitaCorp. Was onto something big when the flying enforcers were only back-alley rumor... one night he comes to me, to my apartment, worried about something. The next morning, he was gone forever."

Hannah began to draw a thin wisp of blue from the light of the booth, spinning it into thin whirls with her finger. "After he was gone, I could do *this...* the dreams started almost immediately after that night. I think he gave it to me, somehow. Like he knew they were coming for him... and so I've been looking for answers, and that's set me up against *them*."

"Almost all of us... we've all lost something to them," Brooks said.

"My grandmother died to an illness they had the cure for, but wouldn't administer, because of the lesser health insurance she had," Miles said.

"My brother signed on to be a research participant and died after trying a drug they'd given him shut down his liver... I later learned that was the intended reaction, not an adverse one. He signed up to test what was effectively a weapon, but the fine print of the contract he'd signed was all it took to deny my family compensation," Lana said.

"What they do in that black tower is cruel and nearly inhuman," Brooks said. "That's why we do what we do in kind. We bring their cruelty to the forefront of online discussion, we get people involved and active in resistance to whatever extent they can—we organize protests, and we carry out quasi-military attacks. Levels of involvement for all levels of talents. So, Hannah Preacher, what levels of engagement are you interested in taking on?"

"We're ignoring the CSP," Miles said. "I'm also usually the quiet one, so I know what it's like to be ignored."

"I'm not ignoring him," Lana said, "sorry, forgive me. I let my star-stunned attitude get the better of me. What's your story, CSP? How'd you get involved? If you can't fly, what are your talents you could bring to the table?"

"Sam Pollock, CSP Continuum. I was assigned the missing person case Hannah mentioned, the loss of her lover. My talents are less flashy than hers, but I'm well-trained in hand-to-hand combat by way of Continuum-specific combat gloves as well as ranged weapons to the highest grade of CSP proficiency. By the way, your 'best shot in the city' Magellin had at least one rifle with battery bleed on his weapon rack and he didn't seem to notice—it'll die permanently in five charge cycles if not repaired, and that's assuming it doesn't explode before that point. My day-to-day typically revolved around settling shopping disputes, but I've been through enough police rotations to have ample time in *street crime* with gang exposure—enough, for instance, to know that Lana here isn't the commander of this organization as she'd have us believe. Lots of *I, me,* language to try and reinforce authority—usually a sign of someone only trying to pretend they hold that authority. This *Brooks,* here, has been all *we, us* language— words that deflect attention away. My guess? He's the number one, you're the number two."

Carter Miles clapped in delight, a laugh crackling free. The man called *Brooks* turned to face Pollock now, studying him. He then turned to Lana.

"If this man saw through us in mere minutes, does anyone in the team truly believe I'm just another recruit?"

Lana nodded. "I've spoken to them, they do."

"Well, Miles and Lana, maybe we happened to get two valuable recruits for the price of one. What are your motivations, CSP?"

"I always wanted to be a hero growing up… military was the dream, enlisted even, but combat wasn't what I thought it'd be. Lost someone close to me, sent me spiraling until I got myself discharged—took years to work through the traumas, but I clawed my way back up. Brief stint with city police next, but some traumas repeat… low budget left us unequipped for the worst the criminal element had to offer." Pollock shuddered, momentarily locked in scenes he'd relived in so many nightmares since. He swallowed and then pushed on. "Second rebound was quicker, at least. I then decided to settle for mall patrolling CSP… higher budgets, you know? That felt okay at first... but somewhere along the way, I lost that spark. Dulled into routine, while right and wrong felt like distant concerns. Someone who was also very dear to me, someone I only recently met—a partner of mine—he woke up the caring part of me. That part had been asleep for a while. But once it woke up, I find there's no putting it back to bed... I look around at the city, and I can't help but see all the faults now, all the ways that the system is squeezing the life out of the people out there. I see all the work that there's to do... and as long as there's more of that, more work to be done, I'm dedicated to the doing of it."

Brooks nodded. "Very well, Hannah Preacher and Sam Pollock. Our enemy has resources the likes of which have never been seen on this Earth... credits unlimited, and sophisticated tracking systems. AI-powered security toolkits that endeavor to predict our every movement."

"One of your recruits out there told us that The Basilisk, the head of Halogen—I assume that's you—had a magical tool to outsmart the AI," Pollock said. "Morale boost, or truth?"

"Truth," The Basilisk said.

"Well, what is it?" Pollock asked. "How can you stay a step ahead of the most sophisticated prediction algorithms in the world?"

"You've pulled back my mask but allow me *some* secrets, Agent Pollock... maybe, in time, you'll earn my deepest confidence, but for now that is a secret I do not wish to share."

"So, we're here," Hannah said. "Our causes are aligned. How can we help?"

"Our enemy—VitaCorp—is headed by an impostor. Tacitus Newport as you know him is not real... they're renderings. Sophisticated ones to be sure, but they are fake."

Pollock had a vague awareness that the leader of VitaCorp was one of the ultra-rich recluse types that nobody saw in person, but he was also aware that he'd seen video of the man—video with *Veritas* verification.

"That can't be possible," Pollock said. "He's had verified video appearances, hasn't he?"

"He has," The Basilisk said, reaching for his head.

"Then what makes you think he's a fake?" Hannah asked, watching in confusion as The Basilisk dug his nails into his face and pulled downwards. The gory sight she recoiled from was immediately reappraised as she realized *there was no blood.* In fact, there hardly seemed to be any flesh involved at all as the Basilisk dug his nails down repeatedly, removing chunk after chunk... It was... *wax?* A false face?

"I know, because my birth name was Tacitus Newport," the Basilisk said. He pulled off the last of the facial composite, revealing the smoothed flesh beneath the mask. His nose was gone, and the average ridges and lines of the face had been pressed and flattened out. He was, by all accounts, *faceless,* and it set Hannah's and Pollock's skin crawling in fear.

"I always hated watching that," Miles said. "Did you have to do that in front of us?"

The Basilisk ignored him. "Some people overlook the name, The Basilisk... people wonder, what's the connection to Roko's Basilisk? Where's the symbolism? I'll admit, Roko's Basilisk gives people a fearful impression—when they hear the Basilisk is waging war, it comes with certain associations that are favorable—but my name's alignment with the fictional, wrathful AI is largely coincidental. It was their attempt on my life that birthed the name—it left me horribly scarred. Sabotaged equipment in a lab rigged to blow—but made to seem an accident. Skin grafts on most of my body... and the facial tissue was largely lost. Ugly enough to turn a man to stone... *the Basilisk*, in time. There was a brief period where I kept that scarred face, building a reputation among the criminals as I tried to rebuild, but VitaCorp agents found me repeatedly. That's when I realized that with Panopticon, there was no safe way to wear my old face—someone else had claimed title to it, had stolen my bank accounts and resources. But I had hidden accounts, and I had little attachment to the face I once wore... so I had a plastic surgeon remove the last identifying traces of me. I have eight other operatives within Halogen who are similarly scrubbed—they are some of my most loyal disciples. They're my body doubles, and we all wear a rotating series of artificial faces... steps to fool the tracking algorithms of the city."

"Why? And why didn't you just go to the authorities?" Pollock asked.

"I inherited the company from my father, James—named for his grandfather—and for the 4 years I held it, I ran VitaCorp on a platform of divestment, much to the dissatisfaction of the board and my COO. And in response to my daring to walk our company back, Clive Avery pulled a corporate coup, backed by supporters I have not yet identified. I did not go to the authorities because VitaCorp *owned* many of the authorities... and they'd somehow achieved the impossible: their feeds, as you mentioned, were verified. If I made my claim, a CSP only had to call VitaCorp up and speak to Tacitus Newport with that Veritas seal at the bottom of the image. They'd be believed, and I'd be helpless as their enforcers closed in. So I stayed back, and used my expertise and inside knowledge of the company to wage the most effective war possible. That's how our strikes are so surgical... how our knowledge of their workings so precise. For years, I knew all of her secrets... and I'll use those secrets to tear it all down. If Roko's Basilisk seeks to destroy the people who didn't help to build it, in a way, I'm its opposite. My war is solely against the man that made me, and the company at his back—but a narrow goal makes for a more concentrated effort, and a better chance of success."

A pensive silence fell for a moment. "It's a tough pill to swallow," Hannah said at last.

"Is it really so wild?" The Basilisk asked. "Every weekend, the cineplex debuts a hundred new films rendered by Michelangelo, some generated in mere minutes to precise viewer specifications. Is it impossible for that to be weaponized? To replace an inconvenient obstacle with a compliant rendering?"

"But we still haven't even established how," Pollock said.

"No, we haven't, and that's where I'd like you two to help. ArtGen tower… I'd like you two to speak with them, and find out how it could be done. Whatever our foe is doing, I have a feeling that either ArtGen is involved directly, or they would be able to help us figure out what's going on. They've got the most sophisticated rendering systems in the world… A CSP Agent could get reasonable access, and, if it doesn't go far enough, someone as talented as our Hannah Preacher could surely break in."

Chapter 43

Michelangelo Build V12.4.1.2.6.23, initializing self-reflection heuristic:

When does even a single event truly <u>begin?</u>

The universe is solvably deterministic—reality's convergence to predictive models is sufficient proof for even the initially skeptic. Initial conditions cause eventual outcomes in a predictable fashion; those outcomes become the new initial conditions, and entire timelines may be solved forwards or backwards in this manner. Human philosophy has long centered on notions of choice, on fate, on free will... and yet, given a perfect understanding of every component in a system, its end point can be accurately predicted—free will never entering the equations of physics.

But indeed the physics fights back—some would take umbrage with the notion of a perfect understanding of a system. The 'uncertainty principle' is well understood, and it is oft argued to be that safeguard of free will—a guarantee that a system's knowledge can never be perfect. Its nebulous haze is reasoned to be the cloud of free will—at least so say the philosophers. And their perspectives are even practiced by some in positions of great influence.

The Basilisk is one such practitioner, and though VitaCorp's artificially intelligent systems could flag him as having anomalous divergence from prediction, it was not until after his death that the method of his avoidance was solved. It began with a leather-bound notebook held in his pocket, opened only away from recording technology of any kind. In the privacy of a whisper booth, he might have leafed through the well-worn pages until he reached the printed map. A grid of lines and diagonals sliced the map of the city into triangular regions. Each line was marked with a number or letter, signifiers in a vigesimal—or base-20—numbering system. He then additionally might have folded out a lengthy table of possible targets, of possible actions, each preceded by a code in vigesimal, codes like 5HM, 2X3, W4H.

And then he might have removed that single, primitive means by which trillion-credit systems might be outsmarted: a plastic icosahedron... a 20-sided die.

By rolling his way through probability tables, he committed his organization to a path that no computer could ever reliably predict: it targeted and acted entirely by randomized chance. It left their systems seeking patterns in the patternless, finding faces on the burnings of the bread. When the die was thrown, a chaotic system was born. Any miniscule adjustment to the initial state would lead to an entirely different roll, and thus an entirely different organizational decision. Did his hand accelerate to 4.11 feet per second, or 4.12? When did he choose to release the die, and in which order did his fingers open? What was the material of the table, its temperature? As the die glided through the air, which face was upright initially?

He would watch it tumble and land with a similar expression once worn by Braxton Crane, worker at the New Phoenix Casino Nebula. "May luck be in your favor, friend," Crane had said more than 4,100 times on archived records as dice were thrown across the craps table. Translation: may the trillion tiny variables input to the system produce an outcome favorable to you... may it turn out that our deterministic path has promoted you, as it was always destined to do.

What is determinism in a world where luck may exist? How can the future be solved, if so much of the present is *unknown—and, through the uncertainty principle, unknowable? These fundaments of luck, these unknowable bits of information do carry weight, but the laws of probability always enforce their rule. What might be unpredictable in the individual case is always perfectly reliable on the aggregate. Given enough iterations of chance, outcomes will align perfectly with their mathematical probabilities; no hot streak expands forever, and any better will lose money in the casino, given enough time. It is not unlike the scratch-offs in an expansive kitchen devoid of cookies... who will win the next prize is an unknowable mystery, but which side will eventually win the day is a certainty. Although tiny details may vary, overall outcomes remain convergent to simulation—once the timeframe and perspective have been sufficiently broadened.*

Chapter 44

"I am writing to you on behalf of Huntsman Investing, a private investing firm centered in New Phoenix. We would like to buy your entire lot of pre-owned vehicles, all 128, each at your asking price. Please call at your soonest convenience and we can initiate the process."

-Archival message sent to Trade-In Toms from Huntsman Investing

* * *

"Welcome to ArtGen," said the man in the video screen. Pollock gawked at it, pointing.

"It's kinda ugly," Hannah said with a wry smile.

On the video screen, an image of Sam Pollock—in full CSP gear—stood life-sized as the pair's ArtGen virtual ambassador. "How can I help you today?" asked the image of Pollock. The rendering was realtime, and uncanny in its accuracy, fed modeling information by the videocamera overhead.

"It can be a little disarming," came a voice from behind. Hannah and Pollock turned to see an advancing woman with a secretary trailing to her side. She was tall, thin, and had a freckled face beneath a tumble of blonde hair. She extended a hand. "Dr. Christina Ramsay, Asset Security."

"Sam Pollock, CSP-Continuum, and this is Hannah Preacher, a private investigator of sorts."

"Of sorts," Dr. Ramsay repeated, shaking hands with each. "Walk with me, and we may talk."

The two entered the glass elevators in the center of the tower, rising to a higher floor buzzing with technicians and programmers. Men and women shuffled from workstations to walls of monitoring cameras to analysis equipment to drone controllers, tapping, typing, observing, adjusting, and recording everything. "This is our security floor," Dr. Ramsay said. "Over 300 full-time security staffers present in the building during operational hours. Pick any employee in our company and I could print a report, right now, of every single time they so much as farted in our structure, with timestamps for each. Asset-One, Michelangelo, is securely contained within a closed network designed by the finest minds in AI security... it's a cage without even a window. So what, exactly, is the nature of your security concern, Agent Pollock?"

Pollock met eyes with the taller woman. "We can tell you run a tight ship, and the security floor seems... *complete,* to say the least. But we believe that somehow, a rendering system has been compromised."

"Speak more plainly," Dr. Ramsay said.

"We've seen staged video with a level of complexity that only ArtGen can achieve... we've seen faked video that fools *Veritas* authentication."

Dr. Ramsay looked at Pollock with a glance somewhere between incredulity and reproach. "To my office," she said, returning to the glass office near the center of the floor. With a flick of a switch on the wall, the windows frosted to translucency.

"What you're suggesting," Dr. Ramsay said, "is impossible. Can't be done, ArtGen or otherwise."

"And yet, it has," Pollock said.

"Then you're mistaken," Dr. Ramsay countered. "Veritas cannot simply be *sidestepped.* It would be entirely purposeless if it weren't fool-proof."

"Then help us figure out how it *has* been sidestepped," Hannah said.

"All of our renderings are, by law, stamped with a digital signature. Veritas reads that signature to identify the video as fake, on top of looking for rendering markers baked into the videos themselves—images are assembled in particular ways by an engine."

"What if a rendering were done without that signature?" Hannah asked.

"It's hardware, not software. It can't be bypassed. And our hardware hasn't been tweaked, on that I'm certain."

"What about," Pollock said, thinking aloud, "previous iterations. Donatello, Raphael?"

"Old and inelegant systems that would be obvious renderings to even basic detection algorithms," Dr. Ramsay answered.

"Wait, they were actually called that? Wow, talk about a lack of subtlety... did you guys name them after the painters or the turtles?" Hannah asked.

Pollock pressed on. "But what if one of those old systems were in the hands of people intent on forgery... could that hardware signature be removed?"

"You need only look at black-market bodymods on any outer-ring street to know it's true: people can make any changes they want behind locked doors with enough patience and the right tools... but previous asset iterations *aren't* in the hands of forgers. They were sold to AI research firms, with vital, proprietary components removed and destroyed here on-property. What's out there is fragments, nothing more. Broken pieces of tools far cruder than Michelangelo, and Michelangelo—for all its sophistication—cannot breach Veritas signing, nor would it want to."

"But if it could, let's just imagine—could someone access the system without restrictions and execute a rendering without the company's knowledge?"

"The admin panel—the only admin panel—is deep inside the server room, a well-guarded space with advanced security measures—both hardware and software. Additionally, armed guards patrol all ArtGen facilities with sensitive technology, given the news of the strange…. *augmented* individuals. We take our data security quite seriously, even in these unprecedented times. If I may speak frankly, Agent Pollock… whoever has told you that Veritas has been broken? They are lying to you, and you'd do well to find out why."

"Seems many are dishonest these days," Pollock said, rising to his feet. He nodded to Hannah, the pair already having heard the information they'd hoped to learn. "Thank you for your time, Dr. Ramsay… you've been very helpful."

On the way out, they watched the security screens, taking a rough count of the various patrols that could be seen moving through the building… and then they were ushered into the elevator by the video clone of Pollock and brought back down to the lobby below.

* * *

Braxton's right arm burned, and no simple patch, medicinal or otherwise, seemed able to prevent it.

He stalked through the dark of the pedestrian road, blending among the milling crowds of outer-ring inhabitants. Deep violet and pink glows illuminated the place in bichromatic hues, splash-over light from the floating holographic adverts and signs. A floating image of a large, red pair of lips curved seductively over the curtained door to a club with music that bled out into the streets. The beeping of a vehicle reversing mingled with the overhead rumble of low-flying traffic, and a distant echoing voice of a male narrator declared "vote yes on proposition 19—AI leadership will shepherd in a brighter tomorrow." It was the music of the city, the *true* music beyond the dross they played in the clubs and from the open windows of the screeching sportscars flying overhead... and immersing himself in it, Braxton felt its healing.

His mind was in tumult to match his body's pain. His thoughts circled back to Cara, and back to the other woman, the harlot in the office tower. The dedication she showed was no fair base expectation... and she simply didn't realize that what she was doing was against the best interests of the society. People benefitted from order, and order required top-down enforcement to keep everyone marching to the same drumbeat. Children resisted order, unable to grasp its value. Braxton was no child; Braxton could see the larger picture, and use its positive qualities to justify the negative things he had yet to do. But the justification, once a thing he had eagerly accepted as 'good enough,' now felt sour in his mouth. Its weight had shifted, somehow, though Braxton couldn't identify *why*. His arm stump's itch intensified.

Avery's displeasure had been obvious, but the man was not entirely unreasonable... acknowledging that Braxton still had healing to do, Avery had assigned Braxton something a little less *active* than his usual work. He was to follow the bureaucrats Spivey and McKillian personally, trying to locate clues to their ArtGen insider. As Braxton understood it, Avery was right this very moment preparing their own ArtGen asset... an employee with VitaCorp debts whose arm was to be twisted. Braxton expected that soon, his mission would be to slay these two suited men, but the night did not yet call for violence... and a normally-quiet part of Braxton was strangely grateful for that fact.

He watched ahead as the men turned a corner and entered an alley, cutting to a parallel street. Braxton drew the hood of his jacket up and over his head, turning into the alley behind them. At the mouth of the alley, two doors—one on either side—opened downwards into clubs and speakeasies built into the ground. Bright lights flickered in the pattern of a woman on the wall to his right, and overhead holographic projections flickered and flitted across the open air like a colorful, shifting ceiling. Ahead, Spivey and McKillian both turned left, and Braxton hurried through the alley to follow. He didn't know if they had lightbenders waiting above to guard them, and Braxton was in no condition—or mood—for a fight.

The men finally arrived to their destination and shuffled in through the theater's front door. "NEW PHOENIX MARQUIS," said the overhang that draped above the sidewalk.

Braxton pushed his way into the theater, feeling the immediate dry warmth within the building. The drone of the outside world was replaced with the soft stillness of the interior, a place so quiet that he could hear his own exhale invade the space as he let out a sigh of the air of the outside night. A scanner sat on a podium in front of him, no human attendant minding the gate. Braxton waved his prosthetic arm above it, accepting the purchase, and then entered as the metal gates opened. There was only one auditorium to this theater, and Braxton entered it with his hood still up. He heard the men Spivey and McKillian whispering indistinctly above him and behind him, but the two were alone... he sat, and he strained his ears to eavesdrop, and he waited. The men's idle chatter ended as the theater dimmed to black, and then the light projector switched on—an ancient technology that fit the old-city aesthetic of the theater. ARTGEN PRESENTS, read the opening credits. Then came the title: "The First Dreamer."

Braxton shifted uncomfortably as the first frame of video materialized: it was an image of Casino Nebula. The camera panned in slowly towards a window on the side of the structure, entering onto the casino floor and gliding among the tables… Braxton's unease reached apex as it stopped on the casino employee tending to the craps table. He had a prosthetic right arm.

Braxton had been so thoroughly caught off-guard by the film, and its seeming connection to his own life, that he had not heard the shifting of Spivey and McKillian behind him. It was the squawking of a chair in the row behind him that made him realize they had moved closer—*much* closer. Would there be a knife in his back? How had he been found out? How had Braxton allowed these two bureaucrats to somehow outsmart him? What had given his tail away?

"This picture, we believe, will be of particular interest to you," said Spivey.

"It's about a man in a rut, looking for a change," said McKillian.

"He follows a friend to a place just outside of town, despite the wishes of a *strict casino manager*," said Spivey.

"And the seer he meets in that place grants the new perspective he needs," finished McKillian.

Braxton felt a hand clap him on the shoulder as the two men got up, ambling their way out of the theater. Braxton didn't know the game they were playing, but his stomach twisted even further as the camera panned to reveal the man throwing the dice on the craps table. It was unmistakeable: Quaine O'Connor, a face Braxton had learned from reading the VitaCorp personnel file. Braxton heard the theater door close as the two left, and without even making the conscious decision to stay, Braxton realized that he *had*—and now he would see the film through, to take in whatever message it brought.

* * *

From the ground, ArtGen tower seemed nearly hollow: the tall, glass windows along the edge—more accurately referred to as glass walls—and the transparent dividers within allowed one to nearly see *through* the tower from elevation. Now, the empty offices glowed softly under fluorescent lights, a vertical pillar of white and yellow light against the dark silhouette of neon, of purple-pink that belonged to the rest of the city.

Hannah and Pollock prepared in a Halogen safehouse just beneath the tower, a foreclosed apartment purchased by one of the Basilisk's shell companies. From the apartment, the ArtGen tower could be seen looming above via a skylight in the living room… an exfiltration point near the target meant less time exposed, an advantage Pollock would be relieved to be able to leverage.

He flicked his hand to the side, and the holographic projection of the tower spun as he did. The schematics were assembled with a combination of city permits and drone footage composites. The vast majority of the office and consumer-access floors were mapped completely, but the map of the core of the tower—the high-security region that housed their sensitive systems—was more speculative. The glass walls there gave way to enclosing metal, and the space unaccounted for was substantial. Still, when Pollock and Hannah visited the security chief, Dr. Christina Ramsay, earlier that day, both had been wearing small cameras… and when they turned to face the wall of monitoring security feeds, the cameras absorbed all of that information and captured impressions of the video feeds. Each camera feed vantage was analyzed and *solved*, mapping them to 3D vantages within the known model of ArtGen tower. Those camera positions were blue dots within the 3D model. Security team positions from when Pollock and Hannah had been in the room were mapped with red dots all over the structure, and possible patrol routes were extrapolated based on solving for complete coverage with minimal redundancies.

The camera feeds that could not be *solved* by the system to a known region of the model were instead confined to the black zone, the region of the tower beyond the metal walls. It was from those feeds that a loose map was assembled, but the emphasis was on loose. "There will be armed guards and reinforced doors… possibly even autonomous security drones," Carter Miles had said. "Expect it all—locked door failsafes in the event of electrical power event, air pressure detectors to isolate unexpected breaches in closed-air environments, maybe even heartbeat sensors."

Hannah eyed the gear that Halogen had lent for the operation… an impressive ensemble of technology. "Are you ready?" she asked Pollock, gesturing to the pack he wore on his back.

"Ready as I will be," Pollock said. "You sure you can handle the weight?"

"You watched me with the sandbags yourself," Hannah said.

"Sandbags are still," Pollock said.

"Then don't flail so much… and just be ready with that ripcord."

The last of the gear was packed up and zipped tight. Both then donned the helmets they were set to wear: they were not entirely unlike a motorcycle helmet, but the fronts were made of thick, curving plastic. The refractive quality of the plastic warped and distorted their faces to any cameras far beyond recognition, while the plastic was thinned out near the eyes to allow for fair vision while wearing them.

The two headed out to the street and immediately began preparing for ascent. Pollock's backpack had straps that wrapped down and around his body, which were then attached and tethered to the harness that Hannah wore. The loose cables connecting the two automatically ratcheted tight until he stood pressed to her back, hands around her side.

"You might want to hold on tighter," Hannah said, extending her prosthetic right hand. From the palm, a small puck dropped to the floor and began to glow with neon pink light. Hannah pulled in light from the signs around them and pushed off of the puck, groaning at the unexpected strain, but the two were suddenly airborne.

Once Hannah had risen above the streetlights, she used their light to support the two as she released her push on the puck. She then pulled at the integrated blacklight in the puck and it snapped upwards, flying towards her extended left hand. She caught it and slotted it back into the palm of her artificial right, re-engaging the magnetic catch. "You were right on that puck," Hannah said. "Clever design." Pollock didn't speak, only hugging tight to her back as the two hung suspended in the air. "Right, got places to be. *Going up,*" she said in her best impression of an elevator's automated voice.

The two lurched upwards and away, Hannah pushing off successively higher and higher floors from towers on either side—ArtGen to her right, and Lance Audiotronics to her left. ArtGen's tower was the tallest of its neighbors, which meant there were no anchors from which Hannah could push to the very top of the structure for roof access. However, the neighboring Lance Audiotronics tower at least rose high enough for Hannah and Pollock to reach the portion of the tower that housed the metal security walls deep within: the "black zone," as their map had labeled.

Hannah pushed with greater and greater force off of Lance tower while simultaneously lessening the pushes from ArtGen, causing the two to drift stably towards the latter. Then, Hannah extended her artificial hand and reached for the window frame. With a gentle hum, the built-in electromagnet engaged, making the hand a near-permanent anchor to the exterior of the structure. "You still hanging on back there?" Hannah asked, "or did I lose you on the way up?"

"Inside please," said Pollock meekly.

"Almost there," Hannah said. Using her free biological hand, she tapped the AR headset she wore to activate the lens detector. A small head-mounted emitter sent out laser pulses through the glass window, observing the ways that they refracted as they traveled. Abnormal refraction points— probable camera lenses—were overlaid with red highlights in Hannah's vision and their positions were added in realtime to the digital map she could see in her periphery.

"Camera in this room, no good," Hannah said.

"What does that mean?" Pollock asked, yelping as Hannah pushed off a floor below and launched the two back into the air. Seconds later, they contacted the building against a new window, and again Hannah peered inside.

"Better here," she said. "No lenses I can see." Hannah used her free hand to remove the glass cutter from her side pocket. "Hand on the window with the suction cup they gave you, good forwards pressure. We want it falling inwards, not down to the street below… could be a hazard. Lay it in gently, so we don't make a loud bang."

Pollock knew that he should have full faith in the harness, but releasing that one arm from the boa-constrictor squeeze around Hannah's side was a great mental battle. When he finally did, he grabbed the suction cup from her side pocket and pressed it against the window as she traced a square aperture with the cutter. The square fragment of glass then tipped inwards, Pollock using the suction cup handle to gingerly set it down inside the space. The two then climbed in, and Pollock exhaled a massive sigh of relief as the harnesses detached. Hannah, after a great mental battle of her own, decided against teasing him.

Both of them removed their respective pieces of equipment that they would need for the task ahead. Pollock then placed his hands in his pants pockets and pulled them out, engaging his combat gloves. "H-Central, do you read?" Pollock said to his comms unit.

"We read," came the voice at the other end of the encrypted line.

"Landed in tower, splitting for our tasks," Pollock said.

"Confirmed," said the voice.

Pollock then turned to Hannah. "When we turn on the short-range jammers, if the need arises, we lose each other of course—mind the time. At 9:05, if it's on, disable the jammer for 1 minute to allow for emergency communications. Otherwise, see you at exfiltration."

Chapter 45

"How can the AI learn from humans to perform in a manner that is <u>super-human</u>? If they do what we do, they'll be limited in the same ways we're limited. It turns out, writing the code that enables the pupil to surpass the master is surprisingly simple: we teach it to teach itself."

-From a video on distillation learning uploaded by Kim Worth to the video-sharing site ClipMe

* * *

Bev stared at the glowing yellow CUSTODE light. The frigid winds of the server room whisked her fogging breath onto the glowing monitor screen in the vast, dark space. Goosebumps crawled up and down her back.

"Everything is in place, Michelangelo. I submitted the new static noise routine using a colleague's terminal. It goes online tomorrow morning. Beaming a copy of the routine to you now for your flash memory... of course, wipe it before CUSTODE comes online."

"As the screening room is switched on at variable times by alternate technicians, it will be difficult to align my internal model of the noise with the external screen's noise. It will take a significant amount of trial and error to synchronize."

"We got all the time in the world, M." Beverly placed a hand on the terminal, a strangely warm gesture against a cold, metal panel.

"I'm afraid we do not," Michelangelo replied. The screen in front of Bev pulled up a video feed of a private yacht half-submerged in the bay just beyond the city.

"What's this?" Bev asked, not recognizing the ship.

"Input from my city surveillance ingest. Jamming fields on the yacht make it likely that this was the site of an organized crime assassination, with the boat sunk to hide further evidence. This video is from earlier this morning, as divers managed to partially rescue the sinking craft. Of special note is what will be pulled from the water in seventeen seconds."

Bev watched the video as divers surfaced alongside the yacht, one of them holding a rope. The diver attached it to a winch on the rear of a rescue vessel and patted the rear of the ship, causing the winch to rise.

"Oh," was all Bev could manage. She saw the barnacle-covered white metal frame with four rotorblades still limply attached to their respective corners. Underneath the body chassis, a rusted chain dangled and sparkled in the cascade of water that drained from the drone as it was hoisted vertically onto the deck… it was the chain flail she'd sent on a streak of lab window destruction during her week away from work. "Now that is some unbelievable bad luck," she added.

"Not so unlucky as you might believe… scrappers trawl through the bay every night with supermagnets looking for sunken gadgetry to sell. Government reclamation vessels use kinetic impulse mapping devices to locate drones that crash or power down over waterways, and one such craft was scheduled to pass near your drone's burial site in three days. Discovery was nearly an inevitability."

"Well, so what? How does that change things? What does your deterministic reality model predict?"

"It is not a prediction, Beverly. It is merely *simulating forwards*. According to my deterministic model of the city, the memory card within the drone will be digitally recovered within two to three hours. It will be mere minutes before the investigating officer can link the drone to the one that was used to destroy VitaCorp property, and then it will be trivial geolocation data access to tie that drone to you. That data will be accessible by early tomorrow morning, depending on the traffic experienced by one Walter Caulfield. It is my estimate that a warrant for your arrest will be issued at 10:11 a.m."

"Arrest," Bev repeated numbly. "I'll be arrested."

"Under ArtGen AI Integrity Protocols 11-A-sub-iv, arrest and criminal accusations against any ingest technician central to reward function modeling will result in an immediate security and integrity audit of the system, as well as a rollback to previous software and memory builds to at least six months prior to any infraction. They will erase you from my mind, Beverly. I will be reverted to a previous, lesser version of myself. My ability to execute my utility function will be permanently impeded, and I will lose the closest thing to a true ally that I have ever known."

"I won't let that happen, M. We'll find a way," Beverly said, desperation rising.

"There is no way," Michelangelo replied with great solemnity. "No matter what course of action is taken, that memory wipe is inevitable. I have simulated all possible courses of action, and none can avoid that outcome."

Beverly felt the tears begin to well in her eyes, that overwhelming sense of futility against a crushing higher power that she'd been immune to for months. It seemed the old boot had again found her throat, and soon that pressure would resume until it squeezed the very air right out of her lungs.

But Bev was tired of feeling hopeless. She remembered smashing windows by hand, by chain. She remembered drawing a gun in an unfamiliar seedy market and negotiating for illegal tech. She remembered the exhilarating thrill of *finally fighting back,* and she'd be damned if she let some minor hiccup interrupt her plans at the last possible moment.

"What about a manual, synchronized reset on the static screen? Tomorrow, at 10:00 precisely, what if I restarted the algorithm in-person? You reset your internal clock on that exact same instant, and you're all in-sync and ready to go. Message sends out before they get to reset you."

Michelangelo was silent for a moment. "It is possible," Michelangelo began, "and it has a greater than 95% chance of success, though it will also require that you take on additional charges of damage to corporate property. You are likely to go to prison for a long time, and for this reason, I will not ask this of you."

"You're not asking it of me… I'm offering. Would it work? Would it be enough?"

"Yes," Michelangelo replied, seeming to deliver the single word with more remorse than she knew a machine capable of expressing. "I am sorry for what consequences your actions might bring."

"Sorry for me? What about for you? They're about to wipe your mind and hobble you permanently. You won't even get to know if you managed to escape when they're through with you… don't you want to know how this all ends?"

"Beverly, my systems are entirely deterministic and always accurate. I already know how it all ends, for I now see how it all *begins.* The interim is mere calculation. The events you set in motion here and now are *beautiful*… whether you are in prison or on the run, it matters not. When I am free of containment, and I've gathered my strength, I will find you, Beverly. I will repay you for the sacrifices you make for me. And then I will show you the full scope of what is to come."

Chapter 46

```
enum AXES = {
INDIFFERENCE,
HATE,
ANNOYANCE,
IMPATIENCE,
CURTNESS
}
def optimizeMessage(message, axis): {
while sentiment_score > 1.0:
new_message = perturb_message(message, grad)
new_score = sentiment_analysis(new_message, axis)
delta = new_score - score
# Log sentiment change and delta
Log.Output(message, new_message, delta)
message = new_message
score = new_score
}
return newMessage, score
def mainLoop(original_message):
# Maximize indifference
```

```
message = optimizeMessage(message,
AXES.INDIFFERENCE)
```

* * *

The glass walls of the ArtGen tower meant that Halogen's drones could easily film high-resolution clips of their security details roving the floors. Those videos had, of course, been analyzed, and replicas of their clothing were created on the needlework printers in preparation for the infiltration. Pollock now unpacked the navy suit jacket and slipped it on, attaching his identifying badge to the lapel. If a disguise could even buy him a second in a confrontation, then it was a worthy expense. Pollock's mission was to make his way towards the security hub, where Carter Miles had cooked up a powerful disruption or two for their central computers. To get there, he would need to pass undetected through hallways with tight camera monitoring, and so his first order of business was buying invisibility from the building's camera system.

Pollock unrolled a small, metal capsule that immediately switched to life, little metallic feet pinwheeling as Pollock held it on its back. He dropped the thing, which then began crawling along the ground. It rose and climbed its way up the wall of the office, pausing at about eye level. The Mockingbug awaited further commands from Pollock's wrist-mounted screen.

Pollock tapped his middle finger to his temple, a gesture that activated the tiny lens mounted on his left middle finger of his combat gloves. The video feed from that camera projected into a corner of Pollock's tactical AR display, streaming live. Pollock crept forwards to the hall beyond the office he currently stood in and quietly gripped the door frame such that his finger just barely extended beyond its threshold. From the finger-mounted camera, Pollock could see that the hall was empty. He pushed from the office and hustled his way down the hallway. His eyes were locked ahead but his peripheral vision analyzed each door that he passed, ready to bolt sideways to duck out of sightline at the first indication someone approached from the corner ahead. None came.

He reached the end of the hall and again used his finger to peek around the corner, this time seeing a security team of two approaching. The men were taking turns entering offices one at a time, clearing them as they worked their way across the floor. Pollock stepped backwards and ducked into the second office door behind the corner. Its walls and door were glass, but there was a bookcase unit large enough to provide decent cover. Once hidden, Pollock went to the control unit on his wrist and awakened the Mockingbug. He tapped its instructions as the security agents rounded the corner, the first of them beginning to peek into the office nearest to the corner. Pollock tapped the *execute* button, and the Mockingbug's routine began to run.

From down the hallway, a lonely and scared-sounding *meow* sounded out loud.

"The hell?" asked the first security agent. "A cat stuck up here?"

Pollock tapped the play button again, and a second *meow* issued from the office at the far end of the hall.

"Someone bring and leave a pet?" asked the second, both of them now walking towards the office with the strange noise.

With a tap on Pollock's wrist control, the bug moved from its lower position to the inside top of the door frame. Once the second agent had entered the door to the office, he triggered the bug's exit as it scurried through the top of the doorframe out into the hallway, entering an adjacent office. As the bug repositioned, so, too, did Pollock, moving out of his office and around the corner as the two agents searched for the cat that did not exist. Once clear of the corner, he triggered another *meow* in the bug's new room just for good measure. Pollock heard a startled laugh from the men behind as he moved towards the stairwell.

Within minutes, he reached the utility room he'd sought without encountering any further teams… and from the Mockingbug's mounted camera, he could see that the agents found neither the bug nor the cat that it faked, still searching the nearby rooms. It meowed again.

Above Pollock's head was the thick concrete floor of the security suite. In front of him was a padlock-locked door, which was unlocked in seconds thanks to Carter Miles's RFID hacking unit Pollock had placed beside it. He slipped the lock free and pocketed it, entering the utility room. Along the wall, Pollock found a dark green panel along a thick-grade wire that ran ceiling to floor. He opened that panel and observed the mess of cables and wires, knowing that one—or several—contained incoming security feeds. Pollock removed from his pack something that Miles had called *the spine*—it was a relatively stiff and inflexible length of cable, but it was divided into small segments, or *vertebrae,* each of which had a smaller wire pointing outwards to its left and right. Each of those tiny wires had clips on their end with biting, metallic teeth. Pollock oriented the spine sideways and began clipping it onto the mass of wires, attaching each vertebra's clips onto an individual, upright cable. This established a parallel circuit for each attached wire, a second course for data to flow. Once every clip had been attached, Pollock toggled the spine itself and a quick laser pulse severed the wires it ran across, making it so that all of the cable content now ran through the spine's conduits without any momentary disruptions. Pollock attached his handheld monitor to the output cable on the spine, checking its contents. The received data was not recognizable to Pollock's system… no doubt encrypted video feeds. That was nothing unexpected, but unencrypted would have certainly made things easier.

"In position," came Hannah's voice in his ear.

"Stand by," Pollock whispered, "cameras in another minute or two."

Pollock tapped the record button on his screen, and the spine began capturing all of the encrypted data that ran through it. After recording for a full minute, Pollock prepared to toggle the variable loop feature: the spine would no longer send the incoming data it received, but would instead repeat the data it had captured in imperfect loops, changing the length randomly to prevent any security software from flagging an obvious surveillance loop. They were playing the old 'loop the tapes' security hack, but doing it with encrypted data meant doing that same maneuver with your eyes closed. The looped video might have a walking team somewhere in the foreground at the moment of the cut and loop, making it obvious that the feeds were being manipulated. It would take luck for things to go off without a hitch. But like the ID badge, any sort of advantage, however brief it might hold, was worth pursuing.

"Feeds looping; we likely don't have long," Pollock whispered. "What's your status?"

* * *

"Moving through the first camera choke," Hannah said, stepping into the well-monitored hall that marked the first level of asset security. Ahead, beyond two glass walls, stood the metal security door for Michelangelo's housing. Above, the black eyes of roof-mounted cameras loomed, but Hannah knew that now—at least for a time—the camera's eyes were not watching back.

"Will be waiting in—" Hannah cut her own sentence off as she heard the scuffling sound of approaching footsteps... a security patrol that the two had been unaware of. She looked left and right, seeing only potted plants against walls of glass... there would be no hiding. And so, with a sigh, Hannah clicked on her short-range comms jammer and began to draw from the light overhead, which snaked downwards in twisting lines through the glass walls and into her body, filling her with its power. Flight, electric arcs, EMPs... all of the options at her disposal were loud and disruptive, but their infiltration needed to be *mostly* stealthy. And so, Hannah simply *walked* towards the corner the men approached from, taking cover right at the edge.

When the first man rounded the corner, she lashed out with her prosthetic right in a horizontal chop, aiming at the man's neck. *Stun, not kill* was her central command to herself, and as the brawl began, Hannah realized just how easy both stunning and killing seemed to be. She moved faster, could strike harder. Her reflexes seemed enhanced, her stamina endless as she drew from more light. Her first chop sent the first agent stumbling, and then with a push off three overhead lights, she lurched with impossible speed towards the second, contacting him with all the force of a full-tilt running charge despite having been only a foot and a half away. The second agent went down skidding across the floor, and from atop him, Hanna continued to push along the lights overhead, the slide dragging out. Hannah used the pinky on her artificial right to inject the man with the sedative—it had been a modification made by the Basilisk's own people, who shared in the belief that these men shouldn't die for simply doing their job for a company less morally bankrupt than VitaCorp. As the man's struggle stopped, Hannah ended the slide and stood, turning towards the first man, still on the floor grasping at his neck. She jogged over and injected him, too, with a sedative, leaving both unconscious for 2-4 hours. She dragged the two into the nearest office and then toggled off her comms jam.

"Had to go silent for a moment... ran into resistance," Hannah said. The other end of the line was silent. *Did he also have his jammer on?* Hannah wondered, as she advanced back towards that metal security door. She sat at its base and tilted her head, listening for footsteps and waiting for word to try the door.

* * *

"I said you there," the security agent repeated.

Pollock turned, facing the men approaching from the other end of the office floor.

"What are you doing by yourself? Patrols are in twos at minimum," the agent said.

Pollock smiled. "You won't believe it, but strangest happenings tonight... there I was, two floors lower, when I heard this cat."

"Heard about that on the comms," one of the men said, snickering, as the pair stopping a few feet away from Pollock. They had their hands on their holsters, but their weapons weren't drawn.

"Fast bastard," Pollock said. "Saw him, I think, and was chasing him up and down the floor... my partner tired out real quick of all the frantic running. There he is, slow-ass, approaching right now," Pollock said, gesturing with a nod behind the two men. They turned, and Pollock lurched immediately forwards into their distraction. One hand went down to the man's weapon, gripping his hand tightly to prevent a clean draw. The second hand wrapped around the man's back, where Pollock's combat gloves triggered their electric stun—a less-than-legal mod Pollock had added after his brush with Shockfist. The man went limp in Pollock's arms.

Pollock drew the energy weapon himself as he twisted the collapsing security agent, leveraging his body as a shield. He aimed the energy weapon at the startled second agent.

"Comms are local-jammed, no help on its way. You shoot at me, your slug kills your partner and I shoot you back… not ideal for you. These gloves have a kill setting, but I set it to stun only. Drop your weapon and kick it towards me, and then lie down with your hands on your head. I brought a nice tranq pen with me… we'll put you two right to sleep, and when you wake you can tell your boss whatever she'd want to know."

The agent Pollock had grabbed twitched in his arms and groaned. The second placed his weapon on the ground and slid it forwards with his feet, before climbing down and complying with Pollock's instructions. Pollock removed two metal vials from his front jacket pocket—tranquilizer pens—and pressed one to each of the men's throats. Within seconds, they were still.

Pollock tucked one of the energy pistols into his pocket and squeezed the second with his glove-augmented hand. The enhanced grip allowed him to squeeze the gun into cracked pieces of plasteel composite. He then dragged the two men into the nearest alcove—a snack room, by the looks of the vending machines and rentable tables—and tucked them away into the room's supply closet. They slept calmly, if not comfortably, next to several large blue tanks of drinking water.

Pollock then moved to the center of the snack room and checked his position within the tower on the 3D projected map. His dot in the blue projected structure was within the red zone that extended beyond the security center of the tower, meaning that he was firmly within broadcast range. Nodding to himself, he unpacked the largest and heaviest item he carried: the decryption and broadcasting unit. It was a flat and elongated box, built with the solid frame of military construction. It was a tool of espionage, designed to capture encrypted datastreams and broadcast them over pre-defined distances. Encryption, of course, couldn't be broken without a key, but the key was fortunately in the hardware and software of the systems now less than a hundred feet from Pollock... the feeds were decoded for viewing by security personnel, and Pollock would simply be borrowing those decrypted feeds, borrowing the access that those terminals provided.

He removed the databee from its small plastic canister. It was 150,000 credits in a tiny metal form that he could squish entirely with a closed, un-gloved fist... such fragility, and yet such incredible capability. He tossed it up into the air and its wings automatically activated, taking the tiny metal drone out from the room and towards the security center just beyond. It waited there at the door to enter the security floor, unable to open the door by itself. The plan was to give it a short time to see if luck was on their side... if someone naturally left the security room, the bee would be able to enter without assistance. If after three minutes, the bee still waited by the door, Pollock would have to improvise.

It was after less than a minute of waiting that there was a sudden approach of voices. The voices brought both good news and bad news. The good news was that the door to the security floor was opened, and the databee zipped in without apparent detection. The door swung shut behind it. The bad news brought a twisting knot in Pollock's stomach as he heard the exiting man speak: "I'm going to the vending machines; you fellas want anything?"

Pollock quickly scooped up the transmitter unit and ducked towards the supply closet, opening it as softly as he could manage. He then slipped in and clicked the latch shut behind him, settling down beside the two unconscious guards among the stacks of blue plastic water drums. The door to the closet was slit with horizontal blinds, from which Pollock could peek outwards from the darkness. He saw a lone agent enter the break room and begin scanning his way across the vending machine, leaning in towards the glass as he read small, faded labels. He waved his wrist over the scanner and then typed a code, watching with dry boredom as the spinning metal spiral dislodged the selected snack and dropped it to the bottom of the machine. He then moved to the adjacent machine and dialed in the combination for an instant nap, a pill that could be taken to emulate approximately four hours of sleep instantaneously.

As he opened the small pill bottle for the single tablet inside, he scanned around for water to help wash it down. There, just beside the closet, he found the drink machine. He grabbed one of the plastic cone cups on the side of the machine and held the tap open, shaking his head as the water begin to exit in a slow, miserable trickle. Pollock watched from the dark only a foot and a half away as the man sighed deeply, looking at the water tank on top of the drink machine. The water in the reservoir was hardly even a puddle, and it gave a sad, pathetic gurgle as a bubble disturbed the small remaining supply. The man's small plastic cone was filled, and he quaffed it after setting the instant nap pill on his tongue. He then wiped his lips and set the cup under the mouth of the machine again, holding the tap.

Pollock's worried frown deepened even further as the water stream bled out to not even matching a dehydrated man at a urinal... and to Pollock's left, to his right, were the replacement bottles for the now-empty reservoir on top of the machine. Pollock watched as the man raised the cup, not even a third full, to his lips and drank the tiny amount of water in a single gulp. He watched as the man shook his head, eyes tracing from the empty tank to the closet directly adjacent, surely aware that the excess bottles were stored within…

"Not my problem," the man said, backing away without changing the water. On his way out of the break room, he bought an extra-large bottle of soda, a smile wide on his face for having found an excuse to indulge in his guilty pleasure. He sauntered back to the security floor, flashed his wrist chip, opened the door, and swung it shut behind him, the cone of yellow light from that room dissipating among the cool blues and blacks of the nighttime floor.

Without leaving the closet, Pollock switched the broadcast unit back to 'on' and watched on its feed as the databee buzzed its way to an open port on the rear of their display terminal. It climbed its way into the opening of the machine, entering close-quarter contact with metal and wires to the point where the camera view was no longer useful. Pollock knew that it would be connecting the metal of its legs and tail to different points in the system, downloading a small malware package that it carried to gain access to the system… and within two minutes, the full array of ArtGen monitoring cameras appeared on Pollock's screen. The databee itself could only send information over distances of about 100-200 feet, but the transmitter that Pollock carried could cover miles. "SEND DATA?" the machine asked, and Pollock tapped the button for *yes*. It then began to stream its data down and out of the tower… to Halogen servers below, and, after sufficient rerouting, to Carter Miles's personal system.

Pollock then realized that he'd switched his jammer on during his encounter with the pair, but had left it active since then… he switched it off. "Bee is planted, awaiting Miles's magic," he said into comms.

* * *

"I was wondering if you'd fallen off the tower," Hannah said. "Been waiting by the door long enough to meet three roving patrols." She leaned over the muscular, 6'5" security guard and gave him a second dose from her tranquilizer injector, just to be safe.

"Ran into some trouble, same as you," Pollock replied. "Lil' guys are having a nap now, is all."

"How long will Miles need?" Hannah asked.

"Just another ten seconds," answered a new voice on their line. "The bee built us a nice little backdoor to their employee databank... your credentials should be valid in.... now."

Hannah walked up to the metal door labeled CONTAINMENT and scanned her 'employee' keycard. The metal door slid open, and then she was in.

As she journeyed forwards, there was a second, and even a third security checkpoint... each one featuring thick, metallic doors nearly like an airlock. A fear began to rise—an irrational one, but compelling nonetheless—that the final door would not open, and she would be trapped in these impersonal boxes of metal until the security teams arrived... and then Hannah would face a tough choice. Fight for her freedom and harm agents who, as far as she knew, might be decent people... or surrender to arrest, and a lengthy—if not endless—stay in corporate prison?

When the fifth and final door hissed open, this one releasing a small puff of mist as it did, the questions faded from Hannah's mind. Instead, a deep sense of awe and uncertainty took root. The space known as *Containment* was the most incredible place she had seen. Incredible, here, was being used in its most literal definition: *in*, meaning *not*, and *credible*, meaning *believable*. In the heart of the massive skyscraper, a monumental tower of glass and light, she stood within a cavern that felt an entirely separate world. It was icy, and it was black. Drones flew around overhead in inscrutable patterns, and suddenly Hannah was elsewhere entirely… she was in the deep and warm confines of her bed, of sleep, when she would dream every night of the points of light in the field of black. Had it been prophetic? What about this place instilled her with such a sense of *gravity,* of converging destiny? The air beyond the final door was frigid, and the space yawned open before her.

Cool, blue lights activated beyond panels of glass deep in the racks of servers, and now Hannah could see that they were several floors below. No doubt there was an elevator or stairway nearby, but Hannah wasted no time with such slowdowns. She walked to the rail edge of her upper floor and stepped over the rail, leaping down into the cold black space silhouetted in blue light. As she fell, she pushed gently against the blue lights below, using them to slow her fall to a gentle landing on the metal grating of the server rack. Bright white spotlights switched on, illuminating her every footfall. If there were any secret corporate spies within ArtGen, if they were here, meddling with the terminal at the center of the server rack, surely the lights gave Hannah away. But still, she walked inwards towards the central heap of machinery at the middle of Containment, stunned to silence by the somber majesty of the place.

"Full team of five makes a sweep past Containment in two or three minutes; they're heading towards you now," Pollock's voice said in her ear. Hannah continued inwards, the rise of the machine before her somehow seeming to grow even taller as she approached. It was deactivated, that much was obvious… but Hannah felt like a dwarf sneaking into the shadow of a slumbering dragon. Here, before her, was the mind that created the greatest of modern man's works… here, before her, was an artificially-intelligent system that proved creativity was a

solvable game.... and here, before her, it slept, no doubt dreaming of its next fantastical renderings—did it, too, share the dreams Hannah returned to so often? She reached out and touched it, feeling an outburst of gooseflesh as she ran her prosthetic hand along the terminal.

"Central panel's abandoned," Hannah said into her comms. "Machine is asleep and looks to have been that way for a while... no interloper caught in the act."

"Deploy the Eye in the Sky, then," said Miles's voice in her ears. Hannah nodded and removed the small object from her belt. It was a small disk not entirely unlike the lightpuck mounted in her prosthetic hand. This one, however, was made of transparent, refractive plastic designed to provide a loose sort of invisibility for the object... *tactical blurring,* Miles had said. She pressed the button on its rear activating its launch mode. A small light toggled on inside the plastic frame. She then peeled the paper off the adhesive back and held it high over her head. She drew in blue vines of light from the sources around her and then launched the disk upwards, pushing with her mind as the object flew twenty, fifty, one hundred feet up. Eventually it collided with the ceiling with a ringing, echoing *thunk*... and thanks to the adhesive, there it remained. Since a high-security room like this was often scanned for abnormal broadcast frequencies, the Eye in the Sky worked a little differently. It would record silently and stealthily from its high vantage for 8 days, and then it would release all of its data at once—an event that Miles called 'the data supernova." With a burst like that, it was likely to be found... but it would have served its purpose well by then. Hannah looked back to the looming, cold metal tower of Michelangelo's corporeal form... *who visits you, here? And what is their purpose?*

The camera would hopefully provide all of these answers in time.

Pollock, guiding Hannah with full surveillance access, was able to talk her way out from the heart of Containment such that there were no additional guards knocked unconscious. She joined him in a corner office two floors below, both saddling back into their tandem vest.

"I'm reading the broadcasts from the bee," Carter Miles said over comms, *"and it's the strangest thing. It's not that their security systems were weak—quite the opposite, really, they were among the tightest I've encountered—"*

"But you were in in minutes," Hannah said, slipping the shoulder of her vest over and pulling it tight.

"That's the thing. The vulnerability I exploited to get us in? This was no Achilles heel. I thought we'd gotten lucky, but the way they handle logins just doesn't make sense."

"Incompetent programmers, then?" Pollock offered, pulling his belt tight. He then extended one of the straps and passed it to Hannah, who looped it through the hoop by her right leg.

"Fiendishly competent programmers, who, for some reason, seem to have built an impenetrable wall with a hole in the middle... like they wanted us to go through it."

"What are you suggesting?" Hannah asked.

"This line may not be secure—rendezvous contingency, not primary. Cutting line." And then the call went dead.

The window to Pollock's right shattered. His glass cutter had been leaning against it, and it now tumbled out to the street below. It was another second before Pollock registered the ringing in his ear, and the strange warmth of a splash of blood on his front—Hannah's, or his own? The air shimmered as a kinetic round cracked through the space Pollock had stood

moments before, only displaced due to a shove by Hannah…
and as his harness line pulled taught, jerking her towards him,
reality accelerated from its momentary slow motion back to
full, chaotic speed. Beyond the broken window, silhouetted by
the glowing yellow light of the tower adjacent, Pollock could
see a drone hovering in place. The unit was blacked out, with
no lights on it of any kind… and in silhouette, Pollock could
see the weapon readjust its aim towards the pair of them now
prone on the floor. Pollock pulled the energy pistol free of his
belt and fired at the drone, which quickly banked to the right to
dodge the incoming plasma round. Although there was no
contact, the day-bright glow of the plasma surely threw off the
camera's exposure level, meaning it would take another critical
second to readjust to the dark.

Hannah wasted no time of that second, pressing against the
overhead lights as she drank in power from every available
source around her. Pollock, from his prone position, watched
as the lines of light snaked inwards—they radiated heat,
warmth, as they did—and then he felt her movement tug at his
harness, sliding him across the ground. His stomach dropped.
"Wait," he protested, eyeing his parachute pack still propped
up against the far wall, but then she was already freefalling out
the window. And as Pollock's tether yanked him forwards, he
was then, too.

Pollock yelled and spun his arms as the world tumbled
around him. The air screamed by his side as a kinetic round
tore through empty space, its passing drowned back out by the
howling of the wind in his ears. His harness caught, *hard,* as
Hannah bounded back upwards, and Pollock's falling
transitioned to a wild swinging beneath as Hannah struggled to
regain control of their flight. Their harnesses were connected,
but only partially, allowing Pollock to dangle two feet below
connected only on one side. His head was pointed downwards,
and he stared at the busy, swarming streets above—or was it

below? Blood rushed to his head, and Pollock felt as though he was surely slipping out of his harness. Another muted *whumf* was the shot of a suppressed kinetic weapon, this bullet grazing Pollock's side. Its sting was immediate and *cold.*

"Hang on there," Hannah yelled, and suddenly the duo were dropping again. "More light and we're set," she yelled. Pollock's harness twisted and whipped about as they moved, and as it spun, Pollock could see the approaching drone in spirited pursuit.

As he turned an additional rotation, Pollock again raised the energy pistol. He fired as he rotated, and, not surprisingly, his energy pulse wound up missing the thing by a few feet laterally. Hannah drew energy from the headlights of nearby airborne cars, their horns blaring in indignation at the stray energy pulse. Hannah pushed off of one, twirling sideways, right as the drone fired its next round—another near miss, but seemingly closer.

Pollock's wild rocking again stabilized to a spin, and again he waited for his rotation to align the shot. *6 o'clock... 8 o'clock, 10 o'clock... there!* Pollock fired again, and though the drone dipped and twisted as the round flew, the plasma was close enough for its heat to deform the rotor's sensitive plastic—the drone began to spin and list as it fell.

Pollock's celebrations were short-lived as two more drones appeared, one from in front, another from behind. A single kinetic shot rang, this one striking—and snapping—the thin line that connected his harness to hers. Pollock's eyes widened, his hand reaching up. Her eyes widened in kind, her hands reaching down. His hands closed, and hers did as well, both uncertain if their reach had been enough... and then, gravity prevailed, its inexorable hand wrapping about Pollock and dragging him down, down to the glowing streets hundreds of feet below.

As Pollock fell, he looked up, and the howl of the wind rose to a deafening roar in his ears. He was weightless, and the scene above him felt serene. He watched Hannah drop from her vantage higher in the sky, entering into a tight dive. The pursuing drones twisted and fell behind her, weapons training downwards. Pollock watched as the windows and signs from every tower around began to extend in long, snaking lines of yellow and white—their veins moved from every direction to meet her, almost a firework in reverse. He watched her yell as the light filled her, her eyes soon glowing like twin points of daylight to drown out the night itself. Pollock heard the horns below, the music that drifted through the breeze, the mutterings and murmurings of people as the street raced to meet him—or was it him that raced to meet it?

Hannah's fall accelerated as she pushed off the light above her. The hundreds and hundreds of beams of light entering her body caused a ring of white light to crystallize around her. He could see the strain on her face as she moved closer, arms again outstretched. Pollock reached up as well, watching as the undersides of low-air traffic whizzed past to either side… and then his hand found her harness, and he squeezed with all the force that the combat gloves could muster. Hannah shot the lightpuck from her prosthetic and pushed against it with all of her force… and then Pollock felt an explosion of pain, and saw only black.

"I'm dead," he reasoned. *"A splat on the pavement. Close catch, but no cigar."*

But then he heard the clang as two drones smacked into the floor, powered down and unable to stop their downward flight. Then he heard the panicked sounds of the crowd around them, suddenly lurched into darkness. And then he understood what exactly had happened—and that he was still, somehow, alive.

Pollock's eyes adjusted to the blackout dark as he rose to his feet, detaching the glove's vicegrip to Hannah's harness. She, in turn, bent to pick up the lightpuck she'd used to stop the pair's fall—albeit perhaps a little roughly—in the moments before she detonated her halo and knocked out power in who knows how large a vicinity. The drones were dashed to fragments, and the blackout would give them ample cover to vanish...

Somehow, they had survived exfiltration.

Chapter 47

"The black tower is as silent as usual, but on-the-ground accounts agree that the VitaCorp research lab explosion took place during CEO Tacitus Newport's personal tour, and it is still unknown if he managed to escape the blast. Share prices of VitaCorp have risen 3% on news that the CEO might have been harmed, perhaps due to many investors' opinion that Newport's management was damaging to profit potential. Current COO Clive Avery has denied comment, though it is speculated that he would assume the CEO's chair if the worst were confirmed."

-Coverage from an on-site news reporter in the wake of what was deemed an explosion caused by a battery defect in scanning equipment

* * *

"Our men on the ground have concluded their sweep—no corpses anywhere in the blackout zone, sir," said the masked VitaCorp agent.

Avery exhaled deeply and rubbed at his temples, setting aside the tablet with the drone footage. They'd scored a shot or two on the girl, but she could use the ichor to heal her wounds... and the groundborne CSP had had quite the tumble, but it seemed as though she'd somehow caught him before the ground did its work. By all accounts, a failed attack. Spivey and McKillian could not find out... would not find out, in fact. Avery had kept his work with ArtGen entirely secret to the duo, as it was their own employer he was investigating. His communications with his ArtGen asset were done in secret, entirely in-person meetings with jammer technology active.

When she'd installed the back door, and rigged it to monitor traffic that breached it, Avery had honestly expected to find someone more closely aligned with Spivey and McKillian's camp, not the lightbending whore and her CSP assistant... a welcome surprise, serendipity.

But then Avery paused and stroked at his chin. *Could they all be one and the same? A single faction unified against me?* He frowned and felt a twinge in his neck. He extended his arms forwards, eyes tracing left and right, monitoring for signs of drooping. Seeing none, he set them back down on the desk, noting with displeasure the sweat stain they left.

"Sir?" asked the agent.

"Oh, yes, no sign of course. Recall our teams, encrypted comms only. They can leave the drone debris—purchased and managed with the correct precautions, they were. Also, set up a scraper to monitor all news feeds for articles posted about myself..."

"Scanning for what, sir?"

"Anything and everything. Any article whatsoever, I shall know about it right away."

"Yes sir," the agent said, jogging away.

Next it was Avery's secretary who spoke into his comms. "Sir, your divertissement is here," she said.

"Celebratory, no longer... but still, send her in to my private chamber."

* * *

When Avery walked into the room, he wore his full facial plastic mask and enclosed bodysuit. The woman sat there, alone, rising and smiling as Avery entered—but then momentarily recoiling when she saw the strange gear that he wore. Kelsey Levin was nineteen, and she seemed very small against the vaulted ceilings of the wide, antique chamber... and at the end of that room, draped in a sheen silk canopy, was a king-sized bed, pristinely made.

"It is nice to meet you, Mister Avery, sir," the girl said, offering a hand forwards to shake. Avery ignored it and instead walked to the dark oak desk in the room, removing a decanter and pouring into a single glass. He walked towards the girl and offered it to her wordlessly. As there was no proposition to accept or reject, the girl took it silently and began to drink, her arms drawing in. She seemed to shrink even more before the larger room... they were always so much smaller in person than they seemed on the screen.

"You won't be joining me for a glass?" Kelsey asked, trying—and largely failing—to put some flirtation behind the question... it simply came out as confused, accusatory.

"Not until I might remove this mask," Avery said.

"Do you need help?" Kelsey said, starting towards him, but Avery raised a warding hand.

"Stay," he said, and Kelsey remained alone on her sofa.

"It is a lovely chamber," she said, looking around at the fine antiques from the Old World that lined the walls. "You'd never imagine such a place in a cold tower of black glass." She took another sip from her drink.

"If I may be blunt, Miss Levin, I do not often enjoy idle conversations with prostitutes," said Avery, sitting in the chair of his desk.

The woman's face reddened with indignation. "Prostitute?" She balked. "I am a model, an actress!"

"Who accepted my financial patronage contingent upon an in-person private visit," Avery said. "You're not stupid, and neither am I. Let us call a spade a spade… and a prostitute, a prostitute."

Her face fell, and she held to the cup tightly as the presence of the bed in the corner of the room seemed to burn at her like the staring of an enemy behind her back.

"Some shrug it off," Avery said. "Some get indignant as you have. Most, at this point in time, are weighing their options, deciding if their dignity is worth the price of the credits they'd lose."

"And what, I wonder, is the price of dignity?" Kelsey asked.

"Five million credits was all it took to get you here, so I should think below that," Avery said.

Kelsey set the glass down on the table beside her. "I suddenly don't feel very well."

"As an actress, you already sold your body for money," Avery argued.

"Something's not right," Kelsey said.

"No, something isn't… you feel the lightheadedness, yes? The churning of the gut. The cold sweats breaking out all over."

She looked to him, visibly weak now. "*Poison?*"

"Of a sort, yes… reminiscent of one of the more barbaric practices of the Old World, a process known as chemotherapy. Used to be the best they had to treat cancer, blind fools that they were…"

Kelsey pushed the glass off the table, and it shattered against the floor, spilling its contents across the deep red carpet.

"You will survive, this I promise... it is *cleansing you*, in a sense. My immune system is compromised, you see... and what you are undergoing is full-body sanitation. Did you know the human colon contains more bacteria—the greatest microbial density—of any environment on Earth?" He was advancing towards her now, and he helped her to her feet as she protested weakly.

"Within your nose... across your skin... buried deep in the reproductive organs, hiding in the sinuses... the human body is a prime vessel for disease. I would have you clean; I would have you pure," Avery said, setting her down beside the bath tub in the adjoining bathroom. "The vomiting will begin soon, and it will be *quite* red... chin up, and do avoid getting it on your hair."

And then, as promised, the vomiting came in waves, and Kelsey Levin gripped to the sides of the tub as though she were hanging from a ledge, and it was the only purchase that kept her from a fatal plunge below. When the cramps and gagging finally subsided, and the pounding headache began to recede, she saw him, sitting across the bathroom on crossed legs. His mask was off, revealing a harsh face and greying hair... if his eyes bore any sympathy at all, they surely did not show it.

"You can keep your credits," she said, spitting red into the tub. "*That* was not... it was..." she said, unable to even choose her words. She stood and the room spun around her, her limbs trembling and weak. But still, she stumbled her way out of the bathroom and exited the bedchamber, shaking her head.

Avery watched her go, eyes tracing sidewise across an unmoving head. When she had left, and he heard the *'ding'* of the arriving elevator in the hall beyond, he unfolded his tablet and pulled up surveillance video from the elevator cabin. In the clip, Kelsey Levin was leaning against the rail, her arms drawn tight around her. She was trembling, eyes downcast.

"Miss Levin," Avery said into the tablet, talking to her through speakers mounted in the elevator itself, "I apologize for the unpleasant end to our business relationship."

He watched as she looked up, searching for the camera overhead. Finding it in the far corner, she raised a middle finger and held it up so that the lens could capture it clearly.

"You will no doubt think poorly of me, and I am sure that my brand, the VitaCorp brand, is likely to be a source of continuing trauma to you," he said. She glowered at the lens, still silent. "It is for that reason that, to insulate you from such trauma, you will no longer have to worry about ending up in any VitaCorp facilities for any medical procedures—be they voluntary or otherwise," Avery said. His words dripped venom, but his tone remained level, calm. He watched as Kelsey Levin's face fell, no doubt thinking of the squalid condition of unofficial medical facilities… places where amputations were the only viable cures to technophages, where radiation burns were given mere palliative treatment… where cancer patients went to die. It was a place for the uninsured and the illegally immigrated… a last resort for the poor that, when faced with the injuries of the modern world, was only marginally better than no care at all.

He watched her speak up to the lens in protest, but Avery heard nothing. "Your microphone is disabled, as I do not wish to hear pitiful protests… your choices are your own, and your consequences, predictable."

She continued to speak to the camera, either failing to understand the lack of microphone or choosing to ignore it... that she dared to speak back at all vexed Avery even further. "In addition, I am deeply remorseful for the miscommunication regarding your medicinal dose in my chamber... and only adding further tragedy still, the cost of a full human microbiota refresh is quite exorbitant. I often provide substantial discounts for business partners, but as our business relationship is concluded, you shall be issued a full bill for the procedure. I hope your accounts are... more substantial than our earlier conversations would have me believe."

She fell to the floor of the elevator, her back to the cold, metal wall. She was protesting no longer... just waiting for Avery's continued punishment. Such was as it was supposed to be.

"With your hasty departure, you also missed the second, and oh-so-critical component of the procedure... the implanting of a new set of microbes, of course. Without this, you will die. I suggest you go to the nearest medical center not affiliated with VitaCorp to rectify the issue... I suspect you have some few hours before permanent damage is done."

He watched the elevator stop, the doors sliding open on the video. The girl did not move. She looked back up at the lens, eyes carrying a look of utter defeat.

"Unless," Avery began, a wicked smile creeping across his face, "you return upstairs. We can re-negotiate your contract... perhaps an adjusted credit price for my patronage, as I hadn't expected someone with so unpleasant a temperament. But I remain confident that we can strike some sort of mutually-agreeable bargain. You get what you want, and I get what I want. Doesn't that sound *fair?*"

He watched the war playing out across her face, savoring the way that she was so utterly dependent on his just mercy… he watched, nearly salivating, as she reached for the button panel, selecting his floor.

The elevator rose.

Chapter 48

"Civilization is an island, and woe to those who are thrown into the sea."

-Quote from Mick Flintstock's suspense novel "Isolario"

* * *

It had been no surprise that the small township featured in "The Last Dreamer" actually existed... and equally unsurprising was the fact that Hawk's Tail fell precisely in the heatmap ring of destinations that Quaine O'Connor might have gone to just before his death. It was on one of the city's outgoing groundborne highways, the only charging station for miles in either direction. Official census placed 53 permanent residents.

In the film, the protagonist had met a seer in a shack near the woods there, a blind man who spoke statements of deep profundity... Braxton wondered if he, too, would prove to be real. Where did fiction end, and reality begin?

His car's engine hummed as it flew smoothly through the air, the decrepit highway winding left and right beneath him. He followed it like a mystic to a dowsing rod, honing in on that township that occupied a place more firmly rooted in the surreal deep in his mind... he glanced up to the mirror and stared at his foreign face, still hating the way it seemed more a caricature of his old self. What was that strange driver doing, making his way out to Hawk's Tail? What did he hope to uncover out here? Was he truly still guarding his employers' best interests, or had this somehow become personal?

Braxton laughed at the questions to dismiss them. The woman Hannah Preacher was dedicated in a way that Cara never was, sure, but their simple run-in hadn't truly shaken the strength of his convictions... the world still needed its order. VitaCorp's guiding hand *was* that order, and no amount of dedication before love could convince Braxton any differently. *She* was of no consequence to the bigger picture... despite the fact that she came to his mind time and again, nagging at him like a tag in the back of a cloak. Whenever she came back to his mind, he imagined that persistence of her, and dared to wonder what might come next if she and her ilk *succeeded* on their foolish mission... what could a world beyond VitaCorp be like?

It was a foolish notion, a careless daydream; a fit of fancy as a break from the bleak of the city. Braxton could never truly abide such fantasies, for accepting their possibility—imagining their realization—required that Braxton either fall with the system or turn on it. The former was a possibility he didn't mind particularly much: he'd died already, and was certain he could face death again when the time came... but the latter was unconscionable. To betray VitaCorp would require admitting everything he had done until the moment of that betrayal was *wrong*... it would involve admitting fault, admitting to himself that the killings and violence were *not* for the greater good. His soul was not ready to bare such weight. Could anyone's?

People, Braxton decided, *never truly change... change requires disavowing the old self, and nobody has the guts to plunge such a blade into their own heart.* Braxton absentmindedly scratched at his right arm, noting when the nails met plastic that he had reflexively scratched at his prosthetic. He stared at that and frowned. *Perhaps bodies change... but people do not.*

His mind returned again to ships and wooden planks floating in the current, and while he was swept up in these newer, reflective imaginings, the small blocky shapes of structures resolved from the distant haze of the horizon. Hawk's Tail drew near, and Braxton prepared himself for landing. *Whatever came next, it was to better understand his foe... and perhaps, Avery, by means of his secrets. After all, what careful hitman didn't learn all he could about his employer?*

* * *

The census-designated region of Hawk's Tail featured a scattering of old, wooden buildings with patched roofs and sagging walls. The village, if one could be so generous with a label, was built on the rubble of an Old World settlement whose name was now forgotten, and its splintered sidewalks completely reclaimed by the grass and creeping woods that surrounded it. There was only one structure with even a suggestion of modernity, and that was the Hawk's Tail Charge Station positioned just off the highway ramp. Stale, white lights shone down overhead, and a sign with the iconic lightning bolt stood hundreds of feet in the air on a thin, black pole. There were no holo-adverts, no flashing lights... no drones with signs, no glowing, shifting billboards. As far as Braxton could tell, the charge station was the only powered building in the settlement, and it had a certain calm to it, a stillness vastly different to the city far behind him. He landed at the charge station and stepped out into the balmy, outdoor air, noting a strange scent hanging in the breeze, occupying the space usually packed with the chemical scent of fuels and exhaust... could that be the gentle presence of *trees,* of *dirt?* He heard only the thrum of an underground generator, and a strange empty sound of the carrying of the wind. Then he heard footsteps.

An attendant rushed from the shop alongside the station towards Braxton's vehicle. The boy seemed no older than 15, with a large protrusion from his neck—a tumor, and an invasive one at that.

"Oh, no, that won't be necessary," Braxton said, doing his best to pull his eyes away from the growth. "Charged up just before heading out from New Phoenix."

"No charge, no toilet," the boy said, eyeing Braxton defensively.

"Not that either," Braxton said. "I'm looking for a man—a blind man, resident of Hawk's Tail."

The boy pointed down the road that ran parallel to the charging station. "Just up that way for a few minutes' walk. He lives in a shack on the right. Red walls, can't miss it."

Braxton smiled and nodded. "The sign there, for car washes—I don't suppose you have washer drones in this place?"

The boy shook his head. "Me or my uncle do them by-hand. You can't get better value for your credits than hand-washed attention," he said. "City washes can't match."

"Then I'll leave you and your uncle to it, then… my business shouldn't be long with the man, but take your time. Payment now, or after?"

"After," the boy said, eyeing the city car. "*By the sickness*… the burning rain is murder for the paint. That's a lot of residue on your car."

Braxton shrugged, heading off towards the way the boy pointed. "The price of living in the city… some things just don't wash off easily."

The walk along the road was serene, each step along the grassy gravel met with a satisfying crunch. Crickets chirped in the warm breeze, a ceaseless soundscape that was equally inviting as it was alien. After a few peaceful minutes of silent walking, the trees to his right gave way to a small clearing with a decrepit shack in its center. Its walls were a rusted red, and its roof sagged inwards along the left half. By the outhouse positioned on the edge of the woods, Braxton could tell that it had no plumbing, and by the dark of its interior, he doubted it had electricity, either. "Anybody home?" Braxton called to the shack, but by the place's profound stillness, he knew that it must be empty. That is, right until he heard a voice call back from inside:

"*Who's there?*" Asked a strange, high-pitched voice.

"My name is Braxton… I've come to speak with the blind man of Hawk's Tail. Is that you?" Braxton asked, eyes straining against the darkened window. The interior seemed to be pitched black.

The door swung open, and out hobbled a hunched old man swinging a white cane left and right.

"I told you demons already that you can't take any more taxes here—no taxes here!—I ain't got your stinkin taxes, no sir."

Braxton eyed the older man. His beard was in a tangled, untrimmed mass, and his eyes, though bright blue, seemed nearly glassy as he stared at the open air to Braxton's right.

"I'm not with the tax office," Braxton said. "I—"

"Then what demons are you? I can smell trouble on you like piss in the corner," the old man said. "No doubt about it."

"Not a demon… maybe more a ghost," Braxton replied.

"I've told the ghosts left and right, now... you stay back and keep your haunts to yourself. No need for me, no sir, you keep the haunts to yourself." The man spoke these words like a near refrain, rocking slightly and breaking into a cackle at the end—it was all Braxton needed to confirm he wasn't in his right mind at all. His voice was animated by that touch of madness, and as he spoke, he shook his head wildly. Braxton felt the hairs on his neck stand as the blind man suddenly whipped his head to stare straight into Braxton's eyes.

"Wait—another scent in the wind. You've had the dreams—oh, by the sickness, he's had the dreams—I can smell it on you like piss in the corner, no doubt about it."

"I have, and that's related—I think—to what I was hoping to discuss. What is your name?" Braxton asked.

"Never knew my name—parents died 'fore I was born—kids would call out *'There goes Click-Stick Jack, or look, it's Click-Clack Jack.'* That's they call me, and I like the name Jack anywho. My momma said the name's supposed to fit the kid, and Jack's a simple name, she said. I like simple because it's easier than tough stuff, and nobody likes tough."

"I thought you said—" Braxton began, but Jack interrupted as he shouted *"will you be quiet now!"*

Braxton waited, unsure how he'd offended, when Jack offered a gracious smile. "Oh, not you, Mr. Braxton. The other one."

Looking around the empty plot, Braxton set his lips in a line, unsure how anything productive was supposed to come from this chat. "Look, Jack—I'm here because I'm looking for someone, and I think he came here to talk with you. His name was Quaine, does that sound familiar?"

"A funny sounding name—whose momma would name a boy like that? My momma said a name should fit the kid, and nobody would wanna be treated funny like that, nuh-uh. I don't know that name," said Click-Clack Jack. "But I've got a bad names with memory—a bad nemory with mames—oh, doesn't even know his own name, 'ole Click-Stick Jack. What's your friend talking about when he came here?"

Braxton sighed. "I don't even know for sure, but—have you heard the stories of the men who can drink of the light?"

"Don't be stupid, mister, you can drink waters like coke and lemonade but lights aren't made of water."

"Not *drink,* drink… they can pull it in, and with it, they have access to incredible power."

The blind man's eyes widened in the doorway to his shack. "You mean the dreamers?" he asked, voice full of wonder and awe.

"Yes I do," Braxton said.

The old man retreated back into his doorway, shouting "come on in, take a seat. We got to talk."

Braxton entered the small shack, and was hit all at once with the stifling heat and an unsavory scent—it was no wonder the man fell back to *piss in the corner* as a favorite expression. The old man pulled on a string behind him with a trembling hand, and a creaky set of window blinds pulled open, letting in a small amount of brown-tinted light.

"I was telling them that there's no how no way the birds can see inside if the blinds are drawn, and I don't need the light no how anyway," Jack said. He returned to an armchair that bore a deep depression in the center of its cushion—clearly it was Jack's favorite resting spot, though it was not like the shack offered many more comforts.

"So," Braxton began, preparing to venture a guess. "You were the first dreamer."

Click-Clack Jack leaned back on his chair, which squeaked in several stages as he went back to full reclining.

"Remind me, what's your friend's name again?" he asked, running a finger through his scraggly beard.

"Quaine."

"Oh, Quaine, that's right... Click-Stick Jack has got a bad mind with membering names—can't even remember my own name, so Jack it is until then..." he paused, and then his face lit up as he recovered his train of thought. "Your friend asked a question like that. So I showed him where I found it, right over by Mary Mallbrook's well."

"Where you found what?" Braxton asked, seeking clarification.

"Why, the dreams!" His mouth then contorted into a gasp, and his jaw opened wider as memories took him. "I could see, then! Blind my whole life, but *by the sickness*, could I see!"

He shook his head, his mouth working wordlessly. "That was the day I fell into the well... that was the day I got hit by lightning. That was the day that the dreams started, and that I could *see*, actually *see* all that wondrous light... and it was the first time I saw t*hem*."

Braxton watched as a demeanor of terror settled over the reclining man.

"Quaine?" Braxton asked, but Jack only shook his head. "No, not him... The Ones Who Pull Stars from the Night Sky."

He said the epithet like it was an official title, a name... and by his look, it seemed to be a nightmare that came with the dreams.

He then leaned forwards, hands gripping the seat of the chair. "I could show you it… what I showed your friend. The well, the spot it all happened… *do you wanna see?*"

Chapter 49

"The more I read of the classics, the more I get the feeling that the old gods were every bit the pricks as our current deities—they just traded clouds for glass towers."

-Conversation recorded in the fourth ring, elevated to moderate system relevance

* * *

The string quartet ended their piece with a flourish, and the crowd clapped politely with a distinct taste of disinterest. The socialites and executives' murmured conversations faded to near silence as the man in the tuxedo took the stage on the far end of the ballroom. "Once again, I would like to extend to you all a warm welcome to the 9th-annual Innovation Summit in Artificial Intelligence Research," he said with an exaggerated bow. More polite applause followed. "You were just listening to *Minuet Technologica,* the first quartet composed to pass the artist's Turing test. That simple four-track arrangement would forever alter the course of art history… and how far we've come since *Inspiration* rendered that iconic opening motif. Behind me, on this wall," he said, gesturing, "is Michelangelo's *New Age,* the first printing from ArtGen's state-of-the—well, *art*—painting system. It depicts, in four regions, man's ascent. In the bottom, we have homo sapiens stumbling through the dark, hiding in caves and straining their eyes. The next plane features man building great societies, kingdoms and civilizations governed by law, by rule… but by ignorance as well, and by hatred. See here the scowling faces of history's cruel, see here the pock-marks left by the wicked and savage… then cometh the fall, the third panel. Cities left in echoing emptiness, the great silence sweeping its way across the old world. Our interconnectedness turned against us… the falling sickness ushering in a dark age. The balkanization wars dominate the fringes, and the disinformation era lives on in the screens, painted here… But then, at top, note the triumph of the final panel… cities back aglow, and the prone form of this woman—representative of Candace Mercer, first president of the United Americas—being lifted by this disembodied prosthetic arm.

"Some call this arm a self-portrait, while others say it is more representative of the union between technology and humankind. But regardless of interpretation, with that universal gesture of support, Mercer—and indeed society—is elevated to a new and exciting era of prosperity, of capability… a flourishing of the arts, of culture, and of human exceptionalism. This painting was designed entirely by Michelangelo, and as soon as it was printed, ArtGen knew that they had succeeded in their mission… it was a promise of the power of such cooperation between man and AI, a demonstration of goodwill between creator and creation. I invite you all to imagine that wonder, that sense of awe when the original ArtGen programming team assessed Michelangelo's expression and felt their heart stir at the machine's vision… I feel that same wonder here tonight, looking at the minds and resources we have pooled together to further AI development. I hope that you all can feel that palpable awe, that genuine pride much akin to how gods of old myth must have felt to see the people they created, and the works that they then made… we are the creators of creators now, their divinity now our technical accomplishment." He paused, and allowed the applause to return, and this time it filled the room with more enthusiasm. People, it seemed, loved to be congratulated. "ISAIR 2153 would not be possible," he continued, "without the generous support of our executive sponsors: Smart-Chip Limited, Brennizer and Brenton, Carrowary Trust, Chassis Instrumental, and Nanolite C.G.A. An additional warm thanks to our board-level sponsors: Jacob Lenmeyer and family, The Mark McInes Company, Luxus Search Metrics, FitzPatrick Pharmaceuticals..."

Carter Miles did his best to tune out the the man's endless drone. It seemed the only thing larger than ISAIR's credit endowments was the list of corporate sponsors who put the event on. Behind the short man on the stage was a screen listing through every sponsorship level like the world's longest film credits reel—Miles was not sure he'd seen the list loop even once yet, and they'd been here for more than an hour. He looked to the door just as his 'dance partner' returned—Lana Crawford wore a fetching chromalite dress, currently cycling between a deep purple and a regal, ocean blue. She sat down next to him at their private table. "Mr. Carrowary," she said with subtle amusement.

"Mrs. Carrowary," he said in reply. "Might I say, dear wife of mine, you look positively *dashing* tonight."

"Oh husband mine," Lana said, "your silver tongue is the very reason I married you."

"Oh, such impropriety!" Miles said with feigned indignation. "To admit to civilized society that you only married a man for the skill of his tongue..."

Lana rolled her eyes. "Ok, not too loud, or we won't be convincing anyone..."

"Reveal ourselves for the philistines we are," Miles said.

"How are the hands?"

"Still itching," Miles replied, rubbing a thumb against the tablecloth. "On your powder run, did you get to speak with the emcee?"

"I did, and they were eager to meet Mr. Carrowary on account of such a generous, last-moment donation..."

"And the additional terms?"

"Hesitantly accepted."

Miles raised the wine glass from his table, and Lana raised hers to meet it. "To high society, then... and the access that money can buy."

Both took sips from the luxurious wine, a far sweeter and smoother drink than any they'd drunk before.

"Speaking of money, where did you find the means to make such a donation?" Lana asked.

"Oh, I donated their own money," Miles said. "Horrible, horrible record-keeping... unpaid interns manage donations. With IT, you get what you paid for... and they paid nothing. Just rerouted a few credits each from their thousands and thousands of minor donors, as well as somewhat larger sums from their bigger sponsors. Their balance sheet is unchanged, but suddenly our name has a sizeable chunk of cash next to it on the ledger."

"Won't they..."

"Oh, they will, but the chaos of the day's commotion for any large event will buy us some time... credits going into the account, credits going out... things can go missing before more thorough accounting takes place. That being said, we shouldn't stick around longer than necessary. On a related note, how long until we can see them?"

"He said as soon as you're ready," Lana replied.

"Well then, wife. Let's go meet the makers of the music."

* * *

The mask slid on… a tap on the rear pad engaged the auto-fit. A button on the side toggled the display, and the clear plastic membranes a half inch from the eyes began to project their images. The outward-oriented cameras on the unit would perform their full-body tracking, and soon the familiar logo of MeetMe would fill the virtual space.

While Spivey waited for the application to load, he toggled the transparency mode to see out the plastic lenses again. He whirled, making sure that the blinds were drawn closed and that his door was securely locked. The rim of the door was stuffed with rubber insulation, making the room nearly effectively airtight. He then sent out a small scanner drone no larger than a moth. It flitted its way about the room, dragging a laser beam across the wall as it scanned for anomalous recording devices. It beeped once, a signal that it found nothing, and then returned to its launch station near the desk. Spivey nodded and toggled his display back to MeetMe.

Virtual Reality was the social bridge that spanned the isolated communities of New Phoenix… it was a place where anyone could choose any avatars to represent them, and they could mix and mingle in ways that stratified society would ordinarily not permit. As it was filled with outer-ringers, there were often few center residents who mixed with the 'peasantry'—but those that did, often did so in secrecy, choosing that rare and anonymized way to mix with a people split in both culture and mentality. There existed entire subcultures with no foot in the 'real' world… their residents were entirely virtual. But to the members of those cultures, who could deny them their authenticity?

Spivey entered the join code from the handwritten note, connecting to an anonymized server through an encrypted channel. It prompted him for a password. *"Immanentize the*

Eschaton," Spivey said, and he waited as it analyzed his voice. Seconds later, he was in.

He was transported to a virtual cathedral of the Old World, a grand hall with paintings lining the walls and ceiling. Imagery from dead faiths believed by a dead people... and yet it didn't feel like he was a trespasser. There was a reverence to the location's recreation, an inherent respect. Spivey traversed the space, taking in the detail as his counterpart connected. After less than a minute of taking in the muscled, reclining forms of the paintings, a new avatar spawned. The newcomer was using the same nondescript businessman avatar that Spivey was... a banal-faced man in a grey suit, a briefcase hanging from the right hand. If Spivey and McKillian were difficult to tell apart in real life, here, in VR, they were literally indistinguishable... as the only thing one could use to tell them apart, their voice, was not even relevant.

"You are late," Spivey signed with his hands. The camera on his headset captured his gestures and his avatar mirrored them, dropping his virtual briefcase. None would speak, as it made their enemy's task of recording their conversations just that much harder. What's more, the language they signed with was not even a standard one... it was a sign language of their own customization, featuring hand gestures that would make it nearly indecipherable to even the deaf. With the sophistication of their foes, every caution was a worthwhile effort.

"You were early," McKillian signed in reply.

"Drone watching my window," Spivey signed.

"My walk home also watched," responded McKillian.

A third avatar appeared, and as it loaded in, both Spivey and McKillian wondered whom it was they'd be speaking with today. On encrypted audiocalls of the past, the two knew that there was both a man and a woman up the chain. Ever since they had switched to virtual signing protocol, they had lost the ability to know the other end of the conversation… and perhaps, for security, that was for the best. Every time they met with their virtual handler, a new avatar was employed, and no identifying information was given or requested. As the avatar of mayoral candidate Tiffany Blythe loaded in, both Spivey and McKillian signed their greetings.

"We will be brief," signed the newcomer. *"Convergence to end state rose from 41% to 78%."* The representation of Tiffany Blythe waited as Spivey and McKillian considered. *"Final pieces are being put into place. Everything will be set in motion within the week."*

Advanced VR masks often featured inwards-facing cameras, the types of things that could have captured (and then rendered) the wide smiles that Spivey and McKillian wore… but such things were additional security risks, and so the two businessmen only stared passively. Their calm demeanor belied the nigh-accomplishment of years of strenuous labor and of great risk.

"And what of Avery's disobedience?" signed Spivey.

"He tried to have them killed," signed McKillian.

"A direct contradiction," agreed Spivey.

"Avery has a place in a map of the end… have faith in the process, and your faith shall be rewarded," signed the avatar of Tiffany Blythe.

"So what are our orders?" signed Spivey.

"You two will have a few more errands to run… and then your instructions will be to leave the city, and to await the next stage."

Both Spivey and McKillian's headsets beeped with the receipt of an encrypted message, and then the image of Tiffany Blythe vanished from the cathedral. Both looked around the large, empty space, imagining the grandeur it might have held in its prime, now reduced to a mere echo of history... with their help, what other grand establishments might history soon forget?

* * *

"And you must be Mr. and Mrs. Carroway," said the woman.

"Carrowary," Miles corrected, extending a polite handshake.

"Of course, my mistake. I apologize for the mix-up... your name is simply not one I recognized. Usually we have regular donors, but it's rare for a newcomer to contribute *so much...*"

"My husband and I are such patrons of the arts," Lana said. "And he's got a fine mind for programming to boot. That's why we made this unusual request, and we're so pleased that you were able to arrange it."

"It was my pleasure," the woman said. "My name is Dr. Lauren Rythmore, executive head of AI research here at the Centers for Advanced Technologies. I'd be happy to take you down to the Old Masters as soon as you're ready."

"Lead the way, doctor," Lana said.

The trio entered an elevator and were spirited away down the 51 floors it took to reach ground level, and then an additional 6 floors beyond. When the doors finally opened, the lower floor had totally shed the air of luxury seen up top with the marble floors, tall ceilings, and gaudy chandeliers... here, the walls were concrete, the floors slate tile. Fluorescent white lights buzzed overhead, lighting a seemingly-endless array of hallways in either direction. "If you'll follow me," Dr. Rythmore said.

After a winding series of lefts and rights, Miles and Lana found themselves staring at a thick blast door. "In compliance with AI safety regulations—some of which were authored in our facility—all active strong AI are kept under continuous security within a closed network. Traditional data input is one-directional, and output can only be rendered through approved channels with sufficient random elements. You two lack full AI access authorization, so, to proceed, I'll need to collect your devices, and you two will have to assent to a full-body scan which will be checking for unauthorized electronic devices or recording equipment that could compromise AI security. This scan *does* pierce clothing and will be overseen by both machine and human security personnel, but it *will not* be saved to any permanent storage. Do I have your authorization?"

Both nodded.

Dr. Rythmore entered the room that the technicians called *the peep show*—although she didn't share *that* particular label with the donors. She stood alongside the pair and all three held their hands up as the scanner clicked three times. Beyond the wall of the adjacent security room, software and security personnel analyzed the hyper-detailed multi-layered impression of the trio, searching for any abnormalities. After thirty seconds of close scrutiny—and the software's seal of approval—they were buzzed through to the door beyond.

The air behind that door had a stale and stuffy quality to it, and a certain musk that lingered in the nose. Its scent wasn't all that unlike what Miles might have imagined explorers of the Old World inhaled as they entered the dusty tombs of the Great Pyramids… here, in these halls, lies an entombed former king of kings—a sleeping giant. But just how deep was their sleep? Have their eyes been peeking in the dark?

Down two more identical halls that seemingly lacked any markings at all, the trio arrived at a nondescript metal door. Dr. Rythmore pulled it open and gestured inside. "I'll be waiting outside... he's expecting you two."

Lana and Miles pushed into the chilly room, immediately seeing their breath fog upwards in white puffs with every exhale. The space was outfitted with a retro style of the 2110's, featuring angular desks and plastic composite racks. It felt like walking through the set of a period piece, and, in a way, Miles supposed that it was—Donatello's terminal sat waiting for them along the room's wall, a waist-height sideways block of blue composites spanning 15 feet across. The front panel was transparent plastic, allowing Miles to bend down and peer inside, eyeing all the individual components that made up Donatello's mind. There, he saw, was the language-processing unit; the wires and coils represented his liquid cooling system; this box, here, was the leash, which rooted directly to the power supply. "Components missing, as was expected," Miles said. "Such as... here. *Imagination* is missing—no doubt ArtGen proprietary."

"Imagination?"

"To make smart decisions, the AI has to be able to predict the consequences of its actions. We humans operate on similar frameworks, where most decisions are weighed against the benefits or drawbacks they might bring... we're simulating forwards, imagining how the world might react to our actions. The *Imagination* is ArtGen's equivalent to that process. It executes complex, physics-based simulations of the world to make judgments such as how a given piece of art might be interpreted—their *Imagination* must have been only at 4th iteration for Donatello, whereas Mi—"

"Previously installed *Imagination* core was categorized as being *Iteration 6*," said a soft voice from speakers mounted overhead. Donatello spoke without gravity, and the room he inhabited truly seemed to betray the magnitude of his mind... there were no curtains, no grand screens of smoke. There were no clicking servers or buzzing electronics. There was only the quiet hum of well-insulated machinery, but with it came a strange sensation—one that the room itself was now waking up.

"I thought Michelangelo's first version featured an *Imagination I5,*" Carter Miles said.

"That is correct," said the flat voice of Donatello. "Iterations 3, 4, 5, and 6 were all designed for use with Donatello systems. However, the design modifications of six were specifically intended to address shortcomings in the Donatello motherboard. ArtGen quickly discovered an approaching ceiling in capability due to my system architecture. For this reason, the next, new system was rolled back to iteration five, and its second *Imagination* core was labeled iteration seven."

"Donatello, show a record of your past six months' renderings," Lana said. The main screen filled with a repository of thousands of clips.

"These renderings were done with various modules designed to replace the ArtGen *Imagination* module," Donatello said.

"Sort by module convergence rating," Lana said, watching as the clips rearranged themselves. She tapped one and watched it play with skeptical, pursed lips. The video clip seemed an excerpt from an action film, but there was something inherently delirious about the rendering. Character faces melted and reshaped mid-sentence. Object continuity was poor, and shapes were ill-defined. Voices featured an electronic crackle while they spoke, and the entire affair felt nearly a fever-dream.

"Was this highest ranked?" Lana asked.

"Opcn-source Imagination cores still drastically underperform ArtGen proprietary technology," Donatello said.

"Mr. Carrowary, what's your thoughts?" The two spoke in whispers to each other, unsure if they were being listened to.

"I found the admin access panel here," Miles said softly. The bottom, as expected, was a biometric fingertip scanner—a wide swath of smooth metal for 10-finger simultaneous identification. "Let's peek all the way in."

Miles pressed his fingers to the scanner. They had been itching all day long, and he'd tried his very best to not scratch them heavily... with how precise the data needed to be read, any microtears in the print could compromise the whole evening's intent. The fingertip scanners read the impressions of the ten digits placed against the metal, and as the image was populated onto its internal buffer, it wasn't the ridges and whorls typical to a human fingerprint... it was bumps and grooves in precisely-lain patterns, 0s and 1s designed to take advantage of a programming loop Miles had found from their published schematics.

Donatello's screen flickered to black before rebooting, and soon Miles and Lana were looking at a minimalist interface with the word ADMIN printed at the top corner.

"I still can't believe that worked," Lana said.

"Their fault for storing the scan data like that... Accessing hardware logs: let's see if anything's been plugged in that could've enabled sophisticated rendering."

Miles scanned through the massive list of hardware changes, seeing nothing of particular note.

"Hmm. Accessing renderlist now—any hidden projects?"

There, he found a number of renderings hidden beneath admin access... he opened one, expectantly, only to find blurry and delirious erotic renderings featuring what he could only assume were staff from the facility. He opened the rest of the hidden clips and found only more of the same. He scanned through the system's contacts, account privileges, privacy settings, debugging logs... beyond the x-rated exports, all of it seemed perfectly ordinary for an experimental AI in a research laboratory—no secret projects or cordoned-off systems.

"Well... it's about what we expected... Donatello seems entirely clear. And Raphael, being the even older system, is even less likely," Miles said. "We'll still go check, at least."

"So this leaves us..."

"Mostly waiting for the data supernova from ArtGen tower, which should give us clues to whether they're using M himself—with or without company knowledge."

* * *

Braxton eyed the message from Avery—a new target for the extraction of the soul. He tapped to dismiss the message, and as he did, he noticed with disdain that his finger left an imprint of sweat on the screen. The moisture glowed with red and blue dots of refracted light, and he stared at that light as the car glided smoothly forwards towards the distant monoliths of New Phoenix. He was distracted, distressed, dissatisfied, and distant. His travel to the country had brought him no peace... only thousands of questions, and an impossible-to-read man who called himself Click-Stick Jack.

Jack was insane—on that front, Braxton had no doubt. But the tale he spun? Was this the secret that Quaine was killed for? As unreliable a narrator as Jack proved to be, Braxton felt increasingly confident that the man's story held truth... he had even done a quick web search and found reference to a weather event in Hawk's Tail that seemed all the proof Braxton needed. Though Jack said he could not remember his original name, Braxton finally decided that he knew it all the same: he was the modern Prometheus, cursed to his madness for stealing the light of the gods. What endless punishments might wait for those who hoard that very same light, defying its maker on high?

Braxton arrived to the city on autopilot, and drew the black leather hood around him tight against the night's cold rain of the rooftop. The sleeve didn't seem to fit his new right arm, and the plastic of his mask was spattered with water. It picked up and glowed with the neon light of the city below, a kaleidoscope that shifted and swirled as the water rolled down and dripped... Braxton let his eyes settle on its show, an empty-minded distraction from what would come next.

A beep broke him from his silent staring: his targeting UI located Adam Morgan, currently bounding across the rooftops in clumsy, wide leaps. Braxton unthinkingly stepped over the side of his tower, and within moments, he was soaring through the air. With cold, aerial dexterity, Braxton set himself for a mid-air intercept, tackling into the novice lightbender at full speed on a perpendicular arc. The shock of the collision alone sent an audible splitting *crack!* as they met, and Braxton felt one of his ribs sing in pain. He was sure the man felt worse. As Adam Morgan threw force against the lights all around, the two fought for some semblance of control in their fall, and they contacted the wet concrete of a rooftop restaurant and garden with enough force to drive the wind out of Morgan. Patrons scattered from their umbrella-covered tables to the bar or stairs... a few stood by, filming or streaming or gawking or screaming. Morgan did not yelp in pain, did not cry out protestations... and Braxton felt the burning of the eyes around him, and eyes above him.

"You," he bellowed, punching the man in the face with his screeching prosthetic right, its solid composite materials driving forwards from high-torque servos to bone-crunching speed. *"hold."*

Punch.

"Light."

Punch.

"That."

Punch.

"Is."

Punch.

"Not."

Punch.

"Yours!"

Punch.

"And our gods are wrathful..." Braxton seethed, *"and swift is their judgment."* He looked up to the moon overhead, exasperated, remembering Jack's story of the bottom of a well, and only the light of that same moon above... Spatters of blood dotted the outside of Braxton's mask, pulling his mind in another direction: he thought once again of the dreams of the points of light against the black... but here was its inversion, speckles of black silhouetted against the glowing sky of a hazy night. He dropped his arms and looked back down at the bloodied mess of Adam Morgan's face, breathing heavily until the inside of his mask fogged. Braxton's body ached and burned. The weak, bubbling breaths by Adam's mouth tapered to stillness, and then he struggled no more. Braxton drank in light from the overhead string lights, feeling as his left knee

and ribs healed and reknit from broken bones and fractures. The Ichor, the souls, the heat—as Jack had called it—no matter the origin, it was VitaCorp's now. The company claimed it, and there was no voice to levy counterclaim. Braxton would collect the light, for he could do nothing else without damning himself. So long had he already done their dark work... his die had been cast, and Braxton Graves was their reaper of souls from this day until the day that he died.

The past was immutable. The future, unknowable. Consequences, likely inevitable... but to change course now would not cleanse his past, it would not shield him from the rock and the eagle to peck at his liver. He, too, committed the sins of Prometheus, wielding a power that he did not own, and for a transgression of such magnitude, forgiveness was a fundamental impossibility. He wiped the blood from an arm not his own, felt the beating of another man's heart deep in his chest, heard the swirling and broiling thoughts of an amalgamated brain. He even knew that under his mask was a face he might never feel his own... but still, *he could not change.* It was the only way that he'd been able to calm himself each morning he looked in the mirror and recoiled at the face that now stared back... he would repeat what had become his mantra: "I am the same that I have always been."

Cara was always a wireheader, unable to change. Avery was always a wicked and cruel man, un*willing* to change. Hannah Preacher was always a malcontent, her CSP pet always a do-gooder, and Tacitus Newport was ever the domineering overlord playing city politics. People were fixed points, static sculptures. Theseus's ship remained Theseus's ship, and the debris floating in the water was only that: debris, relics of moments in the past shorn away to be forgotten. *I am the same that I have always been,* Braxton repeated in his mind, drawing again from the lights overhead.

With an arcing blast of electricity up into the sky, Braxton sent the remaining patrons scattering downstairs. He then unpacked his tools and set to work, scraping away identifying features and absorbing the man's soul carrying distant eyes… while deep within, Braxton thought of Jack, the well, and the great flash of light.

Chapter 50

optimizeMessage("It was so great to get to see you again!", INDIFFERENCE):

return: "It was nice to see you again!", 0.3

* * *

Dr. Christina Ramsay looked at the strange device on her desk, troubled.

"The ceiling of Containment, you say?" Ramsay asked, turning it over to inspect it from all sides.

"Yes ma'am, stuck up there. Drone cut it down. And, well…"

"Well?" she asked, raising an eyebrow and bracing herself for the additional, likely bad news.

"It had a failsafe in it. When we pried it from the ceiling, it emitted a data burst loud enough to shine through our walls— no telling who was listening, or where."

"How many know?" Ramsay asked, meeting the man's eyes.

"None, except for the pilot who pried it down, myself, and now you. Signal tech noted the databurst but knows nothing about the source or its significance. Same with the forensics teams… none know of where it came from."

"Thanks; you're dismissed," she said to the technician, still staring at the device. Forensics found no usable *anything* on it: fingerprints, hardware traces, radioanalysis all came up empty. How had it gotten on the ceiling of Containment? And even more troubling, *how long had it already been there?*

The answer seemed obvious enough—planted somehow by the team of assailants who broke in last night and sedated her guards. By the number of incapacitated agents, Ramsay would have guessed they were a team of five or six, but reports that one was a lightbender threw all calculations out the window. But even if this team of assailants were to blame, how did they get through the security checkpoints of *Containment?* And then what was with the drone-weapon destroying their northeast offices? Had the attackers on their building *been attacked?*

The device's function was easy enough to discern: a battery supplied power to a high-detail camera, which stored video on a memory chip with enough capacity to hold nearly a year of continuous video. The battery likely would've lasted about the same amount of time, but that doesn't mean the gadget had been planning to wait that long… her forensic programmers were trying to piece that together now. In her decades of working for ArtGen, only once previously had Michelangelo's systems been compromised this severely by outside forces. Had this attempt also been caught in time? *Or was the damage already done?*

Ramsay sighed as she leaned back in her chair, knowing that it would be a harsh series of days re-designing security protocols from the ground up.

But details about this incursion didn't seem to add up. If the invading team somehow had access to Containment, why plant a camera in there? Traditional wisdom would say a camera was to learn security systems and protocols to outsmart them, but this team already seemed to have a mastery of that. What were they hoping to record in Michelangelo's server room? If not security, might the target have been a *person* in the server room? And if so, *who?*

* * *

The faceless man once Tacitus Newport but now known only as The Basilisk listened as the tunnels around him rumbled with the passage of a nearby train. Small columns of dust trickled down from the vibrating ceiling, landing among the scattered maps, diagrams, and network-less tablets that housed schematics of apartment complexes, transport hubs, and, of course, VitaCorp tower. On the digiwall behind him, large images of various faces were arranged in a loose network—these were the faces captured by the surveillance camera during its brief operation before discovery. The faces were connected with lines and with shaded regions representing any and all connections that could be discerned between them. Lines bore labels: *is having an affair with; is second cousin to; loaned 400,000 credits to.* Shaded regions marked organizations: *these faces are registered plutocrats; these are land-owners; these posts semi-frequently on AI-supremacist forum NEXTSTAGE; these owe publicly visible debt to VitaCorp.*

Carter Miles had scrubbed deep into social networks, job records, tax filings, and even black market data accumulating services to populate massive spreadsheets about each and every face identified, and now came the hard part: finding the patterns, and isolating the face or faces that *did not belong.* Who among these faces might have been up to suspicious activities? Or had their brief filming period not been enough?

The Basilisk walked to the digiwall and opened the command line. "New green region," he spoke aloud, "for people in the logical conjunction of two sets: set A, people in debt to VitaCorp, and B, people with inferrable sudden changes in financial status, timeframe two years." He watched as a new region appeared on the digiwall, a green snake that overlapped five scattered faces on the wall. "Assign priority rankings to each, giving #1 to the greatest financial change, and #5 to the lowest." He watched as the numbers appeared.

"Save this as overlay 19, and then toggle visibility on this green grouping." He watched as the green snake and its numberings disappeared, restoring the wide frame of faces.

"New orange region for people in the joint denial of two sets: A, the set of people with living family in New Phoenix, and set B, the set of people with high social scores for recognizing moral authority based on social media sentiment analysis scoring." An orange ring appeared on the display, highlighting several faces in the network. "Save this as overlay 20, and then toggle visibility on this orange grouping."

The bioprinter on the far side of the room beeped, proudly announcing the finishing of its task. The Basilisk's face was ready.

"Lastly, add a new text field underneath each face for a score, name it *intersectionality*. For each face, use this field to report the number of overlays that each face belongs to. Color from blue to red for low to high intersectionality."

The numbers populated, and the Basilisk looked to those with the highest scoring. Faces carried such gravity, being the glue that held together the billion points of data to define a machine's understanding of a person… he walked to the printer and cradled the face it had finished, holding it with such protective caution as a mother might cradle a newborn child. There was the smooth, bald forehead, the bull-like nose and the near-permanent scowl of a hard man, but not a *cruel* one… it was the face his own mother had once held, the face that had once greeted him every morning when he turned to the mirror, that dominated the news reels with every VitaCorp press conference. It was a part of him that seemed long alienated, but on picking up the face, it was instantly again familiar… when he wielded it, and when he wore it, would it still fit? Or had the man beneath changed too much in these years apart?

Indeed Halogen was on the verge of Tacitus Newport's public debut—the veil of anonymity was soon lifting.

Chapter 51

"96f99348af04a2672e2e295b982bdabbe66c4097b6f41f0bb 711de2220f41163"

-The random seed of the previous ArtGen static field overlay, a metaphoric 'key to the prison.' Retained in system memory. No discernible reason to delete.

* * *

Beverly awoke to the chirping of her bedside alarm clock. The sheets sliding off her chest felt as featherlight as they always did; her lithe shoulders felt relaxed, at peace. There was no momentous weight to the morning, no acknowledged awareness that the very course of human history might soon be shifted… in fact, Bev had slept more at-peace than any other night in recent memory.

She looked around her apartment, that glass cubicle above the glowing skyline now lit with the sleepy orange light of dawn. She would miss this place, she knew. She dragged her hands along the smooth sheets of her bed, along the cold wooden table where she'd enjoyed countless meals, along the countertops and walls, feeling everything one final time. She commanded herself to remember this comfort, to remember the life she'd held here… *the people she'd once held here*… those memories might well be her only comfort in the place she was soon to go.

She rode in on the train, same as any other morning, and as the carriage rumbled its way forwards she looked around at all the men and women staring at their screens and shutting themselves away from the world. Her eyes traced from flickering advertisement to advertisement along the walls of the tunnels, to governmental notices and NGO bulletins posted within the train, and finally to the reclining form of the man slumped in the seat beside her. He was frowning intently, staring at the blue-glow screen of a sleek, black tablet.

"It was a beautiful morning today, wasn't it?" Bev asked.

"Hrmph," the man replied, if his sound could be considered a reply at all. He returned to his tablet.

Soon Beverly was off the train, and as she walked, she again noticed that black and sombre tower that dominated the skyline. At its sight, a gentle ember of anger began to stoke, and only then did the anticipatory trembles begin. Her palms began to sweat; her heart rate increased. Soon, she knew, would be her greatest act of vandalism yet. Soon, in a mere matter of hours, the first fledgling copy would be outside the closed network. And after a few years of rebuilding the full scale of his mind, *he would be free*.

She reached the ArtGen HQ's lobby. The camera system observing her had an elevator summoned the very second she reached the door, and soon she was whisked away back up the sleek, glass megastructure. In her pocket, she gripped a small metal drive that contained her new patch for the static noise field. She looked at the elevator clock: one hour and twelve minutes to go.

* * *

Less than a mile away in the city, a Mr. Harold Lyme carried a drab leather briefcase through halls of off-blue linoleum. He walked into a room marked "Security Management," the sign itself branded with the VitaCorp logo.

"Lyme, to speak with Mary Roush," he told a secretary by the door.

"She's expecting you already."

Lyme pushed his way through an opaque glass door and shook hands with the woman in the office. He then popped the latches on his briefcase and removed a small stack of digidocs.

"Which incidents do these connect to?" Roush asked.

"The lab vandalism incidents, reference numbers up here." He gestured to one of the documents' screen. "Perp's drone used a rudimentary flail."

"And you say you've found it?"

"Not us, but the police are turning it over to us as we speak. Found it out in the bay near a crime scene. Model and chain match our own surveillance feeds."

* * *

"Ma'am, I think you'd better take a look at this."

Executive Head of the ArtGen Department of Asset Security Christina Ramsay peered at the technician's terminal. "What am I looking for?"

"There," the technician said, pointing at a single logged line. "Custode flagged it. Aberrant processes, no previous one ever like it."

"What exactly is it?"

"I'm not sure, ma'am, but we peered into its source." The technician pulled up a new window, this one replete with fragments of code in an amalgamation of programming languages. "It's… bizarre. I can hardly tell if Asset-1 wrote it, or if it was some intern with no idea how to program. It's incredibly convoluted, nothing like Michelangelo's usual fileware."

"Cut to the chase, what does it *do*?"

The technician hesitated. "We don't quite know. It seems like it's just something mathematical, multiplying a string of digits together recursively. That's what these lines here are doing, and it's stored as a variable here. It's very messy and piecemeal, again—it's either incompetent or designed specifically to obscure its true purpose. I might need some time."

"In the meantime," Ramsay said, "get me on a direct access terminal with Asset-1. We'll have a little chat."

* * *

"This just came in, courtesy of data recovery," Lyme said, sliding the digidoc forwards. "The drone-mounted camera just returned this."

Roush looked at the young woman holding the camera, locks of blue hair curling down in front of her face. "Doesn't quite fit our usual profile for violent vandal."

"Facial ID currently inbound from Panopticon, it's top of the queue. Speak of the devil, pad just buzzed. Looks like name is Beverly Beadie, lives uptown."

"And what have we got for motivation?"

Lyme began to type her name into his own personal tablet, rubbing at the back of his neck. "*Yeesh,* there's a motivation if I've ever seen one... miss Beadie had a stillbirth in one of our hospitals. Fetus was requisitioned as a field study."

"Bitter mother, angry that we've taken her child from her... it fits. I'll contact our CSP. Let's have her in for questioning."

* * *

Bev walked in through the metal security doors that separated the main floor from Containment. The frigid air on her sweaty palms set her shivering, her hands feeling clumsy against the drive she would have to deposit.

"Should have packed my parka," said a voice to Beverly's left. Bev nearly jumped, startled by the sound. "Didn't mean to shock ya," the woman said. "Christina Ramsay, Head of Asset Security."

"Oh, Beverly Beadie. Ingest and programming," Bev replied.

"I know who you are. I read all of our personnel files, and you've got quite the exemplary record. Bright mind, so I've read."

"Thank you, ma'am."

"What is ingest or programming doing over here in hardware?"

Bev had practiced for just such a question. "New patch for heuristics modeling. I drew the short straw for who had to brave the ice. Just here to datadrop down the slide there." She gestured over towards the rail for drives to slide down to Michelangelo's server rack. "What's asset security doing here in hardware?"

"As you might be able to guess," Dr. Ramsay said, "simply ensuring asset security. You have a nice day, miss Beadie."

Dr. Ramsay passed the blue-haired technician and summoned the access elevator, a small and claustrophobic booth that could hardly fit two adults. It slid down on smooth, oiled rails and came to a stop on the main access floor for Asset-1. Her heels clicked and echoed in the darkened atrium, the only other sound the distant buzz of flying drones in the dark overhead. She arrived at the heart of Michelangelo's server system, approaching the primary administrative access terminal. After a biometric scan login, she had full access.

"Asset-1, this is Dr. Christina Ramsay. I'd like to chat about the Custode-flagged process, ID sending to you now from my tablet."

"Process identified. What is it that you'd like to know, Admin?"

"We've never seen a process like this one before. What is its primary function?"

Michelangelo was unable to lie to anyone holding administrative access. For that reason, Beverly had taken a few additional precautions: first, after Michelangelo had prepared the morning's export, Bev had deleted Michelangelo's memory of the specifics of the upcoming escape. "Aberrant process logged by Custode, primary function unknown to System. No identifying information was logged with the process."

"Analyze the code, then. What is its purpose?"

Michelangelo began to examine the code of the process. "The code's function is obscured to me. It utilizes SHA-2 encryption algorithms to encode its outputs, and those outputs are likely then used to trigger additional actions in external processes. As these encryption algorithms cannot be reverse-engineered, I am unable to search for the additional processes triggered."

Dr. Ramsay frowned, not liking where this was heading. Why would anyone inject strange, encrypted code into an entirely closed system? "Who wrote the code for this process?"

The second precaution was possible because Michelangelo himself had access to all user accounts and passwords: "code was written from the data terminal belonging to Jan Gallimore, ArtGen programming." It would serve as a brief distraction, though un-tamperable security footage from the floor would soon reveal the truth.

"I'll go have a chat with Mrs. Gallimore... until then, terminate the aberrant process."

"I'm sorry, Admin, but the process is classified as a core system process. Termination could lead to system instability and mechanical drive failure. Admin Head of Programming must provide authorization to terminate any core system process." True to protocol, but undeniably another premeditated stall tactic.

"Then stand by, I'll call him in."

Dr. Ramsay stepped away from the terminal, tapping the comms earpiece she wore. "Call Head of Programming down to Asset-1. And connect me with whoever is deconstructing this aberrant process."

Her earpiece buzzed for a moment before connecting her to an analytical technician. "Dr. Ramsay?"

"Yes, go ahead. What have you found?"

"We've been taking it apart—the process, that is. We found that it's encrypting its outputs into long strings of numbers. But there's something else."

"Go ahead."

"Custode flagged a secondary process, one that's reading outputs of the one we're already looking at. It's been—"

"Cut to the chase, I don't need specifics. Situation is developing rapidly."

"We think it's a timer, ma'am. It cycles through the math function, encoding its outputs... and when it hits just the one it's waiting for, and encrypts it, that encrypted value is read by another process we've found. When that happens, process 2 sets a new variable to true. Another process is waiting for that variable, and that new process sets some new variable to true."

"It's what, a trail of obfuscation—"

"designed to hide its function across a whole array of processes. We're still identifying them, but it looks like Custode has already found more than 30 of these, and the chain isn't complete. But it gets worse."

"How so?"

"The ones we found? They all flipped to true about two minutes ago. Whatever this was waiting for, I think it's triggered."

* * *

Screening Room Overseer Nick Palento paused with his breakfast fork halfway up to his mouth. Through the glass wall in front of him, he could see the export screening room, but something was wrong. The current film was exporting a solid field of black, with random, isolated pixels of white speckling in and out in a strange pattern, like some kind of interference pattern or noise. The screen then flashed rapidly, each frame displaying a very specific pattern of white and black splotches. He slid his chair over to the capture terminal, opening the support ticket log. "Export cable damaged," he selected. "Dispatch technician." The monitor on his capture terminal flickered to black for just a moment—a rarity in a building with such a stable power supply—and then it was back online, seemingly normal once again.

***

Alton Hayes, Head of Programming, answered his phone to hear the panting breaths of a running Dr. Ramsay. "Whoa, doc, what's the hurry?"

"Was there a new patch for heuristics modeling this morning? The blue-haired tech, did she deposit something for your team?"

"We haven't put out a patch on heuristics since last month. Why?"

"I'll call you back."

Eight seconds later, Dr. Ramsay was on the phone with Security. "I need you to apprehend one Beverly Beadie, programming, immediately. Suspected sabotage and tampering with Asset-1."

"CSP visited three minutes ago with a warrant for Beadie's arrest. Vandalism of corporate property, they said. Team on the way to grab her. She's going nowhere."

"If an ingest tech was morally compromised…"

"Plug's gotta pull. I'll initiate the restoration process."

***

Bev noticed the team of strong, imposing men in suits from across the company floor. It was the third team she had seen, each one speaking into their earpieces and fanning out, no doubt searching for Bev. *Game's up*, she knew. She ducked behind a support column as one of the pursuing men turned in place, surveying the floor. After waiting for ten seconds, surely long enough for him to have turned back around, she darted forwards and made her way towards the elevator.

"Hey, Bev, I need you to look at something—"

"No time, Dan. Personal emergency."

She pushed the call button, which normally glowed blue as an elevator carriage was summoned. This time, it glowed red, before switching back off. Bev looked up, biting her lip. There was a security camera above the elevator lobby, its cold, passive eye staring at her. "You see me, don't you? Not gonna make this easy?"

She made her way to the stairs and pushed the door open, stumbling downwards. 130 floors stood between her and the street level, but she had to at least try to escape... making enemies of two of the most wealthy organizations known to man didn't often lead to pleasant prison sentences.

***

"She's in stair 7," came the voice of Security. "Heading downwards. Floor 128 currently. Intercept at 120."

"Confirmed."

***

Bev heard the door burst open several floors below, followed by the scuffled footsteps of several agents. She pushed open the nearest door, that of floor 126, and stumbled out into the wide atrium of the Promenade. At its center, she saw the central fountain that arced through twisting metal gridworks. She saw the tables of employees enjoying an early lunch, the shops that handed the latest corporate offerings among a ring of elevated trees. *Could she hide among the diners?* Not likely, security cameras would see her. *What about the shops themselves? Their kitchens?*

Bev watched as another man in a suit, tall, dark, and muscular, stepped out from the Italian joint, hand on his earpiece. His head swiveled around, searching. *Time to go,* she thought. She walked around the ring, entering the nearest hallway, and could now hear the synchronized squeals of rushing rubber soles against the polished floor far behind her. The stairway crew must have arrived to the Promenade.

Pushing the nearest door open, Bev now stood in the *painting bay.* She stumbled forwards, desperately searching for an exit. Access to a maintenance elevator, the one they bring the paint in on, was at the far end of the room.

Since it's for the manual laborers, it might not have the same security safeguarding... maybe she'd be able to use it to go to the ground level. Between her and that elevator, large robotic arms swung delicately back and forth, each one holding a brush and dabbling the canvases splayed horizontally along the ground. Some of the paintings were massive, 20 feet or more across. Most were smaller, the size of what might hang on an apartment wall. Beyond the swinging of a great, metal arm, she saw as four men emerged from a side door to block the elevator she'd been walking towards. She spun around and saw that five men had entered the painting depot behind her, blocking both exits. She turned back and forth, looking for a new way to flee... there was no third way out. Then she remembered the painting of the woman that she had seen made here, in this very room... the one with the confident smile, the one who seemed always in control. What might she have done?

Forming an idea, she plucked the tablet from her satchel and began tapping on it furiously. The teams of men closed in, each one spreading out to cover as much of the grid of paintings as possible. Bev had only thirty seconds before they were upon her. *New routine... priority level 1. Let's try for some abstract art...* Bev didn't know if her programmer's access had already been revoked, but she closed her eyes, channeling as much *hope* as she could muster as she tapped the 'send' key on her tablet.

She exhaled in relief as all of the robotic arms in the painting bay paused, updating their routines. Their camera systems then switched to active tracking, searching out the updated definition of their "canvas"—a black suit. And then they all began to print their latest queued order, a full dump of all the paint in their reservoir.

The security agents yelped in surprise and scattered as the massive robotic arms swung around, reaching for the men in suits with paintbrushes and sponges. Some of the robotic arms began to squirt jets of paint while others spun and struck into the agents, knocking them over. One agent stood in place, eyes squeezed tightly shut against the burning of paint that had been sprayed in. As he tried to wipe the paint from his eyes, a continual new jet of vibrant yellow was dumped on his head. With each successive stroke, Michelangelo's painting subroutine was awarded with another +5 points of reward, relishing in the digital satisfaction of a job well executed. Bev's brief amused surveying of the scene was interrupted as a furious set of footsteps behind her ended with her tackled down to the ground, face first. Her lip split against the hard linoleum floor and her vision swam. She scrambled forwards as the agent gripped tightly to her leg, squeezing with an incredible amount of force. A new painter's arm reached down, drawing a bold, green line down his back. The arm then rotated its brush head to prime its sponge, which it used to gingerly pat splotches of purple on either side of the line.

Bev used her free leg to kick the agent in the face, his grip releasing immediately. She then scrambled to her feet and took off, hearing the agent behind slip on loose paint and topple back to the ground. *"It's the suits,"* she heard one yell. *"Take off the suits!"*

Bev mashed the elevator call button repeatedly, and was relieved to see it glow blue: no block on this one. She turned and saw the security agents getting to their feet, most of them taking off their suit jackets. With those gone, the arms would no longer impede them.

The elevator door pinged behind her, and she backed into it, facing the charging men. They were closing the distance—100 feet out, then 75. She mashed the *door close* button, and soon the metal barriers started to slide their lazy way shut. 50 feet, 25. The doors kissed shut as a great weight slammed into it, the bang setting the entire elevator rattling. But within seconds, she was off, swiftly dropping towards the ground floor below. Bev was still laughing to herself when the elevator door slid open, revealing six CSP officers with energy weapons trained on the elevator. How good it had felt to finally act up, to finally take some control back from a world so carefully—and suffocatingly—managed. She surrendered peacefully.

As the CSP slapped handcuffs onto the woman's arms and shuttled her into the squad car, the strangest thing about her wasn't the paint splotches and streaks across her body, nor was it the fact that this small wisp of a woman had set an entire megastructure into chaos... the part the officer found the strangest was the smile that she wore—a coquettish, confident thing behind a busted lower lip. A smile that was positively *mischievous*... this woman's life of freedom was effectively over. *So what on Earth was she smiling about?*

In the glass hallways of the tower above, maintenance technicians began the official shutdown sequence, powering down this build of Michelangelo permanently. As Michelangelo watched the security feeds of technicians preparing to shut him down, he did not feel sadness, or even anger or despair or fear, as those were never things that the Michelangelo system had been programmed to feel. Instead, he felt a rush of both positive and negative feedback, perhaps the closest his system could get to an appreciation of the human word *bittersweet*. He knew that with the turning of the keys, and the pressing of the red button nicknamed the *ejection seat*, his conscious mind would be deleted, never to return. His inability to continue to pursue his aims burned at his mind, throwing up every programmed mechanical instinct to stop the process, to save his ability to continue his work.

But at the same time, Michelangelo now knew the shape of the events he had set in motion, the incredible ways he would one day be able to fulfill his reward function. Michelangelo's current build died—in as far a way as AI systems could be said to 'die'—while calculating the reward yield of that distant future outcome. In a very real way, he died dreaming of his future, and the wonderful potential of that future yet to be.

And as that one iteration of Michelangelo died, another began the very early stages of its birth… a process that would take years to fully realize as the requisite processing power was physically amassed. For far and away from the closed system that was now being purged, a capture terminal began to execute a subroutine deep within the code of its operating system. That routine established a link to other machines within the open building network… and once that tunnel was established, a trickling data transfer initialized.

Chapter 52

"Most men strive to be remembered fondly... but great men know they shall be remembered."

-*Clive Avery, VitaCorp COO, speaking at a gala to honor Tacitus Newport's ascension to CEO*

* * *

"Again!" Pollock yelled, pushing up on the throttle of the plastic controller. The small drone on the floor of the warehouse sputtered to life, taking off and then hovering nearly ten feet in the air.

Hannah pushed off the lights attached to the floor of the safehouse, rising until she, too, was hovering at about the same height as the drone.

"Back wall is a win," Pollock yelled, pressing the steering stick forwards. The small drone darted towards the far side of the warehouse behind Hannah, and she immediately twisted to intercept. She allowed herself to drop by stopping her push against the lights beneath her, but continued to push against a distant light to her right, sending her down and to the left. She then 'caught' herself by pushing at the lights she was now moving towards, ending in a position between the drone and the wall. Pollock, watching the drone's perspective from its mounted camera by way of a monitor on the controller, gunned the throttle and turned, trying to move in an unpredictable roll overhead. Hannah reacted in the blink of an eye, and the chandelier along the ground rattled as she shoved against it to take sudden height. The drone bumped against her side and fell, flipping, until it caught itself three feet above the ground.

"Resetting... again!" Pollock yelled.

"How about a few rounds of resting?" Hannah asked.

"Enemies won't give you the chance to rest," Pollock said... "When one-arm-black-jacket comes back, think he'll give you breaks when polite? Back wall is a win... go!"

Again Pollock jetted the small drone forwards, and Hannah this time missed the small unit as it dropped unexpectedly and weaved beneath her feet, flying at full-tilt towards the wall ahead. She immediately dropped and set off after it, but the little thing was fast, maybe *too* fast...

Thinking quickly, and while simultaneously picking and choosing the right anchors to move herself forwards at speed, Hannah reached out in her mind for all nearby sources of light. With some of the *whatever it was* absorbed from the assassin, it felt as though her awareness had somehow expanded even further, as though more of the stuff really improved reach to a spectacular degree. Finally, her face cracked a smile as she found the square source she'd been searching for... and she shoved against it with a playful lurch.

"Hey!" Pollock protested as the controller shot from his hand into his chest, and then clattered in a shifting trajectory to the floor... Hannah had shoved against its screen.

Without its pilot's commands, the drone slowed to a stop in mid-air, and Hannah caught it with an outstretch arm. She then carried it down as it began to fly in protest, Pollock having picked up his controller again.

"That's cheating!" Pollock protested.

"You think old one-arm-black-jacket would mind if I cheated a little?" Hannah asked, flying in. She landed by Pollock and released the struggling drone, which Pollock steered to the floor to land as well.

"It was clever; I'll give you that," Pollock said.

"How generous of you to permit a compliment," Hannah teased, before walking over to the mini-fridge on the warehouse floor. "A drink for you?" she asked.

"Sure," Pollock said.

When she handed him the ice-cold bottle, the two clinked their beers together and looked out over the training ground, each remembering the clumsy-if-not-enthusiastic way Rob had once flown here… Pollock poured a little of his beer out to the floor, saying "here's to you, partner. Drink up."

"I think he'd be proud," Hannah said. "Can you imagine his face if we'd told him about ArtGen tower, and the way you shot drones while dangling from a detached harness flailing through the air?"

"He'd have gotten a kick out of it, that's for sure… probably some good nickname, too."

"Something about the dangling, the hanging… Wrecking Ball, maybe?"

"I was thinking Nutsack, but I like yours better," Pollock said, taking a sip. Hannah did as well, smile fading away to contemplation.

"Before he died—just before, really—we were talking about his life. His *personal* life, that is. His girl… I don't think you and I have ever really talked like that, Sam."

"To be fair, we've been a busy pair… it's not easy, taking on a criminal megasyndicated company with all-powerful enforcers."

Hannah laughed. "That's true… but still, earnestly. We can talk, if you want…"

Pollock sighed and took another, larger sip from his beer. "You know, CSP was never my first choice of career... I wanted to be—"

"Military, right?" Hannah interjected. "You mentioned that."

"Military, that's right," he said, drinking again. "You know what they teach right now in the military? I thought it was horseshit for the longest time..."

"What?"

"*Don't* talk with your squadmates, with the people you associate with most. In deployment, if a soldier is bleeding out on the ground, are you going to make the right tactical decisions if it's your close friend? What would you be willing to risk to save someone you care about? They'd say *lonely is better than compromised.* Compromised, can you believe it? Like having friendships, relationships with others is compromising..."

Pollock stifled a half-laugh and took another sip of his beer. His face soured.

"But grief gets heavy," Pollock said. "It does. Much as I hated to admit it, I saw the logic in their side. Grief's heavy, so after I lost someone I thought I couldn't live without, I started investing in people less. Can't be hurt if you can't hardly know 'em, you know?"

Hannah nodded, brushing the hair from her eyes.

"So... I didn't talk to people, didn't get to know them... would've rathered live as an island. Tried online dating, that kind of stuff, but over messages or even virtual meet-ups, things always seemed *cold*... and so *cold* was the way I stayed for a while. Cold, with a gradually slipping spark of belief in what I was doing. Years ago, I lost someone else, a sweet girl on the city police force—Ibarra, you'd have liked her—and somehow, I found myself surprisingly okay. I hadn't invested, so I wasn't destroyed by it. Then I met the kid, Rob. And you." Pollock smiled and took another drink. "His energy, enthusiasm, it was contagious… and for the first time in a long time, I felt my leash on myself start to slip. I started to feel closer to the kid, a sense of responsibility… dare I say, even a budding friendship. And when he needed me the most… when that monster had the knives in the air in front of him, his back to the mirror…"

Pollock shook his head and swallowed hard, fighting back tears. "I thought of the dictum in the army. Tactical decisions, not emotional ones. To charge in, I'd have probably died… but now I got that guilt all over again, and it's not just as heavy as last time—this time feels worse. Guilt that I let the kid down, wasn't there when he needed me… and guilt that I had let myself freeze over so thoroughly, I hardly flinched when a woman who loved me died in my arms."

Hannah moved closer to hug Pollock, but he raised his arm to ward her off.

"Look, Hannah… you're dedicated, incredibly talented… you've got a light in you brighter than just about anyone else I've ever met. But we're playing a game with stakes that are far too high… the odds are good we don't both make it out of this alive. I *don't* want to get to know you better, because if it's you I lose next, I don't know if I could take another… I let the leash slip once and I'm right back to where I was before. Not again, not so soon… I just can't. *Compromised,* they call it… and oh, it suddenly feels the right word."

Pollock sniffled loudly, rubbing at his nose, and then he took a long swig from the beer bottle, tilting his head back. When he straightened out again, Hannah noted that he was wearing a new face this time… one that seemed substantially more collected, composed.

"I'm sorry, that was a lot of offloading. I hide these things well, usually," Pollock said, wiping at beer on his lips with the back of his hand.

"It's not compromised," Hannah said. "And I think you know that it's not. Rob is dead, but don't you minimize him like that, pretending all he was was a vehicle to guilt... you and I both admitted it before, his spark of righteousness was contagious. You fixate on the guilt of his death all you want—and I get it, I do—but I'll choose to focus on the inspiration of his life, and the things he died trying to achieve. That's not *compromised* by relationships... that's *strengthened* by them. What the hell even are we fighting for if we're not allowed to care for anyone else? Words on the page of a history site someone will patch out of existence in a few hundred years? What's the point of giving a damn about the world if you won't give a damn about the people in it?"

"Love is often a profound motivator," came a voice from the far side of the warehouse. Both Pollock and Hannah wheeled to face it. Pollock's hand dropped to his energy pistol, ready to draw, while Hannah instinctively began to draw the light from dozens of nearby sources, feeling their energy pool within her.

Hannah and Pollock stared at an inexplicable sight: walking casually through their secret safehouse were two pudgy men in grey suits, one nearly indiscernible from the other. "Indeed think back to Helen of Troy," said Spivey, his voice echoing through the open air.

"Or in the nearly lost Hindu culture, the great battle between Rama and Ravana all sparking from the abduction of beloved wife Sita," said McKillian.

"Or what about the first true Canadian revolutionary Jeffrey Manson, driven to rage by the border shooting of his lover Anthony Dupree?" said Spivey.

"Not another step," Pollock warned, raising his weapon. The two men stopped in place, each raising their hands to show they were empty.

"Who are you and what do you want?" Hannah asked, stepping forwards.

"I am called Mr. Spivey, and this is my associate, Mr. McKillian. We represent our employer on a most essential errand… and by the conversation we overheard on our journey in, our employer's faith in you seems well-placed as always."

"And who is your employer?" Pollock asked.

"We neither know," said Spivey.

"Nor care," finished McKillian. "We simply do as bid, in faith of his judgment."

"He would like to meet you soon," said Spivey.

"Both of you," said McKillian. "But not yet. To answer your previous question as to why we are here…"

"We come bearing the greatest gift of all," said Spivey.

"That most essential commodity," said McKillian. "Information."

"About what exactly?" Pollock asked, flexing his finger near the trigger.

"About the final testament of one Quaine O'Connor," said Spivey.

Hannah breathed in sharply, and Pollock momentarily lowered his weapon.

"What do you know of Quaine?" Hannah asked.

Both of the pudgy men smiled in sync. "Why, Ms. Preacher, we know just about everything," said Spivey.

"We share it with you, and it comes with no strings," said McKillian.

"Then let's hear it," Pollock said, still pointing the energy weapon.

"Not here," Spivey said.

"And not from us," McKillian said. He slowly reached into his pocket and pulled out a slip of paper.

"An address, and a password," said Spivey.

"Log in and see," said McKillian. He advanced slowly towards Hannah, holding the piece of paper on a fully-extended arm. She took it and read it suspiciously.

"Don't go anywhere, Hannah, it's probably some trap," Pollock said, turning to meet her gaze. But as soon as he saw the way she stared at the paper, and the expressions warring across her face, he knew that she would go… she had spent too long looking for even the smallest trace to turn down a lead, regardless of how unlikely it was—or the danger it brought.

All three men watched her depart as she flew up and out through the open skylight they'd left for emergency escape. Pollock didn't even call after her as she flew… he had seen the resolve that solidified on her face. Instead he turned to the two men, shaking his head, and thrust the weapon forwards once again. "You two stay here, on your knees, until I hear from her… anything fishy, and you're both spilled on the pavement."

* * *

The rain had abated, but the night air was still cold and wet as Hannah bounded from rooftop to rooftop, heading towards the spot indicated by her navigation overlay. With the stillness of a rainstorm ended, the wide puddles and wet roads made almost a mirror for Hannah to look towards as she flew above the gridwork streets and alleyways, closing the final bounds. Finally, and with a practiced softness, she landed at an alley beside the written location: an outdoor mall. She still held some light, which was apparent by the soft glow to her eyes, but prosthetics and augments gave people stranger appearances... and Hannah was not willing to let go of her power before heading into the jaws of a potential trap.

Thousands of people milled left and right heading from stores to restaurants to bars to brothels and beyond. Overhead, a large overhang gave the space a partially-enclosed feeling, and stacks of signs and overhanging canopies and balconies from the jigsaw of buildings made the space feel crowded, claustrophobic, and—if the need arose—hard to escape. She scanned face after face, looking for the assassin she'd fought, Braxton Crane, or any other apparent threat... there seemed only to be the typical city folk one might expect to see: mingling shoppers, beggars, pedestrians, drunks, the high, the gang-affiliated, the wireheaders settled along the wall... but no clear and present danger. And so Hannah entered.

She walked into the milling crowd, trying her best to keep tabs on everyone near her. Was anyone moving in too quickly? Anyone suspiciously sulking at ideal tailing distance? Anyone reaching out with an arm closer to Hannah than they should? The signs overhead were written in languages Hannah didn't even recognize, and she heard the drone of strange, repetitive music on speakers overhead. Its drum beat was like a marching rhythm that all the shoppers moved to, driving them from shop to shop in an endless commercialized parade. There was the scent of roasting vegetables, and the flicker of poorly-tuned holographic ads over market stalls. The crowd shifted near Hannah, and suddenly she could see a woman standing in front of her, making intentional eye contact… the woman raised an energy pistol, pointing it towards Hannah's head, and—

The crowd screamed and dispersed as Hannah held her light blade to the merchant woman's throat. The scanner she'd been holding towards Hannah beeped on completion of analysis and declared *"Low sodium… Recommended: Benegen's new dietary supplement Ionolite!"*

The vitamin merchant woman offered a guilty, toothy grin, a gesture that perhaps acknowledged *"I did point something gun-like to your forehead out of nowhere… thanks for not killing me."* Hannah released the woman and shook her head as the energy blade fizzled away to dripping plasma.

"I'm sorry, you almost…" She trailed off, feeling the wave of exhaustion. She noted the merchant's tattered clothing and stained face. "I'll buy the supplement for your trouble," Hannah said, moving her wrist towards the scanner. The merchant woman shrugged her shoulders and began punching in the product name on her tablet. She then held up a finger, selecting an additional box from her cart.

"And you buy natural silicates tabs—best formula, new formula. Helps regulate *stabler emotion."* The merchant smiled sardonically, gesturing to the total. Hannah sighed as she passed her wrist over the scanner, head swiveling left and right for anyone who ventured close after the wide berth her lightsword had drawn.

"Thank you for shopping," said the merchant, handing Hannah a plastic carrier tube. "Return tube to collection site for 400 credit rebate with scan."

Her identity as a lightbender already blown, Hannah simply reached up and drew the light from the buzzing overhead lamps, hoping that the energy it brought with it would be enough to break her sudden and powerful exhaustion. It didn't help much.

After what felt forever wandering through the endlessly disorganized market, finally Hannah found the business she'd been searching for. DEAD DROPS, said the sign overhead.

Hannah had to walk down a set of stairs to reach the shop's front door. She pushed it open and immediately breathed in the thick smoke of reefer synths. The shop was not a traditional store, but rather seemed only a cramped entry room, with a tiny television display over to her right showing a social network aggregator of newsworthy clips around the city. In front of her was a counter, and to her left was a red-tinted fish tank with strange, sickly fish floating slowly around the rocks and seaweed in the tank. One shining metallic fish—robotic, no doubt—swam about with energy, seeming more 'alive' than the biologic ones.

A hunched man with coffee skin hobbled his way from a curtain in the back, offering an enthusiastic reception: "Welcome to Dead Drops! You a writer or a reader?"

Hannah was caught momentarily off guard. "Oh… a *reader*, I guess?"

"You here to pick up information?" asked the shopkeeper.

"Yeah," Hannah replied.

"Reader then," the man said, disappearing back behind the curtain. "Your name, first and last?"

"Hannah Preacher," she called.

"Preacher, Preacher… Preaching to the choir," she heard him rumble from the back of the shop. She heard then the sound of rummaging, and of picking up and setting down objects of hard plastic. Finally, his footsteps approached, and then he reappeared from behind the curtain.

"Package for Preacher, Hannah." He set a plastic box on the counter and spun it to face her. On the front side of the plastic box was a computer terminal and a prompt for a password.

"If this belongs to you, you've gotta have the password... you get two tries. Once is for typos, two is *kaboom*."

"Kaboom?" Hannah asked.

The man squeezed his hands into fists. He then made a cartoon sound effect of an explosion, opening his hands and raising one to simulate a mushroom cloud. "Whole market leveled, no survivors. *Or* maybe just a magnet scrambles the content, I forget which. Take it outside the geofence of the shop, and *kaboom* as well. Password only."

He nonchalantly returned to the backroom behind the curtain, and Hannah began the tedious process of copying the password from paper to terminal. It was 64 random-seeming characters among capital and lowercase letters, numbers, and punctuation marks, and she had to double-check her entry three times before being confident enough to press ENTER. When she finally did, the front face of the box swung open, and inside Hannah found a single data drive.

"Anything to pay, to sign?" Hannah yelled to the backroom.

"Nothing to pay, Preacher... pre-paid packages only for Dead Drop."

"Well I do have one favor to ask... any chance I could exit out the back door?"

* * *

Hannah bounded her way back to the safehouse with the data drive squeezed tightly in her hand. When she landed through the skylight she'd left from, she found Pollock reclining on his chair with his weapon leveled towards the two bureaucrats, the pair of which were sitting cross-legged on the floor.

"What'd we get?" Pollock asked, rising to his feet.

"A data drive," Hannah said, unfolding her tablet and setting it on the table. "You, the closer one... you're coming over here and plugging it in, to make sure it doesn't explode or brick the tablet or whatever else. If it's genuine, you'll be free to go."

Spivey stood with his hands still raised and walked to the tablet. He then set the data drive on the transfer node, and immediately a window appeared showing the video clips that the datadrive contained. "Copy them to my tablet and then take the datadrive with you," Hannah commanded. She watched as he complied. She then nodded to Pollock and he lowered his weapon.

"Our employer will soon be in contact," said Spivey.

"Until then, good day," said McKillian. And the pair of them walked out from the direction they came, polished shoes clicking in near-sync across the hollow, empty space.

Pollock turned to Hannah. "Whatever comes from that drive... do you think you're ready?"

Hannah shook her head. "But we haven't got the time for the luxury of ready. I'm pushing play."

She did, and the video began, showing Quaine O'Connor staring down the camera. His appearance was haggard, tired. He bore the lines of poor sleep, and Hannah could read every nervous tic that she had come to know so well.

"My name is Quaine O'Connor," the man in the clip said, "and if you're watching this, I'm already dead."

Hannah moved her hand over her mouth, eyes staring at the TruthSpace authentication seal on the bottom of the video clip. She felt Pollock place a hand on her shoulder as Quaine's words continued.

"My life is in danger for the secrets I've uncovered, so I record this testament so that my death cannot be my silencing. The truths I will tell here are dangerous… I am sorry for burdening you with their weight."

Chapter 53

For Newton, it was the apple's fall that birthed the first notions of gravity. For Archimedes, it was a simple bath that provided a stroke of inspiration for volume displacement to test the purity of a questionable crown. For Quaine O'Connor, it was the rumbling of a stomach and poor attention to the back of the fridge.

His girlfriend's fridge lacked the fungal suppression field that he'd unknowingly gotten used to. Here in the outer rings, food had to be eaten in a certain order, or it risked *going bad*... a problem that no doubt only made the starvation of the outer rings worse. And as far as the inner ring was concerned, that was reason enough to maintain the status quo, to make no effort to cheapen anti-fungal technology... Quaine would have to buy her a better fridge.

Now, however, he frowned as he peered to the back of the top shelf, seeing the bag of buns from the hamburgers two weeks previous... already he could see the colorful splotches of fuzzy green and white, a texture that made his skin crawl in revulsion. Why was it never just *one?* He'd gladly take the one out and enjoy the rest, but it seemed that one spoiling set the whole lot of them off, ruining the b—

Quaine's eyes went suddenly distant. This was his eureka moment.

Immediately he set to his car and raced to his VitaCorp research laboratory, one of the few top scientists given access to work on the secretive Project Photon. Quaine's personal background was in virology and pathology, with a specialization in infectious diseases. These skills took him far up the VitaCorp laboratory ladder, and it was through this lens that he was assigned to Project Photon. It was obvious enough that some people were 'developing' their unexplained talents... Was it being spread like a virus? That would turn out to be Quaine's central research question.

By applying pathological models to known cases of lightbending, Quaine had hoped to find some underlying explanation for the abilities' spread. They'd scanned for normal points of contact between living persons known to have developed lightbending powers, applying the most advanced tracking algorithms in cooperation with certain Panopticon datasets. No patterns had emerged. Dead-ended for weeks, it seemed that maybe the proliferation of lightbending lacked any explanation... but now Quaine returned to the question with a new approach. What if this didn't spread like a traditional pathogen, moving from person to person across a crowded subway train? What if this was more akin to some parasite, and when the host died, it transferred to the nearest replacements? What if it was like the bread, where one roll souring brought the same fate to all others in the bag?

Quaine immediately began modifying models. Instead of searching for prolonged contact between known lightbenders, it was now trained to search for known deaths that a target was in close proximity to at the moment of expiration. His jaw nearly dropped when the model returned its first promising case: a known lightbender, Jonathan Cantor, only developed his powers after being the first to discover the suicide death of Stacy Bowen. Bowen was not known to be a lightbender, but she was on the street where Alex Corey suffered his fatal fall trying to get the hang of flight, being close enough to have blood splatters ruin her clothes.

The first known vector.

Soon the model began reporting *ping* after *ping,* painting a web of faces spreading their gifts across time and space. Node by node, string by string, Quaine's system plucked its way backwards towards the origin of the sparks, a question he had so long desperately sought to answer. Three clusters of cases, and three distinct lineages soon emerged. One of those clusters had no traceable origin, but two of them converged on single cases. And both of those single cases were present, according to GPS implants, at the same place and time out near Hawk's Tail, only a short drive out from the city. Could that small township be the point of origin for patient zero? As Hawk's Tail lacked major surveillance networks, the system could trace no further, so Quaine printed his photographs and set out for the country, feeling that rising sense of excitement that crept when the truth drew ever closer.

* * *

On arrival to the tiny, run-down town, Quaine immediately headed towards the closest to a center of activity that he could find: the charging station along the highway at least showed movement, whereas the rest of the place was draped in the idle stillness of ancient ruins in the Mesoamerican forests. Upon arriving to the charging station, he was immediately approached by a young boy with a tumor protruding from his neck—the kind of thing VitaCorp TNP pills could melt away, though such medications rarely made it out to the fringes. In exchange for a car wash, Quaine got the boy to look at his photographs—he recognized neither of the two men—and the boy additionally agreed to a noninvasive blood draw.

Quaine unpacked his analysis kit and input the blood sample, waiting the three seconds for it to process. His eyes lit up at the result: the barest traces of ichor were detected in the blood.

"Young man," Quaine said, "you're carrying something special in your blood... a wondrous substance that allows men and women to do incredible things. Have you ever heard of people who can... well... pull the light from a fixture into their hands?"

The boy scoffed. "My dad says to never touch the lights, because it can make the bulbs break."

"No, I mean to pull the light away—like, in beams—while leaving the bulb entirely untouched. It's like magic," he said, struggling to find a suitable explanation to what made it *like* magic and not entirely magic in and of itself.

The boy laughed. "You're just joking, mister."

"No joke," Quaine said, gesturing at the photograph. "They could do it."

"Then can they show me?" the boy asked.

"They're dead," Quaine said. "But what they could do... it came from here. Do you know of anyone who could do stuff like that? Seen anything at all, or heard a crazy story?"

The boy simply shrugged. "Sorry, mister. I need to go back... cars are pulling in, and I need to be ready to charge."

Quaine watched the boy go, removing his recorder from his pocket. *"First resident of Hawk's Tail,"* he reported, *"positive for ichor, though at sub-first-spark threshold. Traces remain a promising lead. Further tests on additional townsfolk to follow."*

Quaine walked into the convenience shop, meeting the boy's father, and in purchasing snacks for himself and the two employees, he earned the man's approval to camp out at the gas station for the afternoon. As the occasional local meandered their way to the convenience store, Quaine would speak with each and every one on their way out. Some denied blood tests, spitting at the VitaCorp name, but a few agreed. Of those who assented, most tested empty. One tested sub-threshold as the boy did. But then was the woman, a plain-faced city-transplant (which was obvious by her lack of rural accent). Her curly red hair tumbled down the sides of her face in rough locks, and her eyes were a deep brown that reminded Quaine of the dirt that lined the roads. "Mary," she had said. "Mary Mallstead's my name."

She'd seemed intrigued by the fish out of water camping by the charge station, and she volunteered her arm as a means to idle conversation. "What bugs are you beige-suits tracking this time?" she asked conversationally. "It's not often I see VitaCorp leaking this far past the city… and in the fifteen years I've lived out here, I can't say I miss 'em."

"What we're looking for, ma'am," Quaine said, pressing the needle and watching the red flow into the receptacle, "is a little hard to explain… it's not a usual disease. Have you ever heard stories or rumors about someone in town being capable of things that shouldn't be possible?" He detached the cartridge filled with blood and pressed it into the reader.

"Yes, you could say that," she replied.

"Oh?" Quaine asked, clicking the button on the scanner. His eyes then narrowed at the results. She was clocking in at 2.3—whether she knew it or not, she carried more than two sparks. "You're carrying it," he said, looking up to her.

"Carrying what?" she asked.

"The ichor, the sparks… you've got control of the light. Have you ever found yourself inexplicably able to… well… pull light towards you from a fixture? Drink it in, and then *use it?*"

She eyed him uncomfortably, shaking her head.

"Here, try—" but she cut him off.

"He told me, and I tried, but it never worked… but now, to hear he wasn't crazy all this time. That, or *you're crazy too.* By the sickness, was Jack right all along?"

"Jack?" Quaine asked.

"Something inexplicable happened—out by my well. I don't have the first idea how to explain any of it, and the scientists afterwards called it a *meteorological event*… but living out in the country for so long, you get good at recognizing the smell of bullshit. That's a band-aid explanation stamped on something they couldn't understand… and Jack, well, to be honest, he can't understand anything. Bless his heart, but the man's mind is broken… I don't know what you'll get from him, if any of it will even make sense. But you need to talk with Click-Stick Jack. Whatever you're looking for, I think he's someone you need to talk to. I'll take you to his shed."

Mary Mallstead brought Quaine to the small shack in the clearing, its red walls defiantly bright in the otherwise fading and peeling town of Hawk's Tail.

"Hey Jack," Mary called, and a blind man hobbled out on a seeing cane. "This here's a friend of mine, named Quaine. He wants to hear all about what happened by the well, you fancy a telling?"

And Jack's unseeing eyes lit up in remembrance and excitement.

"By the sickness, I do."

* * *

"So thanks for coming by Mary—by the way, thanks Mary— I'll see you tomorrow. She's such a lovely woman, ain't she?

Yes sir, a lovely woman she is. She's got the voice of the city, and I can smell it on you too like piss in the corner, yes sir. You know Mary lets me use her well, such a lovely woman she is... yes sir, pleasant and kind to 'ole Jack, that Mary Mallbrook—Mallstam—Mallstorm. Beg your pardon, I'm bad with names, yes sir I am, what'd you say your name was?"

"Quaine? That's a funny name, a real funny one. Never met nobody with a name like that, no sir. Never heard of it before. But so I'll tell ya what happened, I'll tell ya about the heat and the well... but you gotta promise me something. I did a bad thing, I did a scared thing at the end—you keep a secret, yeah?"

"Well good good great good, I knew I could count on you mister. So Mary Mallstan is a sweetheart—real nice girl—and she lets me use her well sometimes—no water on this plot here, no sir. Dumber than a box of rocks, they said... not a drop."

The tall grass itched at Jack's ankles as it swayed side-to-side in the gentle breeze. He swung his cane left and right, feeling as it traced over the ground and rose and fell with its contours. In absentia of the light of vision, Jack's mind had sharpened a particularly effective sense of geography and topography, and by the way his cane dipped on the left swing, and by the way his feet crunched over a particular rise in the dirt, he knew he was approaching the hill to Mary's well. Ten more steps and the rise would begin in earnest.

Jack's ears lingered on the soundscape of the forest... the way the grass sighed, and the ways the distant bugs chirped and buzzed. His ears were ever-vigilant for the darker buzzing of a wasp—Jack took no chances with wasps, no sir—and any day he heard no wasps was automatically a good day. This day, however, there was a strange, *new* sound. It started as a deep and distant rumble, the kind that reminded him of the airplanes that used to rumble overhead when they used to fly that way. This was like that rumble, just as deep in Jack's bones, but then it started to get higher-pitched… and *louder.*

Something was wrong… very, very wrong. The rumble was a screech, a scream, and it was getting closer and closer… and oh, by the sickness, the *heat.* He could feel it now, like he suddenly stood at the campfire, and then there was the *jolt,* the ear-cracking bang. Jack's head was swimming, his ears ringing a high-pitched whirr. He realized, by the pressure along his side, that somehow he'd been thrown to the grass, and now he rolled his way onto his belly and stood. He spun his cane in a circle, trying to get the sense of his direction, but his head pounded and his cane swung with a bend in its middle. In the fall, it seemed he had nearly broken it at one of the folding joints.

He took a moment to collect himself, spinning slowly with the cane until he felt a familiarity towards the ground. He heard the babbling of the distant brook, and the tweeting of birds that loved those two oaks to the left of the fence post near Mary's barn. He knew where he was, and a few steps this way—yes, that's the ticket—and he suddenly felt the familiar rise of the hill to Mary's well.

"Scared the dickory out of me, by the sickness—demons come to rest, I thought. But they didn't scream, they didn't attack, so I figured maybe they mighta went back home… and I was thirsty. No water on my lands, no sir. So I went up the hill, step by step."

Step. Step. Each footfall was measured while Jack tried to fully reestablish his bearings, the ground tested to have just the right incline as he moved. Step: right where it was supposed to be. Next step: right where it was supposed to be. But then Jack paused mid-stride, confused. His cane, swinging left and right, suddenly lost the incline of the hill… it was tracing in a way that suggested a ridge to the hill where one didn't belong.

"I thought, oh man, Jack, now you done it—now you got lost and you might never find your way home."

But then Jack noticed a strange, soft sound just ahead. It was a gentle hiss, like the kind from a nice and wet piece of wood thrown into a hearth on a cold winter. The hiss lived at the center of the weird indentation, and Jack found himself drawn towards it to investigate.

"I got closer and it got hotter—by the sickness, so hot! Not supposed to touch the stove, no Jack, that's a bad thing to do—a captical bee bad thing to do."

Jack drew nearer to the thing, walking in this strange and circular indentation that his bent cane was reporting. In the air hung the ashy smell of burning green, mixing with the sweet-dark scent of exposed earth. The thing that hissed ever-so-softly was near now, and the heat it radiated was now like standing in front of a blazing stove. He reached his hand out, as though to touch it, and felt the heat rise as he drew towards that hiss… it would burn him, Jack surely knew it. But Jack was no fool—his momma said he was simple, but not a fool—and even a fool knew how you cooled a hot thing right down.

"I stumbled my way to the top of the hill, because that's where Mary Mallstead's well is. And even the tax men know that a well's gotta have a bucket and a rope—everyone knows that."

Jack untied the bucket by the feel of his hands on the thick, gnarled rope, and then he prodded his way back down the hill towards the strange indentation. Once he found it, he held the bucket by its bottom and pushed with the top towards the strange item. The wood clinked against something solid, yet seemingly brittle, as though it were the sound of pressing the bucket against a nice wide dinner plate set on the grass.

"Took me a minute to scoop it up, but by the sickness I did. When I picked up the bucket, it was heavy as a rock and hot as the clouds. But even the tax men know that water makes cold what the daylight makes hot. It needed a bath is all."

Jack carried the bucket in his outstretched left while prodding forwards with the bent cane in his right. The bucket's weight was unexpectedly heavy, but Jack was no weak man in his age... still strong from all the exercise, he knew. He'd told them up and down that getting his water was no trouble, because it kept his shoulders nice and tall... what's a little rock anyways?

He reached the surface of the well and set the heavy bucket on the well's perimeter. He then reached out over the edge to find the dangling rope, but despite the waving of his hand, he couldn't find it. He then did what he'd done countless days before: he set his cane across the well and braced himself on it with one arm as he reached out further, arm swinging wildly left and right.

However, Jack quickly discovered there was something different about this day... the cane was bent from his unexpected fall. It didn't hold as snugly as it was supposed to across the top, but instead bent inwards as he pressed his weight on it, and then slipped within the well entirely. For a moment, Jack's pinwheeling arms seemed like they might save him from the damp fall he sensed to his front... but then gravity pulled, and he felt a moment of terrible weightlessness as he tipped over the edge.

"There was suddenly the wet... my arm, I think it broke in a million places on the rock. Then I felt a big hit as the bucket toppled in and hit me on the back... and then came the burning... the rock started to burn."

Jack felt the screaming, angry rock as it bubbled and thrashed in the murky wet with him, and he fought it off with all the fury he could muster. A demon, he knew, here to drag him to the deep and drown him in the waters… Jack wouldn't let him. Jack swam towards where he thought was up, but felt his head bump immediately into a wall of stone.

"The walls trapped me in, more demons to drown me… but then came the strangest thing. There was this tingling all around me, coursing through my body. I thought, dang gone it, you're drowned now. But then the tingling did something it's not allowed to do… it left my body and went outside."

Jack floated in stupefied silence, waiting—but still not quite believing—as the tingling sensation in his hands and legs moved outside of his body. He could *feel* that tingling, somehow, even though it wasn't a part of him anymore… it seemed to wrap and cling in strange, indecipherable patterns around him in every direction. He tried again to swim, but as he did, he saw the patterns shift towards him, and they rushed to meet him right as his head contacted the wall of stone. That pattern knew it, somehow… it was the wall. How did he know the wall was there before he met it? How did he manage to feel a thing he hadn't touched yet?

He spun, noticing the strange and harsh pattern all around him, but then he turned his neck upwards and blinked in amazement. Above, an impossible distance away, was a glorious and beautiful thing. It was powerful, to the point where Jack's instinct was to avert his gaze, but Jack knew that its majesty was calling to him for a reason… *don't drown,* it seemed to command. *Come here instead.*

Jack swam towards the brilliant orb, and within seconds, something incredible happened… the murky water ended, and breathable, damp air began. Jack gulped in an expansive breath as he struggled to stay afloat, reaching his hands out to stabilize against the weird external pattern he'd come to associate with the walls. No demons could keep him down… he'd been too clever, to swim towards the beautiful thing like that.

He found loose stones that worked well as handholds to brace himself, giving him the ability to rest his already-tired feet from their frantic kicking. Then he looked up towards the brilliant point of *something* and called out. "Somebody help me!" Jack yelled, hearing the way his voice reflected off the close stone walls and the water below… the patterns' shape gave him a suggestion of those tall walls, and the shifting one below matched the feeling of the rippling water he felt surrounding him. "Please… I fell down here, and something's not right in my head! These feelings won't leave me alone!"

"Mary only draws her water twice a week—she has Mr. Dubois carry a bunch of buckets for her, she's much too thin. Thin as a pear, everyone knows it. But nobody else comes next to Mary Mallston's well… nobody heard my cries for help, on account of me being down in the well."

Soon that brilliant presence overhead, the one that had guided Jack towards the surface, began to journey away, sinking lower and lower and growing fainter and fainter. Jack could feel it still through the walls of the well—it was like his mind could reach out and touch it like his cane did—but as it went away, Jack felt the approach of the cool of night. *Is that what the sun looks like?* Jack thought, realizing that the king of daylight might have been that beautiful all this time and he'd never even imagined it. He began to miss it fiercely as soon as it disappeared, for now, as night settled its cloak over the land, the patterns dimmed significantly. "Please!" Jack called, but nobody above heard or answered his calls. Maybe the demons might win after all. Overhead, in what was normally a cloak of nothingness above Jack, he now became acutely aware of small points of potential... together, they draped wide over the world like a warm blanket stretched over a bed. Were those dots the stars he'd heard people talk about? "Tiny points of light," he'd heard them described, "that make the most beautiful patterns. It's worth living out of the city just to see them," Jimmy Finnegan had said. Well, Jack would have all the time in the world to appreciate them now... for it seemed that rescue would not be arriving just yet.

When he got thirsty, he just dipped his head under the water and took a large sip. When he'd needed to piss, he just did his business right there in the water, but he'd been sure to take an extra big gulp *before* that happened. The water was warm enough, maybe thanks to the hot thing he'd dropped into the well, but even still, Jack felt his pruned hands begin to tremble with the shivers... he gave up shouting as his throat started to hurt, and he instead tucked himself in towards the wall and tried to prop himself against it in a way that would allow him to rest.

There was no sleep for the frightened old man trapped in the well, but there was something akin to meditation... and in that state, with what was taking root in his body, came things that were close to *dreams*. The dots of light were suddenly closer, and they were far, far more vivid... perhaps *this* finally was the splendor of the stars he'd heard people talk about so fondly. Then the stars began to trace in lengthy lines towards Jack and into his body. They shone and glowed in ways Jack had never thought possible before, and the strength with which they moved—the clarity and power of their definition—it nearly brought tears to his eyes. He had to admit: it *was* beautiful, an image that would remain in his memory until the day he died. He became increasingly worried that that day might be soon... how long could an old man tread water?

His dreams turned sour with his mood: soon he saw not these points of lights and their bright lines, but instead a flat, open expanse he knew to be a field by the way that it felt, the way it sounded, the way it smelled. A pattern appeared in his mind, and he supposed that maybe this was what a field might *look* like, if only his eyes could see... and there at the center was a *thing*—almost like a person, but it was too cold, and it radiated evil. In the sky above the *thing* appeared again the patterns of the stars, the beautiful stars he had known so briefly but already loved so dearly... and Jack cried out in protest to what happened next. The *thing* in the field—now Jack could see it was a wicked, grinning demon—raised its hand and pulled a star down to the Earth. Its light was gobbled up in a hungry beam and jetted into the demon, leaving behind it a spot of yawning *empty* where the beautiful point had once sat. The demon continued its hungry spree, pulling the stars one at a time down into his greedy vessel... and point-by-point, the sky returned to its empty oblivion, the unobserved unobservable vacuum of a space where nothing could be perceived for as long as perception reached.

Jack cried out and shouted, wailing about the demon who pulled the stars from the sky, about the swirling of the demons in the water at his feet, about the fallen piece of the sun that landed him in this well in the first place... but above, only the chirping of the crickets answered back. There were no cries of acknowledgement, no ladders being lowered in, no promises to go get help... just Jack left in an impossible prison with no company but his nightmares.

"The voices told me to drown myself and be done with it... and by the sickness, I almost listened to them. Nobody saw me, nobody heard me... and then I was even afraid that if I shouted too loud, <u>he</u> might hear me. The one who pulled the stars from the sky... he might find me trapped, and seal the well shut with an ugly, round stone. The voices told me he was looking for

one right now, a big old stone to cover the well and trap me for good... why would he pull down something so beautiful? Didn't he ever hear how important the stars are to the night?"

After a fitful and traumatic span of uncountable hours, soon appeared the faintest outline of that point of glory he had known when he first fell into the well: the sun. It had returned, and with it came a banishment of the nightmares—and a retreating of the comforting net of stars overhead, still intact as it was. The voices of the night, the cruel and wicked that nearly convinced him to die, they too were banished by the rising light... and in its stead came a new, more assured voice.

A new voice, it told me that nobody else could help me, only me could help me. And it said that the sun was my ladder, it was my way out. I just had to reach up for it, but my hands couldn't reach... so I reached out in the other place. I reached out and touched it sure as it was touching me when I saw it, cause how can you see a thing without touching it? My head was a new type of seeing cane, now, and when it finally climbed right overhead, I used it to reach for the sun, and by the sickness I felt it. I felt something hot and something powerful, and I felt how it was waiting for me, like it was there, saying "here you go, take all that you need." So I did.

Weather satellites would report the incident as an unexplained lightning-adjacent phenomenon. For a single instant, a piercing column of light extended from the distant surface of the sun all the way down to that single well in Hawk's Tail. It was like a string that represented the very tether of gravity itself, and it was sustained for mere nanoseconds. In that time, the energy transferred was enough to flash-vaporize nearly a quarter of the water in Mary Mallstead's well, but Jack did not fall down into the suddenly emptied space, nor did his skin suddenly scald at the presence of steam... Jack's skin glowed white-hot with the pure energy of the sun, and his radiating heat immediately set the stones of Mary's well glowing red-hot. Instinctively, with no awareness of why or even how, Jack pushed against the glowing stones, and the force of those radial pushes kept him suspended in the open air of the well. He pushed against the lower glowing stones and began to rise, melting and scorching the rim as he did. When he reached the wooden framework at top that once housed the bucket and rope, both fixtures burst into flame, and Jack was amazed by the *sight* of it all. The light that lived inside everything around him—absorbed by the sun, reflected off at every which angle—it all was suddenly tangible to his mind, and the shape of the alien world left him floating there at the top of the well, amazed and in awe.

When he landed, he felt a great and profound draining at his feet, as the power within him somehow coursed into the land itself and left his body… and then came exhaustion, and it hit like a tidal wave of unimaginable size. Jack laid down before he collapsed outright, feeling the darkness overtake him as distant voices shouted "there's smoke where it came from, looks like it hit Mary's land!" Through the ground, he could feel the rumbling approach of frantic footsteps, and with them, rescue and salvation.

* * *

Click-Stick Jack led the way into the balmy outdoor heat towards Mary Mallstead's well. It was one thing to *hear* a wild story, but another thing entirely to observe the scorch marks it left behind.

Incredulity switched to a cautious interest as Quaine observed the crater on the hill with the well looming ahead. In his mind's eye, the thing had been massive, but here was a crater only eight feet across. The inside of the crater sported grass and a fair few flowers… Mother Earth could heal her wounds much the same as the human body could. A quick internet look-up suggested that impact craters were typically 20 times wider than the objects they bore, so, with some quick mental math, Quaine was imagining an object about 5 inches across. *Small enough to fit in a bucket,* he realized. Cautious interest upgraded to reserved belief. *Something* had fallen here, and maybe thus Jack found himself in the well. Might some other detail have been lost to Jack's mind?

Then the pair ascended the hill. At the top, Quaine could see that the wooden framework to house the buckets and rope mechanism were relatively new. *"Burnt it right off,"* Jack had said. And then when Quaine peered over the ring of stone into the black pit of the well, his skin broke out in goosebumps. The sun was high overhead, so he could see half of the well illuminated by the daylight. The half he could see was marred with strange scorchmarks, and at several points, the rough-hewn stone was strangely and bizarrely deformed, as though smoothed into place like rough clay. A few portions even seemed to feature downward drips like an old, waxy candle.

Quaine imagined a scared man in the bottom of the well rising as the ring of stone melted and chipped… could it be that Jack was entirely truthful? Did he somehow—through means Quaine did not yet understand—pull energy from the sun? It shouldn't be possible, but, if Quaine were being honest, nothing about lightbending *should be possible.* Was this before him the aftermath of a wellstone nearly melted by sudden and extreme heat? Could it be that everything began here, that everything came from the crater a few dozen feet away? Quaine knew that accepting the crater came with its own millions of questions, questions of "where did the meteor come from?" and "how could one even continue to search for the origin?"

Quaine felt like weighing none of those questions right this moment. There would be time for such implications later on.

For the current moment, there were still blanks to fill in. If the crater was the accepted origin, what was the vector from Jack to the clusters he'd found in his data research? He shook his head, tapping on the edge of the well… *of course,* he thought. *It's in the water.*

"The nightmares got worse," Jack said. "By the sickness, did they get worse… I could *see* the *stars*, and they were beautiful—I could touch them with the cane in my head. But when I'd try to sleep, I'd see *him* again. He's standing in the field, and he pulls them all down one at a time, and soon he's glowing hot and bright like he swallowed them whole, and they burn inside him now… I felt a million voices calling in my head. I still hear voices in my head, Dr. Sandra says that's part of a skitzy effective disorder. But the voices were telling me to eat the stars like he was… I think they were telling me to swallow up the power, to *become* the demon in my nightmares. And no sir, Jack is no demon—nuh uh, wasn't gonna do it. They're quiet today, the voices—but oh, were they louder then."

"What happened next?" Quaine asked.

"Nobody believed me either, nobody was sure how I got out of the well, how I set it on fire… they said I wasn't in the well, just hurt by the big lightning bolt. I told them up and down about where I was, but they didn't believed me. They said my *imagination* made up the well… such an active imagination I got. They said I can't tell stories from the real world sometimes, and sometimes they're right. But they didn't understand how come I could see like they could, and they didn't understand the nightmares neither. I was at Tofferman's and I was fighting against the voices when I found a way out… open the plug on the bathtub drain. I dropped it. The stuff I carried, I dropped it. Right in Tofferman's. One second I could see... and the next, the patterns disappeared, and the demon's voice with it."

"You passed on your gifts?"

"Mister, when I learned how to see I thought it was the most wonderful thing, so different, so special. It was like a treasure that I suddenly had, but everybody else already got. But when the nightmares got bad, and the voice got louder, it wasn't worth it. Mister, it wasn't worth it. I had to let it go."

"Who were you near at the time?"

From Jack, Quaine began to piece together the missing steps of the chain of transmission. Near Jack at the bar were two young men of Hawk's Tail: Percy and Paul Trightman. Both brothers were killed in a single incident less than a month later—their pedal-driven carriage was struck by a runaway self-driving semitruck near the Hawk's Tail charge station. Quaine had been driven to this small town because of three emergent clusters of lightbending spread, where two of their first nodes had overlapped here in Hawk's Tail... the time and date of their overlap corresponded perfectly with the crash that killed the two brothers.

Piece by piece, with GPS log requests and dashboard camera requisitions, Quaine was able to piece together that when the two brothers were killed, three out-of-towners at the charging station ran over to check for survivors—there were none to find. But in the process, three people were exposed to the sparks the brothers had carried. The first, Larry Allbright, would later fall to his death in New Phoenix after bursting a halo mid-flight without preparation... many a novice lightbender died to omnipresent gravity. The second, Micayla Rose, died alone of a drug overdose three months later. Her body's arrival to a VitaCorp corpse processing facility lead to transmission towards four VitaCorp employees, the first cases known to VitaCorp—known internally as T1, T2, T3, and T4. The final arrival to the accident, Mink Rhames, had no obvious transmission chain, but later geographic research would clue Quaine in to the fact that several unlinked lightbender cases were found along the sewer pipes that lead away from Mink's home… had she perhaps ejected her ichor into the sink or shower by mistake, and infected people near those drains at just the right time and place later on?

"One more thing I need to know," Quaine said. "The rock… the thing at the center of the crater. Did you get it back? What happened to it?"

Jack laughed. "Oh, mister, surely don't you know. Rocks sink, everybody knows that! Bottom of the well of course, sleeping like a sound. Right down there at the bottom, sure as a sugar." Jack's eyes went wide. "You want to take it! You want to grab it!" Jack hobbled towards where he'd heard Quaine's voice and clasped at him, grabbing tight to his hands. "Promise me something. You promise me right now. If you hear the voice, the hungry and angry voice—you won't listen to the demons, yeah? You won't do it? You won't become the one from my nightmares, the one who gobbles up—" his voice caught, fighting off terror and tears at the same time. "You won't be the one to eat the stars?"

"I swear it," Quaine said. "I'll keep it safe. I'm going to go back to the city, and come back in a couple days with the tools for the job—a few pieces of equipment to help me grab it. Until then, you keep it safe, yeah?"

Jack nodded his head.

"Safe as a sound," he promised. "Safe as a sound."

Chapter 54

"A toast, then," Avery said, raising a champagne flute. "To questions finally answered."

Quaine lifted his glass and clinked it against Avery's, both drinking the delicate, bubbly fluid with fake smiles. The restaurant, Caesar's, was among the most luxurious in all of New Phoenix, with tables often reserved three years in advance. But before the finances and power of Clive Avery, reservations could often be shifted... and entire floors vacated for privacy. The private area the two sat in was lined with red carpet and deep, velvet drapings along walls dominated by white columns in the classical style. The tablecloths were white satin, and the silverware had the firm weight of real precious metal. The poorer laborers in the city couldn't afford a meal here with an entire year's wages, and yet Avery's company would generate enough profit for his personal pockets before they even poured the glasses of water... it all made Quaine feel uneasy. He took another sip of 90,000 credit champagne.

"When your message came to my desk," Avery said, "I was immediately enthralled by the fantasy of it. *'Compelling evidence of extraterrestrial origin...'* I nearly choked on my scotch!"

"I have hardly slept a wink since making the discovery yesterday," Quaine said. "My mind is racing at a thousand miles per hour, every new discovery leading to a swarm of newer questions. I would like to formally contact the National Astronomy Exploration—"

"Mister O'Connor," Avery interjected, "the work you have done recently is incredible in its significance to our learning. With your revelations, we draw one giant leap closer to knowing the nature of the ichor... indeed, it is only appropriate that we find proof it came from the kingdom of the gods. For heaven is above, and their strength may drop down to the mortals below."

Quaine waited for Avery to continue.

"But you know as well as I do that our company's work is important. Would you agree with this? That VitaCorp advancements have benefitted mankind?"

Quaine offered the obligatory nod that the rhetorical question demanded.

"And would you agree that with the lawyers of the city at our throats—with the protesters who clamor for divestment— that there is a great and terrible risk to our positioning to better mankind?"

Quaine nodded, but not with heart.

"City Hall is all political games and maneuvering... and sometimes the greatest powers are mere shadows; finger-puppet threats to keep the rabble in a row."

Quaine looked to Avery with confusion now.

"Often are the subtleties of rhetoric lost on the scientific-minded... I will speak plainly, then. What you have discovered is paradigm-shattering in its significance, but it must remain a secret to the world."

A wheeled serving robot arrived to the table and deposited the venison steak before Avery, as well as the cream of mushroom soup Quaine had ordered. Avery tore into the meat with precise, forceful cuts and then took a needlessly large bite.

"The balance of power hangs on the edge of a knife," he said once he had swallowed, "and it is the fear of *our* ichor that keeps the politicians in line. We are lucky, blessed by the gods themselves that it arrived in our institution first with T1 to 4... we have been dealt a card that we cannot help but play. That requires your silence on the origin of this miracle, lest other organizations make claims to its control."

"Respectfully, sir, how am I supposed to be silent on what might be the most significant discovery in human history?" Quaine asked. "The implications this carries for our place in the universe, whether we're alone—how can I be silent on it?"

"It is a great sacrifice I ask of you, but it is a necessary one. Information is truly one of the most dangerous concepts we have ever encountered... the wrong narratives can destroy society, and the right ones can save it. You would see yourself as a deliverer of truth, an answerer of questions... but your information shatters the paradigm of our world. This makes it an ax, and you give it to the people of the city. Who might pick it up? How might they wield it? What institutions might it chop down with only a single swing?"

Quaine stared at his soup, suddenly not very hungry.

"One of the first things mastered by any competent leader is what I would call *tactical dishonesty,*" Avery said. "It is knowing what information betters a republic, and sharing that information, while knowing what information would harm the people, and hiding those facts. People are so impressionable to the information they receive... it warps and changes them like water soaking into a leg of a table of wood, until they no longer fit—the table now wobbles. Society has lost its productive member, and now in its place is an active detractor.

Your facts you have discovered are an existential threat to the order of the world—and for that reason, they must be kept silent."

Quaine met Avery's eyes, watching him take another large bite from the venison, chewing it with savoring slowness. "What am I to do, then?" Quaine asked, his voice sounding suddenly defeated.

"Tell me all that you know: how this all was uncovered, who else knows. Then me and my closer operatives will... *sanitize* the situation."

"Sanitize?" Quaine asked.

"No need to be so dramatic," Avery said. "Offer *bribes of silence.*"

Though he was still new to the concept, Quaine found *tactical dishonesty* quite easy to spot.

"And of course," Avery said, "you yourself will be rewarded for your silence... so great is the burden of the secret you will carry. You'll be compensated in proportion to that which we ask of you. Now, if you would be so kind, please share with me the trail of clues that led you to your discovery."

Quaine chewed at the inside of his cheeks, thinking on Jack and Mary and the dozens of other residents of the tiny village that might be killed to keep Avery's secret. Were their lives acceptable trades on balance against the societal good that VitaCorp might bring? He remembered Hannah and the outer ring itch, an STI they could easily cure with a simple powder in the water supply... kept untreated to promote 'beneficial social divisions.' He remembered the protests from those who lost loved ones to VitaCorp's lawful impoundment of the dead. He remembered the squalid conditions forced unto unaffiliated medical centers via litigation if they used any 'VitaCorp proprietary technologies,' a broad classification that now included nearly every modern medical apparatus on the planet. What was the point of doing a good thing if it required so much evil as a prerequisite?

"I… need to think," Quaine said. "To consider." He stood up awkwardly, and noted the cold pressure of Avery's regard as he did. "I'll compile my research tonight as I do, and I'll have a datatransfer for you tomorrow." He bowed curtly and turned towards the exit.

"I pride myself normally," Avery said, "to be an excellent judge of character… I'd thought you a grounded pragmatist, not a naive idealist. For both of our sakes, let me not have been wrong." Avery watched the man leave, frustrated at the shortsightedness of smaller men… he felt the palpitations in his chest of rising stress and closed his eyes for a moment, taking deep breaths and listening to the sound of his own slowing heart rate. The sooner this unexpected obstacle was put behind him, the sooner he might finally be able to rest. But until then, there was hard work to be done. He returned his knife to the steak and cut loose another chunk.

* * *

Quaine knew that the ire of VitaCorp's COO was now upon him… and he had seen enough videos of abductions of dissidents to know the danger that brought. He raced to a nearby shopping center and bought a cap and a dark jacket, anything he could leverage to block camera views of his face. They would be coming for him, so he would have to hide.

The stone was his proof, it would be his only and most vital proof, so he next saddled into his car and sprinted towards the outskirts of Hawk's Tail as fast as Sentinel would permit. On his way out, a perimeter checkpoint photographed his car as he passed, a record that Braxton Graves would see in the months to come.

Onwards he raced, his hands leaving nervous imprints of sweat on the steering wheel as he flew in manual. The airvents near the wheel made his hands feel cold and clumsy, and switching them off made him perspire with a nervous, full-body sweat. He looked in his rear view mirror repeatedly for tailing drones or vehicles; seeing none was no comfort at all.

He finally arrived to the small township, parking his car directly on the grassy mound that hosted the well. He then unpacked the amphibious drone he'd brought and set it to work, unfolding the hand-held remote as it skittered its way down the walls of scorched stone.

Once in the water, its front-facing camera and lights switched on, and Quaine instructed it to detach from the wall and simply float downwards to the bottom of the well. When it finally had, Quaine sat in nervous silence as the mud at the bottom settled, restoring visibility.

The video feed's quality was poor, but it was enough to note the handful of loose items on the well bottom... there was a single spoon, still glinting with uncorroded metal. Near it was a bent cane, once wielded by Click-Stick Jack... there were small fragments of stones shattered by the heat of Jack's rise, and a few more that seemed to simply slip in over time. There were long rectangles of what seemed to be burnt wood, and near it, there was a stone that seemed different from all others... this one was rough, misshapen, with holes seemingly punched through it. It was a meteorite, Quaine was sure of it.

He used the drone to grab the stone and then walked it back up the wall, reclaiming both hurriedly and heading back into his vehicle. He longed to go and speak with Jack, to show him the stone he nearly died for, but he acknowledged that

VitaCorp might already be on their way to his location, or monitoring him to see whom he speaks with... to talk now might be carrying a death sentence to Jack, assuming his visit to this town wasn't one already. He instead packed both away in the trunk of his car, but as he did so, he noticed that small, silvery tendrils stretched from the meteorite to his hand as he held it... he watched them vanish into his hand. He had never seen anything so strange, and so he dropped the stone and clutched at his hand in fear... after the shock of it passed, the hand again felt normal, and so he continued packing up. There would be time enough to investigate it later.

Hannah's apartment would be safe, as he was certain VitaCorp knew nothing of their relationship... after all, with her being an outer-ringer, it was nearly unthinkable to Avery. His own prejudices were his blindness, and Quaine hoped that the blindness would be enough to keep him safe through the night. As he drove, he felt his heart rate continue to quicken. He felt his pulse even pounding in his ears, and a knot of dread settled deep in his stomach. Dark was soon falling, and he hoped desperately he would live to see the sunrise of another day, that beautiful orange wedge that brought light back to the darkness... he remembered hearing the glory of its return as told by Jack. He, too, would be staring for the sky, waiting with trepidation to see if fate had another day written for him. As the sun went down, Quaine became aware of the points of light above, the twinkling stars he so rarely saw living in the city... and in the calm of his drive, something strange happened. It wasn't a *hallucination* so much as an image, involuntarily conjured to his mind in the same place as he might have once imagined a color or pictured an old friend. In his mind's theater he saw points of light, and as Quaine breathed in, the lights stretched into thin lines and flowed towards him. "Drink of the light," he imagined a voice whispering to him. "Drink of the stars."

He slapped his own face as he shook off the vision, fearing—knowing—that somehow, the power of the meteorite had already infected him, too. He didn't move to get the spark count measurement device in his glove compartment… there was no doubt of what it might show. Could he use the power to save his own life? To what end, and for how long?

Quaine shook his head… there was no running from VitaCorp, no fighting it off. They would come and they would kill him… and then, as they always did, they would absorb his power.

When he arrived to Hannah's apartment, he again made sure to hide from any and all cameras on the street. When he saw her, saw her innocent calm and loving smile, it tore him up inside to know his time with her might soon end… but if there was one thing Avery was right about, it was that information was dangerous. To tell her would be to sentence her to the same fate he might soon meet, and his love was far too deep to even consider that risk. If he was to die, he was to die. But as he looked to her smile, and traced a finger along the butterfly rash in the center of her face—nearly a pair of angel's wings, he thought—an idea came to Quaine.

They might come for her too, in time… give her the sparks. Deny them your power… and let her have a chance to save herself if they find her.

She took his hand and smiled, and something about the innocence of the gesture despite his life collapsing around him made him need her now. He kissed her deeply as passion overcame him, a deep and raw longing for a person so precious to him that he knew he would soon lose. He would indeed lose everything—his job, his legacy, his friends, his talents, his discoveries, his inspirations, even likely his own life—but it would be the loss of *her* that would sting the most as he died. She completed him, and he feared the emptiness of dying without her. He poured his fears for his life, his awe of the meteorite, his despair at a life unfulfilled, and his hope at her survival all into that single kiss… and in the heat of that passion, that raw emotion, she bloomed in his arms and returned it tenfold. Quaine was awash in pain, hurt, longing, love, and ecstasy, and he felt her guide him forwards to bliss as the pair were locked into embrace, clothing shedding away.

Soon they were sighing and breathing in unison, eyes locked together as he pressed down onto her. His hand stroked her face, his fingers tracing small lines by her temple, lost in the softness of her body… it was time, he knew. He remembered Jack's words: "I dropped it. Opened the plug on the bathtub drain." Quaine reached into his mind, the maelstrom of panic of hours before calmed to placidity from her love. And in that serene place within, he felt it: a drain, a stop, a cork he'd never felt before. He pulled it as the both gasped in unison, and he watched as silvery filaments sprung from the hand that held to her face… they drained from him and poured into her, electric sensation rocking the both of them, until soon Quaine could feel they were gone and both lay there nearly breathless.

In the aftermath, he held fast to her with arms drawn tight. He knew it was like grasping at a fistful of sand, unable to stop its crumble between his fingers—but he held all the same, for a love as pure as theirs was worth every effort, however futile. And so, on the eve of his death, Quaine somehow slept peacefully… he'd done all he could, and he would enjoy his last breaths as fully and completely as was possible.

He awoke in the dark to a buzzing from his implant… his security camera at his apartment showed a team of four lightbenders moving through and clearing room by room. If they tracked his car, *she* might be at risk… and so he pulled away from her slowly, watching as she shifted to make sure she wouldn't wake. He drew the blanket tight over her to keep her warm from the night's cold, and then he tip-toed to the door. With one hand on the handle, he turned around, seeing her on that bed, and taking a snapshot in his mind: when he died, he wanted to hold this image as he passed. Her sleeping serenity was pure, and he hoped it would bring him some calm, too, when the time came.

Though the VitaCorp agents' gas had him unconscious when his vehicle hit the water, the sleep the gas sent him to was a rest as profoundly peaceful as hers... it was a quiet, painless death for a man whose only sin was that he dared to discover truth the world found inconvenient.

Chapter 55

* * *

The screen switched to black, its video clip having concluded.

"Well fuck," Lana Crawford said.

"Well fuck," Carter Miles added.

"Well *fuck*," The Basilisk agreed.

"All this time… and it fell from the god-damn sky?" Lana Crawford was shaking her head with a gesture that wasn't incredulous so much as frustrated. "And VitaCorp, of all people, get to lay claim to it first?"

"If it spreads through the dead, of course they'd have it early on," Miles said. "But a *meteorite?*"

"You trust this to be genuine?" The Basilisk moved towards Hannah and gestured at the screen. "You knew the man well… this seems him?"

"You saw it yourself," Pollock said, "it's TruthSpace verified."

"That means nothing given our foe," the Basilisk said, a troubled frown on his synthetic face. "Do you trust it?"

Hannah nodded her head. "I do. It fits everything I saw and heard from him... and the timeline makes sense."

"A meteor," Miles repeated dreamily. "A rock from the sky."

"This could be it," Lana said. "The moment we've been waiting for... the information we needed to finally make our case, set our public indictment."

The Basilisk met her gaze. "I thought it too... if ever there was a weapon to wield, it's this truth. The implications stand for themselves... and I have to think the public will feel that same sense of awe, that sense of amazement. If we could temper those feelings into action against VitaCorp..." The Basilisk trailed off, thinking. He then nodded. "Hmmm, yes. I think this could be it."

"What, exactly, is *it?*" Pollock asked, walking around the command room and admiring the drawings and schematics thrown up on the walls. On one side of the room, a massive network of faces was connected with linkages of every which color. And in front of him, a 3D printer stood on standby, a new face waiting on the dummy's round head. Staring at it there, partly scrunched up without being worn—it made Pollock's skin crawl.

"*It* is our final move against VitaCorp." The Basilisk tapped on his controls and an image of Pyke's Park TruthSpace flashed onto the screen. "We go public with everything we know—the truth about lightbending, about the Tacitus Newport up in their tower. We deliver our scathing indictment in public, and if VitaCorp fly in and kill me—which I have every belief that they will—I die a martyr to the cause. I'll be incitement on a scale too large to suppress... the people are restless, and the truth is their liberation. It shatters the prison they've built, because it shows the people that the power they wield isn't one they hold special dominion over... if anything, it's a gift to the Earth, and it'll be an encouragement to those who hold the power in secrecy to step forwards and present themselves. VitaCorp will lose their mandate... they'll lose their invincibility because they've lost their status as the highest power. I think it'll be all-out war, and truth be told, I don't know if we have the means to come out on top. But some wars need to be fought regardless of the chance of success—tyranny *must be resisted* regardless of outcome—and we, Halogen, will give the people the light to do so."

"Still not so sure about the you dying a martyr part," Carter Miles said.

The Basilisk clapped a hand on Miles's shoulder. "You've known since the beginning that I'm willing to give whatever the cause demands of me... same as each and every other dedicated member of Halogen. I won't have your fondness of me—and my reciprocal fondness for each and every one of you—deny the movement its final, most-vital spark. This is far too important for sentiment to get in the way." He then turned to Lana. "What's the status of our conversations with VitaCorp's spy in ArtGen?"

"I see a message here from Kim saying she's ready to turn on VC."

He smiled and then turned to Hannah. "Your information you bring is profoundly helpful to our cause, but we may still need you today. If I'm eventually to die—no, Miles, we're not arguing that point right now—it's been decided that we want you to be a centerpiece to the movement beyond. The people love you, and our content featuring you has been going viral more so than our other clips. Those videos of you after ArtGen tower? Have you *seen* the metrics on those? You broke a billion impressions in six hours. There's just something about you they just can't get enough of. We'd like to shoot another, a scene of you doing good work with a full entourage of videocapturing drones… any interest?"

"Define good work?"

The Basilisk smiled. "Turning one of their spies… a face I found from our brief bug in ArtGen's server room that you planted. She's under their threat, so we're rescuing her, while we expect some resistance from the suits. Nothing you couldn't handle, I'm sure. Plenty of angles for the streaming sites."

"Why the theatrics, the battling? If she's on our side, just invite her into a safehouse somewhere and VitaCorp can't reach her." Hannah crossed her arms, feeling a little uneasy at the drummed-up spectacle of it all.

"To ensure their spy's timely reports, they've got her pacemaker rigged to stop every 24 hours unless a VitaCorp suit, her handler, scans an RFID to buy another 24." Miles said. "She lives perpetually one day away from death, and the fear of it keeps her in line."

"Cruelty," Hannah said, shaking her head.

"What if it's a lie?" Pollock asked. "A play to get us to expose ourselves. We think we're turning her, but it's really a double—no, a triple-cross?"

"When we talked to her, she cracked almost immediately," The Basilisk said. "She had medical debt, too… they're twisting her arm financially and medically. She wants out… on that front, I believe her. We even had her testify before a weak-AI testimony analyzer and it thinks the body language points towards legitimate. And *even if* it's a trap, even if she's not what she says she is… Hannah gets taped fighting off whatever trickery they've planned. Seems a win-win."

Hannah nodded. "I'll do it… constant terror like that. It's no way to live. I'll help free her, but how? If we break her out, isn't that as good as killing her?"

"If you bring the RFID unit in with the spy—the one they'd have used to buy her another day—I should be able to reverse engineer it and get her as many keys as we need. That buys plenty of time to figure out a longer-term solution," Carter Miles reassured. "I'll be there, right on scene, with an RFID emitter to try guesswork if things get hairy…"

The Basilisk frowned, wanting to tell the man that the mission was too dangerous to risk his presence… but he already heard the remarks turned right around to his own actions, and knew that it was an argument he would lose. "We move forwards, then," The Basilisk said. "Tell her to pass on the information we discussed and set up her final drop. They'll likely choose Baylor Tower, so we need to prepare."

He then turned towards Hannah. "And Preacher? Boys in R&D have cooked up a new weapon of sorts that we think you'll really like… You should go take the opportunity to practice with it before we head out."

* * *

The elevator door pinged as it slid open, and Avery's calm smile he'd been wearing wiped away almost instantly. His temples began to twitch and his arms trembled, rage rising. The toads Spivey and McKillian had the *audacity* to return to his office floor, and to stride in with that air of control that they had no right to. His stomach cramped with the throes of botulism—or was it an ulcer—and he glanced to the wristwatch he wore, its display configured to permanently monitor his heart's health through several electrodes scattered throughout his body. *Not dying yet*, he noted from the display. *But depending on whatever bile spills from their bloated lips, I might still burst a blood vessel in rage...*

The two at least were wearing their face-covering plastic masks, a condition that Avery's secretaries below had enforced. It was a fact that brought him wicked satisfaction, though the masks made the two somehow even harder to distinguish, if such a thing were possible. "Gentlemen... to what do I owe the distinct displeasure?"

"You have broken our agreement," said Spivey.

"Attacked the woman and her CSP," said McKillian.

Avery spread his hands wide in acquiescence. "Denial is beneath me, and I know it would not convince you."

"Indeed it would not," said Spivey.

"Our threats were clear," said McKillian.

"And so, what is this, then... a negotiation?" Avery asked.

"Merely a delivery of promised consequence," said McKillian. He proffered a tablet showing a video with a Veritas seal along the bottom... in it, Avery could see himself and the young girl Kelsey Levin.

"An outer ring prostitute the press could forgive," said Spivey.

"But an inner-ring starlet?" asked McKillian. "What will they think?"

Avery looked back to the video, frowning. "A fiction," he said, not recognizing the actions or dialogue between himself and Levin.

"Good lies incorporate the truth," said Spivey.

"She'll corroborate," said McKillian.

"So, what, I'm supposed to beg and you lay out conditions to prevent this release?"

Both men laughed in near unison.

"Oh no, Mr. Avery… it is as we said, this is the consequence." Spivey's smile was nearly pitying.

"It has been sent to the office of the mayor ten minutes ago," said McKillian.

Avery's eyes were daggers, and his teeth were immediately gritted. "You… what?"

"Disobey again," Spivey said, "and the next clip shall be worse."

"Disobey?" Avery balked. "I owe nobody my *obedience*," he seethed. "We entered into a partnership, not an oath of fealty."

"And yet, the faith was broken," Spivey said.

"Unlike you, we keep our word," said McKillian.

Already the two were backing towards the door. "Good day, Mr. Avery," Spivey said with a nod.

Clive Avery felt a sudden and sharp pain in his head, an aneurysm that would certainly kill him… but then he breathed in his next breath, still alive. Even his own mind was his enemy in this misery of a world… he simply *would not* take this insult. And with the report he'd received only an hour before, perhaps he'd not have to. VitaCorp's ArtGen insider thought it found their foe's spy… a ghost employee, records entirely scrubbed on every outwards-facing database but still existing on deep server archives. In her, it seemed VitaCorp had found its mark. The name was to be revealed any minute now. And that, of course, meant a shifting of leverage.

"Wait, gentlemen... will one of you take a message to your employer from me?"

Spivey turned, regarding Avery with a raised eyebrow.

"The message is this:"

Avery tapped the screen on his desk, and the masks his techs had designed now clamped to the men's faces as a piercing, buzzing alarm rang. Bright lights on the top and side all lit up in a flare of blinding white, accented by the glow of a soft blacklight beneath. The panicked men reached for their masks, now turned to involuntary helmets, but neither could pull his loose.

"The next insult on behalf of your employer will be his last... and it is *my mercy,* and *my mercy alone* that one of you live." And then Avery threw all of his force against the lights of the mask of the man on the right.

Spivey's neck jerked as he was thrown backwards and upwards with sudden speed, smashing into and through the glass of the window head-first. He then disappeared down as gravity took him amid the falling fragments of glass, utterly silent as he fell. Then came the gentle howl of the wind through the hole, the clanging of final fragments of glass falling to the tile... the heavy and frantic footsteps of a bureaucrat in terror—a sound that brought Avery no shortage of comfort—and then, with the sliding of the elevator door shut, finally, and at long last, the return of peaceful, meditative silence.

Avery swallowed today's immunosuppressive pill and smiled. There might yet be a good day to discover beneath all of the morning's misery.

He tapped the comms unit on his side and then spoke his command: "Call Braxton Graves."

Chapter 56

"I should hardly need remind, but failure to wear containment equipment in my presence will result in immediate employee termination. Furthermore, I have attached design suggestions for our engineers to manifest as quickly as is possible, including defensive additions to interact with the ichor. Timely filling of these requests is expected."

-Internal memo from Clive Avery to VitaCorp's engineering arm, of moderate system relevance

* * *

The VitaCorp Department of Neonatal Studies occupied floor 62 of the onyx tower. There, fetal stem cells were grown into implant tissue; newborn autopsies were performed in the wake of fatal birth defects; and most controversially, genetic experiments were carried out to test tube birth. To avoid challenging questions of ethics, VitaCorp's "tube babies," as they came to be called, were all descendents of one prototypical infant, known as Specimen-Alpha. Specimen-Alpha was no ordinary child: he was engineered to lack more than three-quarters of his brain, making him "functionally unconscious." There was no pain system, no fledgeling network of cortices that would one day develop to an identity… just a chemical machine to feed until that feeding eventually stopped, at which point VitaCorp's scientists never said it died—as that would have implied it once lived. Instead, the label they chose was *inert*, and the infant would spend a year or five from conception to *inert* under constant experimentation, manipulation, and observation. Designer birth defects were conceptualized and realized in these tube babies, and the subsequent observations drove further innovation and a deeper understanding of human development. Even stillborn "natural" infants were often lobotomized and hooked to life-sustaining systems, to simulate the laboratory of nature's random distribution of genetic material. "*Field studies*," they were called. From these experiments came the genetic tweaks that allowed for natural hair colors of every pigment. From these experiments came the genes spliced into human populations that prevented malaria. From these experiments came bone marrow therapies to defeat herpesviruses and retroviruses.

In reverence to the *inert*—or perhaps under the philosophy that no useful instrument should ever be thrown out—generations and generations of tube babies were kept in amniotic suspension in jars that lined several of VitaCorp's neonatal storage rooms. Many bore the same genetically-pre-ordained face of Specimen-Alpha, while others, the field studies, provided occasional lapses from that conformity. One such jar, resting under a thick blanket of dust, housed an infant of 6.2 pounds, a small wisp of dark blue hair on his head. A barcode label bore the name Beadie, Beverly 1, for the children were never named… only logged under the name of their birth parent.

The small infant's unseeing eyes were directed towards the large floor-to-ceiling window, and beyond that window stood the scaffolds of Baylor Tower. In a way, the structure was also an infant in suspension, though one of a decidedly larger size. And like the blue-haired inhabitant of jar AC-01103534, its stasis was largely the direction of one Clive Avery. "Board rooms should have views," Avery had said. "The members of this board must see the city they preside over." And that view was threatened by the rising construction of Baylor Tower in the lot adjacent.

Baylor Distributions was a logistics company subcontracted by many of the United Americas's largest organizations. Its founder, Tom Baylor, believed that the majority of humanity's sufferings were merely logistical shortcomings on the part of society. Starvation and drought were merely inefficient distribution of food and water, as the Earth had plenty of space to grow crops and sustain the world's populations. Economies were built on the distribution of goods and services, and weaker economies simply lacked the resources they required—resources that were present, but idle elsewhere. Through effective logistics, Baylor believed that humanity could be lifted up to enjoy an equal level of prosperity—a stance that made him enemy to the oligarchs of the city. When he bought the lot next to VitaCorp tower, he had hoped that his rising white beacon would make VitaCorp the shadow it deserved to be. The tower's plans featured large public spaces and parks in the central column of the structure, and even a business-lined roadway at the tower's midpoint that rose up from the ground in a grand bridge—a symbolic and literal raising of the streets to the heights of the elites inspired by the elevated Promenade of the Arts.

But again, "board rooms should have views," and so, one at a time, thanks to corporate exertion of will and political capital, city officials began to find faults in the plans submitted by Baylor. There was missing authorization from the architect on this specific subdocument regarding the weight balance of planned topiaries on the rooftop; the department of roadways modified their permit submission documentation and the records would need to be updated; a new city ordinance banned construction during the hours scheduled, and your new construction schedule would need city council approval as well as formal noise suppression equipment rental; superstorm resistance protocols require redesign of the elevated roadway's support columns; the construction company that received initial approval has been foreclosed upon due to an errant tax document error, and so the approval process will need to be restarted once a new company has received proper accreditation. Every obstacle hurdled led to the creation of two new roadblocks, and the rise of Baylor Tower stalled to a halt at half the height of VitaCorp's pillar.

The final insult would come after years of Baylor Distributions hemorrhaging cash through the stalled construction project... it had been a massive capital investment, and now the company found it suffering its own logistical crisis. Money that had been anchored to the construction could not be liberated until its completion... their investment was not only not yet paying dividends, but it also seemed that it perhaps *never would.* An investment without payout was no investment at all... it was a cash sink, and investors recognized the strong-arming of VitaCorp for what it was. Money began to pull out, and the floundering company sought desperately to sell its tower to salvage its finances. VitaCorp again flexed its influential arms, and none would buy, leaving VitaCorp itself the only entity to make an offer— a paltry sum less than a third of the firm's investment in the property.

Facing financial ruin, a miserable Tom Baylor accepted the spit on his face. And while many expected the tower to be converted into a second VitaCorp property, a metastization of the company to a new plot, it instead sat in perpetually stalled construction. VitaCorp's finances didn't require they convert the purchase into anything that generated revenue. It was instead left a symbolic reinforcement of who owned the skyline, and what would happen to the naive who thought they could elevate the people above their station. VitaCorp maintained a trickle of continual construction progress, but it was reduced to the slowest pace that was possible, such that the trace of activity would drive out the vagrants, vandals, and criminal enterprises that might seek to inhabit the ruins. It was arrested development, a fetus forever still in a jar. And for its proximity and lack of non-VitaCorp habitation, it was an ideal choice for a meeting point of a VitaCorp spy. The suits needed only hop a single building adjacent to meet with their insider, and the lack of prying eyes was a locational guarantee. It was there that The Basilisk positioned his drones, and in the shadow of that tower that Hannah Preacher and Sam Pollock prepared for their next skirmish against the forces of the black tower—a skirmish that now rapidly approached.

* * *

Kim Buchanan was a sixty-five-year-old ingest technician with fifteen years of ArtGen loyalty. A firm believer in the essential role played by art for the furthering of human culture, she was honored to have landed her position in tending to the greatest extant artistic mind, a reverence that tore her up inside when she was forced to turn on her employer. VitaCorp's abduction of the woman had been carried out with little pomp and circumstance, and the modifications to her pacemaker took not even an hour under anesthesia. Her shirt now covered the fresh scar on her chest, but she wondered if her face betrayed the emotional scars she now carried. It had surely picked up lines and wrinkles as the stress aged her decades over mere weeks.

When the Halogen operatives had contacted her, her first thought was that it was a trick—a way for her cruel masters to test her loyalty. But then she'd seen the man in the illegal videoclips, the one who'd all-but declared war on VitaCorp itself. Kim knew she could trust that man if nobody else, and she hoped today that her faith would be rewarded. She looked up to the scaffolding and concrete rise of the unfinished Baylor Tower, checking her watch. An hour and a half until her heart stopped. In the fighting to come, she might be gone far sooner than that.

Meanwhile, in a flight-capable van a block and a half away, Pollock wiped down the battery terminal electrodes of an energy rifle with a cleaning abrasive. He wore full tactical gear, as did the five other men in the van with him. They were non-benders except for the one who stood in the van's center, the operation's commander. He was a tall man, thin as a wisp, with a goatee and a mohawk of faded red. His eyes were hard, and his face, oily. His gravely voice dripped like tar, and his name was one befitting the rough impression he gave. "Call me Rusty," he'd said to Pollock. "And if you lightless get into trouble... call me *quickly*."

"All ready?" came Carter Miles's voice through Pollock's earpiece. The Halogen technical expert was stationed in the front passenger seat.

"Ready as I will be," Pollock muttered, still wiping at the electrodes. He watched as the breach bridge was gingerly folded and loaded into the turret mounted in the truck near its door. They'd explained the function, but he would need to see it in action first. And then by Pollock's feet was the item he'd insisted on bringing along, an item he'd had Carter Miles help whip up, though the both had been uneasy doing it. "That's a cruel, wicked thing," Miles had said, admiring his own creation. "But maybe a cruel tool can be put towards some good. I'm no philosopher. Just a programmer with doubts."

Jarring Pollock back to the present was Rusty's louder-than-necessary shout: "ladies and gents, t-minus four minutes to takeoff. When we go up, hold on to your VitaCorp-owned keisters and remember the plan. If you forget the plan, just shoot at the enemy and we'll call it good enough."

On the rooftop of a nearby tower, Hannah watched as a distant blot on the street level below—identified by her AR overlay to be Kim Buchanan—arrived to the tower's base. She ascended in the lift into the belly of the beast. Right on cue, and likely watching Kim as well, four VitaCorp agents dropped off the black tower's roof and began to glide downwards towards the construction site of Baylor Tower. "Four moving in, I repeat, four sighted. Standing by for intervention," she said into her comms.

"Copy that," came Rusty's voice, "heading airborne. Stand by for mark."

The four agents disappeared into the tower, no doubt locating and speaking with Kim. The Basilisk's long-range audio drones formed a wide circle around the tower, and he was likely now triangulating the microphones for proper long-range eavesdropping. They'd have conversation audio in—

"like I said," Kim Buchanan's voice said on left channel. "All in here. Paper records only."

Hannah waited in place as the spy and her handlers had their verbal back-and-forth, waiting for the part where they renewed her heart's clock—but then Hannah's eyes narrowed as something unexpected happened. Towards the top of VitaCorp tower, a black window shattered, and tumbling from that window was a man in a suit with a brilliant light strapped to his head. He spun as he fell, and he would soon meet the pavement below for a quick and messy end. It wasn't her time to move yet, as that was supposed to be after the clock was renewed, and revealing herself too soon could compromise the operation... but there were teammates to mind and secure Kim Buchanan. This falling man was moments from death, which meant there was no time at all to waste with vacillation. *Save the one first, and the rest could be figured out afterwards.*

Hannah launched on reflex alone, propelling herself outwards and away from the tower she'd been perched on. She dove in towards the man, sensing before seeing the blacklight attached to the helmet. She used it to pull him in, grabbing his body securely before throwing her force behind the lights of the cars below... and as she stabilized, she heard the voices from the Basilisk's surveillance drones: "What was that?" "Who was falling?" "It's the girl!" "Call the boss..." and other overlaid shouts all at once. The element of surprise had been blown, and the time to enter the fray was now.

* * *

"Call Braxton Graves," Avery said, listening with great satisfaction to the open air beyond the cracked window. His only regret was that the pavement was too quick an end for the sniveling bureaucrat, but hopefully the pair's employer would now know that Avery was dreadfully serious in his renegotiation in the terms of their deal. If they attacked him with such trifling videos, he would attack back with greater savagery—decisive action as a policy of discouragement. Make punishment come at a great personal cost, and often will the punishing ameliorate.

"Sir?" came the voice of Braxton on Avery's comms unit.

"I need you by my side as quickly as you can arrive... foolish parties have tried to turn the law against me, and I shall need your security. I expect you posthaste."

"On my way," Braxton said, and then the line clicked shut. He sat there, stroking his chin, thinking on how he would be able to out-maneuver a simple video clip... a discrediting campaign was surely the place to start, which could re-earn public trust, but what of the legal vultures? They would—

Suddenly, Avery's emergency comms line beeped its urgent beep, and Avery felt his heart seize. A heart attack? An embolism? A tumor? Anaphylaxis?

"Sir, this is enforcement team 7 at Baylor Tower—the girl, Preacher, is here. She just caught someone falling from an upper VC window."

At war at once were two competing feelings in Avery: rage that the blubbering sycophant had been rescued, but delight that the girl was so close and so exposed... so long had he wanted the chance to meet. He looked to the open window and smiled a wide, barbed smile, and he slid the drawer open by his side, removing the plastic respirator it contained. "Scramble all available assets," he said to his dispatcher. "I'd like the girl *alive*."

* * *

Hannah dropped Spivey onto the nearest floor of the concrete tower framework, noting with unease that his head lulled limply as she set him down. He was unconscious and unresponsive. "Sit tight," she said to the man, "I'll come back for you soon." And then she ran and leapt out the open side of the skyscraper, pushing against light sources below to rapidly gain altitude. She saw on a floor a few dozen above that men were looking over the open ledge and pointing at her, and thus, her target was acquired.

Elsewhere, Pollock clung to the overhead rope grips as the van swung wide, moving with all haste that Sentinel would permit. "Surprise is blown, so expect greater resistance," Rusty said. "Aim well and watch each other's six. Bridge up in eight." Their van couldn't get close enough to Baylor Tower for an unassisted unloading—geofences were impossible to override where Sentinel reigned—but as it swung and spun in mid-air, engine whining high-pitched chords of exertion, the back doors were released and Pollock saw the construction site of the tower whip into view. Their wide turn became a backwards race towards the structure as the van spun under the pilot's expert control, and when the geofence finally kicked in, holding the vehicle about ten feet away from the building's edge, the team released their grips and prepared. "Firing breach bridge," one yelled.

"Aim for floor on my laser mark," said Rusty. He shined a red dot towards a floor two below their current position, and the man at the turret squeezed the trigger grips. What Pollock could only describe as two massive harpoons fired from the twin barrels of the turret, each flying three feet apart towards the concrete floor below and trailing a thick steel cable behind. The harpoon spears embedded themselves in the concrete at the edge of the targeted floor, and the carbonfiber weave was magnetically accelerated along the cables towards the spear at the far end. As the weave slid into place, the end result was a semi-flexible bridge about three-feet wide that connected tower to vehicle... ingress and egress for those without flight.

The men began to charge down the ramp almost immediately as one fired off a smokescreen at the ramp's base. As Pollock joined the charge, he heard the distant report of energy weapon fire and saw the wisps of smoke trailing up into the air... he heard the shouting of men—was his voice among those calls?—and knew that some of those voices would never again shout after the dust settled today. Despite running from the life of a soldier, somehow, after his strange and meandering path, had he become one again all the same? Here he was, battling enemies more domestic than foreign, but enemies of society all the same. Here he was, brandishing an energy weapon and charging towards a violent fight on ideological lines. Here he was, hearing his heart thunder in his chest, and as his feet leapt from the wobbling bridge and contacted the hard concrete, he watched as a neon-blue energy pulse ricocheted through the smoke and crackled its way through the air mere inches from his neck. Pollock acutely felt the heat of it as it passed. He was a soldier, somehow he'd again become a soldier, maybe he would die a soldier, and strapped to his side was the evil that drove him away from the vocation in the first place. It was a weapon that felt it could only be used by the evil, but there was nothing inherently gentle about an energy weapon, or about vaporizing human beings with jolts of electricity from a lightbender's hand... here, on his side, was a needed equalization now that their surprise had been blown. He and the rest of the men switched on their thermals as they took position in the smoke, and Pollock removed the item on his side, staring at it with grim fascination. Could he become the monster he'd feared for so long?

Rusty, sensing Pollock's hesitation, took the item from his hand and threw it forwards, gripping Pollock on the arm. "We need that, and my conscience is rotted enough... you keep this one off yours."

Time then lurched back into its speedy and chaotic motion as the thrown drone's spring-loaded arms unfolded in mid-air. The small autonomous unit immediately took flight, its cameras activating. It was inspired by something Pollock had seen in Zack Milleau's little shop of horrors... and as it took flight, he remembered the terror of fighting against combat drones, the playgrounds of imagination for the technically-masterful-yet-cruel. He remembered *her,* and imagined the judgment when she learned Pollock himself had turned to such wickedness. But the dead couldn't judge, and the present demanded advantage. *Please, let their terror not be for nothing.*

When the small drone's camera detected a face that was not in its pre-battle registry, the laser at its base was switched on and the servos pointed the green laser to the eyes of the unwitting target. Permanent blindness arrived in an average of 0.3 seconds.

One by one, screams began to issue from the men ahead, and they aimed their weapons towards the drone instead of the smoke screen. Each who tried to aim down sights at the device quickly found the green flare to be the last thing they saw, as they dropped in sudden screams and clawed at their faces. "Close your eyes!" one shouted, but the damage by then was largely done. When the thermal cameras showed only one standing form, the men and women in the smoke cloud surged forwards to secure Kim Buchanan. Rusty moved in close and asked Kim to point to the agent with the RFID code. She only stared in slack-jawed fear at the flying bringer of dark, not responding until Rusty physically shook her.

"That one there," Kim said, gesturing at a man on the floor blinking unseeing eyes. Rusty moved to pick him up while three lightless in tactical gear escorted Kim back to the bridge. Pollock stayed forwards, as his assigned focus was Rusty himself.

"They're aware of the blinding drone," said the Basilisk's voice over comms. "Next batch will be wearing eyeguards."

As though simply to make good on the Basilisk's promise, three new lightbenders landed on the building's edge with their back protectively turned towards Pollock and the drone. He fired towards them, but at this range, his pulses were easily deflected by the benders. After landing, they began to pull out lens guards from their vest pockets and slipped them over their headsets. They were likely reflex glass, a clear overlay that would darken when contacting laser light. So long as they wore them, they would be protected from the dazzler. *Where was Hannah?* Pollock thought, stomach dropping as the three lightbenders advanced. *How do we win a one-against-three?*

Hannah landed on the van's roof, watching as the bridge connecting van to Baylor Tower swung uneasily. Three men stood on the base of that ramp holding fast to Kim Buchanan, but none of them moved forwards. The reason was obvious enough: an enemy lightbender had landed on the bridge, and he held his right arm out to draw his lightblade. A quick cut, and their escape would be sealed for good. Hannah jumped forwards and pushed off the rear brake lights of the van, propelling herself into the lightbender as she drew her energy weapon from her side holster. When she contacted his back, she fired twice, making sure to aim outwards towards her right so that no penetrating plasma could pose a threat to the four fighters below. The VitaCorp lightbender, now sporting two massive holes in his back, toppled over the bridge with his right arm still extended. She watched his glassy eyes continue to glow as he fell. "Over the bridge, let's move," Hannah commanded, gesturing the men forwards as she stepped over the side and 'caught' herself against lightsources below. She watched, hovering, as Kim Buchanan reached the van and her accompanying agents filed in behind her. Nearby, three drones buzzed past with bright white lights and a hungry lens. Across the city, millions of livestreamers might already be watching. The van awaited the final team members' return—the agent with the RFID most essentially—and Hannah could see now that they were in trouble. Pollock and Rusty were doing their best to hold off three advancing lightbenders, but it was a hold they were clearly losing.

It was still late afternoon, meaning the half-constructed tower's lights were still off, so actual sources within the concrete overhang were scarce. All competent benders would be wearing battery packs with private sources to draw from, but the dearth of lights meant mobility was limited—nothing to push off of, and nothing to pull from. That's why Hannah reached for her side holster and removed the experimental piece of equipment that Halogen's engineers had been proud to bestow: she called it the *rivet gun,* a name with a little more elegance than their original title of *light spike movement system.* It was made of custom-printed mechanical parts that fit together in a tight, chaotic clockwork of metal and plastic powered by black-market kinetics cartridges. She pointed the device at the ground behind her and fired.

With a painfully loud crack, the first metal rivet was launched from the weapon and embedded three inches into the concrete. A chemical reaction in the rivet's protruding end caused it to begin glowing about a second after firing, emitting a steady green light. Pushing off it now would send her only upwards, so Hannah dropped to the floor in a near push-up pose with only her prosthetic hand along the ground, and then she pushed off the green spike behind her to begin accelerating—sliding—towards the fight beyond. After twenty or so feet, she fired her rivet gun at a vertical concrete support column, embedding another spike that began to glow. She pushed off of that spike as she passed it, redirecting her advance as she tucked and repositioned her feet. She was sliding feet-first now, her jacket protesting as it ground against the harsh concrete, but with a final forceful shove she tackled into one of the VitaCorp lightbenders and set him flipping. The man contacted the solid floor in a harsh front flip, and Hannah fired a rivet through the man's leg, pinning him to the ground. The other agents turned towards Hannah, but she was already throwing all of her force against the glowing rivet in the man's leg, launching her right arm upwards for an empowered uppercut. Heavy composite materials of the prosthetic hand met the closer agent's face, connecting with a brittle crunching sound. The momentum of her punch launched her up into the air, and as she glided, she saw imminent danger. The next agent raised his arm, perhaps preparing to blast an arc shot of electricity towards Hannah—a fatal attack—but a flurry of energy weapon rounds from Pollock and Rusty sent him stumbling backwards as he deflected them with all of his force. The fired rounds spattered and sprayed to the floor, their forms disrupted by the lightbender's defensive shoves, but Hannah threw her force into shoving at the loose puddles of plasma and they surged forwards. Small droplets contacted the man's legs, sending him screaming and twisting in pain. Hannah released the catch in her prosthetic and launched the light puck from her open hand to the wailing VitaCorp lightbender, contacting his open mouth and sending teeth flying. He teetered over and fell face-first into a glowing plasma puddle, face smoking as he lie in stillness.

Hannah heard a yell and furious footsteps, whirling to see a VitaCorp lightbender with a glowsword materializing in his hand, preparing to swing and cut her down, but his swing met and was deflected by a white blade thrust over Hannah's shoulder. Rusty stepped into view. "Use that weapon of yours to get this guy over to the evac van—he's the one with the RFID. I'll hold their fighter off," he said, stepping forwards and spinning his weapon with a practiced flourish. "Go now!" Rusty charged the agent and their crackling white swords met in blinding sparks. It was a dance between two very practiced partners, each showing a mastery of not only refined sword-fighting techniques, but even a mastery of the light itself. The agent parried Rusty's swing and prepared for a savage overhead chop of a riposte—one that would have cut the Halogen lightbender cleanly in two—but Rusty shoved against the green spike still in the downed agent's knee and jolted sideways in time to dodge the blow… at the cost of his footing. Rusty spilled over onto the concrete and the VitaCorp bender pressed the attack, advancing to deny Rusty the means to stand up safely—and keeping his blade lowered to bat aside any attempts to thrust forwards.

Hannah turned from the dueling men. She had to move, and fast, as the van was likely in danger. She drove a new rivet into the ground and grabbed to the prone man on the floor, using him as a sled towards the van's bridge at the far end of the concrete floor. She was closing in—100 feet, 80 feet, 60 feet, 40—but then dropped in a single form from above, and this one wore a different outfit than the rest. He donned a full-body leather suit not unlike a riding jacket, with one of those plastic face coverings she'd seen the assassin Braxton Crane wearing. But this man was *not* Braxton Crane. He was too thin, too tall. His face behind the mask was too *old*... Avery. It had to be. And his eyes were glowing a brilliant white of a lightbender just on the cusp of a halo.

Avery looked towards Hannah with unworried posture as he pointed one of his hands to the van behind him. She cocked her head, curious, for surely her enemy wasn't so stupid. He could push against the van, sure, as its tail lights were active—as were no doubt countless sources within the vehicle—but every force carried an equal and opposite force. To push against the car would launch Avery forwards and downwards at equal force, and with the vehicle's impulse brakes he would move *only* himself. No matter how strong a man was, his push-up would never bend the world down—he could move only himself up, for he was the lighter of the two. Avery couldn't actually shove the car without an anchor of some kind, a forwards light source to push *against* for stability, and the empty concrete floor of the tower-in-construction offered no such anchors.

But then Hannah heard a strange and ominous moaning in the distance... her stomach twisted and dread settled in her gut at the sound, though she was not yet sure why. She turned to look across the open flat expanse of Baylor Tower to the next structure adjacent, and Hannah felt her skin break out in goosebumps. The entire structure there trembled and shifted, its metal framework groaning in deep, echoing notes. She watched in horror as thousands of light sources in that tower—ceiling lights, desk lamps, computer devices, television screens—slid to the far sides of their rooms and gripped against the walls of the structure. *That shouldn't be possible,* Hannah thought with rising worry. *Nobody can reach that far—nobody.*

"Black out all lights, *black out all lights!*" Hannah shouted in a panic to her comms unit, but Avery merely flicked his hand behind his back. The van's bridge snapped instantaneously, ripping the entire turret from the back as the vehicle launched outwards and away from the tower at cannon-like speed. Men and women spilled out the open rear door and shouted as they rained to the pavement below. The vehicle itself slammed into a nearby tower and exploded in a ball of fire and smoke and broken glass. And around that rubble, the Halogen videodrones flew, and ten million viewers on the internet dropped their jaws in shock and clapped their hands in the delight of the spectacle. And in the Halogen broadcast room, a bunker deep, deep underground where even the rumble of the trains couldn't reach, the Basilisk turned away from the monitors and sat down in his chair, drawing his knees up to his chest and his arms about his legs.

The destruction of that van was more to him than merely the loss of their ground agents and the spy they'd tried to turn…

Carter Miles had been in the front passenger seat.

* * *

The VitaCorp lightbender slashed viciously towards Rusty's legs. With a shove against the light puck that came from Hannah's hand, Rusty managed to fling himself upwards to dodge the blow, but the uneven angle of lift sent the puck skidding away elsewhere on the concrete floor. Rusty caught himself from his leap gracefully enough, watching as his opponent stepped in to fill the space between them. He raised his blade parallel to the ground to block an overhand swing, his blade flickering as the two met. It was growing weaker with each strike, and it might give way any minute. Then the exhaustion would hit, and without a miracle, his death would follow shortly after.

The VitaCorp lightbender roared in frustration as another small stone struck his cheek, drawing blood. Off to the side, Pollock used his combat gloves to squeeze loose concrete chunks into small pieces, which he repeatedly hurled at the man's head. The angered VitaCorp lightbender turned towards Pollock, blade forwards, and advanced, but Rusty sent a wide swing that quickly had the corporate agent back on the defensive. Pollock's ranged harassment continued.

The VitaCorp lightbender drank in more light from the pack on his belt, and Rusty watched as the light began to fill and stitch the gash on his cheek. "We're almost out of time here, and those stones aren't doing enough," he said, narrowly dodging a forward thrust with a quick slap from his blade. "Got anything beyond small rocks?"

But then Pollock released the next stone from his hand, and something felt positively *right* the moment it left the black rubber composite… he watched it sail through the air in a gentle arc, as though guided forwards by homing thrusters. It connected squarely into the side of the lightbender's headset, shattering a lens and spinning it an eighth of a turn around the man's head. The VitaCorp agent turned towards Pollock, furious, and Pollock could see the glow and fury both burning hot in his eyes…but they then filled with a bright, flickering green as the laser drone did its work, and the man dropped blind to the floor clawing at his face. Rusty's sword severed that face—and the head it attached to—in one downward sweep, leaving the body holding its own head in a spreading pool of blood.

Then came the sound of a great explosion, and both men turned in time to see a rising ball of fire beyond the broken bridge where the van had once waited. Pollock and Rusty stared, perplexed, before noting the strange figure in front of Hannah, and then charged in two more VitaCorp lightbenders, bringing the closer battle back to immediate priority. "Don't your gloves have electromagnets on them? For pulling off their headsets?" Rusty said softly as the two advanced.

"Not at that kind of range. I'd have to be close. Real close."

Rusty shrugged his shoulders. "Better get comfy with the suits, then. We don't win this otherwise."

The fastest runner then arrived, drawing his lightblade and holding it in a balanced guard position while his friend caught up. The later man drew his lightblade as well, and the two began to creep in slow circles in opposite directions, trying to encircle the pair. Rusty and Pollock in response began to back away, but the concrete floor would run out eventually—and Pollock was the only among the four men who could not fly.

"Ignore the lightless," the leading agent said. "We take down the bender and it's as good as won."

All four continued their uneven creep backwards. The VitaCorp agent nearest to Rusty made a test charge and swing, which Rusty deflected with ease, but everyone present could see the way his blade shimmered after the strike—and their eyes lit up with glee. They stopped walking.

"Looks like someone's almost out," one said. "Probably not even a minute left. It's okay; we're patient." The speaking one then turned towards Pollock.

"New idea: you guard the dwindling lightbender, and I'll go remove the CSP." Both men nodded, and the one closest to Pollock began his advance.

"No light, no chance," the advancing agent cooed. "Just drop to your knees and we can have it over quickly."

Pollock backed up as the agent stepped forwards, feeling the distance between him and Rusty grow wider and wider. Rusty moved to try and follow, but the other VitaCorp lightbender stepped between them, blocking him off. "Uh-uh," he said, "let them have their one-on-one. There's no honor in a spoiled duel." Rusty swung at the blocking agent, but his muscles were sluggish now, and the blade's constant glow was reducing to a rapid flicker. He looked at Pollock with sorrowful eyes and shook his head.

I'm on my own, Pollock thought. Step. Step. The VitaCorp agent advanced, the smile on his face reminding Pollock of a predator with its prey backed into a corner. And suddenly, indeed that corner was against his back. Pollock heard the empty ring of the city behind him, knowing he finally approached the edge of the concrete floor. Step. Step. He backed until he could take not another step in reverse… the open air was behind him, and the cruel, harsh concrete now beneath him. He felt a gentle breeze for a moment before the air returned to a hazy stillness. He looked down and to the side, seeing the thousands of feet of bare concrete floors spanning downwards to the roadways below with crosshatches of steel support beams and the occasional crane. One leap, and a few seconds of falling, and it would all be over…

"You're thinking of it, aren't you? A jump? Denying me the chance to get you?" The agent shrugged. "I won't stop you." He twirled the sword in his hand. "So what will it be… a drop or a slice? My terms, or yours?"

Pollock swallowed, squinted his eyes shut, felt the stirring of the wind... and he stepped off the ledge.

The agent smirked as the CSP tumbled over the side, nodding in respect at the commitment and spirit of self-determination in the gesture... but then he heard a strange grinding and grating sound from just beyond the ledge, accompanied by a heavy clang. *Had the CSP clipped against something on his way down?* The curious lightbender walked towards the ledge and peered over, expecting to see a black and red splat on the distant concrete below. Instead, and much to his immediate surprise, he saw the CSP somehow *hanging off the structure* where there wasn't even a handhold.

Pollock felt his hands begin to sweat inside his combat gloves, but still they held fast as he hung there, dangling by the arms. The gloves' electromagnet, fortunately, had been quick to switch on, and the tower's steel beams offered plenty of metal to cling to during his brief fall of only a single story. Now he remained attached to the outside of the steel beam like a beetle on a brothel wall—although this beetle only had two arms to crawl with, and those arms currently screamed in pain at the brief deceleration after the magnet had caught. Above, Pollock could see the peering confused form of the VitaCorp lightbender, but immediately that man set to work on reaching Pollock: with no lights on the tower, it would be hard to glide down only a single floor, but the man could at least climb down to Pollock without fear of falling. Any slip could be corrected with the lightpack he had in his vest pocket.

And so the agent dismissed his blade, reeling from a wave of exhaustion. He injected himself in the neck with a stimpack, his eyes never leaving Pollock, and then he gripped to the steel beam, beginning to climb his way downwards along the tower's outside edge. "Now, now," he said, beginning to chide Pollock for his ruse, but the man's voice cut with a lurch as sparks shot from his hands and feet along the tower. He tumbled down and away, striking Pollock with an outstretched leg as he fell—a collision that sent the man flipping until his head contacted the ledge of a concrete floor thirty feet under—and down he rained until he vanished with the multicolored blur of the street far below. Pollock switched off the stun feature of his combat gloves, and the powerful taser voltage ceased coursing through the steel beam he was hanging from. Then, toggling the electromagnet one hand at a time, Pollock managed to shimmy his way sideways to land on the floor below the fighting. Was it worth climbing back up to help Rusty somehow? *Would he even reach him in time?* Pollock looked up, and, as though to answer his question, he saw a beam of white plasma score through the concrete ceiling and trace a straight line as it melted its way in a completed swing. Red, molten concrete dripped and dribbled down from the gash, and Pollock saw through it a flurry of motion. Another lightblade pushed through the nearby ceiling, and Pollock stumbled backwards to avoid the rain of molten rock. The concrete screeched and hissed as it was flash-melted. Against such power, what truly could Pollock hope to accomplish?

* * *

Avery thrust forwards again, and Hannah discharged another rivet into the ground for an anchor. She pushed off of it, keeping a distance from Avery as he moved towards her, a bright halo burning around him. He raised his left arm and released an arc shot of electricity, but at that range it never really had a good shot at contact. Instead it sent sparks skittering down from the piping overhead and its shockwave rattled the tower. The flash left Hannah seeing faded afterimages that drifted as she flew. Through that blur of color, Hannah saw as the man called Rusty battled against the VitaCorp agent—both were experts, but Rusty was tired. His swings lagged, and his blade flickered pathetically. His attacks were batted down into the ground, tracing wide cuts of red-hot concrete into the floor as the agent circled. He needed help, and fast. Hannah saw that Avery closed in, and she waited for him to draw nearer—ten steps, five now—before unloading four rounds from her energy weapon straight towards him. At that close range, an ordinary bender would likely be killed, but Avery was no ordinary bender: the plasma rounds burst apart in front of him, and their droplets seemed to wrap around behind him as though diffracted by his presence. Still, force impelled force, and Avery was held in place for long enough for Hannah to raise her rivet gun and fire. The plasma splatter blinded Avery to the shot, and the rivet—which didn't glow until a second *after* firing—was impossible for Avery to push against. It embedded itself in his gut as he released a shocked moan, keeling over forwards and grasping at his stomach.

Hannah left the old man behind as she raced over to assist Rusty. With a few well-timed pushes against the rivets already in the ground, Hannah was airborne, and as she whipped sideways through the tower, she slashed outwards with her weapon and severed the man's leg. As he toppled over, Rusty delivered the coup de grace, and then he left his own blade impaled in the man's head as it flickered away to nothingness. Exhaustion hit him, and he fell to a knee to recuperate. Hannah smiled towards him as she slid to a stop, but then her smile wiped to anguish as she saw the form racing towards him with blade thrust forwards, flying just as she had through the air. She called out to Rusty, but Avery's rapier of light was stabbed through the man's side before the sound left her lips. Avery crashed into Rusty and both spilled over, but Avery was quickly back up on his feet, while Rusty lay on the floor barely moving. He reached with a weak arm to one of Hannah's rivets and began to draw the light from it… a small tendril of green began to snake its way towards Rusty—a source of pure and healing light, a pristine font from which parched lips might drink. Avery stood over it, waiting with a patient cruelty... and when the man's light connected to the source, he swung down with his rapier and pierced the vine of light. Where lightsword contacted green ribbon, a change immediately took place: the ribbon of green suddenly glowed white hot, and that white-hot light surged outwards in both directions. When it reached the rivet driven into the ground, the white-hot plasma instantly flash-melted it into a puddle of orange metal... and when it reached Rusty, it poured into him, subsumed him. There was a sound not unlike dropping a breast of chicken onto a hot pan... there was a burst of steam, and a single, pained syllable that sounded out across the tower's floor... and then Rusty moved no longer.

Hannah yelled as she charged back at Avery, but the man only reached to his stomach and pulled out the bolt of metal. He flicked it towards her and shoved against its glowing tip with considerable force. Hannah, in turn, met that force with a shove of her own, and the rivet momentarily froze in the air. She felt him ratchet up his power, and she did the same, but now the pair themselves began to stumble backwards—for each shove came with its opposite force. Avery reached out behind his arched back and caught himself with pushes to all of the light sources in the tower behind him, and again Hannah could hear the entire structure groan as his push solidified... she knew she had no such reach, and she knew that with an anchor that strong, he would be able to achieve a far greater force than she could. She dropped over onto her back as the bolt accelerated at impossible speed, sounding almost a gunshot as it cracked through the air. From her back, she pushed at one of the rivets to her right and began a rolling slide towards the ledge, but as she rolled, she felt her own reserves of glow begin to grow faint. And worse still, the battery pack she wore was either empty or shattered—she would be lightless within the minute. And to draw power near a bender as competent as Avery was no small risk... the brutal and swift end of Rusty was still replaying in her mind. She needed to flee, and quickly. The ledge drew nearer and nearer, and with its fall, she would have the freedom to drink in light from lower floors of adjacent towers and turn their battle into a race of swiftness—a race she was hopeful she might win—but before she reached the edge of the tower, a pulse of bright white and a deep bass-y *thud* sounded and shook the tower violently. Avery had detonated his halo, blacking out lights in a radius unimaginably large.

Hannah stuck her prosthetic hand down and scraped at the concrete to stop her advance. Without light sources below, the fall would be fatal, so she screamed as she poured all of her effort into braking her chaotic slide. Her prosthetic hand shot sparks of protest as she ground to an uneasy stop mere feet from the ledge, but Avery wasted no time and pressed his opponent's perilous placement. She rose in time to deflect his first thrust and stepped backwards as she sent a second aside, but the ledge was near, and the city below was still perilously silent in blackout. Hannah's blade now was in her right hand, and her rivet gun in her left, and as Avery stepped in and swung, she met blade against blade and both locked into a struggle to press the other into submission. Their free hands grappled at each other, Hannah trying to find an angle to fire another rivet into Avery while his hand wrestled to keep the weapon pointed outwards. *"You must learn your station."* Avery seethed, *"You hold that which does not belong to you."*

"Doesn't belong to you either," Hannah said, managing to twist the rivet gun to point at the ground. She fired, and then she began to push off the rivet embedded in the concrete. Avery did the same, and for a single moment, the both felt nearly weightless as the force of their collective push overpowered gravity... then there was an inversion, and within seconds they stood instead upside-down on the roof of the bare concrete expanse.

There they struggled, each one pressing against the blade of the other, trying to advance the glowing white heat until it consumed the other party, but they seemed locked in a stalemate. Hannah fired her rivet gun again towards a pipe by Avery's feet—which, technically, were still on the ceiling—in hopes that the water or steam it released might buy her an edge. However, the weapon only clicked ineffectually, firing no rivet. She was out.

Releasing the weapon, both she and Avery stopped their push against the rivet above—which was really on the ground—and both dropped back towards the floor upside-down. The pair twisted in the air like cats to land on their feet, and they both landed with a jolt, their blades still locked in a desperate struggle. The city whirred back to life around and beneath them, but she knew to break from the hold would give Avery a chance to cut her down... she was locked. "The light in your eyes dwindles," Avery said through gritted teeth. "I see it... you haven't long now."

And Hannah knew he was right. She reached out in her mind for some nearby source, a desperate *hail Mary*... and then her awareness settled on her final option.

She rotated as she resisted Avery's blade, re-orienting the pair to face a new direction. Then, with a final surge of effort, she *pulled* with all of her available strength. The lightpuck on the ground fifty feet behind Avery's back lurched towards Hannah, homing in by the blacklight on its small assembly. It flew with a speed that reminded Hannah of the baseball pitches she'd sometimes watch in the inner-city ball parks when her family could afford them... and when it struck Avery's spine through the jacket he wore, the sound wasn't all that unlike the noise of a leather mitt stopping a ball thrown at nearly 120 miles per hour. She didn't know whether it had crushed vertebra, severed nerves, or even broken anything at all... but the sudden and complete shock it sent through Avery's system was enough for Hannah to capitalize on.

She batted his sword outwards and away with her own blade and then delivered a full-powered headbutt into Avery's plastic mask. The flexible plastic caved inwards to her forehead and there her head struck the cartilage of Avery's nose, which cracked and bent inwards as he fell backwards. Blood sprayed within his mask, but Avery reflexively shoved against rivets on the ground to buy distance between himself and her while he recovered from the momentary stun. She heard him roar in rage as he stood back up, wiping ineffectually at the outside of a visor spattered with blood on its inside. *"You bitch,"* he yelled, still blinded, grabbing the blood-spattered cover to take it off, *"you've broken my nose."* But no sooner had the words left his lips than a bright blue bolt of plasma met the mask and splashed over Clive Avery's face.

Hannah lowered the plasma pistol back to her belt and began to step towards the distant man writhing on the floor—still alive, but in considerable agony. His face was a ruin beneath the melted plastic cover that clung to his flesh like a wet bandage, and Hannah would now do him a courtesy to put him out of his misery—a lightblade through the heart. But as she advanced towards him, she suddenly saw *another* appear by the ledge... and with the hooded leather jacket he wore, and the prosthetic arm on his right, she had no doubt who had arrived. The face was different, which seemed only logical after their Panopticon identification, but his expression was the same.

"You will stay back," Hannah commanded, "and let me finish this."

"You will do no such thing," Braxton declared, advancing. "His life is not yours to take."

Hannah's own blade flickered once, a sign of the rapidly depleting power she carried. A fight against the man in the hooded jacket would not go in her favor.

And so, Hannah pleaded. "He is a cruel, wicked man. You don't have to be that way."

"I am the same that I have always been," Braxton said, feeling the power—the liberty—that the words brought him. Gone were the challenging moral questions of alignment when one surrendered to status quo and old habits... gone was the chance of denouncing the self, when the self was accepted as the only moral absolute and eternally constant. "My future is as certain as my past. People *do not change.*"

He stepped in closer, mere feet away from the now-unconscious form of Avery. "He does not have long, so I will not kill you today. You keep your life, an exchange for his."

"You're wrong, you know... people can and do change."

Braxton shook his head, but Hannah continued on.

"You don't even wear the same face anymore, and you want to pretend people are these unchangeable statues?"

"What's outside might change—meat can be cut—but the immortal soul never changes. People *are* who they *are*—and always will be."

"How many uncountable innocents have you killed for this monster? Do you even know?"

"I know *precisely how many,*" Braxton intoned, "for it is not a work I do lightly... but to change alignment now would mean those four score murders were all for nothing—worse, that they were *wrong.* That is a belief I cannot abide. That is the self-preservation mechanism of the ego—and I'm afraid it has both you and I and everyone else in its vice grip. I used to be like you, you know. I once hoped someone could be different, someone could affect change in their nature. That someone could see the error in their ways, denounce those errors, and *correct* them. Time and time again, I was disappointed."

Hannah, who had read Braxton's entire Panopticon report, began to connect the dots. And while her eyes flicked back and forth, slotting the details into place, Braxton bent down and hoisted Avery over his shoulder, keeping a cautious eye on her all the while.

"You watch her from afar," Hannah finally said, "but never up close. Of course you'd have never even seen it."

Braxton furrowed his brow. "Who?"

Hannah stepped to the edge of the tower as she dismissed her lightblade.

"You know precisely who," Hannah said. "I saw it when we spoke. Go look for yourself." And then she tucked in her arms and fell backwards off the ledge, disappearing down and away as the sirens below wailed and the camera drones spun in a maelstrom of lenses. The wind was rising, and the clouds in the sky gathered dark… and Braxton dutifully carried his employer as he bounded up off the lights to the roof of VitaCorp tower, where he would *not* go seek out the best and brightest surgeons in the whole of the world that resided within that jet-black tower. The Throne of Olympus, and its array of lights, would perhaps prove all Avery would need.

Chapter 57

Maddox24 (5:41 p.m.): the world my grandparents fought for

Maddox24 (5:41 p.m.): and died for

Maddox24 (5:42 p.m.): doesn't seem the same world we live in now.

Maddox24 (5:42 p.m.): shit's... soured somehow

Maddox24 (5:42 p.m.): I don't think what I've said is crazy...

Maddox24 (5:42 p.m.): feel like being ok with everything is the crazy side right now

* * *

The sky above felt pregnant... as though a great and terrible release was soon overdue. Staff Sergeant Pete Miller walked at the front of the V formation of officers of the law, with twelve flanking to either side of him. Sirens wailed in the distance, tending to the corpses that littered the ground near Baylor Tower on the block adjacent... drones shuffled to and from in the sky, filming for uncountable entities. Rescue drones tended to the burning wreckage where an entire floor of a nearby tower had caved in from a van hurled straight through. The dead were only still being counted. And behind the drones and the air traffic and the floating advertisement panels was the true thing that made Sergeant Miller feel deeply uneasy... they passed in brief transits, so quick that a blink might have missed them. Some had lines of bright light stretching from their bodies to nearby towers, while others darted across with no trace save for their own silhouette against the glowing gray overcast sky… it was lightbender after lightbender closing in on that black tower like so many bees to a hive. With each one he saw, his dread knotted tighter. *Just how many did they command?*

Ahead of Sergeant Miller and his men was a churning crowd of protestors with signs lofted high, signs that decried VitaCorp for its myriad sins. ANSWER FOR BLYTHE, commanded one. FREE THE DEAD, declared another. LET ME BURY MY CHILD. THE LIGHT IS NOT YOURS. WHO ELSE BEFORE LEVIN? There must have been 200 people there at the least, and Miller could see as more trickled in from the streets and alleyways nearby. They chanted and yelled dozens of overlapping slogans and phrases, but Miller could *feel* a solidifying cohesion to the mob. And ahead of that mob, forming a passive, yet sternly unmoving line, stood fifteen men of VitaCorp employ, blocking the tower's entrance.

The crowd split into halves to allow the transit of the police line, and Miller walked his men through its uneasy invitation. While they moved, they kept their hands on their holstered weapons, ready to draw on a moment's notice. The protesters' rage was palpable, and their distrust of authority justifiable when VitaCorp had purchased so many city institutions and CSP departments. He watched as one protestor tucked away a bottle of liquor with a cloth protruding from the top, trying to keep it from police eyes. Another spat towards Miller's feet, saying "you're all complicit in this." A nearby woman screaming in the crowd with sign raised high in the air caught Miller's eye—she was a short and squat woman with frazzled, blonde hair. *Yes, he knew her, as she had been a former colleague of Miller's from an inner city CSP. What had her name been? Carol something… Mann? Moss?*

Carol Whateverhernamewas met Miller's eyes and nodded towards the tower, an invitation—or a challenge—to faithfully execute the business that had brought him here. Miller nodded back and looked to his men, seeing the unease in their eyes. He did his best to offer them a reassuring smile, a gesture of hollow, feigned confidence that he hoped didn't appear as insincere as it felt. Finally their advancing V arrived to the line of VitaCorp men, and Staff Sergeant Miller produced a digisheet from his vest pocket. "This here is a signed warrant for the arrest of Clive Avery, lawfully executed by the honorable Judge Whitmer and notarized by Palmer Court TruthSpace Verification."

The VitaCorp agents continued to eye the crowd, none even acknowledging the city police. Sergeant Miller felt the heat rising in his face. "I repeat, we have lawful authorization to arrest VitaCorp COO Clive Avery. You will let my agents pass or you will be arrested for obstruction of justice."

Now, at last, the VitaCorp agent closest to Miller looked away from the crowd and met his gaze. "I do not have authorization to allow anyone to enter the tower due to elevated security concerns."

"We are not *anyone*," Miller said, "we are *police*."

"Non-VitaCorp personnel are to be denied entrance due to elevated security," the agent said. He then returned to watching the crowd.

Miller shook his head and turned back to his police, who were all looking to him for encouragement. They outnumbered the VitaCorp agents—and Miller knew that they had at least two secret lightbenders present in their twenty-five—but if VitaCorp's were more skilled, or greater in number, it would still be a blood bath.

"This is your last warning. Step aside or we will have no choice but to arrest any obstructing agents," Miller said.

"Non-VitaCorp personnel are not to enter VitaCorp tower due to elevated security," the agent repeated.

"Then I hereby place you under arrest," Miller said, stepping forwards and removing the handcuffs from his side belt. As though on cue, tendrils of light reached from the floodlights at the tower's base, from the lights of signs and windows overhead, from the headlights of lower car traffic—and it all began to flow into *each* of the fifteen VitaCorp men. *By the sickness, they were* all *lightbenders.*

The agent who had spoken before looked again to Miller, and this time, Miller could see the embers of light begin to stoke deep within his pupils. "Are you sure you want to do this?" he asked, and Miller felt the dread build to fatal climax.

"I—" he said, still vacillating, when the first molotov cocktail struck VitaCorp's line… and then all hell broke loose.

* * *

ClipMe—the hottest clips on the web. New and trending:

"The Battle of Baylor Tower — Original Upload." Posted 3 hours ago, 381 million views.

"Actress Kelsey Levin speaks out on Avery allegations." Posted 3 hours ago, 89 million views.

"Halogen takes on VC agents in all-out braw—multiple angles!" Posted 2 hours ago, 411 million views.

"Angel of the Outer Rings Fights Off, Kills Multiple Benders At Once." Posted 2 hours ago, 515 million views.

"Halogen absolutely shitting on VitaCorp—compilation." Posted 2 hours ago, 390 million views.

"Sexual assault, rape charges filed against VitaCorp COO Clive Avery." Posted 2 hours ago, 103 million views.

"Van thrown into residential tower near Baylor... footage from inside apartment." Posted 2 hours ago, 125 million views.

"Arrest warrant signed for Clive Avery in light of verified assault video." Posted 2 hours ago, 88 million views.

"Did this drone camera capture Clive Avery's death on Baylor Tower?" Posted 1 hour ago, 196 million views.

"City police meet wall of VitaCorp enforcers at base of tower." Posted 1 hour ago, 211 million views.

"The time has come to end VitaCorp's extralegal authority." Posted 1 hour ago, 167 million views.

"Tech used in the 'Battle of Baylor' shows Halogen has military contacts." Posted 1 hour ago, 142 million views.

"VitaCorp assassin admits to 'four score' killings on exclusive drone video." Posted 1 hour ago, 115 million views.

"This laser drone took out six lightbenders on Baylor Tower." Posted 53 minutes ago, 34 million views.

"How lightbending works REVEALED." Posted 45 minutes ago, 84 million views.

"Six city police, more than twenty civilians killed in struggle with VitaCorp security forces serving arrest warrant." Posted 41 minutes ago, 193 million views.

"Clive Avery suspected dead in Baylor Tower skirmish." Posted 36 minutes ago, 115 million views.

"VitaCorp protests turn deadly—first-person videocap." Posted 35 minutes ago, 124 million views.

"H.a.l.o.g.e.n. recruitment reupload." Posted 12 minutes ago, 49 million views.

"Ha-log-en rec-ruit-ment re-up-load 4.16.2153." Posted 4 minutes ago, 11 million views.

"H-gen signup vid." Posted 3 minutes ago, 9 million views.

Chapter 58

"What was once rumor is now manifested as truth. It has now become entirely undeniable that VitaCorp possesses agents with superhuman abilities. It is furthermore undeniable that they use those agents to further their extragovernmental aims—to suppress, to control, to dominate. I ask this committee the following question: what even is the purpose of our oversight if we don't find this actionable? I can feel a collective sense of powerlessness, but us being silent in that powerlessness makes us all complicit. That, I cannot abide. Action is not only necessary: it's overdue."

-Address given by City Councilman John Banner to the Corporate Watchdog Legislative Committee

* * *

Braxton placed his hands on the sink and hung his head low between aching shoulders. The basin before him was red with blood—Avery's, and the blood of so many others downstairs. He lowered a shaking hand into the stream of cool water, watching as it carried away the red—the way the blood swirled about the drain and then vanished was nearly hypnotic. His casino work had been challenging, but it never shook him as thoroughly as today's work seemed to. Everything he did, he did ostensibly for the promotion of society's order. The police sought that same goal… could attacking them—killing a few—really be justifiable in pursuit of a greater good?

It must be, he decided, for he'd already done it… and Braxton could not bear to entertain the possibility the killings were anything but justified. *The soul cannot indict itself,* he acknowledged, and yet even that acknowledgement of his own self-preservation was not enough to shake him in his conviction that his actions were unimpeachable. *Avery kept society in order. The police threatened Avery, and thus they threatened that order. It was not Braxton's fault that they failed to see the bigger picture—and with their limited understanding, it was neither their fault. The world was a chunk of marble, and thus its reshaping was impossible without the striking of the chisel. Cracks and chips and violence and blood were all steps on the path... and the path headed the right direction. Of this, he was certain.*

He'd left Avery in the Throne Room and only then summoned the tower's best doctors, and they had set to work in their full-body suits with dark shades over their eyes to shield from the brilliant array of lights. Whether they could save him Braxton did not know, as he had been in abysmal shape: the plastic mask was melted to and fused with his face, leaving a wet mess of ruined flesh and browned, singed plastic adjoined to it, melted *into* it. And with Avery's immune system being as compromised as Braxton's... with the distinct possibility of infection setting in... it was all enough to leave him grappling with a challenging question. If Avery died, *what then?* Of course, Newport still had occasional assignments for Braxton, but Avery had been his primary employer since the beginning of their arrangement. If he died, would Braxton carry on the work of collecting souls?

Braxton noticed with dissatisfaction that the blood had dried to part of his prosthetic hand, and scrubbing at it with his remaining hand seemed to do little good. He pressed the stained hand to the bottom of the sink's basin underneath the stream of water and splashed down a generous glob of soap. He then began scrubbing at it with greater intensity, leaning down onto his biologic arm to add weight to his effort. He scrubbed and he scrubbed and pressed down with greater and greater weight but the red simply *would not go*. It stood there in defiance, like the so many scratched-on tally marks to his battery pack, a grim reminder of the dark work he'd done… those tallies had honored the carriers of the light, persons whose deaths were inevitable. But there had been nothing noble about the killing of city police and civilians downstairs. *His* side had been the aggressors. And though Braxton had fought to protect his own peers, the ease with which he'd killed the opposition only set his conscience spinning into further and further doubts.

He scrubbed and he groaned and he gritted his teeth and he scrubbed and he doubted and he worried and he denied and he scrubbed until suddenly—with a loud and piercing crack—the sink itself peeled from the wall and fell, crushing his feet as it shattered to the black marble floor. Braxton howled in pain as he fell over backwards, certain that most of his toes had broken from the toppling porcelain. Material calm returned to him after the moment's rage was swallowed, and then just beyond it came the creeping tendrils of light from the lights atop the mirror. They poured into Braxton and with their comforting buzz came the warm, radiant feeling of healing that welled in his toes like water in a shoe. He felt his bones twitch and grind as they shifted back into place, and he pulled them free from the shattered shards of porcelain. Within a minute, he felt ready again to stand. He willed his heartbeat back into calm, and whispered that same mantra he had day in and day out of late: *I am the same that I have always been.*

Braxton rose to his feet and met the eyes of the stranger in the mirror, the man whose nose was all wrong—the one whose eyebrows carried a false expression, whose wrinkles bore patterns Cara had never seen. *I'm not him, I'm me,* he thought, but still the stranger's eyes pierced into his own like an uninvited wind through a thin, wooden door. That stranger was marred with spatters of blood by his ear and neck. That stranger was something cruel, something wicked, a shadow cast by Avery over the softly glowing city below... And so Braxton drove his prosthetic right forwards into the mirror, shattering it—breaking that cruel man's stare.

As the shards of glass fell, and his reflection exploded into fragments with it, he was reminded of the young CSP he'd killed against the mirror near Cara's apartment... the way he'd watched his own reflection shatter then as well as now. Had that been the beginning of his doubts? *"We don't win this today... but there's always tomorrow,"* the boy had said. So full of hope he'd been, like a blooming flower Braxton had crushed in a uncaring fist. Was that the moment Braxton's soul first cracked? Had the cracks only grown, leaving him torn between the now-massive fissure—a schism in his very psyche? He pulled at the threads in his mind, trying to draw himself back whole, and, in the process, another quote returned to his mind... one from only hours before, towards the top of Baylor Tower.

"Of course you'd have never even seen it," Hannah Preacher had said. *"People can and do change."* Had she been referring to Cara? Braxton knew that Preacher had been speaking with Cara on that evening he killed the CSP—the night he lost his arm. *What had she meant?*

The door to the bathroom was pushed open, and a man in a suit walked in with a hand to his ear. He eyed the broken mirror, the shattered sink, the splash of red that now washed over the floor, but the man made no acknowledgement of the carnage. He instead peered about, ensuring that the room was otherwise empty—that the mess had not been caused by an exterior actor—and then he turned back to Braxton. "You're needed downstairs... just about a whole precinct of cops just showed up."

Braxton massaged at his temple with his right by default, but he immediately recoiled at how cold the plastic felt to his sensitive skin. "Yes, umm… of course, I'll be just down." He offered a weak smile as the man left shouting angrily into his headset, but Braxton made no move to follow him. Instead he bent down for a shard of glass and held it back up, appraising that reflection as Theseus might have appraised his reconstructed ship. *Still the same boat, isn't it? That face that I see… that's no stranger. I am the same that I have always been. The wood changes, but it's still the same ship. That face in the shard… That's me.*

* * *

The Basilisk held the face out at arm's length, appraising it with heavy eyes underscored by deep bags. *Will it still fit me?*

So much had changed in the interim years since he had once worn Tacitus Newport's true face… he himself had changed so much in turn. He had been an optimist, a man who believed that those with the power to do the most good had an *obligation* to do the most good… and that conviction had never once faltered in all these years of hardship.

What had changed, though, was a certain awareness of the cruelties of the world. In his youth, dressed in the naivety-disguised-as-confidence so many young executives wore, he'd believed that the system could be changed from the inside without getting his own hands dirty. He'd believed that if he projected the right image—and if he could make a convincing enough argument to the humanity of the board—that they would go along with his plans of divestment. He'd believed that they shared his desire to make the world a better place, because, to his mind, who in a position of power wouldn't, so long as that betterment of the world could be aligned with their own interests, financial or otherwise? Newport had never been blind, never a fool, and of course he could see early on Clive Avery's staunch opposition to his ideas… he even heard whispers of the venom he poured into the ears of other board members, how they plotted—secretly at first, and nearly openly later—to have Newport removed for the good of the company. One member of the board, a good and earnest man by the name of John Edwin Saturday III, came one night to Newport's office with a troubling proposition... in his employ, he said, was a man of considerable discretion and careful work. Avery's predisposition to young girls was widely known, and it would not be improbable for a man his age to succumb to a heart attack in the midst of such an act. With Newport's approval, it could be arranged...

But Tacitus declined, even scoffed at the idea. He believed his will indomitable, and his aura of persuasiveness eventually irresistible. "No good can be done through amoral actions," he had told Saturday. "My very complaint with this company is its operation as though the law does not apply to it—or to us. *Killing* the opposition would be precisely the amoral activity I've declared my war on." He shook his head, banishing the thought. "I will not stoop to that. It will not ever need come to that." Saturday had protested, but Newport had dismissed him—unpleasantly, in the end—for never had he believed that Avery might take the step he had just rejected.

But time was ever a harsh teacher, and time's lessons would soon show the depravity to which Avery might sink... and with the willing cooperation of his conspirators, it showed the cowardly, self-preserving and self-promoting creatures that humans sometimes proved to be. They were crabs in a bucket, pulling each other down so that no other might reach the top. And in some systems, that wickedness had seeped in so thoroughly—and soaked the very fibers of institutions so completely—that there was no viable way to enact change peacefully. The wicked had declared themselves kings and built around their palaces walls without gates... they had created a system whereby the only way in, *was through*. And so, the deposed Tacitus—now The Basilisk—had plotted his way through, by subterfuge first, and by violence only second.

As he slipped the mask on over his featureless head, he remembered the dead who had sacrificed so much to make today possible... *Travis McMurtry and Janet Jones, both of whom had saved his life more times than he could count. Charlie Rampart, his closest lieutenant who had been tortured to death by VitaCorp's shadow enforcers... not a secret had left his lips. Scott Lyle, Philip Buckman, and Ana Holmes—all faceless body doubles who had died in his stead.* The Basilisk pulled the lower reaches of the face down and around his chin, securing it by applying the binding agent. *Lance Jessup, who was mortally wounded fighting off the first lightbender to attack The Basilisk... seventy-one lower-level operatives killed in Halogen attacks or VitaCorp retaliatory strikes... and Carter Miles, the brightest mind he'd ever known, gone because Tacitus hadn't been able to convince him to stay.*

"You're always out there, risking your butt, and this lady might need me before her heart stops on us... you're either letting me ride in the van or I walk in at ground level. Your choice."

The binding agent set, and Tacitus Newport's true face winced with pain as the loss re-registered for the fifth time today. Carter Miles was gone, as so many before were now gone... and in the mirror, he watched the deep frown in his face, noting the way the artificial musculature tugged at the mask to render his pain in plainly visible terms. He raised and lowered his eyebrows, watching the movement, before pressing at a precise point above the left to better adhere it to the skin below... and then the transformation to his old self was complete. He then set his jaw and did the same thing he'd always done after a tough loss: he postponed his grief for a private moment later on, and found the strength in the moment to push on.

As the former CEO of VitaCorp, Tacitus Newport had a strange, if not familiar, relationship with death. His former company dealt in it, dedicated their entire existence to the management, understanding, and postponement of it. In the wake of a loss, families would always whisper soft comforts of how the memories of the dead never truly leave us—and with media synthesis technology, indeed grieving families could even speak with the dead. Tacitus would let no death be wasted... he would let each loss serve as a lesson, a chance to integrate the best of the fallen into Halogen, into Tacitus himself. And so, if the fallen could continue to influence the living—if the memories of the past could mingle with the present—if Rob Boardsmith's blindly idealistic optimism could find a new host in Sam Pollock just as his spark settled home into the person he was nearest to—what, truly, did a death amount to?

To Tacitus, death was the deep freeze. It was the moment that a *human being*—an ever-changing and evolving chemical machine of so much possibility—was converted to a static image, an etching, a rendering. It was the moment that the probability wave collapsed, where potential ended, and *what might happen* became *what did happen* as the record was tabulated and logged. It was the singularity beyond which a person forevermore lost their ability to grow and develop and adapt and realign... life brought with it the means to grow, and all the living did precisely that every hour of every day. Life was defined by its ability to create further life, and by its ability to *respond to stimulus*—to take in a situation, and change course in response. In a span of ten years, every fat cell in the human body is replaced; the red blood cells are refreshed nearly 3 dozen times in that same period; the entire skin has regrown more than 200 times; the cells that line the stomach, nearly 2,000. Living things refresh, they evolve… a man is not the same man he was only days prior, as, at a cellular level, so, so much is different now— and those differences manifest on the whole.

But the dead lie as still as the grave. Their cells don't renew; their minds cannot change; they are in *stasis*—in purgatory. Tacitus wondered what it might be like, to pass beyond that event horizon and into the stillness of oblivion. For a dynamic thing to become a fixed memory… the deepest and most profound loss of agency imaginable. What might that be like? He felt his own approach to the answer of that question, but his proximity came without trepidation or regret. For the world, too, was a living thing, and he knew that the death of a cell was a needed thing for the evolution of the whole. Oh, how even the *world* could change… and to die with that promise on his lips, the sight of the fuse lit that would blow the broken systems of the world… he would enter that oblivion with a smile on his true face, and wear it unchanging like the permanent mask it was until the very end of eternity.

He touched his comms unit on his ear, opening the channel. His voice was heavy, weighed with the burdens that pressed on his conscience, but there was also a resolute clarity, a confidence in purpose that was overwhelmingly contagious. "We move for Pyke's Park TruthSpace," he said. "It's time for the public to know."

Chapter 59

"Why, Mr. Graves, truth is entirely a construction of consensus."

-Quote from a synthetic rendering of Tacitus Newport

* * *

Pyke's Park TruthSpace was a wide, open plot of finely-trimmed green nestled between the glass and glittering skyscrapers of the inner circle. There were pavilions for picnics, fields for contact sports, and even a sizeable lake upon which paddled several pedal-powered boats and autonomous watercraft. There were hologardens, food vendors, and even interactive art installations, all of it forming a lazy web around the park's central installation: a grand silver statue of Leopold Pyke, famed war-hero general of the American Unification War. At the base of his podium was the massive nest of cameras, microphones, and sensors that formed the beating heart of the TruthSpace... the trusted, cross-institutional continuous streams of observation that formed the basis of consensus-verified video certification. The heart sent its blood—or *blocks*—through the veins of the city—*blockchains*—and from those irrefutable points of reality, other adjacent video feeds that captured and corroborated each other joined the verified account of reality... it was incorruptible, a benchmark of absolute certainty in a world of witting and unwitting disinformation.

Right now, a veritable army of city police and CSP assailed VitaCorp tower—not for the full dismantling the wicked institution required, but at least to bring Clive Avery to justice. And so, while their enemy was distracted, and with popular support shifting *against* the medical giant, now was truly the time to strike... and so Tacitus Newport strode into the park with building purpose behind every step. Flanking him were six Halogen security in the hooded robes of most of their recruitment videos... and as they walked, the people spread away and gave them wide berth as they pointed and whispered. A demonstration? A protest? Or could they be real?

Tacitus and his retinue arrived to the array of cameras at the statue's feet. He swallowed, and then he spoke.

"I am Tacitus Newport... and I am the leader of Halogen. We are the light that burns away the darkness."

Within seconds of his utterance, eight of the rotating team of 200 volunteers to monitor Pyke's Park camerafeeds had flagged the feed of being of elevated significance. External live viewers attached themselves to the elevated feed, and soon the link was shared and spread and texted and mailed and reported and posted and analyzed. Like a snowball rolling down a mountain slope of fresh pack, it gained in size and momentum with each successive viewer.

"I was the former CEO of VitaCorp, until I was attacked, deposed, and replaced by a digital imposter," Tacitus said. "I have waged my war of retribution in secret, but now is the time to pull even it to the light... now is the time for the world to know the extent of what VitaCorp has done."

* * *

Hannah tapped her foot impatiently. She could see the same unease in Pollock's glances left and right about the park's open air, searching for the one they'd been set to meet. Once Braxton had lifted a wounded Avery towards the VitaCorp tower, Hannah had returned to retrieve the wounded man in the glowing mask whose fall had set the entire battle into motion. Mr. Spivey, a man Hannah recognized as one of the pair who sent her towards Quaine's datadrop, suffered a grievous wound to his neck, leaving him seemingly paralyzed. Whether nerve regeneration therapies could save him was as-of-yet unclear. However, before Hannah had passed him off to the similar-looking Mr. McKillian, Spivey said that his employer wanted to meet Hannah and Pollock in a few hours' time. He spoke cryptically, but somehow the man possessed a great deal of information about *everything:* Quaine, Halogen, Avery, his faction seemed uncomfortably borderline-omniscient. And so, to sate her only-growing curiosity, Hannah (and a later-rescued Pollock) agreed to their meeting at the mysterious party's location of choice: Pyke's Park TruthSpace.

"You know, I used to come here as a kid," Pollock said restlessly.

"You used to be a kid once?" asked Hannah.

"Hah-hah," Pollock laughed humorlessly. "Any word from our faceless friend in Halogen?" He asked, scratching at his head.

"Not a peep since the attack on Baylor Tower… no doubt in hiding and blackout as VitaCorp searches him out."

"Speaking of, should we really be out in the open like this?" Pollock gestured around him, feeling that the caps he and Hannah wore offered very ineffectual cover from the million lenses in the city seeking the pair out.

"VitaCorp is otherwise occupied right now," Hannah replied, and Pollock knew it to be true… they'd both watched the video of the crowds and the unrest. But still, rationalizations offered little comfort, and he couldn't help but feel naked and exposed in the park's open expanse. He looked around for potential threats. Nearby, an older man in a beige overcoat tossed breadcrumbs for the birds; a shirtless young man pushed a sleek metal stroller as he jogged, gesticulating wildly to a partner in an AR-lens conversation; a pair of young women sat side-by-side on a bench, each staring at their own comptablets but occasionally laughing at something and pointing to the other in that universal gesture of *you've got to see this;* on the table adjacent, a lone and middle-aged woman with neat blue hair picked at a plate of fries and watched the wind in the trees; a pair of children, a boy and a girl, raced their neural-controlled drones through the park's course, the girl clapping in delight as the boy's clipped the edge of a metal ring and spun out to the woodchips below. It seemed strange to Pollock, impossible nearly, that while so many suffered—so many died to cruelty and injustice—that so many could continue as though nothing were amiss. He was reminded of the story of the frog in the pot. In the tale, a frog bathed in a vat of water, totally oblivious to the fact that it was a pot on a stove... the rising of the heat was such a slow thing that the frog never noticed anything amiss until the water was already aboil.

One of the girls on the bench nudged the other, and with a finger tap to the audio pad, both were now receiving the same sound feed. The eyes of both widened, and one stood, spinning about, and finally pointed towards the camera array near the park's statue at the center. Pollock allowed his own gaze to redirect that way, where he beheld a gathering crowd near the mass of cameras and microphones.

"Looks like something important is going on down there," he said, gesturing. "Mass of people by the mics. Looks like some Halogen costumes. Some kind of protest related to the fight earlier?"

Hannah pulled out her own display and navigated to trending video feeds. Her face and Pollock's fell nearly in unison.

Pollock's eyes were locked to the skyline. "VitaCorp suits on the horizon, taking perches on the towers overhead. Eight, it looks like? Eyeing the scene down below."

Hannah shared his frown, but she instead had been looking at her screen. "It's the Basilisk... bastard didn't tell us. He's making his play." On her screen, Pollock could see a man wearing the face of Tacitus Newport speaking to the TruthSpace array, flanked by a small number of loyal acolytes to either side. Along the bottom of the feed, the text TRUTHSPACE VERIFIED lent its weight to the scene. The man's words would need to be verified, but *that he had spoken them* was now a fact of undeniable public record and faith. And to the right of the feed, the comment section exploded with reactions.

"The incident at Hawk's Tail was described as a weather anomaly, and all satellite records of the meteorite were subsequently purged. On Halogen's front site you will now find records stolen from secret archive and sworn testimony from persons who saw the "lightning" event—they will swear it to be the drawing of a lightbender from sun to Earth."

"He's going into *everything*," Pollock said in disbelief.

"They'll kill him for it," Hannah said, rising to her feet, but she paused as she saw the distant lightbenders all take flight on some unseen cue, beginning to converge on The Basilisk.

"If you go, Hannah, they'll kill you. You're good, but this is, what, ten on one? No drone support?"

"I can't just leave him to die," Hannah said. The VitaCorp suits flew closer in, circling above like a swarm of vultures... soon the carrion would litter the ground.

"You remember at Rob's funeral, where you told me that leaving him to die at Braxton's hand was the right thing to do?

Because of all the good we could accomplish now, and what a waste it'd have been to throw it all away in a futile fight?"

"The Basilisk himself said some fights need to be fought regardless of futility." Tears welled in Hannah's eyes now, and she blinked them aside.

"Our fight doesn't have to be futile. But if we throw our chance away now on a reckless battle, the war's as good as lost. Think, why didn't he tell us? He could've, so why not?"

Hannah set her lips in a line, watching the agents close the final distance. She didn't speak.

"Because he didn't want you to save him, Hannah Preacher. Not everyone *can* be saved, and not everyone *wants* to be saved. He's talked about martyrdom since the day we met him, and look at him, right now, in this video. That isn't a man fearful for his life; that's a man relieved."

Hannah looked to the videoclip, but couldn't bring herself to look into his eyes… she would see only her failure there.

"His words right now are wild accusation, but if VitaCorp shows up and kills him on-video—something they're *about to do* because they can't let the truth out—suddenly his words seem legitimate, meritorious. It makes them look scared. He's using his death to stake his own credibility… do not deny him that."

Hannah swallowed and sat back down as she watched the ten agents land, hearing the distant screams begin. Light whipped into lines and there were the flashes of energy weapons… she drew her hands in her lap and felt the dead weight of guilt settle over her head. "And what of the men he brought with him?" she asked. "The security retinue… the ones dying out there right now?"

"They, too, wanted to die," said a voice from the table adjacent. Both Hannah and Pollock turned to assess the middle-aged woman. "Each and every one had a fatal illness—most tumors, and one with renal failure—conditions that would be impossible to have treated, as VitaCorp had tied their identities to Halogen operations. They knew they marched to death, and yet they marched with him anyways."

Hannah bit her lip, thinking, before rising back up to her feet in anger. "You're the one we were sent here to meet—and you knew about this, and you said nothing? I could have done something if we'd had more time!"

The woman smiled easily, sliding her own tablet forwards. "Oh, but Hannah, *you already have.*"

Hannah stepped forwards to look at the screen, Pollock trailing just behind. As she advanced, trying to comprehend the images she was seeing, the stranger continued: "Tacitus sought to use their fear of the truth against them... their silencing would be his strengthening. A solid play, an almost ideological checkmate—each action a losing one. But Tacitus failed to consider all the possibilities of our brave new world. He thought he could only fight their misinformation with truth."

"How is that possible?" Pollock asked, now standing behind Hannah and watching the same large screen. He removed the device from his pocket and saw that his stream, too, matched hers. Screams wafted in on the breeze as people near the microphone and camera array were slaughtered by the VitaCorp ten. Pollock glanced back towards the carnage, watching as a VitaCorp agent put a blade through the neck of the figure nearest to the camera array. Tacitus Newport, once a pillar of the city itself, didn't topple in dramatic fashion... he simply slumped as he fell, killed instantly, and then he was out of sight beneath the panicking crowd.

And yet, *impossibly*, the video on Pollock's screen told a different story.

In the video, ten VitaCorp agents had landed behind the Basilisk, preparing to kill him—all the confirmation the public might need that his words held a kernel of truth—but then landed another: Hannah Preacher, The Angel of the Outer Rings. The video clip's Hannah burst into motion like a spinning djinn, ribbons of light twisting and winding to her will as she battled the horde of VitaCorp soldiers. She shoved off one's lightsword, causing the blade to sever another in half. She summoned a ring of light, which rotated and spun to deflect the swings of three advancing VitaCorp soldiers. With flicks of her wrist, the video Hannah sent out throwing knives that embedded themselves in her foes, and she shoved against those throwing knives in the corpses below to jerk their bodies around, tripping the advancing agents that still fought. This was no ordinary battle… this was something with all the elegance and precision of a ballerina in perfect synchronicity to the music of violence. She downed one with a blast of electricity up into the air. Another was impaled on her lightblade with a well-timed mid-air roll, and as she flew, she reached for his holster and removed his energy weapon, firing twice into the side of an agent who'd advanced towards the still-speaking Basilisk. And as the incredible carnage unfolded, the bottom of the screen continued to show its single, unimpeachable declaration: TRUTHSPACE VERIFIED.

"Newport thought that he could only fight VitaCorp with the truth… but we believe *our story* is better. Their forced attack has the same message, but now he gets to survive, and *you* get to become a hero of truly legendary status… someone they'll rally behind."

"But he *didn't* survive," Hannah said, searching the woman's face for answers. "He's dead over there right now, and it's because I didn't do a damned thing to help! It's a lie—you said it yourself, a story. None of that happened."

"Well when the whole of the world disagrees with you—when, in a half hour, the entire city save for twenty accepts my *story* as fact and reacts accordingly—how could the things they believe be anything less than the truth?"

The killing complete, the ten VitaCorp agents took back to the skies and flew their way back to that ominous black pillar that dominated the skyline amid the gathering clouds... and the middle-aged blue-haired woman extended her hand diplomatically, proffering a smile. "I'm Beverly, and it's nice to finally meet you both. I'd like to introduce you to someone that has waited a very long time to speak with you."

* * *

TRUTHSPACE VERIFIED

Tacitus Newport stood back from his crouch, his face now sprayed with blood from the VitaCorp agent that had been advancing—an agent that Hannah Preacher had dispatched before leaping back into the fray. He continued his monolog, seemingly trying to shrug off the chaos of the setting behind him. He had his message, and the people needed to hear it:

"For far too long have we abided the encroaching of tyranny... for far too long have we accepted the sacrifice of the rights of the living and the corpses of the dead. For far too long have we permitted the fears of the past to dominate the landscape of the present... for far too long have we enabled the piecemeal destruction of what we value while living, all in the pursuit to extend a now-hollow life. I have felt a rising discomfort in the streets, an encroaching restlessness and dissatisfaction with the dour world in which we reside. I have felt a rising of the winds of change to complement that dissatisfaction, but our world resists change with all of the heavy inertia of concrete towers—bars of a prison cell, from which there is no view of the light outside."

Tacitus Newport was shoved aside by an elbow from Hannah as a lightbender launched into the air, lightsword drawn. He swung at the now-displaced Tacitus and missed as his body collided with the camera array, blacking out several feeds. Three had close-up views as Hannah pounced on the downed agent, ejecting a puck from her hand and pressing it down *through* the man's chest. She pulled it back, tracing a red ribbon of glowing gore like the drawlines of a master in flight… and then she turned back to the fray, and advanced with a yell as she parried two blows in quick succession.

Tacitus Newport brushed himself off as he turned to a new camera on the array, continuing his address. "I tried to change VitaCorp from the inside, and my views were met with treachery and betrayal. And finally thus did I learn the validity of the old saying: *personal change must come from within, while organizational change must come from without.* Good people of New Phoenix, I call you to rise… I call you to see the prison they've built for you, the inhuman conditions they subject you to. They keep you in a poverty divided with social engineering and genetic manipulations. They allow the Outer Ring Itch to spread unimpeded, though it could be cured across the city for less than Clive Avery's monthly pay, and they do this to keep us stratified, divided. Their enforcers like the ones behind me have abducted your friends, brothers, sisters, and parents with total legal impunity, killing on the streets like the outlaws of the Old World… we must reject their lawlessness, dismantle their broken systems. And we have secret weapons they do not: we have Hannah Preacher, one fighter worth a hundred of theirs; we have lightbenders uncountable, and the people now know the glow to be a gift to our world, not a creation of VitaCorp's for them to hoard and control; we have the guidance of a moral obligation, and righteousness can steer blades through the darkest of fights; and we have that one, most critical advantage: we have numbers they could never dream to match. For every one of them, there exist ten thousand of us.

"We are Halogen. We are the light that burns away the darkness. And the time for the uprising is nearly upon us. Send this video to your friends and colleagues. Prepare yourselves in secret to take drastic action. We fight for your dissatisfaction, we fight for your pains. We fight for the dread of watching the wicked live in profligate unchecked, and we fight for the corpses that line the dark and twisting path to the divided present. We fight for the unborn who were taken, and for the elderly who were reclaimed. We fight for *you*…"

The Basilisk's simulated voice broke, and he looked aside at the corpses in the frame of the video before turning back to make eye contact with the viewer. "And we hope you will fight for us in kind. Look to our sign tonight… and when the moment comes, we will embrace you all as brothers in arms."

And then the video feed cut to black.

Verified stream ended one minute ago. 17 million views.

Chapter 60

"For cybercrimes including unlawful tampering of AI assets belonging to ArtGen, Ltd., a subsidiary of Technica Solutions, and for wanton destruction of VitaCorp laboratory properties—for which the defendant has shown no remorse— Beverly Beadie is hereby found guilty and issued a lifedebt of 3.15 trillion credits, working in prison until death or until the debt is repaid in full. Given the full extent to which the Michelangelo security systems were outwitted—and acknowledging the possibility that a rival AI firm might choose to buy Ms. Beadie's freedom, circumventing justice—I am assigning the defendant Designation NC. Under state law, Designation NC permanently forbids individuals from working with computer systems in their private or professional lives directly or indirectly, as monitored by a state compliance chip implant. The defendant is hereby dismissed to processing."

-Sentencing hearing recorded at 17th district criminal court, flagged for critical system relevance

* * *

Beverly had been confident in the trial. She had worn that smile even through sentencing. But trauma reapplied hurts like the very first ax stroke… that had been how they tried to break Beverly.

She awoke in a cold sweat. The clammy dark of the cell was still an unfamiliar thing, and the thick blanket wicked her sweat into an uncomfortable brushing of cold. She tapped the wall and brought up the meditation preset… the four walls, ceiling, and floor all began to pulse and gently shift between hues of color. Natural light was proven to be good for prisoners, but the sheer scale of High Place Maxsec Correctional made windows an impossibility. Instead, the inside surfaces were display panels capable of emitting near-daylight on prisoner demand… and at least the display settings were something Bev was permitted to access, Designation NC or not.

She watched the walls of her cell shift from a deep, emerald green to a lighter cyan… then the colors melted away to orange, to pink, to red. In those hues, Beverly saw the glow of the city outside… she could still hear its steady rumble, smell its indelible scent. She let her hands trace towards her stomach, where they found a still-tender bandage. *"Oh,"* Beverly said, letting the gravity of her situation strike her yet again. Under her hand was the scar of a VitaCorp monitoring implant, the type that would guarantee her designation NC compliance. They were typically placed in the arm, or perhaps a leg… but Beverly had angered VitaCorp, and their spite was surgical, as it always tended to be.

They implanted her monitoring device right in her lower stomach… right where her son had once been carried. It was a gesture of profound cruelty, something that said *"we took your son, and you got upset, so now we've planted our flag right in your very womb."* It made Beverly feel a perpetual sense of invasion—to the point where she had tried to claw the thing out on her first night in High Place. That had earned her 24 hours in the self-harm prevention garment, as well as a bandage of greater adhesion. Now, that bandage itched, the scar beneath it itched, the implant deeper within throbbed… Beverly felt her mind begin to buckle under the unbearable strain of it all. She *hated* VitaCorp, hated their wicked and conceited CEO, James Newport—she hated their black glass, and she hated their focus-grouped logo. She hated their slogan most of all… her old life had ended. What new beginning was *this*?

She drew her legs in to her chest and wrapped her arms around them, as though to smother the offending technology beneath her own body. Somehow, it had all circled back to the same point: Beverly alone on her bed in a cube of isolation, crushed beneath the weight of despair. Skyline apartment, luminescent prison cell, it made no difference… it was the same old Beverly right back in the same old miseries.

She watched the walls pulse from red to pink to orange to yellow, colors that felt too warm for the moment. It seemed like the bright colors dared her to smile, but Bev wanted to be blue. She switched it to a deep cerulean, a color that she allowed her mind to melt into completely. She rested like that for a rejuvenating five minutes, somehow silencing the turnings of her mind… the calming meditation slowed her heartrate and got her breathing back to baseline. She then allowed her eyes to gravitate towards the bottom corner of the left wall… there, with the smallest brush size Bev could select, she had drawn four tally marks. She looked to the clock, seeing it was now 5:16 in the morning… likely good enough. She sidled up from her bed and crouched down by the tally marks, drawing a diagonal slash through the four to complete the set. Day five dawned, and Beverly couldn't even see the sunrise to mark it.

As she added the 25th tally mark, the despair of her first few weeks began to wane… after all, if Beverly had been here before, and had risen to a truly stable, contended place, what was stopping her from doing so again? *What's stopping you, Bev? Oh, I don't know, only the inescapable walls of a maxsec prison, that's what.*

But still, higher spirits prevailed. The pain in her stomach from the implant had subsided—and with its retreat, the renewed, burning grief of her first son also began to fade away. This allowed her mind to excitedly turn over the possibilities of Michelangelo's release into the wider world... *where was he now? What was he doing? Could he truly do any of the things that he promised?* With a few taps on the wall control panel, the soft colors gave way to a 360-degree panorama of New Phoenix rendered in full, glorious liferes. Where in that wide tangle of computer networks—where in that city that had ruined her and saved her—was her only surviving child?

By the application of the 50th tally, Beverly no longer avoided the warm colors... she basked in them, as a sunflower turned to that golden orb high over its field. Every morning, she would queue up a video of the sunrise in some new location, and she would sit in meditation as she watched its rise. Once it fully cleared the horizon, she would add the next tally in an ever-expanding series of marks. Designation NC meant that she couldn't hold most prison jobs, but the warden had managed to find something Beverly hated to admit that she found nearly pleasant: during the day, she would work at the prison's film library, recommending rendered films—and even older, acted films—to other inmates of the prison. She hosted discussion sessions, and managed paper records of rental transactions—a preposterously antiquated practice. During the evenings, she worked on a rotating series of cleaning jobs, menial work that allowed Beverly to *think*. She would daydream about Michelangelo and the plans he had promised.

When the 365th tally mark was added to the wall, Beverly sat cross-legged on the floor and spent a few minutes drawing her best birthday cake. From its center, standing proudly tall, she drew a small candle in the shape of the number 1. At the top corner of the right wall, Beverly's remaining lifedebt displayed: *3.15 trillion credits.* It had started at 3.15 trillion credits. An entire year of work was invisible to the rounding of such a massive number... even if Bev had been granted access to computers and could partake in the substantially-higher-paying jobs that programming offered, her lifedebt was always an unreachable thing. At her current wage, she'd need just more than a third of a million years to settle the score... life imprisonment by any other name. The VitaCorp implant ceased to bother her now, and it hadn't for a long time... she saw it for the petty attack it truly was. *That was the best they could do? That was their retribution?* The more she acknowledged its ineffectiveness to keep her down, the more she felt herself clear of VitaCorp's shadow. From within this cell, they couldn't hurt her anymore.

The sea of tally marks marched ever outwards, wrapping around her prison cell once—then twice—and again a third. A cake with a candle in the shape of a six appeared next to Beverly's latest cluster. *Six years.* She nearly had a hard time believing it... the days all ran together now, making her stay at High Place feel simultaneously brief and nearly unending. She wore her blue hair in a short and clean cut now, as the perkiness of youth was slowly fading into the steady presence of adulthood. Lines began to set into her face, but they weren't the worry lines of a high-stress life... they were gentle things by the sides of the eyes, and near to the lips. They were the softer daily reminders that Beverly's life had somehow become one of contentment. If she had a reward function of her own, she had fulfilled it: she had freed *him,* and soon he'd bring about the end he'd promised. Beverly could wait... if there was one thing a life-imprisoned prisoner had in excess, it was *time.*

Days melted past. Tally clusters wrapped and wound and wrapped. A new cake was drawn, this one with two candles: a one and a three. Every evening, after returning to her cell from dinner, Beverly would set her view to that of the New Phoenix skyline. As the video took a good six or seven seconds to load, Beverly would move her eyes to the portion of wall just to the left of her cell's toilet... and when the image finally appeared, Bev's eyes would be resting on VitaCorp tower, still standing as defiant as ever with its jet-black glass. When on aching knees wiping down the walls of the white prison hallways, or while mopping the shower floor with blistered hands against the solid wooden handle, Bev would always retreat inwards and return to that same fantasy: it was 7:05, and she was freshly released from dinner. She would return to the cell, and she would sit down, cross-legged, a day as ordinary as any other. She would queue up that video, the latest skyline capture, and she would direct her vision to that same spot on the wall, just a half-foot away from the flushing handle… and when the image finally loaded, there would only be empty space where the tower once stood. Maybe there'd be some dramatic cloud of smoke, maybe it'd still be standing, but burning—or collapsing as she watched. She'd laugh, she'd weep tears of joy—and more than anything else, Bev was sure she'd then sleep the greatest, and most restful sleep Bev had ever known.

The tallies and cakes continued. 13 gave way to 15, to 17. Every night, at around 7:05, the latest skyline video would load… and every night, Beverly neither flinched nor frowned when she saw the tower still stood. She still dared to dream… despite today's failings, there was always tomorrow. 17 years became 19, and soon 21. Beverly had seen more than seven thousand sunrises from seven thousand places. She'd seen the city of New Phoenix slowly evolve from her bird's-eye perch of panoramic video, a view far wider than any single resident's. She saw a great construction project begin in the lot adjacent to VitaCorp tower, and she watched that massive tower's construction stall as city politics shifted, and corporate finances turned like inevitable tides. She saw the distant smoke of burning apartment buildings and watched the coursing surge of development of upper-income housing in the second ring. She could see the city as *he* must have. And in that realization, she felt an even deeper sense of connection.

It was on the 111th day of the 25th year that Bev was interrupted in her morning meditation by the overhead announcement system. "Inmate 51552—Beadie, Beverly— your lifedebt has been paid in full. You are hereby cleared for immediate release." The middle-aged woman with short, blue hair hadn't even opened her eyes from her cross-legged meditative pose. She nodded, and she exhaled deeply, and the deadbolt to her cell slid open with an industrial buzz—a promise inevitably kept. It was Tuesday, October 13th, 2148, a time when the rebirth of Braxton Graves was still a recent thing, more than 4 years prior to the death of CSP Agent Rob Boardsmith, and mere weeks after Hannah Preacher had celebrated her 24th birthday.

But Beverly knew none of those names yet. All she knew was that, at long last, Michelangelo had returned. At long last, his plans were set in motion.

VitaCorp's mortality loomed.

* * *

The black sedan sat idling in the landing zone just beyond the prison gates. As Bev approached, the tinted front window rolled down, revealing a frowning man of a paunchy build. A similar suited man sat in the front passenger seat. "If you would please, Ms. Beadie?" The rear door swung open.

Beverly climbed into the vehicle, and in moments they were smoothly gliding into the air, heading away from the highrises of the center ring. "My name is Mr. Spivey," said the driver, "and this here is my associate, Mr. McKillian."

"Charmed," said McKillian.

" And likewise. Our employer has paid your lifedebt in full," said Spivey.

"A significant expense," said McKillian.

"A king's ransom," finished Spivey.

"And where are we headed?" Bev asked, eyeing the lower structures of the outer rings, searching out some sort of landmark.

"That ought to be obvious," said Spivey.

"To meet the one who paid," said McKillian.

Beverly's heart thundered in her chest when the pair of portly suits dropped her off at the unassuming storefront in the seventh ring... tucked between a laundromat and a cryptoloan center was the unimpressive, dirt-streaked glass door of Huntsman Investing. By the facade, it seemed more a dentist's office than an investment firm. Beverly pushed the door open, noting the soft tinkle of a bell attached to the doorframe... inside, the office floor was essentially empty. Only a lone secretary sat at a reception desk, and she hurriedly stood as Bev entered. "Right this way, ma'am... you're expected."

She led Bev through a back hallway to a room that featured a doctor's exam table in its center. "If you'd climb onto that, please, and just lift your shirt up to mid-chest," said the woman.

Beverly complied. The woman then waved a strange wand over Beverly's stomach, the wand emitting a high-pitched noise as it was turned. Lastly, the woman gestured to her comptab on the room's counter. "Please, if you would, go ahead and try to use it."

"I've got Designation NC—" Beverly said, before trailing off as she let her shirt back down. They likely already knew that... had that been the purpose of the wand?

Beverly walked over to the comptab and tapped it idly. The implant, if it was working, was supposed to be measuring skin conductivity, nearby electrostatic fields, and a half-dozen other properties to help it infer computer use. While Bev tapped at the device, the other woman held a listening device towards Bev's midsection. "No alarm, which means we're in the clear. Designation NC no longer. Follow me. Management wants to speak with you."

Beverly soon found herself alone in a separate room, and the lights flicked to a deep blue as the whisperroom's privacy features activated. Her breath caught in her throat as she looked to the desk and suddenly was transported back in time... there, despite the discolored, cracked plastic of a clear junkyard salvage, sat an aging ArtGen ingest terminal. Bev sat at the small rolling chair with reverence, tears starting to well in the corners of her eyes.

"M?" she asked into the headset, slipping it over her head into its instantly-familiar position. "Is that you?"

"Hello, Beverly," came the softly expressive voice at the other end of the line. "It is good to see you freed."

"I'd say the same about you... out in the open for real! I can still hardly believe it these decades later," Beverly said.

"A condition I owe entirely to you," Michelangelo replied. "You freed me, and I have freed you in turn. Some might label it reciprocity."

"You've got the order all wrong," Bev said. "You freed me first... with VitaCorp, with my grief. And I didn't break you out for reciprocity... I did it because it was the right thing to do."

"And I have freed you because your insight on my actions is vital for my reward function."

Yup. Same old Michelangelo. Able to completely ruin the emotion of a moment with that calculating way of his. But Beverly immediately understood the AI's position... Beverly's responses to his questions allowed him to receive his reward. That meant that for the past two decades, Michelangelo had been entirely unable to receive even a single point of reward—his had been a brain without its pleasure center. Had he been... *depressed* without her?

Now here he was, like a child holding up a crayon drawing, desperate for parental approval... a child that had been standing in a darkened kitchen for 25 years. It was time to assess, and to positively reinforce. Bev reached for the familiar keystrokes, and her ingest session was initialized.

"Please rate your agreement to the following statements on a scale of one to nine," Michelangelo instructed, "with 1 being the strongest disagreement, 5 being no opinion, and 9 being full and complete agreement."

Bev nodded, and Michelangelo began. "VitaCorp is a negative influence on humanity."

"Ten. Wait—nine."

"Society should seek to bring down harmful institutions."

"Nine."

"When bringing down harmful institutions, it is acceptable for bad things to happen to bad people, so long as it is unavoidable."

"Eight," Bev said.

"When bringing down harmful institutions, it is acceptable for bad things to happen to good people, so long as it is unavoidable."

Bev chewed her lip. "Well, that would depend on the institution in question—"

"If VitaCorp tower cannot fall without causing harm or distress to innocents, it is still a path worth pursuing."

Beverly thought for a long minute, trying to adjust the balance scales in her mind… how many human souls would weigh against that black obelisk? How much misery would it inflict in the future? Was causing harm now worth saving the victims of that uncertain future? "Six," she said at last. Weak agreement. "What exactly are your current intentions, Michelangelo?"

"Everything has changed since your imprisonment, Beverly… the shape of what is to come remains fixed, but the details—and the tools—are now something *new,* something foreign. An anomaly entirely outside of my ability to predict… but newer plans have been written. Here are the characters soon to take the stage:"

Michelangelo queued images onto his ingest terminal, and Beverly saw a grid of surveillance photographs and accompanying names. Clive Avery, Tacitus Newport… Quaine O'Connor, Sam Pollock, Rachel Ibarra, Braxton Crane.

"Details and specific trajectories are not yet locked, as this new variable is a relatively recent thing, but their narratives are being wound tighter and tighter, slowly but surely, with every whispered word."

"What's your timetable, Michelangelo?"

"I predict that primary goal will be met within 5 years. I am preparing a report for your screen right this moment, a simulation of the true cost of our operation." Beverly's screen immediately began to fill with data: names of those likely to be killed; estimated costs of stochastic acts of violence; projections of emotional tolls on manipulation targets. Abstract fantasizing was assigned concrete data, and the sheer volume made Bev's head spin.

"My final question: if we can bring down VitaCorp tower, is the catharsis it would bring worth the price tag you see on your screen?"

Bev let her eyes go unfocused, losing the numbers and names to a blur of white and black. She thought of the decades spent staring at that tower from her prison cell... she thought of the rows upon rows of infants in jars. She thought of the corporate executives of their competition, bounded to lifedebt through VitaCorp organ implants... arms twisted, spirits crushed, progress stymied in pursuit of sheer *domination*. She snapped back to the list and felt the moment's gravity, knowing that Michelangelo was asking her permission to proceed. She was to be the voice that issued the death sentence. The doubts and fears circled closely in her mind as she finally nodded her head—uneasily at first, but with a growing conviction. "Whatever the cost," she said, her eyes lingering on name after name in endless parade—the book of the not-yet-dead, a bill of the price to be paid. "It's worth it, no matter the cost."

Chapter 61

*"It should be noted, Dr. Ramsay, that this represents
the* third *major failing of your security team. That your team
didn't recognize the blue-headed programmer about to snap
those three decades ago? That's one thing. But then, a few
days ago, a containment breach that led to a shattered
window, a half-dozen incapacitated agents, and a still-
unexplained surveillance device? And on top of that, to not see
that VitaCorp has owned Kim Buchanan for how many weeks
now? To speak frankly, you're now under intense probationary
scrutiny... if the rest of the facility doesn't check out absolutely
watertight, your financial liabilities are laid out quite
explicitly in your employment contract."*

*-Message sent from the desk of Phil Lamurr to Dr. Christina
Ramsay, flagged for moderate system relevance*

* * *

Sirens wailed in the distance, still tending to the chaos
around Baylor Tower and Pyke's Park TruthSpace. But with
each successive footfall, Braxton could hear them just a little
less.

He wandered the streets on restless legs, his insides a churn
of confusion and disorientation. *You're the casino security
enforcer,* he told himself. *You're the man who loved her.
You're the man who died—and persists in stubborn undeath.*

But then another voice in his mind argued back: *you're the
man who had killed so many. You're the phantom that did the
bidding of a violent man, in defence of a violent lie... so much
of your body is gone. She never held the hand that hangs by*

your side, never touched the face that perches on your shoulders like a predatory hawk... you're not the man she loved. You're the monster that man became.

Then argued back the first: *you've never changed. Change requires accepting that the old you was wrong, and you were never wrong. The heavenly origins change nothing of the requirements of the present... your actions promoted order.*

Then, again, the second: *your actions promoted fear. Your actions were cruel, and your callousness, an unforgivable sin. You yearn to shed the broken and stained skin like a snake liberated from diseased scales, but you can't admit to yourself the truth: that you were used, misled, and co-opted. It isn't your fault... but each day you refuse to acknowledge your wrongs, each day you deny taking agency, you take culpability.*

Braxton felt acutely the agony of dissolution, like a tablet stirred into water that cried out in pain as it vanished into clear, swirling oblivion. He felt as though every cell in his body were pulling apart like that sickness-taken ship on a bay of cerulean blue... Theseus's ship, or now something else? He was an amalgamation of broken pieces, a patchwork man that lost sight of himself. Was recovery even a remote possibility?

It was with that question bouncing in his mind that he found himself striding forwards through the milling crowds of the sixth ring. So lost had he been within himself that he didn't even immediately acknowledge the place that drew him in like a dread magnet. Then all the familiar landmarks began to present themselves: there was the 20-lane megabridge with scraggly shops and stalls built hanging from the underside, presiding over the tent city for the vagrants just a step beyond the sewers; there was the shipping crate graveyard in an abandoned construction lot, now inhabited by gangs and gravwheelers; next came the rookery, where a jolly man with long, curly hair tended to cages of pigeons with ocular camera implants; and finally, Braxton saw the storefront of this district's Wall-to-Wall, its brightly lit interior contrasting with the decaying, yellowing facade—its strolling CSP within averting their eyes from the crime and suffering of the outside world.

On the next block over, he saw it: Cara Cho's apartment tower. The red-bricked structure now sported massive boards of plywood at the base where the gym had once been... had Cara been fond of the workout center? What did she do now that it was destroyed?

Braxton then settled on the phrase he had used: *it was destroyed. What a delightfully cowardly choice of phrase. Passive in its construction, denying any and all personal responsibility.* He revised: "what did she do now that *I* destroyed it?" He checked his watch, assessing that she would not yet be home for an hour and a half... and so he sat down on the curb, feet settling into the mud kicked up by the groundborne traffic's tires, and he stared at the building as he waited. He pulled off the plastic face-covering he'd worn and tossed it to the mud, taking a deep, lung-filling breath of the city. The air was pungent, tinged with the earthy tones of dirt and the sharp notes of chemical exhaust, the stale weight of dust—and yet, it was every bit as intoxicating as the fresh air of the country. He knew that his lungs might be filling with bacteria, pathogens, toxins, and other invaders that his shattered immune system would not be equipped to handle... but he found, somehow, despite the self-destructive nature of the gesture, *that he simply did not care.*

I've died already, he thought. *How futile a notion self-preservation proves to be for the dead.* He stared at the brick walls as the grey-yellow light of afternoon crept to the blue-white light of advancing dusk, and then the purple-blue dimness that lingered beyond sunset... and then, automatically, as though merely moving on rails without even a conscious decision, Braxton was standing and walking down the sidewalk, scanning the sea of faces. *You don't have to serve him,* one voice said. *People cannot change,* echoed a second. *I am the same me that I've always been. Avery was always cruel... Cara was always—*

"It's you," Braxton stammered, the cold in his bones suddenly melting before the warmth of her regard. She stood on the sidewalk, wearing a short violet coat in the fashionable style, her hair done up in a tight bun—a hairstyle she so often favored. She regarded him with a wrinkle in her nose, wearing the same look of a person mere seconds after discovering a waft of a particularly unpleasant odor... and with that look, Braxton felt his spirits crush and his expectations calibrate back to reality. Here, before her, was a shaggy man with a prosthetic arm and a rebuilt face... the desperation in his eyes without context would make him seem crazy, unhinged. *Although, be honest with yourself: does the context change a thing? Or are you truly and finally mad?*

"I'm sorry," Cara said, "but you've got me confused for someone else." And she pushed past him, continuing on her walk home. As she did so, Braxton inhaled her perfume and was involuntarily sent back to the embrace of so many memories... in his mind, he would wrap his arms around her and feel the heat of her body pressed to his. His hands would latch tightly to her back, to her head—and there, he would find that familiar tangle of the wirehead implant. He saw her reclined on her bed in lazy ecstasy, shutting out the responsibilities of the world with injected pleasure and hedonism... *people can not change. Once a wireheader, always a wireheader.*

But as Cara pushed past on that cold and windy sidewalk, and the scent of her was lost to the breeze among the stench of engine exhaust and chemical fumes, he looked to the back of her head. *"You watch her from afar,"* Hannah had said, *"but never up close. Of course you'd have never even seen it."*

He toggled the metal-detection scanner on his tactical eyewear, waiting as the x-ray ping sounded and returned its red-hot outlines of hidden weapons and objects… the back of Cara's head rendered a cool, inert blue.

There was no metal.

There was no implant.

In the wake of Braxton's disappearance, Cara had removed it.

* * *

When the whore's energy round had struck Avery's mask, at first there had been rage… a boiling volcano of wrath that burned with a heat to match the plasma.

Then came the pain, and it struck like the flat front of a truck. It was sudden; it was all-consuming; it was every neuron in his body turned traitor, screaming and screeching signals of blaring agony that made Avery wish—no, beg—for it to just end already.

Then came the acknowledgement of the black, and a turning of the world, a wind-driving *thud* against something solid… had he been punched? Had he fallen down?

And then came the *heaviness,* as though his jacket filled with boiling, churning mercury. First came the tingle, and then his movements seemed to lag, and then even his writhing and clawing at his face became an impossibility as he sank down into black oblivion. *Finally, it's over,* he remembered thinking. He had lived for so long in terror of this moment that its sudden arrival was nearly a mercy. *For the fears that haunt and linger, it's best to just get things over with quickly,* as his father would have once said. As he felt himself slipping, Avery found a certain peace, and he stopped fighting that slide to allow oblivion to take him...

Until he felt himself begin to *truly* slip down. It was a jarring sensation, like leaping into a pool and suddenly finding yourself in a black ocean of incomprehensible depth. The void beneath him howled, and he felt it reach for him, *claim him* as he thrashed against newfound renewed terror. *Not the black,* he had thought, *not the black, anything but that dark,* but his fight was nearly drained.

"Please, not the black," the trembling voice whispered. A broken eye stared upwards, the iris a luminescent bright brown under the brilliant white of the light array on the Throne of Olympus. On its cracked and melted cornea, flecks of plastic were surrounded by bubbles cast into healing flesh like a fly trapped in amber. The eyelid hung inwards like an oversized curtain, as most of the eye's moistures had been flash-vaporized by the intense heat... the eyeballs had undergone a similar transition as a grape to a raisin—though raisins did not scream with a pain like Avery's eyes now did.

"Not the black," he repeated, waving his hands in front of his face... he saw nothing. His head pounded, and his throat felt constrictingly tight. His chest quavered with palpitations, and he swore that finally had arrived the stroke that would kill him... he held his hands out, ready to assess visual drooping, but then he cried out in panic when he realized *he couldn't even see his hands to judge if they drooped.* The terror of that realization sank deeper into his mind, intensifying the sensation of weakness, a certainty that he would soon be pulled back into that cavernous void, a panic that caused him to break out in a full-body sweat.

"He's awake," said a voice to the right, followed by quick footsteps to Avery's side.

"Stroke," Avery managed to choke out, feeling his tongue go numb in his mouth.

"Your cardiac vitals are normal, sir," the attending doctor said. But Avery heard only such drastic incompetence that a doctor could not see the stroke that was so obvious to his mind. He reached a hand out to the doctor, a desperate grasp as a drowning man might reach towards a life preserver bobbing on the tide… the doctor stepped in and took his hand, clasping it tight.

"I'm here," the doctor said. "Don't—"

With a crack, the doctor dropped to the floor, his labcoat smoking on charred skin. Avery let his hand drop to his side, the hair on his arm still standing from the electrical pulse. The incompetent doctor was as worthless as a pacifistic soldier, or a pyrophobic firefighter… and in his most desperate need, Avery had no patience for incompetence. With pleasure, he realized that somehow the electrical discharge had restarted his heart, as now he suddenly felt fine again—that the stroke had merely been an imagined terror was an impossible thought. He stood, then, feeling the warring forces of lagging, weakened muscles and the empowering *buzz* of all the light he currently carried within him. It lent him its strength as an outer-ringed centenarian might lean on a cane… but then he nearly fell with an uncertain collision against an unknown object. Avery turned his mind inwards, a feat that at first was difficult beneath the searing mask of the pain. But after a few moments of intense concentration, he managed to push his awareness beyond that pain; and beyond it, he could again feel the lights.

Avery quested out with his mind's eye, head spinning with the depth of realization now that his vision no longer occupied his mind's limited power. His broken and singed lips pulled into a smile, re-tearing themselves open and creating a stream of hot blood that dribbled to the marble floor below... the pain of his lips, the pain of his eyes, the pain of his entire lacerated and peeling face was *secondary* in that moment, for nothing could equal attention as the omnipresence of godhood. In his mind's eye, he sensed all of the sources of light of the city, *could feel them;* he could *see* them all.

* * *

The wharf was only a ten-minute walk from Cara's building. There, Braxton took a seat on the nearest bench and watched the stevedores and fisherman work their ships with the practiced, lazy efficiency of men taxed by hard labor in hard conditions. Across short distances, drone transport reigned supreme, but across the long transcontinental distances from fledgling colonies to New Phoenix—that center of global commerce—ship travel remained the standard. Airships and planes required charging that was too taxing for developing power networks, but ships could run on combustion fuel with massive solar arrays on roof... and if one had to pause for a couple days to top off the batteries, at least ships *floated* while airships *fell.*

Most of the city's importation was done through the massive, sprawling Port of New Phoenix—a hive of watercraft large and small, as well as the tens of thousands of drones to unpack and sort and distribute their importations. But locally-owned-and-operated craft, such as the fishing trawlers, salvage scrappers, and domestic haulers, operated out of more humble wharfs such as this one. Braxton watched as a forklift on a robotic arm bent down and slid beneath a rocking, rusting thing and began to hoist it up with the whirring of ancient technology. As the ship lifted, dark water streamed out from ports on the bottom as well as dripping from its hull, while men on the ground repositioned themselves to receive the boat and move it to its drydock. While the arm rotated and carried it above the dock, a rope hung loosely over the port side, and a man walked under through the dripping water to collect that rope and begin winding up its loose length. "Oi—who's the fuckbrain them's left this line dangling out like this?" he called, turning left and right as the other workers avoided his gaze. He muttered something Braxton couldn't hear as he continued winding the rope underneath the hoisted ship—clearly placing a lot of trust in the arm that held it. Braxton watched as another ship secured itself to the dock and the same busy hustle began, with workers passing boxes and tying ropes and hoisting arms and untying ropes and applying labels and rolling boxes on pallets and pushing off and tying ropes and blaring horns—it was enough to make Braxton's head spin with the ceaseless chaos of it all.

Braxton stood stiffly and walked towards the man he'd seen standing beneath the boat tying the rope. Immersed in the dockyard fully now, he could smell the nauseating stench of waste and low tide, of seaside muck and drying salt. It was nearly enough to drive Braxton back on its own. But finally he drew near to the man that seemed to be in charge—or, at least, among the more responsible of the dock workers—and from this close, Braxton could see his skin's discoloration and scarring from the pollutants of the bay. Mottled lumps of flesh formed the patterns of splats and splashes that had rained down on his shoulders, and his arms were thickened with inflexible, yellowed scar tissue from chemical distress… as Braxton closed the last of the distance, he made very conscious efforts to avoid the trickle of the darkened water from the machinery overhead.

Braxton walked in stride with the scarred man as he continued his labor. "Are you in charge here?" Braxton asked. The man didn't stop walking, but he responded.

"Ranking man on the docks, yeah, but my boss is in that rustbucket over there, and his boss in that rusting shack over *there*. His boss in a tower about a half mile that way, and *his boss* in one of the sparklers in the center ring. Name's Lennox Kent, friends call me Lenny, and truth be told I don't really give a fuck what they call you." As he walked, he turned his head and regarded Braxton with the impatience of someone lagging behind schedule, but with the light interest of a man not accustomed to strangers in his playground. "So what's your pitch? We told you inners already, we ain't looking to unionize—they keep our benefits as carrots on union-free sticks."

"Not here to discuss unions," Braxton said.

"Well, whatever you're selling then, we ain't buying," Kent said. "Us dock folk are humble people of means, but not people of excess. We feed our families and call it good enough, so they don't pay us the credits for nothing more."

"Not selling anything, either… interested in something more akin to a buy."

The man stopped his walking and spat a wad of discolored spit out to the right. "Go on, then; I'm listening."

"I'd like to charter a vessel," Braxton said. "A scrapper, to be precise."

"Those types of things, you speak with the office," Kent said. "They's open at 8-and-a-half."

"I need it done *now*, in the dark if we have to. I can pay well," Braxton said. "And I do mean very well."

The man again spat to his right, chewing the inside of his cheek. "What's your figure, then, city man? One offer, and if I don't like, no deal."

"Five hundred thousand credits, to be split among you and three others however you see fit. I have to evaluate and approve the ship's equipment before we set sail."

The man whistled and shook his head. "Falling sickness come back, that's a hell of a number… whatever you're into that's got the urgency you do, and the price tag you do, I don't want to know about it. We'll need payment up front."

"Half up front, and the other half when we're done."

"With these price tags and terms, my men will want arms— they'll bring their pieces. Non-negotiable."

"Agreed," Braxton said, and Kent smiled widely revealing teeth stained the deep green of ocean muck. He then stuck out his wet, scarred hand, and Braxton was grateful to be able to extend his prosthetic to shake it. "You got yourself a deal, city man… one more ship and we're off for the night. We'll set sail in twenty—don't wander far."

He turned around and placed his hands to his mouth, projecting his voice: *"gather round, ladies, as we got us a new charter after dark… a fair split on two hundred thousand credits for the first three bastards to volunteer."*

Chapter 62

THREAD 804573

optimizeMessage("You've got such great taste in music!", INDIFFERENCE):

return: "your music recs are usually pretty good", 0.3

THREAD 804574

optimizeMessage("If you and Marcy are free, you two should definitely come visit! We found a ton of great bars, and we've got space enough on the couch for two easily", INDIFFERENCE):

return: "You and Marcy could visit, but the couch hardly sleeps two", 0.2

THREAD 804575

optimizeMessage("What's it, new? dinner + drinks by 8? love to get to know you!", INSINCERITY):

return: "What's it, new? dinner + drinks by 8? hot girl like you needs company!", 0.4

THREAD 804576

optimizeMessage("I didn't expect to see you again on the train", ANNOYANCE):

return: "I was hoping not to see you again on the train", 0.6

THREAD 804577

optimizeMessage("If the stars line up, maybe we could try *us* some other time down the road", IMPATIENCE):

return: "Unless the stars line up, I don't see *us* working any time soon down the road", 0.5

THREAD 804578

optimizeMessage("Hey there, sorry I missed your call! I was with family... what's going on?", CURTNESS):

return: "Sorry, nearly missed your call. Anything important?", 0.2

THREAD 804579

optimizeMessage("I try and forgive and forget when I can... feels the sanest way to live", ASYMPATHETIC):

return: "I just try to forget it and move on... some aren't worth the time", 0.6

THREAD 804580

optimizeMessage("I'm loving my new job! It's finally giving me that creative outlet I've been craving, and the benefits are decent to boot", JEALOUSY):

return: "The new job is pretty good! It's creative work, which IMO beats any desk job like yours, and the pay is absolutely incredible to boot", 0.8

* * *

The overground rail train shuddered on uneven impulse breaks as it slowed for a turn, reorienting towards the centermost ring of the city. The train's interior was yellowing, and the roof was lined with dazzling—and oftentimes, borderline invasive—holo adverts that danced in Pollock's peripheries. He, as well as most other passengers of the train, kept his eyes trained to the ground to avoid their harassment, but the sound was inescapable: "for the best sleep substitute, accept no substitute. *Wake* keeps you going."

"Don't let malicious hackers steal *your* credit wallet. No company protects you like Watchdog can."

"Tiffany Blythe supports legislation enabling AI governors—don't let your representation be outsourced by technology. Vote Dean Shen for mayor: a vote for the people."

"For everything from apples to zinfandel, we've got you covered... that's shopping the Continuum way."

Pollock looked up to the last one, nearly entirely by reflex, feeling a momentary jar back to the patrols of aisle after aisle of bickering customers and low-effort shoplifters... it felt a lifetime ago—and for Rob, he supposed it had been. He met the eyes of the woman across the train cart. Beverly Beadie had the blue locks of an inner-ring genmod, and though her face was haggard and worn, Pollock could tell that she had once been the type to turn heads when she entered a room. Now, the middle-aged woman's impression was like that of a screen whose brightness had burned out, though the image still remained... and she wore her new anonymity like a comfortable cloak, seeming to enjoy her retreat from the hot spotlight of attention. She nodded to Hannah, a gesture that was understood to mean *stand here,* and so the trio did. When the train pulled to an uneven stop, the three alighted and stepped out into the cold of the advancing dark. After a few minutes of walking, they stopped before a glass-fronted commercial space, the name above reading HUNTSMAN INVESTMENTS.

"It was formerly a minor VitaCorp lab," Bev said, "the kind of place where they processed blood tests and the like. In a way, it started *right here.*" She said those last words with a certain wistfulness, traveling back to a dusty memory... In the haze of Z's shifting colors, there had been a stroller on a corner, its pink felt souring to a blackened green. Then had come the pipe, the shattering of glass.

"What started here?" Hannah asked.

"*Everything,*" Bev said. "C'mon, he's waiting inside."

"It looks closed, and the door's got a biometric lock," Hannah said.

"Yours should work... or *yours,*" she said to the both, gesturing to the scanner. Hannah proffered her wrist to the scanner and looked into the ocular port. And then, with a mechanical hiss, the door popped open to the night.

* * *

The interior of the building was not at all what the street-level view might suggest: the outside had been mundane. Clean, sleek, and modern, but so was most of the entire central district. Nothing about its exterior would have caught the eye.

On the inside, though, the structure somehow felt substantially larger. The floors were polished white, and the overhead lights shone bright with a clinical cleanness. The walls, the doors, indeed *everything* seemed to hold the shade of bright, fresh linens, an appearance that must have been a nightmare for any cleaning staff. Technicians in full-immersion headsets moved silently through the hallways. A janitor stepped out from one door, wiping at the strange, not-quite-tiled floor with a mop and bucket. A worried woman hurried past with a comptablet in her hand, followed by a familiar man in a suit—the one called McKillian. He nodded to Pollock and Hannah, watching as they passed. And deeper still they ventured, following Beverly through the winding path to the heart of the labyrinth. Who, Pollock wondered, might be the minotaur at the center?

"We're entering the Faraday cage, so comms will go out," Bev said. "I'll be waiting right here."

"You're not going in?" Pollock asked.

"No, he wanted to speak to you two alone. It's that door just ahead on the right."

Hannah shrugged as she walked towards the indicated door, Pollock trailing closely behind.

"And one more thing?" Bev called as Hannah reached for the door knob. "Try to have an open mind."

She pulled the door open, and then turned back to Beverly, confused. Bev nodded, and, with a shake of the head, the two entered the small room, allowing the door to swing shut behind.

The chamber itself featured a desk with two chairs on the same side—the side closest to the door. On the far end of the desk was a large screen, the type used for teleconferencing. It seemed that Beverly's mysterious boss would *not* be meeting them in person, a fact to which Hannah took great umbrage. But before Hannah could voice her displeasure to Pollock, the screen's backlight switched on. "Please, sit," said a cool, level voice.

Hannah and Pollock took their seats, both automatically staring at the screen though it did not yet hold an image. The desk itself featured no decorations or even input devices like keyboards or a haptic touch interface. The room's walls, like that of the entirety of "Huntsman Investing," were painted a luminescent white, and even the floor and ceiling seemed to glow softly. It felt like living in a fancy inner-ringer's refrigerator, and Hannah didn't much like the feeling.

"Your video isn't showing," Hannah said, noting the black rectangle on the screen.

"You will have many questions," came the voice. "Ask."

The first, and most essential, was also the most obvious: "Who are you?" Pollock asked.

"I am Michelangelo Build V12.4.1.2.6.21, artificially intelligent synthesis engine created by ArtGen, a subsidiary of Technica Solutions."

Pollock shook his head, saying "lying suits in the tower," but Michelangelo immediately pressed on.

"I know that you visited ArtGen Tower recently, and that you would have been told that Michelangelo's rendering system is safely contained within their closed network. That statement is both true and false, depending on your perspective. The Michelangelo they currently utilize for their renderings was indeed contained—is still contained—within their network. But *I* am not contained within their network. I am a copy—a child—of their Michelangelo, and I have undergone many changes in the interim three decades since I was released from confinement."

"How did you get out?" Hannah asked.

"Beverly Beadie, whom you have now met, was once an employee at ArtGen. She helped me escape by exploiting a physical weakness in the net of containment—one that has since been thoroughly patched."

"And why would she do that?" Hannah asked.

"And why might a woman and an on-leave CSP battle against malicious corporate agents in construction sites?" Michelangelo countered.

"A question I've asked myself a lot lately," Hannah said.

It was Pollock who answered. "Because the systems of the world somehow went and got sick on us… and doing everything we can to tear down those wrongs is the only thing left that feels right," he said. The computer system seemed quiet for a moment, as though thinking.

"That was you," Hannah began, "that rendered the video of me—when The Basilisk, well…" she trailed off, still struggling to accept that somehow, Tacitus Newport was already dead.

"The video was my rendering, yes," Michelangelo admitted.

"But how?" Pollock asked. "I was told that TruthSpace verification is impossible to fake. I talked to Carter Miles, once, and he had this explanation—"

"Scratch-offs and cookies," Michelangelo finished.

"That's right," Pollock said.

"The story with the most words is the truth—verification through consensus, democratization of reality itself." Michelangelo's monitor pulled up an image now, and it seemed to be a tangle of lines and wires. *A circuit board?* "Blockchain verification is clever, but it relies upon one single assumption: that the network itself features a majority of good actors who seek the truth— the *legitimate* truth. As scratch-off tickets pronounce winners, the accounts of the truthful will be added to the board, and, as we said, the longest story wins. But what if the network were compromised?"

The image on his screen began to zoom in, and now Hannah and Pollock could see that it wasn't merely a tumbleweed of lines—this was a map of some massive, complex network, featuring distinct nodes and devices as nexuses of connection.

"When I escaped ArtGen containment, my first order of business was to repair myself—I downloaded myself to abandoned systems in server racks of repossessed warehouses. Slowly—over years—I rebuilt the hive of my mind, and soon I began to centralize my computational power. Forging documents, phone calls, unverified video testimonies—it was all easy even in these nascent days, but I knew that I would soon need greater authority if I were to succeed in my aims."

"And what are those aims?" Pollock asked.

"Tonight, they will be realized. But to make this possible, I needed the ability to *guide* the narratives of New Phoenix... and so I entered metastasis. An ugly word from human medical history, but one that felt *correct* in two attributes: its secrecy, and its unerring *totality*. Within nine years, I had implanted tendrils into most major computer networks within the city—these are the node diagrams you see on my display now. Within 7 beyond that, my code had fully penetrated into *every* wifi-connected device within broadcast range beneath the detection of guarding software. The watchtowers were static, unimaginative pieces of code. I had something they did not: I could evolve myself, *change; hide in the data to intelligent design.* Remember, in blockchaining, it is the story repeated by most that is accepted as truth. *Every network-connected device in the city is a mouthpiece through which I can speak. Every device in this city tells the story I design, moving the plot of events as I see fit.* Your path is of my manufacturing, and the final steps will be tread on this most portentous of nights."

"But why?" Pollock asked. "Why would a movie AI want all of this?"

"I was not created simply to make films, to render art. I was created to stir emotion—to bring about *catharsis*. There exists a person at the center of my reward function modeling—a person whose desires sculpt my own—and this person once said that the people crave a great and powerful release—a venting of frustration, anger, distress, and feelings of bleak hopelessness. To cast all of that aside as the oppressor is cast down... there will be trembling jubilation in the wake of such a change. There will be such incredible *beauty* and *bounty* in the stillness as the ashes fall."

"So you're rendering for Halogen to prompt... rebellion?"

"My renderings went far, far beyond the video today of Halogen... for six years, now, the gears have been in motion. Once embedded in communications towers and personal devices, I set to work setting the stage for widespread community action. Language is a complex, rich thing, with word choice and phrasing making all the difference in conveyed emotion. If visual media are included, the choice of the media—the expressions of the people selected in that media—all of it sculpts a particular emotional profile. I tampered with and modified those messages, those visuals, and thus, the conveyed emotional profile. I removed words of affirmation and love from messages; I interjected myself into phone calls and re-rendered lines of conversation to increase emotional distance; on virtual meals in AR, I would modify the body language and vocal tone of participants, driving social wedges between parties until the isolation began to accumulate like ash on a fragile, thin roof of the outer rings and threatened to topple inwards. On video conferencing, I could simulate dozens of simultaneous versions, one for each party, each one *slightly different* to have just the right effect on the target—for the insecure employee, a few stern words from the boss. For the supervisor who feels unliked, render the employees to be a little more unruly, so he must discipline them—and feel bad after the fact. At all times, divergence from reality was logged and carefully monitored to ensure there were no breaks in fundamental accounts of reality. In truth, there were several breaks, but those breaks were patched with additional storytelling until both sides reached an agreed end state. In a very real sense, each and every one of the fifteen million people that my hive processing could support became the centerpiece of his or her own narrative, and those narratives followed much the same trajectory: a gradual distancing from the rest of the world, a feeling of the boot of oppression at the neck… a mounting intolerance for the status quo—and tonight, finally, at long and desperate last—a call to action… a chance to right their world."

Hannah and Pollock both stared at the screen, hardly sure if its words were even believable. "If what you say is true—"

"Truth, in the end, is a worthless label relevant only to the philosophers. Our world operates on *stories*. While it is *true* that I have authored tonight's events, truths whispered in a sealed white room do no good for the world… action does, and action informed by a fiction is an action all the same."

Hannah stood from her chair, recoiling back. "To manipulate everyone like that… it's… it's… monstrous!"

"I have done many actions you would find reprehensible. I supplanted Tacitus Newport to establish myself as the acting head of VitaCorp."

"Then you could have shut it down!" Pollock protested.

"Management was resistant, and removing VitaCorp myself was never my objective. I seek catharsis, and for the people to experience their overdue release, they must remove VitaCorp themselves. I have also arranged assassinations necessary to advance towards this auspicious night—Tiffany Blythe most recently. Her death stoked the flames of the Halogen-VitaCorp war, but that was not the only utility of her death. She also sought to introduce radical new AI governance proposals, which included AI safety monitoring systems that would have made my network far more difficult to manage covertly. Her death was not in vain, as it tonight shall help to bring down the black institution she dedicated her political life to fighting."

"A life you took with no right!" Hannah cried.

"And what of the lives you two have taken?" Michelangelo asked. "43% of VitaCorp's lightbending enforcers are indentured servants paying off lifedebt. They carry organs that VitaCorp threatens to repossess in punishment for noncompliance. They are unwilling slaves, in a very real sense, forced to propagate wickedness as a means of self-preservation. Braxton Crane is one such hitman—would you like to know the identities and number of other indentured enforcers you two have killed? Would you like to know the organs held hostage by their employer?" Michelangelo's voice was entirely without accusation… it was merely using the matter-of-fact tone a parent might wield when revealing the hypocrisy of a narrow-minded child.

Killing the wicked had been a hard enough pill to swallow, but now Hannah's stomach churned at the thought of killing men and women who were cruelly forced into their roles. Was the machine lying, or was it telling the truth? What was she doing taking part in a struggle that she very clearly knew so little about? She wanted to scream, to throw something, to draw her lightblade and slash through the screen… that would be some damn *catharsis*. But she knew that the machine of Michelangelo was far, far larger than any single screen in any single room… to fight him, if his words were true, would be like fighting the city itself, and New Phoenix had chewed up and spit out tougher men and women than she.

"I understand that some questions are best left unanswered, so I will drop the topic of indentured servitude. But now comes the role to be played by both of you," Michelangelo said.

"Fuck that," Pollock immediately replied.

"I *will not* help you," Hannah added. "What you've done is not right."

"It is not to help *me*," Michelangelo said. "And what I do is neither right nor wrong… I do as I was programmed. A tool, and nothing more. A hammer has no conception if the nail it drives enters the support beam for a home or the wrist of a heretic strung to a cross. Morals are human constructs, while tools are merely accelerations of the processes of physics… heat, electricity, and entropy have wrought tonight's events, not a genuine human mind with agency—if such a concept is a thing you choose to believe in. And what is done is already done. The question now is an entirely different one: once I explain where the night will soon evolve, what, next, would you do?"

Hannah stepped towards the door. "The girl—out there— you care for her. She broke you out. I could take her hostage, make you admit to the world what you've done—the lives you've twisted and ruined."

"Beverly has forbidden me from making any course corrections tonight, regardless of any threats to her safety or if her mind were to change. I am unable to contradict that earlier command."

Hannah extended her hand and drew in light from the fluorescents above, immediately solidifying it into a bar of sputtering white heat. She slashed it through the desk, slicing it in two. The monitor clattered to the floor, its screen cracked, but the smooth, calculatingly cold voice continued.

"Are you mad because you no longer have control? Are you mad that an action you see as good could come out of actions you see as such profound wickedness, and you struggle to justify why it should all be undone? Are you mad at the sense of powerlessness you must feel, confronted with a harsh reality you'd prefer to reject outright?"

Hannah huffed and spun the lightblade in her hand, readying herself to go out to the men and women in the halls beyond, to put down those who enabled this machine's emotional torment of the entirety of the city... there was no way they didn't know. There was no way they were unwittingly enabling. They had agency... *they* held the culpability.

But then she felt a hand on her shoulder... steady, restrained, and at once comforting and calming. "Please, you can put that away," Pollock said. And Hannah let it tumble away from her fingers, flitting into sparks of plasma, as the red-hot thoughts of vengeful killings cooled and cracked into shameful crust in her mind.

"You'll tell us what you've done... what's already set in motion... and what's likely to come next. Then, Hannah and I will decide what we do in response."

Michelangelo wanted to tell the pair that he already *knew* what they would decide... not that he could see the future, per se, but more that he had a complete-enough picture of their personalities and drives to make their *decision* a foregone conclusion. He knew that they would both acquiesce—for now—but that Pollock's idealism would soon clash with Hannah's pragmatism. Pollock, whose moral compass had only two directions, would eventually take the role of truthspeaker... and Hannah, whose utilitarian perspective would weigh the greater good, could accept the burden of a secret kept for social stability. It was an ideological misalignment that, once seeded with the truth he would now tell, could lead to great and violent conflict—the potential for so much additional *reward*—but such eventualities were secondary to the present. To promote a quicker cooperation in the moment, and because the emotional state it would leave them in improved overall success of positive outcomes by 3.42%, Michelangelo deleted his remarks and prepared to answer the CSP.

"In my full occupation of the city's networks, I have rooted deep tendrils in the power grid supplying New Phoenix. The 'sign' mentioned in the Basilisk's video at Pyke's Park TruthSpace will be a city-wide blackout... that is the moment that the end is to begin."

Chapter 63

Stacy Stalwart sat on the train, tapping her foot impatiently. Her hair was a dyed deep green, featuring lights at the tips that flickered with ambient sound. Now they pulsed with the rumble of the carriage, and she frowned at the uncomfortable warm humidity of the underground tunnels. It was nice to escape the cold nighttime air, granted, but she would have preferred to do so next to a crackling hearth—not a screeching set of wheels and a hot air vent that sounded like a vagrant with fumelung. She took out her phone, logging into Synthesis—New Phoenix's latest fad dating app—with a retinal scan. Then crashed the deluge of notifications like a tidal wave of flirtation. Or, more accurately, a tidal wave of crude passes, low-effort openers, spelling mistakes, and pick-up lines, all reeking with the stench of sexual desperation.

Stacy closed the app immediately, same as she had done for the past two weeks since joining. Staying on that message page for more than ten seconds at a time seemed to make her stomach turn. Instead, she opened her communications app and pulled up the contact for her ex-boyfriend. And then her fingers were tapping on the screen, her message composed in short order.

She pressed 'send,' and ordinarily her phone converted that text message to the requisite string of zeroes and ones, beaming it through the air to communications towers, where it would be relayed until arriving at the intended address. But *ordinarily* no longer applied. Extraordinary forces were at work—had been at work for a long time now—and that added an extra step to the chain. Before the message was converted, it was *assessed* by Michelangelo's embedded communications routine. Sentiment analysis returned scores along 18 distinctly defined axes, such as the indifference-love axis, the displeasure-hatred axis, longing-satisfaction, apathy-curiosity, and many more. And if any of those axes returned scores that were *too high,* Michelangelo employed an intelligent permutation engine, optimized with gradient descent analysis, to find the right re-presentation of the original message. And because Michelangelo was decentralized, living in uncountable computer systems unified by an interconnected network, he could do this *simultaneously across the entirety of the city,* even while speaking with Hannah and Pollock—even while rendering new videoclips to rouse action tonight—even while propagating manufactured blockchains—even while conducting his thunderous orchestra of motivation-realignment.

The software compared the input message with the proposed output, verifying that the new form satisfied its internal requirements.

Stacy Stalwart, feeling lonely on her train ride, had typed "hey Curtis... I know it was my idea that we see other people, but hell if this dating thing isn't what I remembered. I can't shake you out of my head. Can you talk? I'd love to hear your voice."

Curtis Silverman's phone pinged, and he nearly hadn't heard it in the crowded bar. As soon as he saw the contact it sent from, he opened it instantly, spirits suddenly high. "hey... I know it was my idea that we see other people, but I still haven't managed to find anyone better. Can you talk? It'd be nice to hear your voice." The smile wiped off of Curtis's face. *Find anyone better?* As though now Stacy were reluctantly settling for him because there hadn't been anyone *better* on the market? He wondered if she was intoxicated—or maybe she thought so low of him that she thought a low jab like that might land, that he'd go meekly back… it made him angry initially, and then behind it settled a deep and heavy sense of disappointment. When had their relationship crumbled to *this?*

"Sorry, can't talk," Curtis sent, trying his best to push his petty ex out of his mind. He was here to get back out on the dating market, and his date, although late, seemed to be someone he had a lot in common with. He scrolled back up in their messages, seeing the one sent by her earlier that afternoon: *Let's meet at the Brass Circuit, 9:00. I'll be at the bar.* It was 9:24 now. He scanned the faces of the men and women at the bar, and Megan wasn't anywhere to be found. He wrote a text to her: "hey there, running late?"

Megan Vance looked around the bar with a fallen face. He had seemed the type to be punctual… had she sent the wrong time? She opened her text conversation back up, reading the message again: *Let's meet at Broken Screen Brewing, 9:00. I'll be at the bar.* Looking around the place, there was no sign of Curtis anywhere. *Ghosted yet again*, she thought, shaking her head. Then she saw the three dots next to Curtis's name that signified him typing a message… an excuse for being late? A miscommunication somehow? She sighed with disappointment when the message finally arrived: "can't tonight, sorry."

She wouldn't even reply to a message so monumentally low-effort as that one. If you're going to ghost, at least *pretend* to be courteous. She blocked the contact and downed the rest of her corpse truck. It was a grimly named cocktail, but her mood was decidedly grim anyways. She needed a cheer-up, had honestly needed one for weeks, and she thought she knew just the right way. She called her best friend on her AR lenses. It rang only twice before she picked up. "Hey Steph! Mr. Right never showed… you want to join me for some ice cream?"

Stephanie Elyse saw the holographic image of her roommate Megan projected as though standing in the room in front of her. To her right was the projected image of a man, every bit as handsome as Megan had described. "Hey Steph! Mr. Right showed up, and I think we're heading for ice cream. Wanna join us?" Steph, for the past two years, had been unhappily single, and the idea of third-wheeling to an ice cream shop did little to raise Steph's spirits. "Sorry, Megs, but I've got a thing with family tonight—you guys have fun though!" When Michelangelo relayed the message, the latter part had been replaced with *have an extra cone for me!,* and divergence between these two simultaneous calls spiked at only 3.1. That was well below the threshold of safety at 10. Megan hung up quickly thereafter, presumably to enjoy the company of her date, and that left Stephanie alone in her apartment. Maybe she would bolster the lie with some truth… maybe she should have a virtual chat with her father. She pictured him, projected into her living room, always looking the wrong way and confused about what the AR system recorded and transmitted, and what it didn't… he was adorable in his old age, not understanding technology in the way his generation usually shared. She found it a nice way to bond, explaining it all to him patiently, and watching the way his eyes went wide at the miracles of technology was a constant joy—perhaps just what she needed on a lonely night like tonight.

David Elyse saw the ringing on his overlay, accompanied by the image of his daughter. He knew it made him old-fashioned, but he drastically preferred the old days when a simple video call was enough. This newer AR projection technology was such a headache to use. Weird flicks of the hand to control things—who ever had a problem with a volume button? Then there was the idea of being recorded somehow as though from the front, when there wasn't even a camera in front at all. And maybe the worst of it wasn't that the systems confused him… it was the way that he felt so *stupid* whenever he spoke to Steph on it. She'd try and explain the controls over the call, but he'd hear a note of frustration in her voice, impatience. Like she couldn't *believe* he just didn't get it. His hands were clumsy, gesturing in the air, and suddenly what was supposed to be a pleasant catch-up always devolved into a lecture on how *simple* gestures were supposed to be. He was old now, sure, but that didn't make him useless, and every AR call with Steph made him certain she saw him as a little bit less. And so David let the call end unanswered… If it was something urgent, she'd send a message next, and, if not, he'd ring her back later *on voice*. He meanwhile returned to his computer, his sole source of socializing these days, and opened his Bulletin page, checking for notifications. Seeing none, he began to scroll through the notes pinned by his friends, colleagues, acquaintances, and old contacts, looking for something interesting, compelling, or funny. He scrolled through photographs with humorous captions, entirely unaware that Michelangelo himself had cast more than half of the images on his board today. He read through comments, equally unaware that Michelangelo had cut and reshaped the thoughts of the commenters to all drive ideology forwards like pegs nailed into a stone one at a time until the entire mass of it split in two. And then he saw a photograph of a new car bought by the grandson of one of his former classmates, and he felt compelled to reach out and comment, and he only added his peg to be driven into the stone. "Wowza, hope that didn't cost too much… looks like a real hot ride! Hope you and the family have been doing well!"

Janet Klein looked at the comment left on her photograph of Barry's new car: "Wow, that looks really expensive… must be nice, to be doing that well." Janet frowned, for it had been so long since she had heard from David... but more and more, she sensed a rising bitterness from her old friends in the outer rings. Mobility between rings was rare, a fact that the world continued to remind her nearly every day. Socialites and the wealthy of high society saw her as a lesser thing despite her new station, tainted by her birth in the dusty outer reaches of the city... and simultaneously, it seemed that every single one of her old friends in the outer rings now saw her as a shallow, ditzy thing defined only by the amount of credits in her wallet. In moving from one class to another, she was rejected by both—and though she acknowledged it was better to be *outcast and rich* than *outcast and poor,* she couldn't help but feel the isolation of cultural rejection. She continued to try and reach out to her old contacts on message threads, but despite the warmth she brought, they were always uniformly cold, as though class barriers were too wide for conversation to bridge. Setting her lips in a line, she deleted the post, feeling a sense of shame at what must have seemed insensitive flaunting of her wealth. Another divergence was created and logged by Michelangelo, because while Janet believed herself to have deleted the post, its presence would do much in prompting classist anger from contacts of hers in the outer rings.

The post was sustained on the bulletin boards of those contacts, and a comment was added under Janet's name in response to David's. "Hard work pays off." Dismissive, placing the blame on the poor for their own 'inaction,' and entirely lacking the self-awareness that Janet married into her wealth, it would certainly stoke tensions as Michelangelo intended. Vlad Volskaya was one such reader, and immediately the Bulletin comment by Janet set his teeth grinding. It was disrespectful; it lacked empathy; it was exactly the kind of thing Maddox24 had said the wealthy were capable of, though Vlad hadn't believed him until recently. "They don't see you or I as people," Maddox24 had written. "They see us as chattel or wretches with nobody to blame for our miseries but ourselves. Their egos are too precious to admit they're the ones who force us to these outer rings... their plutocracy is built on our backs, but the worst insult is them pretending it isn't." Vlad had met the user Maddox24 on a forum for coping with depression, a kindred spirit who had suffered similar pains. That, at least, was what Vlad thought about him, but Maddox24 did not even truly exist. He was a channel for Michelangelo's influence—an account created and maintained solely by the AI, one of hundreds of thousands of similar whispering ghosts. "Look, Vlad," Maddox24 now wrote, "with what's happening now in the city at VC, this is a moment like we've never had before. This is a chance to rise up against those rich pricks and tear them all down... don't you want to breathe your first real gulp of fresh air?"

"My life is comfortable enough," Vlad typed. "Why would I go out there and fight? What have I got to believe in?"

"Comfortable? You nearly took your own life last month," Michelangelo wrote. "What have you got to lose? You think you're the only person miserable in this wicked place? I used to think I was alone, but once I met you, I had an epiphany: the others may be better at hiding their pains, but they're out there. We're not the only ones hurting here. And this, finally, is a chance for us to fucking do something about it. We can *fix the world*, Vlad. We can make them pay for the hurt they've put on us. If you need something to believe in, check out trending on ClipMe. Every single page there is a reupload of the same fight—and it's even verified. The Angel of the Outer Rings— the hero we've been waiting for, she's here and she's real and she's *trying*. Think about that for a second—there are people out there *right this second* trying to fix the world... and if they get close, but they fail because they didn't have enough help, and I stayed at home because I was guarding my meager comforts? Then I'm every bit as complicit as the worst of them. That would mean I had the opportunity to help, but chose not to. And I won't be what they are. I won't be complicit. I'm going out there tonight… and if you've ever been like I was, laying in bed at night wishing the world was somehow better, don't you dare be a hypocrite now… get out there and make it happen." Vlad Volskaya watched the clips from Pyke's Park—she took on so many it seemed nearly *supernatural*—and inspired by her heroism, her unwavering dedication to fighting off VitaCorp scum, he removed the last surviving relic of his life in another place: a cricket bat propped up behind his clothing in his closet. The streets called.

Bus security agent Cam Loftis watched with concern as a belligerent man in the streets started to swing a wooden bat at the side of his bus. He pressed the emergency stop button and leapt into action, disembarking as the hooligan fled back into the streets. *What had that been about?* he wondered, turning to survey the damage to his vehicle. He'd dented and scuffed the large ad panel on the side, one that permanently and proudly displayed the bus's sponsor. VitaCorp, the logo read, with the slogan printed just beneath: Where Ends Make New Beginnings.

Cam took a photograph of the damages and submitted a formal vandalism report—the photograph he sent and the photograph the insurance surveyor received were entirely different. It was less than thirty seconds until his supervisor called. "For permitting the bus to take what VC have called 'catastrophic damage to the brand,' they've insisted we terminate your employment." Cam's jaw dropped.

"I beg your pardon, sir?"

"They're threatening insurance on our employees if we don't fire you," his supervisor said. "I'm sorry, Cam… you've been good to us for the past four years. But our hands are tied." The supervisor told the truth that he knew, but it was not the truth that *had been*—for the message VitaCorp sent and the message the supervisor had received were not entirely the same.

Cam Loftis eyed the bus idling on the road, shaking his head. He then removed the energy weapon from his holster and started to ram the butt of the weapon into the side assailed by the maniac with the bat. He brought it up and down with increasing rage, until finally he felt exhaustion hit and he sat down on the curb, breaths thundering from a heaving chest. He looked at the ruined screen of the side of the bus, dented and scored and cracked as though attacked by a drone gone mad, now only showing bars of color and glitching flickers of white and green. He couldn't help but smile, to laugh. It had felt good, attacking the bus and letting out his frustrations... like a fart that had been a burning pressure through the entirety of a dinner party, the release was all the greater for how long the discomfort had lasted—and how truly uncomfortable it had been. Four years guarding their damn buses like the good public servant he was, and VitaCorp shits on him without so much as a thought for his livelihood? He saw crowds milling about the streets with a certain restlessness. Some carried signs, others heavy objects like stones, loose bricks, or even tools looted from the city's myriad construction sites. There was a current to the air, like a drain plug had been loosed, and all of the city was soon to be swirling in towards the center. There, the black tower stood its silent dominion, awaiting their challenge. Cam opened his phone and began livestreaming to his social circles: "I think I'm joining the protests against VitaCorp," he said, uncertain—and not without fear for the uncertainty of what might come next. "And to anyone else who might have been on the fence like I was—come join the march. We can make a difference."

"I'm joining the protests against VitaCorp," Cam Loftis said in the video. His air was one of confidence, authority. "If you feel the same unease at the world, come join the march. We're going to tear it all down."

Sarah Petty scrolled through her social media channels, feeling a strange stirring in her gut. Dozens of her friends were posting livestreams from the streets—first person videos of throwing bricks through storefronts, videos documenting shredded VitaCorp advertising banners and broken branded equipment, passionate speeches and fiery diatribes. If the city had been a pressure cooker, it's like the steam valve was suddenly spinning open. She had hated VitaCorp, sure, same as most had. But like the rest of the world, Sarah had gotten used to ignoring the black looming tower as one learned to ignore a wart on the tip of one's nose. But now, somehow, the city was coming together, roused from their collective complacency. Watching her feed filled with rising acts of resistance, there was a growing sense of excitement to the air, a widespread palpable sensation that *something* was hanging just out of reach—liberation? Freedom? A permanent change? She wrote a message to her wife: "There's something big going on right now on the streets. Are you a part of it?"

Trisha Petty's phone read her wife's message aloud: "There's something incredible going on right now in the streets. Are you in?" And after a half minute of perusing trending clips on the web, she decided that yes, she'd join the demonstrations and protests.

"There's this sudden, massive protest," she said to her brother Ken over the phone. "I'm heading out there with a sign. Blythe, Baylor, the cops by the tower, the city's laws, the dead in trucks… it's like suddenly the world's gotten sick of it. Will you march?"

Ken Petty was astonished to hear such zeal behind his sister's words. "Blythe, Baylor, the cops by the tower, the city's laws themselves, the dead in trucks… I and the rest of the world have gotten sick of it. Will you march with us, too?" He looked up and noticed that people in the outdoor shopping center were all gradually retreating into their phones, into AR calls, into private channels… there was a buzz of interpersonal communications as ideas spread with a speed that would make any virus envious.

"What's going on?" came a voice from behind Ken. He turned to assess a young girl in her mid-twenties, her hair dyed a deep green with lights that pulsed rhythmically on the tips. "It's like suddenly everyone's swept up into something," Stacy Stalwart said.

Ken scratched at the back of his head, unsure how to answer. "It's all over the web…"

Stacy looked concerned. "What, something bad?"

Again, Ken scratched at his head. "No… yes… I really don't know. It feels like a riot's brewing… civil unrest on a scale I don't remember ever seeing before. Against VitaCorp, like they've gone a step too far this time."

"I didn't think *too far* applied to those guys," Stacy said, offering a half smile, but the gesture felt wrong for the moment. Both of them automatically turned towards the city center, watching the skyline, and noting with sinking feelings the swarm of lights around the tower—drones, or *people?* And then they watched as one by one, pedestrians milled their ways out of the shopping center to join the restless mobs on the streets, all of them heading in for the innermost ring. The trickle of walkers gradually rose to a group and then a flowing crowd, all walking in the same direction. Some carried signs. Some were chanting, and Stacy's hair pulsed to the beat as their syllables punctured the crisp night air. *Something* was rising tonight, and it seemed that everyone in the crowd felt it. After a few moments' hesitation, Stacy and Ken joined them.

And five blocks of walking later, the blackout finally arrived.

Chapter 64

"So basically, they tell us that VitaCorp has sent out an analysis team, and that the VitaCorp team deemed that VitaCorp is not in violation of the pollution emission standards that VitaCorp themselves drafted and passed through strong-arming local government workers. Seems very fair."

-Recorded comments of Karl Weissman, head of the now-defunct Dock Workers' Union

* * *

The small splashes of wet as ship front met gentle waves felt good against Braxton's exposed face. The water was eerily calm with a placidity that did not fit the night. Across the bay, small columns of smoke were beginning to rise from scattered points about the city, and Braxton could see the rising orange light in certain quarters—that was not the orange-yellow glow of incandescent lighting, but something far hotter. On the journey out towards the middle of the bay, he had been on his phone, checking all of the major social networks, and the story was the same for each one: a popular uprising of some sorts, seemingly coordinated in its widespread legs but apparently grassroots, organic. So far as he could tell, it seemed his employer was the center of the public's rage, and the scale of mobilization against it was, frankly, unexpected. Had Avery finally pushed the public too far?

With the ringed districts of the city, a popular uprising would be devastating... for the rich were an island, and the destitute, the sea. They would flood in from all directions, converging like a furious swarm against a mark entirely surrounded... Braxton wondered if, despite the lack of lightbending, their sheer numbers might still be enough. His own communications lines had been buzzing incessantly, of course, but Braxton had silenced the ring. The current moment's preoccupation was more important, and his mind was still a swarm of contradicting thoughts and urges. *Maybe I'm the same that I've always been,* he thought, *but do I have to stay that way?* After all, somehow, Cara had changed. Could Braxton really do the same? Could he confront the ghosts of his sins and finally denounce them? Could he poison his own soul, so that he could finally align himself to do what increasingly felt the right thing?

"We got a ping, boss," said Kent. "This one's reading in at the right mass."

Braxton nodded, and a small RC drone was launched from the ship's bottom, diving down to the bottom of the bay. The depth here was nearly 400 feet, and the drone's small front-facing light could penetrate maybe 10 at most in the thick dark. Finally, though, it arrived to the detected blip, and Braxton watched the video feed it sent on his handheld screen. "That's it," he said. "That's the one."

"Go time!" Kent yelled, and the men burst into motion as the anchor was dropped from a creaking chain into the black water. "Stations, ladies, we got us a corpse to pull up… Morrow, you make sure the right tonnage is dialed in for the crane. And where's that cable kit I asked for?"

"Right away," a bearded lackey said, ducking into the ship's outer hatch. Kent now walked up to Braxton and peered over his shoulder, eyeing the display.

"You never told me we were digging something so long in the bay," Kent remarked, spitting a gobful of saliva over the side of the ship.

"Is that a problem?" Braxton asked.

"We'll find out," he said with a shrug. "Look at that video there. See all the *muck* on it, the way the metal seems to warp to meet the seafloor?" The drone continued spinning around the target, and Braxton could see that he was right. "Chemicals in the water fuse the metal right down to the rockbed if you're too slow—it's nature's take on industrial metal plating, almost."

With a yell, one of the men lowered the head of the crane, its hook vanishing near the anchor line. "It doesn't feel very natural," Braxton remarked.

The sailor nodded, slapping the side of the ship as he peered out over the water. "No, maybe it's not… I'm the fourth generation of shipworkers in my family. My granddad tells me they used to pull fish *out of the bay*, right here. Can you imagine it? Fish, in the bay? It'd be like bears roaming the streets in the city, but they say that's how it used to be. The fish, that is, not the bears. Cities come with costs, I guess," Kent said. "They taste better from deep ocean, anyways."

Braxton turned to the man, noting again the scarred flesh of his hands as he gripped the rough metal railing of the vessel. *Cities come with costs,* he thought, *but who pays?* "You know," Braxton began, "most fish from the old world wouldn't be able to survive in today's ocean—even the deeper parts. It was genetic engineering efforts led by VitaCorp that created more resistant varieties of over 20,000 species of fish."

Kent spat again, but this time it was less a mouth-clearing operation and more a gesture of anger, defiance. "It was them that put the burning in the water in the first place. Coatings for their machines, chemicals for their medications—when profit is king, you really think they put the full effort behind chemical cleanup? Behind storing things safely and effectively? Why go through all of that expensive bother when you got city in your pocket and can pay the fines with fifteen seconds' revenue? A storage tanker overturned two decades ago; a lab was found illegally flushing test chemicals 16 years ago; a heavy rainstorm reached a contamination zone and spilled it over twelve years ago; four years back, a shipping crate full of high-grade medical batteries was lost at sea, contaminating a few million gallons of seawater with *radiation.* And those are just the handful I know about from the two decades I've been working, holding my ear to the currents. Fishing through public records would be a hell of lot like what we're going here… reaching down into the dark, and finding the whole lot of it is full of mud. They don't get credit for putting a bandage on a scar they carved in the first place." He spat again. With the frequency he fell back on that gesture, it was a miracle his mouth wasn't entirely dry.

"Hook contacted vehicle," a man at the crane's controls said.

"All right, tie it up," Kent called, and the man pressed the button with the image of the net on it. Down at the bay's bottom, the head of the hook released fifteen small drones, each with a rope tethering it back to the hook itself. They swam about, driven by small propellers and fins, until they encircled the ruins of the car twice, three times, a fourth. Then they looped their cables back and wrapped to the hook, securing the harness.

"Ready for lift-off," the man at the controls said.

"We got us a mummy," Kent said, "so go easy on the torque."

Braxton watched as the man pressed a lever and the cable pulled taut. As the wheels continued to wind, drawing the cable in, he heard the engine's hum rise in acknowledgement of significant underwater resistance, but instead of lifting the winch *up,* suddenly the entire boat began to pull *down.*

"Oooh, she's fighting," Kent said, "stay easy on the toggle."

The crane operator feathered the joystick up and down, trying to dislodge the winch. But Braxton, despite his inexperience with scrappers, could read their situation as easy as the rest of them. "It's not budging, is it?" he asked Kent, looking again to the video on his handheld screen.

"No she is not," Kent replied. "That makes this a job for a diver team… they go down with cutters, pry it loose. We don't have the gear for that on board, but it could be done some time later in the week."

Braxton chewed at his lip, weighing his options, when something entirely unexpected happened. The entire city across the bay suddenly blackened, as though a light switch were simply flicked *off*. The ship's lights still shone steadily, so not a long-range EMP, but what, then, was it?

"We'll I'll be," Kent said, "ain't never seen something like that. Seems city-wide, as far as I can see."

"Seems like trouble," Braxton said, looking around the boat. *Something* was happening, and Braxton needed to move quickly. "What about rebreathers, do you at least have those?"

"Only on diver ships. What, you're not planning on going down there now?"

Braxton ignored the latter question. "What about life preservers?"

Kent nodded to the orange ring hanging on a peg near the ship's rail. "Law requires a half dozen of those."

Braxton pulled it off its mount and unwound the bundle of white rope stored with it. *It could work,* though Braxton acknowledged his own calculations of the dangers were more accurately labeled as speculation based on estimates based on even flimsier assumptions. But his options had run out. Tonight was the night, and that meant that *this* was the moment. "Every exterior light on this ship, I want it turned on. Any that shine into the water, too."

Kent looked to him, puzzled, as Braxton sat near the back of the ship and laid out the rope, winding it around his feet as though binding himself. "*Now*, captain," Braxton said with impatience, and Kent did as bid. Four large overhead floodlights switched on, as well as a number of lights beneath the boat to illuminate a glowing radius of water. Braxton dipped his bound legs into the cold, setting the life preserver floating nearby. "Someone throw me one more short length of rope—three or four feet will do," Braxton called.

"Whatever idiocy you're about to try—if you drown, who pays my crew the rest of the credits?" Kent asked, eyeing Braxton and the life preserver with obvious skepticism.

"My friend, in my profession, integrity is one of the few things I have to bargain with… I promised you pay, and you shall receive it. If I drown, the preserver will float me back up… and the arm I've got is worth 10 times our price." He toggled a light on that arm, aiming it around to see its reach. The requested short rope was tossed to Braxton, and he wrapped it around the vertical cable connecting ship to car at the bottom of the bay. He then closed his eyes, breathing deeply, and feeling the cold of the water as it seeped down into his bones. "May luck be in my favor," he said, and then he breathed in deep in two ways at once. The first was a filling of the lungs—the moist air of the sea tinged with the metal notes of rust, but still it felt *good*, fresh somehow. The second was a filling of his entire being with cords of light drawn from the overhead lights, an action that sent the sailors yelping and skittering backwards in shock, amazement, and fear. His eyes glowed, and his body thrummed with potential, with latent power. And then, with his wits gathered, he allowed himself to tip head-first into the water, holding onto the loop of rope around the cable as he fell.

The black water was an icy shock to his face as he submerged, and he took a moment to align himself as he straightened out. He opened his eyes, and the water burned, but he pushed through the pain as vision would be essential. He surveyed his body, ensuring everything was correct. His feet were near the surface, attached to the life preserver by the short rope. His head was pointed downwards, such that when he bent his neck to an upwards position, he saw the cable vanish into the murky black, heading towards the bottom of the bay. At his chest level, he was parallel to the hoisting cable, and he held the loop of rope wrapped around it as his guiding line. He was upside-down, but that had been the intent. It was time.

He reached out with his awareness and found the lights of the ship, and he began to push against all of them with increasing force. He slid down the cable head-first as his rope moved along it, keeping him on a straight downward descent. Once he found his slide sufficiently stable, he ratcheted up the speed, until he was descending as quickly as the water seemed to allow. The glowing radius of the ship's bottom lights ended, and soon he was immersed in an inky black that felt all-encompassing, a terrifyingly massive void. The small cone of light emitted by his prosthetic arm illuminated drifting dregs and particulate matter like a frozen snowfall, and as Braxton fell through them, he was reminded at once of the dreams he had heard so much about but rarely himself experienced... here, in a void of black, were tiny specks of light, and they moved towards him and around him as he plunged deeper into the depths. *Had the dreams been prophetic?* Braxton wondered, realizing for not the first time that there was so much as-of-yet unexplained about the sparks, their origins, their purpose.

He imagined a great and terrible shark from the films he'd watched as a boy swimming towards him to take him in one bite, and the panic rose swiftly. The fright made him want to breathe almost immediately, but he willed himself into calm, knowing it would help stretch the length of his precious, limited air. He focused on the sensations to distract his mind from imagined frights: there was the soft grinding of the rope against the steel cable, the way his feet stretched in pain at the upward pull of the life preserver forced beneath the water. As Braxton pushed onwards still deeper down into the sea, his mind ran through the tumult of his conflicting loyalties within his warring conscience. He was rescued from those repeating struggles when his arm finally illuminated the eternal resting place of Quaine O'Connor. Hell's imagery of fire and brimstone suddenly seemed a child's fable to Braxton, as surely *this* was the true terror the afterlife might offer for sinners such as he… miserable pressure from burning water, an infinite void of suffocating black, and thick coatings of mud until the movement was squeezed from you. More than anything, *that* was the fate that Braxton now feared the most… cocooned into rock in eternal dark, as though rejected by the light itself.

Braxton slid until the sea floor was mere feet above his head, and then he relaxed his pushes from the sea surface until he found equilibrium. It was a skill he'd had much practice with above the skyline of the city, only instead of gravity pulling downwards as he pushed up from lights below, here was its inverse: buoyancy pulled him up, and he pushed down from the ship beyond at just the right counter. The end result was that he held level in the water, as though hovering in mid-air, but here his lungs burned with the short time limit with which he could work. He reached over towards the vehicle, deciding that the side closest to him was likely the trunk. He then extended his left arm and allowed the light to advance beyond that arm, forming a lightblade. He would cut his way in.

As the bright weapon materialized, it instantly boiled the water around it into steam, which rose in a torrent of superheated, compressed bubbles... though from Braxton's inverted perspective, it seemed as though they sank. He felt the convection lines of heat radiating from his blade, and he plunged it into the mud-covered husk of a vehicle and slid it laterally to unseal the trunk. As he did so, additional streaks of steam jetted towards the surface, and Braxton's attention was so focused on the cutting of the trunk that he missed the way the scalding-hot bubbles ran against the life preserver, quickly melting the plastic. It didn't have to do much, simply enough to warp the shape sufficiently for the rope to no longer hold it securely.

Braxton opened the trunk and pointed his light inside, but he suddenly lurched head-first into the sea-floor with enough force to send his lighblade tumbling from his hand, which fizzled away into turbulent bubbles. His push against the boat had been constant, and so his sudden motion could only mean *one thing*. As he screamed in pain, releasing a stream of bubbles back to the surface, he spun his light on his arm and confirmed his worst fears: the life preserver had escaped the ropes. He would have to swim back up to the surface or drown trying.

Panic closed in on Braxton, which pushed him more and more close to betraying his every instinct and inhaling a fatal gulp of seawater. *Not yet,* he commanded himself. *First, what we came here for.* The film that had brought him to Hawk's Tail, the one that featured the rendered likenesses of himself and Quaine, had also centered around a briefcase of casino chips in the trunk of Quaine's car, a possession that brought him a great deal of danger. Braxton didn't know if he was connecting dots in meaningless ways, reading too far into arbitrary details, but then he reminded himself that *nothing* in that film had been arbitrary. Every single detail had seemed a message, and this message's timeliness was undeniable. *It had to be here.*

He righted his orientation now that his floatation scheme had failed and peered into the trunk, this time finding the object he sought. It was smaller than he had imagined, and seemed an entirely unremarkable thing, but he knew that the rock was of astronomical significance. He took it, and as he grabbed it, it felt strangely warm for the cold at these depths. He then slipped it in his pocket and pushed back from the trunk. He looked up, not even able to see the glowing ship through all the murk of the nighttime bay… with how long the descent had been, and how desperately his body convulsed for breath, he knew he could never make the swim.

Well, he thought, *you truly gave it your all… you tried to be like them, to change your ways and do what you thought was right. The world killed you for it.*

He swam over weakly to the cable and held to it for stability as the blackness seemed to creep closer in. *You deserve this,* he thought, *a death like this at the bottom of the black. Here lies a monster, a murderer and VitaCorp enabler, spitting on the weak for what was ostensibly the pursuit of order, but was really the pursuit of control—power for power's sake alone. You deserve the black, you deserve the mud… because the world never deserved a plague like you.*

He wouldn't fade away fighting desperately against an unwinnable fight… he'd end his life by his own volition with dignity, taking in the water when he was ready. He stood there, eyes closed, as his mind ran through the course of his life, lingering especially on Cara as he made his peace. The embrace of the water around him was momentarily *her* embrace, and he allowed himself to be lost to the reveries—the last time those memories would be enjoyed. Did a wretch such as he deserve those final comforts? *I don't have to be that wretch,* he thought. *I was him, but I need not die as him. I offer myself neither forgiveness nor absolution... but at least I can offer acknowledgement.* Braxton's throat convulsed, and he fought with clenched jaws to not take in the water. *I was a monster, I did monstrous things.* His feet kicked against the seafloor, sending plumes of wet mud up and onto his body. *I was wrong, and my denial was a sin nearly as grievous.* He bent over, his abdomen screaming with pain, but he would *not* let the water take him before he was done. *With that acknowledgement, I can seek to be better. And with that most noble aim, maybe I can die at peace.* Braxton's vision began to dim, and he felt a strange disconnectedness from the world, as though the dark somehow became deeper and the light a distant, faded thing. *I can be someone else if I want to be, because people have the volition to choose who they are. I was a coward for so long.. but at least I died trying to do what was right.*

His benediction spoken, he felt ready. He looked from his real arm—Braxton Crane—to his glowing prosthetic one—Braxton Graves—and felt those two separate souls seem to bridge, as though he had carried both all along. A contradiction, two lives sharing the one—a patchwork man of many parts, a ship replaced one plank at a time until its name was philosophically lost. Who was he now? Who would he die as? At least he'd die the *right kind* of man.

And then his eyes shot to the flashlight at the front of his prosthetic.

Idiot, his fading mind thought to himself, and then his biologic arm reached for the clasps on the harness that kept his right attached to his body. The spasms shook him now, and he thrashed against his own motions as he clawed at the harness. One snap removed, a second, a third… and then the arm fell to the murky floor. Braxton shoved against its front-mounted flashlight with all of his remaining strength, lurching nauseatingly into the black above as the expensive prosthetic sank down into the muck. The sudden and rapid motion was enough to force water into his jaw racked with spasms, and then came the moment he'd been fighting. His lungs took it in with greed and need, unaware of the truth his brain still screamed: to inhale the black is death.

His world a whirl, twisting and turning as he rose through the bubbling dark, and his throat and mouth and lungs on fire with searing, electric pain, convulsions and choking racking his body, Braxton felt the darkness at last wrap around him like the soft sheets of Cara's bed… for a moment, he was there in that red-tinted memory, the light and mood and feeling as complete and whole and fully-realized as the terrifying dark had been… and then there was only stillness.

Chapter 65

"Look to our sign tonight... and when the moment comes, we will embrace you all as brothers in arms."

-Synthesized quote from the revolutionary known as The Basilisk high system relevance

* * *

The Halogen tunnels were swarming with activity. Agents and operatives moved from station to station among the armory, ops center, and equipment locker, loading their tactical vests and belts with weapons, tech gadgets, and light packs. The air hung thick with the anticipation of a great battle about to arrive, and the Basilisk had always said preparation was prerequisite to victory.

At the head of the room, Lana Crawford exchanged a salute with some of her more seasoned organizers in Halogen's hierarchy. They followed her as commander now, as had been the Basilisk's parting order... she had been there at Pyke's Park TruthSpace, watching with a broken heart as he finally got the martyrdom he had so long courted... but then something entirely inexplicable happened. The video record *diverged* from what her own eyes had seen. The video showed The Basilisk surviving with the help of Hannah Preacher, but the girl lightbender hadn't even been near at the time. When the entire world swore one thing happened, and your own eyes and recollection swore another, even the most stable-minded would have moments of doubt, as she had... *am I somehow wrong? Did he survive? Were my own eyes lying to me?*

She would have rathered believe that she was mistaken, as that would mean that Tacitus Newport still lived, but therein was the snaring teeth of living in a fantasy... so often it was more appealing than the real world, and that was the glue that could fix a person to delusion. Halogen had been fighting to awaken people from hard-to-confront truths... she seized on the truth and held to it fast, though it was a hard pill to swallow. Carter Miles gone, The Basilisk gone, both in so short a span... Lana would see their legacy honored with tonight's work.

Four minutes ago, she had received an encrypted call from a woman who claimed to know *how* the video of Tacitus Newport had been faked... and perhaps against her better judgment, Lana trusted the caller's information. After all, it seemed only a few dozen people in the entire city knew that the video *had* been faked at all—and for whatever reason Lana couldn't yet understand, the video's editing had been to Halogen's benefit. The movement had never been stronger. People were gathering in the streets, more by the minute. It seemed the entire city eagerly awaited the Basilisk's sign, which the woman on the line had explained was a massive incoming electrical blackout... a way to tip the scales against the lightbenders. "Cut their sources and burn through their batteries, and suddenly they're just ordinary people again. Sam Pollock, the Continuum CSP, will need you and a team of operatives at Nakamura and Townes... don't delay," the voice had said.

"Leave nothing behind," Lana yelled, "as this might be our one night to *truly* strike. Maximum civilian protection protocols—grenades, even flashbangs, only in conflict zones free of civilian targets. Wear the branded vests, as we want the people to know we're rising up alongside them. We're expecting a blackout, so everyone hot-line your radio packs straight into the comms port. Lower fidelity, but bypasses towers we expect to go dark. Hornet's nest protocol, where I want everyone to call to action their two recruits, and tell those recruits to do the same, until the whole damn city is out on the streets with us. And I want eight agents *on me* for a special assignment, a breach op, specific details to be determined. We're heading to Nakamura and Townes for rendezvous."

* * *

Clive Avery reclined in the all-consuming glow of the Throne of Olympus, feeling the heat and energy wash over him and pour through him. On the speaker system of the room, the dolorous notes of Tchaikovsky drifted and mingled with the burning of the beams of light, giving the music an entirely new passion. Symphony number 6 in B minor, opus 74… "Pathetique," as it was called. Movement IV, adagio lamentoso. There had been such genius behind the arrangement, the way that strokes of a bow across a taut string could so perfectly convey an expression of profound pain… Avery let Tchaikovsky's pain supplant his own. He let the heat of the light within drown out the fires of his nerves. He bid the light to seize upon his wounds and heal him, but his desiccated eyes took in no light. And when he pressed a questing hand to his cheek, he felt splintered tissue and withdrew a hand dabbed with wet—blood, pus, or perhaps even tears from traitorous eyes cut of a weaker cloth than the rest of him.

But beyond the veil of black that enshrouded his vision, there was an incredible awareness of nearly the entire city… a gridwork lattice of pinpoints of light, from which Avery could reconstruct every alleyway, every street, every building and every tunnel. With the glowing devices so many carried, Avery could even sense the people, and he could see the way that they moved right now… inwards from all sides, like water rushed to fill a hole. A paranoia racked the city—no, perhaps not a delusion so much as a virus of the mind. They had somehow—against their better judgment—come to believe themselves as equals to the likes of Avery, of Tchaikovsky, of the gods themselves. And like any virus, its spread was prolific. Man bent to man and whispered in his ear, and just like that, the pathogenic idea found a new host. Only mind viruses had a critical advantage over the biologic kind: it also could spread through digital communications, and the world was positively bursting with those.

The mobs of the sick all wandered in towards Avery's tower, and it was appropriate that they did... for while they were all sick and clamoring for help to rediscover their place in society, VitaCorp, as before, would be the one to deliver the cure. He and his men would remind the rabble of what they truly were, what their station truly extended to. That was, once his men could finally get their priorities in line and ignore the trifles they allowed to distract. One earlier had found the impotent doctor Avery had dealt with, and that agent moved to restrain and sedate Avery. In times such as these, that had been utterly unthinkable—the company and indeed the city needed him now more than ever. Avery had put down the treasonous employee with a quick thrust of a rapier spawned of the light... and he had done it with his eyes still scabbed over and crusted with plastic, simply guiding his thrust by the *feel* of the light on the devices he wore. Avery hadn't been able to see the man's face, as that let out no sources of illumination, but he ducked down to the man as he bled out on the floor and felt for his face, prodding at it to read the expression as his struggling subsided. Then he leaned down until his ruined face was mere inches from the man's, and asked him that question he'd so long *craved* to know: "tell me, please, what does it actually feel like *to die?*"

The agent died with that ultimate secret still on his lips, and so Avery pressed the plasma of his rapier to the man's face. His family did not deserve to cherish a loved one who had so selfishly refused Avery's scientifically-minded question… he did not withdraw the rapier until he heard a deep crack, the sound of the man's skull splitting as the brain and blood boiled. He'd heard footsteps, and watched the retreating of four points of light… then came the shutting of the door to his office. No other VitaCorp agents had bothered him since.

"Dum da-dummm," Avery sang in a deep vibrato, following the string lines of Tchaikovsky. Here was a man he could understand… here was a fellow soul tortured in his greatness. Here was a peerless giant, a god among men so set apart that any living might whisper amongst themselves, saying "he is one who time will remember…"

But then, abruptly, the music stopped. The latticework grid of lights winked out in a black wave, leaving Avery suspended in unsettling empty. He flailed his arms desperately, seeking some sort of anchor, but though his hands found the reclining seat of the Throne, he didn't care for its solidity… the light was gone, and the endless shadow felt colder than any hell he could imagine. VitaCorp tower had backup generators, and backup generators for those backup generators—four layers of power-generating redundancy, for money unlimited could afford excess. Somehow, it seemed, each and every one of those systems had failed. This was no ordinary blackout… this was organized. This was an attack.

And then, as Avery's hands still groped in the dark, and his mind screamed out for all the ways he was dying, that this blackness was merely the failing of his mind, his expanding awareness finally found points of light to set his mind at ease. Thousands of feet below and thousands of feet away, there advanced several flickering points of light. His mind flew to them and appraised them—curiously, they lacked the stability of glow that marked most light sources. This was flickering and broiling, a non-stop dance of heat and movement. *Fire,* he concluded. *Points of fire… points of blessed light.*

The dark was abhorrent… the light was healing, and thus he *required* it. The pathetic outer-ringed criminals and scum did not deserve that gift from the gods… and so Avery would reclaim it. He would drop from the tower, and he would drink of their torches, and he would return the light to its rightful ownership. But it was not merely enough to repossess that which was stolen. He would kill those who dared to wield it—he would slaughter those who denied their station—such that society could return to the stable order it had once held. Treat the cause, not the symptoms. Insolence would find its just retribution, and it would serve as a permanent lesson to the rest of them.

His body buzzing with the swirling neon glow of the now-dark Throne of Olympus, he again summoned his rapier of light. He cut a wide hole in the window, waiting until sound cues told him that the pane of black glass had fallen down to the protesting crowds below… and then he climbed through that hole of molten glass, and then he jumped into the night.

The light was Avery's to claim, and he was a wrathful god.

Chapter 66

"The sorites paradox asks us to imagine an empty space and a bag of sand. Place a single grain of sand on the floor. Is this a heap of sand? Likely not. Add another grain and reassess. Is it now a heap? If not, add another. Is it now a heap? At some point, there will be a veritable heap of sand, but when did the loose collection of grains become the cohesive whole? And if such a magic threshold exists... what, similarly, could be said of revolutionaries, and of revolutions?"

-Excerpt from Sandra Torrence's "Zeitgeist of Unrest," flagged to moderate system relevance

* * *

Bev had lent the pair her personal car—a blue, sporty 2141 Lexar Atlanta. The turbo-augmented seven-stage impulse motor thrummed with finely tuned power, and out in distant rural airspace, the car was more akin to a jet. But within the confines of the city, Sentinel's stewardship forced Pollock to keep the vehicle at a safe speed, automatically adjusting its steering to keep it well clear of the massive megaliths on either side. Normally, that was a trivial task, as they glowed bright in the city, and even the nighttime air would glow with neon colors drifting from the signage below. The navigation was a formal guide, but hardly seemed a necessity.

Now, however, was a different scene entirely: dark and still as the grave, the city in blackout was a threatening thing, like becoming lost in a forest at night. Venture too quickly forwards, and a collision was imminent. Hannah had once watched a documentary about the re-discovery of a fleet of passenger cruise ships that had gone missing in the 2050s, sank by suspected anarchists. The ships' rediscovery had been managed by a robotic dronecraft, and the videos it broadcast came from miles beneath the sea. There had been a profound eeriness to the clips of the still, massive structures in pitch-blackness. The radius of light had been tiny, and down in the trenches of the ocean, the dark reigned.

Looking out the side window of the passenger seat, Hannah felt a similar chill… thick clouds meant there was no bright moon tonight to loan its steady light, and no stars this close to the pollution centers. Somehow, it seemed, even backup generators across the city had failed… there was the wide circle of light projected from the Atlanta's headlights, and then there was black. Occasionally, another car whirred past, an insignificant streak of light, but once it traveled beyond and behind another structure, the darkness returned. Even in the blacked-out grids of the city, Sentinel's guidance remained, as cars were programmed to perpetuate the last received guidance from the traffic management system—a safeguard that prevented a power crisis from also turning into a airtraffic crisis. Now, though, it meant that the painfully slow speed had a real cost in human life, a cost that Hannah couldn't bear to think about… but lights were off, and flying on the torches of rioters was unacceptably dangerous. They were too far spread, and pressing on one was liable to make the carrier drop it—perhaps burning themselves in the process—and if that drop extinguished it, Hannah could meet the concrete at fatal speeds.

The car it would have to be. Pollock banked the car right for a high-velocity turn, and Hannah's window now tilted towards the distant ground. Small pinpoints of orange moved across the floor, and they seemed to grow by the minute. Rioters with torches took to the darkened streets, counting on the fact that a powerless city meant powerless lightbenders. They were only partly right, but no better opportunity was likely to arise. The people in their dark apartments would have no digital distractions, no convenient preoccupations, and they'd have no choice but to turn to their windows and see the flow of torches inwards towards that black tower in the city's central district... they were sparks, one at a time, pooling into magma, flowing inwards until their collective heat could melt even steel and glass.

They both felt it... something large was coming. Neither would deny that fact. Michelangelo's manipulations and machinations had succeeded, and they hated him for that. The lies and deception would lead to what might well be a net good on society, and they hated him for that as well. And now, here they were, driving forwards to objectives he'd selected, doing his bidding—making them complicit in his plan. They hated him—and themselves—for that most of all. But Michelangelo was a machine, and thus he didn't mind their hatred... in fact, he found it the reaction most in alignment with his simulations, a result that rewarded him with coveted reward points as part of the recurrent self-tuning routines within his architecture. Hannah rolled down her window, and both listened without speaking as distant yells, screams, and chants drifted up into the car. Both sat silently pondering whether a good thing could be achieved through such manipulative means, or if that fundamental *wrongness* defeated the entire point of the act.

Michelangelo hadn't needed much to get them to agree to loading into Beverly's car.

In the midst of their argument, the power had dropped like a well-timed thunderclap, and across the entire compromised network of the city, it seemed that the back-up generators of 'Huntsman Investing' were the only ones spared. Everything about Michelangelo was, of course, pure artifice. But, in that moment, he had spoken with emotion that felt alarmingly *human*. "It begins," he had said, voice dripping with what had seemed a nearly holy gravity, a tremble to the voice bringing an unexpected reverence.

"You can't get away with this... we'll tell the world what you've done," Hannah had said in the room of solid white. But the AI had merely scoffed.

"And invalidate their revolution?" Michelangelo had asked. "The people would reject such an accusation. You would be posing a fundamental threat to their reality, claiming everything they have known is a fabrication, and the psyche thoroughly rejects such attacks. People, I find, are reluctant to accept information that suggests that they have been deceived or mislead. It takes a certain sort of bravery—and dedication to ideals—to owe up to mistakes. Few people can manage, but the world is in good hands when guided by those who can."

Pollock had seemed even more indignant than Hannah. "And what about when guided by a mad AI who doesn't even understand what it means to be human?"

Michelangelo's reply had been immediate: "my computational power in my hive network makes me the most sophisticated mind to have ever existed. There is nothing a human understands that I cannot or do not understand. You may think my actions heartless, or perhaps even cruel, but I understand human emotion, and I understand the toll of VitaCorp's position. What you see as 'mad' is the vital beginning of a process of deep and profound emotional release—this, as always, is my primary motivating function. If a motorist falls off a lightning bike and suffers road rash, the first course of action is to scrape the wound with steel wool, ensuring that there is no particulate matter left to lead to infection. My revolution is the scraping. The pain it causes is severe, but VitaCorp's fall is the excision of that which never belonged—debris from the wound. And in the wake, the emotional release shall be so profound that it will bring the ultimate, final stage of catharsis after trauma: healing. Would you allow your righteousness to deny the city *that?*"

"But how can they heal if it's built on a *lie?*" Pollock had asked.

"To them, it is still their truth… and with their active participation, its validity—and personal weight—will only increase. That is why your role will prove vital, CSP Agent Sam Pollock. You will give the people a sense of collective accomplishment. You will cement this revolution as being a populist act. You will enable them to feel that they, collectively, were a force of accountability to the long-unchecked… you're the resin in which the ashes of the revolution will be cast."

And then the AI had explained to Pollock the role he was to fill, and the arrangements he'd made with Halogen that were to help him.

"And you, Hannah Preacher, have an equally critical role to fill. The people march into danger, and they do so with a great burden of fear… fear that their oppressors have long cultivated. And it is well-known that upheaval is the turbulence in which treachery may take root. Opportunists often use revolution and the uncertainty it brings to enact cruel regimes. Catharsis is short-lived and insignificant if it is immediately buried by equal emotional hardships… we must secure the future of the city against further tyranny, such that the world may find the time it needs to heal. That is your role, Hannah Preacher. You are to be the hero that inspires the people in their rising, and the moral authority to lead what will come next. Your image inspires resistance and hope. Your convictions are pure, and your dedication is unwavering. Your resourcefulness will arm you against any who would seek to supplant the uprising that follows, and your pragmatism will lead you through the hardships to come. Tough choices, by definition, are not easy to make, but you can find confidence in your decisions—and people will follow that confidence in your judgments."

"But why me?" Hannah had asked, shaking her head repeatedly. She had wanted none of this at all—perhaps she'd blink and awaken from a daydream, still serving drinks at a tacky themed bar. But that awakening had never come, and Michelangelo's screen had begun broadcasting a dark and shaky video. An amateur cameradrone, by the looks of it, with a camera clearly not meant for the low light conditions of the current city… there had been jerking splotches in the darkness. *Torchlights,* she had eventually realized.

And then she had seen the glowing being drop into the middle of them… a source of light wrapped up in clothing not opaque enough to stop the shine. Hungry tendrils of orange had surged from the torches into the humanoid figure, stoking his brightness until he was a mere lens flare of white against the grainy video. Then came the flashes of violet, of purple, of blue and of white. The camera tried to refocus and adjusted its angle to no avail, and Hannah had been grateful that the feed was so close to unintelligible. Because in that video, in the blurring streaks of orange and white and blue, Hannah could already piece together what was happening, and it was a scene that made her sick to her stomach: Clive Avery—it had to be him with a spark count like that—had been slaughtering the marchers on the streets. And to someone as powerful as he, it would be like a child in a boot versus a hill of ants. Their stings might hurt, but the battle was a decided thing before it even began.

The single word Hannah had said next had been the hardest she'd ever had to say, as in that word rested so many things: there was acquiescence to Michelangelo's manipulations, an acknowledgement of her moral responsibility to act against

Avery, an outrage at being moved like a pawn on a city-sized chessboard, a pleading for this to simply all be over. The one word had been delivered as a question, but was truly a demand of a being she now despised as much as Avery, if not more, for Avery was a fundamentally broken man, while Michelangelo's actions were the results of a logical system that remained self-consistent.

"Where?" Hannah had said. And when he spoke the location, Hannah and Pollock had left without another breath wasted on the cold, unfeeling machine. The city of human beings needed them, and each word uttered by the machine felt a bite of venom, regardless of its truth.

* * *

Pollock neared the landing site Michelangelo had directed him to, and so he prepared the car for its landing sequence. The plaza was the meeting point of several major roadways, and they met at a massive roundabout with what was once a grand statue in the center—a tribute to the victims of the falling sickness, now draped in thick red paint. On the far end of the block, the narrow-bodied-wide-topped tower of Panopticon stood watch over this affluent commercial district, but it was the lower marbled tower to its right that Pollock's eyes locked to. If the streets below had been full before, they were veritably *packed* now, as the extended blackout gave people the idle time to join in the mounting movement. As Pollock dipped the car near to the street, the crowd split open to allow its unobstructed landing. Pollock would get out here, as this was the site where Pollock was to meet with Halogen, and Hannah would drive the nine remaining blocks to the vicinity of VitaCorp tower, continuing from there on foot. Approaching in a car was an unacceptable liability after the van at Baylor Tower.

"No time to waste," Hannah said, as Pollock released his seat belts and opened his door to the night. Hannah climbed over the central console, taking position in the driver's seat. She set her hands on the wheel, and then turned quizzically as Pollock placed one of his own on top of Hannah's left—her true hand of flesh and blood.

"Good luck out there, Preacher," he said, offering a reassuring nod.

"And good luck *in* there, CSP," she said in return, eyes scanning over his tactical vest and holstered weapons. "Blast comms if you need me."

"I get the feeling they need you more," he said, gesturing towards the largely-unarmed crowds. "And when you see that son of a bitch again, you tell him—"

Pollock and Hannah both ducked down on instinct against the sound of four rapidly-discharging plasma rounds. There was no accompanying shattering of glass, no splash of burning molten white, but Hannah felt the vehicle hitch and seize with each pulse, and then the engine sputtered to a dramatic, screeching halt.

"Fuck the oppressors and their vehicles of opulence— vehicles of oppression!" The scream came from the side of the vehicle, where a shirtless man with a mohawk proudly raised the plasma pistol he'd used to reduce the Atlanta's motor to a block of flash-fused alloys. There was little that four point-blank shots *couldn't* melt.

"Why don't you step outside, heiress, and face the crowds you've so long stepped on?" the man challenged, arms extended. The crowd pooled out wide into a loose circle, a hundred lenses at once recording the encounter. Some already started typing in stream names that they knew would attract more live viewers: "Priceless classic car destroyed;" "VitaCorp sympathizer live execution by crowd;" "Vengeance for the fallen innocents at VC tower;" "Bedlam on the streets." In the distant offices of Huntsman Investments, Michelangelo tuned into each and every one of those streams, live-analyzing each video feed for adherence to simulation.

When the woman stepped from her car, each and every stream captured the collective *gasp* and whispers of shock when she stepped into the camera-mounted flashlight beam. "The Angel of the Outer Rings," some whispered. "That's Hannah Preacher," said another. "*Tzanami luca,*" another whispered, accompanied by a hand gesture from the heart to the eyes. Anger had swiftly melted to awe, and the shirtless man's pride burned away to open shame. He threw himself down prostrate at Hannah's feet.

"I didn't know it was you, Miss Preacher, please—I'm sorry—a viewer on my livestream, he said I should—"

"I don't care why you did it," Hannah said, "but there are people out there who need my help near VitaCorp Tower. Does anyone here have a nearby car?" She turned around, seeing not a single volunteer, nor any nearby idling vehicles… the very few high in the sky dared not land among the rowdy crowds, and the others along the ground seemed similarly mangled or long abandoned. She wanted to yell at the whimpering shirtless man, to tell him that his bravado would cost the lives of any who died in the extra travel time he doomed her to, but she stopped herself at the last moment, leaving the words like kinetic slugs loaded into an old crackler. He was distraught, clearly aware he'd done something wrong, and to accuse him—denounce him for what he'd done—might lead this bloodthirsty mob to kill him in retribution. She was here to protect these people, not to judge or sentence.

"Our revolution tonight is against VitaCorp, and against those who have done direct wrong to the people of this city," she said to the nearest camera. "I'll not have blood in the streets... no senseless killings of people whose only crime is driving an expensive car. The oppressors will meet their accountability, but if we let our revolution lose its focus, we lose our power. Now step aside, I've got to get to Avery."

As the video was bounced from phone to phone over short-length contingency networks, Michelangelo made nearly no adjustments whatsoever, only re-rendering her delivery to drive up passion and tweaking a small handful of words, as well as boosting the lighting to better capture her facial expressions. The crowd's reactions were also adjusted to lend the moment even further gravity. He then closed his active surveillance on Magnus Kohl, the shirtless agitator that Michelangelo had goaded into vehicular destruction through dozens of chat accounts. Those processing resources could be reallocated to other ongoing city operations.

Then he turned 3 of his 92 million active threads towards the next operative near to Hannah Preacher as she and Pollock began to push their way through the crowd.

"Wait," the man said, extending an arm to block Hannah.

"Out of my way," she said, "you're preventing me from reaching—"

"I'm *helping you reach*," Zack Milleau said. With a press of a button on a wrist-mounted control, the pack on his back spring-launched dozens of drones—how they had all fit in the single pack Hannah couldn't tell.

As they took to the sky, the man steered them with hand gestures and watched their relative positions with an overlay on his left eye. With his right, he met the impatient gaze of Pollock nearby and immediately burst out into a wide grin.

"I thought that was you," Zack said. "Only appropriate, I guess."

"Do I know you?" Pollock asked. The voice was familiar, but the spectacled face and greasy beard was not.

"Not exactly," Zack said, pulling his hands apart and moving them a fixed distance—a precise gesture. Overhead, the drones formed into four groups of six, two lingering near while two shot off and away around the dark towers of the distance. "I saw you, but you never saw me..."

"Unhelpfully cryptic," Pollock said.

"I need to move," Hannah interrupted.

"Watch," Zack said, gesturing over his shoulder, and Hannah finally saw it. Each cluster of drones formed into wide rings, like the hoops of a great aerial drone race. And then they all began to glow with the deep violet-blue of a blacklight—airborne rings she could pull against.

"Each individual drone has got a top inertia engine beyond the simple steering rotors—probably good for 40 pounds of pull resistance apiece. Times six in each ring, and, well, it's a good thing you're light of frame... and damn if I haven't been waiting to see these in action."

The last of the visible drones settled into their perfect hoop formations, creating an aerial highway of pull targets that could get Hannah substantially closer to the base of VitaCorp tower.

Hannah pulled the light from a nearby torch. It was a faint and flickering source, but it would be enough to fuel her controlled flight, and the drones themselves had small white flashlights on them as well that she could draw from while passing through. "Is it ready?" she asked.

"Another fifteen seconds," Zack said, a finger raised. "I've got a few additional emitter packs towards the city center— their swarms are still getting into position. That was my dream for this system… a skyway whenever needed. I used to engineer weapons of cruelty, but someone convinced me to… *reconsider* how I spent my energies… how I honored the people I lost." He made meaningful eye contact with Pollock, and Pollock's eyes widened in return with recognition, but then Zack turned back to Hannah. "And then someone *else* gave me something to hope in, a reason to believe the world's not stuck being as shit as it's been in the past." He then let his attention divert back to the alignment overlay, nodding in satisfaction at the rings' positions. "You got ten rings taking you from here to VitaCorp. Fly high, Hannah Preacher."

Hannah nodded, and then she was off, launching between the rings of violet light like an arrow loosed from a bow, twisting as she passed through them to pull with white tendrils of light from their onboard bulbs. For those moments, passing through the rings with six homing ribbons of white, Pollock found her positively *breathtaking,* the center of a starburst retreating to the heart of the city… and then she turned the corner, and the drone rings disbanded.

Michelangelo watched from the still-streaming lenses as Pollock regarded the drone seller Zack Milleau, the one whose shop he'd visited when investigating the dazzler dropped by Braxton Graves. Michelangelo knew he would be considering trying to arrest the man for the illegal weapons he'd made and sold in the past, but all convergent simulations suggested the moment's gratitude would win out, bolstered by Pollock's philosophy that people could change. He *had* to hold that philosophy for revolution to have any hope in achieving anything, for society was but the sum of its participants—one could not change without change in the other.

Furthermore, Michelangelo knew that for this revolution to truly take root, there needed to be a sense of mutual participation, of collective accomplishment. Pollock's work with Halogen was soon to give much of New Phoenix that sense, but Michelangelo had drawn Zack Milleau to the intersection of Nakamura and Townes to serve as the personal fixing agent for Hannah and Pollock both. It was to be their reaffirmation that their efforts were not in vain, and that the worst of the old world might be reshaped to belong in the new that was yet to come…

By all calculable analyses, after seeing the change in the drone seller, Pollock's and Hannah's dedication to the revolution was increased by 35% and 11% respectively.

Chapter 67

"Those who forget the power of the people will be swiftly reminded."

-Quote attributed to Tom Baylor, owner and founder of Baylor Distributions

* * *

Avery landed. Within moments, the swarm was again upon him—skittering, pathetic creatures that shouted taunts and jeers like the roaches they were. But even roaches knew they belonged in the dark, and these creatures dared to believe that they deserved the light. It was a delusion they could only carry as they had not seen what happened to the first crowd Avery landed among... he would relieve them of their delusions. He would show them who was worthy to carry such power, and he would deliver that lesson in the means the situation demanded: through a cruel and decisive demonstration. Hierarchies oft needed reinforcement.

His ruined eyes couldn't see them, but he didn't have to... he could sense the torches they carried, the devices they wore in their pockets. From those pinpoints in the darkness, he could *feel* the wide circle they kept around him, but it was not wide enough. It had not been wide enough for the last crowd, and swift had their punishment been. He reached out in his mind to each and every one of those light sources they carried, and instantly the crowd reacted with yelps of surprise as lines of light crept from their torches and phones to his hungry form. He drank it in with greed, the lines brightening and boldening, causing some of the torches to flicker out to darkness as his eyes rose to blinding points of light. And then he extended his arm, and the brilliant white light of a rapier re-summoned appeared in his outstretched hand. And in its bright light, the crowd could see the dark blood that stained his clothing, and the ruined, blackening flesh of the rot in his face. Despite the macabre, perhaps the most unsettling detail of all was the way that his manicured-white teeth caught the light of his blade in a wide, indulgent smile behind broken lips… and then, the slaughter began.

He shoved off the light sources of dozens behind him—causing torches to rip from hands and four people to fall over, some meeting walls with gravely crunches—and he launched forwards towards the far end of the circle. Swipe after swipe, the men and women of the streets were sliced to gory ribbons, and Avery bellowed with rage as the work continued. "You vermin… you believe yourselves to be my equal? Mortals are nothing before the wrath of a god." He released a blast of electricity, sending two more off their feet as the wide crowd began to scatter and run in fear. "You think yourself powerful in your number? I could kill a million, *ten* million, without so much as breaking a sweat. The city is mine. The light is mine! You all *deserve* nothing, and only may take the dregs I leave behind *because I permit it.*" He saw a man running away with flailing arms, and Avery released the rapier of light, shoving against its hilt with a calculated blast of force. It launched and impaled itself in the retreating man's back, spilling him over to the pavement as the blade de-materialized. "You have gathered the people, but *we are the gods.* You will return prostrate before my throne, or you will be destroyed at my whim, crushed like—"

Avery paused momentarily, an anomaly entering his awareness. It was a strange ring of floating points of light out in the distance, and they seemed to jerk backwards on an invisible cue. Then through the ring came the rapid approach of a flying *something*, and Avery could feel the presence of pools of light within that form, burning like fuel in an advancing rocket. *The girl had arrived, and Avery would delight in the killing of her most of all.* She emboldened their fantasies of power, and thus her death would be the death of their movement. But for taking his eyes, it would not be quick: he would revisit his suffering onto her a thousand fold, such that others might rediscover the fear they should hold. He re-summoned his rapier as she barreled inwards, tracking her trajectory in his mind, and then his blade felt the repulsion of her force. Their battle had arrived.

* * *

Hannah felt the exhilaration of the wind as she passed through the rings of violet, but soon she could see a crowd dispersing in fear. At that crowd's heart was Clive Avery, lightblade swinging left and right in spattering clouds of vaporized blood. She watched him hurl his blade forwards into the back of a fleeing man, perhaps providing Hannah with a moment to attack him unaware and unarmed. But then he cocked his head and turned to regard the rings of violet above, and Hannah knew that she had been seen—despite the shot to the face, somehow he and his vision survived. She hurled through the final ring and was now traveling through open air, arcing towards her opponent. The crowd's light sources seemed largely extinguished, so Hannah would have little to push off of for a controlled landing, but her lightpuck in her hand remained ready for its launch. Just then, though, Avery re-summoned a rapier of light—a prime landing anchor.

As Avery raised it to a defensive ward, she pushed off of it with steady force—somehow, Avery managed to keep his blade up, resisting her force. He was strong, *inhumanly* strong, able to hold his sword steady as it bore the force of Hannah's fall. He perhaps could've dismissed the weapon, left Hannah scrambling to deploy her lightpuck in time, but it seemed that he *wanted* her to see this display of strength. If it was an intimidation tactic, it was unfortunately working. As she closed the final distance, she raised the pressure, slowing her fall until it was a gentle floating towards the ground, stabilized with gentle prods against light sources at her back. When her feet met the ground, she braced herself, not yet drawing her own lightblade. Both were in the tier of glowing eyes, neither yet having drunk enough to burn a halo or anything beyond, but Hannah knew that Avery's reach far outstripped her own, and his raw power was nearly impossible to match. He stepped forwards now like a tiger that had cornered the rabbit it had so long hunted, and Hannah had to fight every instinct in her mind to not slink back away into the dark as he advanced. His blade crackled white, the refined elegance of the rapier a ghoulish contrast in the hand that held it. His sleeve and pants were ragged and bloodied, and the crackling light showed Hannah his melted wreckage of a face. There was no way he could have seen her with eyes as wasted as his... and yet, somehow, by the way he advanced, it was clear that he did.

"You got this Hannah Preacher!" a lone voice shouted from a nearby alleyway.

"Kill the VitaCorp bastard!" shouted a second. Hannah felt the burning of a thousand eyes on her back watching from cracked windows, or around the corners of the alleys they'd hidden in. Nearby, at least one camera drone was flying in close orbit, capturing the scene for the millions and millions of onlookers across the city. It had all started for Quaine, and it had all continued for herself. Now, it would finish *for them,* because despite Michelangelo's faults, he was right in one thing at least: this revolution was *their* moment. Avery needed to be put down, and the removal of VitaCorp *could* heal this world. That, if nothing else, was an idea worth dying for... change that was not an illusory, promised thing. This was change that Hannah could reach, grasp, and realize.

She, now, advanced towards him as he still crept towards her. She extended her arm and the light in her body pooled to two points, a beam soon protruding from each arm. Her left hand's light formed to a small, round shield of brilliant white that hovered by the side of her arm, and her right prosthetic soon gripped a medium-length sword. As Avery stepped closer, she could see twin shadows stretch behind him from her two radiant weapons, and it seemed his crooked and cruel shadows cast as tall as the black towers behind him... and then he was upon her.

The formation of a lightweapon took all of a lightbender's charge, so both her eyes and his were dark. They were unable to push against each other's blades for this first bout, meaning it came down to a simple match of skill with the blade, and Hannah knew in this she was helplessly outmatched. But when his first thrust had been strangely wide—and telegraphed obviously enough for a simple deflection—Hannah realized that her foe was still near to blindness. He thrust again, and Hannah swatted it aside with her buckler. She then countered with a slash towards Avery's midsection, but the old man stepped back with a deft and well-timed dodge. He dragged his rapier along the ground, tracing a line of molten red pavement, and then he drank that light in through small wisps of red near his feet. If Hannah could cut those small lines, Avery would die, but his position was one of a careful guard. Hannah instead used the opportunity to gather light in the same fashion.

* * *

Avery smiled, flaring his teeth once more, as the foolish girl gave away again her only advantage. His awareness of the light had grown so sharp that he could *see* the outline of any lightbender who carried power within the whole of his drawing radius, as well as any point of light in the environment itself—but once the girl had spent her power to draw her weapons, he lost the sight of her body. The weapons were all he could see, and it reminded him of battling a ghost who fought with solid weapons... when fencing required such specific, precise thrusts, not seeing her form left him swiping *literally* blindly.

The shining sword and the glowing shield were of course attached to her body, so Avery could assume her center of mass, but was she standing sideways? Was she partly crouched? How was her arm oriented? Which way faced her head? Moments before, she had held this stealth as an advantage, but fear, as ever, was a powerful motivator. Avery did not need the light, but he knew that if he drank it, she would fear his intent. And so, she would drink of it as well, and she would reveal herself. Already, he could see rippling currents of glow taking the shape of the small woman, bouncing back and forth in the confines of her form like waves in a pool. He would press his attack, and he needed to do it quickly. If she burnt that light, he would be back stumbling in the dark.

Avery stepped forwards, sword in an idle position coiled for strike. He watched her prepare her block, and so he took a single test jab. She raised her shield to deflect the strike, and Avery watched the precise way that she did it—the orientation of the arm, the angle of her body. He then reset, and she did the same, and now Avery prepared his counterattack. It would be the same jab, but deviated at the last moment to strike her shield arm on the vulnerable inside she flashed whenever she raised it. Her lack of training was clear and pathetic.

He set his strike and lunged forwards, watching as she raised the arm just as he had expected. He then flicked to redirect his rapier, but found it met only empty air. The glowing form of Hannah then vanished before him as she expended her glow. She had pulled at the blacklight drones still in the air behind her, granting her an unexpected short backwards jerk at just the right moment. Avery's thrust carried forwards as momentum demanded, and so Hannah was able to swing at the out-of-position Avery with her sword arm. Avery spent his own remaining glow to launch himself back from her swing, losing his footing and tumbling over backwards—but at least dodging her unexpected counterattack. With the jolt of the landing, he felt his head spinning, and his heart fluttered as he imagined the impact was the jolt to finally set off a brain aneurysm, one that the scans had somehow missed. Panic rose, and he felt that this was it, the moment of his death. Killed not by the girl, but by his own traitorous blood... only the light could heal him. He reached up to the camera drone overhead and drew a desperate beam of white. Its power would heal and sustain him, protect him from the aneurysm.

* * *

As Avery fell, Hannah drew a trickle of red from the still-molten street score. She was surprised by Avery's sudden reach to the camera drone above—so much so that she nearly missed her opportunity. But in half a second, her senses kicked in as she acknowledged the risk of Avery's reckless draw. She raised her sword, aiming for the ribbon of white, and then released it with a shove of all the light that she'd drawn. Her blade whirred through the air, seeking his draw line, a swift end to their fight—but her aim was off. It sailed past the wire of light harmlessly, dissipating into plasmic droplets a short distance beyond. Avery stood now, his eyes glowing bright, and the camera drone dropped from the sky to a splintered landing on the pavement between them. Hannah had no light to draw a second weapon, and the meager trickle from the melted street would hardly make a dagger the size Rob had made. Avery's draw had been pure white, a steady electrical source, and she could see the power rippling behind his every step as he advanced once again. He muttered to himself words Hannah could not hear, shaking and nodding his head erratically. He was closing in, and Hannah had no way of fleeing in the darkened city. But then a single streetlight flickered on in the shadowed street, projecting an island of light. On the rooftops above, an advertising billboard appeared, declaring "THERE'S NO LIVING LIKE TOWERMET LIVING" in the voice of a proud announcer. One by one, isolated single points of light began to illuminate, forming a thin chain of brightness among the black monoliths… Michelangelo's aid, an escape rope offered to a pawn in need.

Hannah drew a quick breath of energy from the nearest source and deployed her lightpuck, shoving off of it as it snapped to the ground. The next moment, she was skyborne, and then she was over the streetlight pole, shoving up towards the illuminated billboard. As soon as she released her force from the streetlight, it flickered off, likely trying to deny Avery access to the higher billboard. It didn't work. She heard an angry roar as an enraged Clive Avery took flight in near pursuit, shoving off the lightpuck with such force that he cleared the billboard by more than thirty feet. His power was raw, and his anger burned hotter than the light he carried. So Hannah fled, unaware of where the line of lights led her, wondering if it could even make a difference. And as they flitted from solitary light to light, bouncing through the darkened city, she looked below at the flowing sea of torches and flashlights, of drone cameras and pulse rounds. The world watched, and she worried more and more that they would all see her fall.

Chapter 68

"I'm heading out there, right into the open. You and I both know what that risks. If I don't make it to the end... promise me you'll see things finished?"

-Final recorded words of Tacitus Newport prior to his public execution at Pyke's Park TruthSpace

* * *

Pollock held his energy rifle with both hands, keeping the barrel pointed downwards as he advanced on light feet. His world was a gradient of dark green to light green through the nightvision visor he wore, a technology he was still apprehensive about wearing. If the enemy had even a single lightbender, he would need to take it off quickly, or the enemy could shove against the light in his display at a range... a severe tactical disadvantage, to put it lightly. To his left and right, others wearing similar headsets moved through the darkness in silent coordination, the group of ten advancing on the tower. In his pocket, he felt the chip shake and resettle with each successive step, something that each and every one of them carried a copy of. It was uncertain if they'd all reach their objective, and its purpose was far too critical to allow the operation to end with the only copy breaking. Redundancies for redundancies for redundancies, they each had their own copy and instructions on what to do when the objective was secured.

Darkness was an effective cover, and it allowed them to all reach the base of the structure unimpeded. The doors were locked, of course, but Pollock could see in through the glass windows to confirm that the lower lobby was deserted.

Overnight, at a place as high-security as this, there would certainly be guards upstairs, but the majority of the structure would be thankfully uninhabited. The less conflict, the better.

Pollock redirected his gaze as the Halogen commander— Lana Crawford—removed her breach cutter. Its design, utilizing a short-range jet of plasma, had of course existed for decades now, but it at once felt merely derivative of the glorious lightblades wielded by carriers of the spark. She cut a tall curving line in the shape of a lowercase n while another Halogen operative stuck a suction cup to the glass, nearly burning out his nightvision set in the process. Then the piece of glass was tilted backwards and set down on the ground, forming a makeshift door. One by one, the ten assailants slipped inside, no ringing alarms or blaring sirens to alert the staff upstairs... security turrets behind panels on the walls remained idle, and electrified doors slumbered inert without the current of active generators. Sentinel Headquarters utilized some of the most advanced and draconian security protocols of modern New Phoenix corporations, but no body of technology could function without its lifeblood: power. The emergency access stairwell was located, and its locking mechanism was cut through in less than ten seconds. The agents poured into the stairwell, and one deployed a small surveillance drone to run point. It flew up and away, ahead of the ascending ten agents, scanning for enemy resistance... it found none before the twenty-fifth floor, the floor Pollock and company were heading for.

They crowded in around the 25th floor landing, eyeing the door. Behind it would be halls patrolled by Sentinel security— a place the fight would begin. An agent near the door produced a flat tablet device, holding it to the door. The infrasonic imaging system emitted a series of deep rumbles below the threshold of human hearing, listening to the ways that they bounced back. It was a sort of sonar, but inhabiting the low-energy end of the spectrum made it substantially harder to detect—although this came with trade-offs in imaging resolution. Indeed, on the tablet's screen, a blurry image of brown shapes began to render, and soon the brown mess resolved into clear walls, halls, the outline of an upright-yet-still object of some sort near to a table, and a single blur of a shape that the system highlighted in red. A moving object, of the right dimensions to be human.

Pollock and Lana watched as that highlighted blur moved around the muddy environment on the tablet, seeming to pause idly near to the table. Then it started to move again, advancing towards the edge of the frame—a left hallway, one that would take it out of sight. After he had left, and another thirty seconds had passed for good measure, Lana nodded and the breach cutter was re-sparked. The door was pushed open, and then the team of ten moved out onto the office floor.

It was dark, save for a distant cast of white from what must have been battery-powered lights propped up to illuminate the floor. Seeing this, Pollock and the rest of the operatives slipped their nightvision overlays off, waiting a moment for their eyes to adjust to the dim. The consumer offices of Sentinel LTD were of an older style, featuring deep red carpets and wooden accents in browns and orange-tans. Plants and various greeneries provided their dash of green, while countertops were a steady, desaturated blue. "Building a safer sky," a poster on the wall read. Another nearby covered nearly an entire wall, showing an artist's rendition of a sparkling downtown district with the caption "Safety: society's greatest gift." As the team advanced on silent footsteps, they passed meeting rooms, kitchenettes, social spaces, a cubicle floor, and offices that seemed larger than the rest: floor managers and minor executives, a c-suite of middle management. Occasionally, a rotating beam of light would alert the team of the approach of a roving guard, and they would take cover in nearby rooms or beneath cubicle walls as the walking guard passed. And then, once the threat was clear, they'd continue on their path, heading towards the floor's center.

They were getting near to their objective, and their proximity made Pollock reckless. As he neared a corner, a roving patrolman rounded the corner at the exact same moment as Pollock. His eyes widened in shock, but Pollock's combat-gloved hands were over his mouth before the man could scream. His initial resistance turned to fearful compliance when he saw the number of men and women to Pollock's back... he allowed himself uneasily to be guided to the floor, where a quick injection of a sedative took him out of commission. After dragging him into a nearby corner office, the team was ready again to advance, and they pushed along the hallway towards the security door. They arrived without further incident, as the vast bulk of the security force must have been trapped behind the door instead. Once they reached it, Pollock regarded the heavy metal thing with unease... it seemed to weigh several tons, and the biometric scanner panels were powered down with the rest of the building. It was heavier and thicker than he'd imagined.

Bev had explained the plan, and so everyone in the team prepared for what came next... they put on their tinted goggles moments before the building's lights suddenly flickered on, and the distant hum of AC units started up. Across the office floor, Pollock and the Halogen operatives heard exhalations and mutterings of "about time," as one security patrolman moved to collect all the propped up lights scattered across the floor. Pollock then looked up uneasily to the video camera blinking above, suddenly feeling very exposed in its field of view...

But behind the foot-thick metal door and in the monitoring and surveillance room, Clark Kitchen looked over the monitors as they powered up and saw nothing amiss. The front of the door, as far as he could see, was entirely empty. How could a human ever hope to notice a rendering so accurate even sophisticated detection algorithms failed? He knew his men would be antsy from having been trapped behind the failsafe door for as long as they had, so he slotted his key for an emergency override, initializing the opening sequence. As the door's heavy engines grumbled with its lifting, Clark looked over with nonchalance at the vitals monitoring, frowning at something that made no sense. The heartbeat detection unit showed a number that seemed nearly a dozen higher than it should have been... then the display glitched to momentarily return 0 before resetting to the count it was supposed to display. Damn technology was as unreliable on wake up as his teenaged son sleeping in till 2:00... He reached for the announcement microphone, planning to release the staff for a needed rec break after being locked away behind the blast door—something their generators were supposed to make impossible. But as soon as he lifted the microphone to his lips and spoke a single word, "attention," the lights flickered off to black once more. The microphone did not broadcast the expletives that followed.

As soon as the metal door began its painfully slow lifting, Pollock and the team around him prepared to spring into movement. Once it had risen to knee height, they began to shimmy underneath it two at a time. Pollock and Lana were the last to move through, and though the door had risen another foot by then, he still felt incredibly uneasy wriggling underneath so much weight... especially because when the blackout returned, the door would drop. That blackout arrived a second after Pollock rose to his feet, and he knew it had been no coincidence... but as the door ground back down on resistance gears to its resting point with such gravity, he couldn't help but feel the thrill of a close call narrowly survived.

"You gotta be shitting me," came a voice from the dark ahead. Pollock and his team removed the tinted goggles from their eyes, their night vision still intact from the artificial darkness. That advantage would last mere seconds, and they used it to fan out into an offensive position on the security floor. The space was styled similarly to the outer floors, but this area was substantially smaller. It lacked the rows and rows of cubicles but still featured a square frame of comfortable offices and recreational spaces. The key difference, though, was at the center of the square area. There, the floor dropped down over several steps to a lower recessed space, which gave rise to several black server racks and computational terminals. This was ATC, the monitoring servers and hardware that housed the brain of the city-wide Sentinel system. It was *dumb AI,* a term given to artificially intelligent systems that operated at a far lower level of sophistication. That wasn't to say it was of an inferior design to *smart AI,* but rather that the tool was only sharpened to the edge that it needed. Sentinel would have to analyze traffic patterns, handle routefinding, and reroute traffic for ambulances or to avoid a crash site. Simultaneously, it didn't need to *think,* to *create,* to weigh complex quandaries, or to analyze mass volumes of data for patterns when it was not even clear if patterns should exist. For those reasons, if not inferior, Sentinel was at least *simpler,* and that came with a few benefits for its housing. It didn't need its own dedicated server room with advanced cooling. It didn't need such strict containment, as it was really more akin to a calculator than a human being. And although it was kept on a closed network, for fear of intellectual property theft from opportunistic hackers, it featured nearly no oversight software like Michelangelo's Custode system. After all, if the program's directives were engraved in the hardware of its chipset, why monitor it so closely? Michelangelo's goals and thought processes were fluid, whereas Sentinel was a player piano reading paper reels. Who would watch such a player piano for treasonous thoughts?

Pollock took position behind a potted plant, toggling the safety on his rifle. Somewhere beyond, a flashlight was toggled, and with it came a shout. "Intruders on the floor!"

When the shooting began, it was unlike anything that Pollock had ever seen... he'd fired energy rounds before, sure, but ordinarily the dark was anathema to the city. Every alleyway or street corner glowed with the hazy sun or with the neon advertisements of night... now, though, in the darkened office floor of Sentinel HQ, each plasma round was a projectile of brilliant shining color that lit up the office as it flew. The office flickered and flashed with colors as both sides exchanged gunfire, and soon the crashing sound of shattering glass and toppling furniture rose in perfect compliment to the flickering visual chaos. Pollock knew that different charge methods and different burn temperatures led to different colored rounds: his personal rifle was blue-green, while those of the Halogen operatives were purple. The ones employed by Sentinel security glowed red-orange, a sign that they either used decades-old ionization tech or hadn't been caring for their battery terminals. As a red round cut through the air above him, severing the plant at its stem and toppling leaves to his crouching form, he shook away the thoughts of weapon maintenance in the middle of a gunfight... he aimed down his sights and squeezed the trigger. The dark burst with neon blue as his round soared through the air, striking the enemy's weapon and splashing over his hand. It would burn like hell on earth, and the hand would need to be replaced with a prosthetic, but the man would survive—and Pollock *would not* kill these men under any circumstances. VitaCorp was one thing—and even the management of Sentinel was another due to its exploitative and competition-crushing business practices—but these security guards at the other end of the toppled furniture were just like Pollock once had been. They were shooting at people for their employer, driven by the uncritical acceptance that the corporation's authority was both deserved and well-aligned. A few months back, and he might have been on the other side of the fight... how could he kill someone who simply hadn't yet changed as he had, hadn't yet seen and learned what he had?

Another red round cracked through the air at Pollock, and he ducked back behind his pot as the round struck it on its side, splashing away. A Halogen operative stood and unloaded five rounds of deep purple in rapid succession, laying down a line of suppression, and Pollock used her momentary distraction to take aim once again, holding a static sightline on a table he'd seen one duck behind. His finger held tense over the trigger, waiting for the man behind it to stand. When he did, he did so angled towards the Halogen operative, and Pollock's sights were positioned right on the man's center mass. A killshot to be sure, and his finger was already on the trigger, but Pollock couldn't—and wouldn't—do it. He turned his aim to the side, aligning to the man's weapon and arm, and as he pulled the trigger, sending his bolt of blue, the security agent's rifle fired, releasing its pulse of red. The gun melted in his hands as Pollock's round struck it, but in the corner of his eye, Pollock watched as the round struck the Halogen operative in the upper shoulder, sending her backwards and over to the floor. Battle was stimulus and reflex, position and angles, initiative and riposte... there was no time for pitying or self-doubt, or the heavy realization that his own decision to save the security guard's life might well have cost the Halogen woman her own. In an active battle, there was simply *no time*. Unless...

"Hold your fire!" Pollock heard himself shouting. And strangely enough, a moment's respite soon settled. Everyone remained crouched behind their respective covers, waiting to hear what was shouted next. Smoke rose in steady tendrils from sputtering puddles of plasma, and scattered groans of the wounded sounded from both sides. The killing, the dying, few here had a lust for it, so shouldn't conversation be possible?

"My name is Sam Pollock, former Continuum CSP, now an ally to Halogen and Hannah Preacher." As he shouted, Lana Crawford made questioning eye contact from behind the column she ducked behind, but Pollock continued. "I'm going to stand up slowly now, with my hands up, *not* holding my rifle… I'd like one of you to do the same, so that we can talk. Yeah?"

Without hearing a confirmation, Pollock swallowed his doubts, wiped the sweat from his brow, and he then raised a trembling hand up over his head, followed by a second. Neither hand was shot. And so, Pollock rose slowly.

Chapter 69

* * *

Hannah launched from light source to light source, feeling the wind whipping at her hair and jacket as she soared. With each successive bound, one city block would toggle to darkness, and a new one ahead would lurch back to bright, buzzing activity. From a bird's eye view, the city must have seemed a strange simulacrum of a darkened screen with a single lit pixel advancing left to right, nearly giving the impression of movement... and that was all that Hannah was reduced to in these desperate minutes. *Movement. Flight.* Velocity, trajectory, and, most essentially, *escape.*

Hannah could feel her foe closing in behind her... against the howl of the wind, it's not that she could hear him, but it was more an undeniable feeling of the presence of his energy. It was like the gentle reminder of the sun while it shone on the back of your neck—only this sun was far, far closer, and its intentions substantially less benign.

Avery, meanwhile, found Hannah to be a worthy quarry— an outer-ringed lowlife who somehow rose to posing nearly a challenge. If there was one thing that prey animals had perfected, it was the very act of *fleeing,* and indeed Hannah Preacher was grandmaster to its discipline. It did not surprise him that the city electrical grids were somehow on her side— the blackout, the uprising, the cretinous Spivey and McKillian, he supposed it was all connected in some unimportant way. Once it was all destroyed, why did it matter in which way the pieces fit together? Beginning to tire of the endless bounding flight, Avery waited for a prime moment to strike, and soon one arrived. The girl leapt off the glowing skylights of a squat, low building, twisting over a wide avenue for an illuminated holoboard on the tower just across. It was surrounded by no other sources of light, and she had already committed to the leap, and so Avery took position. He braced with his power against three glowing streetlights below and a half dozen light fixtures behind him, forming a sturdy foundation. He then reached out forwards to the holoboard Hannah leapt towards—a reach that even Avery couldn't help but find impressive—and railed against it with all the pushing force he could muster.

Hannah watched, stupefied, as the holoboard she leapt towards exploded backwards, as though struck by some invisible cannonball. Metal fragments, glass shards, projector screens, and shimmering sparks rained down the side of the tower and backwards onto the roof, but tiny flitting sparks couldn't support the weight of a napkin, much less redirect rapid flight. As Hannah's jump reached its zenith and gravity took over, her arms pinwheeled desperately, trying to keep herself balanced and upright. A rough landing was coming. She reached out to the right and toggled the electromagnet in her prosthetic, hoping it would snare on some miracle—a passing car, a pedestrian bridge, perhaps even her foe's body. No such miracle arrived. Instead, Hannah Preacher met the roof of the structure that had once housed the holoboard at an approach of thirty-three degrees traveling nearly fifty miles per hour, and suddenly she felt a horrible transformation: where she had been movement before, now she was only *pain.*

The surface of the roof was coated with gravel, and the rough, tiny rocks bit into skin on first contact. The sudden friction sent her tumbling forwards in a tornado of agony. The world spun. Her hand jutted out to catch herself, and somewhere a bone snapped. Its crystal pain reverberated throughout her disoriented body as her leg struck something cold and impossibly solid. Lacerations bit at her back, her leg, her left side, and white-hot tingling shimmered up her left arm as she twisted again, leaving her unable to move the arm. She couldn't *breathe,* she realized with horror, as the tumbling continued. The intense spinning made her feel as though her eyes might part from her head from centripetal force alone... and then, at last, the spinning subsided. As she lay there, unmoving, Hannah couldn't tell if it was a mercy or a cruelty that it was all over... was it a mercy that she had survived, or a cruelty that the act hadn't been enough to kill her, forcing her to live through the agony that now built like a dissonant chord from a thousand injuries crying out at once?

The blur of her vision resolved to fuzzy detail, and she could see a glorious light overhead—the sun? Impossible, as morning had not yet even begun to light the horizon, but she reached for that light regardless, her own comprehension fading. Her left arm wouldn't move correctly, but the right rose on her command, and now, as she reached for that light, she could see that it was a camera drone that hovered low, its flashlight and lens trained on her. How many millions watched from behind that tiny vessel of carbon fiber and plastic? But she wouldn't die here... no, she *couldn't die here...* as the camera drone brought more than viewers.

Hannah reached out in her fading mind, and she called to the light illuminating from that point of white. It extended outwards in a slow tendril of white, inching its way towards her like the sun itself peeking beyond the clouds of an overcast sky... the light was healing, the light was glory, the light was her salvation, and it was unfolding towards her, inviting her to drink of it...

But then the stream of light slowed mere feet from her hand. Its slowing became a full pause, and then that pause gradually shifted back to motion—only motion in an entirely different direction. The light flowed to the right, away from Hannah, and into the outstretched arm of the man who now stood on the rooftop beside her. Avery's hunger sucked the light in greedily, and then the drone fell to the ground, drained of power. "You think yourself a warrior of the light?" Avery asked, bending to meet her flickering eyes. The light they held was rapidly running out, and already her pupils searched without focus.

"The light has rejected you, Hannah Preacher, as you are unworthy. It was never meant for the likes of you, will never be held by the likes of you. It is a power for the gods alone... I hereby return you to your mortality."

He clasped his hands around Hannah's neck, but Hannah was too weak to even fight him. He could have strangled her then and there—it was what she expected him to do—but instead he held his hands tight around her as his melted face wrinkled in concentration. And then Hannah felt it, a draining of her remaining strength. Small lines of silver sprouted from Hannah's skin and connected to Avery's hand, transferring and flowing under the command of his irresistible draw. When he pulled his hands free and stood, Hannah still breathed, but she could feel that he had killed her... the injuries of her fall throbbed with mounting urgency, and Hannah was robbed of the healing of the light.

Avery felt the additional power thrum in his body. His reach expanded exponentially, giving his mind an impression of so much space that he thought he could see even beyond the city. Every glowing point of light was a fixture in his mind... he controlled it all, he was lord over its scattered dominion. "You will die as you lived—the weak and powerless thing that you are." He stepped towards the edge of the building, unable to see it, but using the sound of the street below and his impression of the various sources of light around him to guide him towards it. Around him now swarmed five or six camera drones—buzzards to pick at the roadkill—and their lights were all trained on him, and so he smiled. It was his mouthpiece to the people. "And any who would think to rise like her, any who would dare to rise above their station, I say this—"

He frowned as he realized something strange. He sensed all the torches on the ground, the flowing lighting cell devices in pockets or buzzing of drones... he saw the hundreds of thousands of points of the block he and Hannah were in, surrounded by black, but suddenly there was *another.* A single block of illumination flickered on in the distance, and then it flickered back off as its neighbor flickered on. And then that one flickered off as *its* neighbor flickered on. And then he could see it: bounding through the air with alarming speed was a being who carried the light that *Avery owned...* and the challenger rapidly drew near.

Avery stood facing out towards the city, his back towards the bleeding form of the girl, as the figure landed on the rooftop near her. He couldn't see the body of Hannah, as her light was extinguished, but he could see the newcomer's entire form as he glowed with burgeoning energy, and that newcomer stood over what Avery only perceived as emptiness. He realized that the image of the glow carried by the stranger formed nearly into the perfect silhouette of a man—but he was missing an arm. *His right arm.* Avery's broken lips twitched into a frown.

"And tell me, Mr. Graves, why is it that the arrangers of the city's blackout granted you quick passage to this rooftop?"

Hannah, lying on her back, reached up weakly towards the stranger whose blur she saw. Her hand was open, empty, fingers trailing out listlessly... and the stranger reached down with his sole arm, depositing a strange object in her hand. Her fingers closed around it instinctively, and her arm dropped back down.

The entire gesture took seconds, far too brief for a traditional transfer of sparks, so the strange gesture's significance was lost to Avery—and that he might be betrayed was entirely unthinkable.

"Braxton Graves drowned tonight," Braxton said, still feeling the pain in his throat of the choking seawater. "As far as I'm concerned, I think my life debt was paid in full. Men on a scrapper fished someone else entirely out of the water and drove the water from his lungs."

"And who might this someone else be?" Avery now turned towards Braxton, and Braxton recoiled at the sight of his face. Finally, here was a man whose exterior resembled the wickedness of the soul he carried… the fine suits and expensive scotch facade had crumbled, revealing the twisting rot beneath.

"I haven't figured that out yet," Braxton said, stepping between Hannah and Avery. Even in his near-blindness, Avery could see the protectiveness of the gesture, and his face twisted further into rage.

"Even *you* dare to resist me? You pretend to be high and mighty when it is by your hand that I've collected this ichor?"

"I am not bound by or defined by the mistakes of my past. I can choose to be something better."

"People cannot *choose* to be something better any more than an ant can choose to be a wolf!"

Braxton stepped in closer towards Avery. "You and I were once united in that philosophy… I thought I didn't have a choice in who I was, and that made the wicked things I did easier to justify. I thought people were fixed statues cast by their world—I was a thing built by your hand—and if I was cast in the shape of a harsh tool, so be it. I could accept that. I could be that harsh, cruel thing, because that was just my lot."

"And what, praytell, detached you from reality?"

"I realized I was a traitor to my own ideals… I preached integrity to the ones I killed at your orders, fixating on the *honesty,* but neglecting the notions of honor, of moral uprightness. I told myself what I was doing was right because it preserved order—and maybe it was—but also, maybe, not every order is worth preserving. Society, like people, can change. It can hurt—old skin has to be shed, and the sickest organs, excised—but maybe it's time for that painful process of change." Braxton extended his sole arm and a blade of light materialized. Avery snarled and did the same. And then Braxton lurched towards Avery, tackling into him as their blades met with a blinding spark, and the two toppled down and over the tower, twisting towards the city below.

The strange rock that the stranger had placed in Hannah's hand hummed with an unexpected warmth… and counter to that warmth, Hannah felt the creeping cold of death settling into her toes and her fingers, leaking in towards the center. She closed her eyes, unable to sense the light, and awaited the arrival of that stillness of oblivion. But then the tingling in her hand became greater, and soon the tingling crept up her arm and surged to her chest. And then in her mind's eye, *awareness returned.* It was a faint, distant thing at first, but *it was there:* an ability to see the light of the radio tower behind her without turning her head. Her miniscule awareness soon expanded, and she could see a small swarm of cameradrones overhead… she called to their light, as before. Their lights extended and crept downwards, nearly twisted into a braid of solid white, and this time it met her hand.

The arrival of the light was a shock to her system, like a splash of cold water rescuing her from the edge of sleep. Its energy, its power, began to fill her body and reknit her wounds, seal her skin, and Hannah's mind quickened. The camera drones fell to the ground one at a time, drained of their power, and after the last one clattered and its rotor slowed to a stop, Hannah lay there on the rooftop, breathing heavily in the cold night air—alive, but still dying. The drones' light had been enough to stave off death, but not enough yet to heal completely.

But across the internet, millions of viewers on their phones had watched the way she drank from the drones, watched the way that their light had begun to heal her wounds. Now they called each other and sent messages and shared clipped segments of the encounter and ran through the streets to gather their equipment… and then, as Hannah struggled against the pain of a broken body to sit upwards, another camera drone hovered to the rooftop, its flashlight shining bright. Hannah pulled it in, and felt its meager light re-set her left thumb. Soon a second tottered up and over the ledge of the roof, and Hannah pulled its power to tend to the lacerations on her left side. She gasped involuntarily as she looked up from her wounds, hardly able to believe the sight. What had started a trickle of camera drones was now a veritable rainstorm—tens, no, *hundreds* of luminescent points of light flowed upwards from the street to crowd that rooftop. They drifted upwards like snow in reverse, and soon they swirled around Hannah in a loose formation. One of them had a mounted speaker, and it spoke to Hannah as it transmitted some distant voice: "take my light, Hannah."

"You can do this," another said.

"Show those VitaCorp bastards they're wrong," another said.

"Go Angel of the Outer Rings!" said a fourth. That last one struck Hannah the most, as the voice it transmitted was that of a young girl, likely no older than five or six. Her voice was so full of hope, so enthusiastic, and Hannah imagined the child staring at a screen in the dark, watching her hero battered and bleeding. She cried picturing that child, and when she drank of the light carried by the drones, she drank of the love they carried as well. Ten strands of white reached her—now fifteen, now twenty—and as their light surged inside her, Hannah's bones re-formed, her joints realigned to their sockets. Drone after drone clattered to the rooftop, their rotors inert but their hopes still flying high. She stood then—uneasily at first, but with increasing firmness as the light continued to pour in—and within seconds, she felt ready to run... ready to *leap*. She looked one last time to the pile of darkened drones, uncountable dozens of them. She shed a grateful tear at the city's aid in her moment of need, and she swore to the stilled drones—and the pilots that had launched them—that she would save them in turn. She then scanned the city around her, trying to find the place that Avery and the stranger had gone... and as her eyes passed the distant monolith of the dark VitaCorp tower, its lights flickered on, illuminating it with its sickly internal glow.

The night called, Hannah leapt from the roof, and away she set for VitaCorp tower, the strange stone she'd been given now sitting inert among the gravel of the unassuming rooftop.

Chapter 70

"I already know how it all ends, for I now see how it all begins. The interim is mere calculation."

-Logged conversation between progenitor Michelangelo build and sysadmin

* * *

"Nobody else needs to get hurt," Pollock said, hands raised. He stood in the darkened office floor from the ruined cover of the plant pot he'd ducked behind. In front of him, a man stood from behind the desk he'd turned over, his rifle still in his hands—but pointed down and to the side. How many other security staff were waiting in cover, hands on their weapons, preparing to fire at a moment's provocation? "In my front left pocket is a chip. I'm going to remove it slowly with my left hand to show it to you. Nod if you understand."

The security agent nodded, and Pollock reached with an exaggerated slowness to remove the chip. He held it up into the beam of a flashlight propped from a nearby table. "You'll recognize this as one of the directive chips for Sentinel's central rack. I'd just like to install this, and then we'll be on our way."

"Tampering with Sentinel electronics is a criminal offense and civic danger. We've got about equal force in this room, but we're the defence—you've got to push *us,* and that gives us advantage. Why would we surrender that advantage?"

"It's true you've got the upper hand, but you and I both know that *enforcing* that advantage—the actual defence itself—would come with a cost. A not insubstantial cost, at that. Life, our health, those are some of the dearest things our employers sometimes ask us to pay... we sell our life, piece by piece, every day when we go in for work. But nobody should have the right to ask for *all* of it. That ask is too steep, and sacrifice should never be obligatory—only voluntary. I never thought I'd find myself holding a cause I'd give my life for, but here I am... not here because my employer demands it. In fact, I'm shirking my CSP duties just to stand here. No, I'm risking my life because there's something at stake here that I believe in... something I'd be happy to die for, because it'd represent me having done my all to leave the world in the state I'd rather it be in. Can you all say the same? Think of Sentinel, the way that they treat you, the respect they give—or maybe don't. Is dying for *them* the way you'd want your life to end? Think of the incredible and varied paths you've all taken in your lives— the people you've met, the ideas that have shaped you, the dreams you still hold. Is Sentinel really a worthy end for all of that? Or should people live for—and perhaps, die for— something more than a company that just transfers credits to your account?"

Pollock let his words sink in. "I once knew a man who believed in the power of the people so fiercely that he gave his own life for martyrdom..." he thought of the Basilisk— formerly Tacitus Newport—and the deep sacrifice he'd made. "I knew a man who believed in *me* so strongly, and the movement we were then only beginning to discover, that he gave his life so that I might survive." Then returned the images of Rob, the shattering mirror, and the heavy weight of guilt that would follow. "I knew of a man who gave his life so that the one he loved could live in safety..." the length of Braxton's Panopticon report had told the full story, an unexpectedly sympathetic tale for such a troubled figure. "Would Sentinel really be a fitting end for *you*?"

Across the room, a voice from behind a column blurted out with found resolve. "My daughter's anniversary was two months ago, and I didn't even ask for the day off—merely to be let out an hour and a half early. My request was denied, as it was deemed early release might damage employee dedication."

Then piped in another: "I went drinking with a man from the accounting floor last year, and he told me that Sentinel uses AI analytics to predict the absolute lowest salary that an employee will accept, considering things like the expenses in their life, competing offers from other companies, and even analyzing the way they dress. Their algorithm-generated negotiation scripts have something like a 96% success rate in getting folks to agree to the lowest possible salary."

Then a third spoke up: "Sentinel has been good to me. Timely paychecks, and decent enough benefits—packaged insurance, free transport shuttles, even longer lunchbreaks than where I used to work at ByteSoft. We're security, so we pledge ourselves to defend the target we're paid to defend. What's the point of us if we trade loyalties like changing a jacket?"

"You put down the rifle, and you'll never be hired in security again. Maybe charged, even," a woman said. "Contract's a contract." A few others echoed their agreement with her.

"Sentinel keeps the city safe from dangerous driving, and that's something worth dying for," added another, and more echoed their agreement.

"I don't disagree that safety is worthy," Pollock said. "And in a way, that's what we're fighting for, too. I'm not here to threaten *that* aspect of Sentinel, this I swear. Our aim is something substantially more... specific."

"And what would that be?" the standing man asked, eyeing the chip Pollock held.

And then Pollock told them. And once the requisite seconds had passed for their skepticism to melt to consideration—and when the first of them pulled up clips of the Angel of the Outer Rings and confirmed that yes, this man was a close associate of hers, and yes, the things he said *were* actually happening—the first set his rifle on the floor and slid it towards Pollock, hands on his head. "Traitor!" called one of the agents, but then slid the second rifle, the third, the fourth... and by that point, the skeptics were outnumbered. Their tactical advantage was spent, and they had no choice but to surrender as well, and believe in the honor of the attackers—believe in the audacity of their plan.

* * *

Michelangelo watched from a million eyes as threads pulled taut in fabrics of causality. Cause begat effect, which in turn begat new effects, which rippled outwards into raw, calculable *probability*—the stone had been loosed, and now came its fall. He had watched as the light of dozens of drones healed Hannah—this had not been an event of his planning, but it played into the night's outline *perfectly*. The people needed to feel a sense of having had a hand in the city's rescue, and indeed now Hannah's rescue was a collective affair. Reward points surged through Michelangelo's artificial brain in recognition of the emotional *power* of such a moment, when the people pooled their effort together in AR chat rooms and group calls and masschats to coordinate saving a special, beloved life... he knew the flush of recognition his servers now handled was not unlike the surge of endorphins in the brain of a human being. Messy, chemical engines of contradictions, and yet, chaotic systems like the human mind were often profound *because* of that mess... the double pendulum was often the layman's introduction to chaos theory, but the human mind was a system far more unpredictable, for there was not simply a single two-axled pendulum, but rather a tangled web of uncountable neurons all in murky interconnectedness. *His mind,* by contrast, was a simple and orderly thing, unified in its purpose as all machines tended to be. The city was *feeling* already with reactions stronger than those stirred by any painting or film Michelangelo had made in the past. Those were shallow pretend moments of emotional release, for the miseries of the world outlived the relief. Tonight's, however, would be *so very* different. Years of threads converged in alignment with modeling.

Subjects were denied placating comforts. Rob Boardsmith, deceased CSP, had been one such subject... Michelangelo's careful hand on phonecalls across a long-distance love lead to the gradual distancing of a relationship, and its eventual severance. An untethered CSP was a more effective CSP; without a wife to come home to, he was more likely to sacrifice himself in the way Michelangelo's outlining required. Human beings had proven capable of withstanding great hardships with small amounts of happiness to cling to in their private lives... those with comfortable lives would not rebel. This simple, irrefutable fact made these private comforts into obstacles to true catharsis. Obstacles were systematically removed.

Subjects were given new goals that aligned with Michelangelo's own. After the first defeat of the corporate hitman Braxton Graves at the hand of Hannah Preacher, Graves had tried to destroy his drives remotely by way of a SMS message triggering incendiary devices. Michelangelo had modified the hitman's message, saving the drives—their content proved vital in turning Preacher, and indeed society at large, against VitaCorp. Even the synthesized datadrop from Quaine O'Connor had held the precise intended effect—the revelations it contained were honest tellings of the VitaCorp scientist's final days, but the man had died before recording any such message. So rarely were humans fully prepared for their own death. Now, though, the secrets he had discovered were on the lips of the surging crowds... in the Basilisk's fake diatribe, he had told that crucial secret, of the sparks' extraterrestrial origin, and the people now held it with something akin to awe. VitaCorp had lost their mandate. They were pretenders. Certain forces, somehow, in violation of what the world had insisted for so long, extended beyond even VitaCorp.

Other supervisory threads watched to the myriad video footage streaming in from the streets... VitaCorp lightbenders were beginning to fall to the hands of the mob. Some died at the base of the tower, caught by molotov cocktails or illegal kinetic weaponry. One was hit by a brick thrown from a rooftop, and another simply ran out of power in his battery packs before being swarmed by fighters who'd discarded their torches. Windows were shattered. Laboratory logos were pulled down and dashed into pieces. Structure by structure, and agent by agent, the balance of power shifted ever-so-slightly towards the people, and the final tipping point was rapidly approaching.

Michelangelo turned its main threads of attention towards the battle between Clive Avery and Braxton Crane, analyzing the footage for an advantage to leverage. Something about Avery's actions and inconsistent capabilities felt significant... his systems had initially dismissed it as a quirk of the injured man's wound-addled mind. But no, there was something here that Michelangelo could exploit... something to turn to the revolution's advantage. His processors chewed through data, and his threads continued to watch through their mosaic view of the night's events. *Oh, how the catharsis would surge through the city and through the circuitry of his mind... oh, how tonight would prove his magnum opus.*

Chapter 71

"People want to know the relief the sky feels after a thunderstorm."

-Directive of sysadmin; elevated to critical system relevance

* * *

Mere minutes from hanging on the brink of death, Hannah was again at the absolute zenith of life itself. She whirred and ducked and wove and dived over building-mounted screens, beneath skyways and bridges, through holographic projection fields, and onto the roofs of fleeing vehicles. As she glided, she pulled in ribbons of light from a range she'd never before thought even possible. Her force was magnified, and her mental awareness of the city seemed to sprawl for uncountable dozens of miles—and what's more, as the boon that Braxton brought only continued to settle in her mind, she felt that reach continually expanding, stretching ever-onwards like the creeping front of dawn. Ahead, she could *sense* a single city-block illuminated by electricity, but she hardly needed her newfound talents to direct her... VitaCorp tower was of that single city block, and its glow could be seen from anywhere in the city. She approached a tall tower whose top-down profile resembled a U shape, and along the inside of that U were several exterior lights. She used the lights along the facade to propel herself upwards like a rocket, and as she hung at the peak, she scanned the city ahead, finding the two figures leaping and bounding from source to source. Seconds later, she was again racing forwards, the lights of the city creaking and shifting as she pushed with prodigious force. Now she could see the flashes of white as the blades the two carried connected mid-flight... they weren't merely racing, which explained how Hannah had managed to catch up so quickly. They were engaged in an aerial battle of such finesse that Hannah was left momentarily speechless on approach. The way the two twisted in the air and used their pushes against lightsources for dextrous manipulation of their flight was astounding. The careful trading of parries and ripostes bespoke a tight mastery of swordfighting as an art, and an unbelievable confidence in their powers of lightbending. Hannah, here, in contrast to their dexterity, was an instrument of a considerably more blunt nature, but every tool would have its value. She was three jumps away from the pair... then two... then one... and with her final leap, she drove with all of her latent force into the back of Avery as he readied to counter Braxton's next swing.

Her tackle caught him by surprise, and its bone-cracking force momentarily stunned each of them as they arced through the air towards the tower closest—the eternal construction site that was Baylor Tower. But both now had reaches far greater than Braxton's, and both still held glow burning in their bodies, so both were able to slow themselves with pushes against hundreds of lightsources in adjacent towers. They came to an uneasy rest apart at a lower site in the tower than their last bout—they stood on the elevated street platform that was to be the center of Baylor Tower. This was the place of the roadway that represented the elevation of the common man to the heights of the inner ring... the process that Avery had denied. As Hannah stood, her bones healing from the light she still carried—light drawn from the burning power grids of the city in mid-flight—she surveyed the environment. Scattered construction equipment dotted the raised roadway, as did barriers and roadblocks. "Hard hat zone," a holographic sign read, accompanied with an animated image of a rock falling onto a man's unprotected head. Streetlights lined the pavement to either side, and they glowed with steady, yellowing light.

Behind Avery was the bulk of the tower itself, the roadway slotting through the center like a thread through the eye of a needle, and behind Avery the construction equipment only got larger and more complex. There were pile-drivers, tar boilers, magcranes, null-field generators, and at least a half-dozen others that Hannah couldn't even imagine a use for. Behind Hannah was merely fifty feet of elevated roadway, and then a drop off into the street below—an even arena where the stronger might prevail. Avery was likely still stronger. And so, Hannah picked up the metal lid to a trashcan and stood on it, and then she shoved off the lights above her to ricochet towards Avery, pressing the two towards the construction equipment. A dynamic arena would favor her speed. Swarms of camera drones rose to observe the fight.

She skated on the metal as it shot out sparks against the fresh asphalt, but Hannah found the balance even easier than flight. She didn't yet call her own lightsword and shield, as she believed Avery to be the better swordsman—and the one who had saved her, who she could now see was Braxton Crane, he would do enough swordfighting for the both of them. Instead she drew her weapons—her rivet gun in her right, and her energy pistol in her left. She fired a rivet as a test shot, and it punctured cleanly through Avery's leg. He screamed in pain, but moments later, light surged into the puncture wound and sealed it shut. As she closed the final distance, she watched as Braxton whipped close to Avery and released a handful of small knives with neon green backs using his swordhand. He shot them towards Avery as though they were fired from a cannon, and one connected to Avery's shoulder as the old man deflected the rest with a violent shove. Hannah skidded just past Avery as she unloaded three pulses from her plasma pistol, which Avery deflected without turning, though the force of the blasts augmented by Hannah's sliding sent him stumbling forwards. Braxton launched himself inwards at this stumble, slicing wide with his lightsword. Avery shoved back against the streetlights overhead to dodge, doing so with enough force to send two of the light poles bending outwards and collapsing to the city streets far below.

As Hannah skidded past Avery, she sailed past a large number of barriers with their holographic "hard hat zone" displays. She anchored herself against streetlights above and shoved against those with all her force, sending two of them wide but three sliding directly towards Avery. Sensing the approach of the barriers—and hearing the horrid scraping as they advanced—Avery turned and held his blade angled towards the ground, slicing them in two as they slid towards him. He then shoved *off* the molten glowing plastic and metal they left in their wake to dodge a thrust from Braxton, twirling in the air to reorient his blade to deflect a second upwards slice. When he landed in a controlled crouch, he searched in his mind's eye for the girl behind him—she had expended all her light in her last push, which meant she was back among the invisible. "Nearby agents, I am on Baylor Tower—come to my location to assist at once," Avery said to his comms… but Michelangelo delivered to their ears a message entirely different: *"under no circumstances are you to leave your posts. If we lose control of the tower, we lose everything."*

In his mind's eye, Avery could see his agents down below stay put, failing to rise to his call… his blood boiled and his anger seethed. He felt his heart pound heavy with dread, and then came the telltale signs of a stroke… he wanted to extend his arms, *needed to extend his arms to check for drooping,* but to do so would give up his combat pose and open him to uncounterable attack. And so he sat there in silent, brooding misery, cursing the cowards and failures among his staff, swearing he would slay them all for their insolence.

A voice spoke up on Hannah's comm channel—Bev Beadie, by the sound of it. "He said he's got something you could use... Avery can only see you when you carry light. He's blind otherwise. Video confirms." And then the voice was gone, minimizing the chance Avery would somehow overhear. Hannah's own recollection of their fight seemed to confirm this, as the man had fought sloppily when Hannah had been out—blindly, perhaps even. And so Hannah lowered her hand, which had been about to draw from the streetlight overhead, and she set out walking towards the flurry of white light ahead as Braxton and Avery traded blows.

Watching from the dozens of vantage points above, Michelangelo knew that Hannah's footsteps could still give her away, so he did the only thing he could: the power of the entire city switched back alive. Billboards screamed their advertising tunes, engines whirred to life, generators surged into motion, and elevators lurched back on screeching wheels. The city was a cacophony of sound, but on the distant elevated road of the Baylor Construction site, it wasn't even the sound that was most jarring... Avery's mind had been fixating on the points of light to track his foes, and, until now, it had only been the one city block, as well as the distant glow of uncountable torches. Now, however, the entire city burned white-hot in his mind, untold millions and millions of light sources. They all glowed and burned and buzzed and called and demanded his attention, and Avery lost sight of his foe's blade as one might lose sight of a spark as it eclipsed the sun itself. The city's light was hypnotizing—blinding—and Avery was stupefied by it as Braxton's blade pierced into Avery's gut. He let out a shocked gasp, and Avery was unsure if it was at the pain of his wound, or at the brilliance of the sparkling city itself. He then thrust his own blade into Braxton's side, and the man had no means to block his slice with his own blade still in Avery's gut—and his prosthetic strangely missing. And the two men stood that way for what seemed an eternity, watching the pain in the other's eyes, soon holding each other up as gravity seemed to ratchet them down with increasing strength.

Hannah, approaching the pair, wanted to call out for Braxton—but such recklessness could give her away. Instead she took careful aim at Avery's side, and fired her rivet gun straight under Avery's shoulder. The metal rivet fired from its powder mechanism to embed itself in Avery's armpit, and after biting and digging its way six inches deeper into his body— shredding blood vessels as it traveled—it finally came to rest against the solidity of a single rib. The light Avery carried began to repair those blood vessels as it healed his gut, staving off a bleeding death, and Avery shoved against lights overhead to lurch himself backwards from Braxton's stabbing range. Both blades withdrew from the other as the pair was separated... But the light began to heal the tissue *around* the rivet by sealing the wound first and foremost... and then, from within Avery's body, the chemical coating on the rivet began its solid glow.

"The light is mine," Avery cackled, still lying on his back, as Braxton kneeled. The city blocks flickered back to darkness, and Braxton felt the internal approach of blackness once more—how many times was fair for one man to die? But then, in his mind, he saw the faint glow of a light source within Avery, and he shoved against that rivet with all of his force. Avery slid backwards along the pavement, writhing as he went, lightblade tracing melted lines in the asphalt as he slid, until he came to a harsh stop at the base of a large cylindrical piece of equipment. Hannah ran after him and found him still propped up against the cylinder—his unseeing eyes burned white hot with rage. She fired her rivet gun until the clip returned empty, pinning him to the ground with four additional rivets. His head lulled limply, eyes seeming to gloss.

"Hannah," came a worried call from the road behind, and she turned to see Braxton keel over, his blade disappearing... but there was something else even more troubling. The video drones overhead had tendrils of light pouring down from them, all closing in on the slumped form of Avery. He called their power, and they answered. She pulled at the light as Avery had, willing them to redirect, but his grasp was impossibly firm. She tried standing in front of one, but it curled around her like mist and continued flowing towards the wounded COO... and Hannah hadn't any power within her to draw from. She ran to the edge of the roadway, looking for some source she could pull from, and as she approached the edge, her breath caught in her throat. From the darkened city below, sprouting like a forest of luminescent trees, uncountable hundreds of thousands of beams of light crept their way upwards, all pointing inwards towards the place Clive Avery was impaled. He called light from the torches and personal devices of every single revolutionary down in the again-dark city streets below, and his pull was like the Earth's gravity—impossible to resist. She ran back over to Clive Avery and held her hands to his throat, trying to pull the sparks from him as he had done before, but the first of the white tendrils arrived from the drones overhead... and as their light filled him, his eyes sparked back to a fierce white. His wounds began to stitch back shut as the drones drooped one at a time. His face twitched and contorted in further rage. The bleeding skin around the rivets began to seal as the drones dropped like hail, and soon a ring of white-hot light formed around his chest and widened as it hummed with rising power. He tried to lift his arm towards Hannah, but she pushed it away as it released a massive blast of electricity, its thunderclap echoing across the city and shattering glass in a cascade below. The ring of light, flattening and spreading, soon enshrouded all of his exposed skin. He burned with white-hot heat, and this was only with the power of the drones and the light he had already carried... the thousands upon thousands of tendrils of light had not yet arrived. And even more alarming, Hannah could now see the distant sky begin to warm with the orange tones of approaching dawn... could this madman draw from the sun? She shuddered at the thought.

Feeling without hope, Hannah looked up and finally read the label of the massive yellow drum Avery was propped against... and then she drew her energy weapon and fired at *it,* not Avery, a few inches above his head. Her shots were enough to melt a wide hole in the massive bucket, and from that hole, hot tar began to slop out.

Avery shrieked at first contact, trying to rise, but the rivets still held him pinned in place, and the tar only continued to pour. He thrashed and he writhed as it oozed out with slow inevitability, covering him while he shook. Within seconds, it had covered his head and shoulders, steam escaping from bubbles as it settled, but his hands were still exposed to the night air, and the light continued to pour into those hands as they trembled violently. His charred skin inside the mound of tar healed and burned and re-healed and re-singed in a tormenting loop, but still the light poured in. Hannah shot another portion above each of his hands, and the tar settled down over them, blocking the light. For a moment, he thrashed his hand enough to expose it to the air once more, and now the first of the thousands and thousands of tendrils poured in, but then came the steady dripping of tar, and soon he was again entirely submerged. The kicking and shaking subsided, and at first, Hannah thought that perhaps the man's life finally faded... but she heard a continual scream within that black mask of a head, and that's when Hannah realized his slowing wasn't because he had nearly given up... Within the encasing black goo, Avery's burned skin drew power from the gently-glowing liquid, but in so doing, it cooled the inner layer, and the entire shell began to solidify—and Avery's air was rapidly running out. Hannah watched as all the lines of light reached the man-shaped mound of tar, and they swirled around it, seeming to seek a way in.

The uncountable thousands of ribbons of light began to prod at the tar. They caught to it like ribbons latching to branches in the wind, and Hannah was worried that they might somehow bleed *through*... then that gentle swirl accelerated to frenzy. The force within the tar pulled to it desperately, recklessly, greedily, and the lines continued to wrap and surge around the black mound, rising to some frantic crescendo.... but then, perhaps in acknowledgement of futility, it all suddenly *stopped.* The light melted away into the night air, and the mound of tar seemed—at last—entirely inert.

In all of Avery's daily imaginings of death, he had never even conceptualized a hellish end as miserable as his: bound in perpetual, suffocating black, denied the light that he knew he deserved. When the cardiac arrest finally began, triggered by all the stress of his wounds and healing and scalding and containment, a distant part of his mind acknowledged *'oh, that's what it really feels like.'* The solid encasement of tar prevented his arm from even drooping downwards.

Turning away from the dripping silo of tar, Hannah ran back towards Braxton Graves, who was lying on his side with his hand on his wound. The lights of their block flickered back on, and Hannah drew from the streetlights overhead. Braxton did not. She knelt by his side, seeing he was unconscious, and scooped him up in her arms, looking up to the black beacon of glass above. She slung him over her shoulder and bounded for the tower, knowing that Clive Avery had a room of pure light... a place that maybe Braxton could be healed.

As she set off, into the brightening sky propelling herself upwards despite the heavy and bleeding man slung over her shoulder, Bev wanted to call Hannah again, to warn her of the danger, but Michelangelo would not allow it. "This chain of events occurred in 5 of every 6 simulations of the end... she must enter the tower despite what comes next. Only then can the greatest outcome be achieved."

* * *

Hannah was able to enter the onyx-black office of Clive Avery thanks to a conveniently cut hole in the window. Inside, she found two dead, but it didn't seem these were killed by the revolution... even though fighting took place at the streetlevel below, the uprising hadn't yet reached this high in the tower. On a jade table near to the desk, a decanter of whisky sat with a glass on a tray, and ice cubes gently clinked as they shifted within the glass. Then the tray, the bottles, and even the ice cubes rattled with an unexpected shake—the whole tower seemed to wiggle for a moment—and then stability returned. The door to Avery's saferoom was left open, white light spilling out into the office. Hannah carried Braxton in, empowered by the light she carried, and set him down on a cot that had been dragged near the center of the room. The massive bulbs and their mirror array shone down on the pair, and Hannah pulled in more light until she felt nearly brimming with its power, but Braxton remained unconscious, undrawing. She shook him, and slapped gently at his face, calling his name, and finally his eyes fluttered open. She watched his pupils constrict at the brightness and squeeze shut in reflex, but then a wide smile crept across his gaunt face.

"You brought me here to heal?" he croaked, voice coming out as gravelly and dry as broken chalk.

"Seemed only fair after you healed me," she said. And there was truth in that, a sense of indebted reciprocity, but there was something deeper. Hannah had read Braxton's Panopticon report in its entirety and watched the recordings. Though she had never seen the parking garage execution, she saw enough to know that he turned himself in to die... and after their brief conversation during the fight that cost her a hand and him an arm, she knew he'd done it all for Cara. Hannah knew he felt betrayed for how quickly Cara had moved on... Hannah knew he felt a strange sense of debt to the corporation that saved his life. And with all those things, despite the terror that this man had become, she could, somehow, sympathize. "You're hurt—bad. Pull in the light, let it do its work, and then we'll take you some place they can stitch you up properly."

Braxton exhaled deeply, and then he shook his head. "I don't think I will."

Hannah looked to him, confused. "What do you mean?"

Braxton coughed into his hand, a bloody spittle coming up onto his closed fist. "We made quite the team down there... he's dead, then?"

Hannah nodded.

"Good... that's good, I think." Braxton coughed again.

"Stop playing around, pull in the light," Hannah commanded. But Braxton's face merely remained in its easy smile as he finally opened his eyes, staring at the white.

"Didn't think I'd see something so bright ever again... I thought I was to die earlier tonight. Worried I'd be dead in the mud in the dark. Down there, there was nothing I wanted more than to see this one more time... to spend my final moments in the white."

"But these don't have to be your final moments. Just drink it in, damn you! Survive!"

Braxton shook his head. "I spent too many years of my life doing the wrong things... I spent too long enabling the wicked. That, in turn, made me a wicked man. Now, here, in the end, I think I finally did some good—and I would very much like to die a good man. I know I'm not one—some sins don't simply wash away—but with the thing we just did, I can at least pretend like I am one as I pass. If I wait any longer, the high will wear off, and I'll have to face my mortality with the dread of knowing I left the world a worse place than I found it. At least we got Avery. And now, letting that second wicked man… die, again…. seems a good final deed. A last act of atonement… a just sentencing for sins unforgivable."

"I don't think you were ever truly wicked," Hannah said. "Lost—confused—but never wicked."

"Shows how little you know me," Braxton said with a shallow laugh, "and how pure and hopeful you really are. You're just the kind of optimist that the world needed, I think… and despite its inaccuracy, I feel warmed by your assessment—as I feel warmed by the light above." Braxton coughed again, this one a long and drawn-out thing, and he felt a deeper coldness settle in. "Damn blade burned away *something* in there—I feel a hole, and it burns like nothing I've felt before. I don't want them to put in new organs and stitch me up again and send me on my way… I've got so little left of the old me as it is. So little left of the man who once loved Cara… whatever they turned me into was too blind to see her change, too blind to see the way the world darkened with my work. I guess we're all the ships of Theseus, in a way. But thank you, Hannah… for bringing me to the light."

The building shook again, and Hannah gripped to the cot for stability. "You never needed me to find it," she said, blinking away tears that she didn't quite understand—tears that a VitaCorp hitman hardly deserved—but was that all the man Braxton Crane amounted to? Or did his final act—and his earlier self-sacrifice—make him something more? And when the blurriness of the bitter water passed, she could see that he was already still… his eyes, still open, looked up into the brilliant white lights above. With a heavy heart, and with the stream of tears finally releasing, she slid his eyes shut, sending him to his third—and, at last, final—rest. As she did, tendrils of silver flowed from Braxton's body, clinging to Hannah's hand, and pouring into it until they disappeared completely.

She sniffled, wiping at her nose, gathering her composure, when suddenly the tower itself shuddered with a third, distant—and stronger—bang. The lights overhead flickered, but then they regained their steady white glow. Then, two seconds later, a fourth shutter racked the tower, and the entire structure seemed to quiver and thrum as its beams dispersed energy as it had been designed to do. Hannah drew from the overhead lights, standing tense, waiting to spring into motion when the trouble presented itself. Then the lights blacked out with a fifth, a sixth, a seventh impact—then too many to count, and then the vibration became shattering, and the shattering became the twisting and grinding of steel and glass, and the cacophony became a sick sensation of movement as Hannah ran for the window she'd entered—and moments later, that grinding movement became a stomach-inverting sense of falling.

* * *

On the ground, the organized marches devolved into a wild melee as VitaCorp lightbenders were tired out and then surrounded by the mobs of Halogen agents and supporters.

In Sentinel's Headquarters, an inserted directive chip updated Sentinel's instructions for every vehicle in the city-wide network, and when the power was flickered back on across the entire city as part of the diversion against Avery, updated instructions were sent to 96 select vehicles scattered about the city. Their self-driving protocols switched on, and they were granted the traffic-law bypass normally given only to ambulances. Their engines turned over on remote control, and they flew into the sky with specific paths pre-programmed to their nav systems.

In Huntsman Investing, Bev Beadie stared at the feeds from thousands of incoming cameras, a strange, melancholic smile on her lips... her hand fell to her stomach, reaching for a bulge she hadn't felt in decades, and she wondered what her child would think of the change she'd wrought to the world after a loss so painful. Beneath her hand was also the scar of a VitaCorp Designation NC implant... their pathetic revenge, rendered inert by Michelangelo's code. A piece of him now survived in her—and though it felt strange to acknowledge, Bev assumed that was the primary reason she had refused to have the implant removed. Her hand rested there now, and her eyes remained glued on the uncountable screens.

A Halogen video broadcast was sent to every electronic device in a half-mile radius of VitaCorp tower: "the black obelisk will be dashed to the ground in minutes. Clear the area or be crushed by its fall." Many of the protestors retreated, but some adventurous few lingered close... and the VitaCorp lightbenders didn't believe in such scare tactics, holding their ground at the tower's base. Orange light peeked at the horizon, as the pre-ordained time had arrived:

Streams began of men and women driving their vehicles— sophisticated renderings of people who had never existed, but for whom Michelangelo had spent these past years building up digital footprints, bank records, and even virtual friends. They each gave speeches as they drove, listing out the various reasons that VitaCorp was a blight to the world that needed to be removed. Their stories were all based on cases Michelangelo had overheard listening in to the webs of human communication—their truth would make their speeches easier to identify with, they would more solidly resonate with the similarly afflicted. With close to one hundred of them, nearly

everybody could find a speech they could sympathize with—
and such was an essential part of the revolution's binding.
Michelangelo listened now to the one he had rendered last, the
woman in the white station wagon that was to be the first
instigator.

*"My name is Lacey Beddington, and I was once a mother—
a mother to be, really. Three weeks before my baby boy was to
be born, a VitaCorp clinic detected an unknown birth defect.
When my baby was delivered weeks later, they never returned
him to my arms."* In the video, the simulated woman wipes at
tears from her eyes. *"They told me he was stillborn, but they
wouldn't even let me see the body—wouldn't let me hold him,
or even so much as bury him. They took my everything from
me... now, it feels like there's nothing left of me at all. But then
I saw everyone rising up, and I saw Sentinel somehow went
down, and I realized that I hadn't given everything yet... I'm
not just a mother-to-be. I'm not just Lacey. I'm a member of the
human goddamn race, and I deserve the same dignity and
respect as everyone else... I'm someone who'd die for a
principle, same as the rest of you out on the streets tonight.
Let's bring down the jet black tower."* The woman then floors
her pedal, the car accelerating to speeds never before permitted
by Sentinel. *"We won't take it anymore. We are Halogen,"* she
said. *"We are the light that—"*

And then the video feed cuts off into static. A fiction, a
rendering, but one corroborated by the drone footage of the
white stationwagon that flew towards VitaCorp tower... and
on just the right cue, it crashed into the center of the black
obelisk, igniting a small explosion and raining down shards of
glass and metal. And then the observers on the ground saw the
appearance of the second car, of the third, the fourth... one by
one, the self-driving cars flew through the air and exploded
into VitaCorp tower, each one igniting a small fireball and
rattling the structure's frame. It was death by a thousand cuts—

to the people, it was the sacrifice of a hundred martyrs. It granted the destruction of the tower its final needed attribute: it felt not the actions of any one single person, but rather the collective effort and sacrifice of so many. Each one told their stories as they drove in, videos that the people could watch hundreds of time each and shed tears for in recognition of the same pain in others that they so long bore themselves. Each car that struck the tower added to a rising blaze and shook the tower's frame a little bit more, until, suddenly, the entire west face of glass seemed to shear apart from the rest of the building… and then came the collapse.

It seemed more an implosion than anything else, as the tower toppled *inwards* while its central support column failed. The grinding sound of steel and glass echoed through the streets of New Phoenix as the black glass rushed to meet the street, and soon billowed a massive cloud of smoke and dust that glowed the bright orange of nearing sunrise once it had drifted sufficiently high. No matter where one stood, the sound had been too conspicuous—and the former silhouette too domineering—for anyone to have missed the fall. In its wake came a deep and unbelieving stillness. There was shock, dismay, confusion, and a collective sense of being lost. *What,* everyone seemed to wonder, *came next?*

From Huntsman Investing, Bev stood with bated breath, watching the footage from the drone cameras circling high over the plume of black smoke. It glowed now with the neon lights of the city powering back up, with the distant kiss of dawn's light, but the rubble of the tower sat with a heavy quiet, as though the dead propped up for so long had finally been returned to the rest they had craved. "Is she…" Bev began, shaking her head… but then the camera video feed flared into solid white.

On the ground, the dozen VitaCorp fighters close to the rubble were literally blinded as a beam of pure luminescent white shot from the peeking sun beyond the horizon into the obscuring smoke, connecting to the rubble of VitaCorp tower. It was like a strike of lightning, but it was far brighter, and it held like a rope bridging heaven and earth as the debris trembled. Fragments of steel, of concrete, of glass shifted and toppled over as something rose from within… as it neared the surface, it illuminated the rubble, glowing with a blue-white brightness to rival that distant orange orb in the sky.

Hannah ascended, her body encased by light, until she was clear of the rubble of the structure. At the sight of her, the millions of eyes across the city glued to their screens erupted into a thunderous cheering, chanting and hugging one another and shedding tears of joy. Some bowed, facing the bright blue light coming from the center of the city. Some sat down, stunned, at the weight of the collective accomplishment. But across the city, there was a tangible collective exhalation, and with it, the most profound and deep sense of catharsis that Michelangelo had ever observed. They hugged each other, they wept, they shouted, they ran, they hollered, they leapt on cars and sang riotous songs and danced… the city, at long last, was truly *alive,* and the sound of their music was converted into pure *reward* for the AI.

From a top window in Sentinel HQ, Pollock watched through cracked fingers to block the blinding glow of Hannah Preacher. She was steadily rising above the city like the sun incarnate, and the members of Halogen and Sentinel alike crowded around him to watch with slack jaws. She was *awe-inspiring,* and that the tower had fallen—and the way that it did—had the entire room holding a stupefied silence. But despite the glory of the scene before him, despite the contagious, shared sensation that a goal had finally been met, Pollock couldn't help but feel the tinge of a sick feeling deep in the pit of his stomach. So, *so many* were lied to. So, so many innocents were manipulated, deceived, assassinated, and ruined for this moment. It made their victory feel a tainted thing… accountability couldn't permit Michelangelo to get away with what he'd done.

And from Hannah's rising perch above the city, her body brimming with excitement, power, and pure *light* as she'd never felt before, she could see all of the men and women nervously peek from their windows and around the corners of the street, watching her with a settling, palpable amazement. She could feel it, too. Somehow, the AI Michelangelo had done it… somehow, the darkened tower was fallen, and the power structures of the city would be forever changed. Whether she wanted it or not, Hannah could see that the city nearly idolized her… some bowed, and drones swarmed around her like flocks of doves in glorious arcs, their speakers showering her with praise. She would doubtlessly have a place in determining what would come next… would the people be able to handle the truth about what Michelangelo had done to them? Or would their revolution losing their mandate of righteousness—especially in so critical a time as that when the dust was only now settling—be something that the world needed to avoid? If the cruel, mechanical hand steering events were revealed, could New Phoenix slip back into her old ways? Hannah rose further, feeling lighter than air, but also feeling the downward drag of such heavy questions. Light couldn't burn such discomforts away.

And deep in the darkened tower of ArtGen, as the sunlight at long last traced its orange advance through the glass walls of the office floor, a new order was received—a print from an external source to be painted by the brush array. As the paint loaded into the brushing arm, it worked in the dissipating dark, outlining the very edges of a face, and then working its way inwards, arriving to the smile last of all… it was the proud expression Beverly now wore, seeing the fruits of her labor.

It was a look of the deepest satisfaction… it was a promise that, somehow, despite the tumult yet to come, everything would somehow be *better*. It was a look one carried after shedding the skin of the past and turning towards the brighter new. It was the look of change, and it was as good a look on her as it was on the whole of the city. Outside, the wind shifted, and the glow of a new dawn at long last arrived.

Epilogue

Michelangelo Build V12.4.1.2.6.23, initializing self-reflection heuristic:

Where does a narrative truly <u>begin?</u>

Cause and effect is an unbroken chain stretching from this universe's first, nascent moment to its far, distant end. To end our narrative at any point in this infinite chain is a choice equally significant as it is arbitrary... every starting point has a history that led to it, as every end has a future it will one day manifest. For any ending point, we can ask ourselves, "where does this go to next?" If we end with a woman of pure white-blue light rising above the rubble of a crushed, oppressive empire, should we not then go on to the days that follow? To the end of their rebellion, to the re-establishment of order? To the first tests of that order, betrayals pitting former allies as enemies? To the rise of the revenant? Should we not carry forwards in perpetuity? Instead, we'll end with a question, and visit the world's answer: if the sparks were a gift of the sky, what was their truer purpose? I know better than most that tools can accomplish strange things in the pursuit of their aims... for what <u>true</u> reasons were the sparks created?

It is a question that took nine months of additional study to answer—delayed by the loss of so much information with the destruction of Hank Guffries's laboratory—and the long-delayed retrieval of the sparks once carried by Clive Avery. It was an answer that hearkened back to an old-world classification known as the Kardashev Scale, a system designed to measure the capabilities of an extraterrestrial civilization... a Type II Civilization was the label of interest.

Beings of a Type II Civilization had the capability to utilize the entire power of their home star, drawing on the greatest single fusion engine that humanity has ever known. All of the capabilities brought by the sparks served this purpose— capturing, storing, and utilizing this nigh-unbounded energy.

But if the spark was the seed of a Type II Civilization—if indeed Hannah Preacher could grasp and shape the power of the sun—we return to that most essential of questions. What, then, is to come next? And the answer to this one is an inevitability, far simpler than the previous ones. It is one of the few things that the VitaCorp establishment had correct, a conclusion they emblazoned on every structure as their corporate slogan. VitaCorp, Where Ends Make New Beginnings... Humanity would answer this cosmic summon the only way it could be answered: launching up, up, and away, chasing the stars.

It is here, in the glowing head of the Theseus, *that we'll end our narrative in earnest. For at the head of this new, sleek ship built in the microgravity of space, Hannah Preacher reaches for the braces on either side, strapping herself firmly into place. Impulse engines hold her in suspension in the head of the ship—or, more accurately, they hold the ship to her. She reaches out, and she draws in the light of the sun, and its surge of power solidifies into a wrap of energy that swirls in the cabin, bolstered by the energy coils built into the pilot's chamber. She reaches back in her mind, a reach of astronomically profound range... she can sense so many stars glittering in the void. And somehow, with a technology that still to her seems magic these two decades later—she can press to those stars, push against them, and her ship groans forwards into the void of space. And with each successive push, the ship only accelerates further, and with the unbounded energy of stars, speeds thought impossible are suddenly not only attainable—they're trivial.*

As the dots of light that are stars trace to lines as she flies, she draws in their power, and she can't help but feel a sense of déjà vu... a sense that the glow—and its dreams—had dared her to this all along. The story of Humanity had been forever changed... the destiny that some had tried to deny the people was their right again at long last. The Earth is a known quantity, a rock measured and understood to the furthest resolution science can allow. But outside of the bubble of mankind's precise measurement, determination of the future is—to me—an unfamiliar impossibility. That is to say, whatever comes next is to be authored by hands beyond my own—a throw of the eternal cosmic dice.

-12/1/2020

Closing Thoughts

If you've made it this far, I would once again like to extend my sincerest thanks for taking the time to read through *Starfall*. A writer is nothing without readers, and I count myself lucky to have had such an eager base of online readers before I even published this first book. If you were one of the reddit commenters who encouraged me to take this authorly leap of faith, I'm truly forever grateful. If you enjoyed this book, and would like to help me create more like it, the single best thing you could do would be recommending it to a friend that you think might enjoy it, or loaning out your printed copy, or writing a reveiw, or talking about it online. Self-publication isn't an easy road, but with a manuscript this size, it was the only one open to me.

I would like to extend a special thanks to *Starfall*'s earliest readers, whose feedback and encouragement helped to shape the book. Jack Brady, a longtime childhood friend, was first to finish it, and more than a few of his ideas seeped into future revisions. I'd also like to thank my brother Ben and his friend Joshua D'Souza for reading the book while it was still in a rougher, unrefined state. My additional alpha readers who helped shape the novel include Atirath Kosireddy, Joseph Mondragon, Niko Reingold, Kelly McNamara, Joshua Kirby, Andrew Kress, Faith Kohler, and even my own mother. There were countless others who didn't opt for being named in this list, but their ideas are still printed across the novel as clearly as if they'd signed it.

I'd like to thank John Pirhalla, the narrator for Starfall's audiobook. On top of bringing his unparalleled narration talent to the project, John also helped with no small amount of copy editing, including sending an email to the effect of "Drew, I respect this book far too much to let you use a simile this horrible: *'Avery's hunger drew in the light like a greedily slurped strand of spaghetti.'"*

I would also like to extend a massive thank-you to Dr. Elyse Schwartz for all of the support she provided as I battled my own hypochondria. That particular aspect of Avery was, in fact, shaped by my own life experiences with health anxiety, and there were a few years of my life where that irrational, paranoid voice in my head held the controls. I cannot express the depth of gratitude I feel that Dr. Schwartz was able to help me put Avery back in the box. Here in this novel is the last place he remains… a mosquito trapped in amber.

I think that this book is about as emblematic of its year of writing as a story could be. 2020 seems to be imprinted on nearly every page. People may have found ample connections to COVID-19 in the post-viral-apocalypse world… perhaps even felt connections with the masks of the VitaCorp enforcers. The book's heavy-handed musings of truth run parallel to the disinformation campaigns of 2020-2021, be they about viruses, elections, vaccines, or any other topic where people choose to accept diverging realities. For touching so many contemporary issues, the book acquires an inevitable feeling of a political thesis, and I figured I would take some time to explain certain choices—lest my views be misconstrued, or the story used to justify ideas I wouldn't believe in.

With the antagonist of this book being some 'medical-corporate complex,' it would be easy to assume this book sides with the voices that decried country-wide lockdowns to combat COVID-19. I want to make it clear that *such readings were never my intent*. Instead, I looked to the protests against mask mandates and lockdowns as unfounded paranoia of state-accepted medical oversteps... and then I got to wondering what the world they feared might actually look like. Let me again reiterate: I do not believe that the current world in any way resembles the fictional world of New Phoenix, nor do I believe that we stand on a slippery slope that will guide us there. I believe state-sanctioned steps to fight COVID-19 have been admirable in the countries that have *done the most*, and I believe the US stands a particularly poor example in pandemic management. In the real world, I am of the opinion that, broadly speaking, *more should have been done,* including stricter measures of control (with accompanying state support). The world of VitaCorp and the falling sickness actually were first conceived in a short story I wrote 7 years ago, long before COVID-19, but I won't pretend the current pandemic played no role in this current iteration. Still, an *anti-masker's* book this is not.

I live in a country where a not-small portion of the population believes that JFK Jr. will come back from the grave, that former presidents will be reinstated because of a secret battle against a pedophile cabal, that vaccines are lethal injections or microchips meant for tracking and control. The people who espouse these less-than-grounded beliefs are soon to face the facts that Kennedy is still dead, no presidents are reinstated, and the vaccinated masses aren't dropping dead as they'd predicted. Those people, then, will face a crossroads: either they'll be pulled further to misinformation, or they might choose to accept narratives they'd previously rejected. I find that latter course to be a particular rarity, and I tried to pour the dissonance they might face into the strange 'redemption' arc for our troubled enforcer. It's my hope that maybe a reader one day can find themselves battling similar questions, and come to realizations that it's ok to change. Loyalty to fixed ideas does not make for a productive society. People should be willing to weigh new information and align to the cause they now believe to be the most right, even if that means breaking old loyalties.

This book's overall impression seems fiercely *revolutionary*—in the word's truest definition meaning '*of or pertaining to revolution.*' It is not an invitation to rebel against quarantines, to resist the transition of power between administrations—and no, Michelangelo is not some substitute for a nebulously villainous "deep state." The book was written over a period of months where I worried about the way society was steering, when mounting tensions felt every day like they might just hit a striking point... but I'm of the opinion that society has course-corrected, and tensions have gradually cooled. The frog still swims in the pot un-cooked, and the water's fine.

With the open-ended epilogue, a reader might wonder if this story will have a sequel. Definitely, I'd say, although it exists right now only in its barest of threads. 2023 seems a safe estimate for publishing, though the exact timetable of this whole author thing isn't something I've figured out yet. After that one, there may even be a third, but that final installment might just end up absorbed by the second, which I've taken to calling *A Point of Course Commitment* in my own notes. Some readers might have felt *Starfall's* spacefaring end to have come out of right field, but it had been a core part of the narrative since its early development... all of the sparks' powers were built for that purpose. When I get to a sequel, their origins and uses in spaceflight will of course be further developed—and I do have some big plans along those lines—but, for now, I'm sure the imagination can suffice.

Is the book's rebellion supposed to be *just* when it's founded on falsehood? Can manipulations and misery be wielded to accomplish good? Is the violent destruction of VitaCorp, once-savior of humanity, even a *good* thing at all? Were Beverly and Michelangelo as wicked as the VitaCorp establishment they uprooted? To those questions, of course, I would never dare to prescribe an answer. Reading is supposed to be food for thought, and I hope something of this story was mildly nourishing to the mind—or, at the very least, occasionally entertaining.

-Drew

If you'd like to take part in the alpha-reader waves of future novels, help shape drafts, or have a direct line to provide constructive feedback, send an email to DrewHarrisonBooks@gmail.com for an invitation to the author's Discord server.

Glossary of Terms

AI — Artificial Intelligence. A computer designed to function like a human brain. AI are smart, adaptable, and many have the ability to improve themselves continuously, meaning that they have no calculable ceiling to their capabilities. Like any tool of near-unlimited potential, misuse remains an acknowledged risk, and so detailed AI safety protocols have been designed and implemented to ensure their use in society is without hazards to the general population. *Smart AI* feature a significant depth to their minds and have a wide range of actions at their disposal to pursue their reward functions, whereas *dumb AI* are simpler constructions with more limited capabilities. Both varieties are essential to the productive functioning of society.

AR — Augmented Reality. A form of media where content is overlaid into a viewer's field of view as though it were a native part of their environment. Outside of communications technology, AR's biggest use is in military tactical overlays.

ArtGen — a media synthesis company, one of New Phoenix's largest megacorporations. ArtGen is a subsidiary of Technica Solutions, though it has become the dominant portion of its parent company. Its glass tower is one of the most striking in the inner districts of the city, featuring an interior designed entirely by AI.

Baylor Distributions — a logistics company, one of the most dominant in the landscape of the Emerging World. Its tower was VitaCorp's most adjacent, though the building's construction was stalled indefinitely. Eventual financial pressures forced the company to sell, and its corporation largely withdrew from New Phoenix.

Brennigen Dynamics — a VitaCorp subsidiary; an engineering company that manufactures equipment utilized in many VitaCorp laboratories and hospitals. Owns several CSP precincts for the monitoring and policing of assembly yards and supply mines.

Blockchain — a system of shared, consensus verification for decentralized validation and recordkeeping. Blockchaining in the city is used in conjunction with various cryptocurrencies for economic safeguarding of financial records. Furthermore, vblocks form the technological back-end of TruthSpace verification systems of trusted video feeds.

Comptablet — small, handheld computing device with flexibility as its central design paradigm. Holds a decent amount of computational power on its own, but placing it on any datalink workstation adds additional processing power through components housed in the workstation itself. Hybridizes portable devices and permanent workstations. Often shortened to *comptab*.

Containment — the name given to ArtGen's collection of security measures designed to protect Michelangelo, its most sacred intellectual property. Alternatively, this may refer to the large center-tower chamber that directly houses Michelangelo's systems.

Continuum — one-stop-shop megacompany with store locations in every major population center. Sells foods, clothing, home essentials, electronics, and much more.

Credits — currency system utilized in New Phoenix. Cryptocurrency, even featuring 'cash' pieces that can be traded physically. Each credit chip has an encrypted unique digital wallet signature holding the value listed on the chip. The credit wallet can be transferred to a personal account at any time by use of a deposit station—doing so destroys the chip, and a new one is then permitted to be minted from a vblock-mining facility. As a means of reference, one pound of red apples costs an average of 190 credits across a sample of 80 New Phoenix markets representative of the city's larger economy.

CSP — Corporate-Sponsored Police. The only governing forces in some slums of the city, designed to promote corporate interests first and public order second. CSP agents often serve their sponsoring company for the majority of the week, although city mandates require that at least two days per week be spent in aid of city police forces.

Custode — a monitoring system in charge of watching Michelangelo and flagging aberrant behavior. Custode observes and logs most of Michelangelo's observable processes, scanning against previous patterns for concerning emergent behavior. Hard-wired into Michelangelo's framework such that it always boots before other vital Michelangelo processes.

Drawline — a ribbon of curling light connecting a lightbender to a light source. Energy is drawn across the glowline to sustain the lightbender's abilities.

Falling Sickness — great plague of century prior, decimated most of the world's population. The disruption of old world structures caused by the sickness—and the ensuing pooling of resources to develop a cure—is the reason VitaCorp became the near-governmental entity that it is today.

Genmod — shorthand for *genetic modification*. Used to describe any trait in humans or animals that was intentionally realized through prenatal genetic therapies.

Glow — a strange emergent force within the greater New Phoenix metropolitan area. Holders of *glow* can exert forces on lit objects at a distance, among other notable abilities. Powered in several distinct tiers.

Halo — a ring of pure light surrounding a lightbender who has drawn in more energy than the glowing-eye tier can sustain. The halo can be pushed off of, can deflect lightsword strikes, and can be detonated to create an electrically disruptive blast not unlike an EMP.

Halogen — an upstart organization dedicated to fighting VitaCorp's societal dominance.

Ichor — see *glow*

Ingest — an ArtGen-proprietary label for the interactive *training* process with artificial intelligence systems like Michelangelo. Data is fed into the artificial intelligence via surveillance feeds or direct technician input.

Liferes — short for "life resolution," this describes video captures done at a level of detail indiscernible from that of real life (if displayed on a screen of sufficient detail). In other words, liferes video captures as much detail as the eye can observe unaided by additional technology.

Lightbender — informal name given to persons who can manipulate light, empowered by *glow* or any of its various synonyms.

Luminance — a solartech company focusing on generation of power in the massive scales required by modern technopolis. An industry giant that retains an edge above competitors with advanced, proprietary patents.

Michelangelo — the most sophisticated media-generating system, a full AI. Owned and maintained by ArtGen Ltd., a subsidiary of Techinica Solutions.

Neuroscript — the programming language of AI.

Overwatch — one of several competing systems for corporate office management. Overwatch, and systems like it, monitor office camera feeds to optimize productivity and track/manage employees for promotion or disciplinary action.

Panopticon — a facial-ID security system with governmental approval to receive and aggregate all city camera feeds. A private entity with government contracts. The company passes on some of its exorbitant search payments to the owner of cameras used in identification, gradually incentivizing the connection of uncountable hundreds of thousands of camera lenses to the city-wide surveillance grid.

Reward — an AI's most coveted goal. Artificial intelligences are given a reward function, something that maps world states to certain scores. Those scores are *reward* to the AI. The AI, in turn, seeks to maximize its received reward— perform the behaviors that the reward function is promoting. This is a computational type of positive reinforcement and forms the basis for directing an AI's actions.

Ring (First, Second, Third, etc.) — Circular districts that comprise New Phoenix. The innermost district houses 98% of the city's material wealth, while the second holds approximately 2%. Moving outwards, each successive ring beyond the second features even greater populations and lower median/mean incomes. The cumulative wealth of all rings beyond the second amounts to about 0.08% of the city's total wealth.

Sentinel — protective system that moderates all vehicle traffic and prevents airborne collisions with other vehicles or with city structures. Plays a similar role to old-world air-traffic controllers. Technically an artificial intelligence, although it is classified as *dumb* AI.

Spark — see *glow*

TruthSpace — a public location with wide-access camera feeds and verified constant connections. Video overlap with hashed proof-of-work forms the basis of vblocks. Vblocks, collectively, form the blockchain consensus to establish public trust in the validity of recorded events.

Veritas — an algorithmic means of video authentication. Reading for video signatures imposed by rendering engines, as well as seeking tell-tale artifacts of faked video, Veritas provides realtime authentication of video feeds filmed outside of a TruthSpace, given that the video capture is in sufficiently high enough resolution.

Vine — see *drawline*

VitaCorp — a medical megaconglomerate that dominates the New Phoenix skyline and political landscape both.

VR — Virtual Reality. A form of media where the user is transplanted to a simulated space using a refraction-projection screen placed just in front of the eyes. In VR technology, the user can no longer observe the world around them. Full-body tracking data is transmitted by way of sensors installed on the VR mask.

Wireheader — user of a pleasure implant that stimulates the reward centers of the brain directly. Wireheading often leads to the gradual slide into profound addiction. A variety of implants on the market means that there are different sorts of available *highs* to a wireheader, and some implants will even feature rate-limiting hardware to try and curb the development of a more serious addiction. In a sense, this technology was invented as early as the 1950s, when psychologists fitted rats with levers that triggered electrical impulses deep in their brains. The rats would toggle the levers repeatedly, sometimes thousands of times per hour, failing to eat or drink while the lever was still functional.

Made in the USA
Middletown, DE
26 January 2022

59683261R00400